W9-ANT-090

BEYOND THE LAUGHING SKY

a novel

MICHELLE CUEVAS

illustrated by JULIE MORSTAD

DIAL BOOKS FOR YOUNG READERS

an imprint of Penguin Group (USA) LLC

DIAL BOOKS FOR YOUNG READERS
Published by the Penguin Group
Penguin Group (USA) LLC
375 Hudson Street
New York, New York 10014

USA / Canada / UK / Ireland / Australia / New Zealand / India / South Africa / China

penguin.com

A Penguin Random House Company

Library of Congress Cataloging-in-Publication Data

Cuevas, Michelle.
Beyond the laughing sky / by Michelle Cuevas.   pages cm
Summary: Hatched from an egg and raised by a loving family, ten-year-old Nashville
is more bird than human except for his lack of wings, but he and his classmates
learn that differences need not keep them apart.
ISBN 978-0-8037-3867-6 (hardcover)
[1. Belonging (Social psychology)—Fiction. 2. Individuality—Fiction. 3. Self-acceptance—
Fiction. 4. Family life—Fiction. 5. Orphans—Fiction. 6. Transformation—Fiction.] I. Title.
PZ7.C89268Bey 2014   [Fic]—dc23   2013034416

Manufactured in the USA

1 3 5 7 9 10 8 6 4 2

Designed by Mina Chung
Text set in Caslon

FOR MY LITTLE BROTHER, CHRISTOPHER,

WHO TOLD ME THE ENDING

—M.C.

BEYOND THE LAUGHING SKY

IN A PECAN TREE

N ASHVILLE AND HIS FAMILY LIVED IN A HOUSE perched in the branches of the largest pecan tree in the village of Goosepimple. The tree grew on the top of a high hill, and the hill overlooked the small, perfect village, where the sun always shined, the grass was always mowed, and the men strutted like doves in their gray suits.

The house in the pecan tree, however, was often shrouded in fog like the purple-gray gloom of an aged bruise, causing the old men in town to sit on their porches, drink sweet tea, and gossip.

"That tree on the hill looks like the last feather to be plucked from the pimpled skin of a goose."

"Naw, it looks like the last sprig of hair on an ancient bald head."

"Naw, it looks like the last white ghost seed waiting to fly away from a dandelion."

Tourists often wanted to drive up the one creeping road that led to the top and visit the house, but once they got close realized they had somewhere else to be or something else to do. When they stopped by the town visitor center they would say, "That house in that tree is not like the rest. Was it built there? Was it built like a nest?"

"Oh no, sugar," the old widow working at the visitor center would say. "That house sat on a small street in town for nearly a century. Then, ten years ago, there was a flood the likes of which this area had never seen. It started raining as hard as it could in March, and it didn't stop until June. Can you imagine that?" The widow paused, allowing the visitors to imagine that amount of precipitation. "Needless to say," she continued, "the rivers and swamps and the bayou overflowed. The foundation of the building came loose and the whole place just floated away, bobbing on the water like a toy in the tub. The water rose all the way over that hill, and when the rain stopped, the house was stuck in that pecan tree like a mouse in a hawk's claw."

"Who lives there now?" asked the tourist.

"A sweet young couple and their little girl," replied the widow.

"How precious."

"And also . . ." the widow paused. "And, well, that *boy*."

"What boy?"

"What boy, indeed," replied the widow. "What boy hatches from an egg?"

"Oh, fiddlesticks," a Southern gentleman said to the widow. "A boy can't hatch from an egg. That's impossible"

"What an absurd little word," the widow replied.

"Pardon?"

"You said impossible," the widow pointed out. "There's no such thing. There's things you've seen and things you may not have, but there ain't nothing that's impossible, sugar."

NASHVILLE

IMPOSSIBLE. IMPROBABLE. INCONCEIVABLE. IF the children from far-flung villages who came to catch a glimpse of Nashville had better vocabularies, perhaps these are words they would have used. As it stood, they would ride their bikes to the base of the hill after sunset, their brakes screeching like the call of a night bird, with hopes of seeing something they called just plain *weird*.

"I double-dog super dare you to go up and knock on the door and get a look at him."

And then they'd look and look at the house without moving, their hearts pounding like hoofbeats. They'd imagine they saw a light come on, or a curtain billow out like it had bones.

"I saw him!" they would shout to the wind, pedaling fast. "He's half boy, half bird!"

Had Nashville heard their words it wouldn't have mattered, for he really did look how they said—why, the truth of the matter was, he looked like a bird in almost every way. He was the size of a normal boy, perhaps a tad small for his age, but he had feathers for hair and a beak for his nose and mouth. His eyes were sharp and golden and his legs too long and thin. But when it came to clothing, Nashville was fond of bow ties and hats, and this made him about as alarming as a puppy in a paisley suit. He was, however, extraordinary, and that tended to scare townsfolk, who were hooked on the Ordinary with a capital *O*, and preferred their day-to-day served without any Extra.

Nashville was one of a kind, and he had a way of stirring up whispers in town, causing the old women to sit in the beauty parlor, get their hair curled, and gossip.

"That youngster looks like a dodo bird in a dinner

jacket. What's next? Turtles in tuxedos? Skunks in swimsuits?"

"I'm just glad he doesn't have wings."

"Oh! Can you imagine that? Some whippersnapper flying around, peeping in our windows."

It was true. The only avian attribute Nashville seemed to be missing, much to his disappointment, was a pair of wings. But he had everything else. Why, by the time he was a baby barely out of the egg, Nashville was not only looking like a bird, but acting like one, too—chirping instead of crying for food, preferring sunflower seeds to milk, and only settling down to sleep in the bed his parents had custom made just for him, the one carpenters had been consulted and hired to build. Branches had been soaked, bent, and twisted. The nest was as large as a bed, and made up with pillows and a soft blanket.

"Did you make your nest?" his mother asked Nashville every morning.

"And Junebug," she asked his little sister. "Did you make your bed as well?"

"I want to sleep in a nest, *too*," whined Junebug, with the misguided jealousy of a younger sibling. She was only eight, but Junebug often seemed older and wiser, and Nashville enjoyed her company. And so, from time to time, Nashville would allow his sister, Junebug, to sleep with him in his boy-sized nest.

Sometimes, especially when he was alone, Nashville would stand for a long time at his bedroom window. The interior of the house glowed green due to all the leaves outside, and was like being in the cabin of a ship that sank in an algae pond. Sometimes Nashville felt as if his soul was waiting just under the surface of his skin, ready to leap like a fish into the cool, crisp air above.

But no. Nashville couldn't fly, that was for certain, so there was no reason for his strange desire to leap. Plus, he loved living in a pecan tree. When it was windy, the branches around the house danced and made shadow puppets on the walls. When the birds sang, he and Junebug imagined that from the outside, it must seem like the tree itself was singing.

"If a tree could sing," asked Junebug, "what do you think it would sing about?"

"I suppose," replied Nashville, "it would depend on the tree. A tree starts as a sapling. If it's lucky—if it's not mowed or mocked, chewed or chopped—the tree sets roots. The tree grows branches. The tree sprouts leaves. And every part, down to the smallest speck of bark and the tiniest vein of a leaf, is shaped by the world—the particular world around the tree. One less storm, one more insatiable caterpillar, any twist or turn along the way, and the tree would be changed. The tree would have a different song to sing."

Junebug thought deeply about this. "I wonder," she said finally, "what those pines at the edge of town sing about."

"Junebug," said Nashville. "You know I've never been past those pines."

"Yeah. Me neither," said Junebug. She looked at Nashville who was staring into the distance.

"Nashville?" she continued. "I think I'd like to stay here in our tree for always. Wouldn't you?"

"Of course," Nashville replied, with only the slightest hint of doubt. "I'd like to stay here forever, too." Anything else seemed, well, downright Impossible, Improbable, and Inconceivable.

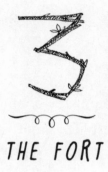

THE FORT

THE BIRDHOUSE HANGING IN THE PECAN tree was shaped like any other. It had a slanted roof, a hole for an opening, and a peg of wood that served as a front porch. The one difference was the size of this birdhouse—it was big enough for two children, and inside, instead of a nest and eggs, were books, crayons, and one small record player.

The birdhouse hung from a giant rope in the midst of leaves and was only accessible by climbing up through the branches of the pecan tree. No one was brave enough

to do this—no one but Nashville and Junebug, that is, for this was their fort.

The fort.

Sometimes, it was just a tree house. But most times it was a ship-like flying contraption with newspaper sails and oars dripping in ink. Junebug would sit in the crow's nest, binoculars to her eyes, looking out for monsters in need of a good slaying. Nashville would, of course, man the wheel. His duties also included waving to pirate kings and throwing the occasional coin to a troll when they'd cross a bridge.

The fort.

Where the pair stored their painted scenes and books of made-up languages, their two-man band, and the tiny matchbox bed plus accessories that they made in case, someday, their experiments in the world of shrinking finally panned out.

The fort.

Where once, on a most heroic adventure, Nashville and Junebug finally traveled all the way to the edge of the map, where the paper was faded yellow and thin.

"What now?" asked Junebug.

So Nashville turned over the page, and there he drew them a new map. They were travelers. They were adventurers. They were treading real dust and pebbles on the surface of an imaginary moon.

HONEYSUCKLE

JUNEBUG AND NASHVILLE WEREN'T ALLOWED to start having adventures first thing in the morning. First things first, the pair had to do their chores. And the start of the day meant taking any trash down the hill and bringing the mail back up.

Most houses in Goosepimple had a trash can on the curb and a mailbox at the end of the drive. This would have also been the case with the house in the pecan tree, except the road that wound up the hill was steep and twisted, and both the mail truck and trash truck couldn't make the trip.

"Truck's too big," explained the trash man.

"Truck's too small," explained the mailman.

"Well then, why don't you walk?" asked Junebug.

To this, neither answered, only laughed loudly.

On the trash and mail mornings, Nashville and Junebug would decide their mission on the way down the hill.

"Okay," said Junebug. "This trash is just a cover. We're picking up a top-secret encoded message in that mailbox. The mailman . . ."

"Is a *spy*," finished Nashville.

"Dum, dum, DUM!" sang Junebug.

They dumped a trash bag in the can, then crept up to the mailbox, looking around to make sure nobody was watching.

"Coast is clear," whispered Nashville.

And so they opened the mailbox. Inside were three envelopes and a coupon flyer for the Goosepimple Grocery. One of the letters was addressed to their parents from Goosepimple Middle School. Nashville suspected he knew the contents, so that one he put back inside the box.

"Come on," he said to Junebug. "I know the secret mission."

The missions were always changing—sometimes collecting jars of rain, paper bags of hiccups, adopting lost moonbeams and folding them into cake batter. Or perhaps investigating glittering slug trails left in the moonlight, finding the owners of abandoned buttons, or playing the sousaphone for caterpillars still in their cocoons.

Today, however, the mission was all about honey.

The honey was trapped inside the honeysuckle flowers, and the honeysuckle flowers were trapped on the other side of their neighbor's wooden fence. The neighbor—who had obviously built a high fence to keep out secret agents—was clearly planning a Goosepimple takeover.

"The honey," said Nashville, "can give you powers. Like invisibility. Or X-ray vision. Or . . ."

"Or it can make you fly," said Junebug, giving her brother a knowing look. Every time they went on a mission, it always seemed to end in Nashville finding, gaining, or otherwise procuring the ability to fly.

Nashville, Junebug thought, didn't seem to need the honeysuckle though. He seemed to be changing all on his own. And she would know. They spent so much time together, and she was so used to their two-headed shadow, that when she saw her own shadow it looked rather strange. But lately, Nashville had been spending time alone. Lately he'd been going for long walks, coming back with his pockets full of feathers he'd collected. Lately she'd find him standing in the yard, looking up, up, up at the sky. He seemed to be stuck in that mysterious morning place—half asleep, half awake, still able to recall a dream.

"Come on," said Nashville, interrupting Junebug's thoughts. "The honeysuckle is through the secret door."

The pair wiggled a board in the fence, loose like Junebug's front tooth, and slipped inside their neighbor's unruly garden. There were bushes growing wild, piles of leaves, and rusty, overturned lawn furniture in the yard. But there, at the far end, almost hidden, was the honeysuckle bush. Its yellow-orange blossoms drew Junebug and Nashville like bees to the flower.

"Remember how I showed you," said Nashville. He

plucked a flower, held the whole blossom in his hands, and turned it upside down.

"First pull off the bottom." He did this, and a silken string emerged from where he separated this piece from the flower. A drop of nectar appeared at the bottom.

"And then . . ." But before he could finish, Junebug swooped in and licked away the honey-tasting treat.

"Then you steal it!" said Junebug.

"Thief," laughed Nashville, and they began collecting more blossoms until they heard a screen door slam behind them and the sound of boy's voice.

"Hey!" he shouted. "My mama said to use my BB gun if I caught you in our yard again!"

Nashville and Junebug looked at each another, then started to run. They made it to the fence, and turned back as they crept through. The boy stood on his porch, arms crossed, no BB gun in sight.

"The honey worked!" cried Junebug, laughing as they ran. "I have X-ray vision! I saw his underpants!"

They collapsed, laughing, their backs against the old, tall fence. They held their hands open, and pulled the flowers apart to get to the honey-like drops hidden inside. Maybe, thought Junebug. Maybe the honey has another power. Yes, she felt sure it could transport her back here any time she had it—to a place that tasted like summer, to a place where two little shadows blended into one.

THE WELCOME CAKE

MOST EVENINGS NASHVILLE AND JUNEBUG baked a cake.

"What's the occasion?" their mother would ask. And of course, they always had an answer; they baked cakes to welcome the first firefly of the season, and cakes to commiserate incurable hiccups. Cakes for well-shaped clouds, cakes for bad hair days, and cakes only to be eaten barefoot in the grass.

"And of course," Nashville explained, "when all else

fails, there are three hundred and sixty-four days of non-birthdays to celebrate each year."

And why was Nashville so interested in cakes? Well, a cake had played an instrumental role in his fate. It's where his life story started. Well, sort of, for it most likely started when the eggs fell to the ground. Or when they were laid. Or, for that matter, when the nest was built in the first place.

Ten years earlier Nashville's mother and father had just been married, and moved into a house with a dazzling, oversized window in a small village called Goosepimple.

It was agreed by all who lived there that Goosepimple was quite simple and quite perfect. The old men sat on the porches drinking sweet tea, the dewy glasses dripping polka dots onto their trousers. Roosters perched on the fence with the red sails on their heads waving in the wind, their eyes dreaming of the sea-blue sky. Pollen-drunk bees hovered around the honeysuckle bushes. The small town held few surprises, and nothing ever changed; time circled like a bug on a glass rim, always returning to where it began.

Then one morning, surprisingly, something *did* change.

A bird—a Nashville warbler to be exact—had started to build a nest in the tree outside Nashville's parents' window. Every few minutes it flew away and returned with a new building block: moss, grass, a twist tie off a bread bag, a long strand of hair. Nashville's mother secretly hoped the hair was hers.

When the bird laid her two eggs, Nashville's mother used paint samples to identify their colors. "Pale cornflower blue," she said, holding up the paint swatch, "with a hint of mint and moss green. And the blotchy spots were a mix of rust and mahogany." She sang to the eggs as well. Nashville's mother had a voice like footsteps in new winter snow. Some say the birds in Goosepimple sang differently after they heard her. Some say they were never the same.

The Goosepimple Library had four books about Nashville warblers, and Nashville's mother checked them all out. She learned that the eggs would hatch two weeks after being laid. When two weeks passed and there were no chicks, she decided to throw them a welcome party. Perhaps it would coax them out.

"Excuse me?" her husband asked. "You're throwing a party for *whom*?"

"The birds," his wife clucked, wiping flour onto her apron. "The birds will be born any day now."

She worked extra hard on the cake. When the two large sheets of chocolate were ready, she gently removed them from the pans and used a sharp knife to cut them into the shape of a bird's profile. Her fingers turned blue mashing berries to color the whipped cream. She spent over thirty minutes drawing the feathers, eyes, and beak with the frosting bag. The cake was perfect.

"Warblers aren't blue, dear," said her husband.

"I know that," said his wife. "But I don't know how to make gray frosting."

Nashville's mother smiled. She smiled the smile of someone who believes a cake can change your fate. She smiled that smile until the morning the eggs disappeared.

"Oh my, oh no!" she cried. She stuck her head out the window and looked at the branches. The eggs and bird were gone. "The eggs," she wept. "What happened to the eggs?"

Her husband did not know. The only thing left in the tree was the nest, surrounded by small white flowers. This made his wife unbearably sad. She went into the kitchen and slid the giant bird-shaped cake into the garbage pail.

A cake. What else has the magic to turn eggs, flour, and sugar into a wish? And a cake never shows up on a bad day; never rings on a humdrum Tuesday to say, "Tough luck. You didn't make the team." No, a cake is there when things are super, when they're better-than-great—always the guest of honor at a birthday or a wedding, always dressed in frosting and wearing its boogie shoes.

Which is why it made her husband heartsick to see the cake his wife had worked so hard to make smeared down the trash bag. Is there anything sadder than untouched joy in the garbage? Her husband did not think so, which is why he immediately took the trash out to the curb.

And there, on the sidewalk in front of the house, was a broken egg.

The egg was open with chipped, white edges. Was there anything sadder than an unhatched egg? Her husband did not think so.

But where was the other egg?

"There you are," said the husband. The egg had rolled off the sidewalk and under the honeysuckle bush. This egg, much like the other, was cracked open. However, what spilled out was not a bird and it was not dead. The man lifted the creature into his hands and pulled the chips of white and blue shell from its face and eyelids. He smoothed the yellow fluid from its hair and across the crease of its mouth.

"Dear," said her husband when he re-entered the house. "I found the eggs. They were cracked on the sidewalk."

"Oh no, no, no," the wife cried. "Are they dead?"

"Not this one," said the man, handing her the creature.

"Why," she whispered. "This is a baby."

And it was. Inside the cracked egg the man had found

a perfect human baby. It was small—as small as a baby chick—but healthy and peach-colored and perfect.

"We'll name him Nashville," said the new mother, as if it were the most natural thing in the world to find a baby in a cornflower blue egg on the sidewalk. "I just wish," she sighed, "that I hadn't thrown out his welcome cake."

THE BIRDBATH

EACH NIGHT, ONCE THE CAKE WAS OUT OF the oven, the bakers both covered in flour and frosting, Nashville and Junebug were sent to take their baths.

"I want to take my bath like Nashville," Junebug pouted. For while Junebug took her nightly bath in a claw-foot tub, Nashville bathed each evening by moonlight in a birdbath in the yard.

Nashville slipped on his striped bathrobe, tied the belt around his waist, and walked to the yard carrying his soap and shampoo and comb. The yard was dark, but Nashville's father had thoughtfully installed a lamp for the evenings when the moon was new. This night, however, the moon was full to the brim, and washed the yard in light.

The birdbath was shaped like any other, only person-size, and to get inside Nashville had to climb a ladder. Once he reached the top, he would take his toiletries from his pocket, lay them out on the edge of the bath, and step into the water. Fed by a hose and heated all day by the sun, the water now reflected the moon.

"Scrubbing behind my ears with moonlight and sunlight in the water, both at once," Nashville liked to say.

After he cleaned his face and feathers with a washcloth, Nashville enjoyed the warm breeze and listened to the odes of insects and the limericks of frogs.

At first Nashville's father had been against the birdbath.

"He can take a bath in the tub like a normal boy," he'd said.

"But he's not a normal boy," his mother had replied. "He's special. Let's just do this one thing," she continued, "to make him feel at home."

Of course, making someone *feel* at home means making where they live feel like their real home. Which was hard, because his parents didn't really know what kind of home Nashville would have lived in had they not found him beneath the honeysuckle bush.

And neither did Nashville. Though sometimes, especially during his baths in the sky, he thought he knew. He thought he could remember coming from a place where everything could fly. A place where a clock's minute and hour hands spread away from its face, flapping like wings. A place where he'd pluck a daisy and watch the petals whirl like the propellers of a helicopter. Where he'd throw a handful of sand, and the grains would buzz away like a swarm of gnats. Where colorful fruits on a tree would burst into flight, and new ones would perch in their place.

"Anything can fly, I think," said Nashville to the pecan tree. "Dandelion seeds can fly. So can whirligig seeds. Why, just yesterday I saw a group of dead leaves fly from a tree and land on a pond. They floated away across the surface like a fleet of ships, the wind tearing at their sails."

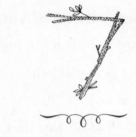

THE TOAST & JAM
TRAPEZE TROUPE

NASHVILLE SPENT A LOT OF TIME ALONE IN
the fort, since it was where he did some of his
best thinking. Sometimes he'd do it lying inside, the
spot of light from the door like a full moon on the floor.
And sometimes he'd think while sitting on the wooden
peg, the rope above creaking like a weather vane changing direction.

On a morning in September, Nashville thought about
the fact that it was autumn, and that meant he was starting middle school. Which meant a new building, with

new students and new teachers. Nashville was no fool. He knew the kids at his old school didn't refrain from calling him a beast or a monster because they liked him; they had just become accustomed over time to the way he looked. He also understood that it's a rare child who *wants* to go to school, but it was perhaps equally rare to dread the event as much as the tender hearts, old souls, and uniquely shaped of the world.

He was not afraid of the classes or the teachers—adults had a way of ignoring his looks in an effort to appear bravely polite. But children were not always so timid. From what he'd seen in the town of Goosepimple, one child might be a little taller, one a little plumper, but really, they looked just like one another. The same freckles, the same grass-stained knees, and the same chewed nails. *What exactly*, wondered Nashville when he saw them, *went so very wrong with me?*

As he pondered this, he heard the tin can scrape across the floor of the fort, and then the tiny voice of Junebug.

"Earth to Bird. Do you read me?" Nashville picked up the can and pulled the string tight.

"I read you, Little Bug."

Junebug spoke into her can in the house. "I have a telegram from kitchen headquarters. Breakfast is ready. Over and out."

By the time Nashville reached the table, everyone was already seated in their perch swings. The swings hung from the ceiling at the perfect height for the table, and made the whole family look like the Toast & Jam Trapeze Troupe. Nashville imagined his family in spandex and sequins, juggling muffins, balancing glasses of fresh-squeezed juice on their noses. He saw his family doing somersault flips, catching one another by gripping on to outstretched cereal spoons.

"Please pass the sugar," said Junebug, taking her seat, pouring milk on her cereal. Nashville climbed up onto his perch as well. The seats had, of course, been his mother's idea, installed to make Nashville more comfortable, and everyone—even Nashville's father, who had fallen out a few times trying to read the paper—had learned to live with, and even like, the arrangement.

"Big day tomorrow," said Nashville's mother. Nashville tried to ignore this, and concentrated on scooping some seeds out of a bird feeder and onto his plate.

"Are you excited?" she asked.

"I am," said Junebug. "I want to get new pencils and notebooks and erasers and a lunch box . . ."

"You know," Nashville interrupted. "I've been thinking. I'm not sure I *need* any more education."

His father peered over the morning newspaper at his son.

"Maybe I could set up shop and be a traveling balloon salesman," said Nashville. "Or a skywriting poet."

His father resumed reading the paper.

"A one-man band?" continued Nashville. "A flea circus trainer?"

"Very funny," said his mother, ruffling Nashville's feathers. "Now hurry up and get dressed. We've got a busy day of errands to run before you start school."

"A cootie cleaner?" Nashville continued, his voice fading as his mother pushed him toward his room. "A star counter? A palm reader? A decoder of alphabet soup?"

NOTHING TO BE FIXED

NASHVILLE, DRESSED IN HIS SUMMER SUIT and hat, set out for town accompanied by his mother, Junebug, and a warm breeze. The family marched together down the winding road, the one that circled the hill like a long, twisted strand of a peeled apple.

"Good morning, Goosepimple," greeted Nashville when they reached the village. Goosepimple was so tiny it was often forgotten on maps, so overlooked that people only seemed to end up there by accident. The village reminded Nashville of an old neighbor forever napping on their porch. But sometimes the neighbor would startle awake, almost knocking over their rocking chair. Sometimes, that is, someone new would catch sight of Nashville for the first time.

Once it had been an out-of-town aunt on a visit. She'd nearly fainted when she saw Nashville, and promptly called the police.

"We're sorry, ma'am," replied dispatch. "But we don't respond to cases of bizarre-feathered boys. Nor do we show up for curiously beaked youngsters or peculiar-shaped lads."

Nashville had made babies cry and dogs bark. He'd made at least two elderly in-laws on a visit get their glasses checked. And to top it all off, there was the issue of the ice-cream truck.

"But *why*?" Protested Junebug on the hottest days each summer, days when the sidewalk sizzled and the pecan tree tried to hunch over into its own shade. "Why does the ice-cream truck go up every street but ours?"

"Who can say," replied her mother, who suspected the snub had more than a little to do with her bizarrely feathered, curiously beaked, peculiarly shaped son.

When they reached the center of the village, Nashville and his family went to the doctor's office for Junebug's yearly checkup. In the waiting room a curious girl stared wide-eyed at Nashville. She looked at his feathers, and she looked at his beak. She looked until she finally had the courage to ask.

"So," she said. "Whatta you got?"

Nashville looked around. He put down the *Audubon* magazine he'd been reading.

"Pardon?" he replied to the girl.

"I mean," continued the girl. "What's the matter with you? Why do you look like that?"

"Nothing's the matter with him," interrupted Junebug. "What's the matter with *you*?"

"Fell off my bike," said the girl, holding up her arm in a cast. She turned back to Nashville. "You think the doctor will be able to fix whatever you've got?"

"I told you," said Junebug. "There's nothing to be fixed." She had just balled her tiny hand into a fist when the nurse emerged and called out her name. The girl's mother pulled her daughter a few seats closer, in the opposite direction from Nashville.

Nashville had been a patient at this same office for exactly one day of his life. Ten years earlier, the day he hatched from an egg, his parents had attempted to take him to this regular doctor.

"I . . . I'm not sure I'm the right doctor for this, er, specific case," the physician had stuttered. He tapped at the newborn's feathers, shined his headlamp at Nashville's beak.

"Well, where exactly do you recommend we go?" asked Nashville's mother.

And that's how Nashville ended up at Dr. Larkin's office, the veterinarian down the street—a veterinarian who, as luck would have it, specialized in ornithology and the general care of birds.

The day of his birth, Dr. Larkin put Nashville's baby X-ray up on the wall and flipped on the light. He studied it, the bones white in the dark like a bleached shipwreck beneath the sea.

"Seems healthy to me," the doctor had said that day.

"But he has feathers," replied Nashville's father. "Can it be fixed?"

"Nothing to be fixed," said the doctor. "Some children

have freckles. Some have interesting birthmarks. Nash-ville happens to have feathers."

"Feathers . . ." said Nashville's father shaking his head, his face still wearing a troubled look.

"So he's healthy?" asked his mother.

"Well, there is this one thing," said the doctor. "Nothing to be alarmed about." He pointed to newborn Nashville's X-ray on the wall.

"See here," said the doctor, pointing to Nashville's shoulders. There seems to be a little extra something." The doctor picked up another X-ray and put it against the light. This X-ray had the unmistakable shape of a bird's wing.

"A wing?" asked Nashville's father.

"Where a bird's wing attaches to the body, it attaches by the same joint that we see here in Nashville." Nashville's mother and father stared in silence, and soon the quiet filled up every part of the room. Why, all the cotton balls in the doctor's glass jar were simply puffed to the poof with silence.

"Are you saying," sputtered his father, "that our son is going to grow wings? That's impossible."

Dr. Larkin smiled and clicked off the light to the X-rays. "Oh, no, no, I think not. But that would be something wouldn't it? Hoo-ee. A boy with wings." He paused in thought, breathed on his stethoscope, and then wiped it like he was shining an apple. "But in the end," he said, smiling, "who can say? I know I for one try my best to never use the word *impossible*."

HAVE YOU EVER SEEN A PLATYPUS?

AND SO, AFTER JUNEBUG'S CHECKUP AT THE doctor, the family made their way down the street for Nashville's checkup with Dr. Larkin, Goosepimple's finest veterinarian.

"Well hello, Nashville," said Dr. Larkin when he walked into the checkup room. "You're growing like a weed."

"Speaking of growing," said Nashville. "Will you be taking an X-ray today, like you did last time I was here?"

"Yes, yes, first let me have a look at you," said the doctor. He turned on his light and looked in Nashville's ears and eyes and beak. He breathed on his stethoscope and directed Nashville to take several deep breaths. He tapped Nashville's knees and watched his legs kick forward.

"Now can you take the X-ray? I can't see back there too well," Nashville explained. "And you're the expert."

"Okay, okay," said the doctor. "Let's have a look."

The veterinary assistant came then and took Nashville into the room next door for an X-ray. After that, Nashville sat patiently waiting for the results. A few minutes later, Doctor Larkin returned, put the X-ray on the wall, and turned on the light that lit it from behind.

"Things look about the same to me," said Dr. Larkin.

"I see," said Nashville. He stared at the X-ray. "But what about the bone? The one that would connect them if I were to grow wings?"

The doctor looked at Nashville. He turned off the light on the wall and the X-ray disappeared.

"Nashville," he asked softly. "May I ask you, why do you want to grow wings?"

"Well, why else would I be this way?" replied Nashville.

The doctor spoke carefully and kindly.

"Nashville, you have an amazing imagination. Truly. And I don't want to disappoint you, but . . ."

"What's the point of being the way I am," Nashville interrupted. "if I'm never going to have wings?"

"Now, now," said the doctor. "None of that." He waved his hands, and the rain clouds that had started to gather in the office dispersed. "Don't waste time wishing to be something other than what you are."

"What am I?" replied Nashville. "When the world made me, it made a mistake."

"A mistake," said the doctor, rubbing his chin. "Every year the leaves change colors and drop to the ground, right?"

"Right," said Nashville.

"Is that a mistake?"

"No," replied Nashville. "That's just fall."

"Well, what about wrinkled elephants? And artichokes?" asked the doctor. "And blowfish and purple sunsets and frill-necked lizards? And platypuses! Have you ever seen a platypus? Hoo-ee. What about spiderwebs and eclipses and star-nosed moles? Are those mistakes?"

"I don't think so," said Nashville.

"Not one thing this world makes is a mistake," continued the doctor. "Including you."

"Including me," repeated Nashville, his voice sounding less than convinced.

"Why yes," said the doctor, tussling the feathers atop Nashville's head. "Especially you."

THE FIRST DAY

THE NEXT DAY WHEN MORNING BROKE,
Nashville could no longer deny it: School was
starting. And while he had tried to store up as much
summer as he could, it was just no use. At some point
during the night, summer had left town, had packed a
suitcase full of fireflies and swimming holes, and whistled on down the road. And so, as Junebug raced around
the house, Nashville dragged his knapsack down the
stairs one at a time. *Plunk. Plunk. Plop.* He conducted
the sound track to his middle school life.

"Hello," said Nashville's teacher, Miss Starling. She

wrote her name in large, loopy letters on the chalkboard. Behind it, Nashville could see the faint ghostly outline of past lessons erased from the board.

"And welcome," continued Miss Starling kindly. "I know most of you don't know one another, coming together from several elementary schools. We have lots to talk about for the new school year, but first things first. I'd like to play a game." The students tittered with excitement.

"Everyone put your chairs in a circle," directed Miss Starling.

There was much scraping and giggling while the students moved their seats. When they were finished, Miss Starling took a chair to the center of the circle and sat.

"My name," she said, "is Miss Starling. And I like sweet tea. Anyone else who likes sweet tea, please stand up."

Six students, including Nashville, stood.

"Now," continued Miss Starling. "If you're standing, quickly switch seats!"

The standing students scrambled to switch seats, but Miss Starling had sat in one of the open chairs, and a red-haired girl was left standing.

"What do I do?" she asked, embarrassed.

"You sit in the middle," said Miss Starling. "And tell us a fact about yourself."

The girl did as she was told.

"My name is Abigail. And I have a little brother."

Only two other students stood this time, and Abigail stole one of their seats. This went on for some time, and Nashville, being quite quick, avoided the hot seat. That is, until a large boy in the middle chair said, "I have a tree fort."

Nashville was the only person to stand, so he and the boy simply switched chairs. Nashville reluctantly made his way to the center, his shoes squeaking on the freshly waxed floor. All eyes were on him, and Nashville wasn't sure what to do with his face. He smiled, a bit too forcefully, and was fairly certain he must look crazy.

"So," said Miss Starling. "What is a fact about you?"

Nashville thought for a moment how to answer.

"My parents," he finally said, "were Nashville warblers."

The class snickered and muffled laughter. Nobody stood.

"Perhaps another fun fact for us, Nashville?"

Nashville thought some more.

"I was hatched from an egg," he stated.

The class had stopped tittering with laughter, and now just stared.

"I sleep in a nest," he continued.

"I bathe in a birdbath."

"I . . . I . . ." he paused, and then quickly proclaimed a final fact.

"I wish I could fly."

The students looked around at one another. Slowly, cautiously, one girl rose, then a second boy, followed by a third. Soon, the entire class was standing. Even Miss Starling rose to her feet. Nashville stood as well, and they all laughed as they bumped and bustled to take one another's seats.

SUPERNOVA

SCIENCE WAS A SUBJECT THAT NASHVILLE never quite grasped.

On the one hand, it was full of things he was intrigued by, things like how to tell the age of a tree, the dances of the moon and tides, and the names of the clouds—like cumulonimbus and nimbostratus—that sounded like magic spells on his tongue.

But science was also full of facts and truths, full of order, genus, and species, where his little life didn't seem to fit. He thumbed through the pages of his science text.

Chapter One: The Solar System

Chapter Six: Water and Weather

Chapter Ten: Earthquakes and Volcanoes

But where was the chapter on being born from an egg? About walking, and talking, but also having feathers? None of that, he knew, would be covered in this text. Or any other.

As he thumbed through the book, Nashville heard whispers to his left. A pair of girls, both larger and older looking than Nashville, whispered loudly enough for him to hear.

"If I looked like that," said the first, "I'd just want to die." She emphasized this last word dramatically like an actress.

The second girl did not answer, only elbowed her friend, and stared at Nashville. He quickly looked away.

"Do you girls have something to share?" asked Miss Starling.

The pair froze.

"No, ma'am," they answered in unison.

Nashville let out the breath he'd been holding, relieved.

"Well then, why don't you read the next paragraph," continued Miss Starling. And so one of the girls—the dramatic one, noted Nashville—began reading in her actress voice.

"'Change is the nature of nature,'" she read. "'For example, stars expand as they grow older. They grow from a star, to a red super-giant, to a supernova. When a massive star explodes at the end of its life, the explosion dispenses different elements—helium, carbon, oxygen, iron, nickel—across the universe, scattering stardust. That stardust now makes up the planets, including ours.'"

"So a star had to die to make us?" Nashville slapped a hand over his mouth. He'd forgotten to raise his hand.

"Yes, Nashville," smiled Miss Starling.

"So we're made of stars?" he asked.

"We were once stars," she answered. "Things are always changing, from one thing to another. And it can happen just like that." Miss Starling snapped her fingers.

"Some magnolias," she continued, "they grow to be trees, but then they can take up to twenty years to blossom. After decades, a silent shift, and one morning *POOF!* The flower is open, bigger than my hand."

Miss Starling closed her book, stood thoughtfully at the front of the room. "Slow, fast, in a minute or a decade. Things are always changing. From a seed to a magnolia, from pollen to honey, from an egg"—she paused, only for a second—"From an egg to a bird. There are no rules. And sometimes there are even miracles."

Nashville looked down at his own hands. He imagined a magnolia blossom twice the size. To his left, he once again heard hushed whispers.

"Like I said," said the girl. "If I looked like that, I'd just want to die."

There was a pause. The second girl tilted her head, considering Nashville.

"I wouldn't," she finally replied.

Her words, thought Nashville, sounded exactly like something made of stars.

HATCHDAY

Happy Hatchday to You.
Happy Hatchday to You.
Happy Hatchday, Dear Nashville,
Happy Hatchday to You!

THE NEXT MORNING WAS NASHVILLE'S birthday, so when his family finished singing, he blew out the ten candles (plus one for good luck) on his sesame-seed cake, wondering the whole time what could be in the big box wrapped in polka-dot paper.

"For you," said his mother, placing the gift in front of Nashville. It was too small for a hot-air balloon, a hang glider, or several of the other things Nashville secretly hoped for. Much too small for a rocket. Perhaps a hero's cape? Perhaps a telescope to see the places he longed to travel?

"Open it!" shouted Junebug, dancing around Nashville's chair, licking frosting off his candles.

When Nashville pulled the lid off the box there was, indeed, something inside that could soar through the air with ease. Its wings were silver, striped with red, and its nose came to a dashing point.

"A plane," said Nashville.

"A remote-control plane," added his father proudly.

Nashville carefully lifted the toy into his hands and turned it over and over. He lifted it to eye level and stared at it head-on. He liked the way it looked, shiny and sleek, but his first thought about it—*it's too small for me to fly in*—was just too strange for him to say out loud.

"I saw it and thought of you," continued his father. "Remember how we used to make paper airplanes for hours when you were small?"

"I remember," said Nashville. He did recall folding the paper over and over, experimenting with interior creases and wing-stabilizing folds. But mostly he remembered sailing the planes out the window. He remembered imagining a small, small version of himself sitting in the paper crease, and all the places he could go—between the boughs of pine trees, under bridges, in one window of the house, then out the other side.

"Come on," said Junebug, grabbing the remote for the plane. "Let's try it."

And so the entire family left the house in the pecan tree, stood on the ground, and stared up at the sky. Nashville's father showed him how to use the simple remote and, sure enough, when he pressed the lever forward, the plane wheeled across the grass then buzzed off into the air. Just like a fledgling from the nest, it took a few moments for Nashville and the plane to get their bearings—the wings tipped from side to side like the wooden balances above a marionette, and the nose jumped forward in jerks and sputters. But soon enough, Nashville was making the plane do loop-de-loops and zipping over his sister's head until she shrieked with delight.

"You're a natural," said his father proudly.

Even after his parents had gone inside to clean up

after the party, even after his sister had yawned her way to bed, Nashville stayed out flying his plane around the yard. He zipped it around fireflies like stars in space, and was having a wonderful time.

And yet . . .

Something was still missing. Controlling the plane, Nashville couldn't help but feel what a conductor must feel using a baton to direct a symphony. But Nashville didn't want to *conduct* the music. Nashville wanted to *be* the music. He wanted to tap-dance across the notes of the page, to visit each black circle on the sheet music like a hummingbird visits each flower. He wanted to *fly*.

Then, suddenly, the hummingbirds stopped humming, the instruments stopped playing, and the audience looked up and gasped. The small plane was hurling toward the ground.

"But how . . . ?" Nashville could only stare. For there was not one plane, but two—two planes, two comets plummeting to the earth.

A DEAD BIRD

THE SMALL BIRD LAY ON THE GROUND BESIDE the broken wings of the plane.

The plane Nashville had been flying.

The plane that had hit—and killed—the bird.

The contrast between the beautiful bird and the sad, hard ground was striking. Nashville looked closer. He saw the kind of beauty yellow flowers have growing over a carpet of dead leaves. The beauty of cracks forming a mosaic in a dry riverbed, of emerald-green algae at the base of a seawall, of a broken shard from a blue bottle. The beauty of a window smudged with tiny prints. The beauty of wild weeds.

"I'm sorry," Nashville said to the bird. His plane had struck the small thing, and now it would never open its eyes again.

"I'm sorry," Nashville said again as he lifted the bird into his hands. He touched the head and it seemed too fragile to exist, not much different from an eggshell.

"I need a small box," Nashville told his mother when he came inside the house. "A fancy one."

His mother rummaged in the closet and found a gold box, probably from the holidays. She handed it to Nashville without any questions.

"Have fun," she said. Nashville left the room. There would be nothing fun about burying a dead bird.

He went into the living room and, after making sure the coast was clear, unzipped a throw pillow on the sofa, and stole some of the soft stuffing inside. He used this to line the box, then went outside to the spot he'd left the bird under the edge of the magnolia bush. He picked some magnolia blossoms, and put the white petals in the box as well.

"I'm sorry," whispered Nashville, and lifted the bird to place her in the box. Perhaps this third sorry worked some magic, because just as Nashville said it, just as his eyes were filling over with tears, the small creature in his hands began to stir. Just a small turn of the head, and a move of the foot, but it shocked Nashville out of his sadness.

"You're alive!" Nashville shouted. It was as if the leaves of fall had flown back up to the tree, or a dead flower had picked up her petals and pinned them back on. Nashville carefully placed the bird inside the box, now an ambulance rather than a coffin, and began to run down the hill to Goosepimple.

"Back so soon?" said Dr. Larkin when he saw Nashville. The doctor had been packing up the veterinary office to head home, and Nashville caught him coming out the door.

"Please," Nashville said quickly. His hands trembled as he held out the box. "Please. I hit it with a plane and it landed in a magnolia bush and I thought it was dead but it's not and—"

"Slow down, Nashville, slow down," said the doctor leading him into the examination room.

"Hmm," said the doctor. He put on rubber gloves, lifted the bird carefully, and laid her on the table under a bright light. Nashville stood back a bit, suddenly remembering to breathe.

"No bleeding," said the doctor. "Heart rate seems good. Although . . ."

"Although?" said Nashville alarmed.

"She has a broken wing," explained the doctor. He exhibited this to Nashville by extending the wing. Instead of folding back tidily as it usually would, the wing dropped on the table, the feathers strangely bent.

"Nothing life threatening," continued the doctor. "I'll bandage it, but I should tell you, it's unlikely she'll ever use that wing again."

Nashville stared at the bird, his guilt overcoming him once more, but infinitely stronger this time.

"Without wings she can't fly," he said.

"No," said the doctor. "Like so many other things in this world, this bird will have to make do with life on the ground."

MAGNOLIA

AND SO MAGNOLIA THE BIRD RECUPERATED in Nashville's fort. Magnolia—so named for two reasons: one, because of the bush she'd landed in, the one that had likely saved her life. And two, because Miss Starling had said some magnolias rest a long time, then bloom overnight. Nashville hoped a miracle like that for the bird's broken wing.

"Magnolia," Nashville would ask in the morning, "what would you like for breakfast?" He'd bring her seeds and nuts. Once he'd brought her a caterpillar he'd found in the yard, but she didn't seem all that interested.

Perhaps they were old friends, thought Nashville.

He would sit with Magnolia on the edge of the bird-house, beyond which only winged-things could go. He greeted the other birds that came to visit his patient, and nodded his head, even though he didn't understand a chirp of what they were saying. It was probably just gossip anyhow, news about worm delicacies and the new hot-spot bird feeder down the street.

"I wish I could understand you," Nashville would tell Magnolia when they were alone. But like the needle-point puzzles of spiders, or the language left in leaves by beetles, Nashville could not decipher a word.

When he wasn't with the bird, Nashville worked with his father, fixing the broken plane.

"A little glue," said his father. "A little Styrofoam, a little wood, almost like new."

"Can't wait to fly it," Nashville lied. He took the plane back to his room and hid it away in the toy chest. He didn't want Magnolia to see the plane and suffer any post-traumatic stress. Nashville couldn't bear to fly it anyhow. He already had one bird injury on his con-science, and no interest in another.

The plane had, however, given him an interesting idea.

"What do you think?" he asked Magnolia. He held up a sketch on paper.

"See here," explained Nashville. "I could *build* you a new wing."

The bird turned her head to one side. Then the other. She looked at the pencil sketch of a wing with feathers sewn onto it, along with a leather strap. She looked from every angle just to be sure she understood the plan.

"I'll take that as a yes," said Nashville. And so he went to work shaping the frame of light wood and Styrofoam left over from the great plane rebuilding. He recruited Junebug to collect feathers outside.

"For what?" she asked.

"No questions," answered Nashville. "But I'll give you a penny per feather."

"Make it a nickel," said Junebug, walking out the door to hunt for fallen feathers.

Magnolia had been recuperating for several weeks in the fort, and it had been near impossible to keep it from Junebug. Nashville wasn't even sure why he was—maybe a mixture of guilt and wanting the bird all to himself.

After Junebug returned with a handful of feathers, and left with a pocketful of nickels, Nashville did the hardest work of all—hand sewing each feather onto the leather wing he'd cut out while she was gone. It was a challenge, and he had to use all his books and knowledge of which type of feathers went where, and how each played a special role in lifting and soaring and gliding on the wind. However, it was all worth it, for when he had finished, the wing was truly a work of art.

Nashville placed the small wing on the floor of the fort. Magnolia hopped around and around it, eyeing it suspiciously.

"Do you like it?" asked Nashville. "Do you think I could fit it onto you?"

Magnolia seemed to understand, and stood perfectly still like she was being measured for a suit at the tailor. Nashville slid the strap around her waist and back, and attached it to the base of her unusable wing.

"Go ahead, try it out," Nashville prodded.

Magnolia moved the wing about a bit, but took several tries before the muscle at the base of her old wing adjusted to the new addition. She moved it on its own, then many times in succession with her good wing. She moved them faster and faster, beginning to hop about.

"Not too bad," said Nashville. "Not too bad at all."

Nashville lifted her to the windowsill, thinking she'd be thrilled to get out into the sky and try out the wings.

"Here you go," he said gently, placing her on the ledge.

But Magnolia was not exactly thrilled. Instead, she shuddered and backed away, tweeting and crying out until Nashville helped her back to the floor.

"Hmm," said Nashville. He inspected the wing, looking at it from every angle, checking and double-checking his calculations.

"Magnolia," he said. "We're pretty good friends by now, right? Well, can you just take my word? I promise you this wing will work."

Magnolia looked at him. He was, as usual, having trouble reading her reaction.

"Trust me," said Nashville.

He lifted the tiny bird in his hands and brought her over to the window once again. This time Magnolia did not struggle or strain, she merely kept her eyes on Nashville.

And so, without fanfare or ado, Nashville tossed Magnolia into the air as if he were a parent at the pool teaching his child to swim. Magnolia faltered for a moment, pausing in the air like a cartoon character run off a cliff, but quickly it all came back to her. She flapped once, twice, and suddenly the little bird was flying.

"It worked," said Nashville. "It's actually working!"

The little bird chirped and flew around the pecan tree. So excited was she, so thrilled to be in the air, it seemed she had forgotten all about the injury. Her wings kept on flapping, and Magnolia kept on flying around the tree.

Finally, she stopped and landed on the edge of the window where she and Nashville had sat so many times gazing at the world beyond.

Nashville bowed. He blew Magnolia a kiss.

And the little bird, well, she flew on out into the cinnamon air, so sweet.

After she left, Nashville looked down at the drawings

of the wing he had built. A wing is certainly a powerful thing, but without flight, it loses its magic like a
wand without a magician. No Alakazam or Alakazoo.
No Bibbidi, Bobbidi, or Boo. *If only*, Nashville thought,
staring at his invention. *If only I had wings big enough for
me* . . .

THE SINGING TREE

THE DAYS OF FALL STRETCHED ON, AS DID THE afternoons in Miss Starling's classroom at school. Nashville waited each day for the short time after lunch when the class was allowed to get outside the walls of school and into the fresh, clean air.

At the edge of the kickball field stood a tree. It was green and perfect, the lowest branches lining up in a way that seemed custom-made for climbing. And so Nashville did just that. Once he was lost in the foliage, he closed his eyes and imagined he was home, not just at recess, and he didn't have to try to be a regular student when everyone knew he wasn't.

Soon, a little brown bird landed on the branch beside him, and was quickly joined by several others. Not wanting to be rude, Nashville tried to strike up a conversation.

"So," he asked, "do you by any chance know a bird named Magnolia? She was a good friend, and I find it a bit curious that she hasn't written a postcard."

The birds only stared.

"Never mind," Nashville continued. "So, were you originally hatched here, or do you come from someplace else?"

The birds stopped staring and went back to their preening.

"Do you think," Nashville said, continuing his one-way conversation, "that you could fly around the world so fast, you could relive your favorite day? Also, do you think wind is fast-moving air, or something moving *through* air? Also, when you are flying and you have to . . . you know . . . do you ever aim for certain people's heads?"

The birds did not reply. And so, to fill the quiet on the branch between them, Nashville began to whistle.

Whistling. Nashville had always loved this simple

act, and had never taken the value of it for granted. Whistling, like cake, was almost exclusively reserved for times of happiness and relaxation—for drawing joy (and dogs) a little bit closer. One never whistled to deter something or because work was just too hard. No, the whistle was pure sunshine through the lips in every regard.

So on that day, with the birds on his branch, Nashville whistled what he hoped was a joyful tune. To his delight, the birds joined along.

Zay-zay-zay-zoo-zee, sang the first little bird.

Tika-tika-swee-chay-chay, sang the second.

Cheerup-cheerup-cheerily, sang the third

And so, Nashville and the birds found a way to converse.

Zay-zay-zay-zoo-zee
Just some birds singin' in a tree
Tika-tika-swee-chay-chay
Gonna sing all night, sing all day
Cheerup-cheerup-cheerily
Gonna sing far and nearily
Wheet-wheet-wheet-eo

Gonna sing so nice and sweet-eo

Seebit-seebit-see-see-see

Zee-zee-zee-zoo-zee

Chick-chick-chickadee

Nashville thought that if someone heard the birds from outside it would seem, once again, as if a tree were singing. But what would this tree sing about? Perhaps, like most, the tree would sing of the wishes she had trouble putting into words. Maybe the tree dreamed of lifting her roots and dancing. Maybe she dreamed of mossy slippers, and each leaf of her tutu buoying her as she spun in a pirouette. When she finished, she would curtsy to Nashville.

"Thank you," the tree would say.

"Any time," he would reply as the other trees fluttered their leaves in applause.

Nashville's daydream was suddenly shattered when the birds stopped singing and exploded from the tree, leaves and feathers flying. Something had alarmed them. Something had made them flee. When Nashville looked down, he realized he was no longer alone.

A MURDER OF CROWS

BELOW THE TREE STOOD A GROUP OF BOYS from Nashville's class.

"Who are you talking to up there?" asked Finnes Fowl, a freckle-faced boy.

Nashville did not reply, only began climbing down the branches, more deftly and quickly than the other students had ever seen anyone exit a tree.

"Was that your flock?" asked Finnes, the others laughing along.

Nashville reached the ground and stood with his back to the tree.

"Well actually," he said, "not all groups of birds are called flocks. It's a common mistake."

The boys raised their eyebrows in unison at the unexpected reply.

"A flock, a gaggle," continued Nashville. "Those are the words for birds that most folks know. But some are surprising, and pretty perfect. A bouquet of pheasants for example." He paused to think. "Oh yes, a caldron of raptors! That one's swell. A charm of hummingbirds. An exaltation of larks. A parliament of owls." He said each name reverently like a spell. "A murder of crows."

"You're weird," said Finnes loudly when Nashville had finished. The students all looked at one another and laughed nervously. All except one large boy, whose name Nashville did not know.

"Really," asked the large boy with his forehead creased in thought. "Are they really called a *murder* of crows?"

"Yes," said Nashville. "I have a book you could borrow."

The large boy was about to reply when Finnes interrupted and pushed him aside.

"So, do you actually think your parents were birds?"

"I don't think it," replied Nashville. "I know it. I have the egg I hatched from at my house. It's cornflower blue with mahogany spots that look like continents."

"Yuck," said a boy in the back of the group.

"Gross," said another.

"You know what I think?" continued Finnes. "I think you're a liar. I think you're a little lying weirdo and you didn't hatch from no egg, and your parents weren't no dumb birds. These probably aren't even real."

And before Nashville knew what was happening, Finnes pushed him against the tree, pinned his chest, and plucked a feather from his head.

"Ouch," whispered Nashville, rubbing his scalp.

"Whoa," said Finnes backing away, dropping the feather like it was on fire. "You really do have feathers."

The recess bell rang and, after one last look, the other students ran toward the entrance to the school. Nashville hung back for a moment. He considered climbing back up the tree and hiding all day. But finally he sighed, picked up his lost feather from the ground, and made his way back to class.

A GADGET, A GIZMO, AN INVENTION

THE FIRST THOUGHT NASHVILLE HAD AS HE
left school that day was a daydream about finding
a tree on the playground tall enough to let him hide
behind the clouds and avoid the boys at school.

The second thought he had was that it would be better to never go back to school at all.

And the third thought he had was just one word, so
lovely he dare not even speak it. Instead, he wrote it on
a small slip of paper.

The word was *Wings.*

He stared at it for a while. *Wings.* He imagined the *W* looked like two bird wings itself, and the rest of the word was in flight, singing along behind it. Finally, not knowing what else to do, he folded the paper, went to the library, and handed it to the librarian.

"Hmm," said the old librarian, pushing up her thick glasses. "Wings." She walked slowly, slowly through the stacks, picking books off the shelves and handing them to Nashville.

"Wings," she repeated. "Wings, wings."

Nashville stayed there all morning reading his way down the stack of books. He learned that bird wings evolved in two ways, that preflight birds were hopping a lot, up into the air to catch and grab things, or away from predators. They were also leaping from tree to tree. Eventually, after many, many, many years of all this hopping and leaping, birds were able to fly. But that was just the scientific answer.

The librarian had also given Nashville other books. Prettier books. Books full of poems and feathers.

Nashville only knew he liked the poems. He understood the poems. He loved the sound when he read *Hope is the thing with feathers/That perches in the soul.* And *I too am not a bit tamed—I too am untranslatable; I sound my barbaric yawp over the roofs of the world.* Poetically speaking, Nashville realized, wings started with a *desire.* The pre-wing birds wanted things; they wanted the tops of trees, or the cloudless skies, or the stars. Who could really be sure?

So Nashville figured he was already on his way, since he certainly had the desire to fly, and hope, and somewhere in him a very barbaric yawp. So now all he needed were the actual materials and tools. Using Magnolia's wing for inspiration, Nashville made a trip to the Goosepimple Curiosity Shop on his way home from the library.

"To help you find what you need," said the wart-nosed proprietor, "I need to know what you're building."

"Oh, you know," said Nashville, not wanting to divulge his plan, "a device. A doohickey. A doodad."

"Eh?" said the owner.

"An apparatus, a gadget, a gizmo. A thingamajig. A whatchamacallit."

"Ah," said the owner finally. "An *invention.*"

Like the librarian, the curiosity shop proprietor walked down the aisles of his shop, poking and pulling items off dusty shelves. Nashville followed at a safe distance as the owner handed him various items: an umbrella, a ship sail, shoelaces, and a hat rack made from bamboo. He handed him a teapot, and one captain's wheel. Nashville teetered to the register with the items.

"Perfect," he said. "Just what I was looking for."

BOX OF QUESTIONS, SUITCASE OF FEATHERS

"S O," ASKED NASHVILLE'S FATHER AT DINNER, "tell us what's been happening at school?"

Nashville was glad when Junebug began prattling about every detail of her day—about the girl with the koala backpack, the pudding fight at lunch, and the freshly painted hopscotch lines on the playground. This gave Nashville time to think of something to say, since he definitely couldn't tell them about the boys on the playground. It was just the kind of thing his mother—or even worse, Junebug—would show up at his school, and make a big stink about.

"And what about you, Nashville?" asked his mother. "Anything fun happening in your class?"

"Well," said Nashville, thinking, "I've been working on this assignment we got."

"Maybe you didn't hear her ask if anything *fun* was happening," said Junebug, crinkling her nose.

"Our teacher," continued Nashville, "Miss Starling, had us each think of a question. And so everyone sat, tapping their feet and pencils, thinking of questions, getting ready to put them into a box. Once they were inside everyone wondered what they said, buzzing there like a box full of bees."

"So what was the assignment?" asked Nashville's father.

"Our assignment," explained Nashville, "is to answer our own question."

"How interesting," said his mother. "And what was your question?"

"My question," said Nashville, "is a secret." He paused. "Well, a secret until I figure out the answer."

"Oh . . ." said his mother. "And? Do you think you'll be able to answer it?" she asked softly.

"Maybe," replied Nashville. "Yes. I think maybe I'll be able to answer it soon."

After dinner, Nashville hurried upstairs to begin work on his wings.

First, he took out his suitcase of feathers. A whole suitcase! Yes, Junebug had proven to be quite the hunter, and Nashville had exchanged nearly his entire piggy bank for the haul of feathers she'd brought him.

Next, he started working on the coat hangers, reshaping the wires until they looked like the skeleton of a bird's wings. He held them against a large, flat piece of leather, and traced the outline. He cut the pieces of leather and some scraps of an old ship's sail into pieces, each fitting into the skeleton, making them resemble bat wings. But they weren't supposed to be bat wings, they were to be bird wings, and for that he'd have to figure out the feathers, and this would be the hardest part.

Feathers, Nashville knew, were more complicated than most folks realized.

"I wonder . . ." Nashville said to the feathers as he emptied the suitcase. "I wonder if you were sad when you fell to the ground. I wonder if you ever thought you'd have a chance to fly again."

ENCHANTED BALLOONS

T HE NEXT DAY WAS SATURDAY, SO
Nashville rode his bicycle down the hill to what
he referred to as his part-time job. This was putting
it a bit loftily, since old Mrs. Craw, the tiny but fierce
owner of the pet shop, didn't exactly pay him. She did,
however, allow him to play with the animals and birds,
which she claimed he had "a real way with" due to his
"unique" looks. Nashville liked the job and figured it was
one place he blended in just fine.

That afternoon, like most afternoons, Mrs. Craw left

Nashville to watch the shop while she went and played canasta.

"You're in charge," she told him as she left. "I have some imperative vocational commerce in town." Mrs. Craw was fond of words that were twice her size.

Nashville liked being alone in the shop. He liked the smell of cedar, and the sound the mice made when they sipped their water bottle. He liked the softness of puppy ears, and the NO FISHING sign in the fish tank. He especially liked the birds—the exotic, bright birds, bopping like jesters in a royal court.

Nashville looked at the birds in their cages, thinking about how odd it must feel to be able to fly, but not allowed. They looked back up at him and seemed to speak with their eyes. The caged birds seemed to all be asking the same exact question.

And their question brought up an idea, an answer, in Nashville.

"It's a bit crazy," he said. "But maybe. Just maybe . . ."

"I think we're ready," announced Nashville two hours later, holding the ends of the strings. "Here goes nothing."

And with that, he flung open the doors to the pet shop. Attached to strings and held by tight knots, the birds flew and spread out. They were like dogs on leashes, except in the sky.

"It's working!" Nashville shouted, dancing below. He looked very much like a salesman holding a colorful bunch of enchanted balloons.

He turned, made sure to be responsible and lock the door to the shop behind him, then let the birds lead the way.

And what joy the birds must have felt, the wind once again running through their feathers. For a moment the strings disappeared, and they were free.

"Now, now," said Nashville. "Be respectful. No tangling, we're not trying to make a maypole here."

One bluebird closed its eyes and imagined dipping down the meadow, past the nest where he had been hatched, the shells now crushed to powder, over the churchyard, straight up, until like rain into a puddle, the bluebird merged with bluest sky.

Nashville took a turn onto the main street of Goosepimple. As he walked, the townsfolk began to take notice and emerge, one by one, from their perfect houses.

"Why I never," a man said as he stood with a hose watering his garden.

"I want one," a little girl said, looking up at her mother.

"Meow," cried a cat, looking hungrily at the birds.

Soon, the entire street was lined with onlookers, and the murmurs and questions danced from freshly cut lawn to freshly cut lawn. Heads started popping out of upstairs windows, and it wasn't long before a reporter for the *Goosepimple Tribune* showed up with his camera.

"Is this some kind of promotional stunt?" he asked, his flashbulbs popping.

"Oh no," said Nashville. "I just feel one should take a stroll on such a fine day, don't you? Even if one happens to be a bird."

He continued past the candy shop and the five-and-dime, where children pressed their faces against the glass. He finally reached the town square, where, storming across the grass, was the squat figure of Mrs. Craw.

"Nashville! What on earth are you doing?"

"I just thought," he said quickly, "that it's such a nice

day with such a warm breeze, perhaps the birds would like to go for a stroll. . . ."

"Have you lost your mind?" Mrs. Craw shouted, trying to untangle the strings. Her face was so red and round, it, too, looked like a balloon ready to pop.

"You . . . you . . ." she was so busy figuring out what to yell, she barely noticed that the birds were dragging her heels off the ground. Yes, for a moment it seemed the wee woman could float away like the basket beneath a hot-air balloon, never to be seen again.

"Nashville!" she shouted as the birds dragged her toward the shop. "Nashville you are absolutely, irrefutably, indubitably *FIRED!*"

FEATHERS DON'T
FIT IN

W HEN NASHVILLE'S FATHER PICKED HIM
up outside the pet shop, Nashville was stand-
ing with a police officer, a reporter from the *Goosepimple
Tribune*, and several of the town's busiest busybodies.

Nashville's father didn't look very happy at all. His
brow was furrowed and creased, the way it always became
when he didn't know what to say to his son. They walked
quietly up the hill to the house in the pecan tree.

"Nashville," he said, finally breaking the silence, "I'm
not mad."

"You're not?" asked Nashville.

"No," said his father. "I don't agree with what you did, but I think, on some level, I can understand why you did it."

"I was trying to be a good friend," replied Nashville.

"And that's great," said his father. "A bit ill conceived in this case, but a tip-top quality in anyone. But . . ."

"But?" asked Nashville.

"But I think," said his father, "maybe you could spend less time with your bird friends, and more time with your classmates. Invite them over to play. Go to the field and get some grass stains."

"The other kids don't like me," Nashville said, nearly whispering. "A boy in my class even plucked one of my feathers."

His father stopped walking and knelt down in front of Nashville. He put his hands on his son's shoulders.

"They just don't know you like we do," he said. "They'd like you if they did. All I'm asking," he continued, "is that you give it a chance. I think you'll be surprised how many friends you'd make if you just try to fit in a little bit. Will you do that? For me?"

"Yes," said Nashville. "I can do that. And I think I know just what you mean."

"You'd like *what?*" asked the barber, an ancient old man with the posture of a jumbo shrimp. Nashville sat in the chair at the barbershop. Normally when he went there he simply requested a preen—a few feathers off the top—but this time he had a new request.

"I'd like you to get rid of my feathers," said Nashville. The barber looked nervous. "You sure?"

"Yes," said Nashville, who didn't seem all that sure. "Cut them. Snip them. Buzz them all off. No more feathers. Feathers don't fit in."

And so, reluctantly, the old man went to work. His scissors clipped and snipped away until the air was full of feathers. The barber's assistant, a young, soundless boy, shuffled around the shop with a broom and dustpan trying to keep up with the storm. Finally, the barber took out his electric razor, and buzzed the last bits of feather from Nashville.

"Ta-da," said the barber, brushing Nashville's neck and shoulders. "You are feather free, my young friend."

When he turned the chair around Nashville gasped—
he had never seen himself without a crown of feathers on
his head, and the sight of his own baldness was alarming.
He ran his hands over the smoothness, and it reminded
him of the way a baby's head looks. It reminded him of
an egg. It reminded him of something he hardly recognized at all.

"How do you like it?" asked the barber.

"Perfect," said Nashville in a small, cracking voice.
"Now I'll fit right in."

WHEN IT RAINS IN
GOOSEPIMPLE

THAT NIGHT IN THE VILLAGE OF GOOSEPIM-ple it began to rain.

It rained sideways and backward, down, and sometimes it seemed to rain up as well. It rained so long and so hard that after three days the news began reporting there was a chance there would be a flood, the likes of which Goosepimple had not seen in over ten years. It rained and rained while Nashville and Junebug stared out the foggy windows, their board games lying exhausted on the carpet, their markers dried up from all work and all play.

Nashville slipped away a few times, opening his toy chest, where he'd stashed the nearly finished wings. He'd worked night after night sewing on each individual feather, and he'd finished attaching the straps that would fit them to his body. He'd finished them except for one thing—one thing was missing, and he wasn't quite sure what it was.

"When will it *stop*?" Junebug asked, staring out the window.

"I don't know," said Nashville. "But it will."

He was right, of course. One day, after a week of storming, the rain stopped falling just as suddenly as it had started.

"See," said Nashville. "No weather lasts forever."

And so Nashville and Junebug put on their galoshes and went out into the world. After so many days of rain, it was cool and cleansed and damp under the pecan tree. Fat water drops fell branch-to-branch, leaf-to-leaf, onto the ground. They fell on Nashville and Junebug, who lay on the ground under the tree, too happy to be outside to care about the wet grass, too excited to see and touch everything as only two children can be after a solid week of rain.

"Hey, Nashville?" said Junebug.

"Yeah?" said her brother.

"Mom and Dad told me not to say anything about it, because you're going through something called 'growing pains.' But I have to tell you . . ." She seemed reluctant to continue in a very un-Junebug-like way. "Well, I preferred you with feathers,"

"Yeah," said Nashville, laughing, the drops from the tree falling on his bare head. "It's been too rainy out for all this fitting in."

They stayed there, watching the raindrops fall down to the ground where they disappeared. But not really, of course, they only vanished to the naked eye. The rain had come, and it had gone, but it would still be there around them; under the ground the roots of the pecan tree would have their share, and the pale threads of the grasses, and the feet of moss. A few drops would enter the mole's tunnel, and eventually, some would even find their way down to stones that, after being buried for thousands of years, would finally be able to feel the sky.

YOU'RE ALL RIGHT

NASHVILLE WORE A HAT TO SCHOOL, BUT
as soon as the bell rang, Miss Starling asked him
to please take it off. He heard murmers and whispers
around the room, but it wasn't until recess, sitting in his
tree, that someone said anything to him about his featherless head.

"Hey." It was, to Nashville's surprise and dismay,
Finnes Fowl standing below the tree.

The large boy wrapped his large hands around a low
branch. After three tries he finally hoisted one leg up as
well, then pulled and grunted himself onto the branch.

Nashville scooted aside to avoid being pushed out of the tree, or worse.

"So why'd you do it?" asked Finnes. "It looked less stupid before." He pointed to Nashville's featherless head.

Nashville was shocked. Finnes seemed to be giving him some sort of . . . compliment? Well, almost.

"That's what my sister said, too," replied Nashville. He could hardly believe he was having an actual conversation with Finnes Fowl. He tried to keep it going. "You really liked the feathers better? I thought you thought they were gross or something."

In response the boy pointed to his own leg.

"Wanna see something gross?" he asked.

Nashville looked down to see Finnes's leg, covered in vicious, red spots. It reminded Nashville of the pictures in their science book of the supernova, the dots meshed together in the center, then spreading over his whole leg.

"I've had it since I was born," explained Finnes. "I've never worn short pants before. But then you came to school, looking like you do, and I thought heck, if that pip-squeak can come to school with feathers, maybe I can show my legs. So I asked Ma to take me shopping."

"And you got yourself some shorts?" asked Nashville.

"Yup," said Finnes smiling. "I got myself some shorts. You should have seen it. Ma tried to act like it was no big deal, but then when she thought I wasn't looking, I saw her wipe her eyes."

Finnes swung his legs. He let the bare skin brush against the cool, green leaves on the tree.

"That's good," said Nashville. "This is a nice time of year for shorts."

"Right," laughed Finnes. He rubbed Nashville's head and jumped from the tree with a thud.

"You're all right, little guy." And with that, Finnes Fowl marched away to his friends, leaving Nashville alone and smiling in his tree.

QUESTIONS AND ANSWERS

SOON, IT WAS TIME FOR THE STUDENTS IN Miss Starling's class to present the answers to the questions they had placed in the box like buzzing bees.

The girl with a freckle on every spare bit of skin made her way to the front of the room.

"Go on," prompted Miss Starling. "What was your question?"

The girl turned red, her freckles merging with the rest of her blushing skin.

"My . . . my question was . . ." She stopped. "I don't really think I should read it."

"Why not?" asked Miss Starling.

"Because," the girl said quietly, "it's about someone in our class."

A look of shock swept over Miss Starling's face, but only for the briefest moment. She took a deep breath.

"Go on," she said.

"It was about Nashville," explained the girl. "But that was at the beginning of school, and I'd never seen anyone like him. But now I don't wonder my question anymore. So I picked a new question, one about how flowers grow."

The girl went on to tell the class about water and sunshine and how the plants could grow.

"The earth laughs in flowers," she said, quoting from her paper.

The next to present was a boy with teeth like loose shutters. He explained about gas and matter and hydrogen and space

"When it is dark enough," he finished, "you can finally see the stars."

Miss Starling smiled. "You can take your seat now."

But the boy kept standing.

"That wasn't my real question," he said, looking down at his shoes.

"Oh?" asked Miss Starling.

"Mine was actually about Nashville, too."

"What was it?" asked Nashville. Everyone turned to look at him.

"I wanted to know if you were, like, a *mutant*. Like a superhero, I mean," the boy quickly continued. The class laughed at this.

"And?" asked Miss Starling.

"I guess he is, kind of," said the boy. "But not in the usual way."

The boy sat down. One by one the rest of the class stood and read their questions from the beginning of the school year. Braver now, they looked at Nashville as they read.

What is he?

Why is he?

Was he a mistake?

Almost all the questions, it seemed, had been about Nashville. But his classmate's answers, Nashville realized, were not really about him at all.

"I hate how tall I am," said a girl taller than the boys. "But it's not that big of a deal."

"It's like, who cares if you have a stupid stutter, or feathers, or whatever," said another boy, hardly stuttering at all. "None of that really matters."

"Actually," said the prettiest girl in school, as she focused her eyes right on Nashville, "I wish we all had feathers," she continued. "I think they're beautiful."

Now it was Nashville's turn to blush.

"Nashville," said Miss Starling, interrupting his thoughts. "I believe it's your turn."

Nashville nodded, stood, and slowly made his way to the front of the class. It was the end of the school day, the air warm. But everyone in Miss Starling's room was wide-awake.

Nashville cleared his throat. He did not have a paper to read from, and instead spoke while looking out at the class.

"My question," he said, "is *why can't I fly?*"

"And?" said Miss Starling. "What is your answer?"

"I don't have one," answered Nashville.

"Why not?" asked Miss Starling.

"Because," said Nashville. He stopped then, looked at his class, the one he'd found so scary at the beginning of the year. The ones that now made him brave with their kind words.

"Because," he said, "I think I *can*."

WHO'S NEXT?

T HE CLASS SAT VERY STILL AFTER NASH-
ville's statement, and for what seemed like an eter-
nity, didn't make a sound. And then, finally, the silence
was broken by none other than Finnes Fowl.

"Prove it," said Finnes, with more joy than mocking
in his voice. "If you can fly, then prove it."

"Okay," replied Nashville. "I will."

And with that statement, Nashville smiled a giant-
sized smile, turned, and ran out the door of the
schoolhouse.

"Nashville!" yelled Miss Starling. "Stop! Come back
here! Where are you going?"

But Nashville did not stop.

He hooted. He hollered. He sounded what could only be called a barbaric yawp.

Nashville ran and ran and ran all the way into the village of Goosepimple. He ran through his favorite park, and around his favorite tree; he waved to the puppets in the puppet shop, the old men gossiping on their porches, and several barking dogs.

He was, in his own way, saying good-bye to Goosepimple.

The last place he stopped was the pet shop. A closed sign hung on the door—likely due to Miss Craw playing canasta—but through the windows he could see the cages hanging around the store, birds hopping from perch to perch, or tossing around seeds, or staring at themselves in the mirror thinking they had a friend.

And then, all of a sudden, he knew exactly what to do. He found himself doing something that, until that day, he would have thought impossible.

Nashville broke into the pet shop.

It wasn't very hard actually. Nobody in Goosepimple

locked their doors, and even when they did, they hid the key somewhere close. Nashville knew the key to the pet shop was under a stone turtle by the door.

The birds started squawking their alarm the minute he walked inside.

"Keep it down," he said. "You can yell all you want once you're out."

First Nashville propped the front door wide open. Next he flung open the large windows to the shop. And then, one by one, he unlocked every birdcage in the store. He stood back, waiting for them all to burst forward, but to his astonishment, not one of them moved.

"Haven't you ever heard the saying free as a bird?" he asked. "What are you waiting for?"

Finally, a small lovebird hopped onto the edge of her cage door.

"That's it. Go on," Nashville whispered. "Be brave. Be bold."

The lovebird puffed her chest once as if making a final decision, then flew out of her cage and out the door of the shop.

"Woohoo!" shouted Nashville.

The birds tilted their heads to the side. What a peculiar thing had just occurred.

"Who's next?" asked Nashville.

The lovebird's mate, not wanting to be alone, was the next to leave his cage.

"Good choice," encouraged Nashville. "Bravo."

It must be true what they say, because those birds of a feather began flocking together, right out the door to the shop. It all happened in one great whoosh! It was like a tornado, the whirlwind of birds and wings and feathers that rushed out the door and window, Nashville in the center of it all, spinning, arms up, yelling like madman.

He followed them, still hooting and hollering, out the door to the shop. He watched them get smaller and smaller as they flew away, like a bunch of balloons accidentally—or in this case quite on purpose—released. He made a mental note to leave instructions on his piggy bank, a note saying that its contents should be paid to Miss Craw for the birds.

"I'm coming, too!" shouted Nashville after the birds. "I'll be right behind you!"

THE FINAL FEATHER

W HEN NASHVILLE ARRIVED HOME, HE could hear his parents once again talking in the kitchen. The phone was ringing over and over, and when his father answered, Nashville heard words like *expulsion* and *school grounds*. Words like *break-in* and *pet shop*. After his father hung up the phone, Nashville heard more clips of conversation. He knew what they were discussing, and he crept around behind the pecan tree to avoid it.

But when Nashville rounded to corner, he found

himself face-to-face with Junebug climbing down the ladder to the fort.

"What are you doing?" asked Nashville.

Junebug smiled her biggest, goofiest smile at Nashville.

"I found your wings," she said. "They're amazing."

"Wh-what?" asked Nashville. He wasn't sure what to say.

"Or," Junebug continued, "I should say they were almost amazing."

"No," Nashville said, climbing up the tree so fast his foot slipped twice and he nearly fell. "What did you do to them?"

When he reached the fort, he saw the wings there, perfect and intact, not decorated with sparkles or glitter or any of the other Junebug crafting fears that had flashed through his mind.

"They're done," said Nashville in awe. He wasn't quite sure why, but the wings seemed like they were perfect.

"But what did you do?" he asked.

"Everyone's looking for you," Junebug replied.

"But what did you *do*?" Nashville asked again.

"I know you have to leave," said Junebug. "I know, and it's okay. I won't tell them to come up until you're ready to go."

"But . . ."

"I added the last feather," said Junebug. "This one." She pointed to a perfect feather at the tip of the wing, one that made it all come together.

"This one," she smiled, "is the one I found after that rainstorm. I looked it up, and wouldn't you know it—this lucky feather came from the wing of a Nashville warbler."

A FAREWELL CAKE

NASHVILLE STAYED IN THE FORT AND GOT things organized while Junebug went downstairs.

"He's in his fort," Junebug told her parents. "But he really wants to be alone for a little while."

"I'm worried," said his mother, her face washed in a rainy-day light. "I wish things were easier for him."

"I know what we should do," chimed Junebug. "We should make him a cake. Just like you did when he was being stubborn and wouldn't hatch from his egg."

"A cake," said her mother. She gave Junebug a knowing look. "Now that just might work."

"But he's in big trouble," protested Nashville's father. "He ran from school. He freed all the birds in town!"

But one look from his wife and daughter, and he went to fetch the mixing bowl. They put in the ingredients—eggs and flour and sugar—and Junebug stirred with ancient eggbeaters. She held out the bowl of batter to her father.

"Put something in," she told him.

"Pardon?"

"It's a Nashville cake, so you need to put in some Nashville. Watch, I'll show you." She held up an imaginary container and turned it over the bowl, pretending to shake the contents into the mix. "I'm pouring in one box of the feathers on his head, looking silly when he comes down for breakfast."

"And I," said her mother pretending to pour, "am putting in a dollop of the way he sings made-up songs when he thinks no one is listening."

"His wonderful taste in hats," added Junebug. "His sense of direction."

They put in every hum and every hiccup; every sun and cloud that had passed across his face; every lovely thing that they loved about Nashville and some, in truth, that they had failed to appreciate, as well.

"I put in every feather," added his father quietly. "I hope he can forgive me someday for telling him to fit in."

They also remembered to add some real sugar, and butter, and flour, and when the batter was finally done, they poured it into the baking pans, opened the oven door, and put everything inside to bake. Slowly the ingredients started to mix, the kitchen and house filling with the delicious smell of cake.

SEND ME POSTCARDS

WHEN THE CAKE WAS FINISHED, JUNEBUG took her mother's and father's hands and brought them to the very top floor of the house—to the dazzling, oversized window. The window his mother had sat at ten years earlier singing, wishing, and waiting for a cornflower-blue egg to hatch.

And there stood Nashville, wearing his homemade wings.

"Oh," said his father.

"My baby," said his mother.

Nashville's parents did not have much more to say.

They knew without words, (in that way parents always seem to know), what Nashville had already decided. Perhaps they had always known—having in their own way willed Nashville into the world—that he could not stay. Perhaps they knew better than other folks that some things are too extraordinary to stay in our world for very long, and so the time they are here should be taken as a gift, as a pause for a moment in front of us, as a hummingbird at the bell of a flower.

"Do you have your good scarf?" asked his father, his hands shaking ever so slightly as he hugged his son and touched his wings. "And your long underwear?" he continued, standing back and looking at his son. "Perhaps you should bring an extra pair of socks. Weather can be . . . very unpredictable."

"Oh, I almost forgot," cried his mother. "We baked you a cake."

There, in her arms, was the finished cake, expertly decorated by his family. It was Nashville all right—same smile. But there was something extra as well. There, frosted and attached to each side of the cake, were wings—two beautiful, beautiful wings.

"Thank you," he said to his family. "It's the perfect cake."

"It was Junebug's idea," they explained.

Nashville's father held his mother as she dabbed her eyes with a handkerchief, and watched Junebug walk her big brother to the window.

The wind blew and the white buds danced outside. Junebug looked at Nashville, and then at the window. She imagined him flying away, farther and farther, his shadow lengthening over the endless ground, until he was just a speck of white and gold wings in the distant sky.

"Will you write me?" she asked.

"I'll send you postcards," said Nashville. "I'll send them on the wind."

And then, as strangely as he'd come into their world, Nashville spread his wings and flew away from his mother, father, and sister; he flew away from the house in the pecan tree into the cinnamon air, so sweet.

THE LEAP

AND SO, WITH THE FIRST GOLDEN GLOW OF sunlight rising over the hills, Nashville glided to a distant treetop. There, in the pine bough, he was out of sight of his family, and able to gather his thoughts.

"On the one hand," Nashville said to himself, "I'll start really flying. Not just floating, but also flapping. On the other hand . . ."

If a scientist could have taken a microscopic cross-section of Nashville's heart at that moment, this is what they would have seen: a map of the sky. A map that had been folded and refolded too many times, like an overdreamed dream, the crease lines becoming soft and fuzzy. The arrow on the map's compass only pointed one way, and that way was the sky.

"Be brave," Nashville said to himself. "Be brave."

And then, to his surprise and delight, he glided on an updraft high, high into the sky.

"I'm doing it," he said, quite shocked. "I'm really flying."

He continued to glide, over the hill and pecan tree, circling like a bird, like a moon orbiting the only home he'd ever known.

A lullaby of clouds encircled Nashville and floated him like a ball across the syllables of a sing-along song in the sky. He tried to think how he'd describe it all to Junebug—piercing the wind and touching nothing but air was like swimming, but not quite. Like freefalling on a roller coaster. But not quite.

Nashville finally began to flap the wings, and that worked as well. He changed direction, and flew over the entire town.

Nashville circled the school, but the school yard was quiet and empty, and he knew they would all be having reading lessons that time of day. He saw all the balls, Frisbees, and toys on the roof. He dipped low, kicking the balls and throwing toys down to the ground, wondering what all his classmates would think if they could see him now. He pictured Miss Starling's smile, and his whole class whooping and clapping for him. He pictured Finnes Fowl in his shorts, shouting "Way to go, little guy."

Nashville felt it all—the singing of the seasons, the warmth of wind, the sailing of ships, the migration of birds, and the simple, perfect smell of the ground after rain. He felt that there was nothing under his skin but light, and were he to ever fall to the ground, he would merely shine.

He felt all these wonderful things until he heard the worst sound—the sound of something breaking.

THE FALL

NASHVILLE HEARD THE SNAP, FOLLOWED by a rip, followed by the feeling of the wings slipping, falling from his body. The wings first broke along the main support—a loud cracking sound like a bone. Next, the smaller pieces of wood all began to shatter, and this sounded more like branches being stepped on in the forest.

When the wings had broken in enough places, the leather material and feathers began folding and buckling like a collapsing umbrella. This meant that Nashville began to fall, hard and fast, the wind whipping against his face.

He was falling, but Nashville did not scream or cry. He knew he would hit the ground, that's how gravity works. But before that could occur, something very strange, and very lovely, appeared to him.

Now, it is worth noting all the things that did not appear. All the things he did not see or hear or recall as he fell.

Nashville did not see the light inside his egg, how dark it was, how the shadows danced, or the sound of his mother's voice singing.

Nashville did not see geese flying south for winter overhead, or catch a glimpse of their perfect V shape.

He did not recall Magnolia, the soft down of her stomach feathers, or how fast her heart beat when he held her.

Nor did he hear the sound of the countless people who had pointed and laughed at him over his ten short years.

He did not see the sky the color of spider tents, or feel the evening as cold as fish scales, or marvel at the sunset glowing like the inside of a ripe plum.

He did not recall his father teaching him to throw a punch, just in case.

He did not remember dusk. A meadow. Long grass, the first buzzes and hums of night insects all around him as he lay on the damp earth with Junebug by his side. He was not covered with vines that had grown so fast, twisting up, diving in and out of each button-hole on his vest.

He did not see artichokes or blowfish or the purple sunset or the frill-necked lizard. He did not see spiderwebs or eclipses or a star-nosed mole. He saw absolutely no platypuses at all.

This is what he noticed:

As he fell, for one simple, splendid, golden moment, he felt nothing but gratitude; gratitude for his old soul and true heart, for his strange looks and strange beginnings, for all the things that made him Nashville. And the moment this feeling flowed through him, something inside him started to blossom. This great leap began to bring about a great change, and Nashville was finally ready to let it transform him.

WAKE UP, JUNEBUG

"J UNEBUG," WHISPERED NASHVILLE. HE stood over his sister in her bed, the night-light's glow beginning to blend into the dawn.

"Junebug, wake up," Nashville said, shaking her small shoulder. Junebug stirred, and then opened her eyes. She looked up at her brother. There, in the first light, Junebug smiled at the sight of Nashville.

"You came back," she said, slowly waking. She put her toes on the cold wood floor, and tiptoed around Nashville.

"The wings," she said, walking around him. "They're different. Did you add feathers? Are they bigger?

They're magnificent, Nashville, like angel wings," gushed Junebug. "They're like nothing I've ever seen."

Slowly, slowly, Nashville began flexing his shoulder muscles.

Slowly, slowly, the wings began to unfold. After a few moments, Nashville was able to extend them both fully.

"They're so beautiful," said Junebug. She inspected them closely, looking at how each feather overlapped perfectly, colored white and brown and gold. "I . . . I just can't believe these are the same wings you built. They are, aren't they?"

Nashville just smiled, and looked to the corner of the room. Junebug followed his gaze into the shadows where something lay against the wall—large and slumped over, shrouded in darkness. Junebug crept closer, closer. Suddenly the truth swept in like the most wonderful breeze.

Junebug smiled.

And she cried.

There in the corner, broken apart and sad, were the remnants of the wings Nashville had built.

BEYOND THE LAUGHING SKY

"THEY'RE REAL," WHISPERED JUNEBUG. "But how?"

"I think . . ." Nashville said with a smile. "I think I had them all along."

Then he took his sister's hand, and led her to the top floor of the house, to the edge of the dazzling, oversized window.

And there, like Peter and Wendy, they stepped out of the window, and up into the never-never land of the air. Junebug clung to her brother at first, but after a few moments she was so entranced by what she saw, she forgot to be afraid at all.

Nashville and Junebug looked below them, and felt the power of seeing a world so familiar from a new, more distant perspective. They flew over the fields where they had run together, and the streams where they had fished and caught frogs. They flew over games they had played, and songs they had sung, marshmallows they had roasted, and sand castles they had built and destroyed. They flew over stacks of books they had read together, and lightning bugs they had caught together; over piles of leaves, and piles of pancakes. They flew over memories of all the years, all the days that seemed so different, but so perfect, when seen from a distance.

Now, here they were flying through chimney smoke and rain-heavy clouds. They flew lower, skimming the tops of houses, and from this place, Nashville and Junebug were able to hear the singing of the trees.

The trees sang of all the things they protected from the cold—of the bluebirds bundled inside together for warmth, and of the hollow nooks where squirrels slept, dreaming, their minds a map of nuts hidden like buried treasure.

They sang songs that tasted of apple pie, of plums and peaches and lemonade grown on the trees. They sang of their grand outfits of moss and mushrooms growing wild. They sang of the rich, dark dirt where the worms and the moles tickled their roots.

They sang of all the trees to go before them and be made into homes and boats, their wood used to make chapels, and doors, and cradles.

But mostly, they sang of a fort in a tree where a boy and a girl would go on grand adventures; they sang of the children swinging, climbing, playing, and building crowns from their leaves. The trees sang softly and sweetly about their branches always being open to little birds. Nashville and Junebug knew the only way was to sing along, and so they joined in with the trees, floating all together for just a little while above the whole, dazzling world.

And what about that world? For Nashville and Junebug were not the only ones awake in Goosepimple.

"Mama. Mama, wake up!" It was a boy standing by his mother's bed.

His mother rubbed the sleep from her eyes, put on a robe, and followed her son. She looked out the window. She rubbed her eyes again.

"Well I never . . ." She ran to the hall, picked up the phone, and called across the street to Mrs. Craw, and Mrs. Craw looked out the window as well.

"Impossible!" cried Mrs. Craw. She picked up the phone and called Dr. Larkin. Dr. Larkin called Miss Starling. And so on and so on, until every woman in curlers and man in slippers were looking up at the sky to get a glimpse of Nashville and Junebug; to hear the faintest, distant, sweet sound of laughter in the sky.

"Impossible," they all said, though the word didn't have quite the huff and puff that it used to.

A SONG TO SING
YOU HOME

THE MORNING WAS THE COLOR OF PALE blue eggshells, the golden yolk of the sun rising in the east. Nashville and Junebug flew low to the ground, where they could hear the last cricket songs of dawn, where they could see their shadows fly along beneath them, the shadows of a boy and girl running along below them, playing and whispering to one another in the long grass. The air was cool—it whipped their hair back and reddened their cheeks. Nashville tried to press the moment into his memory—tried to find a place

he could keep it safe and take it out when he needed it, maybe in the cotton depths of a pocket, or the snap of a locket, or the bottom of a dark trunk. Couldn't he keep all this there—the closeness of clouds, the rooftops and trees like toys below, his sister by his side? He didn't know.

When they returned to the house, they sat on a branch and watched the sun finish rising.

"You could take me with you," Junebug finally said.

"I can't do that," Nashville replied sadly. "Not in a really real way, you know that. You need to stay here."

Junebug thought about this for a moment. There'd be nobody to play with in the fort, and the maps they'd made would yellow and curl with age. Maybe eventually they would replace his nest with a bed or a cradle, the perches with sturdy, normal chairs.

One day, not long from then, Junebug would ask her father, "Where do you think he is now?" And so her parents would take out the globe, and point to a magical place far, far away. And they'd smile, and they'd imagine Nashville flying, soaring, gliding, and seeing the world over the pines. They'd imagine him free.

But for this last moment, her brother was still there.

So Junebug tilted her head to the side as if to listen to the softest music.

"Hey," she asked. "Do you hear that?"

Nashville listened as well. He listened with his whole self, and finally he did hear it. It was the song of a tree. But this one was different—more like it came from inside his own throat, for it was the pecan tree he'd lived in singing, and it was singing a song just for him.

"I do," he smiled. "I do hear it."

Nashville knew that it was time for him to fly away, but no matter where he went, there would always be this: a whisper, a hum, a lullaby. A song singing out over the pines; through the clouds, the lonely hours, and over the rooftops of the world. A song hatched from an egg. A song to sing him home.

THE END OF SPRING

THE HOUSE WAS QUIETER WITHOUT
Nashville.

Well, not *quieter* really, but there seemed to be less of *something*. Junebug felt it, but couldn't put it into words. It was as if some magic had been peeled away like wallpaper.

Perhaps it was because when she looked out the window, Junebug still saw Nashville's birdbath covered in green moss and crawling ivy. Perhaps it was the dust gathering on his bureau and his tin soldier toys. And perhaps, just maybe, it seemed something was missing because someone was; Nashville had been gone for most of the spring, the world turning green, smelling of rain-storms and frogs.

Junebug grew accustomed to this new, quieter house, though odd thoughts did sneak up on her from time to time, the main one being just this: How could she have known? How was she to have known that the last time she saw her brother come downstairs for breakfast with his feathers a mess would be the *last* time? The last card game, the last adventure, the last thumb-fight over the first slice of cake. You rarely know, in the moment, when it's the last time you'll do something. Most of the time, the whole thing just sneaks away in the night, never to be seen or heard from again, not even sending back so much as a postcard to say hello.

Oh, there were stories of course, about where Nashville had gone. People claimed to see him just about every-where, doing just about anything. Some said he'd joined the circus, made friends with the man with webbed feet and the yak girl with horns. Some said they saw him hopping trains like a hobo. Some said he'd never existed at all.

But who would ever *really* know what had become of Nashville?

Junebug would, that's who.

It happened at the end of spring, when the trees had turned from newborn lime to emerald and bottle green. The blossoms were in full bloom. Junebug awoke as always—tangled in her sheets, rubbing sleep from her eyes, rolling over to look out the window and see if there was anything new in the world. There never was. Until, that is, the day the honeysuckle arrived.

It was just a small yellow-orange blossom, nothing too exciting or unusual. What was strange was *how* it was placed, ever so carefully on the edge of her sill. It hadn't blown there, hadn't crept up the wall on its own. The closest honeysuckle bush was at the bottom of the hill, behind the high, high fence.

It could only, she thought, have been flown here.

"Nashville?" she said, though she already knew the answer.

Junebug never told anyone about that honeysuckle that appeared many times at her window that spring. She never told anyone about the bird she would catch glimpses of from time to time, the one that felt so familiar, the one that would appear at the edge of her vision, but be gone by the time she turned her head. She never told anyone that she knew it was Nashville—knew without a doubt that it was her brother, *her brother*, who had been granted the power to transform into what he was always meant to be.

CODA

IMPOSSIBLE

THERE IS A HOUSE. IT SITS PERCHED IN THE branches of the largest pecan tree in the village of Goosepimple. The tree grows on the top of a high hill, and the hill overlooks a small, perfect village, where the sun always shines, the grass is always mowed, and nobody ever, ever, *ever* uses the word impossible.

It's not a law. It's not patrolled or policed. It's just that everyone in Goosepimple remembers that day, much like any other, when the old men gossiping on their porch looked up, up, up to the sky.

"Why, it looks like an angel in an updraft."

"Naw, it looks like some sort of giant bird."

"Naw," said the third old man. "It looks like . . . *Nash-ville*."

Oh, there were tourists just passing through of course, those who stopped in to ask the old widow who worked in the visitor center.

"Is it true?" they asked. "Did a boy in this town grow wings? Did he really fly?"

"Oh, yes," the widow would say. "Nashville grew wings. Nashville could fly."

"Fiddlesticks," a Southern gentleman would say to the widow. "Folks can't fly. That's impossible."

"What an absurd little word," the widow would reply.

"Pardon?"

"You said impossible," the widow would point out. "There ain't no such thing. There's things you've seen and things you may not have, but there ain't nothing that's impossible, sugar."

ACKNOWLEDGMENTS

I am grateful to Brenda Bowen for believing first; Jake Currie for always reading; Nathan Winstanley for always listening; Zach Robbins for laughing with me; Lola Cuevas, Ray Cuevas, Sheryl Bercier, and Rita DeVarennes for cheering; Sarah Wartell for reminding me to see things more beautifully; Carlyle Massey for promising it would get better; Mary and Edward Rossi for a room with a writing desk; Massachusetts Audubon for allowing me to hold a bird to my ear and listen to its heart. And to Nancy Conescu: You believed in Nashville from the very first day he was hatched.

Thank you, thank you, thank you.

ABOUT THE AUTHOR

Michelle Cuevas graduated from Williams College and holds a master of fine arts in creative writing from the University of Virginia, where she received the Henry Hoyns Fellowship. She has worked in the youth education department at The Whitney Museum of American Art in New York, and is now a full-time writer living in Berkshire County, Massachusetts.

ISSUES IN NURSING ADMINISTRATION

ISSUES IN NURSING ADMINISTRATION

Selected Readings

Mary Jane Ward, RN, PhD, FAAN
Professor and Executive Associate Dean
Nell Hodgson Woodruff School of Nursing
Emory University
Atlanta, Georgia

Sylvia A. Price, RN, PhD
Associate Professor
College of Nursing
University of Tennessee, Memphis
Memphis, Tennessee

 **Mosby Year Book**

St. Louis   Baltimore   Boston   Chicago   London   Philadelphia   Sydney   Toronto

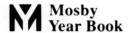

**Mosby
Year Book**

Dedicated to Publishing Excellence

Editor: N. Darlene Como
Editorial Assistant: Barbara M. Carroll
Project Manager: Carol Sullivan Wiseman
Production Editor: Diana Lyn Laulainen
Designer: Susan Lane

Copyright © 1991 Mosby-Year Book, Inc.
A Mosby imprint of Mosby-Year Book, Inc.

Printed in the United States of America

Mosby-Year Book, Inc.
11830 Westline Industrial Drive
St. Louis, MO 63146

Library of Congress Cataloging in Publication Data

Issues in nursing administration: selected readings / [edited by]
   Mary Jane Ward, Sylvia A. Price.
      p.   cm.
      Includes bibliographical references and index.
      ISBN   0-8016-6063-7   : $25.95
      1. Nursing services — Administration.   2. Leadership.   I. Ward,
   Mary Jane.   II.   Price, Sylvia Anderson.
      [DNLM: 1.   Administrative Personnel — organization & administration —
   collected works.   2.   Nursing Services — organization &
   administration.   3.   Personnel Management — collected works.   WY   105
   I86]
   RT89.I87   1991
   362.1'73'068 — dc20
   DNLM/DLC
   for Library of Congress   90-13684
                                                                                     CIP

GW/DC   9   8   7   6   5   4   3   2   1

Contributors

Judith W. Alexander, RN, PhD
Assistant Professor, College of Nursing, University of South Carolina, Columbia, SC

Myrtle K. Aydelotte, RN, PhD, FAAN
Dean Emeritus, College of Nursing, University of Iowa, Iowa City, Iowa

Katherine Pam Bailey, RN, MS
Associate Chief, Nursing Service for Education, Veterans Administration Center, Minneapolis, Minn.

Alan D. Bauerschmidt, PhD
Professor, College of Business, University of South Carolina, Columbia, SC

Corinne L. Bergmann, RN, MS
Lecturer, Department of Nursing, California State University, Los Angeles, Calif.

Rachel Z. Booth, RN, PhD
School of Nursing, University of Maryland, Baltimore, Md.

Marie Annette Brown, RN, PhD
Department of Community Health Care Systems, School of Nursing, University of Washington, Seattle, Wash.

Stephen C. Bushardt, DBA
Professor of Management, University of Southern Mississippi, Hattiesburg, Miss.

Cynthia Flynn Capers, RN, PhD
Assistant Professor, Nursing Department, LaSalle University, Philadelphia, Pa.

Harriett S. Chaney, RN, PhD
Associate Professor, School of Nursing, University of Texas Medical Branch, Galveston, Tex.

Carol Chorba , MBA, RRA
Assistant Professor, College of Health Professions, University of Illinois, Chicago, Ill.

Paula J. Christensen, RN, PhD
Associate Professor and Chair, Department of Nursing, Rockford College, Rockford, Ill.

Luther Christman, RN, PhD, FAAN
Dean Emeritus, College of Nursing, Rush University, Chicago, Ill.

H. Westley Clark
Chief, Substance Abuse Inpatient Unit, Veterans Administration Medical Center, San Francisco, Calif.

Harriet Van Ess Coeling, RN, PhD
Assistant Professor, School of Nursing, Kent State University, Kent, Ohio

Dorothy E. Deremo, RN, MSN, CNAA
Vice President of Nursing Services, Henry Ford Hospital, Detroit, Mich.

Peter F. Drucker, PhD
Clarke Professor of Social Science and Management, Claremont Graduate School, Claremont, Calif.

Sandra R. Edwardson, RN, PhD
Associate Professor, School of Nursing, University of Minnesota, Minneapolis, Minn.

Mary J. Farley, RN, PhD
Assistant Professor, School of Nursing, University of Colorado, Denver, Colo.

Geraldene Felton, RN, EdD, FAAN
Professor and Dean, College of Nursing, University of Iowa, Iowa City, Iowa

Sandra J. Foss, RN, MS
Utilization Review Coordinator, Pacifi Care of Texas,
San Antonio, Tex.

Aubrey R. Fowler Jr, PhD
Chairman, Department of Marketing and Management,
University of Central Arkansas, Conway, Ark.

Cynthia M. Freund, RN, PhD
Associate Professor and Chair, School of Nursing, University
of North Carolina, Chapel Hill, NC

Lois Friss, DrPH
Associate Professor, School of Public Administration, University
of Southern California, Los Angeles, Calif.

Sara T. Fry, RN, PhD, FAAN
Assistant Professor, School of Nursing, University of Maryland,
Baltimore, Md.

Phyllis B. Giovannetti, RN, ScD
Professor and Director, Research Facilitation Office, Faculty of
Nursing, University of Alberta, Edmonton, Alberta, Canada

Robert L. Goldman
Consultant, Health Care Management Consortium,
San Francisco, Calif.

Rosalinda M. Haddon, RN, MSN
President, Symmetry Associates, Dover, NJ

Edward J. Halloran, RN, PhD, FAAN
School of Nursing, University of North Carolina, Chapel Hill, NC

Elizabeth A. Hefferin, RN, DrPH, FAAN
Associate Chief, Nursing Service for Research, Veterans
Administration Wadsworth Medical Center, Los Angeles, Calif.

F. Theodore Helmer, PhD
Associate Professor, College of Business, Northern Arizona
University, Flagstaff, Ariz.

Beverly Henry, RN, PhD, FAAN
James R. Dougherty Jr Centennial Professor of Nursing Admin-
istration, School of Nursing, University of Texas at Austin,
Austin, Tex.

Frederick Herzberg, PhD
University of Utah, Salt Lake City, Utah

Alice S. Hill, RN, PhD
Assistant Professor, University of Texas Medical Branch,
Graduate School of Biomedical Science, Galveston, Tex.

Charlotte B. Hoelzel, RN, MS
Assistant Administrator of Direct Patient Care, Albermarle
Hospital, Elizabeth City, NC

Mary Hoeppner, RN, MS
Nursing Education Coordinator, Association of Public Teaching
Hospitals, University of Minneapolis Hospital and Clinic,
Minneapolis, Minn.

Jo Anne Horsley, RN, PhD, FAAN
Professor, School of Nursing, Oregon Health Sciences University,
Portland, Ore.

Bonnie Mowinski Jennings, RN, DNSc, Lt Col,
USANC
Intergovernmental Fellow, National Center for Nursing Research,
National Institutes of Health, Bethesda, Md.

Susan Brakke Jeska, RN, BAN, MBA
Director, Education Services, Department of Nursing Services,
University of Minnesota Hospital and Clinic, Minneapolis, Minn.

Jo Ann Johnson, RN, DPA
Professor, Department of Nursing, California State University,
Los Angeles, Calif.

Judith Moore Johnson, RN, BA
Associate Director, Health Management Systems,
Minneapolis, Minn.

Cheryl Bland Jones, RN, MS
College of Nursing, University of South Carolina, Columbia, SC

Katherine R. Jones, RN, PhD
Assistant Professor, School of Nursing, University of California,
Los Angeles, Calif.

Fremont E. Kast, MBA, PhD
Professor of Management and Organization, Graduate School of
Business, University of Washington, Seattle, Wash.

Jean Ann Kelley, RN, EdD, FAAN
Professor Emeritus, School of Nursing, University of Alabama,
Birmingham, Ala.

Robert E. Kelley, PhD
Graduate School of Industrial Administration, Carnegie Mellon
University, Pittsburgh, Pa.

Marylou Kiley, RN, PhD
Research Assistant to Senior Vice President and Director of
Nursing, University Hospitals, Cleveland, Ohio

Andrew Kumiega, BS
Research Assistant, Department of Industrial Engineering, University of Illinois, Chicago, Ill.

Jeanette Lancaster, RN, PhD
Professor and Dean, School of Nursing, University of Virginia, Charlottesville, Va.

Wade Lancaster, BBA, MBA
Marketing Analyst, University of Virginia Health Sciences Center, Charlottesville, Va.

Libbie Landureth, RN, MSN
Computer Services Coordinator, Education Department, County Hospital District, Houston, Tex.

Elaine Larson, RN, PhD, FAAN
M. Adelaide Nutting Chair in Clinical Nursing, School of Nursing, Johns Hopkins University, Baltimore, Md.

Helen LeClair, RN, BSN
Director of Nursing Service, Munroe Regional Hospital, Ocala, Fla.

Pat Chikamoto Lee, RN, MN
Director, Personnel Systems in Nursing Services, University Hospital, Seattle, Wash.

Kathleen I. Mac Pherson, RN, PhD
Associate Professor and Associate Dean for Graduate Affairs, School of Nursing, University of Southern Maine, Portland, Me.

Bruce McCain, PhD
Research Analyst, Society National Bank, Cleveland, Ohio

Joanne Comi McCloskey, RN, PhD, FAAN
Professor, Chairperson, Organizations and Systems, College of Nursing, University of Iowa, Iowa City, Iowa

Mary L. McHugh, RN, PhD
Director, Research and Development,
St. Frances Regional Medical Center,
Wichita, Kan.

Afaf Ibrahim Meleis, RN, PhD, FAAN
Professor, Department of Mental Health, Community and Administrative Nursing, School of Nursing, University of California, San Francisco, Calif.

Lawrence J. Nelson
Bioethics Consultation Group, Berkeley, Calif.

Dena A. Norton, MAJ, ANC
Nursing Research Service, Walter Reed Army Medical Center, Washington, DC

Shirley F. Olson, DBA
Associate Professor, Else School of Management, Millsaps College, Jackson, Miss.

Cheryl Patterson, RN, MSN
Coordinator, Patient Classification Project, Department of Nursing, University Hospitals, Cleveland, Ohio

Dottie Perlman, BA, NCC
Director of Human Resources, Centel Federal Systems, Inc., Reston, Va.

Susan K. Pfoutz, RN, PhD
Assistant Professor, Eastern Michigan University, Ypsilanti, Mich.

J. David Pincus, PhD
Assistant Professor, Communications Department, California State University, Fullerton, Calif.

Tim Porter-O'Grady, RN, EdM
President, Affiliated Dynamics, Inc., Atlanta, Ga.

Gaye W. Poteet, RN, EdD
Professor and Assistant Dean of Graduate Program, East Carolina School of Nursing, Greenville, NC

Muriel A. Poulin, RN, EdD, FAAN
Professor, Boston University, Boston, Mass.

Sylvia A. Price, RN, PhD
Associate Professor, College of Nursing, University of Tennessee, Memphis, Memphis, Tenn.

Peggy L. Primm, RN, PhD
Staff Development Associates, Des Moines, Iowa

Karen A. Rieder, CDR, NC, USN
Director of Research, Naval School of Health Sciences, Bethesda, Md.

Carol A. Romano, RN, MS, FAAN
Director, Nursing Information Systems and Quality Assurance Clinical Center, National Institutes of Health, Bethesda, Md.

James E. Rosenzweig, MBA, PhD
Professor of Management and Organization, Graduate School of Business, University of Washington, Seattle, Wash.

June A. Schmele, RN, PhD
Associate Professor, College of Nursing, University of Oklahoma, Oklahoma City, Okla.

Sharon Schneller, RN, MS, CCRN
Critical Care Educator, St. Paul-Ramsey Medical Center, St. Paul, Minn.

Jean E. Schore
Consultant, Healthcare Management Consortium, San Franscisco, Calif.

Judy Shorr, RN, MS
Nursing Personnel Coordinator, University Hospital, Seattle, Wash.

Lillian M. Simms, RN, PhD
Associate Professor, School of Nursing, University of Michigan, Ann Arbor, Mich.

Toni C. Smith, RN, MS
Coordinator, Methods/Procedures and Quality Control, University of Rochester Medical Center, Rochester, NY

Margaret D. Sovie, RN, PhD, FAAN
Associate Executive Director, Hospital of the University of Pennsylvania, Philadelphia, Pa.

Barbara J. Stevens Barnum, RN, PhD, FAAN
Adjunct Professor, Department of Nursing Education, Teachers College, Columbia University, New York, NY

Carol A. Stillwaggon, RN, EdD
Vice President and Director of Nursing, Saint Francis Hospital and Medical Center, Hartford, Conn.

Katherin D. Sudela, RN, MSN
Pediatric Nurse Specialist, Bowden Pediatric Nursing Services, Inc., Houston, Tex.

Judith Szalapski, RN, MS
Director, Educaton and Staff Development Department, Division of Patient Care Services, Hennepin County Medical Center, Minneapolis, Minn.

George J. Takacs, MA
Takacs Techniques, Largo, Md.

Charlene Thomas, MSN, RN
Assistant Professor, School of Nursing, Rush University, Chicago, Ill.

Marlene R. Ventura, RN, PhD, FAAN
Associate Chief, Nursing Service for Research, Veterans Administration Center, Buffalo, NY

Mark Ward, MBA
Assistant Professor of Business and Economics, Trinity Christian College, Palo Heights, Ill.

Phyllis M. Watson, RN, PhD
Vice President for Nursing, Lakeland Regional Medical Center, Lakeland, Fla.

James R. Wilcox, PhD
Associate Professor of Interpersonal and Public Communication, Bowling Green State University, Bowling Green, Ohio

Paul Wowk, FACHE
Senior Manager, Great Lakes Human Resources Practice, Ernst and Whinney, Chicago, Ill.

Deborah Yano-Fong, RN, MSN
Head Nurse Neurology/Neurosurgery Unit, University of California Medical Center, San Francisco, Calif.

Carolyn York, RN, MS
Assistant Director of General Operating Rooms, Johns Hopkins Hospital, Baltimore, Md.

Abraham Zaleznik, PhD
Cahners-Rabb Professor of Social Psychology and Management, School of Business, Harvard University, Cambridge, Mass.

Karen Zander, RN, MS, CS
Organizational Development Specialist, Center for Nursing Case Management, Boston, Mass.

Preface

Nursing administration is a vital component of the health care delivery system. Nurse administrators are responsible for creating and managing environments that provide high quality health care and support and challenge professional nurses. They are accountable for clinical nursing practice, education, and research in a variety of health care settings.

The major challenges facing nursing administrators today and in the twenty-first century stem from the issues and trends that influence the health care delivery system. These include rapid advances in knowledge and technology, necessary changes in nursing education to foster the achievement of full professional status, cost-containment measures, appropriate reimbursement for nursing services, and quality management efforts to promote high quality, client-centered nursing care.

The emphasis on nursing's administration and management roles in the health care system has led to an abundance of published articles addressing various aspects of the roles, responsibilities, and the system itself. These articles are widely dispersed in administration, business, management, and nursing periodicals. The process of locating them is often difficult, time-consuming, and frustrating. This book is a result of our experience, and our students' and colleagues' experience seeking to locate the most relevant and timely articles.

The purpose of the book is to present a comprehensive overview of the theoretical and practical applications of organizational, administrative, and leadership concepts. We have also included issues and trends in health care delivery that influence administrative practice. Our intent is to offer an anthology that will not only be informative but will challenge and broaden the horizons of the reader.

In selecting the topics and articles for inclusion, we undertook extensive literature searches, reviewed topic outlines and reading lists of courses in nursing administration offered by several colleges and universities, consulted with practicing nurse executives and faculty teaching in nursing administration graduate programs, and solicited input from graduate nursing administration seminar students. We were also assisted by several peer reviewers (nursing administrators and practicing nurse executives) who provided valuable comments and suggestions regarding our initial article selections and the book's organization. We began with more than 300 articles. Making final choices became a formidable task.

Criteria for selecting articles were significance and relevance to nursing administration, recent publication in a professionally recognized periodical (except for a few classics), high ratings and recommendations by our students and colleagues, and frequent citations by other authors. We sought articles addressing a broad range of key topics to reflect the entire scope of the contemporary practice of nursing administration. However, space limitations restricted the number of articles we could include.

The readings are grouped under three major headings. Introductions are included to set the stage for each part. The importance of each article in the unit is also briefly described in the Introductions. Part I, The Nursing Organization, includes three units that address important organizational concepts, processes, and practices. Part II, The Nurse Administrator, includes two units, one that examines the roles, functions, and responsibilities of the nurse executive and a second that covers various processes and resources that the nurse executive must manage within the health care setting. Part III addresses the future of nursing and health care delivery and includes four articles. The authors of these articles look ahead to describe what they see as the profession's future, the profession's preferred future, obstacles to that future, and the profession in the emerging health care environment.

The units in the book are arranged in a particular sequence, but the units, subsections, and articles can be read in any order. Because many of the articles are multifaceted and address several concepts, article placement and overall book organization often became arbitrary. Other editors may have organized differently.

This collection of readings will provide a unique survey of the nursing administration literature for graduate students in administration and clinical nurse specialist programs. Upper division undergraduate students and RN students in baccalaureate and master's programs will also find the book useful. Practicing nursing administrators at all levels, those who aspire to careers in nursing administration, teachers of nursing, and nurse researchers will find these readings meaningful and thought-provoking and the book a valuable resource.

ACKNOWLEDGMENTS

During the 2 years we spent developing this compilation of readings, many individuals supported our efforts with their talents and time. We cannot name them all but several deserve special thanks. The first three groups of students admitted to the graduate nursing administration program at the University of Tennessee, Memphis — Sally Aldrich, Kathryn Barnoud, Diane Butler, Betty Sue Cox, Claudia Hamil, Deborah Hooser, Marjorie Martin, Kathleen McCraw, Ruby Miller, Kim Sinclair, Margaret Strong, Marylane Wade-Koch, Bonnie Williams, and Stephanie Winfrey provided valuable input. Our secretaries — Corliss Finlay, Mary Goode, Pat Stone-Goedecke, Patricia Jackson, and Di Patterson, at the University of Tennessee, Memphis; Hope Payne-Butler, Flo Wolf, and Rosemary Fitze at the Nell Hodgson Woodruff School of Nursing, Emory University, Atlanta, helped with photoduplication, word processing, letters, lists, and the many drafts that are part of any such undertaking. Special gratitude goes to Darlene Como, our Mosby–Year Book, Inc. editor, whose interest and belief in the project did much to bring it to fruition, and to the authors and publishers who generously shared their materials with us.

Mary Jane Ward
Sylvia A. Price

Contents

PART I

THE NURSING ORGANIZATION

Scientific and technological advances in health care have dramatically influenced the delivery pattern of nursing services. The majority of these services are delivered within an organizational environment. The goal of the nurse administrator is to orchestrate human and technological resources to create an environment that enhances the practice of professional nursing. It is essential that nurses and most especially nurse administrators, understand the nature of the organizations in which they practice.

Part I includes selections of readings focusing on the nursing organization. The first unit deals with the frameworks and philosophies of a nursing service organization and attempts to provide some insights into the importance of incorporating a theoretical nursing perspective into administrative nursing practice. In their provocative article, Jennings and Meleis emphasize that despite past progress in the development of nursing theory, a common theoretical nursing perspective has not emerged in the nursing administration field. They further state "that such a perspective could serve as a catalyst both to advance knowledge development for nursing administrative practice and to align clinical and administrative practice within a common framework." The authors present a five-item agenda as a guide for future theory development. Poteet and Hill identify the components of a nursing service philosophy. They describe an organizational framework for a nursing service philosophy, identify the essential components of the philosophy, and explore possible content to include in each part.

The second unit deals with leadership and management concepts and theories. Zaleznik notes that managers and leaders are different kinds of people. They differ fundamentally in their world views, goal orientations, work concepts, relationships, and self-perceptions. Managers develop leadership skills through socialization, whereas, leaders develop these skills through personal mastery.

Sovie stresses that exceptional executive leadership is essential to the success and high performance of this nation's diverse health care organizations and educational institutions. Nine priorities for action by exceptional nursing executives who want to shape the future are proposed.

Wowk describes partnering as a new strategy for nursing leadership. He challenges health care executives to think of nurses as fully functioning partners and to help them find an integral place in their organizations. Some intriguing new techniques to promote this concept are also described. Kelley suggests that without good followers to back them up, leaders are irrelevant. Leaders are trained, but followers are expected to grow and develop on their own. Four steps that organizations can take to encourage and develop good followership among their employees are posited.

Because management as a discipline incorporates the principles and guidelines of systems theory and managers function in an open social system, a selection on general systems theory is included in Unit 2. Kast and Rosenzweig discuss the key concepts of general systems theory, the way in which these ideas have been used by organization theorists, and the limitations and dilemmas in their application. They also offer some suggestions for the future.

The third unit examines the following organizational concepts, theories, and processes: ethics and values, culture, communication, power and influence, decision making, and innovation and change. These particular areas were selected because of their significance and relevance to nursing administration. Fry believes that the development of nursing ethics as a field of inquiry has largely paralleled developments within the field of biomedical ethics. She analyzes the value foundations of nursing and proposes a moral-point-of-view theory with caring as a fundamental value for the development of a theory of nursing ethics. Christensen emphasizes that nursing service administrators face myriad decisions each day that reflect moral obligations toward nursing staff within their respective organizations. A six-step approach to ethical reasoning that nursing administrators can use to deal effectively with ethical problems is presented. MacPherson implies that the dominant American values of individualism, competition, and inequality shape American health care policy. Nurses must critically analyze these basic values and address two basic flaws in the current approach to health care policy: (1) the separation of policy creation and implementation from politics and economics and (2) uncritical support of incremental policy changes.

Organizational culture is an important concept essential to understanding what makes organizations function effectively. Coeling and Wilcox state that understanding work culture can assist the nursing administrator in making decisions. The authors report a study that identified the work group culture of two nursing units and suggest that differences between organizational cultures affect a variety of nursing administration decisions. Thomas et al present a quantitative approach to measuring and interpreting organizational culture. They administered the Organizational Culture Inventory (OCI) that was designed to assess quantitatively the ways in which organizational members are expected to think and behave in relation to tasks and other people.

Communication is necessary to achieve the organization's purpose but also may present potential problems. Pincus, in his field study of professional nurses, investigated the effects of organizational communication on job satisfaction and job performance. A number of ways nurse executives can increase the communication effectiveness of their nursing staffs are suggested. Farley asserts that communication problems exist in every organization. Nursing administrators can address these problems by conducting a communication assessment.

Suggestions for developing a tool to assess the communication system of an organization are presented. Data obtained from such an assessment can provide the basis for improving communications.

The readings on power and influence address the sources of power and the status awarded to those who have it. Stevens looks at the power sources of the nurse executive and suggests political strategies and tactics which are important to the nurse administrator. Hoelzel asserts that to be more effective in the health care system of the 1990s, nursing administrators must understand organizational sources of structural power. Three sources of structural power are analyzed and their relevance for nursing administrators is discussed. Henry and LeClair stress that analysis of the language people use at work can help in understanding organizational dynamics. Recognizing the variety, distribution, and relevance of language can help nurse executives understand subtleties of leadership, varying dimensions of power, and paradoxes of organizational life.

Decision making is becoming a more complex process as a result of information overload, the lack of relevant data necessary for complex managerial decisions, and uncertainty in the world. In their article, Lancaster and Lancaster stress the quality of decision making in nursing administration Their practical, descriptive analysis of the decision-making process could improve administrator's effectiveness in this integral aspect of nursing administration. Freund describes managerial and organizational uses of Jung's theory of psychological type as operationalized in the Myers-Briggs Type Indicator (MBTI). This tool is useful not only in identifying individual preferences but also in developing effective managerial and working terms.

Innovation and change are frequently perceived as threatening because individuals often seek stability within their environment. However, change is inevitable and innovation is a necessary element of our culture. To function as an effective manager and leader, the nurse administrator must facilitate change and innovation. Drucker critically examines sources of innovation. Most innovations, especially successful ones, result from a conscious, purposeful search for innovation opportunities, which are found in only a few situations. Drucker analyzes four areas of opportunity within a company or industry and three additional sources found outside a company in its social and intellectual environment. Romano addresses the management of innovations, whether social, organizational, or technical in nature. Opportunities or sources for creating innovation are reviewed, as are the principles that guide the innovation process. Perlman and Takacs state that to cope with change effectively, organizations must consciously and constructively deal with the human emotions associated with it. A model of the change process is presented in their article. The authors discuss how all organization members must cope with the various stages and emotional dimensions of change.

Unit One

FRAMEWORKS AND PHILOSOPHIES

CHAPTER 1

Nursing Theory and Administrative Practice
Agenda for the 1990s

Bonnie Mowinski Jennings, RN, DNSc, Lt Col, USANC
Afaf Ibrahim Meleis, RN, PhD, FAAN

Although nursing's theoretical heritage can be traced to Florence Nightingale, the surge to develop and advance nursing theory did not take place until the mid-1950s. In the ensuing 30 years several milestones have marked the progress in knowledge development within the discipline of nursing.[1] To sustain such momentum it is crucial to identify gaps and omissions in nursing's theoretical development and to refocus the attention of members of the discipline on these underdeveloped areas. The practice of nursing administration, for example, does not appear to have attained a level of theoretical growth commensurate with other nursing specialties.[2-4] Therefore, the central purpose of this article is to discuss the relationship between nursing theory, clinical nursing practice, and administrative nursing practice.

AN INTEGRATIVE THEORETICAL FRAMEWORK: THE RATIONALE
A time for redirection

Knowledge development depends on the degree to which members of a discipline allocate time and energy to develop theory pertinent to the discipline. In keeping with the imperative to develop theory and

Reprinted from *Advances in Nursing Science,* Vol. 10, No. 3, with permission of Aspen Publishers, Inc. © 1988.

knowledge, the 1974 House of Delegates of the American Nurses' Association resolved that for the following decade nursing research and theory would focus on the practice of nursing.[5]

As the thrust of nursing's scholarly endeavors shifted to a strong clinical emphasis, the cornerstone of a scientific basis for patient care was set in place. Concurrently, however, the rather narrow definition of practice as a clinical pursuit contributed to a profound deficit in theory and knowledge development for nursing administrative practice. This gap in nursing theory and knowledge creates problems that are experienced by nurse administrators and nurse clinicians alike. By reconceptualizing relationships between clinical nursing practice and administrative nursing practice and by identifying the potential advantages to all nurses from promoting such a relationship, the nursing discipline as a whole might experience a much needed boost in its quest to develop theory.

Advantages of an integrative framework

First and foremost the relationship between clinical practice and administrative practice is neither artificial nor forced. It is a relationship that becomes more apparent when both areas are viewed within a nursing perspective. Not only do nurse administrators have a direct and potent influence on clinical practice and patient care, but Conway[6] emphasizes that nurse administrators are also in the unique position to bring a nursing perspective to the institutional management group. According to Meleis, "Theory helps to identify the focus, the means, and the goals of practice."[1(p31)] Therefore, nurse administrators may be in a better position to represent nursing care and to become advocates for patients and nurses by framing problems and solutions within a nursing theoretical perspective. In addition, the essence of nursing's theory and research mandates are also binding for nurse administrators, as they create and maintain the climate in which nursing is practiced.[7]

Second, administrative nursing practice is a nursing practice specialty in its own right. The artificial continuum of nursing knowledge, with clinical practice and administrative practice at opposite extremes, can be viewed as a dialectic representing Kuhn's[8] "essential tension." It is now time to nudge the pendulum of interest back to a midpoint, to a synthesis, that can be achieved by considering practice in its fullest sense. Nursing administration may therefore be viewed as another area of nursing practice that can benefit from grounding itself in the concepts central to the nursing domain.

Another advantage to reconceptualizing the relationship between clinical nursing practice and administrative nursing practice concerns knowledge development—both the content and the process. A common core of knowledge relevant to the nursing discipline in general affords a mechanism by which the various factions of the profession may be unified. Such an approach would facilitate injecting a nursing perspective into nursing administration as well. The process of knowledge development would benefit from all members of the discipline subscribing to a similar, more systematic approach. Under such conditions the possibility for accelerated knowledge growth would be considerable.

Using and developing theories for nursing regardless of practice specialty may also enhance communication and collaboration not only for knowledge development but also for patient care. Divergent and dichotomous goals might be realigned as nurses communicate using the same theoretical language and syntax. Nursing as a profession stands to gain more by

unification than by fractionation. Yet, as Styles[9] has suggested, the pressure within the profession that can give rise to splintering may exceed the pressure from external forces. While not a panacea, the use of a common framework such as that provided by the domain concepts may help to solidify the nursing discipline.

Management models: Necessary but not sufficient

Along with addressing the value of viewing both clinical nursing practice and administrative nursing practice from an integrative framework, a slightly different analysis underscores the limitations and inadequacies of existing management theories in guiding the practice of nursing administration. The incongruity between traditional management models and the practice of nursing administration has been explicated by both McClure[10-12] and Stevens.[3,13] They accurately convey, for example, that health care is a labor-intensive industry. The work flow in health care is unpredictable and is punctuated with physical and emotional crises as people—patients, families, and staff—grapple with problems of living and dying.

Additional complexity in the health care milieu is introduced by the workers themselves, who are a heterogeneous mix of individuals: There are both professionals who have acquired advanced knowledge from a variety of settings and paraprofessionals who have developed a more limited but nonetheless vital repertoire of skills. There is also the male-dominated practice of medicine and the female-dominated practice of nursing. These characteristics of the health care industry differ from the inanimate objects and product-line orientation that prevail in the more predictable, assembly line, nuts-and-bolts-filled milieu of the widget factory.[3,10-13]

The human beings who are central to all of nursing practice are at the crux of the inadequacy of using unaltered forms of management theory to guide administrative nursing. It is an issue of people *v* products. The thrust of the management models is largely product oriented: things, goods, commodities. Consequently, the theory or perspective used to drive health care organizations must be modified.

The reformation must take into account the people who seek care as well as the people who provide care.

This is not to suggest that nurse administrators have no need for management theory. On the contrary, for nurse administrators to credibly and effectively interact with other policy makers, the upper echelon of management, and managerial colleagues in other departments, they must be intimately conversant with management perspectives and terminology. However, while familiarity with the management culture and norms is vital for nursing's voice to be heard by the management group, focusing on management alone is insufficient.

As Meleis and Jennings state, "Just as the medical model alone is not suited to the clinical practice of nursing, so the sole reliance on management and administrative theories from other disciplines is not apropos for the practice of nursing administration."[2] To effectively manage the complex problems that are inherent in nursing, because of its focus on human health rather than product generation, traditional management views must be blended and balanced with a nursing perspective.

This condition is exemplified by considering an issue that has come to be a watchword of health care delivery systems in the 1980s — quality patient care. In a factory quality control can be regulated by adjusting the grade of raw materials used to manufacture a product, the skill of the labor, and the speed of the assembly line. Traditional management and economic theories are at the crux of the aggregate of activities that represent quality control from a manufacturer's perspective.

These same managerial and economic perspectives, however, may not be sufficient guides for regulating quality when patients are the focus. Different indicators are needed to provide and assess quality care. For example, as Chance articulated, "Quality care is directly linked to the use of nursing knowledge."[14(p63)] Increased efficiency, productivity, and quality in a people-oriented service setting cannot be controlled by the same parameters as those used in a product-oriented manufacturing plant. Perhaps this accounts in part for why the health care industry continues to grapple with questions about what constitutes quality care, especially in an era of cost containment, and about who defines quality — the patients, the nurses, the physicians, or the financial officer.

The task of actualizing the synthesis of nursing and management perspectives, while essential, will not be easy. First, it will entail a break from tradition in that the nursing perspective has not been routinely incorporated into administrative nursing practice. Such a change will be challenging, demanding, and difficult. The task will require nursing administrators to become trend setters and therefore risk takers. Second, with the present day emphasis on cost-effectiveness, people, those who give care and those who receive it, are often pushed further to the periphery of concern. To ignore the desires and needs of health care consumers and providers represents a form of institutional suicide. It is nursing, both the art and the science, that is equipped to deal with the complex needs of human beings. Similarly, recruitment and retention are among the foremost issues that deplete financial resources and affect the viability and vitality of health care organizations.

The foregoing remarks lead to a serious question. If nursing theory relevant to nursing administration does not evolve, what will become of nursing practice? Because nurse administrators do influence care delivery as well as represent nurses in the management realm, they have an opportunity to effect policy. If the policy is made without a nursing focus, patient care can be compromised, and the intensive efforts to build knowledge for practice may be for naught. Therefore, the entire nursing discipline is at risk if nursing administrators do not practice from a framework that represents a synthesis of both nursing and management. The salient question then becomes, how might theory relevant to nursing administration be developed?

A SHARED DOMAIN: THE VEHICLE TO INTEGRATION
Similar premises, missions, and questions

Because nurse administrators and clinicians share similar premises and focus on similar phenomena, they would ask and investigate related research questions. For example, the premise that all human beings — clients and care providers — are whole entities who are greater than the sum of their parts is fundamental to all of nursing. Furthermore, individuals are biopsychosocial and cultural beings whose responses are influenced by their diversity as well as their environment. Another premise shared by all nurses is that human responses are determined and shaped by perceptions, by experiences, and by the meanings that human beings attach to situations and events.

An additional premise common to nurse clinicians and nurse administrators concerns the purpose of nursing, that is, nursing deals with responses of individuals and environments to health and illness episodes. Clinicians deal primarily with patients who are trying to maintain or regain health. Administrators are not only concerned with the health of patients, but also with the health of the staff and the health of the larger organization. Using a common domain predicated on similar premises such as these to guide research and theory development has the potential to enhance knowledge growth.

While not all goals of nurse clinicians and nurse administrators are congruent, they do share a commitment to some common missions. These parallel missions tend to generate common questions and common concerns. These commonalities between nurse clinicians and nurse administrators form the foundation and provide direction for developing theories relevant to both groups.

The commonalities are evident in the three themes identified by Donaldson and Crowley,[15] who suggested that the boundaries of nursing inquiry revolved around (1) principles that govern human well-being, (2) patterns of human-environment interaction, and (3) processes that enhance health. From these boundaries questions central to the nursing discipline arise. These questions, some of which are enumerated in Table 1-1, underscore two issues. First, they demonstrate that not all questions confronting nurse managers can be answered through existing management theory, thus necessitating the use of a nursing perspective. Second, the questions establish the common concerns shared by all nurses — clinicians, administrators, educators, researchers, and theorists. These questions evolve

from shared premises, and they represent parallel missions.

Although there are some questions unique to clinical practice and others that are unique to administrative nursing, it seems that differences have been overemphasized in the past while similarities have been acknowledged only minimally. Again, Table 1-1 illustrates that questions central to the nursing discipline are equally relevant to nurse clinicians and nurse administrators. The former must focus more intently upon the patient and family, while the latter must take individuals, groups, and the larger organization into account. In both cases, nevertheless, a nursing perspective serves as a framework for considering the human beings who are central to all aspects of health care.

Domain concepts: Common ties

Various domain concepts have been proposed, debated, and finally adopted as representing the questions and propositions that are central to the nursing discipline. Person, environment, health, and nursing are the major features of the nursing paradigm that have been widely accepted.[16-18] Inherent to relationships among these domain concepts is another concept, interaction.[1,15,19,20] More recently, Meleis[1,20] and Chick and Meleis[21] have proposed incorporating the concept of transition into the nursing domain.

The domain concepts therefore provide a vehicle through which blending management and nursing perspectives and uniting clinical and administrative nursing can be achieved; they provide a framework from which theory pertinent to administrative nursing practice can be generated. Administrative goals and responsibilities, however, derive from a context that necessitates redefining the concepts.[2,22] Table 1-2 demonstrates the commonalities and utility of the domain concepts for both clinical nursing practice and administrative nursing practice. The utility of developing theories around central phenomena that are relevant to both nurse clinicians and nurse administrators can be highlighted by briefly presenting four examples — transitions, interactions, environment, and health.

TABLE 1-1
Questions central to nurse clinicians and nurse administrators

CLINICAL FOCUS	ADMINISTRATIVE FOCUS
Understanding responses to health and illness	
How do patients respond to escalating technology in the health care milieu?	How does increased technology affect staffing needs in caring for patients? How does the increased technology affect staff (eg, eyestrain from observing monitors)?
Facilitating adjustments and transitions to health alterations	
What interventions are most efficacious in helping people adjust to experiencing a MI? Does the effectiveness of interventions vary among ethnic groups and between genders?	Which is more beneficial to the patient organization—inpatient or outpatient cardiac rehabilitation programs? What approaches and interventions are most suitable to assisting nurses who have substance abuse problems?
Assisting individuals to enhance their self-sufficiency	
What approaches to education—inpatient/outpatient, group/individual—enhance a patient's ability to manage health problems more independently?	Where in the course of illness is it best to initiate the move from more dependent relationships to more independent care? How can orientation programs more efficiently and effectively increase the new employee's independence within the institution and for a particular patient care area?
Developing and maintaining a healthy environment	
What is the effect of noise in the patient environment on patient recovery?	How does the design of a patient unit affect patterns of caregiving? To what extent is staff health (and subsequently care delivery) enhanced by having adequate supplies and functional equipment readily available?
Coordinating and collaborating for patient care	
How can communication with intubated patients be improved?	How does communication between the nursing staff and the family affect preparation for discharge? How does a decentralized administrative structure influence collaboration and affect patient care?

Transitions

Transitions are defined as those times of passage that are interposed between two more stable phases of life. They are typically periods when common coping styles and normal patterns of response to events and situations may no longer be adequate. Transitions are characterized by new sets of expectations, alterations in former needs and desires, a temporary loss of the familiar, and a sense of disconnectedness.[20] Transitions can be considered according to several continua—planned v unplanned; expected v unexpected; wanted v unwanted. Nurse clinicians may

TABLE 1-2

Nursing domain concepts as defined by clinical practice and administrative practice

DOMAIN CONCEPT	CLINICAL PRACTICE	ADMINISTRATIVE PRACTICE
Person	Patient, family, community	Care providers as individuals and groups as well as the total organization in addition to patient, family, and community
Interaction	Patient-environment interaction	Care provider-environment interaction and other management-environment interaction as well as patients
Transition	Health/illness; patient/family; evolving situations	Same as clinical practice plus nurses in new or different positions and institutional — within and without
Environment	Psychosocial, physical, cultural; family, patient, community; health enhancing	As relevant to the patient; as relevant to the care provider (interpersonal, supplies, equipment); economic, political, legal, ethical; macro and micro levels
Health	Perception of wellness; level of vulnerability; level of functioning	Same as clinical practice but with individual care providers, groups, and the organization at large as the focus

focus on responses of clients in transition, while nurse administrators may focus on client, staff, and organizational transitions.

Client transitions are exemplified by role transitions due to sudden acute illness, such as a myocardial infarction (MI), or the gradual onset of a chronic illness, such as diabetes. For the nurse clinician the interest lies in the synthesis of sick roles, at-risk roles, or well roles in the repertoire of clients' roles. In addition to client transitions the nurse administrator focuses on role transition of the recent graduate, the new employee, the novice clinical specialist, and the neophyte nurse manager, as well as the experienced nurse who is confronting novel situations. The patient care unit may experience transitions such as those that occur when new staff are recruited or when interns and residents rotate services. The entire health care delivery system may undergo transitions: Increased technology and the moves to prospective payment and home care typify these changes.

The questions, then, become (1) how do nurses, clinicians, or administrators facilitate transitions to enhance and to maintain the well-being of the individuals experiencing the passage, (2) how do they create and maintain a healthy environment that is experienced during the transition process, (3) what conditions enhance or impede the transition process, (4) what are the processes, mechanisms, and dynamics by which new roles are incorporated into a person's sense of self, (5) when and how are behaviors related to the role created and manifested, and (6) how are competencies relevant to particular roles developed?

Such a conceptual orientation unites nurse clinicians and nurse administrators by enabling both to use a nursing perspective that considers the wholeness of human beings. In all cases cost-effectiveness, a variable that is central for administrators in planning care delivery, may be an outcome. Patients may achieve an improved health status more quickly; nursing staff may be more satisfied and productive as they are helped to adapt to new situations.

More importantly, a conceptual approach to defining and coping with transitions could provide a reservoir for diverse findings related to responses of nurses, clients, and systems. Although the conceptual questions could bind all nursing specialities, specific research questions and programs would be guided by the particular research population relevant to the particular practice arena. The potential for developing a theory with wider scope, more utility,and greater power may thus be realized. The alternative is to continue to address single, minute questions that are atheoretical. Unless joined by a unifying framework, questions that consider transitions of students, nurses, and patients — parents, children, men, women, young, and old, acutely ill, chronically ill — will remain distinct and unrelated.

Interaction

A second central concept in nursing that may lend itself to similar questions in a variety of areas of nursing specialization is interaction. Individuals are in continuous interaction with their environments.[15] Exchange and reciprocity are inherent to the meaning of interaction, as is the notion of process. Goals of human interactions may include building rapport, validating perceptions, understanding responses, and empathizing. Interaction has been said to epitomize the essence of nursing.[20] Heretofore the context for interactions has been that of nurse-patient relationships. However, the concept of interaction is nonetheless useful to the nurse administrator. Phenomena common to interactions such as communication and power can be used to illustrate these shared properties.

It has been postulated that communication is a critical component of interpersonal competence and nursing effectiveness.[23-25] Communication is at the crux of discharge planning, patient education, nursing assessment, group process, collaboration, negotiation, and all interpersonal relationships. The dynamics of communication come into play as nurses talk with each other, as they relate with patients, and as they engage in exchanges with nonnursing personnel — physicians or chief executive officers. Communication, therefore, is equally pertinent to nurse administrators and nurse clinicians.

Both groups may pose questions about effective communication patterns during different stages of health-illness episodes and with diverse cross-cultural groups. In some cases health may refer to organizations rather than patients, and the culture may be corporate rather than ethnic. Questions derived from

a focus on communication might include (1) what are the properties of effective communication, (2) what impedes or enhances communication, (3) how do different patterns of communication influence relationships, and (4) what characteristics of the environment are most conducive to efficient and effective communication?

The concept of power also elucidates the salience of the concept of interactions to clinicians and administrators. The word power originates from the Latin *potere,* meaning to be able. Power suggests energy and movement. It is through the effective use of power that desired outcomes are attained.[26-28] There are many sources of power, one of which is knowledge. In all relationships a balance of power enables collaboration. Perhaps because of the potential for misuse a negative connotation tends to pervade the phenomenon of power. This negative aura notwithstanding, the effective use of power is crucial to attaining health outcomes whether they are for the patient's health, the staff's health, the organization's health, or the health of the nursing discipline.

Although nurses may not consciously think of power dynamics inherent in the nurse-patient relationship, power is operating nonetheless. When patients are extremely ill the energy and knowledge of the nurse, the nurse's power, are to facilitate recovery. As acute illness subsides, the power gradient between patient and nurse is reduced. Chronically ill individuals may be particularly vocal in realigning the power structure of the nurse-patient dynamics in that they are often highly knowledgeable about the disease with which they must constantly live. Power, nonetheless, is common throughout nurse-patient interactions. Issues surrounding administration of pain medications and control of visiting policies — who can visit? how many? when? — are but a few examples of power in the patient milieu.

Similarly, highly vulnerable members of the nursing staff — those new to nursing, the institution, the position — may feel less powerful in their relationships with others due to their lack of knowledge. Once knowledge expands, the individual may experience an enhanced sense of power. This power will not only facilitate accomplishments but will also require adjustment of preexisting relationships. In a like fashion, the phenomenon of power will operate differently in a healthy department than in one that needs to be revitalized. Power is what facilitates accomplishing goals—in this case goals of nursing. Clinical nurses and administrative nurses alike can benefit from pursuing questions that enhance an understanding of the sociopolitical milieu in which care is delivered and of its attendant power dynamics.

There is a curious circularity that exists with the phenomenon of power. Studying power from an integrative framework has the potential to more rapidly expand knowledge relevant to nursing. Knowledge is a form of power. Therefore, the discipline may experience an enhanced sense of power. By investigating power the negative connotations may fade while the positive potential is highlighted, thereby helping nurses to benefit from the power that exists within the discipline.

Environment

Despite its extensiveness and pervasiveness, environment is a domain concept that has been explicated only minimally.[1,17,29] Chopoorian[29] suggests that the limited conceptual development of environment may be due to regarding it only as immediate surroundings. When the scope is expanded to include social, political, and economic influences, the urgency to better develop the domain concept of environment is apparent. Developing knowledge about the environment may be particularly suitable for those in administrative nursing practice. Such efforts have the potential to contribute substantially to clarifying central questions not addressed by extant theory.[7]

Furthermore, concerns centering on environment are relevant to both nurse clinicians and nurse administrators. For example, health policies may restrict care to the elderly. How, then, can care delivery be modified to meet the health needs of the aging population? Another example concerns cost. The current economic milieu in health care mandates a reduction in the cost of care. What are the effects of cost containment on patients and nursing staff? How can the beneficial effects be maximized and the unwanted outcomes be minimized?[7] Social

support is also representative of the environment; it has demonstrated health-enhancing abilities. How does social support affect patients and staff? Are certain sources of support more efficacious than others? What are the properties of supportive relationships, and do they vary as the nature of the relationship changes?

The influence of environment is memorably demonstrated in a patient study of the effects of preoperative preparation on postoperative outcomes. The findings were not expected: Patient outcomes were more a reflection of the hospital in which care was delivered than a result of therapeutic nursing intervention.[30] This report underscores that the environment and framework within which nursing was practiced did indeed influence patient care. Just as some environments may be healthier for patients, it is also probable that various features of the milieu may also be more health enhancing for nurses. In fact, the organizational climate of health care settings has been found to affect job performance and job satisfaction[31,32] as well as workers' health.[33]

Health

Many individuals have articulated the centrality of health to nursing while underscoring that medical colleagues focus on disease.[15,34-36] Although there are a multitude of ways in which the domain concept of health could be used by nurse clinicians and nurse administrators, one unique aspect will be pursued as an illustration, women's health. Women's health represents not only an area of specialization for nurse clinicians but also a topic of extreme importance to nurse administrators in that women dominate the nursing discipline.

For both groups the focal concern regarding health could be the well-being and functioning of women. The phenomenon would be the part health plays in the repertoire of other facets of a person's life. The questions would be similar for both clinical and administrative nursing practice: How do women maintain mental and physical health? What attributes and conditions help women cope with illness? What is the effect of multiple roles on women's health? Clinicians would address these questions in terms of female patients; administrators would pursue the same queries as they relate to female members of the nursing staff.

In addition to building knowledge for the nursing discipline, answers to questions concerning women's health might have a secondary gain, that is, the discipline of nursing might come to be considered with greater regard by other disciplines. Many researchers have investigated various aspects of women's health. When these studies are viewed critically, however, sufficient flaws are evident, thereby casting doubt on the veracity of the findings. Furthermore, as Haw[37] adduced, it is difficult to discern the combined effects of working and family on women's health, as findings from the many reports are inconsistent and inconclusive. Consequently, nurse clinicians and nurse administrators might not only clarify these dynamics for the nursing discipline but might also make a major interdisciplinary contribution.

NURSING ADMINISTRATION: THEORETICAL AGENDA FOR THE FUTURE

To guide and shape the development of nursing theories that are useful to nurse administrators and that in turn advance theory for the nursing discipline, a five-item agenda for the future is proposed. First, it would be useful to extend and expand this prodromal effort at identifying common ground between clinicians and administrators from which theories may develop. These theories, based upon shared premises, phenomena, concepts, and questions, could be central to both groups. Furthermore, the common focus may help to unite nurses in the process of knowledge development. Collectively there is the potential for the nursing discipline to take a large step forward in theoretical development.

Second, the moratorium on research relevant to nursing administration needs to be lifted. A climate must be created that is conducive to nurturing the development of research programs relevant to nursing administration from a nursing domain perspective. These programs would build and test theory, thereby contributing to knowledge development and a scientific basis for administrative nursing practice derived from a nursing heritage. Nurse administrators need to

make theory development a priority with all the adjustments that may go into such a declaration. The responsibility must be shared between academicians and administrators alike.

A third order of business entails recognizing that nurse administrators must actualize the goal of blending knowledge and skills from both nursing and management.[13] The sole reliance on only nursing views or only management models is less powerful than the multiplicative effect of their combined utility. Both may lead to the development of more powerful, comprehensive theories that may help to clarify and answer questions concerning the human beings who are central to the entire nursing discipline.

Providing effective, quality care in a cost-containment era represents a fourth agenda item that is equally pressing for nurse clinicians and nurse administrators. Neither group can address this crucial concern effectively and efficiently without due consideration of the patient, the nurse, the environment, and their relationships with each other. Therefore, quality care represents an arena for immediate consideration to explicate theories that help deal with questions surrounding quality and to provide models for delivering quality care.

Fifth and finally, as nurse administrators become open to the potential for developing nursing theory, they may consider the utility of extant nursing theory in providing explanations to administrative questions. An example may be found in the interactionist theories of nursing that were developed in the early 1960s. These theories conceptualize nursing as an interaction and provide conditions and strategies to guide nurses as they interact with patients. By reconceptualizing interactions to include all individuals with whom the nurse relates, the existing interactionist theories may prove useful to nurse administrators.

• • •

Theory development is not limited to individuals with a particular area of nursing specialization. In other words, it is not fields of practice that differentiate those who develop nursing theories from those who do not; rather it is skill, commitment, knowledge, and the pursuit of significant domain questions that are conceptually determined. Therefore, nurses who specialize in administrative nursing practice may be as committed to developing nursing theory and advancing nursing knowledge as their clinical practice colleagues.

Similarly, theory utilization is not limited to a particular area of nursing specializations. Rather it is expected that all professional nurses will be conversant with and proficient in implementing theories in their practice. The particular theories are usually selected and used because they answer some central questions to guide a specific area of nursing practice. Consequently, it is plausible that nurse administrators would encounter questions that mandate the use of nursing theories or at least consideration of the nursing domain to answer the questions. In fact, the historical dominance of management models to guide administrative nursing practice makes this a particularly compelling goal.

REFERENCES

1. Meleis AI: *Theoretical Nursing: Development & Progress*. Philadelphia, Lippincott, 1985.
2. Meleis AI, Jennings BM: Theoretical nursing administration: Today's challenges, tomorrow's bridges, in Henry B, Arndt C, DiVincenti M, et al (eds): *Dimensions and Issues in Nursing Administration*. Boston, Blackwell Scientific, 1988, chap 1, to be published.
3. Stevens BJ: *Nursing Theory. Analysis, Application, Evaluation*. Boston, Little, Brown, 1979, pp 113-127.
4. Trandel-Korenchuk DM: Concept development in nursing research. *Nurs Adm Q* 1986;11(1):1-9.
5. Downs FS: Clinical and theoretical research, in Downs FS, Fleming JW (eds): *Issues in Nursing Research*. New York, Appleton-Century-Crofts, 1979, pp 67-87.
6. Conway ME: Knowledge generation and transmission: A role for the nurse administrator. *Nurs Adm Q* 1979; 3(4):29-44.
7. Jennings BM: Nursing theory development: Successes and challenges. *J Adv Nurs* 1987;12:63-69.
8. Kuhn TS: *The Essential Tension*. Chicago, University of Chicago Press, 1977.
9. Styles MM: Anatomy of a profession. *Heart Lung* 1983; 12:570-575.
10. McClure ML: The administrative component of the nurse administrator's role. *Nurs Adm Q* 1979;3(4):1-12.
11. McClure ML: Managing the professional nurse. The organizational theories. *J Nurs Adm* 1984;14(2):15-21.
12. McClure ML: Managing the professional nurse. Applying management theory to the challenges. *J Nurs Adm* 1984; 14(3):11-17.
13. Stevens BJ: Improving nurses' managerial skills. *Nurs Outlook* 1979;27:774-777.
14. Chance KS: Nursing models: A requisite for professional accountability. *Adv Nurs Sci* 1982;4(2):57-65.
15. Donaldson SK, Crowley DM: The discipline of nursing. *Nurs Outlook* 1978;26:113-120.
16. Fawcett J: Hallmarks of success in nursing theory development, in Chinn PL (ed): *Advances in Nursing Theory Development*. Rockville, Md, Aspen Publishers, 1983, pp 3-17.
17. Flaskerud JH, Halloran EJ: Areas of agreement in nursing theory development. *Adv Nurs Sci* 1980;3(1):1-7.
18. Newman MA: The continuing revolution: A history of nursing science, in Chaska NL (ed): *The Nursing Profession: A Time to Speak*. New York, McGraw-Hill, 1983, pp 385-393.
19. Fawcett J: *Analysis and Evaluation of Conceptual Models of Nursing*. Philadelphia, F.A. Davis, 1984.
20. Meleis AI: Theory development and domain concepts, in Moccia P (ed): *New Approaches to Theory Development*, NLN publication No. 15-1992. New York, National League for Nursing, 1986, pp 3-21.
21. Chick N, Meleis AI: Transitions: A nursing concern, in Chinn PL (ed): *Nursing Research Methodology. Issues and Implementation*. Rockville, Md, Aspen Publishers, 1986, pp 237-257.
22. Chaska NL: Theories of nursing and organizations: Generating integrated models for administrative practice, in Chaska NL (ed): *The Nursing Profession: A Time to Speak*. New York, McGraw-Hill, 1983, pp 720-730.
23. Kasch CR:Toward a theory of nursing action: Skills and competency in nurse-patient interaction. *Nurs Res* 1986; 35:226-230.
24. Kasch CR, Lisnek PM: Role of strategic communication in nursing theory and research. *Adv Nurs Sci* 1984; 7(1):56-71.
25. Pincus JD: Communication: Key contributor to effectiveness — The research. *J Nurs Adm* 1986;16(9):19-25.
26. Styles MM: *On Nursing: Toward a New Endowment*. St. Louis, Mosby, 1982, pp 213-223.
27. Kanter RM: Power failure in management circuits. *Harvard Bus Rev* 1979;57(4):65-75.
28. Salancik GR, Pfeffer J: Who gets power — and how they hold onto it: A strategic contingency model of power, in Hackman J, Lawler E, Porter L (eds): *Perspectives on Behavior in Organizations*. New York, McGraw-Hill, 1983, pp 417-429.

29. Chopoorian TJ: Reconceptualizing the environment, in Moccia P (ed): *New Approaches to Theory Development,* NLN publication No. 15-1992, New York, National League for Nursing, 1986, pp 39-54.

30. Hegyvary ST, Chamings PA: The hospital setting and patient outcomes. *J Nurs Adm* 1975;5(4):36-42.

31. Duxbury ML, Henley GA, Armstrong GD: Measurement of the nurse organizational climate of neonatal intensive care units. *Nurs Res* 1982;31:83-88.

32. Lancaster J: Creating a climate of excellence. *J Nurs Adm* 1985;15(1):16-19.

33. Jennings BM: Social support: A way to a climate of caring. *Nurs Adm Q* 1987;11(4):63-71.

34. Ellis R: Conceptual issues in nursing. *Nurs Outlook* 1982; 30:406-410.

35. Payne L: Health: A basic concept in nursing theory. *J Adv Nurs* 1983;8:393-395.

36. Shaver JF: A biopsychosocial view of human health. *Nurs Outlook* 1985;33:186-191.

37. Haw MA: Women, work and stress: A review and agenda for the future. *J Health Soc Behav* 1982;23:132-144.

CHAPTER 2

Identifying the Components of a Nursing Service Philosophy

Gaye W. Poteet, RN, EdD
Alice S. Hill, RN, PhD

An organization's philosophy is a statement of beliefs, concepts and principles containing the ideas, convictions and attitudes of the organization and those directly involved in its composition.[1,2] It serves as a guide for action and an explanation of action. The nursing service philosophy is a statement of beliefs that flows from and is congruent with the institution's philosophy.[3] The belief system of the nursing service philosophy should reflect the nursing division members' ideas and ideals for nursing and should be endorsed by others. The ideas should provide a realistic basis for operating the nursing service department.

THE COMPONENTS OF A NURSING SERVICE PHILOSOPHY

The content of nursing service philosophies varies. Many nursing philosophies include belief statements about the nature of mankind, nursing, health and society.[4] Others include statements about the meaning of health, the nursing service department, or the environment.[5] While these concepts can be related

Reprinted from *Journal of Nursing Administration,* Vol. 18, No. 10, with permission of J. B. Lippincott Company © 1988.

to nursing, they are vague and provide no direct guidance for writing a nursing service philosophy.[6,7] Seventeen typical areas of content in a philosophy were listed by Stevens,[8] covering all the appropriate subject matter. However Stevens does not describe the process of conceptualization; that is, the means by which the nurse manager decides what viewpoint the nursing service philosophy is to represent and how the philosophy is to be used.[3] Once this conceptualization has taken place, the identified content areas can be incorporated into a coherent statement of beliefs.

Three areas which provide a beginning for conceptualizing a nursing department's philosophy are the patient, the delivery of nursing care, and the nurse employee. Cantor[9] noted that philosophies should address the actual concerns of the department and omit other esoteric, idealist goals. Using the concepts of patient, nursing care, and the nurse employee, a conceptual framework for a philosophy can be developed. As Figure 2-1 shows, these concepts are intertwined. They represent vital components of the organization. Therefore, a comprehensive philosophy must address all these areas. Appropriate content in each area is described below, with specific examples, to assist the leader with this process.

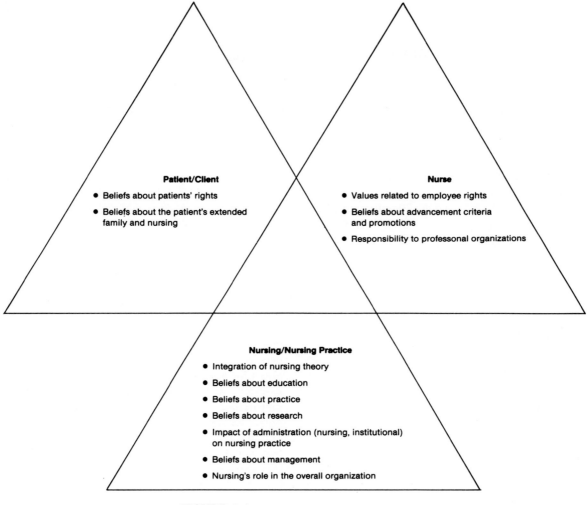

Patient/Client

- Beliefs about patients' rights
- Beliefs about the patient's extended family and nursing

Nurse

- Values related to employee rights
- Beliefs about advancement criteria and promotions
- Responsibility to professonal organizations

Nursing/Nursing Practice

- Integration of nursing theory
- Beliefs about education
- Beliefs about practice
- Beliefs about research
- Impact of administration (nursing, institutional) on nursing practice
- Beliefs about management
- Nursing's role in the overall organization

FIGURE 2-1

Components of a nursing service philosophy.

NURSING/NURSING PRACTICE

Nursing is a health-care service mandated by society; the practice of nursing stems from the beliefs and ideals of the nursing service department. To fully explore this in a nursing service philosophy, the manager should examine content related to nursing theory, education, practice, research, the impact of administration on nursing practice, management, and nursing's role in the overall organization (Figure 2-1).

By examining each of these areas separately, the nurse manager can clarify values and beliefs.

In the first area, nursing theory, the task for the nurse manager is to decide whether and how to incorporate theory. Three different methods may be considered. One method is to use an eclectic approach, selecting ideas and constructs from various nursing theories and incorporating these into the philosophy. For example, the nurse manager may choose to use the ideas about nursing from Orem's Self-Care Deficit of nursing and the ideas on individual development from Maslow. A word of caution, however, when using an eclectic approach, nurse managers must make sure that the theories selected are compatible; otherwise, philosophical beliefs and values may become distorted and in some instances they may be diametrically opposed to one another. Table 2-1 lists some major theorists whose work may be useful in developing a philosophy.

A second method is to use one theory throughout the philosophy. This method requires adoption of the theory by the department members and integration of the concepts and belief systems of the theory into the subject matter of the philosophy. The nurse manager should have a thorough understanding of the theory and be able to relate its intent to the group. The theory would then be incorporated into the department members' beliefs about nursing and nursing practice, as well as their beliefs about the patient/client. Thus all employees, including staff nurses, would use this theory.

TABLE 2-1
Nursing theorists

Client focused
Dorothy Johnson
Sister Callista Roy

Interaction focused
Imogene King
Margaret Newman
Ida Orlando
Josephine Paterson and Loretta Zderad
Joyce Travelbee
Ernestine Wiedenbach

Nursing therapeutics
Myra Levine
Dorothea Orem

Environment/human being interactions
Martha Rogers

NOTE: The classification system used here was first developed by Afaf I. Meleis in *Theoretical Nursing: Development and Progress.* Philadelphia: J.B. Lippincott Company, 1985.

A third approach is for the nursing department to adopt a theory, then attach the entire document describing the theory to the philosophy and refer to the theory at appropriate places in the philosophy. This method requires the nurse manager to understand the theory and be aware of the appropriate areas of application in the philosophy.

A second set of values related to nursing/nursing practice center around practice, education and research. Values or beliefs specific to practice may include the department member's beliefs about the required skill levels for different units and the needs of special care areas. Also, if the philosophy is written for the nursing department as a whole, beliefs about specific practice modalities may be addressed. For example, the philosophy could express a belief that primary nursing is the modality which best meets the needs of the patient for continuity of care, provides the framework in which quality nursing care is delivered, and provides the nurse employee with a professionally and personally satisfying practice environment.

However, if the philosophy is written for a unit, the content may center on a particular theoretical perspective (e.g., the self-care model might be proposed for a rehabilitation unit). The nurse manager may also wish to address the need for advanced preparation (i.e., master's degree or doctorate) for nurses functioning in certain areas or positions. For example, the nursing department may wish to state that it is their belief that master level preparation is necessary for nurses functioning in critical care areas, and the doctoral level preparation is required for research positions.

Values specific to education are essential content for most departments of nursing. The beliefs may focus on the need for continuing education of staff members. For example, if the department is committed to keeping its members up to date on advances in the nursing field, then a statement should be made that expresses this viewpoint. A statement such as "We believe nurses should be given the opportunity to keep current on advances in their field of practice" may be included. Of course such a statement requires a commitment to provide on-going educational opportunities for employees; opportunities may include workshops, formal education, etc.

If the institution provides educational opportunities for students, a statement consistent with this policy may be included, such as, "We are committed to the education of nursing students," or "We will provide appropriate learning experiences and supervision in conjunction with nursing faculty." The latter statement indicates that staff nurses will be responsible, in part, for supervision of student nurses. Such a commitment should be explored in depth by the members of the department.

A third value related to the concept nursing/nursing practice is research. This value may include the department's commitment to applying research findings or supporting others in their research efforts. If the department members believe that it is their responsibility to support research efforts rather than to conduct research, statements similar to these could be used: "We believe research is a vital component for the advancement of nursing practice. We further believe that it is our responsibility to assist with research projects conducted by nurse colleagues." These statements indicate the need for all nurses to become involved with research projects, though the degree of involvement could range from awareness of the project to assistance with data collection.

If nursing research is valued by the department, it is important for all department members to agree on the status to be given to it. Because of the fear aroused by the very idea of nursing research, there is a special need for all members to understand the departmental stance on this issue. Without total commitment and understanding, the belief statement will be nothing more than idle words.

Two other content areas under the concept nursing/nursing practice are the impact of administration (nursing or institutional) on nursing practice and beliefs about nursing management. Quite naturally, the beliefs held about these areas will be influenced by the organizational structure of the institution and the management model followed. Hence it is more important for the nurse manager to keep in mind the administrative values of the institution and the structure of the organization when addressing this part of the philosophy. For example, if the nursing service department functions within a parent department and that parent department's management values are autocratic, then the nursing service philosophy must reflect these ideals. The following statements, although somewhat frivolous, will illustrate these beliefs: "We believe that decisions made about patients and their care should be made by head nurses or their designees. We further believe that these decisions should be carried out without unnecessary questioning." These content areas — the impact of administration on nursing practice and management values — may hold the key to successful operationalization of the philosophy. A nursing service philosophy written out of step with administrative beliefs and management values will be of little or no value in accomplishing the goals of the organization or the department.

The last content area related to nursing/nursing practice is nursing's role in the overall organization. In this particular content area, the nurse manager may wish to identify nursing's responsibilities and contributions to the institution, in accordance with the institution's method of operation. A suitable statement might be: "Nursing is responsible for providing safe care to all patients regardless of their ability to pay." This statement, of course, would be inappropriate for some institutions and would need to be based on the institution's specific ability-to-pay policy. The main idea here is that nursing should identify its responsibilities and carry out these responsibilities within the institution's policies of operation.

PATIENT/CLIENT

The patient is the main reason for the institution's existence. Without patients, hospitals and other agencies would close. Therefore, it is important to be decisive in philosophical notions concerning the patient. The nurse manager may wish to begin by examining patients' rights (see Figure 2-1). Beliefs concerning patients rights will be influenced in part by institutional policies and practices. For example, if the hospital subscribes to certain social or economic policies, realistic beliefs about patients' rights can be meaningful only within the boundaries of those policies. A statement illustrating this is "We believe that each patient should be cared for based on his nursing needs rather than his economic status or other social factors." If the hospital does not provide certain aspects of care in response to social factors (e.g., abortion), then the latter part of this statement would not be appropriate for the philosophy.

Another issue that the nurse manager may wish to consider when addressing patients' rights is the amount of involvement the patient has in his care. Should the nurse take on the maternalistic role and provide all care regardless of the patient's ability to care for self? This philosophical notion will need to be discussed by the group and conclusions drawn based on their discussions. If the group believes that the patient should be involved in his own care, a statement such as "We believe the patient has a right to care for his own needs as far as his health status allows" should be included. This statement signifies a commitment to the patient's right to independence. Furthermore, a statement concerning the patient's involvement in the health care decision-making process should be made, for in this process, the most important element is patient-nurse consensus in the formation of goals.

Another content area related to the patient/client is beliefs about the role of the patient's extended family and their relationship to nursing. The important role that family members play in the recovery of a patient has been documented numerous times. However, some institutions adhere to a strict visiting hours policy, and in some instances only selected family members are allowed to visit. Many of these visiting policies are enforced and/or developed by nurses. If nurses want patients to recover quickly, and if they believe that family members are essential in the recovery process, then nurses must find a way to address this belief. One way would be through stating in the philosophy that patients have the right to visits from extended family members while hospitalized. Nursing's responsibility will be to incorporate the contributions of these family members in the care of the patient.

NURSES

Nurses are essential in the day-to-day operations of the hospital organization. They are the providers of nursing acts which result in quality care. To keep the organization functioning smoothly, it is necessary to address values related to and beliefs about nurses. These values and beliefs center around nurses rights, advancement criteria and responsibilities to other health professionals, as well as professional organizations (Figure 2-1).

When addressing the employee's rights in a nursing service philosophy, nurse managers need to consider the posture of the parent institution. Working within that posture, nurse managers must state their own beliefs about the employee's rights. For example, the statement may be made that nurses have the right to independent decision making in the care of their patients. This statement does not preclude interacting with other health team members, however, it places the responsibility and accountability for nursing acts upon the nurse. A nursing service department making such a philosophical statement will need to be aware of its nurses' abilities and supportive of their actions.

Advancement or career ladder criteria are related to other rights. These criteria are developed and established to guide the nurse preparing for advancement. If the organization has such criteria or plans to develop these criteria, a statement should be made about commitment to staff promotion. For example, the statement could be made that each employee has the same opportunity for advancement based on the institution's criteria; or a statement such as "We believe that promotions should be made from within our organization" may be included.

A third content area is the nurse's responsibility to professional organizations. Traditionally, nursing has allowed its professionals to choose whether they wished to support their professional organizations. While it may not be necessary to make this a major part of the philosophy, managers may want to consider the magnitude of the potential impact professional organizations could have on nursing practice. Hence, managers may want to include a statement such as "We believe that all nurses should belong to a professional nursing organization, and should become involved in fulfilling the goals and objectives of that organization." Such a statement, however, means that nursing service administrators must make time available for all nurses who choose to attend the meetings of their professional organizations.

SUMMARY

A framework for writing a nursing service philosophy provides the nurse manager with a quick and easy reference to identify essential organizers for the philosophy. The framework described here pinpoints three areas of importance, nursing/nursing practice, the patient/client, and the nurse, and describes specific subject matter to be addressed with each area. By organizing the subject matter into three practical areas of concern, the nurse manager can explore each area and develop a realistic and operational philosophy for the Nursing Service Department.

REFERENCES

1. Allen DG. The social policy statement: A reappraisal. Advances in Nursing Science, 1987;10(1):39-48.
2. Yeaworth RC. The ANA code: A comparative perspective. Image: The Journal of Nursing Scholarship, 1985;17(3):94-98.
3. Lusky KF, Macey JC, Rutledge DN. Developing a new philosophy for an established school of nursing. Image: The Journal of Nursing Scholarship, 1985;17(3):91-93.
4. Henry C, Tuxill AC. Concept of the person: Introduction to the health professionals' curriculum. Journal of Advanced Nursing, 1987;12:245-249.
5. Hall BA, Allan JD. Sharpening nursing's focus by focusing on health. Nursing & Health Care, 1986;7(6):315-320.
6. Graham P, Constantini S, Balik B, et al. Operationalizing a nursing philosophy. J Nurs Adm 1987;17(3):14-18.
7. Trexler BJ. Nursing department purpose, philosophy, and objectives: Their use and effectiveness. J Nurs Adm, 1987;17(3):8-12.
8. Stevens BJ. The nurse as executive, 3rd ed. Rockville, MD.: Aspen Systems Corporation, 1985.
9. Cantor M. Philosophy, purpose, and objectives: Why do we have them? J Nurs Adm 1973;1:21-25.

SUGGESTED READINGS

PART I THE NURSING ORGANIZATION
UNIT ONE. FRAMEWORKS AND PHILOSOPHIES

Cantor M: Philosophy, purpose and objectives: Why do we have them? JONA 21-25, 1973.
Christman L: A conceptual model for centers of excellence, NAQ 12(4):1-4, 1988.
Donaldson S and Crowley D: The discipline of nursing, NO 26(2):113-120, 1978.
Drucker P: Management and the world's work, HBR 66(5):65-76, 1988.
Graham P et al: Operationalizing a nursing philosophy, JONA 17(3):14-18, 1987.
Henry B, Woods S, and Nagelkerk J: Nightingale's perspective on nursing administration, Nursing & Health Care 11(4):201-206, 1990.
Lynaugh J and Fagin C: Nursing comes of age, Image 20(4):184-190, 1988.
Murphy E: The professional status of nursing: A view from the Courts, NO 35(1):12-15, 1987.
Nyberg J and Simler M: Developing a framework for an integrated nursing department, JONA 9-15, 1979.
Trexler B: Nursing department purpose, philosophy, and objectives: Their use and effectiveness, JONA 17(3):8-12, 1987.

Unit Two

Leadership and Management Concepts and Theories

CHAPTER 3

Managers and Leaders
Are they different?

Abraham Zaleznik, PhD

What is the ideal way to develop leadership? Every society provides its own answer to this question, and each, in groping for answers, defines its deepest concerns about the purposes, distributions, and uses of power. Business has contributed its answer to the leadership question by evolving a new breed called the manager. Simultaneously, business has established a new power ethic that favors collective over individual leadership, the cult of the group over that of personality. While ensuring the competence, control, and the balance of power relations among groups with the potential for rivalry, managerial leadership unfortunately does not necessarily ensure imagination, creativity, or ethical behavior in guiding the destinies of corporate enterprises.

Leadership inevitably requires using power to influence the thoughts and actions of other people. Power in the hands of an individual entails human risks: first, the risk of equating power with the ability to get immediate results; second, the risk of ignoring the many different ways people can legitimately accumulate power; and third, the risk of losing self-control in the desire for power. The need to hedge

these risks accounts in part for the development of collective leadership and the managerial ethic. Consequently, an inherent conservatism dominates the culture of large organizations. In *The Second American Revolution,* John D. Rockefeller, 3rd. describes the conservatism of organizations:

> An organization is a system, with a logic of its own, and all the weight of tradition and inertia. The deck is stacked in favor of the tried and proven way of doing things and against the taking of risks and striking out in new directions.[1]

Out of this conservatism and inertia organizations provide succession to power through the development of managers rather than individual leaders. And the irony of the managerial ethic is that it fosters a bureaucratic culture in business, supposedly the last bastion protecting us from the encroachments and controls of bureaucracy in government and education. Perhaps the risks associated with power in the hands of an individual may be necessary ones for business to take if organizations are to break free of their inertia and bureaucratic conservatism.

MANAGER VS. LEADER PERSONALITY

Theodore Levitt has described the essential features of a managerial culture with its emphasis on rationality and control:

Management consists of the rational assessment of a situation and the systematic selection of goals and purposes (what is to be done?); the systematic development of strategies to achieve these goals; the marshalling of the required resources; the rational design, organization, direction, and control of the activities required to attain the selected purposes; and, finally, the motivating and rewarding of people to do the work.[2]

In other words, whether his or her energies are directed toward goals, resources, organization structures, or people, a manager is a problem solver. The manager asks himself, "What problems have to be solved, and what are the best ways to achieve results so that people will continue to contribute to this organization?" In this conception, leadership is a practical effort to direct affairs; and to fulfill his task, a manager requires that many people operate at different levels of status and responsibility. Our democratic society is, in fact, unique in having solved the problem of providing well-trained managers for business. The same solution stands ready to be applied to government, education, health care, and other institutions. It takes neither genius nor heroism to be a manager, but rather persistence, tough-mindedness, hard work, intelligence, analytical ability and, perhaps most important, tolerance and good will.

Another conception, however, attaches almost mystical beliefs to what leadership is and assumes that only great people are worthy of the drama of power and politics. Here, leadership is a psychodrama in which, as a precondition for control of a political structure, a lonely person must gain control of him or herself. Such an expectation of leadership contrasts sharply with the mundane, practical, and yet important conception that leadership is really managing work that other people do.

Two questions come to mind. Is this mystique of leadership merely a holdover from our collective childhood of dependency and our longing for good and heroic parents? Or, is there a basic truth lurking behind the need for leaders that no matter how competent managers are, their leadership stagnates because of their limitations in visualizing purposes and generating value in work? Without this imaginative capacity and the ability to communicate, managers, driven by their narrow purposes, perpetuate group conflicts instead of reforming them into broader desires and goals.

If indeed problems demand greatness, then, judging by past performance, the selection and development of leaders leave a great deal to chance. There are no known ways to train "great" leaders. Furthermore, beyond what we leave to chance, there is a deeper issue in the relationship between the need for competent managers and the longing for great leaders.

What it takes to ensure the supply of people who will assume practical responsibility may inhibit the development of great leaders. Conversely, the presence of great leaders may undermine the development of managers who become very anxious in the relative disorder that leaders seem to generate. The antagonism in aim (to have many competent managers as well as great leaders) often remains obscure in stable and well-developed societies. But the antagonism surfaces during periods of stress and change, as it did in the Western countries during both the Great Depression and World War II. The tension also appears in the struggle for power between theorists and professional managers in revolutionary societies.

It is easy enough to dismiss the dilemma I pose (of training managers while we may need new leaders, or leaders at the expense of managers) by saying that the need is for people who can be *both* managers and leaders. The truth of the matter as I see it, however, is that just as a managerial culture is different from the entrepreneurial culture that develops when leaders appear in organizations, managers and leaders are very different kinds of people. They differ in motivation, personal history, and in how they think and act.

A technologically oriented and economically successful society tends to depreciate the need for great leaders. Such societies hold a deep and abiding faith in rational methods of solving problems, including problems of value, economics, and justice. Once rational methods of solving problems are broken down into elements, organized, and taught as skills, then society's faith in technique over personal qualities in leadership remains the guiding conception for a democratic society contemplating its leadership requirements. But there are times when tinkering and trial and error prove inadequate to the emerging problems of selecting goals, allocating resources, and distributing wealth and opportunity. During such times, the democratic society needs to find leaders who use themselves as the instruments of learning and acting, instead of managers who use their accumulation of collective experience to get where they are going.

The most impressive spokesman, as well as exemplar of the managerial viewpoint, was Alfred P. Sloan, Jr. who, along with Pierre du Pont, designed the modern corporate structure. Reflecting on what makes one management successful while another fails, Sloan suggested that "good management rests on a reconciliation of centralization and decentralization, or 'decentralization with coordinated control' ".[3]

Sloan's conception of management, as well as his practice, developed by trial and error, and by the accumulation of experience. Sloan wrote:

> There is no hard and fast rule for sorting out the various responsibilities and the best way to assign them. The balance which is struck . . . varies according to what is being decided, the circumstances of the time, past experience, and the temperaments and skills of the executive involved.[4]

In other words, in much the same way that the inventors of the late nineteenth century tried, failed, and fitted until they hit on a product or method, managers who innovate in developing organizations are "tinkerers." They do not have a grand design or experience the intuitive flash of insight that, borrowing from modern science, we have come to call the "breakthrough."

Managers and leaders differ fundamentally in their world views. The dimensions for assessing these differences include managers' and leaders' orientations toward their goals, their work, their human relations, and their selves.

Attitudes toward goals

Managers tend to adopt impersonal, if not passive, attitudes toward goals. Managerial goals arise out of necessities rather than desires, and, therefore, are deeply embedded in the history and culture of the organization.

Frederic G. Donner, chairman and chief executive officer of General Motors from 1958 to 1967, ex-

pressed this impersonal and passive attitude toward goals in defining GM's position on product development:

> . . . To meet the challenge of the marketplace, we must recognize changes in customer needs and desires far enough ahead to have the right products in the right places at the right time and in the right quantity.
>
> We must balance trends in preference against the many compromises that are necessary to make a final product that is both reliable and good looking, that performs well and that sells at a competitive price in the necessary volume. We must design, not just the cars we would like to build, but more importantly, the cars that our customers want to buy.[5]

Nowhere in this formulation of how a product comes into being is there a notion that consumer tastes and preferences arise in part as a result of what manufacturers do. In reality, through product design, advertising, and promotion, consumers learn to like what they then say they need. Few would argue that people who enjoy taking snapshots *need* a camera that also develops pictures. But in response to novelty, convenience, a shorter interval between acting (taking the snap) and gaining pleasure (seeing the shot), the Polaroid camera succeeded in the marketplace. But it is inconceivable that Edwin Land responded to impressions of consumer need. Instead, he translated a technology (polarization of light) into a product, which proliferated and stimulated consumers' desires.

The example of Polaroid and Land suggests how leaders think about goals. They are active instead of reactive, shaping ideas instead of responding to them. Leaders adopt a personal and active attitude toward goals. The influence a leader exerts in altering moods, evoking images and expectations, and in establishing specific desires and objectives determines the direction a business takes. The net result of this influence is to change the way people think about what is desirable, possible, and necessary.

Conceptions of work

What do managers and leaders do? What is the nature of their respective work?

Leaders and managers differ in their conceptions. Managers tend to view work as an enabling process involving some combination of people and ideas interacting to establish strategies and make decisions. Managers help the process along by a range of skills, including calculating the interests in opposition, staging and timing the surfacing of controversial issues, and reducing tensions. In this enabling process, managers appear flexible in the use of tactics: they negotiate and bargain, on the one hand, and use rewards and punishments, and other forms of coercion, on the other. Machiavelli wrote for managers and not necessarily for leaders.

Alfred Sloan illustrated how this enabling process works in situations of conflict. The time was the early 1920s when the Ford Motor Co. still dominated the automobile industry using, as did General Motors, the conventional water-cooled engine. With the full backing of Pierre du Pont, Charles Kettering dedicated himself to the design of an air-cooled engine, which, if successful, would have been a great technical and market coup for GM. Kettering believed in his product, but the manufacturing division heads at GM remained skeptical and later opposed the new design on two grounds: first, that it was technically unreliable, and second, that the corporation was putting all its eggs in one basket by investing in a new product instead of attending to the current marketing situation.

In the summer of 1923 after a series of false starts and after its decision to recall the copper-cooled Chevrolets from dealers and customers, GM management reorganized and finally scrapped the project. When it dawned on Kettering that the company had rejected the engine, he was deeply discouraged and wrote to Sloan that without the "organized resistance" against the project it would succeed and that unless the project were saved, he would leave the company.

Alfred Sloan was all too aware of the fact that Kettering was unhappy and indeed intended to leave General Motors. Sloan was also aware of the fact that, while the manufacturing divisions strongly opposed the new engine, Pierre du Pont supported Kettering. Furthermore, Sloan had himself gone on record in a letter to Kettering less than two years

earlier expressing full confidence in him. The problem Sloan now had was to make his decision stick, keep Kettering in the organization (he was much too valuable to lose), avoid alienating du Pont, and encourage the division heads to move speedily in developing product lines using conventional water-cooled engines.

The actions that Sloan took in the face of this conflict reveal much about how managers work. First, he tried to reassure Kettering by presenting the problem in a very ambiguous fashion, suggesting that he and the Executive Committee sided with Kettering, but that it would not be practical to force the divisions to do what they were opposed to. He presented the problem as being a question of the people, not the product. Second, he proposed to reorganize around the problem by consolidating all functions in a new division that would be responsible for the design, production, and marketing of the new car. This solution, however, appeared as ambiguous as his efforts to placate and keep Kettering in General Motors. Sloan wrote: "My plan was to create an independent pilot operation under the sole jurisdiction of Mr. Kettering, a kind of copper-cooled-car division. Mr. Kettering would designate his own chief engineer and his production staff to solve the technical problems of manufacture."[6]

While Sloan did not discuss the practical value of this solution, which included saddling an inventor with management responsibility, he in effect used this plan to limit his conflict with Pierre du Pont.

In effect, the managerial solution that Sloan arranged and pressed for adoption limited the options available to others. The structural solution narrowed choices, even limiting emotional reactions to the point where the key people could do nothing but go along, and even allowed Sloan to say in his memorandum to du Pont, "We have discussed the matter with Mr. Kettering at some length this morning and he agrees with us absolutely on every point we made. He appears to receive the suggestion enthusiastically and has every confidence that it can be put across along these lines."[7]

Having placated people who opposed his views by developing a structural solution that appeared to give something but in reality only limited options, Sloan could then authorize the car division's general manager, with whom he basically agreed, to move quickly in designing water-cooled cars for the immediate market demand.

Years later Sloan wrote, evidently with tongue in cheek, "The copper-cooled car never came up again in a big way. It just died out, I don't know why."[8]

In order to get people to accept solutions to problems, managers need to coordinate and balance continually. Interestingly enough, this managerial work has much in common with what diplomats and mediators do, with Henry Kissinger apparently an outstanding practitioner. The manager aims at shifting balances of power toward solutions acceptable as a compromise among conflicting values.

What about leaders, what do they do? Where managers act to limit choices, leaders work in the opposite direction, to develop fresh approaches to long-standing problems and to open issues for new options. Stanley and Inge Hoffmann, the political scientists, liken the leader's work to that of the artist. But unlike most artists, the leader himself is an integral part of the aesthetic product. One cannot look at a leader's art without looking at the artist. On Charles de Gaulle as a political artist, they wrote: "And each of his major political acts, however tortuous the means or the details, has been whole, indivisible and unmistakably his own, like an artistic act."[9]

The closest one can get to a product apart from the artist is the ideas that occupy, indeed at times obsess, the leader's mental life. To be effective, however, the leader needs to project his ideas into images that excite people, and only then develop choices that give the projected images substance. Consequently, leaders create excitement in work.

John F. Kennedy's brief presidency shows both the strengths and weaknesses connected with the excitement leaders generate in their work. In his inaugural address he said, "Let every nation know, whether it wishes us well or ill, that we shall pay any price, bear any burden, meet any hardship, support any friend, oppose any foe, in order to assure the survival and the success of liberty."

This much-quoted statement forced people to react beyond immediate concerns and to identify with Kennedy and with important shared ideals. But upon closer scrutiny the statement must be seen as absurd because it promises a position which if in fact adopted, as in the Viet Nam War, could produce disastrous results. Yet unless expectations are aroused and mobilized, with all the dangers of frustration inherent in heightened desire, new thinking and new choice can never come to light.

Leaders work from high-risk positions, indeed often are temperamentally disposed to seek out risk and danger, especially where opportunity and reward appear high. From my observations, why one individual seeks risks while another approaches problems conservatively depends more on his or her personality and less on conscious choice. For some, especially those who become managers, the instinct for survival dominates their need for risk, and their ability to tolerate mundane, practical work assists their survival. The same cannot be said for leaders who sometimes react to mundane work as to an affliction.

Relations with others

Managers prefer to work with people; they avoid solitary activity because it makes them anxious. Several years ago, I directed studies on the psychological aspects of career. The need to seek out others with whom to work and collaborate seemed to stand out as important characteristics of managers. When asked, for example, to write imaginative stories in response to a picture showing a single figure (a boy contemplating a violin, or a man silhouetted in a state of reflection), managers populated their stories with people. The following is an example of a manager's imaginative story about the young boy contemplating a violin:

> Mom and Dad insisted that junior take music lessons so that someday he can become a concert musician. His instrument was ordered and had just arrived. Junior is weighing the alternatives of playing football with the other kids or playing with the squeak box. He can't understand how his parents could think a violin is better than a touchdown.
>
> After four months of practicing the violin, junior has had more than enough, Daddy is going out of his mind, and Mommy is willing to give in reluctantly to the men's wishes. Football season is now over, but a good third baseman will take the field next spring.[10]

This story illustrates two themes that clarify managerial attitudes toward human relations. The first, as I have suggested, is to seek out activity with other people (i.e. the football team), and the second is to maintain a low level of emotional involvement in these relationships. The low emotional involvement appears in the writer's use of conventional metaphors, even clichés, and in the depiction of the ready transformation of potential conflict into harmonious decisions. In this case, Junior, Mommy, and Daddy agree to give up the violin for manly sports.

These two themes may seem paradoxical, but their coexistence supports what a manager does, including reconciling differences, seeking compromises, and establishing a balance of power. A further idea demonstrated by how the manager wrote the story is that managers may lack empathy, or the capacity to sense intuitively the thoughts and feelings of others. To illustrate attempts to be empathic, here is another story written to the same stimulus picture by someone considered by his peers to be a leader:

> This little boy has the appearance of being a sincere artist, one who is deeply affected by the violin, and has an intense desire to master the instrument.
>
> He seems to have just completed his normal practice session and appears to be somewhat crestfallen at his inability to produce the sounds which he is sure lie within the violin.
>
> He appears to be in the process of making a vow to himself to expend the necessary time and effort to play this instrument until he satisfies himself that he is able to bring forth the qualities of music which he feels within himself.
>
> With this type of determination and carry through, this boy became one of the great violinists of his day.[11]

Empathy is not simply a matter of paying attention to other people. It is also the capacity to take in emotional signals and to make them mean something in a relationship with an individual. People who describe another person as "deeply affected" with "intense desire," as capable of feeling "crestfallen" and as one who can "vow to himself," would seem to have an inner perceptiveness that they can use in their relationships with others.

Managers relate to people according to the role they play in a sequence of events or in a decision-making *process,* while leaders, who are concerned with ideas, relate in more intuitive and empathetic ways. The manager's orientation to people, as actors in a sequence of events, deflects his or her attention away from the substance of people's concerns and toward their roles in a process. The distinction is simply between a manager's attention to *how* things get done and a leader's to *what* the events and decisions mean to participants.

In recent years, managers have taken over from game theory the notion that decision-making events can be one of two types: the win-lose situation (or zero-sum game) or the win-win situation in which everybody in the action comes out ahead. As part of the process of reconciling differences among people and maintaining balances of power, managers strive to convert win-lose into win-win situations.

As an illustration, take the decision of how to allocate capital resources among operating divisions in a large, decentralized organization. On the face of it, the dollars available for distribution are limited at any given time. Presumably, therefore, the more one division gets, the less is available for other divisions.

Managers tend to view this situation (as it affects human relations) as a conversion issue: how to make what seems like a win-lose problem into a win-win problem. Several solutions to this situation come to mind. First, the manager focuses others' attention on procedure and not on substance. Here the actors become engrossed in the bigger problem of *how* to make decisions, not *what* decisions to make. Once committed to the bigger problem, the actors have to support the outcome since they were involved in formulating decision rules. Because the actors believe in the rules they formulated, they will accept present losses in the expectation that next time they will win.

Second, the manager communicates to his subordinates indirectly, using "signals" instead of "messages." A signal has a number of possible implicit positions in it while a message clearly states a position. Signals are inconclusive and subject to reinterpretation should people become upset and angry, while messages involve the direct consequence that some people will indeed not like what they hear. The nature of messages heightens emotional response, and, as I have indicated, emotionally makes managers anxious. With signals, the question of who wins and who loses often becomes obscured.

Third, the manager plays for time. Managers seem to recognize that with the passage of time and the delay of major decisions, compromises emerge that take the sting out of win-lose situations; and the original "game" will be superseded by additional ones. Therefore, compromises may mean that one wins and loses simultaneously, depending on which of the games one evaluates.

There are undoubtedly many other tactical moves managers use to change human situations from win-lose to win-win. But the point to be made is that such tactics focus on the decision-making process itself and interest managers rather than leaders. The interest in tactics involves costs as well as benefits, including making organizations fatter in bureaucratic and political intrigue and leaner in direct, hard activity and warm human relationships. Consequently, one often hears subordinates characterize managers as inscrutable, detached, and manipulative. These adjectives arise from the subordinates' perception that they are linked together in a process whose purpose, beyond simply making decisions, is to maintain a controlled as well as rational and equitable structure. These adjectives suggest that managers need order in the face of the potential chaos that many fear in human relationships.

In contrast, one often hears leaders referred to in adjectives rich in emotional content. Leaders attract strong feelings of identity and difference, or of love and hate. Human relations in leader-dominated structures often appear turbulent, intense, and at times even disorganized. Such an atmosphere intensifies individual motivation and often produces unanticipated outcomes. Does this intense motivation lead to innovation and high performance, or does it represent wasted energy?

Senses of self

In *The Varieties of Religious Experience,* William James describes two basic personality types, "once-born" and "twice-born."[12] People of the former personality type are those for whom adjustments to life have been straightforward and whose lives have been more or less a peaceful flow from the moment of their births. The twice-borns, on the other hand, have not had an easy time of it. Their lives are marked by a continual struggle to attain some sense of order. Unlike the once-borns they cannot take things for granted. According to James, these personalities have equally different world views. For a once-born personality, the sense of self, as a guide to conduct and attitude, derives from a feeling of being at home and in harmony with one's environment. For a twice-born, the sense of self derives from a feeling of profound separateness.

A sense of belonging or of being separate has a practical significance for the kinds of investments managers and leaders make in their careers. Managers see themselves as conservators and regulators of an existing order of affairs with which they personally identify and from which they gain rewards. Perpetuating and strengthening existing institutions enhances a manager's sense of self-worth: he or she is performing in a role that harmonizes with the ideals of duty and responsibility. William James had this harmony in mind — this sense of self as flowing easily to and from the outer world — in defining a once-born personality. If one feels oneself as a member of institutions, contributing to their well-being, then one fulfills a mission in life and feels rewarded for having measured up to ideals. This reward transcends material gains and answers the more fundamental desire for personal integrity which is achieved by identifying with existing institutions.

Leaders tend to be twice-born personalities, people who feel separate from their environment, including other people. They may work in organizations, but they never belong to them. Their sense of who they are does not depend upon memberships, work roles, or other social indicators of identity. What seems to follow from this idea about separateness is some theoretical basis for explaining why certain individuals search out opportunities for change. The methods to bring about change may be technological, political, or ideological, but the object is the same: to profoundly alter human, economic, and political relationships.

Sociologists refer to the preparation individuals undergo to perform in roles as the socialization process. Where individuals experience themselves as an integral part of the social structure (their self-esteem gains strength through participation and conformity), social standards exert powerful effects in maintaining the individual's personal sense of continuity, even beyond the early years in the family. The line of development from the family to schools, then to career is cumulative and reinforcing. When the line of development is not reinforcing because of significant disruptions in relationships or other problems experienced in the family or other social institutions, the individual turns inward and struggles to establish self-esteem, identity, and order. Here the psychological dynamics center on the experience with loss and the efforts at recovery.

In considering the development of leadership, we have to examine two different courses of life history: (1) development through socialization, which prepares the individual to guide institutions and to maintain the existing balance of social relations; and (2) development through personal mastery, which impels an individual to struggle for psychological and social change. Society produces its managerial talent through the first line of development, while through the second leaders emerge.

DEVELOPMENT OF LEADERSHIP

The development of every person begins in the family. Each person experiences the traumas associated with separating from his or her parents, as well as the pain that follows such frustration. In the same vein, all individuals face the difficulties of achieving self-regulation and self-control. But for some, perhaps a majority, the fortunes of childhood provide adequate gratifications and sufficient opportunities to find substitutes for rewards no longer available. Such individuals, the "once-borns," make moderate identifications with parents and find a harmony between what they expect and what they are able to realize from life.

But suppose the pains of separation are amplified by a combination of parental demands and the individual's needs to the degree that a sense of isolation, of being special, and of wariness disrupts the bonds that attach children to parents and other authority figures? Under such conditions, and given a special aptitude, the origins of which remain mysterious, the person becomes deeply involved in his or her inner world at the expense of interest in the outer world. For such a person, self-esteem no longer depends solely upon positive attachments and real rewards. A form of self-reliance takes hold along with expectations of performance and achievement, and perhaps even the desire to do great works.

Such self-perceptions can come to nothing if the individual's talents are negligible. Even with strong talents, there are no guarantees that achievement will follow, let alone that the end result will be for good rather than evil. Other factors enter into development. For one thing, leaders are like artists and other gifted people who often struggle with neuroses; their ability to function varies considerably even over the short run, and some potential leaders may lose the struggle altogether. Also, beyond early childhood, the patterns of development that affect managers and leaders involve the selective influence of particular people. Just as they appear flexible and evenly distributed in the types of talents available for development, managers form moderate and widely distributed attachments. Leaders, on the other hand, establish, and also break off, intensive one-to-one relationships.

It is a common observation that people with great talents are often only indifferent students. No one, for example, could have predicted Einstein's great achievements on the basis of his mediocre record in school. The reason for mediocrity is obviously not the absence of ability. It may result, instead, from self-absorption and the inability to pay attention to the ordinary tasks at hand. The only sure way an individual can interrupt reverie-like preoccupation and self-absorption is to form a deep attachment to a great teacher or other benevolent person who understands and has the ability to communicate with the gifted individual.

Whether gifted individuals find what they need in one-to-one relationships depends on the availability of sensitive and intuitive mentors who have a vocation in cultivating talent. Fortunately, when the generations do meet and the self-selections occur, we learn more about how to develop leaders and how talented people of different generations influence each other.

While apparently destined for a mediocre career, people who form important one-to-one relationships are able to accelerate and intensify their development through an apprenticeship. The background for such apprenticeships, or the psychological readiness of an individual to benefit from an intensive relationship, depends upon some experience in life that forces the individual to turn inward. A case example will make this point clearer. This example comes from the life of Dwight David Eisenhower, and illustrates the transformation of a career from competent to outstanding.[13]

Dwight Eisenhower's early career in the Army foreshadowed very little about his future development. During World War I, while some of his West Point classmates were already experiencing the war first-hand in France, Eisenhower felt "embedded in the monotony and unsought safety of the Zone of the Interior . . . that was intolerable punishment."[14]

Shortly after World War I, Eisenhower, then a young officer somewhat pessimistic about his career chances, asked for a transfer to Panama to work under General Fox Connor, a senior officer whom Eisenhower admired. The army turned down Eisenhower's request. This setback was very much on Eisenhower's mind when Ikey, his first-born son, succumbed to influenza. By some sense of responsibility for its own, the army transferred Eisenhower to Panama, where he took up his duties under General Connor with the shadow of his lost son very much upon him.

In a relationship with the kind of father he would have wanted to be, Eisenhower reverted to being the son he lost. In this highly charged situation, Eisenhower began to learn from his mentor. General Connor offered, and Eisenhower gladly took, a magnificent tutorial on the military. The effects of this relationship on Eisenhower cannot be measured quantitatively, but, in Eisenhower's own reflections and the unfolding of his career, one cannot overestimate its significance in the reintegration of a person shattered by grief.

As Eisenhower wrote later about Connor, "Life with General Connor was a sort of graduate school in military affairs and the humanities, leavened by a man who was experienced in his knowledge of men and their conduct. I can never adequately express my gratitude to this one gentleman. . . . In a lifetime of association with great and good men, he is the one more or less invisible figure to whom I owe an incalculable debt."[15]

Some time after his tour of duty with General Connor, Eisenhower's breakthrough occurred. He received orders to attend the Command and General Staff School at Fort Leavenworth, one of the most competitive schools in the army. It was a coveted appointment, and Eisenhower took advantage of the opportunity. Unlike his performance in high school and West Point, his work at the Command School was excellent; he was graduated first in his class.

Psychological biographies of gifted people repeatedly demonstrate the important part a mentor plays in developing an individual. Andrew Carnegie owed much to his senior, Thomas A. Scott. As head of the Western Division of the Pennsylvania Railroad, Scott recognized talent and the desire to learn in the young telegrapher assigned to him. By giving Carnegie increasing responsibility and by providing him with the opportunity to learn through close personal observation, Scott added to Carnegie's self-confidence and sense of achievement. Because of his own personal strength and achievement, Scott did not fear Carnegie's aggressiveness. Rather, he gave it full play in encouraging Carnegie's initiative.

Mentors take risks with people. They bet initially on talent they perceive in younger people. Mentors also risk emotional involvement in working closely with their juniors. The risks do not always pay off, but the willingness to take them appears crucial in developing leaders.

CAN ORGANIZATIONS DEVELOP LEADERS?

The examples I have given of how leaders develop suggest the importance of personal influence and the one-to-one relationship. For organizations to encourage consciously the development of leaders as compared with managers would mean developing one-to-one relationships between junior and senior executives and, more important, fostering a culture of individualism and possibly elitism. The elitism arises out of the desire to identify talent and other qualities suggestive of the ability to lead and not simply to manage.

The Jewel Companies Inc. enjoy a reputation for developing talented people. The chairman and chief executive officer, Donald S. Perkins, is perhaps a good example of a person brought along through the mentor approach. Franklin J. Lunding, who was Perkins's mentor, expressed the philosophy of taking risks with young people this way:

> Young people today want in on the action. They don't want to sit around for six months trimming lettuce.[16]

This statement runs counter to the culture that attaches primary importance to slow progression based on experience and proved competence. It is a high-risk philosophy, one that requires time for the attachment between senior and junior people to grow and be meaningful, and one that is bound to produce more failures than successes.

The elitism is an especially sensitive issue. At Jewel the MBA degree symbolized the elite. Lunding attracted Perkins to Jewel at a time when business school graduates had little interest in retailing in general, and food distribution in particular. Yet the elitism seemed to pay off: not only did Perkins become the president at age 37, but also under the leadership of young executives recruited into Jewel with the promise of opportunity for growth and advancement, Jewel managed to diversify into discount and drug chains and still remain strong in food retailing. By assigning each recruit to a vice president who acted as sponsor, Jewel evidently tried to build a structure around the mentor approach to developing leaders. To counteract the elitism implied in such an approach, the company also introduced an "equalizer" in what Perkins described as "the first assistant philosophy." Perkins stated:

> Being a good first assistant means that each management person thinks of himself not as the order-giving, domineering boss, but as the first assistant to those who 'report' to him in a more typical organizational sense. Thus we mentally turn our organizational charts upside-down and challenge ourselves to seek ways in which we can lead . . . by helping . . . by teaching . . . by listening . . . and by

managing in the true democratic sense . . . that is, with the consent of the managed. Thus the satisfactions of leadership come from helping others to get things done and changed — and not from getting credit for doing and changing things ourselves.[17]

While this statement would seem to be more egalitarian than elitist, it does reinforce a youth-oriented culture since it defines the senior officer's job as primarily helping the junior person.

A myth about how people learn and develop that seems to have taken hold in the American culture also dominates thinking in business. The myth is that people learn best from their peers. Supposedly, the threat of evaluation and even humiliation recedes in peer relations because of the tendency for mutual identification and the social restraints on authoritarian behavior among equals. Peer training in organizations occurs in various forms. The use, for example, of task forces made up of peers from several interested occupational groups (sales, production, research, and finance) supposedly removes the restraints of authority on the individual's willingness to assert and exchange ideas. As a result, so the theory goes, people interact more freely, listen more objectively to criticism and other points of view and, finally, learn from this healthy interchange.

Another application of peer training exists in some large corporations, such as Philips, N.V. in Holland, where organization structure is built on the principle of joint responsibility of two peers, one representing the commercial end of the business and the other the technical. Formally, both hold equal responsibility for geographic operations or product groups, as the case may be. As a practical matter, it may turn out that one or the other of the peers dominates the management. Nevertheless, the main interaction is between two or more equals.

The principal question I would raise about such arrangements is whether they perpetuate the managerial orientation, and preclude the formation of one-to-one relationships between senior people and potential leaders.

Aware of the possible stifling effects of peer relationships on aggressiveness and individual initiative, another company, much smaller than Philips, utilizes joint responsibility of peers for operating units, with one important difference. The chief executive of 'his company encourages competition and rivalry among peers, ultimately appointing the one who comes out on top for increased responsibility. These hybrid arrangements produce some unintended consequences that can be disastrous. There is no easy way to limit rivalry. Instead, it permeates all levels of the operation and opens the way for the formation of cliques in an atmosphere of intrigue.

A large, integrated oil company has accepted the importance of developing leaders through the direct influence of senior on junior executives. One chairman and chief executive officer regularly selected one talented university graduate whom he appointed his special assistant, and with whom he would work closely for a year. At the end of the year, the junior executive would become available for assignment to one of the operating divisions, where he would be assigned to a responsible post rather than a training position. The mentor relationship had acquainted the junior executive firsthand with the use of power, and with the important antidotes to the power disease called *hubris* — performance and integrity.

Working in one-to-one relationships, where there is a formal and recognized difference in the power of the actors, takes a great deal of tolerance for emotional interchange. This interchange, inevitable in close working arrangements, probably accounts for the reluctance of many executives to become involved in such relationships. *Fortune* carried an interesting story on the departure of a key executive, John W. Hanley, from the top management of Procter & Gamble, for the chief executive officer position at Monsanto.[18] According to this account, the chief executive and chairman of P&G passed over Hanley for appointment to the presidency and named another executive vice president to this post instead.

The chairman evidently felt he could not work well with Hanley who, by his own acknowledgement, was aggressive, eager to experiment and change practices, and constantly challenged his superior. A chief executive officer naturally has the right to select people with whom he feels congenial. But I wonder whether a greater capacity on the part of senior officers to tolerate the competitive impulses and

behavior of their subordinates might not be healthy for corporations. At least a greater tolerance for interchange would not favor the managerial team player at the expense of the individual who might become a leader.

I am constantly surprised at the frequency with which chief executives feel threatened by open challenges to their ideas, as though the source of their authority, rather than their specific ideas, were at issue. In one case a chief executive officer, who was troubled by the aggressiveness and sometimes outright rudeness of one of his talented vice presidents, used various indirect methods such as group meetings and hints from outside directors to avoid dealing with his subordinate. I advised the executive to deal head-on with what irritated him. I suggested that by direct, face-to-face confrontation, both he and his subordinate would learn to validate the distinction between the authority to be preserved and the issues to be debated.

To confront is also to tolerate aggressive interchange, and has the net effect of stripping away the veils of ambiguity and signaling so characteristic of managerial cultures, as well as encouraging the emotional relationship leaders need if they are to survive.

REFERENCES

1. John D. Rockefeller, 3rd., *The Second American Revolution* (New York: Harper-Row, 1973), p. 72.
2. Theodore Levitt, "Management and the Post Industrial Society," *The Public Interest,* Summer 1976, p. 73.
3. Alfred P. Sloan, Jr., *My Years with General Motors* (New York: Doubleday & Co. 1964), p. 429.
4. Ibid., p. 429.
5. Ibid., p. 440.
6. Ibid., p. 91.
7. Ibid., p. 91.
8. Ibid., p. 91.
9. Stanley and Inge Hoffmann, "The Will for Grandeur: de Gaulle as Political Artist," *Daedalus,* Summer 1968, p. 849.
10. Abraham Zaleznik, Gene W. Dalton, and Louis B. Barnes, *Orientation and Conflict in Career,* (Boston: Division of Research, Harvard Business School, 1970), p. 316.
11. Ibid., p. 294.
12. William James, *Varieties of Religious Experience* (New York: Mentor Books, 1958).

13. This example is included in Abraham Zaleznik and Manfred F.R. Kets de Vries, *Power and the Corporate Mind* (Boston: Houghton Mifflin, 1975).

14. Dwight D. Eisenhower, *At Ease: Stories I Tell to Friends* (New York: Doubleday, 1967), p. 136.

15. Ibid., p. 187.

16. "Jewel Lets Young Men Make Mistakes," *Business Week,* January 17, 1970, p. 90.

17. "What Makes Jewel Shine so Bright," *Progressive Grocer,* September, 1973, p. 76.

18. "Jack Hanley Got There by Selling Harder," *Fortune,* November, 1976

CHAPTER 4

Exceptional Executive Leadership Shapes Nursing's Future

Margaret D. Sovie, RN, PhD, FAAN

An executive may be defined as a person or group having administrative or managerial authority in an organization. A leader is a guide or person who leads others along a way (Morris, 1971). Many individuals can and do serve as leaders. However, executive leadership limits the universe of possibilities and narrows the focus to the leadership roles required of those individuals with administrative or managerial responsibilities. For members of the nursing profession, executive leadership positions (based on these definitions) include head nurses, supervisors, coordinators, directors, chiefs, clinicians, managers, faculty members who manage courses, and students, deans, vice presidents, presidents, and chief nurse executives under whatever title might be created next.

Excellence in executive leadership is essential to the success and high performance of this nation's diverse health-care organizations and the educational institutions that prepare the care givers, teachers, and researchers required to provide effective and efficient health-care services to society.

The leadership activities of these executives direct the present and shape the future, creating paths on which we can move together and correcting directions along the way. I believe that exceptional executive leadership will move us towards a future where nurses

are recognized as full partners in the health enterprise. But before discussing exceptional executive leadership, let us examine the health enterprise more closely.

HEALTH CARE — THE NATION'S THIRD LARGEST BUSINESS

Health care has become the nation's third largest business (Rutigliano, 1985). Rising health-care costs have provoked increasing attention from the business communities as well as from the federal and state governments. In 1985, despite intense efforts to control costs, health-care expenditures totaled $425 billion, representing 10.7% of the gross national product (GNP), up from 10.3% in 1984 and almost double the 1965 health expenditures. Hospital care represented almost 40% of the total 1985 health expenditures ("Health Spending," 1986). Yet hospital admissions dropped 4.6% in 1985 with the biggest drop in the over-65 population, which had 5% fewer admissions in 1985 than in 1984. Average length of stay also dropped 1.1% ("Admissions Drop," 1986).

Effects of prospective payment. The Medicare prospective payment system (PPS) has had a decided effect on hospitalization rates as well as lengths of stay. In fact, the American Association of Retired Persons, Gray Panthers, American Medical Association, American Hospital Association, and American Nurses'

Reprinted from *Nursing Economics,* Vol. 5, No. 1, with permission of Anthony J. Jannetti, Inc. © 1987.

Association have joined forces to support the monitoring of the effects of PPS on the quality of patient care. In the April 1986 Prospective Payment Assessment Commission (ProPAC) Report to the Secretary of Health and Human Services, four major areas of concern were identified:

1. Patients are discharged sicker and quicker.
2. Beneficiaries and providers have misconceptions about PPS and Medicare benefits.
3. Alternative care may not be available and/or accessible.
4. Quality monitoring mechanisms for alternative health-care delivery modes are not in place or are beyond the scope of the professional review organizations.

These concerns emanate from the radical changes in payment mechanisms that have been implemented and the resulting changes in the health-care system. These national groups are encouraging the establishment of mechanisms to ensure access to quality care for all people.

Business initiatives to control costs.   Accompanying the federal actions have been a series of initiatives implemented by business and industrial leaders to cut health-care costs and to help employees understand that the costs of health benefits must be controlled. Rutigliano (1985) reported that employee health insurance will cost more than $100 billion this year and that expenditures for health-care services have climbed to 8% to 10% of payroll.

These spiraling costs have precipitated new approaches to reducing and controlling costs. These "intervention plans" include: (a) requiring the health-care provider to get authorization prior to rendering care, (b) contractual arrangements with preferred provider organizations, (c) providing incentives to employees who select less costly approaches to care, (d) establishing deductibles and coinsurance to encourage prudent buying, and (e) performing utilization review on hospital claims. In terms of audits, A.S. Hansen, Inc., a Chicago benefits consulting firm, estimates that savings up to $3 can be realized for every $1 invested in employees' hospital bills' audits (Naisbitt & Aburdene, 1985). Some companies now provide incentives to their employees to monitor their own health-care costs. For example, Uniroyal, Inc. of

Connecticut employees receive half of any overcharges that they identify on their health-care bills.

These types of actions by the government and business sectors are producing an industrialization or economic transformation of the U.S. health-care system. Competition, product pricing, and prudent buying have come to be expected and are encouraged and supported. The results speak for themselves. For example, Joseph Califano, former Secretary of Health, Education and Welfare, is credited with helping to cut Chrysler Corporation's health-care expenditures by 15% over the past 2 years. Chrysler, with Califano's leadership, now views health care as any other product, and buyers conduct hard negotiations to get the best price (Rutigliano, 1985).

Increase in alternative delivery methods. Such efforts to control health-care costs have produced increasing emphasis on alternative methods of health-care management. Ambulatory surgical centers and emergicenters are common. Health-care problems are managed in the home; office; clinic; or hospital, a setting of last resort. Today, hospitals are used when no other approach will do. Prospective payment systems using diagnosis related groups (DRGs) to determine price have created the phenomenon identified as "sicker and quicker." Patients enter hospitals sicker and leave quicker, returning home with care and treatment demands that were considered high tech and at the cutting edge of hospital treatment just a few years ago. Home care and alternative care services are in great demand. Multiple types of providers are vying for market share, and competition based on price is encouraged.

Challenges presented by technological advances.   Advances in science and technology have added to the complexity by creating new demands that must be met by our health systems. From birth to death, we have new problems and concerns with which to deal. The extremes of age present particularly taxing challenges — from the 500 gram neonate to the increasing numbers of citizens 85 years of age and older. Technological advances have occurred at such a rapid rate that for example, in less than a decade, heart and liver organ transplants have moved from experimental status to accepted therapy for patients meeting the qualifying criteria. Increasingly, providers and payers will have to face the questions of who shall live and at what costs.

Economic pressures, changes in care delivery approaches (including corporate restructuring of health-care institutions), new societal expectations and demands, increasing numbers of aging citizens, growing enrollments in health maintenance organizations (HMOs), and prudent buyer concepts in health-care services are signs of systems in transition; it will never again be business as usual.

LEADERSHIP FOR THE FUTURE

Indeed, these are turbulent times in the health-care industry, times marked by the rapidity of the changes and increasing uncertainty. Traditional approaches and practices are being challenged, and many are yielding to the scrutiny—eroding and disappearing. New clinical practices and patterns are being created. Effective leadership is critical. Exceptional executive nurse leaders are needed on every front of the health-care business as well as in all of the educational institutions preparing the practitioners of tomorrow.

Burns (1978) describes leadership as getting things done and making things work. The leader is viewed as a pragmatist. Power and leadership are measured by the degree of production of intended results. However, leadership is also much more, and Burns (1978) describes it as "transforming leadership"—the process by which the leader and led affect each other, raising one another to higher levels of motivation and morality. Transforming leadership ultimately becomes moral in that it raises the level of human conduct and ethical aspirations of both the leader and led.

Mahoney (1984) states that leaders must respond to the needs and hopes of people, reconstruct and reorder priorities, control excessive expectations, and integrate individual and factional objectives for the benefit of the whole. This requires giving definition to individual expression and resolving the dichotomy between individual and institutional goals.

Exceptional executives enable the process of reciprocation to unfold—the carrying out of a psychological contract between a person and the work organization in which mutual expectations are fulfilled and mutual needs satisfied (Levinson, 1968). Levinson captures the essence of this type of transforming leadership with quotes from Emerson and Goethe:

> In "Considerations by the Way," Emerson wrote: "Our chief want in life is somebody who shall make us do what we can." Goethe expressed the same thought somewhat differently in *Poetry and Truth from My Own Life:* "If you treat a man as he is, he will stay as he is, but if you treat him as if he *were* what he *ought* to be and *could* be, he will become that *bigger* and *better* man." (p. 244)

Each of us can want no more from our leaders than that they will help us, one and all, to become all that we are capable of being.

What are the priorities that exceptional nurse executives must address in order to honor the trust invested in them by nurses in their organizations and by the nursing profession? What are the agenda items that must be dealt with on our way to a desired future?

NINE PRIORITIES FOR ACTION BY EXCEPTIONAL NURSE EXECUTIVES WHO WANT TO SHAPE THE FUTURE

1. Address and solve the nurse shortage. Promoting and preserving health, preventing disease, and treating illness are activities that this society holds in high regard. In fact, care givers probably should be considered a national resource with measures instituted to ensure that sufficient quantities of this resource are available to meet the health-care needs of Americans. However, this is not the case and neither health policymakers nor society have yet viewed professional nurses as a scarce national resource. This country and its policymakers usually react with policies shaped in response to local, state, and national dilemmas.

We are approaching such a dilemma with another nursing shortage on the horizon. At this time of increasing demand for professional nurses from the many new as well as traditional sectors of the health industry, our nursing educational programs have declining enrollments. Vigorous action must be taken now, and consistent attention must be directed toward strengthening the image of the nursing profession and increasing the numbers of individuals entering professional nursing education programs.

Part of the reason for the dilemma is the plethora of attractive careers attracting bright young women and men, and the career of professional nursing has not been faring well in the competition. Why? Part of the answer is obviously the economic benefits that accrue over a nursing career as compared to other potential careers. Lockhart (1985) succinctly describes the problem as follows: A new baccalaureate-prepared nurse enters the work force at a salary competitive with that of an engineer; in 5 years, the nurse will be earning 51% less than the engineer.

High unmet demands for nurses by the health-care industry and low nursing salaries are factors that should produce change in the marketplace. Unfortunately, however, nurse salaries have not responded to nurse supply and demand in the past. We have experienced shortages in cycles yet nurses' salaries remain low.

We must have exceptional nurse executives who can analyze the problem, identify alternatives, and help produce the required changes. The shortage of critical care nurses may be the driving force that will help us invent a new future without the old problems. Nursing salaries must be raised so that the future nurse and the future engineer are not so drastically different in earning power at the end of 5 years.

We must attract and retain bright and talented men and women in the nursing profession. We need to educate the public as well as teachers and guidance counselors of professional nurses' multifaceted roles and the tremendously diverse career opportunities that are available in nursing. We need to increase the visibility of nurses in all sectors of society and sharpen the image. This is a challenge for us all.

2. Promote vision and clarify values. We need leaders with vision — nursing leaders who occupy executive positions in health-care agencies and organizations and who can help nurses achieve their personal and professional goals while simultaneously meeting organizational goals and objectives. Executive nurse leaders must have a vision of what nursing and nurses can become in this transforming health-care system. Not only must they as executive leaders have a vision, but they must be able to describe it with such vividness, enthusiasm, and energy that it inspires other nurses and engenders their excitement as well as their confidence in the ability to work collaboratively to make the vision a reality. The vision becomes a motivating force, and the work becomes the path to the vision.

Executive leaders must be able to dream, to encourage others to dream, to create, to take risks, and to do things differently and better. Nurses are the high touch carers as well as the high tech care givers. "We care" attitudes, compassion, and patient/family advocacy are attributes that need to be preserved, nurtured, and promoted. Patients and families who have experienced serious illnesses appreciate the therapeutic caring and curing of nurses. Now, it is time for health-care organizations to demonstrate in direct and measurable ways how much professional nurses are valued as care givers, teachers, coordinators, and managers.

Several changes will be required to ensure that society will have the necessary nursing resources to meet this country's care needs. Recognition and value can and must be demonstrated in multiple ways, including appropriate financial compensation and new kinds of benefits.

Hospitals can no longer be silent with the knowledge that nurses are the glue of the health-care system. Nurses must be recognized along with the physicians and administrators as *partners* in the business of care giving and as partners in meeting the health-care institution's mission, goals, and bottom-line targets.

Nurses must be recognized as key image emissaries of the organization. According to Hafer and Joiner (1984), "Since the nurse is the most visible health-care professional to both the patient and the patient's family, the nurse has a substantial impact on the patient's image of the hospital, the type of care being received, and the word-of-mouth image created by the patient's family throughout the community" (p. 26). Recognition of the nurse as central to meeting the organizational goals must become a health-care institutional norm.

Furthermore, nurses must become economically as well as professionally accountable for their nursing care to patients (Covaleski, 1981). This means that a price must be established for nursing care rendered to patients. Coming out of the room rate and charging for nursing care increase the visibility of nurses and move nursing from a cost center to a revenue center. This too should become a new norm. Patients and third party payers have a right to expect that they will be charged only for services actually delivered, including nursing care.

Additionally, nurses must be recognized as essential partners in achieving the cost-quality balance. In order to effectively fulfill the partnership expectation, nurses need to have significant knowledge and information about the corporation and its fiscal status. Nurses need to be made aware of the costs of the multiple products used in delivering care and need to participate in decision making related to ensuring the quality of that care while controlling costs.

The vision for the future also must include new types of compensation programs invented to recognize the unique contributions of the professional nurse members of the organization. Because nurses are key players in achieving the projected bottom-line of institutional performance, they deserve to share in some type of incentive program through which their annual salary can be augmented. If the agency or institution exceeds its goals, nurses should be rewarded for their contributions to this margin. In addition, nurses who succeed in developing new product lines that become profitable should benefit materially through annual bonus programs or their equivalent.

Indeed, these are new norms for many settings — the nurse as a valued partner, participating in decisions affecting the delivery of care and the business of the organization as well as the nurse as a care giver, responsible for providing quality, compassionate care to patients and families. Nurses need to be prepared for these new norms, and executive nurse leaders must see that the job gets done. This vision expresses the value of the professional nurse — a value that must be made increasingly explicit if the desired future is to unfold.

3. Empower and commit to excellence. A third priority for high-achieving executive nurse leaders is to empower other nurses to act, produce, create, and excel. Mahoney (1984) states that a responsible leader disperses power rather than clings to it. An effective leader encourages leadership at all institutional levels while providing clear goals that enable others to assume responsibility and to grow. Empowerment is absolute recognition of the value of your colleagues. Empowerment encompasses helping others to become all they are capable of being and assisting the human assets in the environment to appreciate in value.

Garfield (1986) believes that the more leaders empower, the more they can achieve and the more successful that the whole enterprise becomes. Empowerment is a part of team building and team playing. Exceptional nurse executives recognize the energy unleashed with empowerment and skillfully serve as coaches, cheerleaders, and developers.

Executive leaders have a commitment to excellence for themselves, their staffs, and their organizations. They are capable of doing great work. They want to excel and expect others to do likewise. Most importantly, effective executive leaders love their work, approach it with intensity and passion, and demonstrate their own capacities to excel at what they do. Leaders must know what they and their followers want and then go after it.

4. Enable participative management. The fourth priority is to enable participative management. Appreciating the power of knowledge, executive nurse leaders will ensure that the nurses with whom they work have the knowledge required to perform effectively in the organization. These leaders will ensure that information flows in every direction so that nurses throughout the organization will be well informed and prepared to engage actively and effectively in organizational decision making.

Professional nurses are knowledge workers who expect to participate in the decisions that affect their practice. Exceptional nurse executives will promote participative management because it recognizes the professional's expertise and enhances productivity through a culture of shared ownership. In this model of shared ownership or partnership, administrators, nurses, and physicians collaborate in making decisions related to management and care giving. Organizational structures are flattened. Relationships are collegial and frequently matrixial.

Participative management and partnership behaviors will result in high performing health-care organizations. Shortell (1985) describes these high performing organizations in terms of their ability to provide high-quality, cost-effective care, to innovate, to grow, and to enjoy excellent reputations in their communities and among their professional staffs and employees. Shortell has identified the following 10 characteristics of high-performing health-care organizations:

1. They stretch themselves. They are committed to doing better, no matter how good they are.

2. They maximize learning and emphasize effectiveness over efficiency. They have many employees whom Garfield (1986) would describe as peak performers with constructive restlessness who never stop searching and learning.

3. They take risks. Creativity and entrepreneurial efforts require moving forward in unfamiliar territory. Failures are viewed as learning opportunities.

4. They exhibit transforming leadership. People within the organization give and take meaning from each other and the organization. Individual and organizational goals are integrated.

5. They exercise a bias for action. They create opportunities to serve and meet their objectives.

6. They create chemistry. The whole is more than the sum of its parts, and individuals within the organization complement rather than compete with each other.

7. They manage ambiguity and uncertainty.

8. They exhibit a loose coherence. The professional and organizational cultures are harnessed together.

9. They exhibit well-defined cultures. They have their own personalities.

10. They reflect a basic spirituality. People have a sense of the organization's wholeness.

Nurse leaders should examine the characteristics of their own organizations in light of Shortell's 10 correlates. Exceptional nurse executives will pursue the challenge of integrating these characteristics within their organizations and their leadership behaviors.

5. Acquire business savvy. The fifth priority involves acquiring competence in the business aspects of health care. Its necessity should be self-evident. Nurse executives are responsible for budgets ranging from $1 to $50 or more million. Such big business requires knowledge of accounting and financial management techniques as well as basic business and personnel management principles. Exceptional executives realize that not only must they have such knowledge but they must also extend this knowledge to those practicing nurses with whom they work. The continuing development of the organization's human resources becomes a top priority for exceptional nurse executives who are committed to helping their organizations succeed and excel.

Nurses must become more knowledgeable about the health-care consumer marketplace and the roles that nurses can and should play in marketing their particular organizations. Guest relations training programs have become commonplace in hospitals. The focus is on serving our customers — whether patients, families, or students. Competition abounds for the best and brightest students and for the business brought by patients and families to our health-care organizations. A customer orientation is critical. Quality programs in both patient care and professional undergraduate and graduate education will provide the competitive advantage we need.

Market surveys help us discover the kind of health services that our potential patients want. We must make certain that we will have the resources to deliver them. We need to package and price services so that they meet consumer needs and are affordable to multiple buyers. We must determine how much of the market share we need to break even and to be profitable. In addition, we know we will have bad debts and charity patients. What type of payer mix will allow the organization to meet its objectives? How will the organization achieve such a payer mix?

It is interesting and exciting to see the marketplace influence our educational programs as well as our patient care programs. The registered nurse (RN) student has finally captured the attention of even the most conservative and traditional academicians. The RN student represents a large potential market for baccalaureate and higher degree nursing programs, especially at a time of increasing competition from multiple careers attractive to high school graduates. It marks a real opportunity to advance the knowledge and skills of many nurses while they meet their professional objectives for earning their baccalaureate and graduate degrees.

Nurses need help to develop bimodal thinking that combines the macro and micro approach. The macro view is the bird's eye view from which one can see the organizational whole, whereas the micro view is the worm's eye view from which one can identify the specific details of a situation or problem (Garfield, 1986). Executive leaders must plan strategies to help nursing staff members and nursing faculty acquire corporate knowledge and a corporate view so that, as necessary, they can wear institutional hats versus unit, department, discipline, or school hats.

Product line orientations. Prospective payment systems have forced a product orientation in health services with DRGs as one product line. Product line management or strategic business units are concepts borrowed from the business world and now applied to the health-care industry. These concepts have forced a product pricing approach that has stimulated increased competition and new corporate ventures under the rubric of vertical integration.

Corporate restructuring enables an organization to control the gamut of health-care delivery options from home care services to long-term care institutions. With control of all levels of care, patient care management is facilitated, and quality care at controlled costs is a more likely outcome. Where ownership and control of such diverse organizations are not feasible, new alliances with varying types of care delivery organizations and new collaborative arrangements are developed to accomplish similar results. Exceptional nurse executives are already planning for how they will manage nurses who may have the opportunity to move among different types of health-care delivery organizations without ever having to change employers.

Productivity management is another concept borrowed from the industrial world. However, patients are not widgets, and performance standards for productivity measurement must be carefully established by each discipline in each setting in order to ensure that quality care standards are integrated into the units of measurement. An effective nurse executive will be aware of the need for variable productivity standards dependent on patient diagnoses, types of services provided, nursing acuity, and severity of illness indices.

Quality of care and risk management. Quality care must be the standard. However, we must discover more effective and descriptive ways of measuring quality of care. We also need to develop a language for differentiating levels of quality, a language that can be understood by the consumer of care and also by the multidisciplinary team involved in patient care. Mortality rates are too gross and final as measurements for quality. Yet many of the indices used to measure quality seem to measure the reverse, such as infection rates, medication errors, or falls. Perhaps it is because we have not developed either the knowledge, indices, or descriptors to discuss quality in more positive ways. This is certainly a challenge for our nurse researchers as well as for our nurse managers and administrators.

The language of risk management is another area in which today's nurses must become fluent. The delivery of quality patient care by competent professionals is the first line of defense in risk management. Attention to patient and family complaints must be immediate and comprehensive. Incidents that could result in adverse effects for patients must be carefully addressed. Standards of nursing care and performance must be explicitly stated, and nurse managers must monitor and direct activities to ensure that these standards are met.

The complex patients requiring high technology treatments and extensive expert nursing care in an industry with rising malpractice claims are all factors influencing nurse executives to move their organizations to a predominantly RN staffing pattern. These same forces are also contributing to the increasingly responsible roles for master's prepared clinical specialists and nurse practitioners. It has become clear that the best prepared professional nurse offers the greatest flexibility to the health-care system and its patients.

As a final part in this priority of acquiring business savvy, nurses at all levels in this changing economic environment are expected to participate in the essential fund-raising activities of organizations. Grateful patients and families need the right advice and direction. These new business competencies must become priorities and must be integrated with nursing clinical and management skills in order to ensure a future where quality care will be available to all and where each citizen has an opportunity to reach and maintain his or her unique health potential with our help.

6. Shape the corporate culture. The sixth priority relates to shaping the corporate culture. Blake and Mouton (1986) believe that executives in an organization create the corporate culture that produces the bottom line consequence. To shape this culture, leaders: (a) project corporate vision, (b) provide role models, (c) establish values that followers embrace, (d) set or condone the reward system that compensates people, (e) set policies by which the organization is conducted, (f) create systems to get work done, (g) establish norms regarding attitudes toward customers, (h) demonstrate in decisions and attitudes toward excellence how much mediocrity will be tolerated, and (i) stimulate involvement and teamwork and promote sound use of human resources.

These investigators have concluded that the most effective organizations demonstrate high concern for both production and people.

7. Develop and test new approaches in nursing practice. Effective executive leadership for the future calls for new approaches in nursing practice. One of the first areas for focus must be an examination of clinical practices and their outcomes.

What differences do specific nursing interventions make, and what are those differences? What practices should we continue? Which practices should we delete? What practices should be expanded or revised? What nursing interventions prevent iatrogenic disorders? What new strategies might be tried? What should the nurse's role become in the use of new technology? What are the possibilities for dealing with ventilator-dependent patients other than in intensive care units? What should nursing's policy be toward patients who do not want to be treated? What about the ethical dilemma of patients whose treatments are so complex that they pull resources away from other patients equally in need? Exceptional executive nursing leadership is needed to help address these issues.

The value of the professional nurse and nursing contributions to an evolving system of health care must be articulated. The role of the nurse in alternative delivery sites must be delineated. Nurses are the best prepared to act as case managers. How can we seize the opportunities and allow nurses to demonstrate how they can excel in this role? What is the nurse's role in emerging health-care and wellness programs? Certainly, this must be a central role because most often, the nurse is the best prepared professional to deliver the instruction and direction on how to modify lifestyles and gain control of one's health. What should be the titles of such nursing positions, and where will they fit in the organizational structure? What can we as nurses do to improve patient care in long-term care facilities? What kinds of programs can we invent to help the frail elderly remain in their homes and avoid institutionalization? What kinds of rehabilitation programs are required for the increasing numbers of trauma cases?

New products and new models of care delivery will require full participation of nurses who occupy a central partnership role in the enterprise. Nursing leaders must help ensure that role. Nurse leaders must help us survive the nurse shortage and ensure that nurses achieve different and better positions than they currently hold or held in the past. This time, with strategic maneuvering, the nurse shortage must be used to our advantage to improve the economic status of practicing nurses. We must seize the "now" opportunity to market the nurse's role as a primary care giver and coordinator of patient care. We must help the public and policymakers see that nurses are indeed the carers as well as the care givers and that their role is valuable, valued, and worthy of increased compensation. The shortage of critical care nurses presents us with the opportunity to put nurses and nursing care in the spotlight. Let's do it, and keep nursing's contributions at a heightened level of consciousness.

8. Educate nurses for the information age. Schools of nursing must have a commitment to forge new partnerships with nursing practice organizations. The entry into practice issue must be finally resolved. Styles and Holzemer (1986) have proposed a course correction in education in order to meet the future needs for professional nurses. Collectively, we should work to ensure the desired course correction and to ensure that the baccalaureate degree in nursing will be the minimal requirement for entry into professional nursing practice.

Undergraduate nursing curricula must be revised to include an introduction to the business of health care, ethics, politics and policy-making, institutional governance, organization, and management in addition to the programs' current clinical content.

The graduate curricula must also change with more graduate study opportunities available to prepare nurses for positions in critical care, long-term care, geriatrics, management, and administration. We need both generalists and specialists.

There is a critical need for postgraduate leadership training. How are we to become knowledgeable in the priorities required to direct our future? Postgraduate opportunities for study as well as continuing education offerings may provide some answers.

Clinical nursing research offers hope of helping us to do it differently and better. Linda Amos (1985) stated that nurses are the ones who will provide crucial information to resolve such clinical problems as complications associated with prolonged bed rest, nosocomial infections, insomnia, pain, fatigue, incontinence, and adherence to treatment regimens. Solutions for these and similar problems could reduce the federal health-care bill by lessening the length of hospital stay, minimizing the need for additional treatment, and preventing unnecessary or premature institutionalization in long-term care facilities. To resolve the clinical problems delineated by Amos, nurses need a uniform minimum data set to document and study the nursing process and its outcomes. Nurse researchers should also take the lead in studying health activities and ways to help individuals maintain or secure healthier states.

9. Seek and form new coalitions. The ninth and final priority is a focus on new coalitions. Executive nurse leaders, nurses, and the professional nursing organizations must form new coalitions with other important professional, business, and societal organizations and groups. Through such coalitions, health policy can be shaped and new policies created that will ensure that the professional nurse will be appropriately recognized and compensated as a valued primary provider of health-care services for this nation's people.

I believe that it is only when physicians, administrators, business leaders, and federal and state legislators appreciate the delicate nature of this human resource called professional nursing that we will have the required support to end the nursing shortage permanently. We are at a critical period in our history. This scarce national resource may not be sufficiently available to meet future demands, and exceptional executive leadership in nursing is essential to ensure that it is. I am confident that nurses and the profession of nursing will be established firmly as essential partners in the successful and thriving health-care organizations of the future. The charge to exceptional nurse executives is to make it happen.

REFERENCES

Admissions drop 4.6 percent in 1985, says AHA economic 'Year in Review.' (1986, August 29). *Hospital Week, 22*(35), p. 2.

Amos, L.K. (1985). Influencing the future of nursing research through power and politics. *Western Journal of Nursing Research, 7*(4), 460-470.

Blake, R.R., & Mouton, J.S. (1986). Executive achievement. *Making it at the top.* New York: McGraw-Hill.

Burns, J.M. (1978). *Leadership.* New York: Harper & Row.

Covaleski, M.A. (1981). The economic and professional legitimacy of nursing services. *Hospital and Health Services Administration, 26*(5), 75-91.

Garfield, C. (1986). *Peak performers. The new heroes of American business.* New York: William Morrow and Company.

Hafer, J.C., & Joiner, C. (1984). Nurses as image emissaries: Are role conflicts impinging on a potential asset for an internal marketing strategy? *Journal of Health Care Marketing*, *4*(1), 25-35.

Health spending gets bigger slice of 1985 GNP. (1986, August 1). *Hospital Week, 22*(31), p. 1.

Levinson, H. (1968). *The exceptional executive: A psychological conception.* New York: New American Library.

Lockhart, C.A. (1985). Nursing's future in a shrinking health care system. In G.E. Sorensen (Ed.), *The economics of health care and nursing* (pp. 19-29). Atlanta: American Academy of Nursing.

Mahoney, M.E. (1984). *Leaders. The president's report.* Reprinted from the 1984 Annual Report of the Commonwealth Fund. New York: Harkness House.

Morris, W. (Ed.) (1971). *The American Heritage Dictionary of the English Language.* Boston: American Heritage Publishing and Houghton Mifflin Company.

Naisbitt, J., & Aburdene, P. (1985). *Re-inventing the corporation.* New York: Warner Books.

Prospective Payment Assessment Commission [ProPAC] (1986). *Technical appendices to the report and recommendations to the Secretary. Department of Health and Human Services.* Washington, DC: U.S. Government Printing Office.

Rutigliano, A.J. (1985). Surgery on health care costs. A checklist for health activism. *Management Review, 74*(10), 25-32.

Shortell, S.M. (1985). High-performing health care organizations: Guidelines for the pursuit of excellence. *Hospital and Health Services Administration, 30*(4), 7-35.

Styles, M.M., & Holzemer, W.L. (1986). Educational remapping for a responsible future. *Journal of Professional Nursing, 2*(1), 64-68.

ADDITIONAL READINGS

American Nurses' Association, Cabinet on Nursing Research. (1985). *Directions for nursing research: Toward the twenty-first century.* (Report No. D-79). Kansas City, MO: Author.

Fahy, E.T. (1986). Keying in on the business of graduate education in nursing. *Nursing and Health Care, 7*(4), 203-205.

Kanter, R.M. (1983). *The change masters: Innovation and entrepreneurship in the American corporation.* New York: Simon and Schuster.

Korn, E.R., & Pratt, G.J. (1986). Workaholism: Often a sign of success. *The Hospital Manager, 16*(1), 2.

Medicare. Physician incentive payments by hospitals could lead to abuse. (1986). Report to the Chairman, Subcommittee on Health, Committee on Ways and Means, House of Representatives (Report No. HRD-86-103). Washington, DC: U.S. General Accounting Office.

St. John, S. (1985). Attitude can create success. *Hospital Manager, 15*(6), 1-2.

Sovie, M.D. (1986). Nursing management considerations — Doing things differently and better. *Nursing Economic$, 4*, 201-203, 205.

With ICUs filling up, hospitals are searching high and low for more critical care nurses. (1986). *American Journal of Nursing, 86*(8), 960, 966-967.

5

Partnering
A new strategy for nursing leadership

Paul Wowk, FACHE

Healthcare executives still tend to view nurses as caregivers rather than partners in the delivery of care.

As the nursing profession grows in confidence, credibility and expertise, executives ironically grow more perplexed about the appropriate role of nursing in today's complex and competitive healthcare market.

Since patient-care delivery models that offer the highest quality at the least cost are of utmost concern to executives, there's a continuous search for new approaches to attract and retain a high-quality nursing staff. Even though the long-term solution to this nursing dilemma is not simple, there's a basic principle you can immediately apply to gain the cooperation, support and involvement of nurses in your organization: Think of nurses as fully functional partners and help them find an integral place in your organization. In addition, keep in mind that nursing is far more than a department or function like materials management, pharmacy or laboratory. Nursing represents 50 percent of everything we do.

This article suggests some new techniques that help position nurses to become equal partners in the

Reprinted from *Health Care Executive*, Vol. 4, No. 2, with permission of American College of Health Care Executives © 1989.

delivery of care. These techniques build on basic, proven management practice and can be applied quickly at minimal cost.

INFLICTING CULTURAL CHANGE

Paradigm shifts in relationships can never be executed through edict, fiat or a weekend management retreat in the country. Instead, they involve an intricate and extended process of cultural change in which you, the executive, must assume a key role. Partnering involves nothing less than a merger among physicians, nurses and management. In this new and powerful triumvirate, all parties come together to set budgets, explore strategy, review financial figures and discuss marketing. No longer are nurses handed a bound notebook and told, "This is our plan for the next fiscal year." And no longer does a product-line manager hand nursing a final draft of the strategic plan and say, "Let us know if you have any input" or "Here's what we're doing. Do you have any objections?" In the partnering model, healthcare professionals discuss, debate , and make to work from the same data base, managers see the intrinsic worth of optimal patient care, and physicians and nurses recognize the value of cost control and charge capture.

If you want to bring partnering into your

organization, give these recommendations full consideration:

1. **Become a role model for partnering and set the tone for the rest of the organization.**

   Partnering with nursing begins with the relationship you develop with the people closest to you. Demonstrate your willingness to partner with your own management group by fostering a climate of give and take, candid scrutiny of strengths and weaknesses and a humble recognition that no single person has all the answers. Setting the standard for partnering will create credibility and acceptance of the partnering concept in the lower levels of your organization.

2. **Assume the stance of coach and build a team geared to partnering.**

   Surrender the role of director general and become a coach and advisor instead. Only then will you assess and maximize your organization's true potential. The 1990s will be the era of continuous improvement with quality as the focus. Start now by assembling a team of partners who are willing to look beyond the artificial boundaries of functions, specialties and departments to the root causes of patient-care problems.

3. **Invest time in goal-setting.**

   Sit down with team members and define tasks — what will be done; how, when and with whom it will be done; and how results will be measured. Make sure every team member discusses and approves goals before you proclaim them adopted.

4. **Take time to get to know each other.**

   Working together as a team of partners means getting familiar. Invest time in learning about each other — as individuals and as working professionals. Unless team members understand each others' quirks, foibles and strengths, they will never become partners. In the process, don't forget to pinpoint roles and responsibilities and agree on complementary areas of expertise.

5. **Develop a structure for getting things done.**

   Set out a process and structure to accomplish your work — especially how you plan to communicate and make decisions. Before resentments begin to smolder, call a time out to discuss how you'll handle potential conflicts. People will be less inclined to hide their feelings and brood in silence.

6. **Get your medical staff actively involved.**

   Gain the support of the chief of staff and department chairmen in creating new partnerships with nurses. An unfortunate but popular stereotype is that physicians couldn't care less about nurses. The reality is that most physicians find it difficult to respect an organization that leaves its nurses feeling chronically frustrated, resentful and alienated. Satisfied nurses usually mean satisfied patients and that's important to physicians.

7. **Reach a meeting of the minds and build unity.**

   Define the results you want to achieve — what you want to measure and how to measure it. Be prepared to give nursing the support it needs to sort through responsibilities, functions and levels and decide what is optimal for your patient mix. Consider a task force for each clinical service as well as an umbrella nursing task force to evaluate levels of nursing support and determine staffing patterns.

8. **Develop a hospitalwide program to encourage communication about nursing's new role.**

   Boldly assert that nursing is a full partner in everything the organization is and does, and that nursing will subsequently collaborate on all decisions important to the organization's future. Reinforce this message in meetings, interoffice memos, employee communications and community publications.

9. **Work to build a culture of quality.**

   At present, the issue of quality is highly clinical. An alternative approach is that quality is everything an organization does and that every action defines it. The executive's battle cry then becomes, "Our culture is that we want to achieve the highest quality possible as perceived by our patients and care givers."

10. **Emphasize long-term nurse retention as well as recruitment.**

     If nurses are supported and respected, they will stay with your organization. Even if your pay is average, you can remind nurses that they're important by offering valued benefits such as day-care service or career ladders. If possible, develop incentive compensation systems that allow nurses to share in the achievement of organizational goals. Trips to Hawaii or tuition waiver programs will never produce long-term results unless nurses are made to feel like partners.

11. **Develop pre- and post-evaluations of the partnering process.**

     In cooperation with the medical staff, develop a survey to look at nursing turnover, patient satisfaction and selected quality indicators. Administer this survey twice: before initiating the change process and again six months later.

CHANGING BEHAVIOR

If these are the broad strategies for introducing partnering into your organization, how do you need to change as an executive? Following are behaviors that work against partnering and suggestions for how to change them:

1. **Making statements that are too general or excessively firm.**

     How many times do you catch yourself saying, "You're always handing in variance reports late," or "You never get those meetings started on time." Instead, try for a more tentative statement of your point and use examples to support your conclusions.

2. **Repeatedly telling your "partner" what to do.**

     If you operate with the persona of a South American dictator, then make a concerted effort to give your partner fewer answers. Depersonalize the problem and discuss it as if it could belong to anyone. Avoid phrases like "your problem" and "you need to" and experiment with questions such as, "In what way does this situation cause problems?"

3. **Talking down to your partner.**

     "I'm surprised at you." "You should have known better." "I want you in here right now." This is not your teenage son you're talking to, but a 40-year-old clinical supervisor. Make an effort to talk to your partner like an equal, not like an irresponsible child. Stick to statements that focus on the problem and a responsible solution, not on personality quirks or character disorders. Instead of telling your partner what to do or how to be, encourage a discussion of what makes sense and how to achieve it.

4. **Making premature comments and evaluations.**

     If your middle name is "Yes But," then you might as well plead guilty to this communication foible. The solution: Save your comments until you've gathered all the important information. Also ask clarifying questions such as: "I'm not sure I understood your point, could you say a little more about it?" "Could you give me a couple of examples?" "Could we review it once more?" Without sounding like a $90-an-hour psychologist, make sure that you can describe your partner's main points before adding your own comments and views. Use phrases such as "Let's stop for a minute and check all the key points in the discussion" or "In essence, you've said . . . ."

5. **Administering punishment through sarcasm.**

     There's a little of Don Rickles in all of us. We may think we're above it, but how many times have you heard: "I could have done it with my eyes closed. What were you doing, watching the birds?" "You're so bright; you figure it out." "You're clever. Ever think of doing it the way I told you?" Instead of resorting to sarcasm, state your point in a simple, direct way. Also consider your intent. If you want a situation or condition to change, it may be to your advantage to be less sarcastic and personal and more direct and to the point.

6. **Placing emphasis on blame.**

   You don't have to point a finger or shake your head to encourage guilt. Words are just as devastating, especially when delivered in the form of comments such as: "This is your fault." "I suppose you realize you made a mistake." "You know you're to blame for this." "I hope you learned something from this." "You're wrong and you know it." It takes an incredible amount of self control, but focus on asking questions that might help improve future performance: "What can we learn from this situation that will help us manage the problem in the future?" "What steps could be taken to prevent this from happening?" "Let's see if we can't project a few more ways for handling situations like this." "What recommendations and suggestions would you make to someone in a similar situation?"

7. **Nonconstructive arguing.**

   Voices rise. Faces redden. Words hurtle across the room like rocket salvos. Save your energy by taking another tack: Ask clarifying questions and give examples to clarify points — focusing not on who's right, but on the right issues and ideas. When you sense you're be-

coming angry, stop and take a deep breath. Try to paraphrase or at least make some sense of your partner's position. Then back up to the assumptions or feelings that may have caused the conflict to go out of control. Say something like, "I'm getting confused. Let's back up and clarify our ideas. Tell me about what's happened to make you say that?"

8. **Asking loaded questions.**

   Some day executives will need a permit for carrying a loaded question. How many of us have heard, "Don't you agree that missing this opportunity was a result of poor planning?" "You don't think I'd do a thing like that, do you?" "You made a mistake, didn't you?" Instead, open your mind and heart and ask an open question: "How do you see this situation?" "Could you tell me what happened last month?" "What's your view on how the slip-up happened?" "Why do you feel that way?" In other words, make your point in a statement rather than hiding it in a question.

Executives willing to improve their partnering skills will find immediate bottom line results. By focusing on the situation and not on the person, executives can quickly outline alternative solutions to previously confusing scenarios. By saying, "Let's work this out together," instead of "Do you know what you're doing here?" executives will develop willing participants dedicated to continuously improving the quality of patient care — which is after all the primary reason healthcare organizations exist.

CHAPTER **6**

In Praise of Followers

Robert E. Kelley, PhD

We are convinced that corporations succeed or fail, compete or crumble, on the basis of how well they are led. So we study great leaders of the past and present and spend vast quantities of time and money looking for leaders to hire and trying to cultivate leadership in the employees we already have.

I have no argument with this enthusiasm. Leaders matter greatly. But in searching so zealously for better leaders we tend to lose sight of the people these leaders will lead. Without his armies, after all, Napoleon was just a man with grandiose ambitions. Organizations stand or fall partly on the basis of how well their leaders lead, but partly also on the basis of how well their followers follow.

In 1987, declining profitability and intensified competition for corporate clients forced a large commercial bank on the east coast to reorganize its operations and cut its work force. Its most seasoned managers had to spend most of their time in the field working with corporate customers. Time and energies were stretched so thin that one department head decided he had no choice but to delegate the responsibility for reorganization to his staff people, who had recently had training in self-management.

Despite grave doubts, the department head set them up as a unit without a leader, responsible to one another and to the bank as a whole for writing their own job descriptions, designing a training program, determining criteria for performance evaluations, planning for operational needs, and helping to achieve overall organizational objectives.

They pulled it off. The bank's officers were delighted and frankly amazed that rank-and-file employees could assume so much responsibility so successfully. In fact, the department's capacity to control and direct itself virtually without leadership saved the organization months of turmoil, and as the bank struggled to remain a major player in its region, valuable management time was freed up to put out other fires.

What was it these singular employees did? Given a goal and parameters, they went where most departments could only have gone under the hands-on guidance of an effective leader. But these employees accepted the delegation of authority and went there alone. They thought for themselves, sharpened their skills, focused their efforts, put on a fine display of grit and spunk and self-control. They followed effectively.

To encourage this kind of effective following in other organizations, we need to understand the nature of the follower's role. To cultivate good followers, we need to understand the human qualities that allow effective followership to occur.

THE ROLE OF FOLLOWER

Bosses are not necessarily good leaders, subordinates are not necessarily effective followers. Many bosses

Reprinted by permission of *Harvard Business Review*. In Praise of Followers by Robert E. Kelley, November/December, 1988, 46(6). Copyright 1988 by the President and Fellows of Harvard College; all rights reserved.

53

couldn't lead a horse to water. Many subordinates couldn't follow a parade. Some people avoid either role. Others accept the role thrust upon them and perform it badly.

At different points in their careers, even at different times of the working day, most managers play both roles, though seldom equally well. After all, the leadership role has the glamour and attention. We take courses to learn it, and when we play it well we get applause and recognition. But the reality is that most of us are more often followers than leaders. Even when we have subordinates, we still have bosses. For every committee we chair, we sit as a member on several others.

So followership dominates our lives and organizations, but not our thinking, because our preoccupation with leadership keeps us from considering the nature and the importance of the follower.

What distinguishes an effective from an ineffective follower is enthusiastic, intelligent, and self-reliant participation — without star billing — in the pursuit of an organizational goal. Effective followers differ in their motivations for following and in their perceptions of the role. Some choose followership as their primary role at work and serve as team players who take satisfaction in helping to further a cause, an idea, a product, a service, or, more rarely, a person. Others are leaders in some situations but choose the follower role in a particular context. Both these groups view the role of follower as legitimate, inherently valuable, even virtuous.

Some potentially effective followers derive motivation from ambition. By proving themselves in the follower's role, they hope to win the confidence of peers and superiors and move up the corporate ladder. These people do not see followership as attractive in itself. All the same, they can become good followers if they accept the value of learning the role, studying leaders from a subordinate's perspective, and polishing the followership skills that will always stand them in good stead.

Understanding motivations and perceptions is not enough, however. Since followers with different motivations can perform equally well, I examined the behavior that leads to effective and less effective following among people committed to the organization and came up with two underlying behavioral dimensions that help to explain the difference.

One dimension measures to what degree followers exercise independent, critical thinking. The other ranks them on a passive/active scale. Figure 6-1 identifies five followership patterns.

Sheep are passive and uncritical, lacking in initiative and sense of responsibility. They perform the tasks given them and stop. Yes People are a livelier but equally unenterprising group. Dependent on a leader for inspiration, they can be aggressively deferential, even servile. Bosses weak in judgment and self-confidence tend to like them and to form alliances with them that can stultify the organization.

Alienated Followers are critical and independent in their thinking but passive in carrying out their role. Somehow, sometime, something turned them off. Often cynical, they tend to sink gradually into disgruntled, acquiescence, seldom openly opposing a leader's efforts. In the very center of the diagram we have Survivors, who perpetually sample the wind and live by the slogan, "better safe than sorry." They are adept at surviving change.

In the upper right-hand corner, finally, we have Effective Followers, who think for themselves and carry out their duties and assignments with energy and assertiveness. Because they are risk takers, self-starters, and independent problem solvers, they get consistently high ratings from peers and many superiors. Followership of this kind can be a positive and acceptable choice for parts or all of our lives — a source of pride and fulfillment.

Effective followers are well-balanced and responsible adults who can succeed without strong leadership. Many followers believe they offer as much value to the organization as leaders do, especially in project or task-force situations. In an organization of effective followers, a leader tends to be more an overseer of change and progress than a hero. As organizational structures flatten, the quality of those who follow will become more and more important. As Chester I. Barnard wrote 50 years ago in *The Functions of the Executive,* "The decision as to whether an order has authority or not lies with the person to whom it is

Independent, Critical Thinking

Alienated Followers		Effective Followers
	Survivors	
Sheep		Yes People

Passive ← → Active

Dependent, Uncritical Thinking

FIGURE 6-1

Some followers are more effective.

addressed, and does not reside in 'persons of authority' or those who issue orders.''

THE QUALITIES OF FOLLOWERS

Effective followers share a number of essential qualities:

1. They manage themselves well.
2. They are committed to the organization and to a purpose, principle, or person outside themselves.
3. They build their competence and focus their efforts for maximum impact.
4. They are courageous, honest, and credible.

Self-Management. Paradoxically, the key to being an effective follower is the ability to think for oneself—to exercise control and independence and to work without close supervision. Good followers are people to whom a leader can safely delegate responsibility, people who anticipate needs at their own level of competence and authority.

Another aspect of this paradox is that effective followers see themselves—except in terms of line responsibility—as the equals of the leaders they follow. They are more apt to openly and unapologetically disagree with leadership and less likely to be intimidated by hierarchy and organizational structure. At the same time, they can see that the people they follow are, in turn, following the lead of others, and they try to appreciate the goals and needs of the team and the organization. Ineffective followers, on the other hand, buy into the hierarchy and, seeing themselves as subservient, vacillate between despair over their seeming powerlessness and attempts to manipulate leaders for their own purposes. Either their fear of powerlessness becomes a self-fulfilling prophecy — for themselves and often for their work units as well — or their resentment leads them to undermine the team's goals.

Self-managed followers give their organizations a significant cost advantage because they eliminate much of the need for elaborate supervisory control systems that, in any case, often lower morale. In 1985, a large midwestern bank redesigned its personnel selection system to attract self-managed workers. Those conducting interviews began to look for particular types of experience and capacities — initiative, teamwork, independent thinking of all kinds — and the bank revamped its orientation program to emphasize self-management. At the executive level, role playing was introduced into the interview process: how you disagree with your boss, how you prioritize your in-basket after a vacation. In the three years since, employee turnover has dropped dramatically, the need for supervisors has decreased, and administrative costs have gone down.

Of course not all leaders and managers like having self-managing subordinates. Some would rather have sheep or yes people. The best that good followers can do in this situation is to protect themselves with a little career self-management — that is, to stay attractive in the marketplace. The qualities that make a good follower are too much in demand to go begging for long.

Commitment.   Effective followers are committed to something — a cause, a product, an organization, an idea — in addition to the care of their own lives and careers. Some leaders misinterpret this commitment. Seeing their authority acknowledged, they mistake loyalty to a goal for loyalty to themselves. But the fact is that many effective followers see leaders merely as coadventurers on a worthy crusade, and if they suspect their leader of flagging commitment or conflicting motives they may just withdraw their support, either by changing jobs or by contriving to change leaders.

The opportunities and the dangers posed by this kind of commitment are not hard to see. On the one hand, commitment is contagious. Most people like working with colleagues whose hearts are in their work. Morale stays high. Workers who begin to wander from their purpose are jostled back into line. Projects stay on track and on time. In addition, an appreciation of commitment and the way it works can give managers an extra tool with which to understand and channel the energies and loyalties of their subordinates.

On the other hand, followers who are strongly committed to goals not consistent with the goals of their companies can produce destructive results. Leaders having such followers can even lose control of their organizations.

A scientist at a computer company cared deeply about making computer technology available to the masses, and her work was outstanding. Since her goal was in line with the company's goals, she had few problems with top management. Yet she saw her department leaders essentially as facilitators of her dream, and when managers worked at cross-purposes to that vision, she exercised all of her considerable political skills to their detriment. Her immediate supervisors saw her as a thorn in the side, but she was quite effective in furthering her cause because she saw eye to eye with company leaders. But what if her vision and the company's vision had differed?

Effective followers temper their loyalties to satisfy organizational needs — or they find new organizations. Effective leaders know how to channel the energies of strong commitment in ways that will satisfy corporate goals as well as a follower's personal needs.

Competence and Focus.   On the grounds that committed incompetence is still incompetence, effective followers master skills that will be useful to their organizations. They generally hold higher performance standards than the work environment requires, and continuing education is second nature to them, a staple in their professional development.

Less effective followers expect training and development to come to them. The only education they acquire is force-fed. If not sent to a seminar, they don't go. Their competence deteriorates unless some leader gives them parental care and attention.

Good followers take on extra work gladly, but first they do a superb job on their core responsibilities. They are good judges of their own strengths and weaknesses, and they contribute well to teams. Asked to perform in areas where they are poorly qualified, they speak up. Like athletes stretching their capacities, they don't mind chancing failure if they know they can succeed, but they are careful to spare the company wasted energy, lost time, and poor performance by accepting challenges that coworkers are better prepared to meet. Good followers see coworkers as colleagues rather than competitors.

At the same time, effective followers often search for overlooked problems. A woman on a new product development team discovered that no one was responsible for coordinating engineering, marketing, and manufacturing. She worked out an interdepartmental review schedule that identified the people who should be involved at each stage of development. Instead of burdening her boss with yet another problem, this woman took the initiative to present the issue along with a solution.

Another woman I interviewed described her efforts to fill a dangerous void in the company she cared about. Young managerial talent in this manufacturing corporation had traditionally made careers in production. Convinced that foreign competition would alter the shape of the industry, she realized that marketing was a neglected area. She took classes, attended seminars, and read widely. More important, she visited customers to get feedback about her company's and competitors' products, and she soon knew more about the product's customer appeal and market position than any of her peers. The extra competence did wonders for her own career, but it also helped her company weather a storm it had not seen coming.

Courage.   Effective followers are credible, honest, and courageous. They establish themselves as independent, critical thinkers whose knowledge and judgment can be trusted. They give credit where credit is due, admitting mistakes and sharing successes. They form their own views and ethical standards and stand up for what they believe in.

Insightful, candid, and fearless, they can keep leaders and colleagues honest and informed. The other side of the coin of course is that they can also cause great trouble for a leader with questionable ethics.

Jerome LiCari, the former R&D director at Beech-Nut, suspected for several years that the apple concentrate Beech-Nut was buying from a new supplier at 20% below market price was adulterated. His department suggested switching suppliers, but top management at the financially strapped company put the burden of proof on R&D.

By 1981, LiCari had accumulated strong evidence of adulteration and issued a memo recommending a change of supplier. When he got no response, he went to see his boss, the head of operations. According to LiCari, he was threatened with dismissal for lack of team spirit. LiCari then went to the president of Beech-Nut, and when that, too, produced no results, he gave up his three-year good-soldier effort, followed his conscience, and resigned. His last performance evaluation praised his expertise and loyalty, but said his judgment was "colored by naiveté and impractical ideals."

In 1986, Beech-Nut and LiCari's two bosses were indicted on several hundred counts of conspiracy to commit fraud by distributing adulterated apple juice. In November 1987, the company pleaded guilty and agreed to a fine of $2 million. In February of this year, the two executives were found guilty on a majority of the charges. The episode cost Beech-Nut an estimated $25 million and a 20% loss of market share. Asked during the trial if he had been naive, LiCari said, "I guess I was. I thought apple juice should be made from apples."

Is LiCari a good follower? Well, no, not to his dishonest bosses. But yes, he is almost certainly the kind of employee most companies want to have: loyal, honest, candid with his superiors, and thoroughly credible. In an ethical company involved unintentionally in questionable practices, this kind of follower can head off embarrassment, expense, and litigation.

CULTIVATING EFFECTIVE FOLLOWERS

You may have noticed by now that the qualities that make effective followers are, confusingly enough, pretty much the same qualities found in some effective leaders. This is no mere coincidence, of course. But the confusion underscores an important point. If a person has initiative, self-control, commitment, talent, honesty, credibility, and courage, we say, "Here is a leader!" By definition, a follower cannot exhibit the qualities of leadership. It violates our stereotype.

But our stereotype is ungenerous and wrong. Followership is not a person but a role, and what distinguishes followers from leaders is not intelligence or character but the role they play. As I pointed out at the beginning of this article, effective followers and effective leaders are often the same people playing different parts at different hours of the day.

In many companies, the leadership track is the only road to career success. In almost all companies, leadership is taught and encouraged while followership is not. Yet effective followership is a prerequisite for organizational success. Your organization can take four steps to cultivate effective followers in your work force.

1. Redefining Followership and Leadership. Our stereotyped but unarticulated definitions of leadership and followership shape our expectations when we occupy either position. If a leader is defined as responsible for motivating followers, he or she will likely act toward followers as if they needed motivation. If we agree that a leader's job is to transform followers, then it must be a follower's job to provide the clay. If followers fail to need transformation, the leader looks ineffective. The way we define the roles clearly influences the outcome of the interaction.

Instead of seeing the leadership role as superior to and more active than the role of the follower, we can think of them as equal but different activities. The operative definitions are roughly these: people who are effective in the leader role have the vision to set corporate goals and strategies, the interpersonal skills to achieve consensus, the verbal capacity to communicate enthusiasm to large and diverse groups of individuals, the organizational talent to coordinate disparate efforts, and, above all, the desire to lead.

People who are effective in the follower role have the vision to see both the forest and the trees, the social capacity to work well with others, the strength of character to flourish without heroic status, the moral and psychological balance to pursue personal and corporate goals at no cost to either, and, above all, the desire to participate in a team effort for the accomplishment of some greater common purpose.

This view of leadership and followership can be conveyed to employees directly and indirectly — in training and by example. The qualities that make good followers and the value the company places on effective followership can be articulated in explicit follower training. Perhaps the best way to convey this message, however, is by example. Since each of us plays a follower's part at least from time to time, it is essential that we play it well, that we contribute our competence to the achievement of team goals, that we support the team leader with candor and self-control, that we do our best to appreciate and enjoy the role of quiet contribution to a larger, common cause.

2. Honing Followership Skills. Most organizations assume that leadership has to be taught but that everyone knows how to follow. This assumption is based on three faulty premises: (1) that leaders are more important than followers, (2) that following is simply doing what you are told to do, and (3) that followers inevitably draw their energy and aims, even their talent, from the leader. A program of follower training can correct this misapprehension by focusing on topics like:

> Improving independent, critical thinking.
> Self-management.
> > Disagreeing agreeably.
> > Building credibility.
> > Aligning personal and organizational goals and commitments.
> > Acting responsibly toward the organization, the leader, coworkers, and oneself.
> > Similarities and differences between leadership and followership roles.
> > Moving between the two roles with ease.

3. Performance Evaluation and Feedback. Most performance evaluations include a section on leadership skills. Followership evaluation would include items like the ones I have discussed. Instead of rating employees on leadership qualities such as self-management, independent thinking, originality, courage, competence, and credibility, we can rate them on these same qualities in both the leadership and followership roles and then evaluate each individual's ability to shift easily from the one role to the other. A variety of performance perspectives will help most people understand better how well they play their various organizational roles.

Moreover, evaluations can come from peers, subordinates, and self as well as from supervisors. The process is simple enough: peers and subordinates who come into regular or significant contact with another employee fill in brief, periodic questionnaires where they rate the individual on followership qualities. Findings are then summarized and given to the employee being rated.

4. Organizational Structures That Encourage Followership. Unless the value of good following is somehow built into the fabric of the organization, it is likely to remain a pleasant conceit to which everyone pays occasional lip service but no dues. Here are four good ways to incorporate the concept into your corporate culture:

> In leaderless groups, all members assume equal responsibility for achieving goals. These are usually small task forces of people who can work together under their own supervision. However hard it is to imagine a group with more than one leader, groups with none at all can be highly productive if their members have the qualities of effective followers.

> Groups with temporary and rotating leadership are another possibility. Again, such groups are probably best kept small and the rotation fairly frequent, although the notion might certainly be extended to include the administration of a small department for, say, six-month terms. Some of these temporary leaders will be less effective than others, of course, and some may be weak indeed, which is why critics maintain that this structure is inefficient. Why not let the best leader lead? Why suffer through the tenure of less effective leaders? There are two reasons. First, experience of the leadership role is essential to the education of effective followers. Second, followers learn that they must compensate for ineffective leadership by exercising their skill as good followers. Rotating leader or not, they are bound to be faced with ineffective leadership more than once in their careers.

Delegation to the lowest level is a third technique for cultivating good followers. Nordstrom's, the Seattle-based department store chain, gives each sales clerk responsibility for servicing and satisfying the customer, including the authority to make refunds without supervisory approval. This kind of delegation makes even people at the lowest levels responsible for their own decisions and for thinking independently about their work.

Finally, companies can use rewards to underline the importance of good followership. This is not as easy as it sounds. Managers dependent on yes people and sheep for ego gratification will not leap at the idea of extra rewards for the people who make them most uncomfortable. In my research, I have found that effective followers get mixed treatment. About half the time, their contributions lead to substantial rewards. The other half of the time they are punished by their superiors for exercising judgment, taking risks, and failing to conform. Many managers insist that they want independent subordinates who can think for themselves. In practice, followers who challenge their bosses run the risk of getting fired.

In today's flatter, leaner organization, companies will not succeed without the kind of people who take pride and satisfaction in the role of supporting player, doing the less glorious work without fanfare. Organizations that want the benefits of effective followers must find ways of rewarding them, ways of bringing them into full partnership in the enterprise. Think of the thousands of companies that achieve adequate performance and lackluster profits with employees they treat like second-class citizens. Then imagine for a moment the power of an organization blessed with fully engaged, fully energized, fully appreciated followers.

7

General Systems Theory
Applications for organization and management

Fremont E. Kast, MBA, PhD
James E. Rosenzweig, MBA, PhD

Biological and social scientists generally have embraced systems concepts. Many organization and management theorists seem anxious to identify with this movement and to contribute to the development of an approach which purports to offer the ultimate — the unification of all science into one grand conceptual model. Who could possibly resist? General systems theory seems to provide a relief from the limitations of more mechanistic approaches and a rationale for rejecting "principles" based on relatively "closed-system" thinking. This theory provides the paradigm for organization and management theorists to "crank into their systems model" all of the diverse knowledge from relevant underlying disciplines. It has become almost mandatory to have the word "system" in the title of recent articles and books (many of us have compromised and placed it only in the subtitle).

But where did it all start? This question takes us back into history and brings to mind the long-standing philosophical arguments between mechanistic and organismic models of the nineteenth and early twentieth centuries. As Deutsch says:

Both mechanistic and organismic models were based substantially on experiences and operations known

Reproduced from *The Journal of Nursing Administration*, Vol. 11, No. 7, with permission of J. B Lippincott Company © 1981.

before 1850. Since then, the experience of almost a century of scientific and technological progress has so far not been utilized for any significant new model for the study of organization and in particular of human thought.[2]

General systems theory even revives the specter of the "vitalists" and their views on "life force" and most certainly brings forth renewed questions of teleological or purposeful behavior of both living and nonliving systems. Phillips and others have suggested that the philosophical roots of general systems theory go back even further, at least to the German philosopher Hegel (1770-1831).[3] Thus, we should recognize that in the adoption of the systems approach for the study of organizations we are not dealing with newly discovered ideas — they have a rich genealogy.

Even in the field of organization and management theory, systems views are not new. Chester Barnard used a basic systems framework:

A cooperative system is a complex of physical, biological, personal, and social components which are in a specific systematic relationship by reason of the cooperation of two or more persons for at least one definite end. Such a system is evidently a subordinate unit of larger systems from one point of view; and itself embraces subsidiary systems — physical, biological, etc. — from another point of view. One of the systems comprised within a co-operative system, the one which is implicit in the phrase "cooperation of two or more persons," is called an "organization."[4]

And Barnard was influenced by the "systems views" of Vilfredo Pareto and Talcott Parsons. Certainly this quote (dressed up a bit to give the term "system" more emphasis) could be the introduction to a 1972 book on organizations.

Miller points out that Alexander Bogdanov, the Russian philosopher, developed a theory of "tektology" or universal organization science in 1912 which foreshadowed general systems theory and used many of the same concepts as modern systems theorists.[5]

However, in spite of a long history of organismic and holistic thinking, the utilization of the systems approach did not become the accepted model for organization and management writers until relatively recently. It is difficult to specify the turning point exactly. The momentum of systems thinking was identified by Scott in 1961 when he described the relationship between general systems theory and organization theory.

> The distinctive qualities of modern organization theory are its conceptual-analytical base, its reliance on empirical research data, and above all, its integrating nature. These qualities are framed in a philosophy which accepts the premise that the only meaningful way to study organization is to study it as a system . . . Modern organization theory and general system theory are similar in that they look at organization as an integrated whole.[6]

Scott said explicitly what many in our field had been thinking and/or implying—he helped us put into perspective the important writings of Herbert Simon, James March, Talcott Parsons, George Homans, E. Wight Bakke, Kenneth Boulding, and many others.

But how far have we really advanced over the past decade in applying general systems theory to organizations and their management? Is it still a "skeleton" or have we been able to "put some meat on the bones"? The systems approach has been touted because of its potential usefulness in understanding the complexities of "live" organizations. Has this approach really helped us in this endeavor or has it compounded confusion with chaos? Herbert Simon describes the challenge for the systems approach:

> In both science and engineering, the study of "systems" is an increasingly popular activity. Its popularity is more a response to a pressing need for synthesizing and analyzing complexity than it is to any large development of a body of knowledge and technique for dealing with complexity. If this popularity is to be more than a fad, necessity will have to mother invention and provide substance to go with the name.[7]

In this article we will explore the issue of whether we are providing substance for the term *systems approach* as it relates to the study of organizations and their management. There are many interesting historical and philosophical questions concerning the relationship between the mechanistic and organistic approaches and their applicability to the various fields of science, as well as other interesting digressions into the evolution of systems approaches. However, we will resist those temptations and plunge directly into a discussion of the key concepts of general systems theory, the way in which these ideas have been used by organization theorists, the limitations in their application, and some suggestions for the future.

KEY CONCEPTS OF GENERAL SYSTEMS THEORY

The key concepts of general systems theory have been set forth by many writers and have been used by many organization and management theorists.[8,9] It is not our purpose here to elaborate on them in great detail because we anticipate that most readers will have been exposed to them in some depth. The box on pages 62 and 63 provides a very brief review of those characteristics of systems which seem to have wide acceptance. The review is far from complete. It is difficult to identify a complete list of characteristics derived from general systems theory; moreover, it is merely a first-order classification. There are many derived second- and third-order characteristics which could be considered. For example, James G. Miller sets forth 165 hypotheses, stemming from open systems theory, which might be applicable to two or more levels of

Key Concepts of General Systems Theory

Subsystems or Components

A system by definition is composed of interrelated parts or elements. This is true for all systems — mechanical, biological, and social. Every system has at least two elements, and these elements are interconnected.

Holism, Synergism, Organicism, and Gestalt

The whole is not just the sum of the parts; the system itself can be explained only as a totality. Holism is the opposite of elementarism, which views the total as the sum of its individual parts.

Open-Systems View

Systems can be considered in two ways: 1) closed or 2) open. Open systems exchange information, energy, or material with their environments. Biological and social systems are inherently open systems; mechanical systems may be open or closed. The concepts of open and closed systems are difficult to defend in the absolute. We prefer to think of open-closed as a dimension; that is, systems are relatively open or relatively closed.

Input-Transformation-Output Model

The open system can be viewed as a transformation model. In a dynamic relationship with its environment, it receives various inputs, transforms these inputs in some way, and exports outputs.

System Boundaries

It follows that systems have boundaries which separate them from their environments. The concept of boundaries helps us understand the distinction between open and closed systems. The relatively closed system has rigid, impenetrable boundaries; whereas the open system has permeable boundaries between itself and a broader suprasystem. Boundaries are relatively easily defined in physical and biological systems, but are very difficult to delineate in social systems such as organizations.

Negative Entropy

Closed physical systems are subject to the force of entropy which increases until eventually the entire system fails. The tendency toward maximum entropy is a movement to disorder, complete lack of resource transformation, and death. In a closed system, the change in entropy must always be positive; however, in open biological or social systems, entropy can be arrested and may even be transformed into negative entropy — a process of more complete organization and ability to transform resources — because the system imports resources from its environment.

Steady State, Dynamic Equilibrium, and Homeostasis

The concept of steady state is closely related to that of negative entropy. A closed system eventually must attain an equilibrium state with maximum entropy — death or disorganization. However, an open system may attain a state where the system remains in dynamic equilibrium through the continuous inflow of materials, energy, and information.

Feedback

The concept of feedback is important in understanding how a system maintains a steady state. Information concerning the outputs or the process of the system is fed back as an input into the system, perhaps leading to changes in the transformation process and/or future outputs. Feedback can be both positive and negative, although the field of cybernetics is based on negative feedback. Negative feedback is informational input which indicates that the system is deviating from a prescribed course and should readjust to a new steady state.

---

systems.[10] He suggests that they are *general* systems theoretical hypotheses and qualifies them by suggesting that they are propositions applicable to general systems *behavior* theory and would thus exclude non-living systems. He does not limit these propositions to individual organisms, but considers them appropriate for social systems as well. His hypotheses are related to such issues as structure, process, subsystems, information, growth and integration. It is obviously impossible to discuss all of these hypotheses; we want only to indicate the extent to which many interesting propositions are being posed which

Key Concepts of General Systems Theory—cont'd

Hierarchy

A basic concept in systems thinking is that of hierarchical relationships between systems. A system is composed of subsystems of a lower order and is also part of a suprasystem. Thus, there is a hierarchy of the components of the system.

Internal Elaboration

Closed systems move toward entropy and disorganization. In contrast, open systems appear to move in the direction of greater differentiation, elaboration, and a higher level of organization.

Multiple Goal-Seeking

Biological and social systems appear to have multiple goals or purposes. Social organizations seek multiple goals, if for no other reason than that they are composed of individuals and subunits with different values and objectives.

Equifinality of Open Systems

In mechanistic systems there is a direct cause and effect relationship between the initial condition and the final state. Biological and social systems operate differently. Equifinality suggests that certain results may be achieved with different initial conditions and in different ways. This view suggests that social organizations can accomplish their objectives with diverse inputs and with varying internal activities (conversion processes).

might have relevance to many different types of systems. It will be a very long time (if ever) before most of these hypotheses are validated; however, we are surprised at how many of them can be agreed with intuitively, and we can see their possible verification in studies of social organizations.

We turn now to a closer look at how successful or unsuccessful we have been in utilizing these concepts in the development of modern organization theory.

A BEGINNING: ENTHUSIASTIC BUT INCOMPLETE

We have embraced general systems theory but, really, how completely? We could review a vast literature in modern organization theory which has explicitly or implicitly adopted systems theory as a frame of reference, and we have investigated in detail a few representative examples of the literature in assessing the state of the art.[11] It was found that most of these books professed to utilize general systems theory. Indeed, in the first few chapters, many of them did an excellent job of presenting basic systems concepts and showing their relationship to organizations; however, when they moved further into the discussion of more specific subject matter, they de-

parted substantially from systems theory. The studies appear to use a "partial systems approach" and leave for the reader the problem of integrating the various ideas into a systemic whole. It also appears that many of the authors are unable, because of limitations of knowledge about subsystem relationships, to carry out the task of using general systems theory as a conceptual basis for organization theory.

Furthermore, it is evident that each author had many "good ideas" stemming from the existing body of knowledge or current research on organizations which did not fit neatly into a "systems model." For example, they might discuss leadership from a relatively closed-system point of view and not consider it in relation to organizational technology, structure, or other variables. Our review of the literature suggests that much remains to be done in applying general systems theory to organization theory and management practice.

SOME DILEMMAS IN APPLYING GST TO ORGANIZATIONS

Why have writers embracing general systems theory as a basis for studying organizations had so much difficulty in following through? Part of this difficulty may stem from the newness of the paradigm and our inability to operationalize all we think we know about this approach. Or it may be because we know too little about the systems under investigation. Both of these possibilities will be covered later, but first we need to look at some of the more specific conceptual problems.

Organizations as Organisms

One of the basic contributions of general systems theory was the rejection of the traditional closed-system or mechanistic view of social organizations. But, did general systems theory free us from this constraint only to impose another, less obvious one? General systems theory grew out of the organismic views of von Bertalanffy and other biologists; thus, many of the characteristics are relevant to the living organism. It is conceptually easy to draw the analogy between living organisms and social organizations. "There is, after all, an intuitive similarity between the organization of the human body and the kinds of organizations men create. And so, undaunted by the failures of the human-social analogy through time, new theorists try afresh in each epoch."[12] General systems theory would have us accept this analogy between organism and social organization. Yet, we have a hard time swallowing it whole. Katz and Kahn warn us of the danger:

> There has been no more pervasive, persistent, and futile fallacy handicapping the social sciences than the use of the physical model for the understanding of social structures. The biological metaphor, with its crude comparisons of the physical parts of the body to the parts of the social system, has been replaced by more subtle but equally misleading analogies between biological and social functioning. This figurative type of thinking ignores the essential difference between the socially contrived nature of social systems and the physical structure of the machine or the human organism. So long as writers are committed to a theoretical framework based upon the physical model, they will miss the essential social-psychological facts of the highly variable, loosely articulated character of social systems.[13]

In spite of this warning, Katz and Kahn do embrace much of the general systems theory concepts which

are based on the biological metaphor. We must be very cautious about trying to make this analogy too literal. We agree with Silverman, who says, "It may, therefore, be necessary to drop the analogy between an organization and an organism: organizations may be systems but not necessarily *natural* systems."[14]

Distinction Between Organization and an Organization

General systems theory emphasizes that systems are organized—they are composed of interdependent components in some relationship. The social organization would then follow logically as just another system. But, we are perhaps being caught in circular thinking. It is true that all systems (physical, biological, and social) are by definition organized, but are all systems organizations? Rapoport and Horvath distinguish "organizations theory" and "the theory of organizations" as follows:

> We see organization theory as dealing with general and abstract organizational principles: it applies to any system exhibiting organized complexity. As such, organization theory is seen as an extension of mathematical physics or, even more generally, of mathematics designed to deal with organized systems. The theory of organizations, on the other hand, purports to be a social science. It puts real human organizations at the center of interest. It may study the social structure of organizations and so can be viewed as a branch of sociology; it can study the behavior of individuals or groups as members of organizations and can be viewed as a part of social psychology; it can study power relations and principles of control in organizations and so fits into political science.[15]

Why make an issue of this distinction? It seems to us that there is a vital matter involved. All systems may be considered to be organized, and more advanced systems may display differentiation in the activities of component parts—such as the specialization of human organs. However, all systems *do not* have purposeful entities. Can the heart or lungs be considered as purposeful entities in themselves or are they only components of the larger purposeful system, the human body? By contrast, the social organization is composed of two or more purposeful elements. "An organization consists of elements that have and can exercise their own wills."[16] Organisms, the foundation stone of general systems theory, do not contain purposeful elements which exercise their own will. This distinction between the organism and the social organization is of importance. In much of general systems theory, the concern is primarily with the way in which the *organism* responds to environmentally generated inputs. Feedback concepts and the maintenance of a steady state are based on internal adaptations to environmental forces. (This is particularly true of cybernetic models.) But, what about those changes and adaptations which occur from *within* social organizations? Purposeful elements within the social organization may initiate activities and adaptations which are difficult to subsume under feedback and steady-state concepts.

Open and Closed Systems

Another dilemma stemming from general systems theory is the tendency to dichotomize all systems as open or closed. We have been led to think of physical systems as closed, subject to the laws of entropy, and to think of biological systems as open to their environment and, possibly, becoming negentropic. But applying this strict polarization to social organizations creates many difficulties. In fact, most social organizations and their subsystems are "partially open" and "partially closed." Open and closed are a matter of degree. Unfortunately, there seems to be a widely held view (often more implicit than explicit) that *open-system thinking is good* and *closed-system thinking is bad*. We have not become sufficiently sophisticated to recognize that both are appropriate under certain conditions. For example, one of the most useful conceptualizations set forth by Thompson is that the social organization *must seek* to use closed-system concepts (particularly at the technical core) to reduce uncertainty and to create more effective performance at this level.

Still Subsystems Thinking

Even though we preach a general systems approach, we often practice subsystems thinking. Each of the

academic disciplines and each of us personally has a limited perspective of the system we are studying. While proclaiming a broad systems viewpoint, we often dismiss variables outside our interest or competence as being irrelevant, and we only open our system to those inputs which we can handle with our disciplinary bag of tools. We are hampered because each of the academic disciplines has taken a narrow "partial systems view" and find comfort in the relative certainty which this creates. Of course, this is not a problem unique to modern organization theory. Under the more traditional process approach to the study of management, we were able to do an admirable job of delineating and discussing planning, organizing, and controlling as separate activities. We were much less successful in discussing them as integrated and interrelated activities.

How Does Our Knowledge Fit?

One of the major problems in utilizing general systems theory is that we know (or think we know) more about certain relationships than we can fit into a general systems model. For example, we are beginning to understand the two-variable relationship between technology and structure. But, when we introduce another variable, say psychosocial relationships, our models become too complex. Consequently, in order to discuss all the things we know about organizations, we depart from a systems approach. Perhaps it is because we know a great deal more about the elements or subsystems of an organization than we do about the interrelationships and interactions between these subsystems. And, general systems theory forces us to consider those relationships we know the least — a true dilemma. So we continue to elaborate on those aspects of the organization which we know best — a partial systems view.

Failure to Delineate a Specific System

When the social sciences embraced general systems theory, the total system became the focus of attention and terminology tended toward vagueness. In the utilization of systems theory, we should be more precise in delineating the specific system under consideration. Failure to do this leads to much confusion. As Murray suggests:

> I am wary of the word "system" because social scientists use it very frequently without specifying which of several possible different denotations they have in mind; but more particularly because, today, "system" is a highly cathected term, loaded with prestige; hence, we are all strongly tempted to employ it even when we have nothing definite in mind and its only service is to indicate that we subscribe to the general practice premise respecting the interdependence of things — basic organismic theory, holism, field theory, interactionism, transactionism, etc . . . . When definitions of the units of a system are lacking, the term stands for no more than an article of faith, and is misleading to boot, insofar as it suggests a condition of affairs that may not actually exist.[17]

We need to be much more precise in delineating both the boundaries of the system under consideration and the level of our analysis. There is a tendency for current writers in organization theory to accept general systems theory and then to move indiscriminately across systems boundaries and between levels of systems without being very precise (and letting their readers in on what is occurring). James Miller suggests the need for clear delineation of levels in applying systems theory: "It is important to follow one procedural rule in systems theory in order to avoid confusion. Every discussion should begin with an identification of the level of reference, and the discourse should not change to another level without a specific statement that this is occurring."[18] Our field is replete with these confusions about systems levels. For example, when we use the term "organizational behavior" are we talking about the way the organization behaves as a system or are we talking about the behavior of the individual participants? By goals, do we mean the goals of the organization or the goals of the individuals within the organization? In using systems theory we must become more precise in our delineation of systems boundaries and systems levels if we are to prevent confusing conceptual ambiguity.

Recognition that Organizations are "Contrived Systems"

We have a vague uneasiness that general systems theory truly does not recognize the "contrived" nature of social organizations. With its predominant emphasis on natural organisms, it may understate some characteristics which are vital for the social organization. Social organizations do not occur naturally in nature; they are contrived by man. They have structure; but it is the structure of events rather than of physical components, and it cannot be separated from the processes of the system. The fact that social organizations are contrived by human beings suggests that they can be established for an infinite variety of purposes and do not follow the same life cycle patterns of birth, growth, maturity, and death as biological systems. As Katz and Kahn say:

> Social structures are essentially contrived systems. They are made up of men and are imperfect systems. They can come apart at the seams overnight, but they can also outlast by centuries the biological organisms which originally created them. The cement which holds them together is essentially psychological rather than biological. Social systems are anchored in the attitudes, perceptions, beliefs, motivations, habits, and expectations of human beings.[19]

Recognizing that the social organization is contrived again cautions us against making an exact analogy between it and physical or biological systems.

Questions of Systems Effectiveness

General systems theory with its biological orientation would appear to have an evolutionary view of system effectiveness. That living system which best adapts to its environment prospers and survives. The primary measure of effectiveness is perpetuation of the organism's species. Teleological behavior is therefore directed toward survival. But, is survival the only criterion of effectiveness of the social system? It is probably an essential but not all-inclusive measure of effectiveness.

General systems theory emphasizes the organism's survival goal and does not fully relate to the question of the effectiveness of the system in its suprasystem — the environment. Parsonian functional-structural views provide a contrast. "The *raison d'etre* of complex organizations, according to this analysis, is mainly to benefit the society in which they belong, and that society is, therefore, the appropriate frame of reference for the evaluation of organizational effectiveness."[20]

But, this view seems to go to the opposite extreme from the survival view of general systems theory — the organization exists to serve the society. It seems to us that the truth lies somewhere between these two viewpoints. And it is likely that a systems viewpoint (modified from the species survival view of general systems theory) will be most appropriate. Yuchtman and Seashore suggest:

> The organization's success over a period of time in this competition for resources — i.e., its bargaining position in a given environment — is regarded as an expression of its overall effectiveness. Since the resources are of various kinds, and the competitive relationships are multiple, and since there is interchangeability among classes of resources, the assessment of organizational effectiveness must be in terms not of any single criterion but of an open-ended multidimensional set of criteria.[21]

This viewpoint suggests that questions of organizational effectiveness must be concerned with at least three levels of analysis. The level of the environment, the level of the social organization as a system, and the level of the subsystems (human participants) within the organization. Perhaps much of our confusion and ambiguity concerning organizational effectiveness stems from our failure to clearly delineate the level of our analysis and, even more important, our failure really to understand the relationships among these levels.

Our discussion of some of the problems associated with the application of general systems theory to the study of social organizations might suggest that we completely reject the appropriateness of this model. On the contrary, we see the systems approach as the new paradigm for the study of organizations; but, like all new concepts in the sciences, one which has to be applied, modified, and elaborated to make it as useful as possible.

SYSTEMS THEORY PROVIDES THE NEW PARADIGM

We hope the discussion of general systems theory and organization provides a realistic appraisal. We do not want to promote the value of the systems approach as a matter of faith; however, we do see systems theory as vital to the study of social organizations and as providing the major new paradigm for our field of study.

Thomas Kuhn provides an interesting interpretation of the nature of scientific revolution.[22] He suggests that major changes in all fields of science occur with the development of new conceptual schemes, or paradigms. These new paradigms do not just represent a step-by-step advancement in "normal" science (the science generally accepted and practiced) but, rather, a revolutionary change in the way the scientific field is perceived by the practitioners. Kuhn says:

> The historian of science may be tempted to exclaim that when paradigms change, the world itself changes with them. Led by a new paradigm, scientists adopt new instruments and look in new places. Even more important, during revolutions scientists see new and different things when looking with familiar instruments in places they have looked before. It is rather as if the professional community has been suddenly transported to another planet where familiar objects are seen in a different light and are joined by unfamiliar ones as well . . . Paradigm changes do cause scientists to see the world of their research-engagement differently. Insofar as their only recourse to that world is through what they see and do, we may want to say that after a revolution scientists are responding to a different world.[23]

New paradigms frequently are rejected by the scientific community. (At first they may seem crude and limited — offering very little more than older paradigms.) They frequently lack the apparent sophistication of the older paradigms, which they ultimately replace. They do not display the clarity and certainty of older paradigms, which have been refined through years of research and writing. But, a new paradigm does provide for a "new start" and opens up new directions which were not possible under the old. "We must recognize how very limited in both scope and precision a paradigm can be at the time of its first appearance. Paradigms gain their status because they are more successful than their competitors in solving a few problems that the group of practitioners has come to recognize as acute. To be more successful is not, however, to be either completely successful with a single problem or notably successful with any large number."[24]

Systems theory does provide a new paradigm for the study of social organizations and their management. At this stage it is obviously crude and lacking in precision. In some ways it may not be much better than older paradigms which have been accepted and used for a long time (such as the management process approach). As in other fields of scientific endeavor, the new paradigm must be applied, clarified, elaborated, and made more precise. But, it does provide a fundamentally different view of the reality of social organizations and can serve as the basis for major advancements in our field.

We see many exciting examples of the utilization of the new systems paradigm in the field of organization and management. Several of these have been referred to earlier[25], and there have been many others. Burns and Stalker made substantial use of systems views in setting forth their concepts of mechanistic and organic managerial systems.[26] Their studies of the characteristics of these two organization types lack precise definition of the variables and relationships, but their colleagues have used the systems approach to look at the relationship of organizations to their environment and also among the technical, structural, and behavioral characteristics within the organization. [27] Chamberlain used a system view in studying enterprises and their environment which is substantially different from traditional microeconomics.[28] The emerging field of "environmental sciences" has found the systems paradigm vital.

Thus, the systems theory paradigm is being used extensively in the investigation of relationships between subsystems within organizations and in studying the environmental interfaces. But, it still has not advanced sufficiently to meet the needs. One of the major problems is that the practical need to deal with comprehensive systems of relationships is over-running our ability to fully understand and predict these relationships. *We vitally need the systems paradigm but we are not sufficiently sophisticated to use it appropriately.* This is the dilemma. Do our current failures to fully utilize the systems paradigm suggest that we reject it and return to the older, more traditional, and time-tested paradigms? Or do we work with systems theory to make it more precise, to understand the relationships among subsystems, and to gather the informational inputs which are necessary to make the systems approach really work? We think the latter course offers the best opportunity.

Thus, we prefer to accept current limitations of systems theory, while working to reduce them and to develop more complete and sophisticated approaches for its application. We agree with Rapoport, who says:

> The systems approach to the study of man can be appreciated as an effort to restore meaning (in terms of intuitively grasped understanding of wholes) while adhering to the principles of *disciplined* generalizations and rigorous deduction. It is, in short, an attempt to make the study of man both scientific and meaningful.[29]

We are sympathetic with the second part of Rapoport's comment, the need to apply the systems approach but to make disciplined generalizations and rigorous deductions. This is a vital necessity and yet a major current limitation. We do have some indication that progress (although very slow) is being made.

WHAT DO WE NEED NOW?

Everything is related to everything else — but how? General systems theory provides us with the macro paradigm for the study of social organizations. As Scott and others have pointed out, most sciences go through a macro-micro-macro cycle or sequence of emphasis.[30] Traditional bureaucratic theory provided the first major macro view of organizations. Administrative management theorists concentrated on the development of macro "principles of management" which were applicable to all organizations. When these macro views seemed incomplete (unable to explain important phenomena), attention turned to the micro level—more detailed analysis of components or parts of the organization, thus the interest in human relations, technology, or structural dimensions.

The systems approach returns us to the macro level with a new paradigm. General systems theory emphasizes a very high level of abstraction. Phillips classifies it as a third-order study[31] that attempts to develop macro concepts appropriate for all types of biological, physical, and social systems.

In our view, we are now ready to move down a level of abstraction to consider second-order systems studies or midrange concepts. These will be based on general systems theory but will be more concrete and will emphasize more specific characteristics and relationships in social organizations. They will operate within the broad paradigm of systems theory but at a less abstract level.

What should we call this new midrange level of analysis? Various authors have referred to it as a "contingency view," a study of "patterns of relationships," or a search for "configurations among subsystems." Lorsch and Lawrence reflect this view:

> During the past few years there has been evident a new trend in the study of organizational phenomena. Underlying this new approach is the idea that the internal functioning of organizations must be consistent with the demands of the organization task, technology, or external environment, and the needs of its members if the organization is to be effective. Rather than searching for the panacea of the one best way to organize under all conditions, investigators have more and more tended to examine the functioning of organizations in relation to the needs of their particular members and the external pressures facing them. Basically, this approach seems to be leading to the development of a "contingency" theory of organization with the appropriate internal states and processes of the organization contingent upon external requirements and member needs.[32]

Numerous others have stressed a similar viewpoint. Thompson suggests that the essence of administration

lies in understanding basic configurations which exist between the various subsystems and with the environment. "The basic function of administration appears to be coalignment, not merely of people (in coalitions) but of institutionalized action—of technology and task environment into a viable domain, and of organizational design and structure appropriate to it."[33]

Bringing these ideas together we can provide a more precise definition of the contingency view. The contingency view of organizations and their management suggests that an organization is a system composed of subsystems and delineated by identifiable boundaries from its environmental suprasystem. The contingency view seeks to understand the interrelationships within and among subsystems as well as between the organization and its environment and to define patterns of relationships or configurations of variables. It emphasizes the multivariate nature of organizations and attempts to understand how organizations operate under varying conditions and in specific circumstances. Contingency views are ultimately directed toward suggesting organizational designs and managerial systems most appropriate for specific situations.

But, it is not enough to suggest that a "contingency view" is based on systems concepts of organizations and their management is more appropriate than the simplistic "principles approach." If organization theory is to advance and make contributions to managerial practice, it must define more explicitly certain patterns of relationship between organizational variables. This is the major challenge facing our field.

Just how do we go about using systems theory to develop these midrange or contingency views? We see no alternative but to engage in intensive comparative investigations of many organizations following the advice of Blau:

> A theory of organization, whatever its specific nature, and regardless of how subtle the organizational processes it takes into account, has as its central aim to establish the constellations of characteristics that develop in organizations of various kinds. Comparative studies of many organizations are necessary, not alone to test the hypotheses implied by such a theory, but also to provide a basis for initial

exploration and refinement of the theory by indicating the conditions on which relationships, originally assumed to hold universally are contingent. . . . Systematic research on many organizations that provides the data needed to determine the interrelationships between several organizational features is, however, extremely rare.[34]

Various conceptual designs for the comparative study of organizations and their subsystems are emerging to help in the development of a contingency view. We do not want to impose our model as to what should be considered in looking for these patterns of relationships. However, the tentative matrix shown in Table 7-1 suggests this approach. We have used as a starting point the two polar organization types which have been emphasized in the literature — closed/stable/mechanistic and open/adaptive/organic.

We will consider the environmental suprasystem and organizational subsystems (goals and values, technical, structural, psychosocial, and managerial) plus various dimensions or characteristics of each of these systems. By way of illustration we have indicated

TABLE 7-1

Matrix of patterns of relationships between organization types and systems variables

ORGANIZATIONAL SUPRA- AND SUBSYSTEMS	CONTINUUM OF ORGANIZATION TYPES	
	CLOSED/STABLE/MECHANISTIC	OPEN/ADAPTIVE/ORGANIC
Environmental relationships		
General nature	Placid	Turbulent
Predictability	Certain, determinate	Uncertain, indeterminate
Boundary relationships	Relatively closed; limited to few participants (sales, purchasing, etc.); fixed and well-defined	Relatively open; many participants have external relationships; varied and not varied and not clearly defined
Goals and values		
Organizational goals in general	Efficient performance, stability, maintenance	Effective problem-solving, innovation, growth
Goal set	Single, clear-cut	Multiple, determined by necessity to satisfy a set of constraints
Stability	Stable	Unstable
Technical		
Structural		
Psychosocial		
Managerial		

several specific subcategories under the environmental suprasystem as well as the goals and values subsystem. This process would have to be completed and extended to all of the subsystems. The next step would be the development of appropriate descriptive language (based on research and conceptualization) for each relevant characteristic across the continuum of organization types. For example, on the "stability" dimension for goals and values we would have high, medium, and low at appropriate places on the continuum. If the entire matrix were filled in, it is likely that we could begin to discern patterns of relationships among subsystems.

We do not expect this matrix to provide the midrange model for everyone. It is highly doubtful that we will be able to follow through with the fieldwork investigations necessary to fill in all the squares. Nevertheless, it does illustrate a possible approach for the translation of more abstract general systems theory into an appropriate midrange model which is relevant for organization theory and management practice. Frankly, we see this as a major long-term effort on the part of many researchers, investigating a wide variety of organizations. In spite of the difficulties involved in such research, the endeavor has practical significance. Sophistication in the study of organizations will come when we have a more complete understanding of organizations as total systems (configurations or subsystems) so that we can prescribe more appropriate organizational designs and managerial systems. Ultimately, organization theory could serve as the foundation for more effective management practice.

APPLICATION OF SYSTEMS CONCEPTS TO MANAGEMENT PRACTICE

The study of organizations is an applied science because the resulting knowledge is relevant to problem solving in ongoing institutions. Contributions to organization theory come from many sources. Deductive and inductive research in a variety of disciplines provide a theoretical base of propositions which are useful for understanding organizations and for managing them. Experience gained in management practice is also an important input to organization theory.

In short, management is based on the body of knowledge generated by practical experience *and* eclectic scientific research concerning organizations. The body of knowledge developed through theory and research should be translatable into more effective organizational design and managerial practices.

Do systems concepts and contingency views provide a panacea for solving problems in organizations? The answer is an emphatic *no;* this approach does not provide "ten easy steps" to success in management. Such cookbook approaches, while seemingly applicable and easy to grasp, are usually shortsighted, narrow in perspective, and superficial—in short, unrealistic. Fundamental ideas, such as systems concepts and contingency views, are more difficult to comprehend. However, they facilitate more thorough understanding of complex situations and increase the likelihood of appropriate action.

It is important to recognize that many managers have used and will continue to use a systems approach and contingency views intuitively and implicitly. Without much knowledge of the underlying body of organization theory, they have an intuitive "sense of the situation," are flexible diagnosticians, and adjust their actions and decisions accordingly. Thus, systems concepts and contingency views are not new. However, if this approach to organization theory and management practice can be made more explicit, we can facilitate better management and more effective organizations.

Practicing managers in business firms, hospitals, and government agencies continue to function on a day-to-day basis. Therefore, they must use whatever theory is available, they cannot wait for the *ultimate* body of knowledge. (There is none!) Practitioners should be included in the search for new knowledge because they control access to an essential ingredient—organizational data—and they are the ones who ultimately put the theory to the test. Mutual understanding among managers, teachers, and researchers will facilitate the development of a relevant body of knowledge.

Simultaneously with the refinement of the body of knowledge, a concerted effort should be directed toward applying what we do know. We need ways of making systems and contingency views more usable.

Without oversimplification, we need some relevant guidelines for practicing managers.

The general tenor of the contingency view is somewhere between simplistic, specific principles and complex, vague notions. It is a midrange concept which recognizes the complexity involved in managing modern organizations but uses patterns of relationships and/or configurations of subsystems in order to facilitate improved practice. The art of management depends on a reasonable success rate for actions in a probabilistic environment. Our hope is that systems concepts and contingency views, while continually being refined by scientists/researchers/theorists, will also be made more applicable.

REFERENCES

1. An entire article could be devoted to a discussion of ingenious ways in which the term "systems approach" has been used in the literature pertinent to organization theory and management practice.
2. Deutsh, K.W. Toward a Cybernetic Model of Man and Society. In Buckley, W. (Ed.) *Modern Systems Research for the Behavioral Scientist.* Chicago: Aldine, 1968, p. 389.
3. Phillips, D.C. Systems Theory — A Discredited Philosophy. In Schoderbek, P.P (Ed.) *Management Systems,* New York: John Wiley, 1971, p. 56.
4. Barnard, C.I. 1938, p. 65.
5. Miller, R.E. The new science of administration in the USSR., *Admin. Sci. Quart.,* Sept. 1971.
6. Scott, W.G. 1961.
7. Simon, H.A. The Architecture of Complexity. In Litterer, J.A. (Ed.) *Organizations: Systems, Control and Adaptation,* vol. 2, New York: John Wiley, 1969.
8. Boulding, K.E. 1956. Buckley, W. 1968. Easton, D. *A Systems Analysis of Political Life.* New York: John Wiley, 1965. Hall, A.D., and Eagen, R.E. Definition of System. *General Systems, Yearbook for the Society for the Advancement of General Systems Theory,* vol. 1, 1956. Miller J.G. Living systems: basic concepts. *Behavioral Sci.,* July 1965. Parsons, T. *The Social System.* Glencoe, Ill.: Free Press, 1951. Thompson, J.D., 1967.
9. Churchman, C.W. *The Systems Approach.* New York: Dell, 1968. Emery, F.E., and Trist, E.L. 1960. Kast, F.E., and Rosenzweig, J.E. *Organization and Management Theory: A Systems Approach.* New York: McGraw-Hill, 1970. Katz, D., and Kahn, R.L., 1966. Litterer, J.A. *Organizations: Structure and Behavior,* vols. 1,2. New York: John Wiley, 1969. Miller, E.J. and Rice, A.K. *Systems of Organizations,* London, 1967. Schein, E. *Organizational Psychology,* rev. ed. Englewood Cliffs, N.J.: Prentice-Hall, 1970.
10. Miller, J.G. 1965.
11. Kast, F., and Rosenzweig, J.E. 1970. Katz, D., and Kahn, R.L. 1966. Litterer, J.A. 1969. Rice, A.K. *The Modern University,* London: Tavistock, 1970. Scott, W.G. 1961.
12. Back, K.W. Biological models of social change. *Am. Sociological Rev.,* Aug. 1971, p. 660.
13. Katz, D., and Kahn, R.L. 1966, p. 31.
14. Silverman, D. *The Theory of Organizations.* New York: Basic Books, 1971, p. 31.
15. Rapoport, A., and Horvath, W.J. *Thoughts on Organization Theory.* In Buckley, W. 1968, pp. 74-75.
16. Ackoff, R.L. Towards a system of systems concepts. *Management Sci.,* July 1971, p. 669.
17. Murray, H.A. Preparation for the Scaffold of a Comprehensive System. In Koch, S. (Ed.) *Psychology: A Study of a Science,* vol. 3. New York: McGraw-Hill, 1959, pp. 50-51.
18. Miller, J.G. 1965, p. 216.
19. Katz, D., and Kahn, R.L. 1966, p. 33.
20. Yuchtman, E., and Seashore, S.E. 1967, p. 896.
21. Yuchtman, E., and Seashore, S.E. 1967, p. 891.
22. Kuhn, T.S. *The Structure of Scientific Revolutions.* Chicago: University of Chicago Press, 1962.
23. Kuhn, T.S. 1962, p. 110.
24. Kuhn, T.S. 1962, p. 23.
25. Buckley, W. 1968. Easton, D. 1965. Katz, D., and Kahn, R.L. 1966. Litterer, J.A. 1969. Miller, E.J., and Rice, A.K. 1967., Rice, A.K. 1970. Thompson, J.D. 1967.
26. Burns, T., and Stalker, G.M. *The Management of Innovation.* London: Tavistock, 1961.
27. Miller, E.J., and Rice, A.K. 1967.
28. Chamberlain, N.W. *Enterprise and Environment: The Firm in Time and Place.* New York: McGraw-Hill, 1968.
29. Buckley, W., 1968, p. xxii.
30. Scott, W.G. 1961.
31. Phillips, D.C. 1971.
32. Lorsch, J.W., and Lawrence, P.R. *Studies in Organizational Design.* Homewood, Ill.: Irwin-Dorsey, 1970, p. 1.
33. Thompson, J.D., 1967, p. 157.
34. Blau, P.M. The comparative study of organizations. *Industrial and Labor Relations Rev.,* April 1965.

SUGGESTED READINGS

UNIT TWO. LEADERSHIP AND MANAGEMENT CONCEPTS AND THEORIES

Ellis R: Organizational leadership in turbulent times, Management Review 59-61, 1973.

Lundborg L: What is leadership? JONA, 32-33, 1982.

Miller K: Nurse executive leadership: A corporate perspective, NAQ 13(2):12-18, 1989.

Tannenbaum R and Schmidt W: How to choose a leadership pattern, HBR 51(3):1-10, 1973.

Affleck J: The constructive orchestration of chaos, JONA 10(3):16-20, 1980.

Alidina S and Funke-Furber J: First line managers: optimizing the span of control, JONA 18(5):34-39, 1988.

Kotter J: What leaders really do, HBR 68(3):103-111, 1990.

McClure M: Managing the professional nurse. I. Organizational theories, JONA 14(2):15-22, 1984.

McClure M: Managing the professional nurse. II. Applying management theories to the challenges, JONA 14(3): 11-17, 1984.

McClure M: The nurse executive role: A leadership opportunity, NAQ 12(1):45-51, 1989.

Unit Three

ORGANIZATION CONCEPTS, THEORIES, AND PROCESSES

CHAPTER **8**

Toward a Theory of Nursing Ethics

Sara T. Fry, RN, PhD, FAAN

The development of nursing theory to explain and predict the nature of phenomena as they occur within the range of nursing interests in health care has been a consistent theme in the nursing literature over the past 25 years. In the attempt to conceptualize the role of theory in nursing practice and research as well as to formulate some structure for theorizing about nursing, scholars enlisted the help of philosophers Dickoff and James. The outcome of this collaborative effort was the proposal of Practice Theory.[1-3]

Under Practice Theory, nursing theories could be classified as either factor-isolating, factor-relating, situation-relating, or situation-producing and would represent the conceptual frameworks utilized by the nurse in carrying out nursing interventions.[1] As originally conceived, Practice Theory assumed that theories of nursing already existed within the thought processes and strategies that the nurse employed at the bedside with the patient, and it simply organized these theories as they became apparent in the plans and activities of the nurse to bring about the desired patient or nursing goals.

Not surprisingly, these inductive classifications of nursing theories were strongly criticized and did not receive wide support within nursing. Many scholars agreed on the need for prescriptive (situation-producing) theories in order to bring about change.

Reprinted from *Advances in Nursing Science*, Vol. 11, No. 4, with permission of Aspen Publishers, Inc. © 1989.

Few, however, accepted Practice Theory as the way to classify all nursing theories or agreed that theorizing by nurses was limited to the thought processes and strategies used by nurses in carrying out patient care interventions. Indeed, one of the more well-known critics of Practice Theory claimed that the system was simply not needed in nursing.[4-6] Arguing that knowledge used by the nurse is not different from the knowledge of science and ethics, Beckstrand concluded that nursing should utilize scientific and ethical theorizing, not Practice Theory, to bring about change in practice.[5]

Over the years, serious consideration of Practice Theory in nursing has gradually dissipated, while Beckstrand's argument for the use of scientific theory in nursing practice has been overwhelmingly accepted. Yet her argument for the development and use of ethical theory in nursing has largely gone unheeded by nurses. Why are there no formal theories of ethics for nursing practice? If one could be proposed, what would its structure be? Would a theory of nursing ethics simply be the application of a general ethical theory to nursing practice? Would it resemble or even mirror a theory of ethics for medical practice, or would it be unique to the range of moral judgments and/or actions used by nurses?

The purpose of this article is to begin to answer these questions by the careful description and analysis of the types of ethical theorizing currently beginning to emerge in the nursing literature. The author is of the opinion that the articulation of a theory (or theories) of nursing ethics is on the horizon and that ethical theory will become an essential part of a yet-to-be-formulated philosophy of nursing. The particular form that any theory of nursing ethics will finally take is, of course, unknowable at present. This situation is probably advantageous, as it allows the nursing community and would-be ethical theorists to learn from the recent and important theoretical developments within the related disciplines of ethics and biomedical ethics. These developments will certainly influence how a theory of nursing ethics is eventually conceptualized and may raise important theoretical and methodologic issues for any theory.

WHAT IS NURSING ETHICS?

In order to begin theorizing about nursing ethics, one must first be clear about the world view one brings to a consideration of the ethics of nursing practice. Veatch,[7,8] for example, notes that the term "nursing ethics" is, in itself, controversial. While some might argue that nursing ethics is a unique field of inquiry separate from medical ethics, Veatch claims that "there is really very little that is morally unique to nursing."[7(p17)] The same moral issues emerge in the health care setting whether one is a physician, nurse, or patient. Thus Veatch concludes that "nursing ethics" is a legitimate term only insofar as it refers to a subcategory of biomedical ethics. A branch of applied ethics, biomedical ethics addresses the ethical judgments made within the biomedical sciences; nursing ethics is the ethical analysis of those judgments made by nurses, and physician ethics is the ethical analysis of those judgments made by physicians. According to this view, if nursing ethics is a specific form of inquiry under the more general category of biomedical ethics, then any theory of nursing ethics will necessarily follow from biomedical ethics theory.

Contrary to Veatch's view, Jameton[9] argues that nursing ethics is not another form of applied ethics, and especially not of biomedical ethics. Since there appears to be a "rich and complex relationship between the moral conventions of nursing practice and the philosophical imagination,"[9(pxvi)] nursing ethics cannot simply be the application of philosophical principles to a new set of facts, according to

Jameton. For him, nursing ethics is a form of philosophical study that raises questions about the aims of theory formation, the meaning of philosophical principles, and the nature of philosophical solutions to ethical problems. It is a form of inquiry that contributes to progress in philosophical ethics and influences the work and thought of philosophers in general. Because the study of ethics in nursing is philosophical in nature, it should not be viewed as a form of inquiry independent of ethics. Nursing ethics uses traditional and contemporary forms of philosophical analysis to describe the moral phenomena found in nursing practice. To assess critically the language and theoretical foundations of nursing practice, and to raise normative claims about the aims of nursing practice. Although Jameton does not propose a framework for a theory of nursing ethics, his overall view tends to support the notion that if nursing ethics is a form of ethical inquiry that is primarily philosophical in nature, then a theory of nursing ethics will necessarily be an ethical theory as generally accepted within the discipline of philosophy.

It is interesting that the views of Veatch and Jameton are congruent with the models of nursing ethics proposed by White[10] (Figure 8-1). Model #1 depicts nursing ethics as a form of inquiry that is equal to medical ethics within the general field of biomedical ethics. This construct is similar to Veatch's view of nursing ethics. Model #2 depicts nursing ethics as being equal to biomedical ethics and business ethics among the forms of ethical inquiry. This construct is similar to Jameton's view of nursing ethics. Both models depict nursing ethics as a separate form of inquiry within philosophy and ethics, yet only the second model clearly depicts nursing ethics as separate from biomedical ethics, rather than as a subcategory of the larger field. While White stated no preference for the conceptual location of nursing ethics in relation to biomedical ethics and medical ethics, she did note that the location should be of concern to those working within nursing ethics, and it would be of interest to those articulating a theory of nursing ethics as well.

During the past ten years, most efforts to describe nursing ethics have tended to adopt Model #1.[8,10-14] Accordingly, they have applied biomedical ethics to

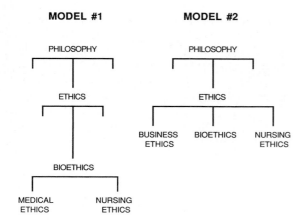

FIGURE 8-1

Two models of nursing ethics. *From White G: Philosophical ethics and nursing—A word of caution. In Chinn PL, editor: Advances in nursing theory development, Rockville, Md, Aspen Publishers, 1983.*

the practice of nursing using frameworks from bioethical theory,[15] theologically based contract theory,[16] the secularly based pluralistic theory of human rights,[17] and a well-known liberal theory of justice.[18] This influence on the development of nursing ethics has been quite extensive. Current discussions of nursing ethics tend to revolve around comparisons of deontologic and utilitarian theories, the weight of bioethical principles and rules in nurses' decision making, and the relative importance of nursing's contract with society and individual patients. Empirical studies in nursing ethics have almost exclusively used justice-based theories of moral reasoning from cognitive psychology to interpret their findings about nurses' moral behavior, judgment, and reasoning.[19-23] In addition, biomedical ethics guides most normative discussions of ethics in nursing.[24,25] The result is a trend in nursing ethics that does not take into consideration the role of nurses in health care, the social significance of nursing in contemporary society, or the value standards for nursing practice. By focusing on the terms of justification, gender-based considerations of justice, and the language of principles and rules, nursing ethics has come to be viewed primarily as a species or application of biomedical ethics. Jameton's view of nursing ethics has

not been widely discussed, and a theory of nursing ethics based on his view (or any other view) has yet to be articulated.

TRADITIONAL VALUE FOUNDATIONS OF NURSING ETHICS

Despite the lack of clear conceptual underpinnings for nursing ethics, several individuals have attempted to identify the moral foundations of nursing and the central value(s) important to any theory of nursing ethics. For example, empirical studies of the clinical decision making of nurses have pinpointed autonomy as a fundamental value affecting the moral dimensions of nursing practice.[26,27] The results of another study have suggested that subjective values, such as producing the greatest good for the greatest number, are basic to nurses' ethical decision making.[28] Unfortunately, the results of these studies were interpreted in terms of these values as predetermined ideologies for nursing practice. What was assumed to be the case in biomedical ethics was assumed to be the case in nursing ethics as well. In other words, autonomy and producing good were categories that the researchers expected to find because autonomy and producing good are prominent features of biomedical ethics.

This should not be a surprise. Both of these values—autonomy and producing good—are indeed prominent features of theories of biomedical ethics. Engelhardt,[17] for example, posits autonomy as the foundational value of secular bioethics, and Pellegrino and Thomasma[29] urge the restoration of beneficence as the fundamental principle of medical ethics. As used in these theories, autonomy and producing good constitute idealized value components of a social ethic for the practice of medicine, and they function within a structured framework of ethical principles and rules for physician decision making. Both secular bioethics and medical ethics rely on traditional interpretations of their central principles and use traditional patterns of moral justification as articulated by leading bioethicists. The same views of autonomy and beneficence have even been claimed by some nurses to form the moral basis for needed social reform of the institutional setting in which nursing is practiced.[30]

However, there is no good reason to assume that autonomy and producing good are, de facto, the appropriate value foundations for nursing ethics simply because they are accepted moral foundations for biomedical ethics. While no one would dispute that nurse autonomy and producing good are related to the practice of nursing, neither of these values derived from theories of biomedical ethics has been convincingly demonstrated to be the primary moral foundation of nursing ethics.

Other approaches to identifying the moral foundations of nursing have been both analytical and normative. For example, Stenberg[24] analyzed the value concepts of several theoretical frameworks in biomedical ethics in terms of their relevance to the practice of nursing. She found the concepts of code, contract, and context, as discussed in the works of May[31] and Fletcher,[32] to be inadequate as bases for the nursing ethic. On the other hand, Stenberg judged the concept of covenant, as discussed by Ramsey[33] and May,[31] to be adequate as an "inclusive and satisfying model for nursing ethics."[24(p21)] Covenant, interpreted as a binding agreement, was viewed as the foundational value for such health worker actions as fidelity, promise keeping, and truth telling in patient care. On the basis of this analysis, the medical ethical interpretation of covenant was adopted without alteration by Stenberg as a sound moral foundation for the practice of nursing. Because covenant was a moral foundation for the physician-patient relationship, it was seen to be similarly valid for the nurse-patient relationship as well. This tendency to adopt medical ethical frameworks as valid moral foundations for the practice of nursing is repeated in more recent analyses of the moral foundations of the nursing ethic.[34,35] However, it is important to question whether the values appropriate to the practice of medicine or the moral foundations for the physician-patient relationship are necessarily applicable to the practice of nursing or the nurse-patient relationship.

THE MORAL VALUE OF CARING AS A FOUNDATION FOR NURSING ETHICS

A few individuals have attempted to articulate values other than medical values as foundational for the moral practice of nursing. Gadow,[36] for example, argues that the value of caring provides a foundation for a nursing ethic that will protect and enhance the human dignity of patients within the health care system. Viewing caring in the nurse-patient relationship as a commitment to certain ends for the patient, Gadow analyzes existential caring as demonstrated in the nursing actions of truth telling and touch. Through truth telling, the nurse helps the patient to assess the subjective as well as objective realities of illness and to make choices based on the unique meaning of the illness experience. Through touch, the nurse assists the patient to overcome the depersonalization that often characterizes a patient's experience in the health care setting. To touch the patient is to affirm that he or she is a person rather than an object and to communicate the value of caring as the basis for nursing actions. This approach thus identifies a moral foundation for nursing ethics based on the reality of the nurse-patient encounter in health care and has been supported by those who wish to articulate caring as a foundation of the nurse-patient relationship and its meaning.[37-39]

Watson built on the ideas of Gadow to propose a slightly different view of caring as the foundation of "nursing as a human science."[40(p13)] Viewing nursing as a means to the preservation of humanity within society, Watson posits caring as a human value that involves "a will and a commitment to care, knowledge, caring actions, and consequences."[40(p29)] Such a view of caring requires a commitment on the part of the nurse to protect human dignity and preserve humanity. Caring becomes a professional ideal when the notion of caring transcends specific acts of caring between nurse and patient to influence collective acts of the nursing profession, at which point it takes on important implications for human civilization. Like Gadow, Watson views caring as a moral ideal that is rooted in our notions of human dignity. Unlike Gadow, however, Watson sees human caring as constituting a philosophy of action with many unexplained metaphysical and spiritual dimensions. This view of caring supports Watson's abstract philosophy of nursing, but it does not adequately support caring as a moral value that ought to serve as a foundation for the nursing ethic. The value of caring remains an ideal rather than an operationalized aspect of nursing judgments and/or actions.

Nonetheless, both Gadow and Watson posit caring as a value of central importance to the nature of the nurse-patient relationship.[36,40] First, like Griffin,[37] they consider caring to be a mode of being, a natural state of human existence in which individuals relate to the world and other human beings. This is not unlike Heidegger's[41] notion of care as a fundamental mode of human existence in the world and Noddings's[42] view of caring as a natural sentiment of being human. As a mode of being, caring is natural—a feeling or an internal sense made universal in the whole species. It is neither moral nor nonmoral; it is simply one's way of being in the world.

Second, caring is considered to be a precondition for the care of specific entities, whether things, others, or oneself.[37] In other words, a conceptual form of caring must exist as a structural feature of human growth and development prior to the point at which the process of caring actually commences.

Third, caring is identified with moral and social ideals. For example, Watson[40] views caring as occurring in society to serve human needs, such as the need for protection from the elements or for love. Similarly, Gadow[36] views caring as a means of protecting the human dignity of patients while their health care needs are met. Thus, as a phenomenon of human existence, caring gains moral significance because it is consistently reinforced as an ideal by those who have the responsibility of serving the needs of others.[37] Because practice of nursing is socially mandated to assist with the health needs of individuals, and because the nature of the nurse-patient encounter is viewed as having important moral dimensions, caring becomes strongly linked to the moral and social ideals of nursing as a profession.

THREE MODELS OF CARING RELEVANT TO A THEORY OF NURSING ETHICS

Given these attributes of caring as defined by accounts of the nurse-patient relationship, at least three models of caring are relevant for a theory of nursing ethics that posits caring as a foundational value.

Noddings's Model of Caring

The first model is found in the work of Noddings[42] and is theoretically based on ethics and social psychology. Building on the work of Gilligan,[43-45] Noddings combines a knowledge of ethics with perspectives on moral development in women. She states her purpose to be "feminine in the deep classical sense, rooted in receptivity, relatedness, and responsiveness,"[42(p2)] yet she is careful to develop her notion of caring as applicable to both females and males.

Caring is a feminine value in that the attitude of caring expresses our earliest memories of being cared for—that is, one's store of memories of both caring and being cared for is associated with the mother figure. However, caring is also masculine, in that it involves behaviors that have moral content and that can be adopted and embraced by men, even though it may not be their natural tendancy to adopt such notions.[42] In defining care, Noddings states that "to care may mean to be charged with the protection, welfare, or maintenance of something or someone."[42(p2)] Rather than an attitude that begins with moral reasoning, caring represents the attitude of being moral or the "longing for goodness."[42(p2)] Caring is thus not an outcome of ethical behavior, in Noddings's view, but itself constitutes ethics. As such, it is not necessarily gender-dependent but is gender-relevant.

Central to this view of caring are the aforementioned notions of receptivity, relatedness, and responsiveness: the acceptance or confirmation by the caregiver of the one cared for (receptivity), the relation of the caregiver to the one cared for as a fact of human existence (relatedness), and commitment from the caregiver to the one cared for (responsiveness). Ethical caring, which is not necessarily either masculine or feminine, is simply the relation in which we meet another morally. Motivated by the ideal of caring in which we are a partner in human relationships, we are guided not by ethical principles but by the strength of the ideal of caring itself, claims Noddings. Thus, instead of the notions inherent in conditions for traditional moral justification,[15] Noddings's ethic of caring depends on "the maintenance of conditions that will permit caring to flourish."[42(p5)] It is a person-to-person encounter that ultimately results in joy as a basic human affect within relationships bound by ethical caring.

Scholarship on the caring phenomenon in general has been strongly influenced by Noddings's model of caring, which stresses the ethics and morality of caring from a perspective that is definitely gender-related, although Noddings herself would undoubtedly deny that she is advocating a feminist model of caring. The model's relevance to the practice of nursing, however, remains largely unexplored. For those who recognize the limitations of theories of biomedical ethics as bases for a theory of nursing ethics, Noddings's model is a rich resource for future discussion of nursing ethics. It may also prove to be an acceptable model for the descriptive study of ethical decision making in nursing practice. While its focus on the ethic of caring as inherently feminine might not be attractive to nurses who are not female, its foundations in the notions of receptivity, relatedness, and responsiveness between the caregiver and the one cared for make it a viable theoretical framework that realistically represents the nature of the nurse-patient relationship.

Pellegrino's Moral Obligation Model of Caring

Pellegrino, a humanist and a physician, has written extensively on caring as a derivative value of the physician's obligation to do good.[29,46] When discussing the role of the physician vis à vis the patient, Pellegrino notes that there are at least four senses in which the word "care" is understood by the practice of medicine. The first sense is care as compassion or concern for another person. This is a feeling of sharing someone's experience of illness and pain or of simply being touched by the plight of another person. To care in this sense, according to Pellegrino, is to see the person who is ill as more than the object of our ministrations. He or she is "a fellow human whose experiences we cannot penetrate fully but which we can be touched by simply because we share the same humanity."[46(p11)]

The second sense of caring is related to doing for others what they cannot do for themselves. This entails assisting others with the activities of daily living that are compromised by illness (eg, feeding, bathing, dressing, and meeting personal needs). Pellegrino recognizes that physicians do little of this type of caring but that nurses do a great deal. Interestingly, he also contends that nurses do much less of this type of caring than they used to do and that nurses' aides do most of it in contemporary nursing practice.[46]

The third sense of caring discussed by Pellegrino is taking charge of the medical problem experienced by the patient. It is a type of caring that assures that knowledge and skill will be directed to the patient's problem. It includes inviting the patient to transfer responsibility and anxiety about what is wrong to the physician, and recognizes that the patient's anxiety calls for a specialized type of caring that is presumed to be available from a physician.

Pellegrino's fourth sense of caring has to do with ensuring that all necessary procedures (personal and technical) in patient care are carried out with conscientious attention to detail and with exemplary skill. He regards this as a corollary of the third sense of "care" but argues that it is differentiated from the previous sense by its emphasis on the craftsmanship of medicine. Together, the third and fourth aspects of caring make up what most physicians understand to be competence.

Pellegrino does not find these four aspects of caring to be separable in clinical practice. Care that conforms to all four definitions is called "integral care." This type of care is, for Pellegrino, a moral obligation of health professionals, not an option that can be exercised or interpreted "in terms of some idiosyncratic definition of professional responsibility."[46(p13)] The moral obligation to care in this manner is created by the special human relationship that brings together the one who is ill and the one who offers to help.

In assessing whether the caring model is foundational for medical practice, Pellegrino reexamines the relationships of physicians with their patients and concludes that "to care for the patient in the full and integral sense requires a reconstruction of medical ethics."[46(p17)] What is needed, he claims, is an ethic that attends to the concept of care in its broadest sense and that makes caring a strong moral obligation between patient and professional. Instead of a relationship of curing between physician and patient, a relation of caring is needed to express the nature of the obligation between physician and patient.

Central to Pellegrino's notion of care is the good of the individual (ie, patient good), which is prior to any other notion of good within the practice of medicine. Within a human obligation model of caring, it is patient good that ultimately guides a physician's decision making in regard to a patient's health and illness. Hence, while the various aspects of caring engender desirable physician behaviors toward the patient, the physician's decision making is primarily guided by the notion of patient good. In the final analysis, then, Pellegrino's integral caring is reduced to being a derivative value of patient good as it conforms to typical biomedical ethical theorizing by utilizing a more general (and traditional) value as the foundational value for a theory of medical ethics. Therefore, rather than a theory of caring, Pellegrino actually proposes a theory of patient good that simply uses caring to operationalize patient good.

While Pellegrino's ideas about caring generally fit in with the realities of nursing practice, the subordinate role assigned to caring within his medical ethical theory of patient good limits the theory's usefulness for the development of a theory of nursing ethics. For nursing, caring seems to be more than a mere behavior between nurse and patient, and it might not always be derived from a notion of patient good. For example, even when the good of the patient is undecided or unknown, the nurse carries out interventions designed to care for the patient. Conversely, even when the patient's good has been made evident, nursing interventions may be carried out that do not in fact contribute to this restrictive sense of patient good. The value of caring, for the nurse, extends beyond the notion of patient good as conceived by Pellegrino, because the nurse's caring relates to the patient's status as a human being.[36,37] For this reason, Pellegrino's moral obligation model of caring may not be appropriate to the development of a theory of nursing ethics.

Frankena's Moral-Point-of-View Model of Caring

The third existing model of caring that is relevant to the development of nursing ethics is the moral-point-of-view (MPV) model. As described by Frankena[47] in his critique of other MPV theories,

it entails adopting a certain point of view by defining its moral principle or central moral value. The MPV model is a type of ethical theory for which Frankena is a major advocate.

In essence, one takes a moral point of view by (1) subscribing to a particular substantive moral principle (or value) and (2) adopting a general approach, perspective, stance, or vantage point from which to proceed. Whereas most MPV theories contain views about moral judgments and principles, the differences between them and nonmoral principles, and the general nature of their justification, taking a moral point of view in itself simply means adopting a moral principle or value and the methodology to argue for that principle. It entails the endorsement of a general outlook or method by someone seeking to reach conclusions in a particular field.[47]

According to Frankena, various moral principles have served as the central principles or values of MPV theories. Mill, for example, accepted a principle of utility that was pivotal to his MPV theory.[48] Mill started with a particular outlook (his moral point of view) and accepted the principle of utility as the focal principle that indicated the kinds of facts about which he would make moral judgments. Frankena, however, argues for going farther than simply accepting a certain view of morality. For him, taking a moral point of view entails not only acceptance of a particular view of morality but entering the moral arena oneself, "using moral considerations of the kind defined as a basis for evaluative judgments."[47(p70)] It means subscribing to a particular view of morality and living that morality in one's life, rather than merely accepting a certain view of morality and the relevant criteria for separation of the moral from the nonmoral.

Frankena thus takes a significant step in establishing the crucial difference between his conception of taking a moral point of view and the approaches of others who espouse MPV theories. Like Hume, who argued for sympathy as his "sentiment of humanity,"[49] Frankena believes that there is always something that "moves us to approve or disapprove of persons."[47(p70)] It is an attitude or precondition that is ultimately the source or motivating factor in a person's taking a moral point of view. In other words, it is not so much the setting forth of any particular fact as a reason for deciding what is good and right, but rather it is what generates the setting forth of that particular fact (and not some other fact) that is important to taking a moral point of view.

For Frankena this attitude or precondition has to do with the fundamental status of persons and their human dignity. While he never explicitly defines this attitude or precondition, he does eventually claim that it generates a moral point of view of caring or, as he puts it, "a Non-Indifference about what happens to persons and conscious sentient beings *as such.*"[47(p71)] Frankena's substantive moral value is the value of caring, which takes the form of Kantian respect for persons or Christian love. The result is a moral point of view that includes direct caring about (or nonindifference to) what goes on in the lives of sentient beings beyond oneself. It includes the making of normative judgments and a concern with being rational in those judgments. It is a moral point of view that does not entail the acceptance or use of any particular test of justifiability, validity, or truth. A judgment based on caring is assumed to be morally justifiable because it "would be agreed to by all who genuinely take the MPV and are clear, logical, and fully knowledgeable about relevant kinds of facts (empirical, metaphysical, or whatever)."[47(p72)]

Frankena's view of caring is quite different from that of Pellegrino. Whereas Pellegrino's notion of patient good provides the basis for the physician's evaluative judgments, Frankena posits caring as the basis of normative human judgments in general. His focus on caring is direct and involves taking a moral point of view toward caring as a fundamental moral value or principle for normative judgments involving persons, unlike the indirect focus on caring (through patient good) that is characteristic of Pellegrino's medical ethics. Like Noddings, Frankena eschews both the structures of moral justification that typify traditional biomedical ethical theories and the separation of the conditions for justification from the context of ethical decision making in regard to persons. Whereas much of moral philosophy defines a moral point of view as simply acting on principle or out of duty, Frankena's moral point of view requires a human response in the form of respect for persons or Christian love. In other words, it requires an identifiable form of response on the part of the caregiver to the person cared for.

Unfortunately, Frankena makes no attempt to define respect for persons, and he certainly does not discuss his principle of caring in terms directly relevant to the practice of nursing. However, he does indicate that adopting the moral point of view of caring stems from an undefined, preexisting attitude toward personhood and human dignity. This is not unlike the notions of receptivity, relatedness, and responsiveness that anchor Noddings's view of ethical caring. While it would not be appropriate to interpret Frankena's view of caring as identical or even similar to Noddings's, his method of arriving at caring as a lived principle for a system of morality (taking the MPV) certainly bears some relevance to Noddings's views and to the consideration of a theory of nursing ethics.

• • •

Given the models of caring proposed by Noddings, Pellegrino, and Frankena and the views on caring that have been developed by nurses, several recommendations for the future development of a theory of nursing ethics seem appropriate.

First, theories of biomedical ethics, as currently formulated, are not directly applicable to the development of a theory of nursing ethics. The context of nursing practice requires a moral view of persons rather than a theory of moral action or behavior or a system of moral justification. Present theories of medical ethics tend to support theoretical and methodologic views of ethical argumentation and moral justification that do not fit in with the practical realities of nurses' decision making in patient care and that, as a result, tend to deplete the moral agency of nursing practice rather than enhance it. Any theory of nursing ethics should consider the nature of the nurse-patient relationship within health care contexts and should adopt a moral point of view that focuses directly on this relationship, rather than on theoretical interpretations of physician decision making and their associated claims to moral justification for this decision making.

Second, the value of caring ought to be central to any theory of nursing ethics. There is a commitment to the role of caring in several conceptions of nursing ethics and nursing science. There also appears to be an important link between the value of caring and nurses' views on persons and human dignity. As proposed by Frankena, taking a moral point of view entails adopting a view of caring that is rooted in an attitude of respect for persons. If a theory of nursing ethics is to have any purpose, it must espouse a view of morality that not only truly represents the social role of nursing as a profession in the provision of health care but also promises a moral role for nursing in the care and nurture of individuals who have health care needs. For theory to achieve this purpose, its view of morality ought to turn on a philosophical view of caring that posits caring as a foundational, rather than a derivative, value among persons.

Third, taking a moral point of view and developing an MPV theory need not necessarily include the acceptance or use of any particular test of moral justification. Thus, a theory of nursing ethics need not endorse typical frameworks of justification contained in theories of biomedical ethics. It is true that judgments must be justified within the moral point of view and must pertain to the sorts of facts that are considered relevant according to the MPV theory. However, the moral point of view of the theory of nursing ethics itself should not be defined by reference to any external system of justification.

A final point: To the extent that any theory of nursing ethics takes seriously the claims of the MPV model and the role of caring as a central value within its framework, there is reason to believe that the discipline of biomedical ethics will benefit as well, for such a theory cannot develop apart from the practice of medicine and nursing or from the evolution of biomedical ethics as a discipline. The links between all three types of theorizing are probably more important than is currently realized. When the role of a theory of nursing ethics within a philosophy of nursing becomes articulated, the links between the various types of theorizing will, of course, become clearer.

REFERENCES

1. Dickoff J, James P: A theory of theories: A position paper. *Nurs Res* 1968;17(3):197-203.

2. Dickoff J, James P, Wiedenbach E: Theory in a practice discipline. Part I: Practice oriented theory. *Nurs Res* 1968;17(5):415-435.

3. Dickoff J, James P, Wiedenbach E: Theory in a practice discipline. Part II: Practice oriented research. *Nurs Res* 1968;17(6):545-554.

4. Beckstrand J: The notion of a practice theory and the relationship of scientific and ethical knowledge to practice. *Res Nurs Health* 1978;1:131-136.

5. Beckstrand J: The need for a practice theory as indicated by the knowledge used in the conduct of practice. *Res Nurs Health* 1978;1:175-179.

6. Beckstrand J: A critique of several conceptions of practice theory in nursing. *Research in Nurs and Health* 1980; 3:69-79.

7. Veatch RM: Nursing ethics, physician ethics, and medical ethics. *Law Med Health Care* 1981;9:17-19.

8. Veatch RM, Fry ST: *Case Studies in Nursing Ethics.* Philadelphia, Lippincott, 1987.

9. Jameton A: *Nursing Practice: The Ethical Issues.* Englewood Cliffs, NJ, Prentice-Hall, 1984.

10. White G: Philosophical ethics and nursing—A word of caution, in Chinn PL (ed): *Advances in Nursing Theory Development.* Rockville, Md, Aspen Publishers, 1983, pp 35-46.

11. Benjamin M, Curtis J: *Ethics in Nursing,* ed 2. New York, Oxford University Press, 1986.

12. Davis AJ, Aroskar MA: *Ethical Dilemmas and Nursing Practice,* ed 2. New York, Appleton-Century-Crofts, 1983.

13. Muyskens JL: *Moral Problems in Nursing: A Philosophical Investigation.* Totowa, NJ, Rowman & Littlefield, 1982.

14. Thompson JB, Thompson HO: *Ethics in Nursing.* New York, Macmillan, 1981.

15. Beauchamp TL, Childress JF: *Principles of Biomedical Ethics,* ed 2. New York, Oxford University Press, 1983.

16. Veatch RM: *A Theory of Medical Ethics.* New York, Basic Books, 1981.

17. Englehardt HT: *The Foundations of Bioethics.* New York, Oxford University Press, 1986.

18. Rawls J: *A Theory of Justice.* Cambridge, Mass, Harvard University Press, 1971.

19. Crisham P: Measuring moral judgment in nursing dilemmas. *Nurs Res* 1981;30:104-110.

20. Ketefian S: Critical thinking, educational preparation, and development of moral judgment among selected groups of practicing nurses. *Nurs Res* 1981;30:98-103.

21. Ketefian S: Moral reasoning and moral behavior among selected groups of practicing nurses. *Nurs Res* 1981;30:171-176.

22. Munhall P: Moral reasoning levels of nursing students and faculty in a baccalaureate nursing program. *Image* 1980;12:57-61.

23. Murphy CC: *Levels of Moral Reasoning in a Selected Group of Nursing Practitioners,* dissertation. Columbia University, Teachers College, New York, 1976.

24. Stenberg MJ: The search for a conceptual framework as a philosophic basis for nursing ethics: An examination of code, contract, context, and covenant. *Milit Med* 1979;144:9-22.

25. Silva MC: Ethics, scarce resources, and the nurse executive: Perspectives on distributive justice. *Nurs Econ* 1984;2:11-18.

26. Alexander C, Weisman C, Chase G: Determinants of staff nurses' perceptions of autonomy within different clinical contexts. *Nurs Res* 1982;31(1):48-52.

27. Prescott PA, Dennis KE, Jacox AK: Clinical decision making of staff nurses. *Image* 1987;19:56-62.

28. Self DJ: A study of the foundations of ethical decision-making of nurses. *Theor Med* 1987;8:85-95.

29. Pellegrino ED, Thomasma DC: *For the Patient's Good.* New York, Oxford University Press, 1988.

30. Yarling RB, McElmurry BJ: The moral foundation of nursing. *Adv Nurs Sci* 1986;8(2):63-73.

31. May WF: Code, covenant, contract, or philanthropy. *Hastings Cent Rep* 1975;5:29-38.

32. Fletcher J: *Situation Ethics: The New Morality.* Philadelphia, Westminister, 1966.

33. Ramsey P: *The Patient as Person.* New Haven, Yale University Press, 1970.

34. Bishop AH, Scudder JR: Nursing ethics in an age of controversy. *Adv Nurs Sci* 1987;9(3):34-43.

35. Cooper CC: Covenantal relationships: Grounding for the nursing ethic. *Adv Nurs Sci* 1988;10(4):48-59.

36. Gadow S: Nurse and patient: The caring relationship, in Bishop AH, Scudder JR (eds): *Caring, Curing, Coping: Nurse, Physician, Patient Relationships.* Birmingham, Ala, University of Alabama Press, 1987, pp 31-43.

37. Griffin AP: A philosophical analysis of caring in nursing. *Adv Nurs* 1983;8:289-295.

38. Huggins EA, Sclazi CC: Limitations and alternatives: Ethical practice theory in nursing. *Adv Nurs Sci* 1988;10(4):43-47.

39. Packard JS, Ferrara M: In search of the moral foundation of nursing. *Adv Nurs Sci* 1988; 10(4):60-71.

40. Watson J: *Nursing: Human Science and Human Care.* New York, Appleton-Century-Crofts, 1985.

41. Heidegger M: *Being and Time.* Macquarrie J, Robinson E (trans). New York, Harper & Row, 1962.

42. Noddings N: *Caring: A Feminine Approach to Ethics & Moral Education.* Berkeley, Calif, University of California Press, 1984.

43. Gilligan C: Woman's place in man's life cycle. *Harvard Ed Rev* 1979;49:431-446.

44. Gilligan C: *In a Different Voice.* Cambridge, Harvard University Press, 1982.

45. Gilligan C: Gender difference and morality: The empirical base, in Kittay ER, Meyers DT (eds): *Women and Moral Theory.* Totowa, NJ, Rowman & Littlefield, 1987.

46. Pellegrino ED: The caring ethic: The relation of physician to patient, in Bishop AH, Scudder JR (eds): *Caring, Curing, Coping: Nurse, Physician, Patient Relationships.* Birmingham, Ala, University of Alabama Press, 1985, pp 8-30.

47. Frankena WK: Moral-point-of-view theories, in Bowie NE (ed): *Ethical Theory in the Last Quarter of the Twentieth Century.* Indianapolis, Hackett Publishing Co, 1983, pp 39-79.

48. Mill JS: *Utilitarianism.* 1863. Reprint. Gorovitz S (ed). Indianapolis, Bobbs-Merrill, 1971.

49. Hume D: *An Inquiry Concerning the Principles of Morals.* Indianapolis, Bobbs-Merrill, 1957.

CHAPTER **9**

An Ethical Framework for Nursing Service Administration

Paula J. Christensen, RN, PhD

Nursing service administrators face a myriad of decisions each day that reflect moral obligations toward nursing staff within their respective organizations. As nurses these administrators come from a humanistic profession that emphasizes the respect for individuals, including each other. As administrators these nurses are charged with achievement of organizational goals within given constraints. Thus nurse administrators have a particularly unique responsibility to promote the welfare of other nurses — and their clients — while meeting obligations to the institution as well.

WHY ETHICS?

Ethics provides a helpful foundation for developing a framework that creates a work environment consistent with the nursing profession's beliefs about human beings. Issues of morality and moral problems not only arise in clinical practice but also in managerial practice. Implicit in morality is the use of reasoning and critical thinking that goes beyond the acceptance of traditional rules to guide actions. Value systems and personal moral codes develop out of society as those actions or characteristics that are desirable or useful and that are accepted customs

of conduct and right living. The individual is viewed as an autonomous agent with the freedom to make decisions resulting in rational self-guidance and self-determination. Nurse administrators have significant influence over daily practice and policy decisions that influence the kind of environment in which nurses work. Applying humanistic values such as caring, autonomy, equality, and connectedness creates a more ethical organizational climate. Thus respect for the dignity and well-being of others is promoted.

Ethical Foundations

Jameton[1] differentiates ethics from morals by referring to ethics as a publicly stated and formal set of rules or values, such as a code of ethics. Ethics also includes the systematic study of theories, principles, and values that are used to examine beliefs and behaviors. Morals are more informal and personal. They reflect a set of values or principles people are committed to and thus follow and defend in their daily lives.

Two major theoretical approaches provide the basis for principles and rules that guide judgments and behaviors.[2] These theories attempt to determine what is right or wrong by judging (1) the worth of actions by their consequences (utilitarian) or (2) the kind of actions that are chosen (formalist). Most people use

Reprinted from *Advances in Nursing Science,* Vol. 10, No. 3, with permission of Aspen Publishers, Inc. © 1988.

both utilitarian and formal considerations during moral discussions.[1]

Ethical principles derived from these theories are more tangible for giving direction and guiding actions. First, the principle of respect for persons gives direction for treating people as unique individuals yet also recognizes them as part of a community.[3] Autonomy and self-determination are subsumed within this principle, which promotes individuals' involvement in decisions affecting their well-being. Accepting this principle also implies rights to being informed prior to making those decisions.

Second, the principle of beneficence guides nurses to avoid infliction of harm as well as to promote good.[4] One must try to balance harms and benefits in a given situation; yet the duty to not inflict harm takes precedence over the duty to promote good. Harms refer to risks to health or welfare, whereas benefits are considered positive values that promote health or welfare.

Finally, the principle of justice refers to the fundamental equality of human beings.[1] One treats others according to what they deserve or can legitimately claim in a given situation.[2] The context of a specific circumstance influences whether people are treated equally or according to individual need, effort, contribution, or merit. All these factors are important to the fair treatment of individuals.

Moral rules are also derived from the major ethical principles.[2] Veracity refers to the duty of telling the truth and of not lying or deceiving others. This rule is based on the values of respecting persons, keeping promises, and developing trusting relationships between human beings. The rules of confidentiality and privacy are linked to the respect for autonomy of others. The right to self-determination involves giving people moral authority to determine what others may know about them. Finally, the rule of fidelity includes promise keeping and faithfulness to others. Justification for fidelity comes from ideas of its inherent rightness as well as its utility for promoting human interaction and trust.

These basic ethical principles and their derivative rules are all subject to conflicts with each other given differing role obligations of professionals and the institutions in which they work.[2] Principles and rules

are duties that may be overridden in cases of conflict. Thus close examination of each specific ethical situation is needed to enhance the rightness of decisions made.

Nursing Ethics

Nurses in professional practice make judgments about what is right and wrong, express ideals and aspirations, and establish minimal expectations of conduct as a part of determining what ought to be done to create a desired image of health care delivery. The Code for Nurses is a collection of statements reflecting the nursing professional's conscience and philosophy.[5] It provides general principles that are used to guide and evaluate nursing actions.

Nursing as a profession is fundamentally concerned about respect for the dignity of persons. As the basic moral principle of the nurses' code, nurses have an absolute duty to fulfill the best interests of their clients.[6] This emphasis on the human welfare of clients has slowly and justifiably been integrated into understanding nursing's needs for freedom, respect, and integrity,[7] that is, nurses' well-being is also an important element in creating a health care system sensitive to the human dignity of all persons.

Several authors, however, question the freedom of nurses to practice nursing within bureaucratic settings, which threatens their professional and personal well-being. Most recently Yarling and McElmurry stated that "nurses are often not free to be moral because they are deprived of the free exercise of moral agency."[8(p65)] Nurses as moral agents of clients experience a basic conflict between honoring their obligations to clients and upholding their responsibilities to institutions and their power structure. Yarling and McElmurry[8] indict institutions that systematically create formidable obstacles to nurses' responsible action. Nurses are free to be accountable to clients insofar as their subsequent actions do not threaten the power structure that controls their professional and economic future.

Davis and Aroskar[3] identify nurses' primary ethical obligation to clients yet point out that others exist toward physicians and organizations. These authors question whether nurses can be ethical in a hospital setting and, if so, ask what the risks are for being ethical. Within the realm of ethics, multiple accountability is a "logical nightmare."[9] When two or more authorities conflict, one must prioritize, and the choice is not usually an obvious one.

Ethical autonomy — or the freedom to choose or to independently endorse a given course of action — is basic to the practice of professional nursing.[10] Autonomy involves thinking for oneself, not unconditional freedom of action. Professional competence includes both practical and ethical dimensions. Thus nurses cannot be totally competent — or autonomous — until they are able to be more ethical.[1] A challenge faces nurses today to develop a professional model of practice within health care systems that respects the autonomy of all practitioners.

Ethical nursing practice has yet to be clearly described within the context of nurses' social contract with their employing agencies, physicians, and society in general.[11] The American Nurses' Association's (ANA's) Social Policy Statement explains that nursing grew and is evolving out of society.[12] Because of this nursing has a responsibility to promote a health-oriented system of care that incorporates respect for the dignity and autonomy of human beings. This principle applies to humanity in society as a whole, to clients receiving care, to other health care providers, and to nurses themselves. Yet individual nurses' views about the purpose and function of the health care system and opinions regarding the nature of nursing itself affect how ethical practice is defined. Those who see health care as a series of medical cases, as a commodity, or as a client's right to be free from pain view nurses as means to others' ends. When health care is identified as promoting well-being in a cooperative environment, nurses are seen as active participants with clients and others in decision making.[11]

Nursing Administration

The fundamental principle of respect for every person applies to a variety of people in a multidisciplinary setting.[13] Nurse administrators are responsible to several groups to which the principle of respect can be applied: clients and families, nursing staff and other employees, medical staff, institutional board,

community and society, and the profession. As a basis for decisions about ethical concerns, the nurse as administrator must examine his or her own principles, philosophy, or beliefs and also be able to support those of the institution.

Each institution has its own system of priorities from which values can be inferred.[14] Efficiency and economic stability are often the focus of complex health care systems. Yet continuing this trend and avoiding positive humanistic values may lead to less efficiency as individuals themselves are devalued.[15] Values such as caring, autonomy, professionhood, diverse knowledge base, and responsibility to clients and society can be integrated into organizations. Individual responsibility and freedom thrive under these conditions, while the organization experiences success as well.

Moral and ethical issues underlie the argument for comparable worth for nurses.[16] Nursing units in hospitals have historically been labeled "cost centers," indicating a debit relationship to the overall organization's economic status. But since nursing services have not traditionally been itemized, hospital administrators have not recognized the economic contribution of the nursing department. More recently studies have shown nursing to be a revenue producer. Even with increasing numbers of registered nurses as a percentage of personnel, payroll as a percentage of costs has decreased. Styles[16] states that ignoring equitable compensation for nurses violates moral and ethical principles.

Clatterbuck and Proulx[17] emphasize the ethical allocation of human and financial resources for nurse administrators. They describe the ethical exercise of power through desired professional values of professionalism, position, prestige, and politics. These concepts are important in day-to-day decisions as well as in those regarding staffing and budgeting over time. Professionalism is the adherence to a code of conduct; it is moral concern for other human beings. The position of nurse administrator carries with it the "authority and responsibility for establishing nursing objectives; determining departmental policies, procedures, and practices; and developing and administering a nursing service budget."[17(p11)] The administrator's personal ethic and prevailing organizational values influence how one's position is enacted. Prestige or status is necessary to be heard and is included in decision making at the organizational level. Education and the judicious application of knowledge are the key ingredients to exercising skill in dealing with situations and people. Last, the nurse administrator is involved in politics as a part of everyday work. Professional unity and improvement of health care are mentioned as outcomes of nurses' involvement in politics. Ethical action of nurse administrators implies client advocacy, equitable allocation of scarce resources, and consideration of the nursing staff.[17]

Management Ethics

Heightened concern for managerial ethics is a product of social transformation within management, institutions, and society. Previously growth of organizations led to increasing bureaucratic systems that depersonalized people. Since people need to relate to each other, some norms of behavior are sacrificed under sanctions and pressures experienced in large bureaucracies.[18] Even with the guidance of a professional code of ethics, conflicts force people to fall back on their own resources and ability to deal with difficult situations.

Bureaucracies exert forces on employees and clients that create and maintain subordination and uniformity.[19] Men and women are socialized into supportive, dependent, and attentive roles that are isolated and depersonalized to deal with the constraints placed on their behavior. These behaviors may lead to the destruction of personal relationships and thus may threaten the foundation of self-identity. Ferguson[19] calls for embracing the values of care and connection, making a commitment to equality, and actively participating in public life. She encourages the formation of "a community that recognizes the dialectical need for connectedness within freedom and for diversity within solidarity . . . to nurture the capacity for reflexive redefinition of self."[19(p197)] Some tension would still exist in this type of organization, but differences could be worked out within a concern for the humanness of others.

Powers and Vogel[20] describe business and managerial ethics as a concern for human welfare and the conduct to promote it. Corporate management has considerable discretion over management policies and practices regarding the dignity and well-being of employees. Managers are viewed as agents for making the institutional character more ethical by facing difficult issues, by ordering (ethical) concepts correctly, and by reasoning with them. As ethical agents managers must have the freedom to choose among alternative actions to promote welfare within a given context. There is potential for conflict between the individual manager's conscience and the policies and practices of an organization. However, managers must attempt to reconcile this difference while maintaining their own integrity.

New values and economic necessity are forcing managers to change their behaviors toward an equal emphasis on profits and people. Naisbitt and Aburdene state that "working for most companies is so demeaning to the human spirit that many talented people are forced out the door."[21(p82)] They call for creating a nurturing work environment that fosters a positive attitude and makes work fulfilling and fun. For organizations to survive, social, political, and moral principles must be considered to form a new ideology of business.[22] The narrow focus of economic principles is no longer adequate to satisfy social demands. There is a need for a genuine and deep morality that focuses on respect and concern for people.

This overview of nursing and management ethics reveals a critique by both disciplines of the current treatment of humans in organizations. Both disciplines express a concern for the dignity and well-being of all people and provide some suggestions for promoting human welfare. These criticisms and ideas form some of the foundation upon which an ethical framework for nurse administrators is built.

DIMENSIONS OF AN ETHICAL FRAMEWORK FOR PRACTICE
Components

An ethical framework for nurse administrators stems from the theoretical underpinnings of ethics and the critique by nursing and management ethics of human treatment in organizations. The components of this framework include ethical awareness, the use of a principled reasoning process, a moral commitment to the profession and to each other, and a primary consideration for human welfare with strategies to promote it. The nurse administrator uses these dimensions to create an ethical organizational climate in which nurses work.

Ethical awareness is the result of increased sensitivity to ethical issues. Conscious self-reflection on values, beliefs, thoughts, and feelings creates a personal ethic upon which the nurse administrator thinks through issues and eventually acts. A sincere concern for human well-being and the meaning of the human experience leads to having integrity and using one's abilities in a balanced way.[1]

The use of a principled reasoning process provides a systematic approach to analyzing ethical problems. Having a moral basis for judgments, actions, duties, and obligations is preferred over ready-made answers and gut-level feelings.[3] Appeals to conscience are often not adequate in ethical situations. Defending the rightness or wrongness of decisions involves more than expressing personal opinions.[23] Principles and rules such as respect for persons, autonomy (self-determination), beneficence (promote good), nonmaleficence (avoid harm), veracity (tell truth), confidentiality, fidelity (keep promises), and justice (fair treatment) are used while thinking through an ethical problem to promote conscious attention to morality.[5] Analyzing and ordering these concepts is an integral part of the principled reasoning process.

To effectively deal with ethical problems, nurse administrators can use a six-step approach to ethical reasoning.[1] First, one identifies the problem itself. Since all choices are not moral choices and all problems are not ethical ones, the nature of the problem is examined. Ethical problems can usually be described using the following characteristics: (1) the problem does not fall within any specific science and cannot be resolved by using empirical data; (2) the problem is inherently perplexing, involving value conflicts and uncertainty regarding data needed to make a decision; and (3) the answer to the problem will have long-range effects on one's own perceptions and will have relevance to other areas of human concern.[24] Other aspects to consider are the agent's relationship to the problem and time parameters involved.

Second, one gathers data and describes the situation giving rise to the problem. Relevant facts are obtained and irrelevant ones determined. The views and interests of key people in the situation, including health care professionals, are identified. Thus a case study is mapped out showing the main characters and events. The third step is to identify optional courses of action and their likely consequences. Future decisions based on current actions must also be ascertained.

Thinking the ethical problem through is the fourth step. At this point one considers basic principles and rules to see if they address the current issue and help resolve the problem. An in-depth knowledge of nursing, administration, and ethics is needed to effectively apply principles and rules to ethical inquiry of complex administrative decisions. By employing ethical judgment, nurse administrators can construct a point of view defending right action.

The fifth step in this approach is to make a decision based on one's judgment. Others' opinions are solicited to make the best decision possible. Yet a time comes when one must "cease pondering and make a choice."[1(p68)] Last, one carries out the chosen action and evaluates its effects. Anticipated as well as unanticipated outcomes are identified. The information gathered at this point is used to improve the efficiency, sensitivity, and sophistication of future decisions.

Nurses have a moral commitment to the profession and to each other that is necessary for collective and individual competence and growth. This sense of loyalty is fundamental to meeting the criteria of being professional: maximal competence, significant social value, and autonomy.[1] This commitment also enhances nursing's common goals of providing health-oriented services to individuals and groups in society.[12] Nurturance of nurses and others is a quality that can lead to rethinking and reformulating ways to better serve human interest and health.[25]

Consideration for human welfare applies to nursing staff as well as to clients. Nurse administrators and managers are agents for enhancing nurses' dignity and well-being. Strategies to promote human welfare provide ideas for incorporating more nurturing and pro-people values into an organization. The use of this framework acknowledges an ethical component to administrative practice and the importance of nursing's strong humanistic heritage.

Strategies for Promoting Nurses' Welfare

Strategies for attending to nurses' well-being and human welfare cluster into five major categories: (1) autonomy of nursing practice, (2) professional nursing system, (3) environment for ethical reasoning, (4) personnel management policies and practices, and (5) management style.

The nurse administrator enhances autonomy of nursing practice by developing a perspective that views health care as the promotion of well-being in a cooperative community.[11] Philosophy statements, goals, policies, and practices incorporating this view benefit nurses, as they lead to respecting nurses' unique contribution to health care and to promoting their involvement in decision making.

A professional nursing system exists when a department of nursing adheres to the ANA's Standards for Organized Nursing Services.[26] Seven standards with criteria and 19 components give direction to administrators for developing a professional climate for practice. The concepts of autonomy and respect for persons as well as direct reference to using the code of ethics are incorporated into these documents.

Nurse administrators have a moral obligation to create an environment for ethical reasoning. This involves thinking about ethical issues and being aware of how one's own values fit into the conflicts nursing staff face regularly.[27] Brooten[27] relates that nurses must also be encouraged to think rather than react to ethical problems. This can be done informally by making thoughtful statements to staff that reinforce a desired approach. More formal means to an ethical work atmosphere include disseminating and using the code of ethics[28]; educating staff regarding bioethics and ethical practice[17]; and ensuring intradisciplinary and interdisciplinary discussion of ethical concerns through ethics rounds[29] and institutional ethics committees.[30] Open discussion about these concerns may prevent the burnout phenomenon so prevalent in nursing today.[31]

Personnel management policies and practices are developed and evaluated using an ethical component.

The principles of respect for persons, beneficence, and justice can be used during policy formation and review and while examining daily practices. This includes policies that protect patients from professionals impaired by substance abuse without harming the professional through abandonment.[32] Access to treatment programs is also important to preserve nurses' functioning in their roles. Nurse administrators can ensure equitable wages to nurses by examining their organizations' practices regarding job segregation, pay disparity, and the presence of discrimination.[33] On the basis of these extensive analyses (not only market analysis), corrective action can be taken toward eliminating unjustifiable disparities. Organizations can create a bill of employee rights that is written and enforced.[34] There should also be a procedure for due process that is visible, predictably effective, relatively permanent in the institution, perceived as equitable, easy to use, and applicable to all employees.[34]

Management style that incorporates ethical principles empowers nurses as people. Promoting nurses' increased participation in decisions that directly affect them ensures that nurses are treated with respect and consideration.[35] People usually want to make a commitment, express themselves and their values, make a difference in society, and fit in harmoniously with other priorities. Managers can promote this contribution by opening communication channels, developing their subordinates, and changing their own roles toward professionals and planners, rather than being watchdogs.[36]

These strategies are dynamic entities that change as the contexts of the ethical issues themselves change. Since values and norms are influenced by the society and the specific organization in which they occur, nurse administrators must be creative in determining which strategies are appropriate for given situations. The underlying ethical foundation of these strategies, however, does not change as readily, that is, the principles of respect for persons, beneficence, and justice, along with their derivative rules, remain relatively constant forces for enhancing nurse administrators' moral behavior.

• • •

The application of ethical theories, principles, and rules to nursing administration creates a framework for moral responsibility toward nursing staff. Concern for the dignity and well-being of nurses in organizations is justified throughout the nursing ethics and management ethics literature. Through the use of an ethical framework for practice nurses as administrators have the opportunity to create an ethical organizational environment by increasing ethical awareness, using a principled reasoning process, establishing a moral commitment to the profession, and promoting the dignity and well-being of all people in an organization.

REFERENCES

1. Jameton A: *Nursing Practice: The Ethical Issues.* Englewood Cliffs, NJ, Prentice-Hall, 1984.
2. Beauchamp TL, Childress JE: *Principles of Biomedical Ethics,* ed 2. New York, Oxford University Press, 1983.
3. Davis AJ, Aroskar MA: *Ethical Dilemmas and Nursing Practice,* ed 2. Norwalk, Conn, Appleton-Century-Crofts, 1983.
4. Frankena WK: *Ethics,* ed 2. Englewood Cliffs, NJ, Prentice-Hall, 1973.
5. American Nurses' Association: *Code for Nurses with Interpretive Statements.* Kansas City, Mo, ANA, 1985.
6. McCullough L: The code for nurses: A philosophical perspective, in American Nurses' Association: *Perspectives on the Code for Nurses.* Kansas City, Mo, ANA, 1978, pp 35-43.
7. Curtin LL: The nurse as advocate: A philosophical foundation for nursing. *Adv Nurs Sci* 1979;1(3):1-10.
8. Yarling RR, McElmurry BJ: The moral foundation of nursing. *Adv Nurs Sci* 1986;8(2):63-73.
9. Newton LH: To whom is the nurse accountable? *Conn Med Supp* 1979;43(10):7-9.
10. Benjamin M, Curtis J: *Ethics in Nursing.* New York, Oxford University Press, 1981.
11. Aroskar MA: Are nurses' mindsets compatible with ethical practice? *Top Clin Nurs* 1982;4(1):22-32.
12. American Nurses' Association: *Nursing: A Social Policy Statement.* Kansas City, Mo, ANA, 1980.
13. Goertzen I: A nurse administrator's view of ethics in practice, in American Nurses' Association: *Ethics in Nursing Practice and Education.* Kansas City, Mo, ANA, 1980, pp 17-22.
14. Purtilo RB, Cassel CK: *Ethical Dimensions in the Health Professions.* Philadelphia, W.B. Saunders, 1981.
15. Binder J: Value conflicts in health care organizations. *Nurs Outlook* 1983;1(2):114-119.
16. Styles MM: The uphill battle for comparable worth. *Nurs Outlook* 1985;33(3):128-132.
17. Clatterbuck SE, Proulx JR: *A Framework for Ethical Action in Nursing Service Administration.* New York, National League for Nursing, 1981.
18. Emmet D: *Rules, Roles and Relations.* Boston, Beacon Press, 1966.
19. Ferguson KE: *The Feminist Case Against Bureaucracy.* Philadelphia, Temple University Press, 1984.
20. Powers CW, Vogel D: *Ethics in the Education of Business Managers.* New York, The Hastings Center, 1980.
21. Naisbitt J, Aburdene P: *Re-inventing the Corporation.* New York, Warner Books, 1985.
22. Silk L, Vogel D: *Ethics and Profits: The Crisis of Confidence in American Business.* New York, Simon & Schuster, 1976.
23. Muyskens JL: *Moral Problems in Nursing: A Philosophical Investigation.* Totowa, NJ, Rowman and Littlefield, 1982.
24. Curtin LL, Flaherty MJ: *Nursing Ethics: Theories and Pragmatics.* Bowie, Md, Brady, 1982.
25. Heide WS: *Feminism for the Health of It.* Buffalo, Margaretdaughters, 1985.
26. American Nurses' Association Commission on Nursing Services: *Standards for Organized Nursing Services.* Kansas City, Mo, ANA, 1982.
27. Brooten DA: *Managerial Leadership in Nursing.* Philadelphia, Lippincott, 1984.
28. Hacker LJ: The code for nurses: A nursing administration perspective, in American Nurses' Association: *Perspectives on the Code for Nurses.* Kansas City, Mo, American Nurses' Association, 1978, pp 23-26.
29. Davis AJ: Helping your staff address ethical dilemmas. *J Nurs Adm* 1982;12(2):9-13.
30. Aroskar MA: Institutional ethics committees and nursing administration. *Nurs Econ* 1984;2(2):130-136.
31. Davis AJ: Ethical decision making: Considerations for future activities, in American Nurses' Association: *Ethics in Nursing Practice and Education.* Kansas City, Mo, American Nurses' Association, 1980, pp 23-27.
32. Daniel IQ: Impaired professionals: Responsibilities and roles. *Nurs Econ* 1984;2(3):190-193.
33. Sape GP: Coping with comparable worth. *Harvard Bus Rev* 1985;63(3):145-152.
34. Ewing DW: *Freedom Inside the Organization.* New York, EP Dutton, 1977.
35. American Academy of Nursing: *Magnet Hospitals: Attraction and Retention of Professional Nurses.* Kansas City, Mo, American Nurses' Association, 1983.
36. Kanter RM: *Men and Women of the Corporation.* New York, Basic Books, 1977.

ETHICS AND VALUES

CHAPTER 10

Health Care Policy, Values, and Nursing

Kathleen I. Mac Pherson, RN, PhD

Health care policy is currently a central issue in nursing theory, research, education, and practice. Professional nursing organizations have provided guidelines for nurses to follow:

- The American Nurses' Association has issued a social policy statement[1] and has produced a videotape that provides basic direction for nurses who want to participate in the health policy process.[2]
- The American Academy of Nursing has published the proceedings of scientific sessions that addressed nursing and health care policy.[3-5]
- The National League for Nursing has created a handbook for nursing instructors on integrating public policy into the curriculum[6] and a student workbook that offers key concepts in public policy.[7]
- Several books have been written by nurses on various aspects of health care policy[8-12] as has a handbook for political action.[13]

During this period of heightened interest in nurses' involvement in health care policy, there is a need to step back and think clearly about what needs to be accomplished. Questions must be asked such as:

- What are the basic value premises underlying current health care policies?

Reprinted from *Advances in Nursing Science,* Vol. 9, No. 3, with permission of Aspen Publishers, Inc. © 1987.

- How are these policies linked to major structural aspects of American society?
- Is there an existing model that can be used to analyze health care policies that will address the above questions?

PUBLIC POLICY, SOCIAL POLICY, AND HEALTH CARE POLICY

Many writers on health care policy seem to assume that the concept is self-explanatory, conveys the same meaning to every reader, and therefore requires no definition. It is also rare to find a distinction made among the three concepts of public policy, social policy, and health care policy.

Public Policy

Although there is no consensus on how to define the concept, public policy has been defined most simply by one political scientist as "whatever governments choose to do or not to do."[14(p2)] The important word here is governments. This definition is useful because it focuses not only on government action but also on government inaction. Health is one of the substantive areas public policies deal with, along with housing, education, unemployment, urban development, and so on. Medicare and Medicaid are examples of government action. They were enacted in 1965 as amendments to the basic Social Security Act. An example of government inaction is the lack of vigorous health programs to deal with the vast difference in mortality rates between white infants (10.1 per 1,000) and either black (19.6 per 1,000) or Hispanic (17.3 per 1,000) infants.[15]

Social Policy

The concept of social policy also lacks a universal definition, as social scientists and policy analysts differ in their views concerning "the domain and functions of social policy, and concerning the key processes through which social policies operate."[15(p3)] In this article, social policies will be considered "guiding principles or courses of action adopted and pursued by societies and their governments as well as by various groups or units within societies, such as special interest groups (eg, the American Nurses' Association and the American Medical Association), business corporations, labor unions, voluntary organizations, family groups, and individuals."[16(p12)] Social policies tend to, but do not need to, be codified in formal legal documents and address life in a society and "the intra-societal relationships among individuals, groups, and society as a whole."[16(p13)]

Health Care Policy

Health care policy is one type of social policy as defined above. This definition can be useful to nursing as it calls for a macroanalysis that addresses how a proposed policy would influence the quality of life and human relations in a society. Such an analysis would, of necessity, reveal the overt or covert value premises behind a given health care policy.

VALUES AND HEALTH CARE POLICY

A value is a quality having intrinsic worth for a society, and American society's dominant values significantly influence all decisions concerning health care policies. The following interrelated value continua[16(p27)] can be used to examine the influence of American values on policies:

- individualism . . . collectivism;
- competition . . . cooperation; and
- inequality . . . equality.

Individualism lies at the very heart of American culture. In a recent study of American character, Bellah et al[17] found that the fierce individualism that has created self-reliant heroes like explorers and cowboys also has undermined the capacity of Americans for commitment to one another. It is natural then, in a country like the United States, which stresses individualism, pursuit of self-interest, and competitiveness, that health care policies tend to promote structured inequalities. On the other hand, a society like Cuba, which stresses collective values and cooperation, has developed health care policies that ensure equal access to health care resources. In two decades, Cuba has transformed its rudimentary and crisis-ridden medical services into a dependable and accessible health care system.[18]

While values appear to be of central importance for health care policy development and analysis, it must be noted that public discussion of health care policies in the United States tends to ignore this crucial variable. The emphasis, instead, is usually on technical matters or on the means of implementing a policy.[16(p28)] As a result, evaluation of policies commonly focuses on technology and means of providing health care by using a cost-benefit or cost-effectiveness framework.[19] Although this type of evaluation remains important, it does not reach the underlying value premises behind a policy such as the "naturalness" of unequal access to health care.

ELITES AND POLICY FORMATION

Unless our dominant American values can be changed, significant improvement in our system of health care policies is highly unlikely. But changing values is not easy. One has to start by asking, who in American society profits most from these values? We can start by looking at cultural and political elites who tend to shape and guard the values that reflect and support their interests.

These elites are active as executives and directors of large health-related corporations such as the

Humana Corporation or the Hospital Corporation of America[20] and of health insurance firms such as Blue Cross/Blue Shield. They also include powerful politicians such as Senator John Heinz, chairman of the Senate Special Committee on Aging, and political appointees such as Carolyne K. Davis, RN, PhD, the former director of the Health Care Financing Administration (HCFA), which controls Medicare and Medicaid. Directors of large foundations such as the Carnegie Mellon and Rockefeller Institutes have an enormous influence on shaping many aspects of health care policies, including the education of professionals. Finally, directors of multinational pharmaceutical companies[21] should not be overlooked in this nonexhaustive list.

Americans tend to deny the existence of social classes and inequality of wealth and how these factors create power for the roughly 0.5% of the American population who constitute the social upper class.[22] Policies are created within a health policy-planning network that the various interests join together to create. This network of elite corporate executives, government officials, private foundations (who provide money for research), and blue-ribbon presidential commissions (who legitimate the policies to the general public and present them formally to the president)[22] join with research institutes and think tanks to map out health care policies. Finally, influential newspapers (*The New York Times, The Washington Post*) and magazines (*Time, Newsweek*) bring views of the elite policy makers to the attention of the public. Policies thus trickle down from the top and are rarely presented for public debate.

The values of individualism, competition, and inequality, which benefit American elites, profoundly influence health care policy formation and implementation. Their influence can be analyzed by using a conceptual model that identifies the basic processes used to create policies.

THREE PROCESSES OF HEALTH CARE POLICY CREATION

This discussion relies heavily on the work of Gil,[16] professor of social policy at Brandeis University. According to Gil, all social policies, including health care policies, can be understood and evaluated by looking at three basic processes: resource development, division of labor, and rights distribution.[16(pp15,16)]

The first process, resource development, involves "decisions and actions related to the type, quality and quantity of all health care related material and services generated by a society as well as the ordering of priorities in this sphere."[16(p18)] Policies concerning who will be the preferred health care providers in the future are a case in point. The emerging preferred provider organizations (PPOs), a hybrid of the fee-for-service and prospective payment systems, provide nurses with the opportunity to promote a health care policy that will allow them to market their services as autonomous health care providers to employers, hospitals, and insurers.[23] The nurse-controlled PPOs can provide society with a life-enhancing alternative form of health care.

The second process is concerned with the division of labor in the health care system, the allocation of roles (nurse, physician, social worker), and the allocation of statuses with their differential degrees of prestige. The struggle of the nurse midwife to be an alternative to obstetrical care illustrates how health care policies (certain state licensure laws) perform a gate-keeping function to prohibit midwives from practicing their specialized nursing role.[10]

The third process concerns the distribution of rights to health care resources, goods, and services through entitlements, rewards, and constraints. Rewards are rights provided for the performance of roles and include salaries, wages, and titles. The income differential between nurses and physicians, for example, illustrates differential financial rewards.[24] Entitlements are rights assigned by virtue of membership in a society or in a specified social group. Thus, all members of American society are entitled to public health services and all elderly persons are entitled to Medicare. Constraints take the form of specific or general limitations on the level of rights distributed to individuals or social groups as rewards or entitlements. The health care policy of the prospective payment system (diagnosis related group [DRG]-based payment) for Medicare and Medicaid was an effort by HCFA and the Department of Health and

Human Services to contain rising health care costs. Hospitals are now constrained from unlimited increases for patient care. If a hospital's cost for providing Medicare services exceeds the DRG rate, the hospital will lose money.

By using Gil's conceptual model to analyze a proposed or actual health care policy, nurses can also demystify the value premises implicit in the policy. We need to ask, does the policy support the dominant American values of individualism, competition, and inequality or move toward the more humane values of collectivism, cooperation, and equality?

NURSING'S FLAWS IN HEALTH CARE POLICY CREATION AND ANALYSIS

Based on the analysis above, it appears critical for nurses to consider value premises when creating health care policy or supporting policies made by other groups. Because we have not, with rare exceptions,[25,26] questioned covert values in health care policies, nursing literature on this topic is characterized by two major flaws.

The Separation of Health Care Policies from Politics and Economics

Irrespective of whether nurse-authors subscribe to a narrow or a comprehensive conception of health care policy, they tend to consider political and economic issues as a separate policy domain. Implied in this conceptual separation of politics and economics from health care policies is a view of politics and economic development as ends in themselves rather than as means for attaining socially beneficial humane goals. Furthermore, viewing health care policies apart from economic policies deprives nurse policy analysts of an important tool. One does not ask, who benefits?

Health care policies are commonly taken at face value as a way of dealing in a reactive and ameliorative manner with the fallout or backlash problems created by economic policies. The economic policies of the Reagan administration that emphasize increased military and defense spending (aid for the Contras, "Star Wars" research projects) cannot be logically separated from decreased federal funding for health care.

The health care policy of prospective reimbursement to hospitals for Medicare recipients legislated in 1983 can be used to illustrate how the majority of nurses have generally accepted uncritically the potentially harmful measure that discharges patients "sicker and quicker." In an effort to cull some professional benefit, or merely to survive, nursing administrators, clinicians, and educators are generally scrambling to make professional adjustments in line with policy changes.[27] As one nurse gerontologist has written, "Most of us have already jumped or been pulled onto the bandwagon and are committed, to some extent, to this change." [28(p260)] Since then, cost containment, nursing as a cost center, DRGs, and PPOs have become common terms in the nursing literature. The comments above do not mean that some reforms were not necessary. The objective is to point out that the reforms were driven and shaped by economic policy and not by a coherent, internally consistent health care policy that explicitly valued an equal distribution of health care services.

In terms of nursing and health care policy, most telling is the term "nurse entrepreneur," which is widely used in nursing literature.[29] As health care policies are being shaken up and revised, nurses, understandably, want "a piece of the action" that includes both more professional autonomy and increased income. Few could argue against these goals. But why use the word entrepreneur? According to *Webster's New World Dictionary* the word means "a person who organizes and manages a business undertaking, assuming the risk for the sake of profit."[30(p467)]

In an odd reversal of nursing's usual rejection of the link between economic issues and policies, the profit motive is made central in the name chosen to describe an independent nursing practice. It is even more ironic when one considers that in a colloquial sense the word entrepreneur means someone who has an extensive and highly profitable business. Given the fact that the income of most nurses in private practice would be far below the $100,000 average income of physicians, who have not called themselves super capitalists or entrepreneurs, this choice of name appears strange and does not convey the value premises of personalized, humane quality care that an independent nursing practice can provide.

Nursing education must also concern itself with the separation of health care policies from politics and economics. In a recent article on health policy and nursing curricula,[31] health policy formation was placed in opposition to politics, as if the two concepts operate separately in the real world. Certainly they can be separated theoretically, but it would be counter-productive for nursing educators not to give students tools for a critical analysis of the mutual reinforce-ment of politics, economics, and health care policy. In that article it was stated that: "Politics is reactive, policy is proactive."[31(p422)] This statement must be juxtaposed to Dye's definition of public policy as "whatever governments choose to do or not to do."[14(p2)] Health care policy as a form of public policy can, on the contrary, be reactive or proactive, and instead of being separate from politics it is created and maintained through complex political-economic alliances discussed earlier in this article. Public policies are actually institutionalized political values and beliefs about what is right and good for society. These policies are created by a process in which a power elite formulates policies on large issues such as health care. "It is within the policy-planning network that the various special interests join together to forge, however slowly and gropingly, the general policies that will benefit them as a whole."[22(p61)]

In Gil's view, social policies are expressions of political conflicts within societies aimed at reshaping or preserving social structures. The processes of social policy evolution continue "as a result of ceaseless conflicts of interest among individuals and social groups who control different levels of resources and who differ consequently in rights and power."[16(p26)]

A recent health care policy decision made by a nursing organization illustrates the lack of a critical analysis of external economic and political forces that shaped this decision. The Nurse's Association of the American College of Obstetricians and Gynecologists (NAACOG) was recruited by Ayerst, the manufac-turer of Premarin (most popular trade name of estro-gen), to take an active role in their public relations campaign linking menopause with osteoporosis.[32] Representatives of Burson-Marsteller, a public rela-tions firm hired by Ayerst, approached NAACOG, an

18,750-member organization for obstetric, gyneco-logic, and neonatal nurses founded in 1969. Fran Weed, then NAACOG director of education, in de-fending NAACOG's decision stated, "It's [the Burson-Marsteller package] a clean bit of information — women will have more information to make choices."[32(p8)]

Burson-Marsteller developed a two-tiered seminar approach — nurse to health professional and nurse to public. These seminars were designed for presenta-tion by nurse members of NAACOG, but the content was developed by an osteoporosis education advisory board. The three members of the board were Dr. Robert Lindsay, medical researcher and educator, Jeri Winger, president of the National Federation of Women's Clubs, and Kathleen Goldblatt, dean of the University of Missouri School of Nursing and an NAACOG member.

The advisory board materials were tested in seven trial seminars in six states beginning in April 1985. Burson-Marsteller contributed $200 to each trial group to cover the expense of speakers. In the past, NAACOG had accepted grants from other drug com-panies such as Johnson and Johnson and Searle but had never been funded before for a consumer program.[32] This acceptance of financial support from a drug company for consumer education illustrates how easily nursing organizations can be manipulated into creating policies that are for large transnational pharmaceutical companies and against the best in-terest of their consumers. The value premise beneath this policy favors support of a drug company over an even-handed presentation of the issues related to osteoporosis. If other nursing organizations adopt this approach, the public will eventually distrust nurses as it now distrusts many physicians.

Lack of Criticism of Incremental Health Policy Changes

The second major flaw in nursing's involvement with health care policy is that incremental policy changes are uncritically supported, in most instances, without an analysis of their limitations. The incremental model, one of several conceptual models used by political scientists,[14] focuses on how policy changes build upon past policies with only minor modifications. Supporters of incremental policy changes defend this method by saying that it is quicker and safer, and causes less social dislocation, and is usually more politically expedient than radical innovation.[14] According to Lindblom,[33] a political scientist, policy makers do not use a rational model of decision making that includes annual review of existing policies, identification of social goals, or research into the cost-benefit ratios of competing policies in achieving goals, and so on. Instead, various constraints, including time and cost, limit perceived policy choices. This incrementalism model is innately conservative, basically supporting the status quo since most policy makers accept the legitimacy of established programs and the existing social structure.

In Gil's view, the incremental model for social policy leads to fragmentations and inconsistencies. These fragmentations and inconsistencies in the policy formation process "reflect their political nature, that is, their roots in conflicts of real or perceived interests of diverse groupings within society at large."[16(p214)] Gil goes on to add that the values implicit in this incremental model correspond to the dominant value premises of American society: pursuit of self-interest, competitiveness, and defense of social and economic inequalities. A basic underlying assumption of this model is that the existing social, political, and economic systems of the United States are structurally sound and should therefore be left untouched, even if they are the sources of social and economic disorders.

In Gil's view, social policy must address structural changes based upon a different set of values, eg, equality of social, economic, civil, and political rights and liberties. Structural change can only be effected by focusing on the major issues, eg, reallocating resources, reallocating statuses, and redistributing rights. Such policies would avoid futile programs offering "BandAid solutions" and would focus instead "primarily on restructuring society as a whole, so that all members and groups would live in circumstances conducive to the fullest possible development of their innate human potential."[16(pp220,221)]

While the above policy changes would enhance the health of American citizens and are therefore of interest to nurses, they are long-term possibilities and will not occur overnight. Meanwhile, nurses need to act immediately to create and support ameliorative health policy reforms when they provide immediate relief for suffering and oppression. Most importantly, however, nurses must, at the same time that they use incremental health policy reforms, expose their "inadequacies and faulty assumptions, and their futility in terms of overcoming systemic causes of suffering and oppression."[16(p173)] Nurses can thus openly criticize incremental health care policies while using them to their limits. By employing this strategy, nurses could turn incremental policies, designed to defend the status quo, into tools for social change.[34] In other words, nurses could use the system to help change itself while taking from it the incremental policies that offer immediate health relief for clients.

WHICH NURSING VALUES SHOULD SHAPE HEALTH CARE POLICIES?

Up to the present time, nursing leaders and nursing organizations have primarily focused on health care policies that would enhance the profession of nursing. Examples are abundant: revision of Nurse Practice Acts to reflect current concepts of the expanded role of the nurse,[35] entry into practice legislation,[36] the Community Nursing Centers Bill,[37] and federal funding for nursing education,[38] to name a few.

Instead of looking at structural problems in the health care system that will require long-term, sweeping changes, nursing leaders, on the whole, tend to concentrate on enhancing the power of nursing.[26] While no one can fault the good intent of this policy thrust, the time has arrived to incorporate a broader vision. Returning to Gil's[16] conceptual model, one must question if nursing's health care policies emerge from the dominant societal values of individualism, competition, and inequality.

It is the central belief of this author that the value premises underlying nursing's involvement with health care policy need to consist of the opposite values of collectivism, cooperation, and equality. If these values could underly nursing theories, research, practice, and education, the focus would extend from the nursing profession and individual clients to inequalities and forms of oppression in the United States and elsewhere. What can we as nurses do with our rage when we read that one out of every four children under six years of age lives in poverty,[39] that 70% of the elderly poor are women, and before the Nicaraguan revolution (which the Reagan administration is attempting to destroy) 60% of children under four years of age were malnourished. This nursing rage, spurred by a changed set of value premises, could be directed toward health care policies that address sweeping structural changes in American society that would help to create a more humane society here and in other countries under American influence.

The need for social policies that will lead to fundamental structural changes in American society in order to provide adequate health care for all citizens is being addressed in the literature by a small number of nurses. In 1978, Davis linked fundamental change in the health sector of society to major changes in the larger social system and its power structure.[26] She encouraged nurses to ask such philosophical questions as, "What should be the nature of the relationship between a health care system and a profit-oriented economy? What, if any, effective safeguards can be instituted to preserve a desired balance between these systems?"[26(p7)] She believes that many of the health care system's problems arise out of class struggles and economic inequities and that workable solutions would have to come about at some expense for the capitalist order.[26(p10)]

Recently, Moccia and Mason,[25] in addressing the increasing number of poor Americans, emphasized the need for nursing policy to work for structural change rather than merely accepting incremental policies that reinforce the status quo.

In discussing the need to reconceptualize the concept of environment in nursing theory, Chopoorian implied that nurses generally do not see promotion of health care policies for changing, adjusting, or altering environments as part of their role. Instead, it is the client or family who is expected to adjust, assimilate, or accommodate while nurses support them in this process.[40] Thus persons, not societal structures, are seen as the focus for change or adaptation through social policies.

Nursing in the late 1980s and 1990s must address the two basic flaws in its current approach to health care policy — separating policy creation and implementation from politics and economics and uncritically supporting incremental policy changes. These two flaws have mutually reinforced each other in the past. As nurses are becoming increasingly involved in policy creation and implementation, they need to be constantly aware of the covert values beneath each health care policy. If this can be done by nursing, the result will be a contribution to a more equitable and humane health care system. Nurses must also ask, what would it be like to practice nursing in a society characterized by values of collectivism, cooperation, and equality, and what do the current structures do to promote or inhibit such a society?

REFERENCES

1. American Nurses' Association: *Nursing: A Social Policy Statement.* Kansas City, American Nurses' Association, 1980.
2. American Nurses' Association: *Nurses, Politics, and Public Policy,* videotape. Kansas City, American Nurses' Association, 1985.
3. American Academy of Nursing: *Nursing's Influence on Health Policy for the Eighties.* Kansas City, American Academy of Nursing, 1979.
4. American Academy of Nursing: *From Accomodation to Self-Determination: Nursing's Role in the Development of Health Care Policy.* Kansas City, American Academy of Nursing, 1982.
5. American Academy of Nursing: *The Economics of Health Care and Nursing.* Kansas City, American Academy of Nursing, 1985.
6. National League for Nursing: *Integrating Public Policy into the Curriculum.* New York, National League for Nursing, 1986.
7. Solomon SB, Roe SC: *Key Concepts in Public Policy: Student Workbook.* New York, National League for Nursing, 1986.
8. Aiken L (ed): *Health Policy and Nursing Practice.* New York, McGraw-Hill, 1981.
9. Aiken L, Gortner S (eds): *Nursing in the 1980s: Crises, Opportunities, Challenge.* Philadelphia, Lippincott, 1982.
10. Kalisch B, Kalisch P: *Politics of Nursing.* Philadelphia, Lippincott, 1982.

11. Milio N: *Promoting Health through Public Policy.* Philadelphia, FA Davis Co, 1981.
12. Wieczorek R (ed): *Power, Politics, and Policy in Nursing.* New York: Springer, 1985.
13. Mason D, Talbott S (eds): *Political Action Handbook for Nurses.* Menlo Park, Calif, Addison-Wesley, 1985.
14. Dye TR: *Understanding Public Policy,* ed 5. Englewood Cliffs, NJ, Prentice-Hall, 1984.
15. Children's Defense Fund: *The Data Book: The Nation, States and Cities.* Washington, DC, Children's Defense Fund, 1985.
16. Gil DG: *Unravelling Social Policy,* ed 3. Cambridge, Mass, S Chenkman Books, 1981.
17. Bellah RN, Madsen R, Sullivan WM, et al: *Habits of the Heart.* Berkeley, University of California Press, 1985.
18. Waitzkin H: *The Second Sickness: Contradictions of Capitalist Health Care.* New York, Free Press, 1983.
19. Hicks, LL: Using benefit-cost and cost-effectiveness analyses in health-care resource allocation. *Nurs Econ* 1985;3:78-84.
20. Wohl S: *The Medical Industrial Complex.* New York, Harmony Books, 1984.
21. Braithwaite J: *Corporate Crime in the Pharmaceutical Industry.* Boston, Routledge & Kegan Paul, 1984.
22. Domhoff GW: *The Powers that Be: Processes of Ruling Class Domination in America.* New York, Vintage Books, 1978.
23. Griffith H: Who will become the preferred providers? *Am J N,* 1985, 85:538-542.
24. Navarro V: *Medicine under Capitalism.* New York: Prodest, 1976.
25. Moccia P, Mason D: Poverty trends: Implications for nursing. *Nurs Outlook* 1986;34:20-24.
26. Davis AJ: Nursing's influence on health policy for the eighties, in American Academy of Nursing Scientific Session: *Nursing's Influence on Health Policy for the Eighties.* Kansas City, American Nurses' Association, 1979.
27. Harrell J, Frauman A: Prospective payment calls for boosting productivity. *Nurs Health Care* 1985;6: 535-537.
28. Cieplik C: Prospective payment, diagnosis related groups and elder care. *Geriatric Nurs* 1985;6:260-263.
29. Felton G, Kelly H, Renehan K, Alley J: Nursing entrepreneurs: A success story. *Nurs Outlook* 1985; 33:276-280.
30. Guralnik D (ed): *Webster's New World Dictionary,* ed 2. Cleveland, William Collins Publishers, 1979.
31. Diers D: Health policy and nursing curricula — a natural fit. *Nurs Health Care* 1985;6:420-433.
32. Dejanikus T: Major drug manufacturer funds osteoporosis public education campaign. *Network News* 1985 (May-June): 1, 38.
33. Lindblom CE: *The Policy-Making Process.* Englewood Cliffs, NJ, Prentice-Hall, 1968.
34. Gorz A: *Strategy for Labor.* Boston, Beacon Press,. 1967.
35. Mixon PR: Public policy making on a nursing issue, in Wieczorek RR (ed): *Power, Politics and Policy in Nursing.* New York, Springer, 1985.
36. American Nurses' Association: Maine law is first to call for two education levels. *Am Nurse* 1986;1(May):18.
37. McGivern D: The community nursing centers bill, in National League for Nursing: *Legislation Challenges for Nursing in the '80s.* New York, National League for Nursing, 1985.
38. Solomon SB: Federal funding for nursing education, in National League for Nursing: *Legislative Challenges for Nursing in the '80s.* New York, National League for Nursing, 1985.
39. Tobier E: *The Changing Face of Poverty.* New York, Community Service Society, 1984.
40. Chopoorian TJ: Reconceptualizing the environment, in Moccia P (ed): *New Approaches to Theory Development.* New York, National League for Nursing, 1986.

CHAPTER **11**

Understanding Organizational Culture
A key to management decision-making

Harriet Van Ess Coeling, RN, PhD
James R. Wilcox, PhD

An understanding of organizational culture offers a key to effective management interventions involving work group norms and values.[1,2] Understanding the intricacies of work group culture can assist the nursing administrator in making decisions regarding hiring personnel, orienting newcomers, facilitating organizational change, and promoting learning.

Each organizational culture is probably a pattern of work group subcultures that vary in similarity to one another. Van Maanen and Barley-suggest the work group is a useful level of cultural analysis because this is where people discover, create, and use culture.[3] The value of studying organizational culture by examining work groups is supported by both organizational[4-6] and nursing scholars.[7-10]

Culture is defined in this study as a set of solutions devised by a group of people to meet specific problems posed by the situations they face in common.[11] Schall has demonstrated that a study of informal work group rules is an effective way to clarify the work group culture. Work group rules are the behaviors (verbal and nonverbal) that group members consider to be the appropriate responses to given situations. They are established by the work group members themselves. These behaviors describe the typical ways

Reprinted from *The Journal of Nursing Administration*, Vol. 18, No. 11, with permission of J. B. Lippincott Company © 1988.

of acting on a given unit.[12] Louis, in studying these typical behaviors or rules, notes that just as individuals have unique personalities, so also do groups.[13] Although in any group there is room for individuality, work group members tend to demonstrate similar behaviors which mutually are perpetuated and strengthened over time.

These work group rules are seldom, if ever, written down or presented formally to newcomers. Rather they are inferred from what members say and do. Organizational scholars suggest that these work group rules be inferred or identified by "listening" to such verbal and nonverbal behaviors as stories, metaphors, rituals, use of space and time, maintenance of relationships, and calls to accountability.[14-17]

This article reports the findings of a study conducted to identify the unique work group cultures of two nursing units in a Midwestern medical center. Behaviors and questions used to identify the cultures are presented. The implications of these cultural differences for nursing administrators are also discussed.

THE STUDY
Method

The anthropologic, ethnographic method was used in this study.[18] The researcher functioned as a participant-observer to gather the data necessary to compare the day shift cultures of two medical-surgical units. On each unit, the researcher observed the personnel as they interacted in the nursing station, utility areas, and break rooms for 112 hours. The researcher also conducted 25-minute, semistructured, taped interviews with each participant. Participants (head nurses, staff nurses, and unit clerks) included 20 personnel on Unit A, a urology-renal unit, and 15 personnel on Unit B, an oncology unit (total N = 35). At the conclusion of the study, the researcher met with participants in small groups to share the findings and solicit feedback to determine whether participants felt the findings accurately reflected behavior on their unit.

Data Collection and Analysis

Data was collected and analyzed in three stages. In Stage One the researcher spent 2 weeks observing the verbal and nonverbal behaviors listed in Figure 11-1 and asking questions similar to, but not limited to questions suggested in Figure 11-2. The behaviors and questions listed in these figures are examples of items that could be used to identify the work group culture of any unit. Additional questions and behaviors relating more directly to the specific unit could

and should be added. This information was recorded on data sheets which included the time, setting, code

---

General Questions

Describe the nurse who "fits in" on this unit.
Describe a nurse who does not "fit in."
What makes this unit a good place to work?
How does this unit differ from other units?
What would you miss most if you were to leave?

Specific Questions

Rules For Working Together

When do they ask each other for help?
How do they respond when asked to help someone?
How do they describe the way they work together?
What do they say about nurses who often or seldom help others?
Describe the competition between them.

Rules For Telling Others What To Do

What attitude is shown regarding being in charge?
How directly and frequently are commands given?
How do they describe any hierarchy among themselves?

Rules For Following Established Standards

How is a desire for standardization or creativity shown?
How do they justify deviations from policies and procedures?

Rules for Organizing and Using Time

What nursing priorities do they list for their unit?
What activities can be omitted if time is short?
How highly do they value efficiency?

Rules For Taking The Patient's Perspective

How do they describe nurse-patient relationships?
How do they interpret patient complaints?
To what degree do they focus on psychosocial needs?

Rules For Change

Under what conditions do they attend classes?
How often do they seek out learning experiences?
What attitude regarding change is expressed?

Verbal Behaviors

Attacks	Directives	Names
Complaints	Explanations	Reassurances
Compliments	Gossip	Slogans
Defenses	Justifications	Statements
Descriptions	Metaphors	Taunts

Nonverbal Behaviors

Activities	Intonations
Decorations	Pictures
Drawings	Speed
Dress	Touch
Facial Expressions	Voice

FIGURE 11-1

Behaviors to observe in identifying organizational cultures.

FIGURE 11-2

Questions that identify unit cultures.

names of participants, description of the action, and suggestions for future observations. The content analysis technique was then used to establish initial categories and associated content of work group rules as described in Figures 11-3 and 11-4.

In Stage Two the researcher spent an additional 3 weeks on each unit continuing to observe, question, and record data. In addition, interviews were conducted with each participant. These additional observations and interviews were also content analyzed and used to either confirm or invalidate the initial impressions. The participants agreed that many of the researcher's initial impressions of work group rules were indeed rules which should be followed if group members wanted to "fit in" and be accepted by the group. However, it was also noted that some of the researcher's initial impressions were held by only some of the group members. Those rules that were not agreed upon by the group as a whole were removed from the initial list. This condensed the

categories into the six sets of work group rules listed in Figure 11-5. These are the rules that were considered very important on both units.

Stage Three involved one more week of observation and questioning during which the researcher looked for behaviors that would not support the six categories and their associated rules. In addition, the researcher met with participants in small groups to describe the rules identified and ask them to agree or disagree with the findings. During this period the participants agreed with the rules presented and the researcher found no evidence to reject any rules.

Findings

After the agreed-upon rules for each group were identified, they were compared to highlight cultural differences between the two units. The following presentation of the findings demonstrates how these rules reflect different work group cultures.

The *rules for working together* suggested that Unit A preferred to work more as a team whereas Unit B worked more independently. On Unit A, a sense of family unity prevailed and contributed to getting the

---

Family: We know, help, support, tease, defend, accept, and correct each other.

Organization: It's very important to be organized here.

Standardized care: We don't make mistakes here.

Paternalism: We take care of and protect our patients.

Physicians: We know how to get doctors to write the orders we need.

Work: We help each other to get the work done.

Personal life: We talk freely about what goes on at home.

Patient's emotional needs: We listen a lot; we've learned how to support patients without hurting ourselves.

Time: It's not too important to do things exactly on time.

Conflict: If you're upset with someone, you take them to your "office" and talk to them.

Change: Thank goodness we won't be getting cardiac monitors for a while yet.

Hierarchy: The charge nurse is in control.

FIGURE 11-3

Initial impressions of Unit A work group rules after 2 weeks of observation.

Relations with patients: That's why we're here, to help them.

Relations with patient's family: They're part of the patient.

Openness: We greet everyone who comes into the station.

Education: We can't get enough of it.

Fun: We try very hard to have fun.

Conflict: It's often expressed by teasing.

Standardized care: We bend it for the good of the patient.

Helping each other: Well, we try.

Hierarchy: Everyone can give orders.

Personal life: Sometimes we discuss it.

Physicians: We're here to help them help the patient.

Time: Medications must be on time, they're so important.

FIGURE 11-4

Initial impressions of Unit B work group rules after 2 weeks of observation.

work done. The nurses on this unit viewed all the work as "our work" rather than seeing a specific assignment as a certain individual's work. At the end of the shift everyone pitched in to complete the work that remained. The researcher observed the following example of working together:

> One day two nurses were trying to fix a blood pressure cuff. As they succeeded, one said, "It took two of us. I tried to do it myself and couldn't."

Frequent stories were told of how they worked together to survive various crises. Several nurses described the value of these rules:

You come in with a better attitude knowing you won't be overwhelmed. Hospitals are scary places to work. It's nice to know there are other people to help you out.

This view of the work as "our work" was associated with a very low level of competition among the nurses. One work group rule specified that competition was unacceptable. For example, they were uncomfortable when management attempted to motivate them toward higher levels of excellence by asking them to vote for the best nurse in such areas as helpfulness, friendliness, and professional behavior. A sizeable number responded by not voting at all.

UNIT A	UNIT B
Working Together	
• See work as our work • Work together • Finish together • Avoid competition	• See work as my work or your work • Work independently • Finish on their own • Compete among themselves
Telling Others What To Do	
• Avoid telling others what to do • Recognize no staff nurse hierarchy	• Use their authority to persuade others • Recognize hierarchy based on skills, knowledge, and assertiveness
Following Established Standards	
• Desire to follow traditional procedures • Prefer standardized guidelines	• Desire to use their own judgment regarding procedures • Prefer individual decision-making
Organization and Use of Time	
• Value efficiency and organizational skills • Clearly identify priority activities	• Limit emphasis on efficiency • Identify numerous activities as priorities
Psychosocial Perspective-Taking	
• Attend to obvious psychosocial needs • Show concern for a period of time	• Actively look for psychosocial needs • Show concern indefinitely
Change	
• Prefer the status quo • Attend certain classes	• Prefer a changing situation • Attend as many classes as possible

FIGURE 11-5

Comparison of salient work group rules showing cultural differences between two units.

In contrast, the nurses on Unit B preferred working more individually. These nurses did not expect others to provide a lot of help with the care of their patients. They saw work as assigned to individual nurses, not to the entire group. They explained that they did not want to be obligated to help others because this might "make them lose track of their continuity in the relationship with their patients."

Unlike Unit A, the rules here allowed and even promoted competition. As one nurse said, "Everyone here is fighting to be the best nurse."

Unit A staff nurses did not try to *tell each other what to do.* That was the role of nursing management. These nurses disliked being charge nurse for then they had to tell their peers what to do. One nurse explained it thus:

> "It's difficult when you have peers on the desk for they're telling you to do something that the next day they would be doing. This may lead to a conflict."

Another added, "We don't try to push others around and tell them what to do for us." When asked if there was a hierarchy among staff nurses, they denied such.

On Unit B, the unwritten rule said that nurses were free to tell others what to do. One nurse said, "I'm on the desk today. I'm the assertive nurse." When asked if the desk nurse was allowed to be more assertive, she replied, "You have a better chance to be." Complaints were voiced when some nurses were allowed to be at the desk more often than others. When asked if a staff nurse hierarchy existed, they listed criteria used to establish the hierarchy.

Attitudes toward following policies and procedures demonstrated Unit A's relatively greater *desire to follow established standards.* Unit A nurses suggested they almost always followed policies and procedures:

> One noted, "I've never seen anyone really not follow policy. Here you're expected to follow policies and procedures. Use the book! We have a very thick book that you have to know."

Another nurse described how the head nurse wrote policies to solve problems, kept them informed of policies, and kept the unit running well by enforcing the policies.

In contrast Unit B, when asked if they followed traditional procedures, described themselves as being "freer than other units to deviate," and used the metaphor of the unit being an island within the hospital. The head nurse here made this statement: "There's a lot I don't know about what happens on this unit; it's their system." Nurses on Unit B indicated that they liked this freedom to make their own decisions.

Work organization and use of time rules also reflected different work group cultures. On Unit A it was mandatory to be well-organized. One nurse explained it by saying, "If you're not organized, you don't make it up here." Rolling of the eyes and loud sighs communicated the nurses' reactions to the less organized new graduates. These extremely efficient nurses knew how much time to allot to each activity and still finish on time. They were able to list which patient care activities were priorities and focus their attentions on these efforts.

In contrast Unit B did not value organizational skill as highly. One nurse made this comment:

> Basically we've accepted the fact that we're not going to get out on time. We don't skip anything. We stay and do it all. We take as long as the patient needs.

They valued providing comprehensive care even when it took a great deal of their time to do so.

Psychosocial concerns also revealed cultural differences between these two work groups. Unit A nurses attended diligently to psychosocial concerns when the need was obvious but they did not look for hidden concerns. They demonstrated a high level of empathy for a period but if the patient had not resolved the concern after a reasonable time, their empathy decreased. This behavior is likely related to the chronicity of health problems on this unit. Patient requests for help (e.g. requests for food or comfort measures) were always attended to at once in a very helpful and caring manner, giving this unit a reputation for being among the most caring units in the hospital. However, there was no group rule that mandated the nurse analyze the situation to determine whether the external complaint represented a more internal, psychosocial concern. Such analysis was optional, not mandatory. Thus Unit A attended to psychosocial concerns but not to the extent that Unit B did.

On Unit B, the nurses consistently saw complaints and requests as potentially asking for both physical and psychosocial assistance. On this unit it was obligatory to understand how the patient was feeling both physically and emotionally. Nurses often made comments such as the following:

> Here you have to understand these patients. If you don't understand them, you can't work here.

For these nurses it was mandatory to try to understand the patient's perspective and to use this insight to enable them to relate to patients in a very individual manner.

Finally, differences were noted regarding attitudes towards learning experiences and changing. *Change rules* suggested that Unit B was relatively more desirous of changing their nursing practice to conform with the latest thinking in nursing than was Unit A. This was especially evident in Unit A's rules regarding attitudes toward attending classes dealing with psychosocial concerns. Participants on Unit A commented thus regarding these classes:

> If you work here you should know that already. We're, I think, (pause) just smug enough, and we may be wrong, to think that we don't need these classes. Classes don't really change our behavior.

Classes dealing with technological advances, however, were well received. Thus they saw some classes as important.

Unit B, however, saw all classes as important. They explained, "We stress classes to try to decrease any tunnel vision we might have." They verbalized their frustration when they did not have time to go to classes. When asked about the importance of attending class, answers ranged from important to very important. The atmosphere of this unit was one of constant learning, constant change. They took advantage of journal articles, professional meetings, physicians' lectures, and new job opportunities to enrich their knowledge and skills.

IMPLICATIONS FOR NURSING

It should be noted there is neither reason to suppose that an ideal unit culture exists,[19] nor reason to suppose that Unit A is "better" or "worse" than Unit B. Both are considered excellent units and patient and employee satisfaction on each is consistently high. However, they differ from each other. Differences are not identified to make judgments as to whether a culture is good or bad, but rather to identify different outcomes.[20] The following paragraphs identify four areas in which different cultures necessitate different management strategies. These areas include hiring personnel, orienting newcomers, facilitating organizational change, and promoting the learning experience.

Hiring Personnel

One way to maintain a culture is by hiring people who are able and willing to "fit in" or "buy into" the group's norms and values. In this study both head nurses were able to list characteristics they looked for in interviewing potential employees. The behaviors they reported corresponded very closely to the rules identified on each unit. For example, the head nurse on Unit A looked for nurses who were well-organized and able to work well with others. In contrast, independence and a desire to move ahead professionally were considered more valuable behaviors on Unit B.

Participants in this study noted that those group members who did not buy into group rules, at least the salient rules, ultimately left the unit. The nurses often described these people as weeding themselves out. Participants saw it as better for the unit and better for the person if they left. They indicated this voluntary leaving usually occurred within the first year. Thus turnover from the group's point of view was seen as a self-correcting adjustment for the benefit of group maintenance. However, the money lost in orienting this person is not beneficial to the organization. This financial loss, in addition to the emotional stress which ensues before the person finally leaves, highlights the value of carefully hiring people likely to fit in with the work group. Walters has recently proposed an innovative method of finding the right person for the right position based on the candidate's values and skills.[21]

In contrast, a desire to change the culture could be facilitated by hiring persons with different cultural norms which would fit in better with the desired new culture. In this case one would have to identify the desired culture and specify the desired characteristics in potential employees. This new culture can be brought about most effectively when a large number of new personnel with new norms and values are hired at one time. A group of seven nurses on Unit A often referred to their impact on the unit when they were hired together for this unit immediately after graduating from the same class.

Orienting Newcomers

Differences in unit cultures also impact on orienting new employees. Louis writes that voluntary turnover during the first 18 months on the job is increasing among college graduates in first career jobs. She notes that assisting new orientees adjust to their work group culture by helping them to identify work group norms is essential to alleviate this rapid turnover.[22] Vestal describes the failure of newcomers to identify cultural norms as falling into "culture pits."[23] Del Bueno and Freund note that often newcomers demonstrate a pattern of violating group norms, receiving unfavorable reactions to these violations, and then experiencing the stress of not fitting in with the group.[24] The researcher frequently witnessed this pattern as several newcomers were being oriented during the course of the study. On Unit A, eyeballs rolled when new nurses were unable to finish their work on time and did not ask for help in doing so. Eyebrows rose on Unit B when too much help was requested from others or a progressive attitude was not demonstrated.

Louis[25] and Van Maanen and Barley[26] note that the orientation process is facilitated by helping the newcomer learn the skills associated with identifying work group rules. Training employees to observe for the behaviors listed in Figure 11-1 would help newcomers to identify important rules on their units.

In addition, preceptors could be trained to increase the orientee's awareness of the work group rules. These preceptors could clarify some of the important work group rules for the new employee and identify situations in which the employee might be violating the rules, thus hindering their integration into the work group.

Facilitating Organizational Change

It is important to identify differences in work group culture to facilitate the process of change. Deal and Kennedy comment that often, the hidden cultural barriers are overlooked when attempting change. This is unfortunate because in most cases "culture is *the* barrier to change."[27]

Yet the error of many of the early cultural change projects must be avoided. Gregory addresses this error as she notes that early corporate culture studies had culture control as a goal. The goal of many early researchers was to encourage lower-ranking employees to accept a new set of values.[28] Wilkins and Patterson add that early cultural change projects were seen as a "quick fix" to cure the ailing American corporation. This resulted in considerable disillusionment when many of these cultural change projects failed.[29]

Miner summarizes the effectiveness of management or cultural innovations, such as participative management and management-by-objectives, by noting that sometimes they appeared to improve organizational functioning and sometimes they did not.[30,31] Perhaps one variable in determining whether or not these changes improved organizational functioning was the initial nature of the work group culture. In this study participative management could be predicted to impact differentially on the two units studied. Unit A preferred an autocratic leader, someone to direct them. They gave evidence of desiring policies and procedures which told them what to do. In contrast, Unit B preferred to exercise their own initiative; they preferred a more democratic leader. They preferred to make their own decisions based on the needs of their patients. Thus, Unit A demonstrated a culture receptive to a more autocratic leader and only limited participative management, whereas Unit B gave evidence of being more receptive to democratic leadership and participative management. More recent studies have also identified the importance of considering the work group culture in the change process.[32,33]

Current writers are therefore suggesting that the honeymoon phase of organizational culture, which expected cultural change to quickly solve organizational problems and increase productivity, is over.[34-36] Frost comments that organizational culture as a quick fix is *passé,* but organizational culture as a way to understand organizations is just beginning.[37]

Wilkins and Patterson view understanding of the current work group culture as an essential step in bringing about change. They suggest that acceptance of cultural change can be facilitated by formulating a plan that includes answers to the following questions:

1. Where do we need to be going strategically as an organization?
2. Where are we now as a culture?
3. What are the gaps between where we are and where we should be?
4. What is our plan of action to close those gaps?[38]

Del Bueno and Freund add that culture change can also be facilitated by a successful manager who is able to understand the organizational culture enough to be able to "tailor" new strategies to comply with existing norms and values.[39] This tailoring will help close the gap between the current culture and the desired culture. Hofstede refers to this tailoring as performing a "cultural transposition" which involves altering the proposed change to fit the culture of the work group, individualizing the change process, and introducing an idea in such a way that it will mesh with the rules of the particular work group and fit the values of their subordinates.[40] Cultural transposition facilitates the change process because participants (change agents and staff nurses) each bring to any interaction a different repertoire of experiences and values. The final outcome of the change process is a function of the experiences and values of both parties and of the interaction between them.[41]

Promoting the Learning Experience

It is also important to understand how differences in these work group cultures suggest different teaching methods. Unit A preferred having an authority tell them what to do. For them it would be best for their trainer to spell out specifically what behavior changes were expected. Unit B preferred making their own decisions. A better strategy with them would be to give general guidelines and help them to identify what changes they wanted to make.

Unit A preferred operating according to the clock. They would be most comfortable with a teaching schedule that specified how long each learning segment would take. Unit B, however, would do better with a more loosely organized curriculum allowing a flexible amount of time on each segment.

A focus on priorities and tangible activities characterized Unit A. Concentrating on tangible tasks such as the new way to make assignments would hold their interest. Unit B was more interested in the less tangible, more psychosocial aspects of care. They would prefer focusing more on individualizing the relationship.

Finally, Unit A preferred to maintain the status quo. Showing how the innovation was similar to the old way of doing things might assure them that much of their work life would stay the same. In contrast, Unit B would enjoy seeing how the innovation was new and progressive.

SUMMARY

Current organizational literature suggests that understanding a work group's culture (personality), as revealed in work group rules, can assist the nursing administrator in decisions regarding hiring, orienting, changing, and teaching. This article presented a study demonstrating how the work group culture of two nursing units was identified so that management understanding could be enhanced and effective decision-making could take place.

REFERENCES

1. Kramer M, Schmalenberg C. Magnet hospitals; Part I. institutions of excellence. J Nurs Adm 1988;18(1):13-24.
2. del Bueno DJ, Freund CM. Power and politics in nursing administration: a casebook. Owings Mills, MD: National Health Publishing, 1986;15-25.
3. Van Maanen J, Barley SR. Cultural organization: fragments of a theory. In: PJ Frost, LF Moore, MR Louis, CC Lundberg, J Martin. Organizational culture. Beverly Hills, CA: Sage, 1985;31-53.
4. Deal TE, Kennedy AA. Corporate cultures. Reading, MA: Addison-Wesley, 1982.

5. March JG, Olsen JP. Ambiguity and choice in organizations. Bergen, Norway: Universitets for laget, 1976.

6. Weick KE. The social psychology of organizing, 2nd ed. Menlo Park, CA: Addison-Wesley, 1979.

7. McClure ML. Managing the professional nurse: Part II. applying management theory to the challenges. J Nurs Adm 1984;14(3):11-17.

8. Bopp KD, Hicks LL. Strategic management in health care. Nurs Econ 1984;2:93-101.

9. Allen D, Calkin J, Peterson M. Making shared goverance work: a conceptual model. J Nurs Adm 1988;18(1): 37-43.

10. Coyne C, Killien M. A system for unit-based monitors of quality of nursing care. J Nurs Adm 1987;17(1):26-32.

11. Van Maanen and Barley, 31-53.

12. Schall MS. A communication-rules approach to organizational culture. Admin Sci Q 1983;28:557-581.

13. Louis MR. Surprise and sense making: what newcomers experience in entering unfamiliar organizational settings. Admin Sci Q 1980;25:226-251.

14. Pacanowsky ME, O'Donnell-Trujillo N. Organizational culture and culture performance. Communication Monographs 1983;50:126-147.

15. Smircich L. Concepts of culture and organizational analysis. Admin Sci Q 1983;28:339-358.

16. Henry B, LeClair H. Language, leadership, and power. J Nurs Adm 1987;17(1):19-25.

17. del Bueno and Freund, 27-32.

18. Spradley JP. The ethnographic interview. New York: Holt, Rinehart & Winston, 1979.

19. del Bueno DJ, Vincent PM. Organizational culture: how important is it? J Nurs Adm 1986;16(10):15-20.

20. Leininger MM. Ethnography and ethnonursing: models and modes of qualitative data analysis. In: MM Leininger. Qualitative research methods in nursing. New York: Grune & Stratton, 1985:33-71.

21. Walters JA. An innovative method of job interviewing. J Nurs Adm 1987;17(5):25-29.

22. Louis, 1980;226-251.

23. Vestal KW. Management concepts for the new nurse. Philadelphia, PA: JB Lippincott, 1987;195.

24. del Bueno and Freund, 15-25.

25. Louis MR. An investigator's guide to workplace culture. In: PJ Frost, LF Moore, MR Louis, CC Lundberg, J Martin. Organizational culture. Beverly Hills, CA: Sage, 1985;169-185.

26. Van Maanen and Barley, 31-53.

27. Deal and Kennedy, 158-159.

28. Gregory KL. Native-view paradigms: multiple cultures and culture conflicts in organizations. Admin Sci Q 1983;28:359-376.

29. Wilkins AL, Patterson KJ. You can't get there from here: what will make culture-change projects fail. In: RH Kilmann, MJ Saxton, R Serpa, et al. Gaining control of the corporate culture. San Francisco, CA: Jossey-Bass, 1985;262-291.

30. Miner JB. Theories of organizational behavior. Hinsdale, IL: Dryden Press, 1980;270-271.

31. Deal and Kennedy, 158.

32. Allen, Calkin, and Peterson, 37-43.

33. Coyne and Killien, 26-32.

34. Wilkins and Patterson, 262-291.

35. Sathe V. How to decipher and change corporate culture. In: RH Kilmann, MJ Saxton, R Serpa, et al. Gaining control of the corporate culture. San Francisco, CA: Jossey-Bass, 1985;230-261.

36. Lundberg CC. On the feasibility of cultural intervention in organizations. In: PJ Frost, LF Moore, MR Louis, CC Lundberg, J Martin. Organizational culture. Beverly Hills, CA: Sage, 1985;169-185.

37. Frost PJ. Does organizational culture have a future? In: PJ Frost, LF Moore, MR Louis, CC Lundberg, J Martin. Organizational culture, Beverly Hills, CA: Sage, 1985;379-380.

38. Wilkins and Patterson, 264.

39. del Bueno and Freund, 15-25.

40. Hofstede G. Culture's consequences: international differences in work-related values. Beverly Hills, CA: Sage, 1980;380.

41. Barnlund DC. Toward an ecology of communication. In: C Widler, JH Weakland, Rigor and imagination. New York: Prager, 1981;87-126.

CHAPTER **12**

Measuring and Interpreting Organizational Culture

Charlene Thomas, MSN, RN
Mark Ward, MBA
Carol Chorba, MBA, RRA
Andrew Kumiega, BS

The concept of "culture" is an important tool for understanding and changing the behavior of individuals in organizations. Academic journals devote entire issues to the subject, organizational consultants develop culture change programs, and books on the topic are best sellers. Peters and Waterman view the dominance and coherence of culture as "an essential quality of excellent companies."[1] The Joint Commission on Accreditation of Health Care Organizations, while not proposing to directly measure this variable, now recognizes culture as one dimension important to the provision of high quality patient care.[2]

The concept of organizational culture has its roots in several disciplines including psychology, sociology, anthropology and management. While these diverse perspectives add richness to the concept, they have resulted in numerous and sometimes conflicting approaches to defining culture. This article examines the usefulness of this multi-faceted concept and highlights one method for measuring and interpreting culture in healthcare organizations.

Reprinted from *The Journal of Nursing Administration,* Vol. 20, No. 6, with permission of J. B Lippincott Company © 1990.

UNDERSTANDING CULTURE
Multifaceted Nature of Culture

Smirich identifies two basic perspectives on the meaning and application of culture. These perspectives, derived from different understandings of culture, are evidenced in the way researchers and managers address culture, approach its measurement, interpret results and apply the information. The first perspective identifies culture as a variable. The variable is perceived as an unchangeable external constraint which must be accepted or alternatively, as an internal control mechanism, unique to each organization, which can be manipulated by the manager. When culture is viewed as a variable, emphasis placed on how it impacts organizational outcomes. The second perspective presents culture as a root metaphor for understanding organizations; culture helps explain why people behave as they do in organizations. Culture is seen as a system of cognitions, symbols, and unconscious interactions. In this framework, the emphasis is on understanding what creates the culture.[3]

The confusion resulting from the multifaceted nature of culture can be reduced by examining the potential practical utility of each of these perspectives.

First, while there are some aspects of culture that are clearly beyond the control of managers (e.g., cultural differences due to geographical location), managers are primarily interested in the aspects they can control. Perceiving and treating culture as an internal variable that can be molded and shaped is applicable and useful. Secondly, understanding the cognitive aspects of culture is more easily accomplished than understanding the symbolic or unconscious aspects. Asking individuals what they are thinking (cognitive approach) is more likely to elicit an accurate response than asking them what symbols they see around them or what assumptions they are operating under. Therefore, managers can approach culture as a system of knowledge and beliefs that can be developed and shaped to impact the outcomes of an organization.

CULTURE AS A CONTROLLABLE VARIABLE

Viewing culture as a cognitive, controllable variable is compatible with a recently proposed quantitative approach to its assessment.[4] By defining culture as "the ways of thinking, behaving, and believing that members have in common," this approach is based on the assumption that the measurement of culture is an important component in the organizational change process.[5] Shared thoughts, behaviors and beliefs can be identified by asking individuals to comment on the norms and behavioral expectations in their specific organization. Norms and expectations reflect both the substance and continuous reinforcement of shared values. From the employee's perspective, norms and expectations are guides that provide direction, communicate what is important for "survival and success," and provide a framework for choosing appropriate behaviors. From the manager's perspective, norms and expectations are cognitive processes that can be molded to positively impact both the organization and its members.

There is considerable variation across organizations regarding their cultures. Some cultures are strong in a positive direction and promote constructive behavior (e.g., teamwork and goal setting). As a result, they tend to produce behaviors and outcomes typically associated with individual and organizational effectiveness. Other cultures are strong, but negative. For example, unnecessary competition and conflict are reinforced or defensiveness is implicitly encouraged. In yet other organizations the culture is weak. A sense of shared values and expectations is missing or very limited. Members do not clearly know what is valued and are uncertain about what is expected of them.

Organizational culture assessed in this way should not be confused with the related, but distinct, concept of organizational climate. Climate is a measure of individual perceptions or feelings about an organization. Culture is a measure of common thoughts, behaviors, and beliefs. To relate the two concepts, when an employee's personal beliefs and values are consistent with the prevailing culture, he tends to perceive the climate as "good." However, a perception of a "poor" climate results when the beliefs and values are in conflict.[6]

Culture in the Context of Nursing

The concept of organizational culture has been applied to nursing in several ways. Specifically, the socialization process to organizational norms has received considerable attention.[7] As new employees enter a nursing department, there is the natural feeling of discomfort related to the unfamiliarity of the environment. The adequacy of the orientation they receive has great implications for their adjustment. Del Bueno discusses how new employees might feel not only uncomfortable, but alienated as well.[8] The value of trained and energetic preceptors who work closely with orientees is unlimited. Together they can identify taboos, sacred cows, and behaviors that are desirable and have proven successful in the organization. The earlier new employees learn the informal group rules, the sooner they can feel that they "fit in" the organization. This in turn can increase their level of comfort and the likelihood of their staying with the organization. This presupposes, however, that the culture is reasonably strong and that norms support behaviors that can be recognized and adopted by new members.

Munroe applies the concept of socialization to part-time employees. Many nursing organizations rely heavily on part-time personnel for whom the orientation process is often abbreviated. This has potentially negative ramifications for both the individual and the organization.[9] Brief orientations along with reduced exposure to the organization render it difficult for employees to adjust to the organization's culture, especially if norms and expectations are weak and ambiguous. As a result, part-time employees may become increasingly uncomfortable and choose to terminate.

In addition to learning the culture, there must be a "fit" between the employee's personal needs and expectations and those of the organization. Experienced, career-oriented nurses deliberately learn an organization's culture in pursuit of personal goals. They identify what is rewarded in the organization and structure their objectives and behaviors to achieve success.[10] Nurses often feel that they "fit better" in certain environments because of the culture. The quality of "fit" affects both individual and organizational performance. It also directly impacts the organization's ability to attract and retain nursing personnel.

MEASURING CULTURE

Attempting to provide a complete description of a particular organization's culture is a monumental undertaking. Intensive interviews and lengthy observations would be required. However, for the manager interested in organizational change and development, a survey-based approach can generate information on such aspects of culture as beliefs, values or norms. Quantitative methods, which are conducive to statistical analysis, allow the responses of different individuals, subgroups, and groups to be profiled. Results of different groups can be statistically compared with each other as well as to an ideal nursing culture.[5]

The Organizational Culture Inventory (OCI)

One survey which measures behavioral norms and expectations associated with shared values and beliefs is the Organizational Culture Inventory (OCI).[4] The OCI is designed to quantitatively assess the ways in which organizational members are expected to think and behave in relation to their tasks and to other people. Respondents are given a frame of reference in which to answer the questions. Although there are several possibilities, a unit-level frame of reference facilitates interesting groupings and comparisons. Participants answer 120 questions describing behaviors or personal styles that might be expected of members in their organization (eg, "compete rather than cooperate"). The questions produce twelve scales corresponding to the cultural styles summarized in Table 12-1. Participants plot their own results on a "circumplex" (Figure 12-1) to visualize their personal impressions of their work culture. Aggregate results are also profiled to depict the group's assessment of the culture.

The results profiled in Figure 12-1 represent the "ideal" nursing culture as described by a small group of nurses representing several hospitals. These nurses completed the OCI in terms of behaviors that should be expected to maximize organizational performance, quality of care, and individual motivation and satisfaction. The culture they describe is Constructive (emphasizing members' higher-order or "satisfaction" needs) and would promote Achievement, Self-Actualizing, Humanistic, and Affiliative behaviors on the part of nurses.

Concurrently, the culture would minimize expectations for Passive/Defensive and Aggressive/Defensive behaviors (associated with lower-order or "security" needs). This ideal culture is generally consistent with the "ideal profiles" identified by members of various for-profit organizations in the manufacturing and service sectors.[11] The extensions along the Constructive styles are basically the same. Organizations that are successful along various criteria (eg, growth, sales, and member satisfaction) tend to demonstrate significant extensions along these styles. This relationship is not surprising. The Achievement style promotes high motivation, the Humanistic style facilitates good client relations, and the Affiliative style encourages teamwork and coordination. With respect to Defensive styles, the nurses' ideal culture is slightly

TABLE 12-1
The cultural styles

Constructive styles

Emphasize members' satisfaction needs (e.g., higher-order needs for achievement and affiliation) and encourage them to interact with people and approach tasks in ways to meet needs.

Achievement culture

Organizations that do things well and value members who set and accomplish their own goals. Members are expected to set challenging but realistic goals, establish plans to reach those goals, and pursue them with enthusiasm.

Self-actualizing culture

Organizations that value creativity, quality over quantity, and both task accomplishment and individual growth. Members are encouraged to gain enjoyment from their work, develop themselves, and take on new activities.

Humanistic-encouraging culture

Organizations that are managed in a participative and person-centered way. Members are expected to be supportive, constructive, and open to influence in their dealings with one another.

Affiliative culture

Organizations that place a high priority on constructive interpersonal relationships. Members are expected to be friendly, open, and sensitive to the satisfaction of their work group.

Aggressive/defensive styles

Promote members' security needs (e.g., lower-order needs for power) and require them to approach tasks in forceful ways to protect their status and position.

Oppositional culture

Organizations in which confrontation prevails and negativism is rewarded. Members gain status and influence by being critical and thus are reinforced to oppose the ideas of others.

Power culture

Nonparticipative organizations structured on the basis of the authority inherent in members' positions. Members gain status and influence by being critical and thus are reinforced to oppose the ideas of others.

Competitive culture

Winning is valued and members are rewarded for outperforming one another. Members operate in a "win-lose" framework and believe they must work against (rather than with) their peers to be noticed.

Perfectionistic culture

Organizations in which perfectionism, persistence, and hard work are valued. Members must avoid mistakes, keep track of everything, and work long hours to attain narrowly defined objectives.

Passive/defensive styles

Promote the security needs of members (e.g., lower-order needs for acceptance and avoiding failure) and implicitly require them to interact in self-protective ways to meet those needs.

Approval culture

Organizations in which conflicts are avoided and interpersonal relationships are superficially pleasant. Members should agree with, gain the approval of, and be liked by others.

Conventional culture

Organizations that are conservative, traditional, and bureaucratically controlled. Members conform, follow rules, and make a good impression.

Dependent culture

Organizations that are hierarchically controlled and nonparticipative. Centralized decision making in such organizations leads members to do only what they are told and to clear all decisions with superior.

Avoidance culture

Organizations that fail to reward success but nevertheless punish mistakes. Members shift responsibilities to others and avoid any possibility of being blamed for a mistake.

Source: Organizational Culture Inventory. Adapted with permission from: Cooke RA, Lafferty JC. Organizational Culture Inventory. Plymouth, MI: Human Synergistics, 1989.

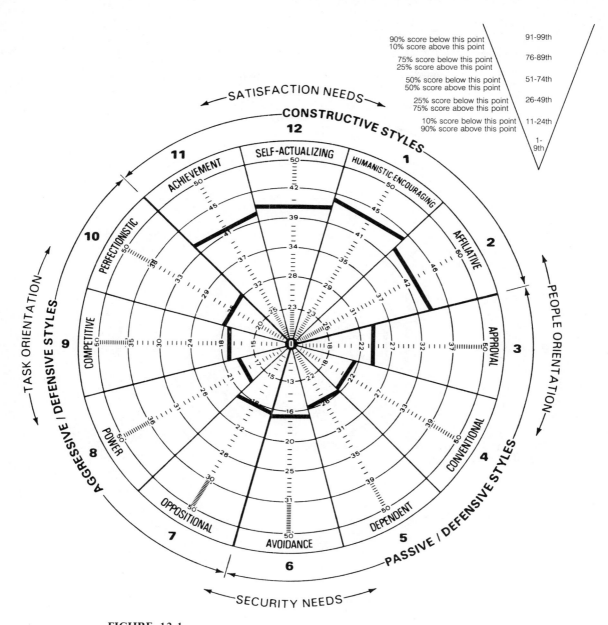

FIGURE 12-1

Ideal culture profile (n = 26 registered nurses). *From Cooke RA and Lafferty JC: Organizational culture inventory, Human Synergistics, 1989.*

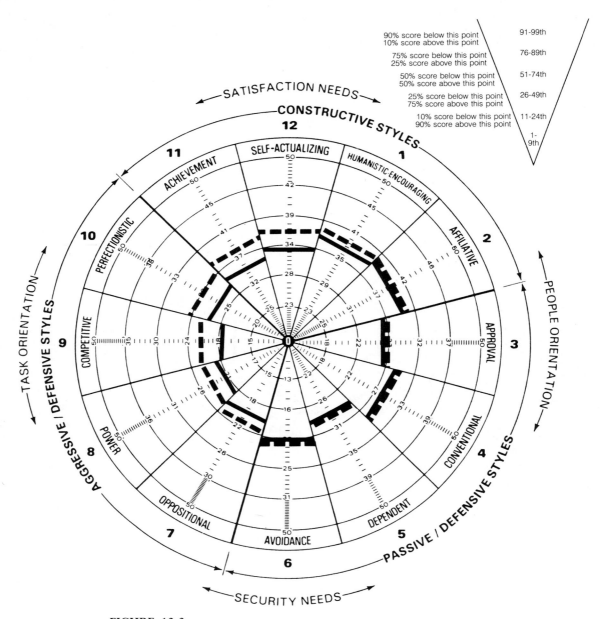

FIGURE 12-2

Culture profile: staff nurses versus nursing administrators. Staff nurses ($38 \leq n \leq 41$):————; administrators: ($13 \leq n \leq 15$):- - - - -. *From Cooke RA and Lafferty JC: Organizational culture inventory, Human Synergistics, 1989.*

weaker along the Oppositional, Power, and Competitive styles as compared with that of members of other organizations.[11]

"Ideal" nursing profiles of this type provide a useful benchmark against which actual cultural profiles can be compared. The styles for which the differences or "gaps" between the ideal and actual are the greatest indicate potential targets for organizational change and development efforts. These gaps can signal the need for changes in several areas, including: (1) the way values are communicated, (2) the organizational structures that are promoting the undesired norms, and (3) the human resource management practices that are reinforcing these norms. Gaps might also signal the need for an examination of the values, beliefs, and basic assumptions held by members at different levels of the organization.

Measuring Culture with the OCI

The OCI has been used in various healthcare organizations, including a metropolitan community hospital with approximately 225 nursing personnel. Fifty-six nurses at this site completed the inventory. These responses, while not intended to provide a complete picture of the nursing culture, illustrate how norms can be measured and interpreted.

The responses of these nurses taken in total or in subgroups (divided by position, unit, shift, etc.) indicate that the culture at this hospital is weak. Nursing personnel do not report strong norms and expectations for any of the twelve cultural styles. In addition, the level of agreement among the nurses regarding these norms and expectations is low, further indicating a weak culture. Compared with the "ideal" profile, these nurses report higher expectations for Aggressive/Defensive and Passive/Defensive behaviors and lower expectations for Constructive styles. Assuming the administration of this hospital is interested in moving toward this particular concept of the ideal nursing culture, changes would be warranted to establish and reinforce norms that are more satisfaction-oriented.

Further insights can be gained by looking at sub-groups in this hospital such as staff personnel versus administrative nurses (Figure 12-2). The administrators report slightly higher expectations for satisfaction-oriented behaviors such as Achievement and Self-Actualization. It is possible that job design contributes to these findings. Administrative nurses (head nurses upward to the Director of Nursing) are given authority and responsibility for a delineated work unit, including goal setting, planning and risk taking. These responsibilities promote Achievement-oriented behaviors. Personal goals are integrated into the process and this provides for Self-Actualization.

One could argue that staff nurses are also personally achievement-oriented and motivated toward self-actualization. However, in this particular organization, these styles do not seem to be strongly encouraged (Figure 12-2).

The most significant differences between the nurse managers and the staff nurses are along the Aggressive/Defensive styles. Staff nurses report substantially weaker expectations for Competitive and Power behaviors than do the administrators. The managers may be successfully shielding staff personnel from some of the pressures they experience, encouraging them to behave in an aggressive, security-oriented manner.

Figure 12-3 displays the responses for day shift versus nurses on "other" shifts. Day-shift personnel report norms and expectations closer to the "ideal" with stronger Constructive norms and weaker Aggressive/Defensive and Passive/Defensive norms.

Given the nature of "daytime" work, these results are not unexpected. During daytime hours there are more people present, including nursing administrators, to facilitate communication, exchange ideas and provide feedback. Traditionally, off-shift personnel have less communication with co-workers and nursing administrators. Although mechanisms are in place for communication, spontaneity is limited and much information is transferred via memoranda. This temporal separation hinders the development of a 24-hour culture via reduced communication regarding norms and expectations. This situation is not unique. In most nursing organizations, administrators must devote considerable creative energy to build a strong culture on a 24-hour basis.

The concept of organizational culture is abstract, yet potent. Today, in the presence of declining financial resources, reduced staffing levels and a

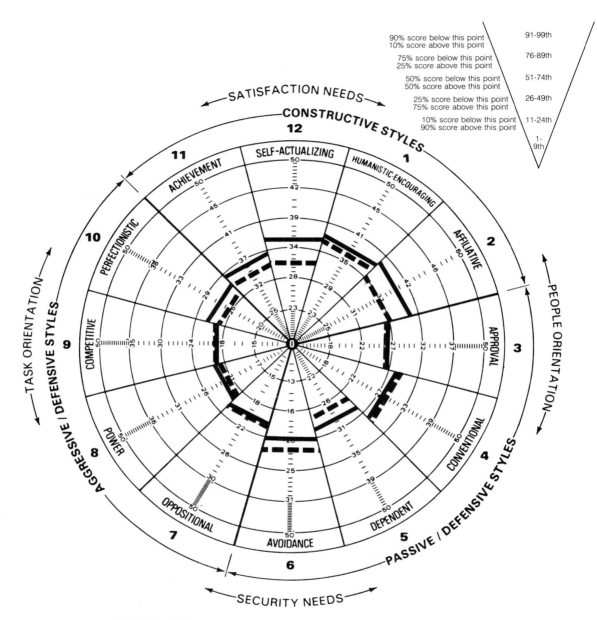

FIGURE 12-3

Culture profile: day shift versus nurses on other shifts. Day shift
(31 ≤ n ≤ 35):- - - -; other shifts (18 ≤ n ≤ 20):- - - -. *From Cooke RA and
Lafferty JC: Organizational culture inventory, Human Synergistics, 1989.*

consumer demand for high quality nursing care, nursing administrators must demonstrate insight into their organization's culture. An awareness of the underlying forces can help them understand personnel behavior, identify necessary organizational changes, and help develop the organization to function more efficiently.

While there is no simple prescription for achieving the "ideal" nursing culture, valid and reliable assessments of the existing nursing culture are critical so that the nursing administrator may identify the most important targets and strategies for organizational change. To develop a "picture" of the current culture, nurse executives can use quantitative methods such as the Organizational Culture Inventory to compliment their observations and other qualitative strategies. These complimentary methods, in combination, provide substantial insight into the highly abstract culture of organizations.

REFERENCES

1. Peters TJ, Waterman RH. In search of excellence. New York, NY: Harper & Row 1982; p. 75.

2. Principles of organizational and management effectiveness for health care organizations. Chicago, IL: JCAHO, 1989.

3. Smirich L. Concepts of culture and organizational analysis. ASQ 1983;28(3):339-358.

4. Cooke RA, Lafferty JL. Level V: Organizational culture inventory. Plymouth, MI: Human Synergistics, 1987, 1989.

5. Cooke RA, Rousseau DM. Behavioral norms and expectations: A quantitiative approach to the assessment of organizational culture. Group and Organizational Studies 1988;13(3):245-273.

6. Schwartz H, Davis SM. Matching corporate culture and business strategy. Organizational Dynamics 1981;10 (Summer):33.

7. Coeling H, Wilcox JR. Understanding organizational culture: A key to management decision making. J Nurs Admin 1988;18(11):16-23.

8. Del Bueno DJ. Organizational culture: How important is it? J Nurs Admin 1986;16(10):15-20.

9. Munroe DJ. Commitment of part time nursing personnel: A challenge. Nurs Manage 1988;19(12):59-61.

10. Smith MM. Getting ahead in the corporate culture. AJN 1987;87(4):513-514.

11. Cooke R. Personal Communication, July 18, 1989.

CHAPTER **13**

Communication: Key Contributor to Effectiveness — The Research

J. David Pincus, PhD

As hospital markets become increasingly competitive and profit-driven, nurse and hospital executives are intensifying the search for ways to enhance nursing effectiveness. This industry-wide trend is reflected in the thrust of recent nurse-related research, which has focused on effectiveness measures such as job satisfaction, job performance, and turnover rates.

Few studies of hospital nurses, however, have attempted to explain how and why communication activities, which affect every facet of nurses' working lives, influence nurses' job satisfaction and job performance. Nursing supervisory personnel, particularly those at executive levels, must be cognizant of the crucial contribution positively perceived communication can make to nurses' morale and productivity.

This void of communication-related research is puzzling in light of Georgopolous and Mann's conclusion more than 20 years ago that nursing performance — particularly those aspects related to patient care — is enhanced by the "free flow" of both "general information" and "specific, task-relevant information" through formal hospital communication channels.[1] Within the broader body of organizational research, communication has been extensively

studied as a contributor to job satisfaction and, to a lesser degree, to job performance.[2] Nevertheless, few research efforts have concentrated solely on linking empirically certain types of organizational communication and organizational effectiveness variables among nurses in a hospital setting.

The purpose of this study was to explore the relationships between different types of organizational communication and job satisfaction and job performance among hospital nurses.

SUMMARY OF PRIOR RESEARCH

The study of job satisfaction — the factors that cause it and its impact on organizational life — has evolved over the years. Within the nursing field, several trends in job satisfaction research are discernible. Early studies revealed the importance of personal factors, such as family and education, as contributors to nurses' job satisfaction.[3,4] Results of more recent job satisfaction studies, however, suggest nurses' growing concern with work and organizational issues, such as autonomy,[6] supervisory style,[7,8] interpersonal relationships with superiors and co-workers,[9,10] organizational climate,[11] and self-esteem/recognition.[12] An increasing number of researchers have attempted to categorize and explain these various causal factors of job satisfaction using Herzberg's two-factor theory of motivation.

Reprinted from *The Journal of Nursing Administration,* Vol. 16, No. 9, with permission of J. B. Lippincott Company © 1986.

Herzberg's Theory

In his series of studies of engineers and accountants, Herzberg found that the causes of job satisfaction and job dissatisfaction are quite different; that is, each is affected by a different range of factors. For example, job satisfaction is enhanced by the fulfillment of intrinsic human needs, alleged motivators, such as achievement, recognition, responsibility, the work itself, and advancement. Job dissatisfaction, on the other hand, is caused by the deprivation of extrinsic environmental needs, called hygiene factors, such as salary, working conditions, interpersonal relationships, and company policies.[13]

In general, nursing studies applying Herzberg's theory have yielded mixed results.[14-17] The essence of these findings is that the determinants of nurses' job satisfaction are far more complex and situation-specific than the two-factor theory posits.[18] This conclusion was reinforced in a recent study of the difficulties associated with measuring job satisfaction among nurses, which revealed that job expectations and the importance placed on job factors can also affect satisfaction scores.[19]

Communication Aspects

Although several factors identified by Herzberg and other researchers (e.g., recognition, interpersonal relationships) contain inherent communication components, communication variables per se have rarely been investigated by researchers as contributors to nurses' job satisfaction. Interestingly, the body of non-nursing organizational literature demonstrates clearly the important contribution of different types of organizational communication to job satisfaction.[20] Interpreted broadly, communication, which encompasses both information exchange and relationship-building elements, touches — and can affect — all the factors comprising job satisfaction. Nurse and hospital executives, therefore, must be sensitive to the communication atmosphere in their organizations because of its potential impact on nurses' job satisfaction and job performance.

The few nursing studies incorporating communication and job satisfaction or job performance variables[21-24] suggest, in general terms, that positively perceived communication contributes to nurses' job satisfaction and job performance. However, this evidence is weak and difficult to interpret. Existing studies are not easily compared as they use varying research methodologies and different operational definitions of communication and effectiveness variables. For example, communication has been operationalized in nursing studies as general communicative effectiveness[25] and downward communication,[26] while job performance has been defined as subordinates' perceived performance[27] and global self-reports of productivity.[28]

Research Questions

Research to date suggests that the communication–job satisfaction and communication–job performance relationships are extremely complex. Nevertheless, most studies have found some viable evidence that open, credible communication positively affects nurses' job satisfaction and performance. However, several important questions facing nurse managers and hospital administrators are yet to be investigated thoroughly. Three of those questions comprised the focus of this study:

1. What specific types of organizational communication have the strongest impact on nurses' job satisfaction and job performance?
2. How do the communication–job satisfaction and communication–job performance relationships differ, if at all, within a nursing population?
3. Is it possible to predict which types of organizational communication are likely to have the greatest influence on hospital nurses' job satisfaction and job performance, regardless of organizational setting?

A CONCEPTUAL FRAMEWORK AND COMMUNICATION MODEL

Communication has been defined and operationalized in field research in a host of different ways.[29] Emerging from this body of communication research are two major categories of communication variables: (1) information flow variables, and (2) perceptual, or relationship, variables. These categories offer a broad framework for examining the dynamics of communication systems in organizations.[30]

Communication Satisfaction

One integrative communication construct — communication satisfaction — has been described by its developers, Downs and Hazen, as a "summing up" of an individual's satisfaction with information flow and relationship variables.[31] A series of factor analyses encompassing a pool of 88 communication items yielded eight dimensions to this construct:

1. *Communication climate* (general satisfaction with communication environment)
2. *Supervisor communication* (e.g., immediate supervisor's openness to ideas, guidance in solving job-related problems)
3. *Media quality* (written and verbal channels, e.g., meetings, memos, newsletters)
4. *Horizontal communication* (e.g., grapevine, informal communication with peers)
5. *Organizational integration* (information relevant to performing job)
6. *Personal feedback* (information about performance and how performance is judged)
7. *Organizational perspective* (information about organization as a whole, e.g., policies, procedures, competition)
8. *Subordinate communication* (refers to supervisors only, e.g., response to downward communication)

Based on these dimensions, Downs and Hazen developed a 46-item Communication Satisfaction Questionnaire, which has been found to be internally consistent in its subscales and dimensionality.[32]

Several recent studies have reported evidence as to the impact of perceptions of communication between employees and top management on employee job satisfaction.[33,34] In addition to the above eight dimensions of communication satisfaction, a ninth dimension was created for this study:

9. *Upper management communication* (top management's direct communication with employees, listening to employees, credibility)

A number of studies have examined communication satisfaction's relationship with job satisfaction and, in a few cases, performance or productivity within different types of organizations.[35-38] One communication satisfaction study examined a nursing population in Kansas.[39] Results of these studies suggest the existence of a general positive relationship between communication satisfaction and job satisfaction variables.

In an effort to synthesize the major findings in previous research and to organize the specific research questions in this study, the "Comm Sat-Outcomes" Research Model was developed[40] (Figure 13-1). This model graphically depicts the expected relationships between the specific dimensions of communication satisfaction, grouped according to each dimension's dominant informational or relational characteristics, and job satisfaction and job performance.

Implicit to the model are several key concepts: (1) the communication–job satisfaction relationship is stronger than the communication–job performance relationship, (2) information variables are more closely tied to job performance, while relationship variables are more tightly linked to job satisfaction, and (3) specific types of communication (e.g., supervisor communication, communication climate, and personal feedback) will have the strongest influence on both job satisfaction and job performance. The study reported below was developed as a test of this model.

METHODOLOGY
Sample

The sample consisted of 327 professional nurses in the nursing department of a large, urban, teaching hospital on the east coast of the United States. Representing 66% of the nursing population, this sample included nursing supervisors, head nurses, assistant head nurses, registered nurses, and licensed practical nurses. The nursing staff was not unionized. The lines of communication between nursing managers and staff were quite traditional, relying on a mixture of hospital publications, the "grapevine," and periodic face-to-face meetings. The performance

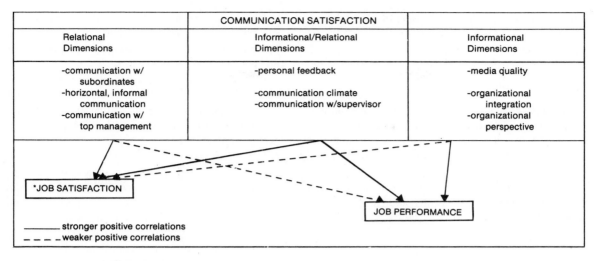

	COMMUNICATION SATISFACTION		
Relational Dimensions	**Informational/Relational Dimensions**	**Informational Dimensions**
-communication w/ subordinates -horizontal, informal communication -communication w/ top management	-personal feedback -communication climate -communication w/supervisor	-media quality -organizational integration -organizational perspective

*JOB SATISFACTION

JOB PERFORMANCE

———— stronger positive correlations
— — — weaker positive correlations

FIGURE 13-1

"Comm Sat-Outcomes" research model. The overall comm sat-job satisfaction linkage is hypothesized to be *more* positive than the overall comm sat-job performance linkage (represented by difference in distance).

appraisal system was largely informal, void of a system for measuring specific job behaviors.

Instrumentation

Data were collected using three instruments: (1) the Communication Satisfaction Questionnaire, which was modified to include a top management communication dimension, (2) a version of the Job Description Index (measures job satisfaction) modified for a nursing population,[41] and (3) a Nursing Job Performance Evaluation Questionnaire developed from a synthesis of nursing and general performance evaluation measures for use in this study.

Each of the three key variables were measured by global and multidimensional scores. Each instrument was modified to use a 0–100 probability scale. Several open-ended "write-in" questions were also included. The instruments were pretested among a cross-section of nurses and nursing managers at four medical facilities. Only minor language changes were made as a result of the pretest.

Reliability of Instruments

Each of the scales was found to be internally consistent, using .80 as an acceptable guideline on the overall scales. The Cronbach's alpha reliability scores on the three scales were: job satisfaction, .85; communication satisfaction, .95; and job performance, .93.

Data Collection

The major data collection occurred on-site during a 24-hour period. All nurses were given sealed packets containing communication and job satisfaction questionnaires. They were asked to complete them during their shift that day and return them to the sealed drop-box on their floor. Job performance evaluation questionnaires were distributed to nursing supervisors and head nurses several hours later. A follow-up effort occurred 3 weeks later. Questionnaires were returned by mail in postage-guaranteed envelopes.

During initial data collection, 496 questionnaires were distributed, and 298 usable questionnaires were returned. An additional 29 were obtained during follow-up, for a 66% return rate.

RESULTS
Profile of Sample

Demographic data revealed that 84% of the sample consisted of non-supervisory staff nurses: 61% RNs and 23% LPNs. The sample was overwhelmingly female (96%), full-time nurses (79%), and most nurses were between 20 and 40 years of age (68%). Most respondents were experienced nurses; that is, 44% had been in nursing between 4 and 10 years, and another 38% for more than 10 years.

The Communication–Job Satisfaction Relationship

As predicted, the strength of the communication–job satisfaction bond was confirmed — and a more precise understanding of the factors influencing it uncovered. Each of the nine communication satisfaction dimensions was found to be positively and significantly correlated with global job satisfaction (p = .001). The three communication types most strongly correlated with job satisfaction were, as outlined in the model, communication with supervisor (r = .43, p = .001), communication climate (r = .39, p = .001), and personal feedback (r = .38, p = .001). Less strongly correlated but significant at the .001 probability level were communication with top management, horizontal communication, organizational integration, media quality, and organizational perspective.

More powerful statistical tests revealed that nurses' job satisfaction was strongly influenced by nurses' perceived communication with several important groups in the hospital. Canonical correlation, which analyzes the influence of all facets of independent and dependent variables simultaneously, was used to test the multidimensional relationships between communication and job satisfaction. The first of three statistically significant and the strongest canonical correlation (.69, p = .001, explained 48% of the variance in job satisfaction) pointed up the importance of communication activities to the superior–subordinate

relationship. Communication with supervisor and satisfaction with supervisor formed the strong basis of this critically important relationship between nurses and their immediate supervisors.

The second strongest canonical correlation (.42, p = .001, explained 17% of the variance in job satisfaction) suggested the substantial impact of nurses' perceived communication with top-level management on nurses' job satisfaction.

The third canonical correlation (.36, p = .003, explained 13% of the variance in job satisfaction) pointed up the vital role peer relationships play in nurses' working lives. Horizontal communication and satisfaction with co-workers were the major contributors to this correlation.

Analyzed together, these results indicate that different types of communication, particularly those types contributing to building human relationships, substantially affect nurses' levels of job satisfaction. Interestingly, this link between interpersonal relationships and job satisfaction seems to contradict Herzberg's two-factor theory, which categorizes interpersonal relationships as a hygiene factor, tied directly to job dissatisfaction.

The Communication–Job Performance Relationship

For the most part, the data confirmed the model's prediction that this relationship would be weaker than the communication–job satisfaction bond. Correlation analysis of the nine dimensions of communication with global job performance yielded only two statistically significant communication types: communication with supervisor (r = .21, p = .002) and personal feedback (r = .12, p = .04).

A stronger overall communication–job performance relationship was found when all dimensions of both factors were evaluated together via canonical correlation analysis. For example, in the one statistically significant correlation (.44, p = .05, accounting for 19% of the variance in job performance), each of the nine communication types and the quality component of performance were positive and significant (p = .001) contributors to this relationship. Once again, communication with supervisor was the major influence on this relationship, followed by communication climate, media quality, organizational integration, and personal feedback. These findings demonstrate the pervading importance of supervisor–subordinate communication on the communication–job performance relationship. Also noteworthy is the influence of information–oriented communication factors, as outlined in the research model, on this relationship.

Comparing Nursing Studies

Striking similarities among comparable results of this study and Thiry's study of Kansas nurses[42] were discovered. The same three types of communication — communication with supervisor, communication climate, and personal feedback — were ranked highest in both studies. This finding supported projections in the "Comm Sat-Outcomes" model.

A statistical test (Kendall's coefficient of concordance) that compares the amount of agreement of rank ordered data across studies was applied to the communication–job satisfaction correlation rankings. Data from the two studies exhibited a very high degree of concordance (coefficient of concordance = .94, p = .005). Table 13-1 contains full results.

This finding suggests that certain types of communication may have the strongest effects on nurses' job satisfaction, regardless of work setting or geographic location.

DISCUSSION

The major implication of this study to nurse executives is that positively perceived communication activities can substantially affect nurses' attitudes toward their work environment and, to a somewhat lesser degree, their performance on the job. Nurse executives should consider developing formal, ongoing communication programs (i.e., incorporating both written and interpersonal media) within their nursing department and between the nursing department and other hospital departments, if these programs are not already in place. Several areas of communication (supported in both the studies of nurses analyzed

TABLE 13-1

Kendall's coefficient of concordance rank order comparisons of communication satisfaction-job satisfaction correlations in two nursing studies

COMMUNICATION DIMENSIONS	RANK ORDER OF CORRELATIONS	
	PINCUS, 1984	THIRY, 1977
Communication w/ supervisor	1	3
Communication climate	2	1
Personal feedback	3	2
Organizational integration	4	5
Media quality	5	4
Communication w/ subordinates	6	7
Horizontal communication	7	6
Organizational perspective	8	8

Coefficient of Concordance = .94 (p = .005)
Coefficient of Rank Correlation = .88 (p = .006)
Note: Communication with top management, which ranked 4th in the Pincus study, could not be included because it was not measured in the Thiry study.

here) appear especially critical as contributors to nurses' job satisfaction and job performance:

(1) Communication between head nurses and staff nurses was the most important influence in this study. Nurses' perceptions of their jobs and organizations were substantially influenced by their relationship with their immediate supervisor. And that relationship was found to be heavily dependent on nurses' perceptions of their communication with their immediate supervisor. Moreover, results of this study clearly suggest that a nurse's communication with her/his immediate supervisor is the primary influence on that nurse's job satisfaction *and* job performance. One way to perhaps emphasize the importance of nurse managers' communication role is to incorporate this responsibility into their job descriptions. Nurse executives may also be able to help their supervisors better understand how to build relationships with

their staff nurses through advanced training in small group and interpersonal communication strategies, and conflict management techniques.

(2) This study argues for the need to establish a positive communication atmosphere within the nursing department and the hospital. This climate may be the result of many factors. Results of this study indicate that two factors in particular may affect a nursing department's communication environment: nurses' perceptions of their communication with top management and nurses' desire to participate in decisions affecting them.

Nurses and hospital executives, by their words and actions, set the tone of the communication atmosphere in which their employees work. And, as this study showed, the subordinate–top management communication relationship (apart from the subordinate-immediate supervisor relationship) has a strong influence on nurses' job satisfaction. Nurses in this study, for example, through their personal written comments urged their top-level executives to be more accessible to and initiate contact with them regularly — with candor and sincerity. Some specific suggestions are shown in Figure 13-2.

Another aspect of this two-way communication relationship is nurses' expectations of being integrally involved in the decision making process, where appropriate to do so. Feedback systems, such as quality circles, confidential "rap" sessions with key executives or suggestion boxes, can signal top management's public commitment to opening the channels of communication throughout the organization and involve staff nurses more intensely in the organization. If these programs are perceived as genuine "employee-driven" programs that can influence how the hospital operates, desirable outcomes such as increased job satisfaction and job performance, and reduced turnover and absenteeism are more likely results. Figure 13-2 shows the nurses' comments.

(3) Nurses reported a strong need for frequent, constructive personal feedback on how they are doing in their jobs. This information may not only provide them with input for improving their performance, but may also help fortify nurses' relationships with their immediate supervisors, who are usually best qualified to supply this feedback.

One suggestion for bolstering the feedback process

Nurses were asked to respond in their own words to the question: "What areas of communication do you feel are most in need of improvement in your hospital and how would you suggest they be improved?"

Based on a content analysis of the 247 nurses (75% of sample) who offered written comments, the following statements, presented exactly as offered, represent the tone and content of the total response.

"Communication is lacking between top management and the nursing staff. Quite often, the grapevine is our only real communication."

"We're not allowed as much input into changes affecting us as we'd like."

"We don't get information about what's going on here, especially regarding changes."

"We need more meetings. We have to have more direct communication between nurses and upper management. We don't think management is honest with us most of the time."

"A gap exists between management's knowledge of what's happening in the units and what's actually happening. They need to talk to the nursing staff directly and learn the major sources of our discontent."

"We should have a quarterly newsletter just for the nursing staff. It should discuss subjects of concern to us."

FIGURE 13-2

Nurses' written comments and suggestions on improving communication.

might be to provide nurse managers with or involve them in developing appropriate, usable performance evaluation criteria. In addition, they should receive training in how to administer performance appraisals effectively. Largely a communication activity, regular performance evaluations may assist both supervisor and subordinate in identifying problems early, jointly generating reasonable objectives, and assuring them of regular face-to-face communication sessions.

Communication activities, particularly those that help improve organizational relationships, are one of many factors contributing to nurses' job satisfaction and performance. However, communication is inextricably linked to all areas of nurses' working lives. And, as this study demonstrates, nurses who perceive their communication with other organizational members positively will be more satisfied with their work, co-workers, and supervisors, and perform their jobs more effectively.

REFERENCES

1. Georgopolous BS, Mann FC. The Community General Hospital. New York: The Macmillan Co., 1962, p 543.

2. Goldhaber GM, Porter DT, Yates MP, et al. Organizational communication: 1978. Human Communication Research 1978;5(1):76–96.

3. Diamond LK, Fox DJ. Turnover among hospital staff nurses. Nursing Outlook 1958;6(7):388–391.

4. Saleh SD, Lee RJ, Prien EP. Why nurses leave their jobs: an analysis of female turnover. Personnel Administration 1965;25–28.

5. Maryo JS, Lasky JJ. A work satisfaction survey among nurses. Am J Nurs 1959;59(4):501–503.

6. Slocum JW, Susman GI, and Sheridan JE. An analysis of need satisfaction and job performance among professional and paraprofessional hospital personnel. Nurs Res 1972;21(4):338–341.

7. Gruenfeld L, Kassum S. Supervisory style and organizational effectiveness in a pediatric hospital. Personnel Psychology 1973;26:531–544.

8. Jain HC. Supervisory communication and performance in urban hospitals. J Communication 1973;23:103–117.

9. Everly GS, Falcione RL. Perceived dimensions of job satisfaction for staff registered nurses. Nurs Res 1976; 35(5):346–348.

10. Rump EE. Size of psychiatric hospitals and nurses' job satisfaction. J Occupational Psychology 1979;52:255–265.

11. Lyon HL, Ivancevich JM. An exploratory investigation of organizational climate and job satisfaction in a hospital. Academy of Management Journal 1974;17(4):635–648.

12. McCloskey J. Influence of rewards and incentives on staff nurse turnover rate. Nurs Res 1974;23(3):239–247.

13. Herzberg F, Mausner B, Snyderman B. The Motivation to Work. New York: John Wiley & Sons, 1959.

14. White CH, Maguire MC. Job satisfaction and dissatisfaction among hospital nursing supervisors. Nurs Res 1973;22(1):25–30.

15. Cronin–Stubbs D. Job satisfaction and dissatisfaction among new graduate staff nurses. J Nurs Adm 1977; 7:44–49.

16. Ullrich RA. Herzberg revisited: factors in job dissatisfaction. J Nurs Adm 1978;8:19–24.

17. Munro BH. Job satisfaction among recent graduates of schools of nursing. Nurs Res 1983;32(6):350–355.

18. Everly GS, and Falcione RL, 1976;346–348.

19. Larson E, Lee PC, Brown MA, et al. Job satisfaction assumptions and complexities. J Nurs Adm 1984;31–38.

20. Pincus JD, Rayfield RE. Organizational communication and job satisfaction: an analysis of research and prospects for future study. Presented at the Western Communication Educators Conference, San Jose, CA, November 1985.

21. Jain HC, 1973, 103–117.

22. Sims HP, Szilagyi AD. Leader structure and subordinate satisfaction for two hospital administrative levels: a path analysis approach. J Appl Psychol 1975;60(2):194–197.

23. Anderson J, Level DA. The impact of certain types of downward communication on job performance. J Bus Comm 1980;17(4):51–59.

24. Thiry RA. Relationship of communication satisfaction to need fulfillment among Kansas nurses. Unpublished Doctoral Dissertation, University of Kansas, 1977.

25. Jain HC, 1973, 103–117.

26. Anderson J, Level DA, 1980, 51–59.

27. Jain HC, 1973, 103–117.

28. Thiry RA, 1977.

29. Porter LW, Roberts KH. Communication in Organizations. In: Dunnette MD, ed. Handbook of Industrial and Organizational Psychology. Chicago: Rand McNally, 1976, pp 1553–1590.

30. Goldhaber GM, et al., 1978, 76–96.

31. Downs CW, Hazen MD. A factor analytic study of communication satisfaction. J Bus Comm 1977; 14(3):63–73.

32. Crino MC, White MC. Satisfaction in communication: an examination of the Downs-Hazen measure. Psychol Rep 1981;49:831–838.

33. Goodman R, Ruch RS. In the image of the CEO. Pub Rela J 1981;(Feb):14–19.

34. Foehrenbach J, Rosenberg K. How are we doing? J Organ Comm 1982;12(1):3–9.

35. Clampitt PG. Communication and productivity. Unpublished Doctoral Dissertation, University of Kansas, 1983.

36. Wippich BJ. An analysis of communication and job satisfaction in an educational setting. Unpublished Doctoral Dissertation, University of Kansas, 1983.

37. Jones JW. Analysis of communication satisfaction in four rural school systems. Unpublished Doctoral Dissertation, Vanderbilt University, 1981.

38. Downs CW. The relationship between communication and job satisfaction. In Huseman RC, et al., eds. Readings in Interpersonal and Organizational Communication, 3rd ed. Boston: Allyn and Bacon, 1979.

39. Thiry RA, 1977.

40. Pincus JD. The impact of communication satisfaction on job satisfaction and job performance: a field study of hospital nurses. Unpublished Doctoral Dissertation, University of Maryland, 1984.

41. Smith PC, Kendall LM, Hulin CL. The Measurement of Satisfaction in Work and Retirement. Chicago: Rand McNally, 1969.

42. Thiry RA, 1977.

CHAPTER **14**

Assessing Communication in Organizations

Mary J. Farley, RN, PhD

The recent emphasis on recruiting and retaining qualified registered nurses while providing high quality cost-effective nursing care places immense pressure on nurse administrators. The majority of solutions suggested for retention and quality care include recommendations for implementing a variety of different nursing care delivery systems or practice models. While these suggestions offer exciting new horizons for the future of the nursing profession, they may not contribute to the retention of experienced nurses if nurses are dissatisfied because communication problems exist within the organization, department or unit.

Communication problems are frequently mentioned as a source of job dissatisfaction.[1-7] Pincus[8] found three components of organizational communication systems to be related to job satisfaction: 1) positive communication atmosphere, 2) positive communication between staff nurses and their immediate superiors, and 3) personal feedback on job performance. If retention of nursing staff is to be increased, nursing administrators cannot afford to ignore the communication needs of employees.[9]

In addition to influencing a person's satisfaction with his or her job, organizational communication systems are seen as powerful determinants of a

Reprinted from *The Journal of Nursing Administration,* Vol. 19, No. 12, with permission of J. B. Lippincott Company © 1989.

hospital's effectiveness.[10] As Wolf[11] noted, "effective communications are the bricks in the road to corporate excellence." With so much at stake, nursing and hospital administrators ought to be exceptionally concerned about the quality of communication interactions occurring within the organization.

This article focuses on a systematic assessment of the formal organizational communication system that can be initiated by nursing administration. If communication problems are identified through the assessment, the nurse administrator will have data to use as a basis for making necessary changes in the nursing department or the organization. When improvements are made in the communication system, possibilities exist for increased job satisfaction of the nursing staff and greater effectiveness of nursing administration.

The conceptual underpinnings for a communication assessment are found in rules-based theory of communication.[12-15] A communication rule is generally believed to be a standardized communication behavior that is shared by members of an identified group of interacting individuals. Shimanoff[16] defined a communication rule as a followable prescription that indicates what behavior is obligated, preferred or prohibited in certain contexts.

Each organization has its own set of communication rules that affect communication interactions and govern the conditions under which information exchange takes place. These rules may be explicit or implicit. An explicit rule is one that is codified in some permanent fashion and is disseminated to those individuals whom it affects. Explicit rules govern formal activities, such as access to superiors or the choice of documents to be used for specific types of communication. Generally, specific organizational sanctions exist for violation of explicit rules.

Implicit rules are similar to norms and are the behavioral expectations that evolve over time. They are unspecified, generally accepted forms of behavior which are non-codified and mutually shared by members of the organization.[17]

Communication rules are observed because there are penalties for violation and because they have a stabilizing effect on communication behaviors. Penalties include such things as ostracism and criticism from organizational members and being passed over for promotions. The stabilizing effect of rules help employees know what kind of communication is expected from them and the type of communication that can be expected from others.[18] When organizational members conform to communication rules, dissonance is reduced and stability in the environment is maintained. Communicating without rules would be similar to rush hour traffic without traffic lights.

Understanding the rules of the formal communication system is essential for the nurse administrator. This knowledge serves as a foundation for assessing and analyzing the communication processes within the organization.

Determining the effectiveness of organizational communications may be viewed as a herculean task, and the various standardized communication audits that are available[19,20] tend to be expensive, time consuming, and not specific to nursing or health care. These barriers often keep the nurse administrator from conducting communication assessments.

However, for a small amount of money, a task force can be appointed to develop a communication assessment questionnaire that is specific to the health care organization. Nurse administrators can then critique the questionnaire, make modifications as necessary and distribute them to employees.

Results obtained from the questionnaires can be analyzed fairly easily. A cardinal rule for any

information-obtaining strategy is to inform the respondents or participants about the results and what is planned to rectify any deficiencies found. If this feedback is not forthcoming, respondents will be unlikely to participate in further data gathering procedures.

Many aspects of the formal communication system within the organization need to be assessed. From an administrative perspective, at least six areas are of critical importance: 1) accessibility of information, 2) communication channels, 3) clarity of messages, 4) span of control, 5) flow control/communication load, and 6) the individual communicators. A communication assessment should include questions from all six categories. Elaboration of each of these categories follows. Figure 14-1 provides sample questions that could be included in a communication assessment questionnaire.

ACCESSIBILITY OF INFORMATION

Accessibility of information refers to the availability of specific details necessary for job performance. Employees at all levels must have the requisite information in order to do their jobs. If a patient or client has special needs, the staff nurse must either know how to meet these needs or know where to get this information. If a staff nurse wishes to know about obtaining additional leave days, or if a nurse manager wants to check a proposed policy with the philosophy statement of the organization, knowledge of where this information can be obtained should be readily available.

Determining the accessibility of information is accomplished by asking questions about the ease or difficulty in receiving information necessary to do the job, and if organizational members know who to contact in order to obtain requisite knowledge.

COMMUNICATION CHANNELS

Communication channels are closely related to accessibility of information. These channels are the links between members of the organization through which news normally passes. Sometimes the channels are similar to the organizational chart. At other times, and

Please circle the number representing the extent to which you believe the statement is true for you in your work environment.

1 = the statement is not at all accurate

5 = the statement is completely accurate

1. I have the information I need in order to do my job in the most effective and efficient manner.	1 2 3 4 5
2. I know where I can get the information I need in order to do my job well.	1 2 3 4 5
3. I receive information about my job from	
a) my immediate supervisor	1 2 3 4 5
b) my co-workers	1 2 3 4 5
c) notices posted on bulletin boards	1 2 3 4 5
d) personnel from departments other than nursing	1 2 3 4 5
4. I receive the information about any changes that might affect my job in a timely manner.	1 2 3 4 5
5. The communications I receive are clear and understandable.	1 2 3 4 5
6. I am satisfied with the frequency of communications I have with my immediate superior.	1 2 3 4 5
7. I receive too little information about things that are happening in this organization.	1 2 3 4 5
8. I believe that nursing administration shares critical and pertinent information with nursing personnel.	1 2 3 4 5
9. People in administration effectively communicate with employees.	1 2 3 4 5

FIGURE 14-1

Communication assessment questionnaire.

in some organizations, there is very little resemblance between the organizational chart and the actual channels of communication. When there is a disparity between the informal and the formal communication systems, the nurse administrator needs to be aware of the key people involved in the informal (grapevine) communication system and the accuracy of information passed through these channels.

In addition to determining congruence between the formal and the informal channels, the linkage of the formal channels should be assessed. This linkage is especially important to assess in health care agencies where off-shift and part-time employees comprise a sizeable portion of organizational members. To determine this linkage, it is important to

know the amount of time it takes for both written and verbal information from nursing administration to reach a part-time night shift nurse. It is also important to determine the channels the information went through in order to reach him or her.

Survey questions could inquire about how and when information is received, as well as from whom it is received. A comparison can then be made between the formal organizational chart and the actual channels of communication. Responses to these questions may provide data upon which to base changes for improving the formal lines of communication and the use of informal channels. Observations and interviews could also help in determining the extent to which messages sent downward obtained the type of responses or behaviors desired.

Many nursing units use a "message book" to communicate messages from administration. Every nurse is expected to read this message book during his or her shift assignment. Sometimes nurses are asked to write their initials beside each written communication indicating that they have read it. This practice reinforces use of the formal communication channels.

The channels used to send messages from staff nurses and middle management upward to administration also needs to be assessed. Frequently, staff nurses believe that administration does not "hear" their needs or requests, and these perceptions result in feelings of frustration and anger.

CLARITY OF MESSAGES

Message clarity refers to the extent to which those who read or hear messages interpret them in the way they were meant to be understood. Misunderstandings are common. Adams and Munn[21] identified three communication problems related to communication messages: 1) multiple definitions for the same word, 2) personal interpretation of words, and 3) dual messages.

Messages may be written or verbal. Regardless of the type, those which consistently deviate from established grammatical rules decrease the effectiveness of the message. Concise messages, whether written or verbal, are more likely to be heard and remembered than are long elaborate messages.

The type of messages sent directly affect the amount of trust and confidence that exists between departments and levels of employees. If the results obtained from analyzing the assessment data indicate problems in message clarity, the nurse administrator has a basis for implementing staff development in the area of written memos and messages as well as verbal feedback techniques.

Questions related to message clarity should ask nurses for their opinions about the clarity of the written messages received from nursing administration. It is also helpful to know precisely why the messages were unclear.

SPAN OF CONTROL

Span of control refers to the number of people for whom a supervisor is directly responsible.[22] Small spans of control occur when a supervisor has a few individuals for whom she or he is responsible. In these situations, there is more time and more opportunities for interpersonal communication to occur because the supervisor has only a few people with whom it is necessary to interact on a regular basis. Small spans of control are expensive and often have many levels of decision making.

Large spans of control occur when one individual is responsible for many employees. In these situations, direct communication between superior and subordinate is usually at a minimum; there simply is not enough time or opportunity for multiple one-to-one communication. Subordinates in large spans of control often feel that they receive an inadequate amount of information and believe that they cannot be fairly evaluated due to the lack of adequate interaction with superiors.

There is no single span of control that is best in all situations; dysfunctional communication could result if either extreme is operant. Large spans of control are more likely to be successful when the majority of employees are professionals. Organizations employing professional nurses should consider moving in the direction of large spans of control that reflect the autonomy and professional nature of nursing practice. Assessment questions related to the span of control could address feelings of satisfaction with the type and frequency of communications between administration and staff nurses.

FLOW CONTROL AND COMMUNICATION LOAD

Flow control and communication load are intricately related. Flow control refers to the ability of managers to regulate the dissemination of a message to other employees. Communication load refers to the amount of information received by an individual within a specified period of time.[23]

Communication underload is a result of high flow control and occurs when information is inaccessible or highly controlled by administration. If needed knowledge is not provided, peak productivity and performance is impossible. When flow control is high, rumors occur within the organization and encourage the overuse of the informal communication system.

High flow control exists when an administrator has the power to make clear cut decisions about when and in what form a message will pass through his or her office.[24] There are occasions when it is necessary and appropriate for administration to control information. However, continued high flow control often contributes to dysfunctional organizational communication and feelings of distrust if employees believe that important information is being withheld. In popular terms, "information is power,"[25,26] and individuals with a high need for power may control dissemination of information to increase their power base.[27]

When flow control is too low, employees may be bombarded with large amounts of irrelevant information, and communication overload becomes a problem. Low flow control exists when the administrator wants employees to "know everything." When a person receives too many messages within a short period of time, adequate processing is difficult, and consequently much information is lost. Verbal messages may be forgotten or "never heard," inappropriate or incorrect responses may be given, or memos may be found a week later under a pile of other mail. Farace and associates[28] argue that any organization experiencing widespread communication overload among the members is probably exhibiting a high level of error.

Often, it is difficult for an administrator to determine whether or not employees would be interested in certain information. Color coding written messages sent to employees, such that each color represents a specific kind of message is useful. After this practice is operant for a period of time, it is easier to get feedback about the usefulness of sending out various types of information.

A thin line exists between low flow control/communication overload and high flow control/communication underload. Individual differences play an important part in this distinction and these perceptions need to be assessed. Existence of either extreme often results in employee dissatisfaction with the work environment.

The communication assessment should include questions about the rationale for and use of information control. Additional questions might address perceptions of organization members about the amount and appropriateness of the information they receive.

COMMUNICATOR EFFECTIVENESS

The communicator's ability to communicate effectively involves the skill of accurately encoding and decoding messages, seeking information and engaging in communication activities that have positive outcomes. Communicator effectiveness occurs when the outcome of a message can be accurately predicted and when recipients of messages feel satisfied with the communication. Positively perceived communication activities can influence nurses' attitudes toward their work environment and, to a somewhat lesser degree, their performance on the job.[29]

Communicator effectiveness is directly related to the skill of actively listening to another's verbal communications. Good listeners contribute to organizational performance by encouraging others to express their views and by communicating a sense of concern for each employee. Effective listening skills are the links that enable employees of diverse backgrounds and interests to work together in building a successful organization.[30]

McGregor[31] contends that communicator effectiveness has two positive outcomes: it facilitates high production and it fosters a greater personal commitment to the organization. Interpersonal competence is believed to be the best predictor of organizational success.[32]

Assessing communicator effectiveness may be difficult because people are often perceived differently than they perceive themselves. Also, personalities of the communicators influence perceptions. Nevertheless, questions can be asked about feelings of satisfaction with interpersonal communications between peers, between staff nurses and members of other departments and between staff nurses and administrators.

The six areas of organizational communication discussed in this article do not include all dimensions of communication interactions within an organization. They do, however, contain most of the critical indicators of communication problems and provide some direction for nurse administrators who wish to conduct a communication assessment.

Since a large percentage of all activities taking place in organizations are in the form of communication events, effective communication bears a strong relationship to the organization's ability to transform the resources it acquires into the outcomes it desires.[33] These outcomes could be increased retention of experienced nurses and high quality cost-effective care provided to patients.

REFERENCES

1. Weisman CS, Alexander CS, Chase GA. Determinants of hospital staff nurse turnover. Med Care 1981;19(4): 431–443.
2. Haw MA, Claus EG, Durbin-Lafferty E, Iversen S. Improving nursing morale in a climate of cost containment. Part I. organzational assessment. J Nurs Adm 1984; 14(10):8–15.
3. Sanger E, Richardson J, Larson E. What satisfies nurses enough to keep them? Nurs Mgmt 1985;16(9): 43–46.
4. Pincus JD. Communication: Key contributor to effectiveness — The research. J Nurs Adm 1986;16(9):19–25.
5. Buccheri RC. Nursing supervision: A new look at an old role. Nurs Adm Q 1986;11(I):11–25.
6. Prescott PA and Bowen SA. Controlling nursing turnover. Nurs Mgmt 1987;18(6):60–66.
7. Wolf GA. Communication: key contributor to effectiveness — a nurse executive responds. J Nurs Adm 1986;16(9):26–28.
8. Pincus, 19–25.
9. D'Aprix R. Organizational communication. Hospital Forum 1983;26(3):24–34.
10. Edwards BJ, Brilhart JK. Communication in nursing practice. St. Louis: C.V. Mosby, 1981.
11. Wolf, 26–28.
12. Cushman DP. The rules perspective as a theoretical basis for the study of human communication. Communication Quarterly 1977;25(1):30–45.
13. Donohue WA, Cushman DP, Nofsinger RE Jr. Creating and confronting social order: A comparison of rules perspectives. The Western Journal of Speech Communication 1980;44(1):30–45.
14. Shimanoff SB. Communication rules: Theory and research. Beverly Hills, CA: Sage Publications, 1980.
15. Cushman DP, Whiting GC. An approach to communication theory: Toward a consensus on rules. Journal of Communications 1972;22(9):217–238.
16. Shimanoff, 1980.
17. Cushman and Whiting, 217–238.
18. Farace RV, Taylor JA, Stewart JP. Criteria for evaluation of organizational communication effectiveness: Review and synthesis. In: Communication yearbook II. New Brunswick, NJ: International Communication Association, 1979;271–292.
19. Goldhaber GM. Organizational communication, 2nd Ed. Dubuque, Iowa: Wm. C. Brown, 1981.
20. Wiio O. Auditing communication in organizations: A standard survey — the LTT communication audit. Paper presented at a meeting of the International Communications Association, 1974.
21. Adams R, Munn HE. Communication: Say what you mean. Hospital Topics, 1983;61(3):18–21.
22. Sullivan EJ, Decker PJ. Effective management in nursing, 2nd Ed. NY: Addison-Wesley, 1988.
23. Farace, 271–292.
24. Farace, 271–292.
25. Farace, 271–292.
26. Kanter RM. Men and women of the corporation. NY: Basic Books, 1977.
27. Kantor, 1977.
28. Farace, 271–292.
29. Pincus, 19–25.
30. Brownell J. Listening: The toughest management skill. The Cornell Hotel and Restaurants Administration Quarterly 1987;27(4):65–71.
31. McGregor D. The human side of enterprise. NY: McGraw-Hill, 1960.
32. Argyis C. Interpersonal competence and organizational effectiveness. Homewood, IL: Irwin-Dorsey, 1962.
33. Farace, 271–292.

CHAPTER **15**

Power and Politics for the Nurse Executive

Barbara J. Stevens, RN, PhD, FAAN

The terms *power* and *politics* are used together so frequently in nursing circles that it is difficult to separate them. It may be useful, however, to make that intellectual differentiation. Plato equated power with knowledge, while Aristotle saw power as the ability to produce change. The early Romans equated power with public control, coming close to our present association of power and politics. For practical purposes, we can view power as the *capacity* to modify the conduct of others in a desired manner, while avoiding having one's own conduct modified in undesired ways by others. In this definition, the focus is that of power as a state of being, as an end-in-itself, separate from the act of exercising that capacity.

Politics, on the other hand, is viewed as a process rather than as a capacity or end-in-itself. Politics is the *act* of influencing the decision of others; it is the process of exercising control over the course of events. Politics, then, is a means-to-an-end. Clearly, effective use of process (politics) is one source of power. Conversely, the state of holding power provides one with certain resources that make for effective politicking. A reciprocal relationship exists between power and politics: the state of power enhances the resources available for political

process, and effective politics enhances the amount of power held.

POWER

It is common to define power as interactional control of another. In this conception of it, A's power over B rests in B's dependency on him. A may control B's access to a skill he desires (e.g., a nursing procedure) or to other goals (e.g., job raises). The strength of A's power depends on availability to B of other potential sources for satisfaction of his desire. Additionally, A's power depends on the cost to A of exercising the power. Many head nurses, for example, retain a deficient employee rather than pay for the cost of the time required to document poor performance.

Note that this definition of power focuses on the psychological or sociological interaction of dyads. This is a common perspective on power but one that calls for interpretation if applied to an organizational or political context. Sources of power frequently are approached from a similar psychological/sociological perspective.

Sources of Power

Perhaps the most commonly cited reference on power is the French and Raven work that categorizes power as: referent-, expertise-, position-, reward-, or

Reprinted from *Nursing and Health Care,* Vol. 1, No. 4, with permission of the National League for Nursing © 1980.

coercion-oriented [1]. The categorization assumes a psychological/sociological approach to understanding power. This scheme differentiates power on the basis of its source. While these categories are meaningful, they may not be of major significance to the nurse executive who is acting from a positional as well as psychological power base.

In looking at the power sources of the nurse executive, one might propose a list of options that relate to the organization executive. The nurse executive may derive power from the following:

1. Knowledge (expert power)
   a. of nursing technology and/or trends, e.g., of vanguard nursing practices
   b. of managerial technology, i.e., techniques or knowing how to make things happen in an organization
2. Network relations and linkages
   a. informal channels within or outside of the institution, e.g., knowing the "right people" to contact for getting results
   b. public relations expertise and ability to use mass media effectively
   c. positional access to diverse communications networks
3. Resource control
   a. power to distribute or withhold organizational resources
   b. knowledge of resources that fit needs or knowledge of how to get access to appropriate resources
4. Decision-making or problem-solving ability
   a. right to determine what the problem is
   b. ability to make effective decisions in problematic situations
   c. positional authority to dictate one's decisions
5. Vision and statesmanship in one's craft
   a. ability to identify professional goals and to challenge others to pursue them
   b. ability to communicate vanguard goals and practices effectively.

These sources of power combine personal, professional, and organizational dimensions. Mintzberg offers a similar list of power skills. These power skills may be viewed as political processes that serve as sources of power accumulation. Mintzberg identifies skills of:

1. Establishing and maintaining a network of peer contacts
2. Leadership
3. Conflict resolution
4. Information processing
5. Defining and solving problems in ambiguous situations
6. Resource allocation
7. Entrepreneurial enterprise
8. Introspection [2]

Claus and Bailey have a similar list, including executive abilities to:

1. Obtain and share accurate information
2. Use high level expertise
3. Use positional authority
4. Promote subordinate identification
5. Use rewards and punishments
6. Manipulate behavior
7. Control the work environment [3]

These sources, unlike many, look at power from an institutional perspective, from the viewpoint of the manager in the institution. Clearly, a position of authority enhances one's opportunity to accumulate power. Indeed, the nurse executive has two distinct sources of power: the functional and the formal. Functional power relates to those elements of leadership based on charisma, ability to guide and direct subordinates, accurate assessment and interpretation of situations within the nursing division and/or institution. These functional leadership skills are highly individual, but most nurse executives achieve top management positions by virtue of their functional skills.

Formal sources of power include elements built into the job, such as the reporting relationships of the nurse manager, the membership on critical organization committees granted to the role incumbent, the rewards and status accorded the nurse executive position in a particular organization. Formal power rests in the structure of the position rather than in the unique abilities of the incumbent. There are great individual differences in how various nurse executives use these two sources of power [4]. For any nurse executive seeking to enhance her power in the organization, it is important to selectively use and manipulate the power potential vested in these formal and functional sources.

The Nurse Executive in Professional Activity

Typically the nurse executive is interested in the power potential that exists in professional nursing activities as well as the power she exercises in her employment setting. She may be interested in the use of power to advance professional nursing, nursing education, or other internal nursing discipline interests. She also may be interested in the activities by which organized nurse professionals try to influence the political process in local, state, and federal levels.

Consideration of power in these settings shifts from that of a situation with control by a single individual (executive in her own job) to a situation where shared power exists. Indeed, there is no power professionally or governmentally except through organized bodies who represent a significant constituency. Principles of power are more complex in these settings. Shared power calls for shared goals, agreements as to tactics, and shared effort. Principles that pertain to joint efforts at power will be discussed in detail later under consideration of political processes.

Nurse executives share professional and political power with other nurses who do not hold executive positions. The support base broadens to include others from the clinical domain and from educational settings. Often these professional and political activities are the developing grounds for future nurse executives.

Sources of a Profession's Power

When a profession seeks power, it finds several prerequisites that must be attained before power is vested in the group. Attaining the prerequisites depends on agreement among the professional membership. First, the profession must have a clear *identity*, both among its own people and among others who are sought as political advocates, allies, or publics. The profession must stand for something that is clear, unambiguous, and understood. Sometimes the public understanding of that identity is necessarily oversimplified, but that identity must be someway conveyed.

The profession seeking power also must exhibit *unity* — on its definition of self, on its goals, and on its methods for achieving goals. The inability of nursing to reach unity on these elements accounts for much of its present political ineffectiveness. *Utility* is the next prerequisite to political power: a profession must be able to assert the usefulness of its goals to society — or at least to the elements of society from which it seeks support. *Visibility* is the last prerequisite; a profession must be recognized in the channels of power. And those channels are not always the obvious ones. Often one may gain access to such inner circles of power by learning the real power structures and their entry points. Public visibility also is necessary in assuring that a profession will advance politically. A profession without a strong constituency will not claim the attention of the politically astute for long.

Politics is addressed as a means, and power is seen as an end-in-itself. Nevertheless, it is important to note that power is, or should be, an instrumental end, i.e., an end achieved for what it may bring. Power is an instrument for the attainment of other goals. If a profession has not defined those goals, it has little need for power. In nursing, unfortunately, our goals still are diffuse and even contradictory. No specific goal content for the nursing profession is addressed here but, it is evident that nursing must find a way to reach agreement on goals if it is to amass political power. To date, the profession has not succeeded in this respect. Most nursing groups act independently, and there is no forum for joint decision-making. If each professional body (and every informal group of nurses) claims a different agenda, there is little chance to join forces, producing a united front on any issue. Indeed, it is well known that nurses make up the largest number of health care workers, yet no nursing group constitutes a meaningful quorum in relation to those numbers.

The nurse executive's goals for organizational and professional power may differ, but she usually is visible in both domains. This is true because those nurses in leadership positions in organizations tend to hold leadership positions in the profession simultaneously. While a professional body often seeks democratic representation, it is not surprising that leadership falls on those who have honed their leadership skills in their daily job performance.

POLITICS

Politics involves influencing powerful individuals or groups to act as one wishes they would. Politics are practiced within one's work setting, within the profession, and within government at various levels. Sometimes nurses have a psychological problem with the connotation of politics. Politics is seen as manipulative and therefore not quite respectable. It is important to recognize that political influence is the basis for our democratic form of government. Groups who hesitate to develop political skills may be virtuous to the extreme, but they never will influence society to accept their goals, no matter how valuable those goals may be.

Politics is the pragmatic art of producing agreement on what is to be done. In spite of the fact that political groups have diverse goals, agreement (and politics) works for several reasons. First, though perhaps least common, different parties may be brought to see the innate value of a given goal. Alternately, parties may be brought to see specific values that the goal achievement will bring to their respective groups. Additionally, different parties may agree on a single set of acts because those acts will achieve several goals, thus satisfying different ends-in-view. Further, some parties will trade off interests, supporting some goals to which they are basically indifferent to win support of others (coalitions) in goal achievement where their own interest is high.

Politics clearly involves the possible, not the ideal. Indeed, nursing has lost many a crucial political battle because some part of its constituency has held out for an even loftier goal, one that may not have a chance in the political arena. Sadly, many nurses are not able to understand the nature of political action. Politics is the art of the possible, not of the best. To hold out for the ideal often sacrifices an improvement in the real. Compromise is the name of the political game.

This is how groups with divergent interests arrive at agreements for action. Nurses who understand the political process often are frustrated when they must fight both those who oppose a generally recognized improvement for reactionary reasons and those who oppose it because it offers less than the ideal.

Political Strategies

Political strategies, then, include trade-offs, compromise, negotiation (where one gives up a lesser value to achieve a greater one), coalition (joining with others holding corresponding positions on an issue), and cultivation of the power players in the situation. That cultivation must take into account the goals of those cultivated as well as the goals of the group that seek to be influential. The author knows of one instance where a licensed practical nurse constituency had a lobbyist who periodically dropped off home-baked bread at the desks of influential legislators. Some of the registered nurse peer lobbyists viewed this act as an old-fashioned display of feminist subordinancy as well as viewing the act as unprofessional. One should not be surprised to hear that at the first disagreement between LPNs and RNs on a proposed law, the LPNs carried the day. This is not to say that lobbyists should all race out and bake bread, but that one must consider the nature of the persons one seeks to influence as well as the justice of one's political positions.

Political strategies and tactics are important for the nurse executive in her own institution as well as in professional and governmental actions. While the same principles apply in all settings, the nurse executive must be particularly cautious in use of her individual power. In her organization, the executive must determine when and when not to use the power of her position (or personality). For a given situation, she must determine if exercise of her power will achieve the desired results. It is futile to exercise power against overwhelming forces. Alternately, the nurse executive will not want to use overkill, bringing stronger forces of power to bear than are necessary. Force should never be used where influence will suffice, and influence should not be used if persuasion will win the case. The nurse executive learns to accurately assess her power resources, and she learns to assess the cost of power moves. In some situations, the cost may be creation of permanent enemies or destruction of open lines of communication. It would need to be a serious issue for a nurse executive to exercise her power in such a case, at such a price.

Before making any power move the nurse executive asks the following questions:

1. What is the real issue? Have I discriminated the issue from surrounding issues and methods of approach?
2. Who is involved? Who will be proponents? Opponents? Who will be indifferent?
3. What are my resources of power? Are they superior to the resources of the opposition?
4. What are the consequences if I win? Lose? Take this stand at this time?

Advice to Power Seekers

If the nurse executive is trying to extend her power, what advice may be given? The following cautions may help:

1. Pay the entry fee. Often hard committee work, long time investment in a job, or other strenuous effort is required in the accumulation of power. Don't expect power to be achieved by slick and quick maneuvers.
2. Have a voice. One must have access to communication channels to achieve power. Power demands interaction. Interaction requires communication. Communication with people involves extensive network building; communication through media involves developing the skills of writing and speaking.
3. Have something to say. Power cannot be abstracted from its context. Power is over something or someone in the interest of something or someone. Hard work and building of communications channels only have meaning if one has something of importance to convey.
4. Look upward and outward, not just downward. A nurse executive who focuses exclusively on the nursing department beneath her misses opportunities within top management of her

institution. Similarly, a nurse executive who fails to enter professional channels fails to link her institution with the rest of the nursing world.
5. Act like a powerful person. Know who's who. Act assertively. Do favors for other powerful persons, and start accumulating those psychological debts to be paid when you need them.

For the nurse executive seeking power in her employing institution, it is especially important that she interact with other top management outside of the nursing division. She must learn to speak their management language; she must translate the concerns of her nursing division into language that they can understand. The nurse executive also must be sensitive to attempts to coopt her departments, and she must not use cooperation in situations that call for managerial competitiveness. She must learn to build appropriate allies and coalitions.

The nurse executive must be sensitive to connotations of power. She should be aware that titles, environment, personal appearance, and behaviors all contribute to power acquisition. Some nurse executives, for example, prefer soft terms for their nurse managers such as patient care coordinator, nursing facilitator. Terms like these indicate to other managers positions with staff rather than line responsibility. The executive who elects such modern titles over the old-fashioned, hard-line titles of supervisor, assistant director, or head nurse, may be paying an unexpected price in the overall power of her division.

Some nurse executives overlook the effect on others of their environment. If her office lacks carpeting, for example, it may tell of her position in the pecking order. Or positioning of the nurse executive in a building far removed from the organization president may be an indication that she is literally and figuratively out of the action. Personal appearance also speaks to power. If the nurse executive is the only major administrator in a uniform, she may be giving a message that she is more in tune with labor than with management.

These indirect indices of power may be equally as important as those formal indices such as membership on major executive committees. Similarly, inclusion in the informal activities of the power group marks an important achievement for the nurse executive. This may be even more difficult if she is the only female executive and most informal events are viewed as masculine activities by her boss.

Power and politics are new concerns for many nurse executives. To acquire skills in these domains, as with any skill building, requires practice and diligence. Nurse executives have much to learn, but they also have much to gain. Indeed, nursing as a profession has much to learn if it wishes to become politically effective. The challenge is an exciting one, however, and it will not be the first or last new domain that nursing has conquered.

REFERENCES

1. French, J.R.P., Jr. and Raven, B., The Bases of Social Power, in Cartwright, D. (ed.) *Studies in Social Power,* Ann Arbor: University of Michigan, 1959, pp. 150–167.
2. Mintzberg, H., *The Nature of Managerial Work,* New York: Harper & Row, Publishers, 1973.
3. Claus, K.E. and Bailey, J.T., *Power and Influence in Health Care,* St. Louis: C.V. Mosby Company, 1977.
4. *Ibid.,* pp. 11–12..

BIBLIOGRAPHY

Banfield, E.C., *Political Influence,* Glencoe, Illinois: Free Press, 1961.

Banfield, E.C. and Wilson, J.Q., *City Politics,* Cambridge, Mass.: MIT and Harvard University Press, 1963.

Bell, D.V., *Power, Influence, and Authority,* New York: Oxford University Press, 1975.

Bernal, H., Power and Interorganizational Health Care Projects, *Nursing Outlook,* 24(7):418, 1976.

Boyarski, B. and Boyarsky, N., *Backroom Politics,* New York: Hawthorne, 1974.

Cantril, H., *Human Nature and Political Systems,* New Brunswick, New Jersey: Rutgers University Press, 1961.

Claus, K.E. and Bailey, J.T., *Power and Influence in Health Care,* St. Louis: C.V. Mosby Company, 1977.

Cotton, C.C., Measurement of Power-Balancing Styles and Some of Their Correlates, *American Science Quarterly,* 21(2):307, 1976.

Courtade, S., The Role of the Head Nurse: Power and Practice, *Supervisor Nurse,* 9(12):16, 1978.

Davies, J.C., *Human Nature in Politics; the Dynamics of Political Behavior,* New York: John Wiley, 1963.

Diers, D., A Different Kind of Energy — Nurse-Power, *Nursing Outlook,* 26(1):51, 1978.

Easton, D., *A Framework for Political Analysis,* Englewood Cliffs, New Jersey: Prentice-Hall, 1965.

Eulau, H., *The Behavioral Persuasion in Politics,* New York: Random House, 1963.

Fenn, D.H., Jr., Finding Where the Power Lies in Government, *Harvard Business Review,* 57(5):144, 1979.

Froman, L.A., Jr., *The Congressional Process: Strategies, Rules and Procedures,* Boston: Little, Brown & Company, 1967.

Gruberg, M., *Women in American Politics,* Oshkosh, Wisc.: Academic Press, 1968.

Hacker, A., *The Study of Politics: The Western Tradition and American Origins,* New York: McGraw Hill, 1963.

Hall, D.R., *Cooperative Lobbying — The Power of Pressure,* Tucson: University of Arizona Press, 1969.

Hart, H.H.L., *Strategy, 2nd Ed.,* New York: Praeger Publishers, 1967.

Hott, J.R., Nursing and Politics: The Struggles Inside Nursing's Body Politic, *Nursing Forum,* 15(4):325, 1976.

Jaquette, J.S. (ed.), *Women in Politics,* New York: Wiley, 1974.

Kalisch, B.J., The Promise of Power, *Nursing Outlook,* 26(1):42, 1978.

Kalisch, P.A. and Kalisch, B.J., The What, Why, and How of the Political Dynamics of Nursing, in Marriner, A. (ed.) *Current Perspectives in Nursing Management,* St. Louis: C.V. Mosby, 1979.

Kanter, R.M., Power Failure in Management Circuits, *Harvard Business Review,* 57(4):65, 1979.

Kotter, J.P., *Power in Management: How to Understand, Acquire, and Use It,* New York: Amacom, 1979.

Lawrence, J.C., Confronting Nurses' Political Apathy, *Nursing Forum,* 15(4):363, 1976.

Lippitt, G.J., Power Begins With You, *Assuring a Goal Directed Future for Nursing,* New York: National League for Nursing, 1980.

Longest, B.B., Jr., Institutional Politics, *Journal of Nursing Administration,* 5(3):38, 1975.

McClelland, D.C. and Burnham, D.H., Power is the Great Motivator, *Harvard Business Review,* 54(2):100, 1976.

McFarland, D.E. and Shiflett, N., *Power in Nursing,* Wakefield, Mass.: Nursing Resources, 1979.

McMurry, R.N., Power and the Ambitious Executive, *Harvard Business Review,* 51(6):140, 1973.

Mintzberg, H., *The Nature of Managerial Work,* New York: Harper & Row, 1973.

Mintzberg, H., Strategy-Making in Three Modes, *California Management Review,* 16(2):44, 1973.

Mullane, M.K., Nursing Care and the Political Arena, *Nursing Outlook,* 23(11):699, 1975.

Peterson, G.G., Power: A Perspective for the Nurse Administrator, *Journal of Nursing Administration,* 9(7):7, 1979.

Powell, D.J., Nursing Politics: The Struggles Outside Nursing's Body Politic, *Nursing Forum,* 15(4):341, 1976.

Riker, W.H., *The Theory of Political Coalitions,* New Haven, Conn.: Yale University Press, 1962.

Shiflett, N. and McFarland, D.E., Power and the Nursing Administrator, *Journal of Nursing Administration,* 8(3):19, 1978.

Stevens, B.J. , Development and Use of Power in Nursing, *Assuring a Goal Directed Future for Nursing,* New York: National League for Nursing, 1980.

CHAPTER **16**

Using Structural Power Sources to Increase Influence

Charlotte B. Hoelzel, RN, MS

Power is often considered an unattractive human characteristic, associated with aggression and coercion.[1-3] Some nursing administrators feel that in the caring and supporting world of nursing, power is an alien concept. Others assert, however, that power is an essential component of effective managerial behavior.[2] Access to and willingness to use power increases an administrator's ability to acquire the resources needed to improve patient care.[4] This idea is not new; Peterson[5] says if the nursing administrator does not seek and use power effectively "the nursing service, at best, maintains the status quo, and the sphere of influence of the nurse administrator is diminished." Employees working with bosses who have influence experience an increase in pride and self-esteem.[2]

Nurses prefer to work with supervisors who can get things done, who have influence both upward and outward. Also, employees with an influential supervisor usually have a more positive outlook. Nursing administrators who understand and use power tend to improve their effectiveness within the nursing department and the hospital organization. The many definitions of power usually center around an individual's ability to influence others or the behavior of others.[5-10] Power is also defined in terms

of its potential to achieve goals.[1-4,11-14] This more comprehensive view of power brings together the concept of influence with achievement of organizational goals.

Most of the nursing literature on power focuses on personal power[5-10] and discusses ways nursing administrators can behave so that they can attain more power. Along with personal strategies for achieving power, administrators must develop strategies to use structural sources of power. To do this, nursing administrators must understand structural sources of power and ways to tap these sources. In the end, administrators must be able to integrate the use of behavioral measures to obtain power with organizational sources of power.

There are three main structural sources of power: 1) centrality—participation in the major function of the organization and interconnections with all or most aspects of the system; 2) control of uncertainty—influencing organizational goal attainment through coping with the organization's uncertain environment; and 3) control over resources—access to and control of manpower, information and other critical resources of the organization.[12,13,15] Using the organizing framework of Smith and Grenier,[13] these three sources of power are examined in light of the structural factors that define them and their availability to the nursing administrator.

Reprinted from *The Journal of Nursing Administration*, Vol. 19, No. 11, with permission of J. B. Lippincott Company © 1989.

CENTRALITY

Centrality is the degree to which activities are connected within a system.[15] A subunit is seen as central if the activities performed are linked with the other activities of the organization (workflow pervasiveness) and if the activities performed by that subunit are critical to the workflow of the organization (workflow immediacy).[15] It is hypothesized that the higher the pervasiveness and immediacy of the workflows of a subunit, the greater the subunit's power within the organization.[15]

Nursing certainly has a high degree of centrality within the hospital organization. As Ashley[16] has stated, "without the pooled energies of individual nurses, health care facilities across the nation would be forced to shut down or offer a far different kind of service than they do at present." The workflow pervasiveness of the nursing department is evident when examined in light of the services offered by a hospital—patient care. Patients are admitted to the hospital nursing department by the admitting department. The physician sees the patient on the nursing unit and leaves treatment orders with the nursing staff of that unit. The dietary, X-ray and laboratory departments receive treatment orders through communication from the nursing staff. The purchasing department receives requests from the nursing units for needed patient supplies. The business office compiles patient charges from information documented by the nursing personnel. If members of the nursing department ceased to function, the effect would be immediately evident and would substantially impede the workflow of the organization.

Chain of Command

Several structural factors determine centrality. Nursing administrators with knowledge of these factors may be able to use them when developing strategies to increase the influence of the nursing department and or their position. The first factor is "chain of command." A department head with direct access and responsibility to the top manager has more power than the department head whose communications and recommendations to top management filter through others. The higher one is in the chain of command, the greater one's chances of being involved in critical activities and decisions of the organization. To have more influence on hospital operations, it is imperative for the nursing administrator to have direct access to the chief executive officer in order to clearly communicate the values, goals and objectives of nursing and the nursing department. To have an impact on the hospital's long range strategic planning, the nursing administrator must have direct dialogue with the Board of Trustees.

In total hospital operations, the degree of influence of the nursing administrator depends upon being included in the hospital strategic management decision process. A nursing administrator may have power in the nursing department but have minimal power in the hospital as a whole. Being a part of the decision making body of the hospital increases a department head's access to power. Nursing administrators involved in hospital-level decision making have greater prospects of initiating nursing goals such as primary nursing or budget allocations for parking expense reimbursement for nurses.[14]

Specialization

Specialization is the second structural variable determining centrality. Departments which participate directly in the production of the primary output of the organization are critical because their specialized activities generate a high degree of centrality.[17] Because nursing participates in all aspects of patient care, the nursing department is centrally linked with other hospital departments and is critical to the workflow of the hospital organization. If Hickson's hypothesis[15] that the greater the subunit's centrality, the greater its power is accepted, any decrease in centrality would lead to a decrease in power. When highly specialized positions are grouped together into a new department and removed from the authority and responsibility of their original department, the power and influence of the original department is diminished because of a decrease in the breadth and importance of the impact of its workflow within the organization. In the past, nursing personnel performed most of the activities within the hospital. With increased specialization, separate departments have been established which encompass responsibilities that, in the past, were part of nursing, ie, respiratory therapy or patient education. Nursing administrators cannot overlook the power consequences of specialization in relation to centrality when considering further specialization.

Separating Line and Staff

The last structural determinant of centrality is the separation of line and staff in organizations. Power is usually located in line positions where activities are carried out that are critical to the organization.[18] Supportive (staff) positions are usually not as powerful as line positions. Departments central to the workflow of the organization are more powerful than support departments. In the hospital organization, nursing departments and administrators usually have more power than that found in the business office or in purchasing. The latter are seen as necessary adjuncts to the task of the hospital, but not essential in the every day, every hour operating sense.

The unusual structural situation in hospitals is the addition of the medical staff who, even though not in line positions, have a great deal of power. Because of professional responsibility for directing the patients' medical care, physicians are able to give orders to those in work production positions. Physicians also control the supply of patients, which gives them economic power over hospital staff. Nursing administrators must develop strategies to deal with conflict resulting from these overlapping lines of authority.

Nursing may determine that a patient can be cared for just as well on a less expensive unit, eg, a Medical Step-down unit instead of a coronary care unit for a patient with chest pain but no documented M.I. after 24 hours. The physician may resist moving the patient. The conflict arising from different priorities can be aired in a forum established between nursing and the medical staff to discuss just such conflicts. The forum could be used to share such things as hospital cost information and quality assurance statistics concerning outcomes of patients at different levels of care. Discussions between these two groups which share the common goal of patient welfare will,

hopefully, lead to a better understanding between the groups and the negotiation of some win-win compromises.

CONTROL OF UNCERTAINTY

Not knowing with assurance what will occur in the future is a state all individuals and organizations experience. In organizations, the ability to correctly predict or deal with the future, may spell the success of one organization over another. The subunit of an organization that most effectively copes with the uncertainty in the organization has the most power within that organization, since "coping by a subunit reduces the impact of uncertainty on other activities in the organization."[15] Coping with uncertainties occurs in different ways. Correctly predicting the future is one method of coping; prevention of the unsure future and planning ways to respond to the uncertainty are other coping mechanisms.

The ability of the nursing department to cope with uncertainty has a great impact on the power of the nursing department and the nursing administrator. The nursing department which is able to more accurately forecast patient occupancy and needs, such as nursing care hours and supplies, provides a critical service to the hospital. Prevention of the unsure future by the nursing department may include assuring high quality of nursing care and communicating this to the community so that patients ask to come to that hospital. It might include building a reputation of fair employment and innovative nursing so that staff shortages do not occur. Coping with uncertainty through planned reaction could be illustrated by having a nursing part-time on-call staff to cope with an unusually high census or by making prior agreements with staff to use personal days or part days off to cope with an unusually low census. Uncertainty cannot be eliminated, but a department can cope more successfully if more "what ifs" are considered and planned for. Uncertainty within the environment must also be considered and plans made to successfully cope. For example, how will the nursing department react if the phone system becomes inoperative, or a snow storm prevents normal transportation? An ability to quickly react and use available personnel will positively affect the nursing department's power.

Formalization

Several structural factors affect the ability to cope with uncertainty. Understanding these factors enhances the nursing administrator's (and thereby the department's) ability to cope. The degree of formalization of the department affects flexibility and the ability to cope with uncertainty. A department with a high degree of formalization-written rules, policies, and specific work procedures-usually has a low degree of human flexibility. In many nursing departments, formalization is high, illustrated by a large policy and procedures manual. For any situation, there is usually a rule to dictate behavior. For instance, the ambulatory surgery department is open between 6 AM and 6 PM. The nurse manager may enforce these hours, because that is how the department was originally organized. Following predetermined rules and ignoring requests for longer or different hours may influence the surgeons to take their business elsewhere. The nurse who is able and willing to make an independent decision and change practice has more power than the nurse just following rules. A nursing department with a high degree of formalization has less flexibility to cope with uncertainty.

Task Routine

Task routinization is the second structural indicator that must be explored when looking at controlling uncertainty. Positions with repetitive task activities become more standardized and formalized.[19] If tasks are nonroutine and must be continually adjusted, those who make decisions concerning these tasks have control over the impact of uncertainty for others in the organization and thereby acquire power.[13] Patient care is nonroutine, but often through formalization and standardization is made routine. The nursing administrator may want to consider this when developing the position of the staff nurse and structuring continuing education for staff nurses. The degree of formalization and standardization must also be considered when structuring the nursing policy and procedure committee.

Lastly, nursing administrators should examine the implications of task routinization when assessing their own position. If the task is routine, does it belong in the administrator's role? Routine procedures such as compiling data from Quality Assurance studies can be performed by less skilled personnel. Inherent in administrative positions are uncertainties with which only innovative, creative leaders and managers can cope. If nursing administrators' time is taken up by routine tasks, they will not have time to devote to controlling uncertainties.

Environmental Complexity

The degree of environmental complexity is another indicator of uncertainty in an organization and therefore must be considered when examining sources of power.[13] A highly uncertain environment with a great deal of change demands that the organizational structure be flexible and adaptive. An organic management system, with less formal definitions of duties, authority, and techniques, is more able to effectively deal with environmental complexity.[19] A decentralized organizational structure is more compatible with an organic management system. In the organic system, interactions occur horizontally as well as vertically and it is not assumed that the head of an organization has infinite knowledge.[19] Sources of power become more diffuse in an organic, decentralized system. The health care system of the '80s and '90s is certainly a complex and uncertain environment. The future demands a decentralized organizational structure that can respond in new and innovative ways. The nursing administrator in such a decentralized system, aware of the availability of power and willing and able to acquire that which is available, will become more powerful than the administrator who is unaware of or unwilling to tap the sources of power.

CONTROL OF RESOURCES

The last structural source of power to be explored is the control of resources. Resources can be grouped into tangible and intangible resources. Tangible resources are raw materials (patients) and workers. Intangibles are the information and knowledge necessary to plan, organize and run the business and the necessary support of organizational goals by suppliers and workers. Organizational subunits that control these critical resources have access to this structural source of power. Subunits that contribute more critical resources to the organization have more power over the organization in reaching its goals than subunits that contribute few or less critical resources.[12] In a hospital, patients are a critical resource supplied by physicians. A physician who admits 20% of the hospital's patients has more available power than a physician who admits only 2% of the patients.

Nurses, on the other hand, are the resources needed to care for patients the physician admits. Nurses are the largest group of personnel in the hospital.[20] As Bowman and Culpeper[21] say, "Nursing's greatest resource is people. For too long nurses have underestimated the power they have in being the largest group of health professionals in the nation." Not only does nursing control human resources, nurses also have access to the greatest amount of information about the patient. The nurse is with the patient 24 hours a day and therefore has information not available to the physician from any other source. The power of nursing has been recognized at the patient care level but not at the organizational level of strategic and financial planning.[7] The nursing administrator interested in increasing access to and control of critical resources and, thereby, power, must be knowledgeable in structural determinants of critical resources.

Chain of Command

The chain of command is the first structural determinant to analyze when reviewing control of resources. A position high in the chain of command has access to more resources because of the number of employees and their related resources which are under the authority of the position. Access to resources, information, and support necessary to carry out a program increase the probability of acquiring power.[18] Subordinates and peers can provide information not available through formal communication lines. Gathering and compiling information from different levels and departments of the organization gives the nursing administrator a view of the organization as a whole. The higher the position in the chain of command, the better the opportunity to understand and respond to the total picture of the organization. Subordinates can be developed to relieve some of the administrator's duties and to provide a larger voice to promote the philosophy of the nursing department. Support from peers and important figures in the organization is also necessary. Supportive physicians and hospital executives can provide approval, prestige, and backing for objectives and goals of the nursing department. These supportive sponsors can also function as a resource for upward mobility for the nursing administrator. The nursing administrator with subordinate, peer, and sponsor support has access to considerable power sources.

Span of Control

Span of control is the second structural indicator of resource control. The larger the span of control, the greater the potential to develop a power base of subordinates and peers. Nursing administrators must relate effectively with the nursing staff both individually and as a group if they are going to successfully fill their administrative position. Information available to the staff nurse from patients, physicians, and visitors may be very helpful to the nursing administrator. The collective support of the nursing staff provides powerful backing for the nursing administrator. However, this collective action can also be a negative force, if administrators are viewed as uncaring bosses who don't know or care about what is really going on. Nursing administrators need to identify with those they represent, keep communication lines open, and cultivate a supportive power base among the nursing staff. When the common purpose between the nursing administrator and the nursing staff is lost, the administrator suffers from a kind of powerlessness.[18] A common reaction to powerlessness is to increase control and decrease the power available to staff. In the long run, the administrator and staff lose in this situation. Support and backing by a large group of subordinates increases the power advantage of the nursing administrator.

Formalization

The last structural indicator of access to resources is formalization. Formalization—written rules and regulations—can either facilitate or hinder access to resources. Rules that limit the availability and use of resources to an administrator necessarily decrease the power of that administrator. Relying on written rules to bring about action may be perceived by others as powerlessness[22]—that is, the administrator who does not have the personal or positional influence to bring about action must fall back on a rule or regulation for power. The nursing administrator needs to share information with staff, delegate responsibility downward and be more flexible about organizational rules, to ensure that formalization does not hinder access to resources.

To succeed in the hospital organization, the nursing administrator must understand the nature of the organization. To grasp the nature of the organization, its structure must be analyzed and it must be determined how the structure delimits power and the ability to meet organizational goals. To succeed, nursing administrators must first understand power and willingly "acquire and use it, like, it, and most of all admit they like it."[2] Applying structural and behavioral sources of power, the nursing administrator can then act rather than react, proceed rather than retreat, direct rather than be directed.

REFERENCES

1. Willey EL. Acquiring and using power effectively. Journal of Continuing Education 1987;18(1):25–28.
2. Booth RZ. Power: A negative or positive force in relationships? Nursing Administration Quarterly 1983;7(4):10–20.
3. Gorman S, Clark N. Power and effective nursing practice. Nurs Outlook 1986;34(3):129–134.
4. Carter MA. The self-serving goals of professional nursing. J Prof Nurs 1988;4(3):149.
5. Peterson GG. Power, a perspective for the nurse administrator. J Nurs Admin 1979;9(7):7–10.
6. Curtin LL. Watch your language. Nursing Management 1987;18(8):9–10.
7. Harrison JK, Roth PA. Empowering nursing in multihospital systems. Nursing Economics 1987;5(2):70–76.
8. Courtemanche JB. Powernomics: A concept every nurse should know! Nursing Management 1986;17(7):39–41.
9. Singleton EK, Nail FC. Developing relationships with the board of directors. J Nurs Admin 1986;16(1):37–42.
10. Lamar EK. Communicating personal power through nonverbal behavior. J Nurs Admin 1985;15(1):41–44.
11. Johnson JA, Bergmann CL. Nurse managers at the broker's table? J Nurs Admin 1988;18(6):18–21.
12. Salancik GR, Pfeffer J. Who gets power—and how they hold onto it: A strategic contingency model of power. Organizational Dynamics 1977;5(Winter):3–21.
13. Smith HL, Grenier M. Sources of organizational power for women: Overcoming structural obstacles. Sex Roles 1982;8(7):733–746.
14. Cavanaugh DE. Gamesmanship: The art of strategizing. J Nurs Admin 1985;15(4):38–41.
15. Hickson DJ, Hinings CR, Lee CA, et al. A strategic contingencies' theory of intraorganizational power. Administrative Science Quarterly 1971;16(2):216–227.
16. Ashley JA. This I believe about power in nursing. Nurs Outlook 1973;21(10):637–641.
17. Perrow C. Departmental Power and Perspective in Industrial Firms. In Zald M (ed). Power in Organizations. Nashville, TN: Vanderbilt University Press, 1970.
18. Kanter RM. Power failure in management circuits. Harvard Business Review 1979;57(4):65–75.
19. Jackson JH, Morgan CP. Organizational theory: A macro perspective for management. Englewood Cliffs NJ: Prentice-Hall, 1982.
20. Maas ML. A model of organizational power: Analysis and significance to nursing. Res Nurs Health 1988;11(3):153–163.
21. Bowman RA, Culpepper RG. Power: Rx for change. Am J Nurs 1975;74(6):1053–1056.
22. Larsen J. Nurse power for the 1980s. Nursing Administration Quarterly 1982;6(4):74–82.

CHAPTER 17

Language, Leadership, and Power

Beverly Henry, RN, PhD, FAAN
Helen LeClair, RN, BSN

The administrative environment is a highly verbal one. It is a milieu in which people use language to interpret information based on what they see, hear, and do.[1]

Powerful executives are as fluent with the technical language of management systems as they are with the aesthetic verse of poetry. Judging from Peters and Waterman's research, in America's best run organizations, the language people use is different: it is riveting. Words rich in meaning engender excitement, special languages communicate information and a sense of fun, and metaphors give meaning to work.[2]

Effective leadership involves renewing the languages used in organizations. As environments change, vocabularies evolve that describe new ways of doing things. Administrative effectiveness may well be contingent on being in the vanguard of change — seeing, labeling, talking about new phenomena, and establishing shared understanding that strengthens commitment. Effectiveness may be based, too, on the ability to help groups build special vocabularies defining them as unique and on finding a language that cuts across the entire organization.

From our observation and study of nurse administrators, we think attention in nursing to the use and subtleties of language is an essential endeavor. Educational programs that emphasize development of

Reprinted from *The Journal of Nursing Administration*, Vol. 17, No. 1, with permission of J. B. Lippincott Company © 1987.

strong linguistic skills, sensitivity to the values implicit in varying lexicons, and appreciation of the subtlety of language in all its verbal and written forms are needed in higher and continuing education to enhance nurse executives' performance.

Blair states,

> The language of nursing and nursing knowledge and skills are no longer sufficient to interpret the goals, scope and standards of nursing in the administrative, economic and political arenas. . . . Nurse administrators along with administrators from other health care disciplines must learn to speak a common administrative language. . . .[3]

SIGNIFICANCE OF LANGUAGE

Everyday life is as it is because of the language we share with other people. We speak as we think; language makes our experiences real to others and to ourselves.[4] Without words, there are no concepts or clear thoughts.[5]

Language is comprised of written and vocal signs that convey ideas, emotions, and experiences. However inaccurate our words may sometimes be, language is the most highly developed form of symbolism providing instruments to accomplish work, methods to express feelings, and directives to influence events.[6]

English, with its huge vocabulary (approximately 750,000 words), enables us to convey ideas in an unusually wide range of logical, sophisticated, yet subtle ways.[7] Through the vocabulary, grammar, and syntax of language, we converse scientifically in some situations and personally in others. To illustrate, as administrators we do not use words that describe managerial systems to give meaning to what we say when we talk with our children. We take into account the prevailing parlance for our organization in the one instance and our family members in the other, and match our language accordingly. We adjust words and their nuance to others depending on what it is we wish to know, asking probing technical questions in complex professional jargon in some circumstances and making casual comments in general everyday expression in others.

Recognizing that words have different meanings for different people, eminent organization researchers are paying increasing attention to language in an effort to understand leadership and power, key elements of effective administration. Communication is widely discussed in nursing. But language and the part it plays in leadership and life in organizations has been largely neglected. Our purpose therefore is to analyze the usefulness for nurse executives of research-based theories of language in organizations, particularly those developed by Pondy, Daft, Wiginton, and Pettigrew.

LEADERSHIP AND LANGUAGE

To enlarge understanding of leadership in organizations, Pondy suggests that we view organizations as language systems and conceive of leadership not merely as changing behavior (improving performance or increasing compliance, for example) but as giving meaning to the work people do.[8]

Visionary leaders with linguistic skill do more than alter behavior: by conveying shared values they help others transcend the mundane and find added meaning in their lives. Leaders gain power who themselves make sense of things, then put what they perceive into coherent language, using simple words and phrases meaningful to large numbers of people. Articulating what others feel about the work they do or hope to do, about the ideals they hold and the goals toward which they strive, amplifies understanding and meaning. Sentiments, feelings and aspirations, put into words, become accessible social facts that can be

acted on. As Pondy notes, Martin Luther King's power, "was not only that he had a dream but that he could describe it, that it became public and therefore accessible to millions of people."[9]

Viewing organizations as language systems, Pondy further hypothesizes that leaders are effective when the language they use overlaps with that of others. Sharing a common language enhances the likelihood of improved understanding and increases the probability that the behavior of another can be influenced. People who are most likely to have an impact on our actions are those who talk languages we understand.[10]

NATURAL AND SPECIAL LANGUAGES

Articulating new ideas and talking one's own language, as well as the language of others, is not a simple task particularly in large, complex, highly specialized health care systems. According to Daft and Wiginton (Figure 17-1), the array of languages that can be found in organizations range from the ambiguous language of art and poetry to the precise special language of computers and mathematics.[11]

Nurse executives work with a wide range of groups that often times have significantly different modes of expression. Consider for example, the differences in the words and meanings used by consumers, nurses, and finance officers. "Quality care" may mean timely and courteous service to clients; holistic assessment and family education to nurses; and appropriate per case cost and reimbursement to financial experts. Consumers in our organizations use general verbal expression; each of the many professional groups in hospitals uses its own special jargon; and highly skilled technologists rely heavily on the language of mathematics. In today's hospitals with their many specialized groups, each with its own vocabulary, executives who engender willing cooperation and build cohesive groups may well be the most highly skilled at speaking many special languages and at translating ideas captured in specialized, sometimes esoteric vocabularies into a common language that all organizational constituents can understand.

Understanding, speaking, and translating different languages may also contribute to commitment and the ease with which people are socialized into organizations. Socialization is the comprehensive and consistent induction of an individual into society or a sector of it. Primary socialization is the first induction we undergo in childhood; during this experience, we learn our natural "mother tongue." Secondary socializations are subsequent experiences whereby we are inducted into organizations. During these experiences, we learn additional, special purpose vocabularies.[12]

Secondary socialization into health care institutions for example, requires acquisition of special vocabularies for the specific, unique roles organization members will play. Consider for a moment, how inexperienced nurse managers learn new meanings for terms such as strategic priorities, patient management, and intensity measurement; and how newcomers to critical care learn the special purpose language of invasive monitoring and cardiac arrhythmias.

Orientation programs and internships are mechanisms for secondary socialization. Through these mechanisms, new information is internalized through new language. We learn a second language by building on our "mother tongue." Exposed for the first time to unfamiliar language, we consciously translate and integrate new words into our existing vocabulary to give the unaccustomed words meaning. As socialization proceeds, we increasingly forego translation and think in our newly acquired language.

Sensitivity on the part of nurse administrators and educators to the natural and special vocabularies of incoming personnel may well be an essential element of successful, satisfying orientation programs. A task for nurse administrators is finding ways to assess natural and special languages used by incoming personnel and integrating these with the unique vocabularies that typically exist in today's highly differentiated health institutions. Orientation programs in which language differences are attended to can potentially shorten orientation time and reduce the trauma, isolation, and loneliness people new to organizations and special languages frequently feel. Figure 17-2 depicts how language may be related to individuals and groups in organizations. Summarizing to this point, emerging theory suggests that natural and special vocabularies exist in organizations, that they convey feeling, information, understanding and

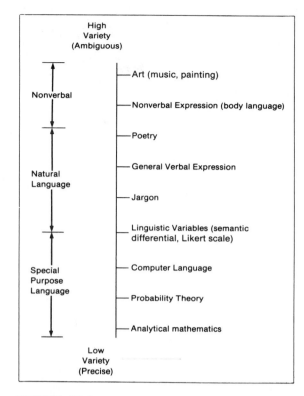

FIGURE 17-1

Continuum of languages for describing organizational reality. *From Daft RL and Wiginton JC: Language and organization, Acad Mgmt Rev 4(2):181, 1979.*

meaning, and that skillful articulation and translation strengthen individuals and groups.

POLITICAL LANGUAGE

According to Edelman et al., language skill also adds to an executives' power.[13] Morris states, "Sharing a language with other persons provides the subtlest and most powerful of all tools for controlling the behavior of other persons to one's advantage."[14] Based on the premise that politics involves the exercise of power (defined as influence and control) and that language is a mechanism for influence and control, then language is a key aspect of political activity and as such, is worth the attention of nurse administrators at work in todays politically charged health care organizations.

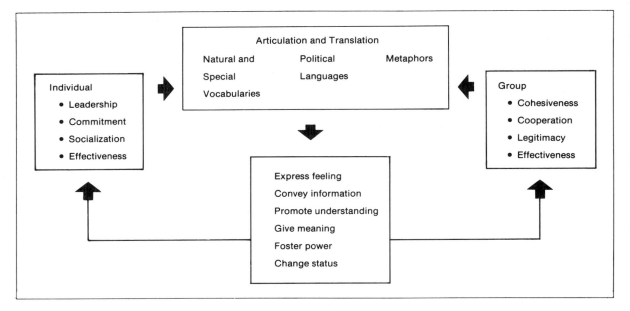

FIGURE 17-2

Languages, individuals, and groups.

The political process in organizations works like this: Administrators who exercise power in organizations identify issues, label the phenomena involved in words constituent groups find meaningful, prescribe actions that should be taken, and develop consensus by legitimating activities and points of view.[15] Politically astute executives generate committed collective action inside organizations and look outside organizations, to society, to legitimize their action.

In the nursing profession as a whole, there is graphic evidence to illustrate the political ramifications of language. Take the movement of nursing into institutions of higher education, for example. Changing nursing education from training in hospitals to academic endeavor in universities was underway in earnest about the same time as publication of Thomas Kuhn's, *The Structure of Scientific Revolutions* in the early 1960s, and the scurrying in every field of the social sciences to find a "paradigm." Consensus was built by nurse leaders and legitimized in terms of societal need, to change nursing from a technical vocation to a theory-based profession. In the course of this undertaking and in view of the emphasis on research in the scientific community at large, new language in

nursing emerged: paradigms, models, theories, and quantitative research became part of nursing's lingua franca. Words representing scholarly activity in higher education were used politically to align and legitimize nursing with powerful scientific disciplines already firmly entrenched in the country's most prestigious academic institutions.

Consider too, the more recent effort to reach consensus about language that articulates nursing's unique contributions. Pridham and Schutz state unequivocally, "If nursing is to make clear its contribution to health care, a language that is equal to the task is a necessity."[16]

Nursing administration job titles provide a further example of how language can be used politically to mobilize support, justify action, and upgrade status. As administration of health services has grown more and more complex, we have changed the words in use to describe our positions in organizational hierarchies. Judging from the highly observable shift, from the term "nurse administrator" to "nurse executive"; from the title "director of nursing" to "administrator of patient services" or "vice president of nursing," it seems safe to say that we are using words politically to portray the magnitude of our responsibility and enhance our power.

METAPHORS

Acquiring and holding power must be worked at linguistically and never-endingly.[17] Based on the premise that language enpowers and enpowered nurses better serve the public, questions worth contemplating are, how do nurse administrators become masters of the languages spoken in organizations?

Linguistic mastery, never an easy undertaking, is even more of a challenge in an era of financial constraint and demand for efficiency, both of which dictate changes in language: consider for example, terms such as lower-cost product, contraction of demand, and discretionary spending. Roethlisberger notes that the precise language of efficiency can convey feelings of dismay.[18] Talk of cutbacks, reductions, and lay-offs communicates insecurity.

Much of the language in today's price-driven environment must of necessity, be in the cold, calculated financial, and actuarial genre that, while by no means riveting in the linguistic sense, is necessary for intelligent decision making. But equally essential for effective administration is the ability to use language that is less literal and more figurative — metaphorical for instance.

Metaphors take several particular ideas and make a single term of them in a poignant and understandable way.[19] Weick and March note that the metaphor is a subtle but highly important use of language.[20,21] It shuts out or opens up new ways of solving problems and seeing opportunities. Fagin and Diers say that metaphors "influence not only language but also thought and action" and suggest that metaphoric analysis in nursing is an important activity.[22] We agree and recommend elucidation of nursing administration metaphors as well.

As nurse administrators, we often talk the language of the military metaphor using its vocabulary of loyalty and obedience: Nurse administrators are "chiefs" responsible for a "service"; nurses "battle to fight disease"; patients, "attacked by disease" are given "shots"; employees "on duty" are "in uniform," and so forth. When we use language like this, the force of the metaphor powerfully conveys our values, past

experiences and what we consider legitimate. As Athos puts it, "the truth lurks in the metaphor."[23]

Metaphors enable us to create expectations and make some forms of behavior seem more natural than others.[24] Here are two examples in nursing administration. Nurse as administrator (note the root component "minister" in the word administrator) connotes ministering parent, nurturent care giver; nurse as executive connotes executing, canny business person. Carried a step further, using the language of organization theory, nurse administrator as organization developer connotes ministering caregiver, initiator of change, increasing an organization's capacity to satisfy employee needs. Nurse executive as negotiator and manager of resource dependence, on the other hand, connotes tough, savvy, business-like action oriented less to individual needs and far more to efficiency and cost effectiveness.

Metaphors like these are powerful because of their capacity to focus attention and generate new ways of thinking about what is going on. Nurse as good soldier is old metaphor. Nurse as advocate and nurse as executive are newer metaphors that have captured our imagination and changed the way we view our work. But a word of caution: Metaphoric thinking as Sontag and Wilensky note, can cloud issues and divert attention away from what is actually happening in a situation.[25,26] Metaphors can be overused, and there is the danger that leaders will become captive of their own rhetoric. Nevertheless, we believe that developing powerful metaphors in nursing that convey our mission to the public and other professionals, is as important to our success as are special vocabularies and politically sensitive language.

STUDY OF LANGUAGE IN ORGANIZATIONS FOR NURSING ADMINISTRATION AND EDUCATION

As nurse executives search for ways to encourage individual leadership and creativity, they can strike new veins of thought about practice by finding new language. Per Peters and Waterman,

> We need new language. We need to consider adding terms to our management vocabulary: a few might be temporary structures, ad hoc groups, field

organizations, small is beautiful, incrementalism, experimentation, action orientation, imitations, internal competition, playfulness, the technology of foolishness, bootlegging, skunk words, shadow organizations and cabals.[27]

What is relevant to us is apparent from the phonetics, semantics, and syntax of our language. In the course of communicating, we find others interesting, and in turn are found interesting when what we say and the words we use are relevant. Our language tells colleagues about our values and through transference of information about values we intersect with others. If the unconscious are "vegetables," the unusual are "fruits," least preferred co-workers are "turkeys," and employees are "bodies," the way we view and value people is apparent because of our words.

Educators in health-care agencies can hasten incoming employee's confidence and understanding with language that conveys an organization's shared history and values. Pettigrew suggests that organizations create a sense of exclusiveness and commitment in employees through development of distinctive organizational vocabularies.[28] Commitment is earned, it is not automatic. Part of the way executives may undoubtedly earn employee commitment is by developing distinctive language that conveys a vision of the height to which work can attain.

Karl Weick notes, "No one is ever free to do something he can't think of."[29] A task for nurse educators is finding ways to help nursing administration students become knowledgeable about using words, elucidating old metaphors, and making new relevant ones. Emphasizing language skills in nursing administration curriculums is especially appropriate in view of Mintzberg, Kotter, and Gronn's research of administrative activity.[30,31] Consistent among their findings is that at least three quarters of an administrator's day is spent talking with others, using language.

FUTURE RESEARCH

Leading organizational researchers suggest that language, a concept widely studied in sociology and anthropology, be used for analysis of organizations and as a basis of new organization theory.[32] According to Pettigrew:

> The study of organizational vocabularies is long overdue. Analysis of their origins and uses and in particular their role in expressing communal values, evoking past experiences, providing seed beds for human action, and legitimating current and evolving distributions of power, represent key areas of inquiry in research on the creation and evolution of new organizations.[33]

Argyris says that statistical studies merely touch on the complexities that exist in organizations.[34] And Weick recommends that rather than doing purely quantitative studies of large organizations, we find ways of getting into small organizations to study relationships and the reasons for them.[35]

A way of improving understanding of how people relate to one another is by analyzing languages they use. Daft and Wiginton's continuum depicting the range of organization languages from the ambiguous languages of poetry and art, to the precise computer and mathematical languages can be useful in future investigations that address these propositions:

- A wide variety of languages is spoken in today's health care organizations.
- The greater the number of languages spoken in an organization and the greater their complexity, the more challenging and taxing a nurse executive's job.

A sample of research questions nurse administrators can ask to test these propositions are as follows:

- What are the non-verbal, natural, and special purpose languages used in health care organizations?
- How many and what kind of languages do nurse executives use?
- What jargon do nurses use that administrators, physicians, and consumers find foreign and mystifying?
- What languages are shared in hospitals? Where are words the same, but the meaning attached to words different? Where are the mismatches in meanings of words between physicians, nurses, and consumers, and how are the mismatches problematic?
- What metaphors are used in nursing administration? What language is used in our metaphors and what is the effect?

Our view of the world, the way we identify problems, and the choices we make are delimited by our language.[36] Vocabularies give us categories for distinguishing experience.[37] Knowledge and understanding of language in organizations enlarge insights about ambiguous phenomena and enable us to combat parodoxical problems with imagination.

The facility to use words well enables nurse executives to be tolerant of eccentric goings on in organizations that are actually rich wells of creativity. New language that describes what looks like aberrant organizational behavior to casual observers, but in fact is extraordinary creativeness — the "technology of foolishness" of brilliant nurses' minds — can have a profound effect on the future of nursing.

REFERENCES

1. Roethlisberger FJ. The executive's environment is verbal. In: Dubin R. Human relations in administration. Englewood Cliffs, NJ: Prentice Hall, 1974.

2. Peters TJ, Waterman RH. In search of excellence. New York: Harper and Row, 1982:,241.

3. Blair EM. Needed: nursing administration leaders. Nursing Outlook 1976;24(9):550–4.

4. Berger PL, Luckman T. The social construction of reality. New York: Anchor Books, 1966;36–8.

5. Ohashi JP. The contributions of Dickoff and James to theory development in nursing. Image J Nurs Sch 1985;17(4):122–6.

6. Hayakawa SI. Language in thought and action. New York: Carcourt, 1949:27.

7. Why English is so easy to mangle. U.S. News and World Report 1985;99(3):53.

8. Pondy LJ. Leadership is a language game. In: McCall MW, Lombardo MM, eds. Leadership where else can we go? Durham, NC: Duke University Press, 1978:94–5.

9. Pondy LJ. Leadership is a language game. In: McCall MW, Lombardo MM, eds. Leadership where else can we go? Durham, NC: Duke University Press, 1978:94–5.

10. Pondy LR. The other hand clapping: an information-processing approach to organizational power. In: Hammer TH, Bacharach SB, eds. Reward systems and power distribution in organizations: searching for solutions. Cornell University: New York State School of Industrial and Labor Relations, 1977.

11. Daft RL, Wiginton JC. Language and organization. Acad Manage Rev 1979;4(2):178–91.

12. Berger PL, Luckman T. The social construction of reality. New York: Anchor Books, 1966:130–3.

13. Edelman JM. Political language. New York: Academic Press, 1977.

14. Morris CW. Signs, language and behavior. New York: Prentice Hall, 1949:214.

15. Pfeffer J. Power in organizations. Boston: Pitman, 1981.

16. Pridham KF, Schutz ME. Rationale for a language for naming problems from a nursing perspective. Image J Nurs Sch 1985;17(4):122–6.

17. Gronn PC. Talk as the work: the accomplishment of school administration. Adm Sci Q 1983;28(1):1–21.

18. Roethlisberger FJ. Communication and symbols. In: Dubin R, ed. Human relations in administration. Englewood Cliffs, NJ: Prentice Hall, 1974.

19. Miles MB, Huberman AM. Qualitative data analysis: a source book of new methods. Beverly Hills: Sage, 1985.

20. Weick KE. The social psychology of organizing. Reading, MA: Addison-Wesley, 1979:9.

21. March JG, Simon HA. Organizations. New York: Wiley and Sons, 1958.

22. Fagin C, Diers D. Nursing as metaphor. N Engl J Med 1983;309(2):116–7.

23. Peters TJ, Waterman RH. In search of excellence. New York: Harper and Row, 1982:101.

24. Winslow GR. From loyalty to advocacy: a new metaphor for nursing. The Hastings Center Report 1984:32–40.

25. Sontag S. Illness as metaphor. New York: Farrar, Straus and Giroux, 1977.

26. Wilensky HL. Organizational intelligence. New York: Basic Books, 1967.

27. Peters TJ, Waterman RH. In search of excellence. New York: Harper and Row, 1982:106.

28. Pettigrew AM. On studying organizational cultures. Adm Sci Q 1979;24:570–80.

29. Weick KE. Educational organizations as loosely coupled systems. Adm Sci Q 1976;21(2):193.

30. Mintzberg H. The nature of managerial work. New York: Harper and Row, 1973.

31. Kotter JP. The general managers. New York: The Free Press, 1982.

32. Pfeffer J. Organizations and organization theory. Boston: Pitman, 1982.

33. Pettigrew AM. On studying organizational cultures. Adm Sci Q 1979;24:575.

34. Argyris C. The applicability of organizational sociology. Cambridge: Cambridge University Press, 1972.

35. Weick KE. Amendments to organizational theorizing. Acad Manage J 1974;17(3):485–502.

36. Chinn PL. Debunking myths in nursing theory and research. Image J Nurs Sch 1985;13(2):45.

37. Silverman D. Theory of organizations: a sociological framework. New York: Basic Books, 1971.

CHAPTER **18**

Rational Decision Making
Managing uncertainty

Wade Lancaster, BBA, MBA
Jeanette Lancaster, RN, PhD

In the story of Alice in Wonderland, Alice was confronted with a problem, so she pleaded with the Cheshire Cat, "Would you tell me, please, which way I ought to walk from here?" "That depends a good deal on where you want to get to," the cat wisely responded [1]. Just like Alice, each person is daily confronted with finding answers to a variety of problems. These range from what to wear or eat to major administrative and personal decisions. Decision making and problem solving are also integral aspects of nursing administration. In truth, the factor that weighs most heavily in the success or failure of nursing administrators is the quality of the decisions they make. This is especially true in an era fraught with rapid changes that necessitate a rational, systematic approach to making decisions. Decisions based largely on intuition, hunches, or past experiences are becoming less effective for resolving contemporary problems because circumstances, resources, and constraints are changing at too rapid a pace; yesterday's experience may not accurately mirror today's problems.

Too often the decision-making process is taken for granted. Because it is a frequent and universal activity, administrators often fail to recognize that it is also a

systematic process, one that can be approached from varying points of view. Decision making is often defined as the act of choosing among alternatives, but this definition is deceptively simple. Although brief, easy to understand, and focusing on the essential element of decision making, it is incomplete in that it fails to emphasize that actually making the decision is only one of several interrelated steps. Decision making is instead a sequential process. Each decision is based on certain assumptions and depends heavily on the environment in which the decision is being made. This sequential process involves the need to implement the decision by translating it into a course of action.

The process of decision making consists of several elements, including the problem, the decision maker, the process, and the decision itself. These elements and the factors that make up the decision-making environment are depicted in Figure 18-1. Generally, people approach decision making by using one of two possible models as a framework for their actions. The first approach, a normative or prescriptive view of the process, emphasizes the way people *should* make a choice. The descriptive or behavioral view, on the other hand, discusses how people really go about making decisions and solving problems.

Reprinted from *The Journal of Nursing Administration*, Vol. 12, No. 9, with permission of J. B. Lippincott Company © 1982.

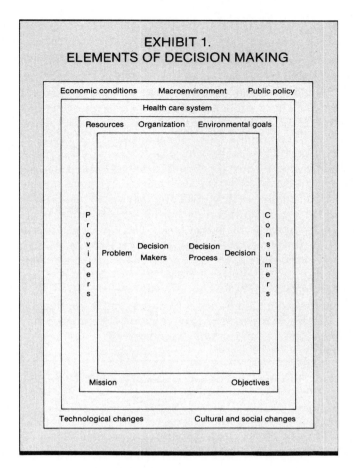

FIGURE 18-1

Elements of decision making.

THE NORMATIVE MODEL FOR DECISION MAKING

The normative decision making model was proposed at least 200 years ago by Adam Smith. It is based on classical microeconomic concepts and contains two primary assumptions. The first is that the objective of all decisions is to maximize satisfaction. The second, called the "perfect knowledge assumption," is that, in any given situation calling for a decision, all possible choices and the consequences and potential outcome of each are known [2].

Based on these two assumptions, the normative model of decision making characterizes the decision maker as a completely rational, all-knowing, hedonistic calculator who begins with a predetermined good or desired value and approaches any given problem in the following manner:

1. Define and analyze the problem.
2. Identify all available alternatives.
3. Evaluate the benefits and disadvantages of each alternative.
4. Rank all alternatives in the order in which they are likely to meet the desired value or objective.

5. Select the alternative that maximizes satisfaction.
6. Implement the decision.
7. Follow up the decision.

Although the normative model is analytically precise, its assumptions have been criticized as being unrealistic. While these are valid criticisms, administrators should recognize the model for what it is, a prescriptive approach to decision making. As such, it prescribes a specified objective and provides guidelines that greatly facilitate the application of analytical techniques in problem solving.

DESCRIPTIVE MODEL FOR DECISION MAKING

The major quarrel with the normative model for decision making is its "perfect knowledge assumption," as few people actually know all of the possible alternatives. Herbert Simon recognized the limitations of the normative model and developed a descriptive model, based on a set of alternative assumptions [3]. The descriptive model has considerable potential for nursing administrators. Its assumptions are that decision makers are subjectively rational people who make decisions on the basis of incomplete information and that they are more likely to be "satisfiers" than "optimizers." Satisfiers tend to look for an acceptable solution, while optimizers seek the best possible solution. The descriptive view emphasizes that problems are not always clearly and correctly defined and that people do not always make the one best choice, and that it is not always possible or feasible to try to secure complete information because of limitations of time, money, or people. In short, the premises underlying the descriptive model view the decision maker as a person who logically solves problems on the basis of known or easily retrievable information.

Simon contended that, if people always attempted to arrive at optimal solutions, they would make few decisions. They would expend too much time and money in gathering information about the problem ever to arrive efficiently at a solution. Therefore, instead of seeking optimal solutions, people tend to establish a set of minimal objectives that they will seek

to accomplish and that they can comfortably consider as acceptable alternatives. Figure 18-2 illustrates this descriptive model whereby the decision maker

1. Establishes a satisfactory or acceptable goal
2. Defines the subjective perceptions of the problem
3. Identifies acceptable alternatives (The decision maker may either identify several alternatives before proceeding to the next step or identify and evaluate alternatives sequentially.)
4. Evaluates each alternative in terms of its ability to solve the problem satisfactorily
5. Selects a satisfactory alternative (This may be the first one encountered or the one that produces the most favorable outcomes.)
6. Implements the decision
7. Follows up.

We will discuss the descriptive model as a framework for decision making that nursing administrators can readily implement.

THE DECISION-MAKING PROCESS

The decision-making process is a systematic series of sequential steps. The steps include

1. Recognizing the problem
2. Gathering and processing information
3. Evaluating alternatives
4. Deciding, selecting, or choosing
5. Implementing postdecision activities.

The first necessary condition for a decision is a problem. Problems exist where goals are to be attained and uncertainty exists about an appropriate solution. A problem must also suggest more than one alternative solution. The decision-making process is then a sequential and reiterative series of psychological and physical activities in which the decision maker seeks and evaluates information to achieve the required level of confidence to reach a decision.

The process is not rigid; it allows a person to move backward or forward or to skip stages. For example, in some instances gathering and processing information may precede problem recognition, for nurse administrators may be seeking information to arrive at one decision only to learn of a need for additional related decisions. For example, when using forms to

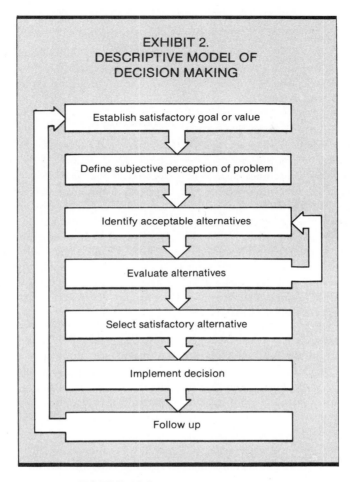

FIGURE 18-2
Descriptive model of decision making.

collect data and attempting to tabulate information and write a quarterly or annual report, the administrator may realize that the form circulated did not satisfactorily request the needed information. The situation then requires new, unexpected decisions. For organizational reasons, we will discuss decision-making steps in their listed sequence.

Recognizing the Problem

Identifying a problem is an essential prerequisite for decision making. Although this step at first glance appears simple, it is actually the most complex, for it involves a perception of the current state of affairs. Because people view reality differently from one another, each holds a slightly different preference about what an ideal state, situation, or outcome should be. One might postulate that a perfect situation would exist whenever the actual and the ideal were totally congruent, but this seldom occurs, as both actual and ideal are in a continuous state of flux. Incongruence between actual and ideal does not alone constitute a problem; rather the incongruence must be of sufficient magnitude to provoke problem recognition.

It is easy to get caught up in symptoms and never really identify the real problem. Thus, it is helpful to state specifically what is wrong and what improvements seem feasible. Then, the nursing administrator can gather facts, investigate possible causes, and determine the real problem.

Nursing administrators, who are continually faced with limited resources, must establish priorities about the importance of various problems. For example, a problem involving inadequate office space may be irritating to a nursing supervisor or clinical specialist, yet it may not be recognized or perceived as a problem by those in upper levels of hospital administration. The nursing administrator must therefore choose either to ignore the unsatisfactory situation or to gather sufficient information to convince the hospital administrator that a problem does exist. The decision will depend on the amount of time and energy that can be devoted to the issue at a given time, after the nursing administrator has taken other demands and priorities into consideration.

When evaluating a problem, the decision maker needs to look at both the problem's priority and its potential for being solved. Nursing administrators will occasionally encounter high-priority problems that have limited potential for being solved. The nursing administrator faced with high staff turnover might find, for example, that the problem largely stems from the unusual demands of one surgeon who insists on beginning a surgical schedule at 4 A.M. The hospital administrator, while acknowledging the nursing problem, refuses to intervene in the physician's control of the hospital schedule because the physician brings a large number of patients to the hospital. In this case, the problem, although important to the nursing administrator, may be unsolvable.

Faced with such situations, nursing administrators must often establish priorities for dealing with problems. Reitz suggests three possible ways of choosing priorities.

1. The first problem encountered is the first problem solved. In other words, deal with problems in the order in which they appear.
2. Problems that can be dispensed with immediately are given priority over more time-consuming ones. That is, give the easiest problems to solve first priority.

3. Give crisis or emergency problems priority over all others.[4]

Once a nursing administrator has arranged problems according to priority and degree of solvability, it is time to begin gathering and processing information.

Gathering and Processing Information

Gathering and processing information are separate yet interrelated actions. Information gathering, which occurs in the second stage of the decision-making process, includes mental and physical actions devoted to gathering information about the problem, identifying possible alternatives, estimating the relative merits of each alternative, and speculating about potential consequences of each alternative. Information processing occurs in both the second and third stages. At stage two, it involves appraising the data to determine whether to continue.

The information-gathering process

Information gathering either can be instantaneous, or it can involve intensive exploration over a prolonged period of time. Regardless of the extent of the search, the process is normally a series of steps; these include an internal and an external search.

The internal search begins with an individual's memory examination. This may call forth such information as organizational policies, prior experience, training, education, or the experiences of others. Because of the constant flux of most organizations, an internal search must be combined with additional data from the external environment. The volume of information that nursing administrators processed daily means that it is not usually possible or even desirable for them to rely on their internal sources.

During an external search, administrators devote conscious mental and physical activities to gathering data. The external search process begins with a preliminary search to identify alternatives and compare the attributes of these alternatives with a desired set of attributes. This preliminary sampling ordinarily allows nursing administrators to reconcile what they desire with what they find available. As decision makers they make concerted efforts to match their desired sets of attributes with those actually available. To accomplish this goal, they seek information from a variety of sources. One such source in organizational setting is the data base information system, which provides management with a timely flow of relevant information. While these systems do provide up-to-date and accurate information, the need for judgment on the part of the decision maker still remains [5].

This process is illustrated by the case of the nursing administrator who wanted to have an RN in charge of each nursing unit around the clock. An examination of the administrator's information system, which included cards indicating shift preferences, revealed, however, that there were not enough nurses willing to work the night shift. Consequently, the administrator had to reconcile the desired staffing level with the resources available, resulting in assigning one RN to each set of two physically adjacent units and an accelerated recruitment program to expand the nursing staff and eventually reach the desired staffing level.

Determining how much to search

The extent of any search is affected by three factors (1) the perceived value and cost of the search, (2) individual search capabilities, and (3) situational variables. The potential value of a search must be measured in time, effort, and money that are likely to be entailed. Often the cost of a thorough search will not be consistent with the minimal benefits anticipated. However, a thorough information search may be needed for correct diagnosis of the problem.

Less apparent but equally important are the psychological costs of frustration, tension, and annoyance associated with acquiring information. In addition, the delay incurred from information gathering may be frustrating or may cause the decision maker to experience a time pressure or miss an important deadline. Further costs associated with search include information overload, which occurs when anyone gathers too much information or gathers it too rapidly.

The perceived value of a thorough search is also influenced by the type and amount of information stored in the decision maker's memory, the quality of this stored information, and the ability to recall it. Another determining factor is often decision makers' personal confidence in their decision-making abilities. In general, search for outside information becomes more important when a person has less confidence in the ability to make an accurate decision. Less-experienced administrators, who may question their decision-making abilities gather considerable information to support their choices. In contrast, seasoned administrators who may have made many similar decisions, feel comfortable in predicting the possible outcomes of their decisions with minimal supporting information.

The degree of risk the administrator perceives in making a decision also influences the extent of information search. Perceived risk may be financial, psychological, social, or physical, but in general, the greater the anticipated risk, the more information the person is likely to gather. A second factor in the extent of information the decision maker seeks is the individual's ability to engage in such efforts. Some people become bored and restless, or are unable to tolerate the tediousness of a thorough search.

Finally, situational factors also affect searching; those include the urgency of the problem, the type of problem, (whether long-range and strategic or routine and administrative), and the availability of information. People may, for example, want information to stay hidden to cover up certain aspects of organizational functioning, or information may be ineffectually stored and therefore difficult to retrieve.

Evaluating Alternatives

Before making a decision, the decision makers should develop feasible alternatives so that they can evaluate the potential consequences of each. This step is actually a continuation of information processing, where relevant internal and external factors determine the cost and time constraints associated with each potential alternative. For each decision, the goal is to determine the extremes among the decision outcomes. Administrators should ask, what is the best possible outcome, the worse possible outcome, and the choices that fall in the middle of the outcome continuum.

A basic assumption of descriptive decision-making theory is that the goal often results from a compromise among the influential parties. For example, nursing administrators usually hold as a patient care goal that their staffs provide each patient with the best possible nursing care, skilled and reflective of the patient's physical and psychological needs. However, if the hospital is significantly understaffed and each nurse has responsibility for ten patients who are acutely ill, the goal may be compromised, and providing safe, acceptable care may be the reasonable alternative.

The evaluation process is either sequential or comparative. In the sequential approach, the decision maker determines the first alternative (A), analyzes it carefully to evaluate potential consequences, and compares the outcome to what is considered a satisfactory level of performance. If the outcome of (A) seems acceptable, then it is chosen. If (A) is rejected, then a second alternative is critically evaluated, and so on until the decision maker exhausts the store of alternatives. In contrast, other decision makers evaluate multiple alternatives simultaneously by comparing the relative merits of all identified alternatives. Of course, the number of alternatives any one person can identify is finite, and there may be an alternative that offers a perfect solution but has not occurred to the administrator.

Reitz points out that thorough determination and evaluation of alternatives potentially leads to effective decision making. He recommends

1. Identifying all possible outcomes, both positive and negative, from each alternative.
2. Assessing the positive and negative value of each outcome, as well as determining how effectively it will accomplish the objectives or requirements of a satisfactory solution.
3. Estimating the likelihood of each outcome for each alternative [6].

Each alternative will have both advantages and disadvantages that must be carefully weighed. Identifying disadvantages, while often difficult to do, is an essential step in that it helps to determine the amount of risk involved in each possible outcome.

Selecting an Alternative

Rarely are the solutions to problems clear-cut black or white choices; most tend to reflect shades of gray. The difficulty encompassed in making a decision depends on a variety of factors, including the number and quality of alternatives, risks, and the interaction

effects. March and Simon have described the quality of alternatives as good, poor, bland, mixed, or uncertain [7].

Clearly, selecting an alternative from some combinations will be more difficult than others. For example, if one alternative is good and the others are bland, mixed, poor, or uncertain, then the choice is straightforward. If none of the alternatives are good, however, then the selection becomes more difficult. Not only is the selection of an alternative affected by the number and quality of potential solutions, but it is also influenced by the element of risk. Part of the difficulty in making a decision stems from the constantly changing environment that injects uncertainty into the probable success or failure of a prospective solution.

Finally, choosing an alternative solution is complicated by the interaction of one activity on another. In few situations does one activity singularly achieve the desired goal or objective without having some positive or negative influence on another goal. This is especially true in organizational settings, where a multiplicity of objectives exist and short-run objectives often affect long-run objectives. This sort of situation is illustrated by the hospital superintendent who attempts to keep a tight rein on maintenance costs at the expense of the hospital's long-run objective of high-quality patient care [8].

Postdecision Activities

Once the decision maker has selected an alternative, it must be converted into action. Obviously, any decision is worthless if it is never implemented. Thus in the final phase of the decision-making process, implementing postdecision activities, the effective decision maker uses knowledge and skill to transform the solution into behavior through skillful implementation, effective communication, and evaluation through individuals and groups. Unfortunately, evidence of postdecision activities indicates that few decision makers are either careful or unbiased in following up their decisions [9]. Postdecision activities are extremely important, for there is virtually no difference between an ineffective decision and no decision at all. Because good decisions lose their effectiveness if they are improperly implemented, the nursing administrator should raise the following questions:

1. What must be done?
2. In what sequence must it be done?
3. Who should do it?
4. How can the necessary steps be most effectively accomplished?

Equally important is communicating the decision effectively to everyone who will be directly or indirectly affected by it. Clear, concise language is essential. Administrators should point out the logic of the decision and state the reasons for making it. Such communication will add a measure of success to the decision, since it helps the administrator determine the degree of commitment on the part of those who must participate in the implementation. Clearly, even the most technically sound decision can easily be undermined by those who are dissatisfied and not committed to following through.

Once a decision has been implemented, the decision maker cannot assume that the outcome will meet the original objective. Instead, effective management involves a monitoring system that measures the actual results and compares them to the planned results. If deviations between the actual and planned results exist, then modifications in the solution, its implementation, or the objective is necessary. Obviously, measurable objectives are important components of the evaluation and control process, for without them judging performance is difficult. Consider the following example.

During the past five years, Woodbrook, a proprietary hospital located in a major metropolitan area, has experienced increasing difficulty in hiring staff nurses. The chief administrator and the director of nursing service have reviewed their current recruiting program, evaluated several new approaches, and decided on hiring professional recruiters to recruit new nursing graduates from NLN-accredited schools across the nation. In order to bring the nursing staff up to an acceptable level, both the administrator and the nursing director agree that a 15-percent increase per year for the next three years would be desirable, but at the end of the first year, employment increases by only five percent. (1) The administrators therefore examine a number of possibilities: the original objective was overstated, (2) the use of professional recruiters (the selected alternative) to achieve the objective was not appropriate, (3) the wrong recruiters were selected (implementation) or (4) there is more to the problem than was identified.

If the problem had been inadequately defined, the original objective too high, or poor implementation had occurred, the entire decision-making process should be reactivated. Going back to step one of Figure 18-2 shows that the first step is to establish goals. Perhaps here the pool of nurses to be recruited from the surrounding area is insufficient to provide a 15-percent annual increase. It would also be extremely important to determine what nurses like about the hospital and what those who leave dislike. It may be for example, that the organizational atmosphere, once nurses are recruited, is unfriendly and impersonal. Unless administrators clearly define the real problem, no alternatives will provide a solution. Once they identify the problem, however, each alternative (to have a recruiter or not) must be carefully weighed until a satisfactory choice can be made to guide the implementation strategy.

DECISION MAKING FOR NURSING ADMINISTRATORS

Decision making is the core of successful administration. The quality of an administrator's decisions largely affects administrative effectiveness. Of two models providing frameworks for decision making, the descriptive model describes a process in which people actually make decisions. Decision making is not, as the normative model would suggest, always a clear-cut choice among identifiable alternatives. A nursing administrator is usually weighing a variety of interrelating factors in an environment characterized by scarcity of time and resources.

Decision making therefore requires a conscious systematic process, that can in turn be defined as a series of sequential steps. The nursing administrator who (1) identifies the problem, (2) gathers and processes information, (3) evaluates alternatives, (4) selects an alternative, and (5) implements the final choice will be a more effective administrator.

REFERENCES

1. Lewis Carroll, *Alice in Wonderland* (New York: Arcadia House, 1950), p. 53.
2. Jack W. Duncan, *Decision Making and Social Issues* (Hinsdale, Illinois: The Dryden Press, 1973), pp. 1-19.
3. Herbert A. Simon, *Administrative Behavior,* 3rd ed. (New York: The Free Press, 1976).
4. Joseph H. Reitz, *Behavior in Organizations* (Homewood, Illinois: Richard D. Irwin, 1977), pp. 154-199.
5. Henry L. Sisk, *Management and Organizations,* 2nd ed. (Cincinnati: South-Western Publishing, 1973).
6. Joseph H. Reitz, *Behavior in Organizations,* pp. 154-199.
7. James G. March and Herbert A. Simon, *Organizations* (New York: John Wiley, 1958), pp. 113-114.
8. James L. Gibson, John M. Ivancevich, and James H. Donnelly, *Organizations: Structure, Processes, Behavior,* revised ed. (Dallas: Business Publications, 1976), pp. 341-362.
9. Joseph H. Reitz, *Behavior in Organizations,* pp. 154-199.

CHAPTER **19**

Decision-Making Styles
Managerial application of the MBTI and type theory

Cynthia M. Freund, RN, PhD

Managerial potential and competence are currently matters of concern, and nowhere is the concern greater than in the health field, particularly in nursing. The focus on managerial training and development in hospitals and health systems reflects concern about managerial effectiveness. Many factors contribute to this heightened concern, including the attention focused on the critical role of the nurse executive by the Institute of Medicine[1] and Commission on Nursing,[2] as well as recognition of the pivotal role that nurses in first-line and middle-management positions play in maintaining the delicate balance between clinical effectiveness and cost-efficiency. As the nature and scope of responsibilities and performance expectations for all levels of managers have expanded, assessment centers and training and development programs have been developed to identify future managers and to help current managers meet new expectations.

A variety of tools and methods are used to help managers assess their capabilities, strengths, and limitations, and to help them increase their effectiveness. The Myers-Briggs Type Indicator (MBTI) is one such tool. The MBTI has been used in industry for a long time and is gaining popularity in the

Reprinted from *The Journal of Nursing Administration,* Vol. 18, No. 12, with permission of J. B. Lippincott Company © 1988.

health care sector.[3,4] Although it is categorized as a "psychological test," it is nondiagnostic and non-evaluative; furthermore, it is relatively easy to understand. These characteristics make it an ideal tool for use in managerial assessment and development programs.

The MBTI measures the way people use their minds — how they take in information (perception) and how they come to conclusions about that information (judgment). Because almost any human activity involves either perception or judgment in action or ideas, the potential applications of the instrument cover a broad range of human experiences and situations. In all instances, the MBTI is used to help individuals understand and accept their own strengths and limitations. Because there are no right or wrong ways to perceive and judge, only different ways, the MBTI is used to help individuals appreciate and understand the *valuable* similarities and differences between themselves and others. In work situations, the MBTI has been used to help individuals learn how to "talk the language" of and work with different people, to create a climate where differences are seen as valuable rather than problematic, and to construct working groups with sufficient diversity to solve problems and learn from each other.

The MBTI and the theory it is based on provide a useful framework for studying individual decision-making styles and for examining other issues that are important to managers and executives. They are useful in looking at how one works with one's subordinates, peers, and superiors; how one can delegate appropriately; and how one can put together effective working groups.

Unfortunately, the MBTI is sometimes used inappropriately and the theory underlying it, called type theory, is not fully understood. Consequently, the MBTI can be misinterpreted. This article briefly describes type theory and then discusses how individuals and organizations can use the MBTI. (A more extensive discussion of type theory can be found in Freund's article.[5])

TYPE THEORY

Type theory refers to C. G. Jung's theory of psychological type as interpreted by Isabel Myers and Katharine Briggs and operationalized through the MBTI. Jung observed patterns in the way people prefer to perceive and make judgments, and he called these patterns "psychological types." According to Jung, all conscious mental activity involves four cognitive processes—two perception functions, sensing and intuition, and two judgment functions, thinking and feeling. Everyone uses all four processes, but individuals differ in their preference for and skill in each process and function, as well as in the attitude with which they use each process.[6] Myers and Briggs identify four dimensions of psychological type: a perception function, a judgment function, an attitude toward life, and an orientation to the outer world.[7]

The four dimensions of psychological type are based on concepts of polarity and balance. All four dimensions have polar opposites: there are two opposite basic mental functions, perception and judgment; two opposite perception processes, sensing and intuition; two opposite judgment processes, thinking and feeling; two opposite attitudes toward life, extraversion and introversion; and two opposite orientations toward the outer world, perceptive and judging (Figure 19-1). Along each dimension, strength and competence are developed in one of the

- Basic Mental Functions:
  Perception—Sensing (S)
  Intuition (N)
  Judgment—Thinking (T)
  Feeling (F)
- Attitude Toward Life: Extraversion (E)
  Introversion (I)
- Orientation Toward World: Perceptive (P)
  Judging (J)

FIGURE 19-1
Type dimensions.

polar opposites, while the other polar opposite is less well developed.[7,8]

Perception and Judgment Functions

Perception is the process of becoming aware of something—people, things, events, or ideas. It includes gathering information and choosing the information to attend to. It is the process of taking information into consciousness, either by sensing or by intuition.[8]

Sensing

Sensing is the perception of the observable by use of the senses—sight, hearing, touch, and other senses. Managers who use sensing as their predominant perception process (sensing types) focus on the present and have acute powers of observation, a memory for details, a desire for accuracy, and a sense of realism and common sense.

Intuition

Intuition is the perception of meanings, possibilities, and relationships by way of insight. Managers who use intuition as their predominant perception process focus on future possibilities rather than the present; they have the capacity to deal with complex and abstract relationships.

The second dimension of psychological type is the judgment function—the process of making a decision about what has been perceived. This involves analysis, evaluation, choice, and selection of an action. The two processes of judgment are thinking and feeling.[7-9]

Thinking

Thinking involves coming to conclusions on the basis of logic. Decisions are made by ordering choices in terms of cause and effect, logical connections, and impersonal analysis. Thinking type managers are objective, analytical, and critical; they value fairness and justice.

Feeling

Feeling involves coming to conclusions on the basis of relative values. Decisions are made by ordering choices in terms of personal values and the effect of decisions on others. Feeling type managers are warm and compassionate and attend to what matters to others; they value harmony and affiliation with others.

Use of Perception and Judgment

All conscious mental activity involves perception and judgment. The first step is to use a perception function — either sensing or intuition — to take in information about or observe a situation. The second step is to use a judgment function — either thinking or feeling — to decide on the appropriate action or arrive at a conclusion. Both are critical elements of managerial and executive responsibilities. All persons use both sensing and intuition for their perception functions and both thinking and feeling for their judgment functions — but not at once and not with equal preference or skill.

Through a developmental process, individuals develop a preference for and strength in one process. Type theory assumes that children during early life develop a predisposition toward one of the four processes and the preferred process is used most often. Consequently, most skill is developed in the use of the preferred process; continued use of this process then leads to increased competence with it. Such constant reinforcement leads to the development of a dominant process.

In order to avoid a one-dimensional cognitive style, an auxiliary process is also developed. The dominant process occurs in one function — either perception or judgment — but because all mental activity involves both functions, the auxiliary process is in the other, nondominant function. For example, if sensing or intuition is the dominant process (a perception function), the auxiliary process will be either thinking or feeling (a judgment function).

During youth, then, individuals develop command over the perception and judgment functions by developing mastery of their dominant and auxiliary processes. While individuals are striving for excellence in their dominant and auxiliary processes, they also develop at least passable skill in the other, less preferred, third and fourth process. Gaining greater command over the less preferred processes is a developmental objective of midlife. However, even though greater skill in the less preferred processes can be developed, the dominant process remains dominant, continues to be the preferred process, and is the most highly developed of all the processes. Likewise, the auxiliary process continues to be the individual's second best and second preferred process. Individuals use their dominant and auxiliary processes most often. Only a few exceptional people can use all four processes with equal ease and skill as the situation requires.[9]

When the various dominant processes are combined with the various auxiliary processes, different patterns of how individuals process and use information result. These combinations are referred to as "types," and reflect basic differences in the cognitive style of individuals, managers, and executives. In addition to the dimensions of perception and judgment, Jung described a third dimension of personality structure, attitude toward life, and a fourth dimension, orientation to the outer world.[6]

Attitude Toward Life

Jung identified two attitudes toward life, "extraversion" and "introversion," and defined them quite specifically: extraversion means outward-turning and introversion means inward-turning.[6] Like sensing-intuition and thinking-feeling, extraversion and introversion are opposite poles or attitudes. Also, like the perception and judgment processes, individuals use both attitudes, extraversion and introversion, but not simultaneously and not with equal preference or skill.

In the *extraverted attitude,* attention and energy flow out to the objects and people of the environment. There is a desire to act on and in the world. Managers who prefer the extraverted attitude are action-oriented, get their stimulation and energy from events and people in the environment, and tend to be social.[8]

In the *introverted attitude,* attention and energy are focused on the inner world of ideas and concepts. There is a desire to turn into oneself and reflect. Managers who prefer the introverted attitude are contemplative, get their energy from their own inner world of thoughts and ideas, and enjoy privacy and solitude.[8]

Thus, extraverts use their dominant process in the outer world and, consequently, show their best to the world. Introverts, on the other hand, show their second best, their auxiliary process, to the world, reserving their best for their most preferred place — their own inner world. Consequently, introverts are less well known and may often be underestimated. It is important *not* to assume that extraverts never like to be alone and that introverts never like to be with others, or that extraverts are all action without reflection and that introverts are all reflection with no action. Everyone must live as both an extravert and an introvert, particularly in work situations. Many individuals achieve competence at both, but every individual prefers one attitude.[9] Furthermore, equally important to note, both introverts and extraverts can be effective managers and executives.

Orientation to the Outer World

The fourth dimension of personality or type structure reflects a preferred way of dealing with the outer world. Individuals live in the outer world with either a perceptive orientation or a judging orientation.

When a *perceptive orientation* is used to run one's outer life, one strives to keep things open, to receive new and additional information. Regardless of the favored perception process (sensing or intuition), managers with a perceptive orientation are characteristically spontaneous, flexible, and adaptable, and they strive to keep plans to a minimum; they are always open to new ideas.[7]

When a *judging orientation* is used to run one's outer life, one seeks organization and closure. Managers with a judging orientation, whether they are thinking or feeling types, desire plans, organization, order, purposefulness and decisiveness; they want to regulate and control situations and events.[7]

Summary

The four dimensions put together result in 16 combinations which represent a complex set of dynamic relationships between the four mental processes, attitude toward life, and orientation to the outer world. These 16 combinations are known as psychological types, they describe cognitive structure, the way people prefer to use their minds to take in information and draw conclusions, and the way people prefer to live in the world. The 16 combinations reflect the valuable differences among people.

ASSESSING MANAGERIAL DECISION-MAKING STYLE

In recent years, the MBTI has been used in a variety of ways. The Myers-Briggs Type Indicator is an instrument designed to test type theory and put it to practical use.[7] Although the instrument was originally used as a research instrument, Myers and Briggs noted that its ultimate purpose was to make the theory of psychological type useful in practical applications. The objective of the MBTI is to identify individual preferences for one of the poles of the four type dimensions. As noted in the MBTI manual,

> The intent is to reflect a habitual choice between rival alternatives analogous to right-handedness or left-handedness. One expects to use both the right and left hands, even though one reaches first with the hand one prefers. Similarly, every person is assumed to use both poles of each of the four preferences, but to respond first or most often with the preferred functions or attitudes.[7]

In regard to managerial assessment, as noted previously, results from the MBTI can be used to help individual managers: examine the strengths and limitations of their own decision-making style; enhance their working relationships with others; and develop effective working teams.

Individual Assessment

Although it is human to recognize the strengths associated with one's type, it is also natural to be reluctant to admit and accept the weaknesses associated with one's type. However, in decision situations it is important for managers to realize that their type preferences will lead them to a tendency to process only certain kinds of information, to attend to certain kinds of data, and to draw conclusions based on certain kinds of criteria. Alert to these tendencies, they can either draw upon others of opposite type to fill their gaps or they can make a conscious effort to pay attention to the kind of information they would not naturally consider in drawing their conclusions.

The mutual usefulness of opposite types is an important concept for decision makers. A sensing manager focuses on the present, on pertinent facts, essential details, and realism whereas an intuitive manager focuses on the future, signs of change, the larger picture, and possibilities. Each performs well in what he or she does, but seldom sees or minimizes what the other sees. The same is true for thinking and feeling types. Feeling type managers need thinkers to help them analyze, organize, weigh the facts and evidence, hold consistently to a policy, and fire people if necessary. Thinkers need feeling types to assess how others will feel and react, persuade others, conciliate, maintain flexibility, and appreciate others.

Opposite types can complement each other. However, too much oppositeness makes it difficult for people to work together. They see the world too differently and cannot hear each other. If they have two or three preferences in common, they have a basis for understanding and communicating with each other while at the same time respecting each other's differences and learning from each other.

In assessing decision-making styles, the most important consideration is the strengths and weaknesses associated with one's type and preferences. Decision makers thus can assess which kinds of decisions they can make well and with confidence, which kinds of decisions they should "think twice" about, and when they should seek the input of others, preferably those of opposite type.

Work Relationships with Others

Type theory can be useful in helping managers work with others—subordinates, peers, and even superiors. People of the same type or those with three preferences in common quite easily understand each other. However, frequently there is friction between people of opposite types, though an understanding of type can lessen the friction.

Identifying the type preferences of others is not easy and must be done with caution. Even though with practice individuals may develop skill in identifying the type of others by observation, observation is a less reliable and valid measure of type than the MBTI. However, with practice and deliberate effort, one can develop skill in identifying the type preferences of others.

The key to this is deliberate, systematic, effort. It cannot be done spontaneously, sporadically, or randomly. The observer must keep in mind the characteristics of all of the preferences, ruling in and ruling out preferences based on observation of *consistent* patterns and tendencies. The observer must also keep in mind the dynamic nature of type theory, remembering that for introverts, the auxiliary process is the most observable and that their orientation to the outer world (J-P preference) points to their second-preferred function. In work settings, further caution is necessary because observable patterns and tendencies may reflect the demands of the work situation rather than true preferences.

Knowledge of the type of others can be very useful. As noted above, this can reduce interpersonal friction, and it can also help managers delegate more appropriately. For example, extraverts can be given jobs that involve variety and a lot of people; long, slow jobs should be avoided. On the other hand, introverts can be given jobs that require concentration, working alone, and a long time to complete. Judging types do better when they can plan their work and follow the plan; perceptive types do better in situations that require flexibility and adaptability; they prefer not to be bound to a plan. Judging types will follow a plan through to completion but tend to ignore interruptions, even urgent ones. On the other hand, perceptive types take on too many things at once and have difficulty completing any of them, tending to all interruptions, even insignificant ones. Thus, knowledge of subordinates' type preferences and the characteristics associated with various types can help managers match the requirements of a job with the strengths of individuals.

Knowledge of type can also help in dealing with one's superior(s). The success of a proposal for a new program, project, or budget request can be enhanced by presenting it in terms that appeal to a superior's preferences. Of course, any proposal should be complete in its analysis and justification. However, if the person acting on the proposal is a feeling type, emphasis can be placed on the program's effect on the people in or served by the organization; if the person is an intuitive type, future possibilities might be emphasized, and so on.

Working Groups

Critically important to executives and managers is an effective managerial and working team. "Good teamwork calls for recognition and use of certain *valuable differences* between members of the team."[10,2] The value of the differences between team members is that they bring something different to a problem, situation or project, and what they bring in sum is more than people of the same type would bring. They will see quite different aspects of a situation and direct action toward quite different ends. What would be boring and dull to some types (and thus not done well) will be interesting and rewarding to other types and thus handled well. A variety of types on any team will contribute to greater effectiveness, more informed decisions, and greater satisfaction.

Teams of opposite types can run into difficulties, however. Opposite types often disagree on what should be done, how it should be done, or whether anything at all should be done. Forceful members,

particularly judging types, are likely to maintain that they are right, while less forceful members will resent being overpowered. Communication may suffer because what seems a perfectly reasonable and clear statement to one type may seem preposterous to another type. Morale and effectiveness may be at stake in composing teams of opposite types.

Morale and effectiveness will survive, however, if team members recognize that both kinds of perception and judgment are necessary for sound problem-solving, if they respect and value each others' differences, and if they learn to tailor their communication to others of opposite type. There are no "golden rules" about the proportion of team members that should be of the same or similar type (three or four preferences in common), near-similar type (two preferences in common), and opposite or near-opposite type (one or no preferences in common). It is probably important that the "head" of the team have at least one preference in common with all team members and that she or he have three preferences in common with several members. It is also important that members of the exact same type not be a majority.[10]

The goal is to achieve a balance between preferences, but the balance may be tipped depending on the nature and purpose of the team. For example, an executive team might have more thinking than feeling types and more judging than perceptive types. On the other hand, a team concerned with patient care would probably need more feeling types. In any case, there are no formulas. The objective is to have all type preferences represented in relative proportion to the nature and purpose of the team.

Summary

Type theory can be useful for managers and executives. Type theory describes how people use their minds — how they perceive or take in information and how they use information or draw conclusions. Type theory can enhance a manager's or executive's decision-making powers, which represents a large part of what a manager does. Knowledge of one's own type can help one capitalize on strengths and minimize weaknesses. Knowledge of type theory and the type of others has usefulness in working with others throughout an organization. It can be used to motivate others and to maximize human resources; to gain cooperation; and to persuade and get support.

USE OF THE MBTI IN ORGANIZATIONS

An understanding of type theory and its potential for helping managers is only a preliminary step in using type theory and the MBTI in organizations. To be maximally effective, an organization, department, work group, and the individuals comprising each, must commit themselves to a better understanding of themselves and others through administration, interpretation, and discussion of MBTI results.

It is important to remember that the MBTI is not a diagnostic or evaluative tool. The results do not indicate that respondents are more or less normal, based on some standard of normalcy. Rather, they indicate important patterns and preferences in the way people take in information and make decisions.

Extensive work has been done on construction of the MBTI items and scales and on the reliability and validity of the instrument. Consequently, there is an impressive amount of evidence on the MBTI's reliability and validity, which can be found in the MBTI manuals[7,9] and the scientific literature on the theory of psychological type.

Appropriate Use of the MBTI

Unfortunately, when the MBTI first became popular, it was frequently used inappropriately. Because of this, the Association of Psychological Type, a professional association of persons interested in psychological type theory, developed a Code of Ethics for practitioners of psychological type theory and for the administration and interpretation of the MBTI.[10] Two issues are worth emphasizing. First, the MBTI should be administered only by those qualified to administer it. Second, the results of the MBTI should be provided in a face-to-face situation where the interpreter and respondent can interact.

There are many reasons why these guidelines are important. The beauty of type theory is that its general principles can be summarized so that people who do not have extensive or formal training in psychological theory can understand it. However, type theory is not simple; it is complex and dynamic. MBTI results are meaningless to a respondent unless an explanation of the theory is provided. Anyone interpreting the MBTI needs to understand the theory in all its complexity so that the explanation can be both accurate and tailored to the individual's or group's needs, questions, and issues. In addition, the MBTI is a psychometric tool. As such, accurate interpretation of results depends on an understanding of psychometric tools in general and of the psychometric properties of the MBTI in particular.

Verification of MBTI results ultimately rests with the respondent. In other words, an individual's type as determined by the MBTI should be confirmed by the individual's own sense of himself or herself. This verification, however, does not come automatically. For some people, there is instant recognition of the accurateness of the MBTI results. For others, there may be doubts — doubts caused by confusion or lack of differentiation for the preferences. Negative connotations associated with some terms — for example, the assumption that introversion implies neurotic, that judgment implies judgmental, or that feeling implies overemotional — may cause some people to reject those preferences. Thus, a true interpretation of the MBTI and an understanding of type theory cannot be provided by merely giving someone his or her type results (ESTJ, ENTP, *etc.*) or providing him or her with written material. Interpretation and verification, to be meaningful and useful, depend on a thorough understanding of type theory, knowledge of the psychometric properties of the MBTI, and interpreter-respondent interaction.

Once individuals understand and accept their own type, they can begin understanding and respecting others of different types. The MBTI is best used in small groups or work teams, with people who work together frequently. It opens up new avenues of communication and understanding, and not only enhances the problem-solving process, but also improves outcomes and decisions. With so much emphasis currently on productivity, cost, and quantitative issues, all of which are important, type theory and its application provide a relatively inexpensive way of increasing effectiveness by emphasizing the qualitative issues in organizations.

REFERENCES

1. Institute of Medicine. Nursing and nursing education: public policies and private action. Washington, DC: National Academy Press; 1983.
2. National Commission on Nursing. Initial report and preliminary recommendations. Chicago: The Hospital Research and Educational Trust, 1981.
3. Mitroff II, Kilman RH. Stories managers tell: A new tool for organizational problem solving. Mgmt Rev 1975; 64(7):18–28.
4. Hirsh SK. Using the Myers-Briggs type indicator in organizations: A resource book. Palo Alto, CA: Consulting Psychologists Press, 1985.
5. Freund CM. Assessing decision-making style with type theory. In: Henry B, Arndt C, Vincenti D, Marriner A, eds. Dimensions and issues in nursing administration. Boston: Blackwell Scientific Publications, Inc., 1988.
6. Jung CG. Psychological types. London: Rutledge and Kegan Paul, 1923.
7. Myers IB, McCaulley MH. A guide to the development and use of the Myers-Briggs type indicator. Palo Alto, CA: Consulting Psychologists Press, 1985.
8. Myers IB, Myers PB. Gifts differing. Palo Alto, CA: Consulting Psychologists Press, 1980.
9. McCaulley MH. Introduction to the MBTI for researchers. Gainesville, FL: Center for Application of Psychological Type, Inc., 1980.
10. Myers IB. Type and teamwork. Gainesville, FL: Center for Applications of Psychological Type, Inc., 1974.
11. Association of Psychological Type. Code of ethics. Bull Assoc Psychol Type 1987;7–8.

CHAPTER **20**

The Discipline of Innovation

Peter F. Drucker, PhD

Despite much discussion these days of the "entrepreneurial personality," few of the entrepreneurs with whom I have worked during the last 30 years had such personalities. But I have known many people — salespeople, surgeons, journalists, scholars, even musicians — who did have them without being the least bit "entrepreneurial." What all the successful entrepreneurs I have met have in common is not a certain kind of personality but a commitment to the systematic practice of innovation.

Innovation is the specific function of entrepreneurship, whether in an existing business, a public service institution, or a new venture started by a lone individual in the family kitchen. It is the means by which the entrepreneur either creates new wealth-producing resources or endows existing resources with enhanced potential for creating wealth.

Today, much confusion exists about the proper definition of entrepreneurship. Some observers use the term to refer to all small businesses; others, to all new businesses. In practice, however, a great many well-established businesses engage in highly successful entrepreneurship. The term, then, refers not to an enterprise's size or age, but to a certain kind of activity. At the heart of that activity is innovation: the effort to create purposeful, focused change in an enterprise's economic or social potential.

SOURCES OF INNOVATION

There are, of course, innovations that spring from a flash of genius. Most innovations, however, especially the successful ones, result from a conscious, purposeful search for innovation opportunities, which are found only in a few situations.

Four such areas of opportunity exist *within* a company or industry:

Unexpected occurrences.
Incongruities.
Process needs.
Industry and market changes.

Three additional sources of opportunity exist *outside* a company in its social and intellectual environment:

Demographic changes.
Changes in perception.
New knowledge.

True, these sources overlap, different as they may be in the nature of their risk, difficulty, and complexity, and the potential for innovation may well lie in more than one area at a time. But among them, they account for the great majority of all innovation opportunities.

Unexpected Occurrences

Consider, first, the easiest and simplest source of innovation opportunity: the unexpected. In the early 1930s, IBM developed the first modern accounting machine, which was designed for banks, but banks in 1933 did not buy new equipment. What saved the company—according to a story that Thomas Watson, Sr., the company's founder and long-term CEO, often told—was its exploitation of an unexpected success: the New York Public Library wanted to buy a machine. Unlike the banks, libraries in those early New Deal days had money, and Watson sold more than a hundred of his otherwise unsalable machines to libraries.

Fifteen years later, when everyone believed that computers were designed for advanced scientific work, business unexpectedly showed an interest in a machine that could do payroll. Univac, which had the most advanced machine, spurned business applications. But IBM immediately realized it faced a possible unexpected success, redesigned what was basically Univac's machine for such mundane applications as payroll, and within five years became the leader in the computer industry, a position it has maintained to this day.

The unexpected failure may be an equally important innovation opportunity source. Everyone knows about the Ford Motor Company's Edsel as the biggest new car failure in automotive history. What very few people seem to know, however, is that the Edsel's failure was the foundation for much of the company's later success. Ford planned the Edsel, the most carefully designed car to that point in American automotive history, to give the company a full product line with which to compete with GM. When it bombed, despite all the planning, market research, and design that had gone into it, Ford realized that something was happening in the automobile market that ran counter to the basic assumptions on which GM and everyone else had been designing and marketing cars. No longer did the market segment primarily by income groups; suddenly, the new principle of segmentation was what we now call "life-styles." Ford's immediate responses were the Mustang and the Thunderbird—the cars that gave the company a distinct personality and reestablished it as an industry leader.

Unexpected successes and failures are such productive sources of innovation opportunities because most businesses dismiss them, disregard them, and even resent them. The German scientist who around 1906 synthesized novocaine, the first nonaddictive narcotic, had intended it to be used in major surgical procedures like amputation. Surgeons, however, preferred total anesthesia for such procedures; they still do. Instead, novocaine found a ready appeal among dentists. Its inventor spent the remaining years of his life traveling from dental school to dental school making speeches that forbade dentists to "misuse" his noble invention in applications for which he had not intended it.

This is a caricature, to be sure, but it illustrates the attitude managers often take to the unexpected: "It should not have happened." Corporate reporting systems further ingrain this reaction, for they draw attention away from unanticipated possibilities. The typical monthly or quarterly report has on its first page a list of problems, that is, the areas where results fall short of expectations. Such information is needed, of course; it helps prevent deterioration of performance.

But it also suppresses the recognition of new opportunities. The first acknowledgment of a possible opportunity usually applies to an area in which a company does better than budgeted. Thus genuinely entrepreneurial businesses have two "first pages"—a problem page and an opportunity page—and managers spend equal time on both.

Incongruities

Alcon Industries was one of the great success stories of the 1960s because Bill Connor, the company's founder, exploited an incongruity in medical technology. The cataract operation is the world's third or fourth most common surgical procedure. During the last 300 years, doctors systematized it to the point that the only "old-fashioned" step left was the cutting of a ligament. Eye surgeons had learned to cut the ligament with complete success, but it was so different a procedure from the rest of the operation and so incompatible with it that they often dreaded it. It was incongruous.

Doctors had known for 50 years about an enzyme that could dissolve the ligament without cutting. All Connor did was to add a preservative to this enzyme that gave it a few months' shelf life. Eye surgeons immediately accepted the new compound, and Alcon found itself with a worldwide monopoly. Fifteen years later, Nestlé bought the company for a fancy price.

Such an incongruity within the logic or rhythm of a process is only one possibility out of which innovation opportunities may arise. Another source is incongruity between economic realities. For instance, whenever an industry has a steadily growing market but falling profit margins — as, say, in the steel industries of developed countries between 1950 and 1970 — an incongruity exists. The innovative response: minimills.

An incongruity between expectations and results can also open up possibilities for innovation. For 50 years after the turn of the century, shipbuilders and shipping companies worked hard both to make ships faster and to lower their fuel consumption. Even so, the more successful they were in boosting speed and trimming fuel needs, the worse ocean freighter's economics became. By 1950 or so, the ocean freighter was dying, if not already dead.

All that was wrong, however, was an incongruity between the industry's assumptions and its realities. The real costs did not come from doing work (that is, being at sea) but from not doing work (that is, sitting idle in port). Once managers understood where costs truly lay, the innovations were obvious: the roll-on and roll-off ship and the container ship. These solutions, which involved old technology, simply applied to the ocean freighter what railroads and truckers had been using for 30 years. A shift in viewpoint, not in technology, totally changed the economics of ocean shipping and turned it into one of the major growth industries of the last 20 to 30 years.

Process Needs

Anyone who has ever driven in Japan knows that the country has no modern highway system. Its roads still follow the paths laid down for — or by — oxcarts in the tenth century. What makes the system work for automobiles and trucks is an adaptation of the reflector used on American highways since the early 1930s. This reflector shows each car, which other cars are approaching, from any one of a half-dozen directions. This minor invention, which enables traffic

to move smoothly and with a minimum of accidents, exploited a process need.

Around 1909, a statistician at the American Telephone & Telegraph Company projected two curves 15 years out: telephone traffic and American population. Viewed together, they showed that by 1920 or so every single female in the United States would have to work as a switchboard operator. The process need was obvious, and within two years, AT&T had developed and installed the automatic switchboard.

What we now call "media" also had their origin in two process need-based innovations around 1890. One was Mergenthaler's Linotype, which made it possible to produce a newspaper quickly and in large volume; the other was a social innovation, modern advertising, invented by the first true newspaper publishers, Adolph Ochs of the *New York Times,* Joseph Pulitzer of the *New York World,* and William Randolph Hearst. Advertising made it possible for them to distribute news practically free of charge, with the profit coming from marketing.

Industry and Market Changes

Managers may believe that industry structures are ordained by the Good Lord, but they can — and often do — change overnight. Such change creates tremendous opportunity for innovation.

One of American business's great success stories in recent decades is the brokerage firm of Donaldson, Lufkin & Jenrette, recently acquired by the Equitable Life Assurance Society. DL&J was founded in 1961 by three young men, all graduates of the Harvard Business School, who realized that the structure of the financial industry was changing as institutional investors became dominant. These young men had practically no capital and no connections. Still, within a few years, their firm had become a leader in the move to negotiated commissions and one of Wall Street's stellar performers. It was the first to be incorporated and go public.

In a similar fashion, changes in industry structure have created massive innovation opportunities for American health care providers. During the last 10 or 15 years, independent surgical and psychiatric clinics, emergency centers, and HMOs have opened throughout the country. Comparable opportunities in telecommunications followed industry upheavals — both in equipment (with the emergence of such companies as ROLM in the manufacturing of private branch exchanges) and in transmission (with the emergence of MCI and Sprint in long-distance service).

When an industry grows quickly — the critical figure seems to be in the neighborhood of a 40% growth rate over ten years or less — its structure changes. Established companies, concentrating on defending what they already have, tend not to counterattack when a newcomer challenges them. Indeed, when market or industry structures change, traditional industry leaders again and again neglect the fastest growing market segments. New opportunities rarely fit the way the industry has always approached the market, defined it, or organized to serve it. Innovators therefore have a good chance of being left alone for a long time.

Demographic Changes

Of the outside sources of innovation opportunity, demographics are the most reliable. Demographic events have known lead times; for instance, every person who will be in the American labor force by the year 2000 has already been born. Yet, because policymakers often neglect demographics, those who watch them and exploit them can reap great rewards.

The Japanese are ahead in robotics because they paid attention to demographics. Everyone in the developed countries around 1970 or so knew that there was both a baby bust and an education explosion going on; half or more of the young people were now staying in school beyond high school. Consequently, the number of people available for traditional blue-collar work in manufacturing was bound to decrease and become inadequate by 1990. Everyone knew this, but only the Japanese acted on it and they now have a ten-year lead in robotics.

Much the same is true of Club Mediterranee's success in the travel and resort business. By 1970, thoughtful observers could have seen the emergence of large numbers of affluent and educated young adults in Europe and the United States. Not comfortable with the kind of vacations their working-class parents had enjoyed — the summer weeks at Brighton or Atlantic City — these young people were ideal customers for a new and exotic version of the "hangout" of their teen years.

Managers have known for a long time that demographics matter, but they have always believed that population statistics change slowly. In this century, however, they don't. Indeed, the innovation opportunities that changes in the numbers of people, and their age distribution, education, occupations, and geographic location make possible are among the most rewarding and least risky of entrepreneurial pursuits.

Changes in Perception

"The glass is half-full" and "the glass is half-empty" are descriptions of the same phenomenon but have vastly different meanings. Changing a manager's perception of a glass from half-full to half-empty opens up big innovation opportunities.

All factual evidence indicates, for instance, that in the last 20 years, Americans' health has improved at unprecedented speed — whether measured by mortality rates for the newborn, survival rates for the very old, the incidence of cancers (other than lung cancer), cancer cure rates, or other factors. Even so, collective hypochondria grips the nation. Never before has there been so much concern with health or so much fear about health. Suddenly everything seems to cause cancer or degenerative heart disease or premature loss of memory. The glass is clearly half-empty.

Rather than rejoicing in great improvements in health, Americans seem to be emphasizing how far away they still are from immortality. This view of things has created many opportunities for innovations: markets for new health care magazines, for all kinds of health foods, and for exercise classes and jogging equipment. The fastest growing new U.S. business in 1983 was a company that makes indoor exercise equipment.

A change in perception does not alter facts. It changes their meaning, though — and very quickly. It took less than two years for the computer to change from being perceived as a threat and as something only big businesses would use to something one buys for doing income tax. Economics do not necessarily dictate such a change; in fact, they may be irrelevant. What determines whether people see a glass as half-full or half-empty is mood rather than fact, and change in mood often defies quantification. But it is not exotic or intangible. It is concrete. It can be defined. It can be tested. And it can be exploited for innovation opportunity.

New Knowledge

Among history-making innovations, those based on new knowledge—whether scientific, technical, or social—rank high. They are the superstars of entrepreneurship; they get the publicity and the money. They are what people usually mean when they talk of innovation, though not all innovations based on knowledge are important. Some are trivial.

Knowledge-based innovations differ from all others in the time they take, in their casualty rates, and in their predictability, as well as in the challenges they pose to entrepreneurs. Like most superstars, they can be temperamental, capricious, and hard to direct. They have, for instance, the longest lead time of all innovations. There is a protracted span between the emergence of new knowledge and its distillation into usable technology. Then, there is another long period before this new technology appears in the marketplace in products, processes, or services. Overall, the lead time involved is something like 50 years, a figure that has not shortened appreciably throughout history.

To become effective, innovation of this sort usually demands not one kind of knowledge but many. Consider one of the most potent knowledge-based innovations: modern banking. The theory of the entrepreneurial bank—that is, of the purposeful use of capital to generate economic development—was formulated by the Comte de Saint-Simon during the era of Napoleon. Despite Saint-Simon's extraordinary prominence, it was not until 30 years after his death in 1826 that two of his disciples, the brothers Jacob and Isaac Pereire, established the first entrepreneurial bank, the Crédit Mobilier, and ushered in what we now call "finance capitalism."

The Pereires, however, did not know modern commercial banking, which developed at about the same time across the channel in England. The Crédit Mobilier failed ignominiously. Ten years later, two young men—one an American, J.P. Morgan, and one a German, Georg Siemens—put together the French theory of entrepreneurial banking and the English theory of commercial banking to create the first successful modern banks, J.P. Morgan & Company in New York and the Deutsche Bank in Berlin. Another ten years later, a young Japanese, Shibusawa Eiichi, adopted Siemens' concept to his country and thereby laid the foundation of Japan's modern economy. This is how knowledge-based innovation always works.

The computer, to cite another example, required no fewer than six separate strands of knowledge:

Binary arithmetic; Charles Babbage's conception of a calculating machine in the first half of the nineteenth century; the punch card, invented by Herman Hollerith for the U.S. census of 1890; the audion tube, an electronic switch invented in 1906; symbolic logic, which was created between 1910 and 1913 by Bertrand Russell and Alfred North Whitehead; and the concepts of programming and feedback that came out of abortive attempts during World War I to develop effective anti-aircraft guns. Although all the necessary knowledge was available by 1918, the first operational computer did not appear until 1946.

Long lead times and the need for convergence among different kinds of knowledge explain the peculiar rhythm of knowledge-based innovation, its attractions, and its dangers. During a long gestation period, there is a lot of talk and little action. Then, when all the elements suddenly converge, there is tremendous excitement and activity and an enormous amount of speculation. Between 1880 and 1890, for example, almost 1,000 electrical apparatus companies were founded in developed countries. Then, as always, there was a crash and a shakeout. By 1914, only 25 of these companies were still alive. In the early 1920s, 300 to 500 automobile companies existed in the United States; by 1960, only 4 remained.

It may be difficult, but knowledge-based innovation can be managed. Success requires careful analysis of the various kinds of knowledge needed to make an innovation possible. Both J.P. Morgan and Georg Siemens did this when they established their banking ventures. The Wright brothers did this when they developed the first operational airplane.

Careful analysis of the needs and, above all, the capabilities of the intended user is also essential. It may seem paradoxical, but knowledge-based innovation is more market dependent than any other kind of innovation.

De Havilland, a British company, designed and built the first passenger jet airplane, but it did not analyze what the market needed and therefore did not identify two key factors. One was configuration — that is, the right size with the right payload for the routes on which a jet would give an airline the greatest advantage. The other was equally mundane: how the airlines could finance the purchase of such an expensive plane. Because De Havilland failed to do an adequate user analysis, two American companies, Boeing and Douglas, took over the commercial jet aircraft industry.

PRINCIPLES OF INNOVATION

Purposeful, systematic innovation begins with the analysis of the sources of new opportunities. Depending on the context, sources will have different importance at different times. Demographics, for instance, may be of little concern to innovators in fundamental industrial processes like steel making, although Mergenthaler's Linotype machine became successful primarily because there were not enough skilled typesetters available to satisfy a mass market. By the same token, new knowledge may be of little relevance to someone innovating a social instrument to satisfy a need that changing demographics or tax laws have created. But — whatever the situation — innovators must analyze all opportunity sources.

Because innovation is both conceptual and perceptual, would-be innovators must also go out and look, ask, and listen. Successful innovators use both the right and left sides of their brains. They look at figures. They look at people. They work out analytically what the innovation has to be to satisfy an opportunity. Then they go out and look at potential users to study their expectations, their values, and their needs.

To be effective, an innovation has to be simple and it has to be focused. It should do only one thing; otherwise it confuses people. Indeed, the greatest praise an innovation can receive is for people to say: "This is obvious! Why didn't I think of it? It's so simple!" Even the innovation that creates new users

and new markets should be directed toward a specific, clear, and carefully designed application.

Effective innovations start small. They are not grandiose. They try to do one specific thing. It may be to enable a moving vehicle to draw electric power while it runs along rails, the innovation that made possible the electric streetcar. Or it may be the elementary idea of putting the same number of matches into a matchbox (it used to be 50). This simple notion made possible the automatic filling of matchboxes and gave the Swedes a world monopoly on matches for half a century. By contrast, grandiose ideas for things that will "revolutionize an industry" are unlikely to work.

In fact, no one can foretell whether a given innovation will end up a big business or a modest achievement. But even if the results are modest, the successful innovation aims from the beginning to become the standard setter, to determine the direction of a new technology or a new industry, to create the business that is — and remains — ahead of the pack. If an innovation does not aim at leadership from the beginning, it is unlikely to be innovative enough.

Above all, innovation is work rather than genius. It requires knowledge. It often requires ingenuity. And it requires focus. There are clearly people who are more talented as innovators than others but their talents lie in well-defined areas. Indeed, innovators rarely work in more than one area. For all his systematic innovative accomplishments, Edison worked only in the electrical field. An innovator in financial areas, Citibank for example, is not likely to embark on innovations in health care.

In innovation as in any other endeavor, there is talent, there is ingenuity, and there is knowledge. But when all is said and done, what innovation requires is hard, focused, purposeful work. If diligence, persistence, and commitment are lacking, talent, ingenuity, and knowledge are of no avail.

There is, of course, far more to entrepreneurship than systematic innovation: distinct entrepreneurial strategies, for example, and the principles of entrepreneurial management, which are needed equally in the established enterprise, the public service organization, and the new venture. But the very foundation of entrepreneurship — as a practice and as a discipline — is the practice of systematic innovation.

CHAPTER **21**

Innovation

The promise and the perils for nursing and information technology

Carol A. Romano, RN, MS, FAAN

For most people the word "innovation" calls to mind thoughts of technology, new products, and new ways of making them. The word creates the image of an invention such as the microprocessor, or a computer-related device. An innovation, however, represents the process of bringing a new problem-solving idea into use and can be social, organizational, or technical. Unfortunately, often in the health care system, technical innovations are reviewed and analyzed without the necessary complementing social and organizational changes that are required to reap the full benefits of the innovation. This is particularly true with computerization or information technology as an innovation. This article reviews the concept of innovation and the ongoing search for a theory to explain it; it examines strategies for managing innovation; and finally, it addresses the principles and practices of innovation as they relate to health care.

The period between the late 1970s and 1980s has been referred to as the "information age." This term draws attention to the nature of the changes taking place in society, but few, if any clues, are given to nurses regarding how to respond in this information age. Nursing as a discipline is not concerned with

Reprinted from *Computers in Nursing,* Vol. 8, No. 3, with permission of J. B. Lippincott Company © 1990.

producing computers, telecommunications, or databases; it is not in the business of selling, transmitting, or storing information. Rather, the modern nursing role is to take the explosion of new information and find new and better ways to deliver care. Nursing has the role of innovator in the 1990s.

CLARIFICATION OF CONCEPTS

It is important to differentiate innovation from invention. Although they are related terms and frequently used interchangeably, they are very different concepts. To invent is to conceive of an idea. Every invention is a *new* combination of *preexisting* knowledge which satisfies a *need.* Innovation, on the other hand, is a more subtle concept. To innovate is to convert an idea into use or action. It refers to technology being used for the first time. It is the transfer of knowledge applied to practical purposes.

Utterback (1982) views innovation as a process with four phases or components. The first stage involves the *generation of ideas,* and involves the synthesis of existing information about a need or alternate ways to meet a need. This phase includes recognizing the technical feasibility of an idea as well as the consumer demand. Information and creativity are very important in this phase. The second stage is *problem solving,* which includes setting goals and designing alternative solutions to meeting them. Thinking, gathering information, and politicking are very important during this stage. *Implementation* is the next phase and consists of "start up" costs and the energy required to bring an original solution or invention to its first use. *Diffusion* takes place in the environment and begins after the innovation is introduced.

Studies have noted there is an 8–15-year lag time between the time technical information about an idea is generated and the time it is used or diffused in the environment as an innovation (Utterman, 1982). This lag time varies with the type of innovation, the market to which it is directed and the resources needed to implement it. It is noted, however, that lag time is shortest for mechanical innovations. Chemical and pharmaceutical innovations have longer lag times. Electronic innovations take the longest. This lag time is shortened when the inventor himself tries to innovate, when the innovation is directed toward consumers, and when innovations are developed by the government as opposed to those from industry (Enos, 1962).

LITERATURE REVIEW

The literature offers some help in understanding the diffusion of innovation. It contains one well developed classical theory concerned with the adoption of innovation by individuals. The literature also contains a body of knowledge concerned with organizational traits as they influence organizational innovations; finally there are a few first steps toward understanding the political decision making process used by health institutions who confront opportunities to innovate (Greer, 1977).

Classical Theory

Classical diffusion theory addresses how responsible individuals receive and adopt innovative ideas. It focuses on the process through which a new idea is communicated from one person to another, the networks through which information passes, and how influence is exerted by opinion leaders. Social traits of motivation, attitudes, competencies, and leadership are studied (Mohr, 1969; Becker, 1970; Kaluzny, 1974). It explains the diffusion of low risk or readily acceptable innovations, especially in organizations where resources are available. This theory suggests that diffusion occurs in response to the values of professional groups and that professional norms view innovation as good. Classical theory falters, however, in explaining or encouraging the diffusion of disruptive or risky innovations (Greer, 1977).

Organizational Theory

Classical theory lacks the ability to explore those aspects of organizations which constrain or facilitate the implementation of innovation. Thus, one turns to organizational theory for assistance in determining factors that influence an organization's response to innovation. It is believed that the complexity of an organization, or the diversity of its tasks, yields diverse employees. This complexity results in the circulation of diverse ideas, which in turn may spark the innovative process. However, while the proliferation of ideas is encouraged, complexity handicaps the implementation of any one idea. Thus, the innovation process becomes stifled in phase one (Wilson, 1977).

Centralization of decision making is thought to inhibit innovation by reducing the flow of information and thus the spread of ideas (Zaltman, 1973). However, contrasting studies have noted that decentralization and the inclusion of many people in decision making slows the speed with which an innovation is brought to use (Mansfield, 1973). Formalization is also thought to inhibit the communication and awareness of new ideas. Highly formalized rules limit the consideration of alternatives and emphasize routines. However, conflicting studies note that from a positive perspective, formalization increases an organization's ability to implement new ideas by decreasing conflict, ambiguity, and uncertainty as to how an innovation will affect one's job (Zaltman, 1973).

Political Theory

Relatively little scholarly attention has been paid to how the politics of decision making in health organizations affect the representation of interests and values of an innovation. Questions relevant to innovation and decision making include: What are the competing goals of different groups? Who controls the resources used to persuade others? and whose ideas prevail? For example, a physician sees the goal of hospitals as that of catering to the needs of his private patients; medical schools view the role of hospitals as providing quality medical education and research; and government agencies see the goal of hospitals as providing access to quality care at an efficient cost (Greer, 1977).

Political processes suggest that the adoption of innovations involves not only consideration of individuals with certain inclinations, and organizations with certain properties, but also groups with special interests. Although studies have been grouped into these three theoretical frameworks, (Greer, 1977) many aspects of innovation remain virgin territory for study. These areas include exploration of the medical and social consequences of an innovation, the cost effectiveness of adopting an innovation, and the specific attributes of innovations as they affect diffusion.

MANAGEMENT OF INNOVATION

Coexisting with the state of evolving theories of innovation is the present reality of continual confrontation with the need for change and innovation. It comes in the form of new demands and expectations from consumers, providers, governments, standards setting bodies, and the technologies of today's health care environment (Tushman & Moore, 1982). It is recognized that change has always been a constant in human affairs; for to stand still is to move backwards. Change is a generic concept that deals with any modification, whereas innovation is defined as any idea or practice perceived to be new to an organization, work group, or individual. Thus, all innovation is considered change — but not all change is innovation. (Kaluzny & Hernandez, 1981). Therefore, the effective management of innovations in meeting the changing needs of society is essential. Kanter (1983) views change as a disruption of existing activities, and a redirection of energies. Innovation is the exploration of that change for opportunities to provide new

services, businesses, methods, or products. To move an invention or technology to its first use or to the realm of an innovation requires a transfer of three things: information about technology, enthusiasm for the technology, and the authority to use the technology (Quinn & Mueller, 1982).

This transfer itself requires change. To understand the interrelationship of the three prerequisites, consider the following simile paraphrased from Quinn & Mueller (1982):

> A new technology or invention is like a baby. You can't just bring it into the world and expect it to grow and be successful. It needs a mother to love it and keep it going when things are tough. The mother is enthusiasm. It needs a pediatrician or nurse to solve the problems the mother can't cope with alone. The pediatrician or nurse being expert information and technical skill. It needs a father to feed and house it. The father being authority with resources. Without any one of these the baby or the new technology may still turn out all right but its chances of survival are very slim.

A new set of skills is required to effectively manage in the innovation age. First, we are challenged to use power skills in persuading others to invest information, support and resources in new ideas. Second, we are challenged with the complexity of managing participation because grass roots involvement in generating ideas and defining needs is critical. Third, we are challenged to understand how to design and construct change as an opportunity for innovation (Kanter, 1983).

Power Skills

To initiate and implement innovation, people need that extra bit of power to move a system off the course on which it seemed to be irrevocably running. An innovative accomplishment is very different from merely doing one's job. It is different in scope, in impact, and in the energy required to carry it out. That is why power, the capacity to mobilize and influence people and resources, is so important.

Power skills include gathering information and expertise and maintaining open communications. Open communication provides the airwaves for innovation. An open door policy for accessing information and asking questions is critical if we want ideas to spark. To get support and resources, coalition building — a network of people support — needs to be established. This process involves "clearing" an idea with those persons in authority and then lobbying for peer support. The skill of mobilizing an idea into an innovation involves an action oriented perspective. Action tasks involve handling criticism or opposition, maintaining momentum, redesigning or bending the rules in midstream if needed, and "managing the press" or the external communication to create favorable and up-to-date impressions of the innovation.

Managing Participation

Next, participation is essential in managing innovation. But managing participation is a balancing act between having management control and providing opportunities to team members. There are no rules or formulas for making participation work because it is the skillful engagement of many talents in the mastery of change. And although participation is encouraged, innovators still must maintain leadership. This leadership consists of keeping all minds focused on the vision of success, of defining non-negotiable areas, of monitoring group processes and pressures, and of keeping the time factor controlled.

Construction of Change

Finally, the management of innovation requires the ability to design and construct change. Efforts at change have to mobilize people around what is not yet known, what is not yet experienced. There are no logical steps or how-to approaches. Plans may exist more as an outline to be modified, than a blueprint to be followed to the letter. Constructing change involves selecting the right people — the ones with the ideas that move beyond established practices. It involves creating the right places — the integrative environments that support innovation and encourage teams to support and implement the visions. Constructing change encompasses determining the right times — the moments in an organization's history or in a society when one can reconstruct reality in order to shape a more productive and successful future.

OPPORTUNITIES FOR INNOVATION

The practice of innovation involves purposefully searching for sources that portend opportunities for success (Drucker, 1985). These sources are reliable indicators that changes have occurred or can be made to occur with little effort. First, the unexpected outside event offers rich opportunity for successful innovation with low risk involved. The irony here, however, is that unexpected successes or consequences are almost always neglected or viewed as nuisances. Such was the case with the unexpected discovery of penicillin. The "unexpected" should be taken seriously. The incongruity between reality as it is and reality as it "ought to be" is the second invitation to innovate. But incongruity does not necessarily appear on management charts or tables. It doesn't appear as quantitative data but rather as a qualitative discrepancy that is clearly visible to people in an organization or market. Here again, incongruity is usually overlooked or taken for granted.

Need as a source of innovation relates to the phrase "necessity is the mother of invention." With these innovations everyone knows the need exists, but usually no one does anything about it. When the innovation finally appears, however, it is immediately accepted as "obvious." Next, changes in the structure of industries or markets are sources of innovation. These changes are highly visible and predictable to outsiders but are perceived as threatening changes to insiders. Such changes usually result from rapid growth in an area or from the convergence of two technologies. For example, when telephone technology and computer technology were combined they spurred the need for new products and new ways of doing business.

These first four sources of innovation are visible and show up in one's internal environment. The next three, defined by Drucker (1985), are external and reflect changes in the social, philosophical, political, and intellectual environments. Changes in populations, ie., in size, age, composition, and economic structure have the most predictable consequences for change. However, although the importance of demographics has always been acknowledged, population changes are thought to occur so slowly and over such a long time span that little attention to demographics is given in day-to-day corporate decisions. Next, changes in perception are seen as sources for innovation. One needs only to consider the difference between the glass "half-full" and the glass "half-empty" as a classic example of perception difference. In mathematics there is no difference here; however, great differences exist in perception and consequence. When people's perceptions change from seeing "half-full" to seeing "half-empty," opportunities for innovation exist.

And finally, new knowledge in science and technology is the "superstar" of the sources for innovation. It requires the longest lead time of all innovations and possesses the highest risks — especially in the currently hot areas of personal computing and biotechnology. Here innovators do not get a second chance; they must be right the first time because the environment is harsh and unforgiving. A knowledge-based innovation brings about change, but it is hard to predict whether the user of such an innovation will be receptive, indifferent, or resistive; there in lies the risk. Stories abound about the acceptance of knowledge-based innovations; ie., when the railroad was introduced in Prussia it was felt that no one would pay money to get from Berlin to Potsdam in 1 hour when he could ride his horse in 1 day for free! And when the computer appeared, there was not a single expert who imagined that business would ever want such a contraption (Drucker, 1985).

PRINCIPLES OF INNOVATION

Given the many sources of innovation, one may turn attention to several principles in confronting innovations (Drucker, 1985). The first principle of innovation is to analyze the opportunities or sources. Different ones have different importance at different times. The search for opportunity has to be organized, and done on a regular, systematic basis. The second

principle is that innovation is both conceptual and perceptual. It requires use of both the right and left sides of the brain. Successful innovators look at figures and they look at people. It's imperative to look, to ask and to listen so that innovation can meet the expectations, values, and needs of users. The third principle notes that for an innovation to be effective it has to be simple and focused otherwise it confuses people. If it is not simple it will not work. It's as simple as that. Next, effective innovations start small and they aim to do one specific thing. Grandiose ideas do not work because they require too much money or manpower resources. Starting small allows time to make the adjustments and changes needed for the innovation process to proceed. Finally, successful innovations aim at being the best from the very beginning, nothing less is tolerated.

The principles acknowledge that innovations have to be handled by ordinary people; anything too clever in design or execution is almost bound to fail. In addition it is recognized that innovations which try to do too many things at once become diffuse and remain ideas that never make it off the drawing board. That is, successful innovations need the focused energies of a unified effort. In addition, one needs to innovate for the present, not the future, because an innovation may not reach its full maturity until 20 years after development. Such was the case with computers which began to assert their impact 25 years after the first working model. However, from day one, computer technology had immediate application. Unless there is an immediate application, an innovation is likely to remain a "brilliant idea" whose day never came.

Despite the guidance offered by principles of innovation, sometimes the obvious is ignored. For example, innovation is hard work which makes demands on diligence, persistence, and committment. To succeed, innovators must build on their strengths, on what they are good at, and must focus on an area important enough to invest in the frustration and work required. And because innovations effect a change in the behavior of people and how they work or produce, they need to be driven by the consumer or market need.

SUMMARY

An author once explained the rise and fall of nations in terms of the challenges they confronted and the responses they made. As we enter the last decade of this century, it is expected that the challenges in health care delivery will change and thus the previously successful responses must also change. Nightingale cautions us that no system endures that does not march (Rogers, 1985). Developing technical, social, and organizational innovations are the prerequisites for survival in tomorrow's health care system. Therefore, we need to march into the next century with powerful ideas, acknowledgment of the need for social, organizational, and technical innovations, and we need to march being comfortable with the unfamiliar. But as we journey into the discovery of the innovation age, and embark on the challenges it brings, most importantly we must march embracing nursing as the future of human health.

REFERENCES

Becker, M.H. (1970). Sociometric Location and Innovativeness: Reformulation and Extension of the Diffusion Model. *American Sociological Review 35,* 267–282.

Drucker, P.F. (1985). *Innovation and entrepreneurship-practices and principles.* New York: Harper and Row.

Enos, J.L. (1962). In R.R. Nelson (Ed.), *The role and direction of Inventive Activity: Economic and Social Factors.* Princeton: Princeton University Press, 298–322.

Greer, A.L. (1977). Advances in the Study of diffusion of innovation in health care organizations. *Milbank Memorial Fund Quarterly Health and Science, 55*(34), 505–532.

Kaluzny, A.D., Gentry, J.T., & Veney, J.E. (1974). Innovation of health services: A comparative study of hospitals and health departments. *The Milbank Memorial Fund Quarterly: Health and Society, 55,* 51–82.

Kaluzny, A.D. & Hernandez, S.R. (1981). Organizational Change and Innovation. In S. Shortell, & A. Kaluzory, (Eds.), *Health Care Management.* New York: John Wiley and Sons, 379–417.

Kanter, R.M. (1983). *The change masters.* New York: Simon and Schuster.

Mansfield, E. (1973). Speed of response of firms in new techniques. *Quarterly Journal of Economics, 77,* 290–311.

Marquis, D.G. (1982). The anatomy of successful innovations. In M.L. Tushman, and W.L. Moore (Eds.), *Readings in the management of innovation,* Boston: Pitman, 42–50.

Peters, T. & Austin, N. (1985). *A passion for excellence.* New York, Random House.

Pinchott, G. (1985). *Intrapreneuring* New York: Harper and Row.

Quinn, J.B. & Mueller, J.A. (1982). Transferring Research Results to Operations. In M.L. Tushman and W.L. Moore (Eds.), *Readings in the management of innovation,* Boston: Pitman, 60–83.

Rogers, M. (1982). Beyond the Horizon. In N. Chaska (Ed.), *The nursing profession: A time to speak* New York: McGraw Hill, 795–800.

Tushman, M.L. & Moore, W.L. (1982). *Readings in the Management of Innovation.* Boston: Pitman.

Utterback, J.M. (1982). Innovation in industry and the diffusion of technology. In M.L. Tushman & W.L. Moore (Eds.), *Readings in the management of innovation.* Boston: Pitman, 29–41.

Wilson, J.Q. (1966). Innovation in organization: Notes toward a theory. In J.D. Thompson (Ed.), *Approaches to organizational design.* Pittsburgh: University of Pittsburgh Press, 193–218.

Zaltman, G., Duncan, R., & Holbeck, J. (1973). *Innovations and organizations.* New York: Wiley.

CHAPTER **22**

The 10 Stages of Change

Dottie Perlman, BA, NCC
George J. Takacs, MA

Organizations spend a considerable amount of time, money, and effort trying to change and yet are never fully satisfied with the results. A major reason for this is that organizations rarely deal consciously or constructively with the human emotions associated with organizational change. Unfortunately, there are no exterior "fix-it" time tables or mechanical means available to help them. Resources and energy from within individuals are necessary to help accomplish change. "All change is a kind of death, and all growth requires that we go through depression."[1] To cope with and work through the changes which affect them, organization members must deal with the emotional process of "letting go," of letting the past die, and of experiencing the depression.

The model presented by Elizabeth Kuebler-Ross in her book, *On Death and Dying,* is useful in dealing with one major aspect of change: grief.[2] While Kuebler-Ross deals with death and dying on an individual level, the stages she presents are strikingly similar to those encountered in organizational change. However, the authors added five phases to Kuebler-Ross's original five to help explain more fully the problems associated with change. The purpose of this article is to enable executives, managers, and supervisors to face some of the more personal and emotional issues which change

Reprinted from *Nursing Management,* Vol. 21, No. 4, with permission of S-N Publications, Inc. © 1990.

produces, and to offer them certain tools which will help them make conscious choices about how they will deal with change in their organizations.

PHASE ONE—EQUILIBRIUM

(See Table 22-1 for summary of phases) Many employees, especially those in management positions, have set and met personal and professional goals within the organization as it is now. Both consciously and unconsciously they are vested in the status quo. With both personal and professional goals in "sync" with the organization, they are comfortable and contented. The employees identify with the organization; they are emotionally and intellectually in a state of equilibrium.

When external events begin to put pressure on the status quo, the organization changes. Financial reverses may lead to reductions in force which cost some people their jobs and build up insecurities for others. Reorganizations due to mergers, acquisitions and corporate takeovers lead to political struggles, transfers, promotions, new management, and policy changes. New technologies in and of themselves alter job responsibilities and relationships. Employees who are heavily vested in the status quo, who benefited from it, enjoyed it, created it, and nurtured it, have a very hard time letting go of it. Loss of the status quo presents not only logical, intellectual problems, but also the emotional problems associated with grief.

TABLE 22-1

Growing with change: The emotional voyage of the change process

	CHARTED SUMMARY	
PHASE	**CHARACTERISTICS/SYMPTOMS**	**INTERVENTIONS**
1. Equilibrium	High energy level. State of emotional and intellectual balance. Sense of inner peace with personal and professional goals in sync.	Make employees aware of changes in the environment which will have impact on the *status quo*.
2. Denial	Energy is drained by the defense mechanism of rationalizing a denial of the reality of the change. Employees experience negative changes in physical health, emotional balance, logical thinking patterns, and normal behavior patterns.	Employ active listening skills; e.g., be empathetic, nonjudgmental, use reflective listening techniques. Nurturing behavior, avoiding isolation, and offering stress management workshops also will help.
3. Anger	Energy is used to ward off and actively resist the change by blaming others. Frustration, anger, rage, envy and resentment become visible.	Recognize the symptoms, legitimize employees' feelings and verbal expressions of anger, rage, envy and resentment. Active listening, assertiveness, and problem-solving skills needed by managers. Employees need to probe within for the source of their anger.
4. Bargaining	Energy is used in an attempt to eliminate the change. Talk is about "if only." Others try to solve the problem. "Bargains" are unrealistic and designed to compromise the change out of existence.	Search for real needs/problems and bring them into the open. Explore ways of achieving desired changes through conflict management skills and win-win negotiation skills.
5. Chaos	Diffused energy, feeling of powerlessness, insecurity, sense of disorientation. Loss of identity and direction. No sense of grounding or meaning. Breakdown of value system and belief. Defense mechanisms begin to lose usefulness and meaning.	Quiet time for reflection: Listening skills. Inner search for both employee and organization identity and meaning. Approval for being in state of flux.
6. Depression	No energy left to produce results. Former defense mechanisms no longer operable. Self-pity, remembering past, expressions of sorrow, feeling nothingness and emptiness.	Provide necessary information in a timely fashion. Allow sorrow and pain to be expressed openly. Long-term patience, take one step at a time as employees learn to let go.

TABLE 22-1—cont'd
Growing with change: The emotional voyage of the change process

| | CHARTED SUMMARY | |
PHASE	CHARACTERISTICS/SYMPTOMS	INTERVENTIONS
7. Resignation	Energy expended in passively accepting change. Lack of enthusiasm.	Expect employees to be accountable for reactions to behavior. Allow them to move at their own pace.
8. Openness	Availability to renewed energy. Willingness to expend energy on what has been assigned to individual.	Patiently explain again, in detail, the desired change.
9. Readiness	Willingness to expend energy in exploring new events. Reunification of intellect and emotions begins.	Assume a directive management style: assign tasks, monitor tasks and results so as to provide direction and guidelines.
10. Re-emergence	Rechanneled energy produces feelings of empowerment and employees become more proactive. Rebirth of growth and commitment. Employee initiates projects and ideas. Career questions answered.	Mutual answering of questions. Redefinition of career, mission and culture. Mutual understanding of role and identity. Employees will take action based on own decisions.

People grieve for the old organization, the old people, the old ways.

Concrete methods of facilitating change, such as outplacement, retraining, office automation, team building, and strategic planning are, by and large, mechanical and intellectual. The overt technical, mechanical and intellectual methods of handling change are well treated by the organization because they are easier for administrators to conceptualize and implement. They focus on observable tasks but do not address the emotions aroused by the change. Change produces a sense of uneasiness, a lack of direction, a sense of unfinishedness, insecurity, and a lack of closure. For employees, organizational change involves a continuous process of "letting go" of the status quo. However, organizational change efforts usually ignore the psychological impact of grief, and techniques for helping managers address the emotional aspects of change are largely unexplored.

Employees at all levels are anxious about what is happening, yet the response to their free-floating and unstated anxiety usually is a lecture about productivity and competition. The emotional pain contained in the employees' questions is easily ignored. Progress in change is then blocked because employees will not let go of the old ways as they struggle to maintain equilibrium.

PHASE TWO—DENIAL

The more organizational power the employees have, the easier it initially is to hold onto their familiar patterns. However, as external changes and internal pressures continue to build, their ability to maintain their equilibrium wanes. People in an organization use organizational power to keep the world looking as they see it and this provides them with a sense of certainty, security, and power. The only drawback is that, as pressures build, it takes more and more energy and power to keep the world operating as they view it. The energy the employees used to use to maintain the status quo now has to be channeled to actively resist the change.

During the denial phase managers must acknowledge the legitimacy of employees' feelings and make themselves available to discuss the change(s). Employees may not show up to participate in training sessions which are meant to help facilitate change, and the reasons are usually "valid:" an accident or illness (theirs or others) or some other acceptable-sounding reason. Issuing edicts to the effect that "by such and such a date all discussion on the issue will be over" will not help. Rather, the change agents should use active listening skills, e.g., mirroring back to the employees both the content of their expressions and the feeling they communicate. However, care must be taken to do so in a way which implies neither acceptance nor rejection of what the employees feel and think. Even though care must be taken to avoid sending the message that the change process will come to a halt because of what the employees think or feel, if administrators clarify and confirm their perceptions of the employees' communication they will convey to them that their rational and emotional messages are getting through.

To help both managers and employees work through this second phase, it is important to learn what part of the change they are accepting and then build on that. So, set up a hotline, schedule regular meetings and actually *hear* what people say. When employees begin to deny the current reality, they must neither be isolated and judged nor agreed with. Acknowledge their statements and then reinforce the reality of the change. Stress management training seminars may help everyone involved.

PHASE THREE—ANGER

When employees begin to recognize that the current reality no longer meets their expectation and they don't have enough energy to maintain the *status quo* anymore, they will begin to blame others for their predicament. Elizabeth Kuebler-Ross notes: "When the first stage of denial cannot be maintained any longer, it is replaced by feelings of anger, rage, envy and resentment."[3] How true! Almost universally, employees feel that "administrators" should know what makes them angry and do something to help. The past is glorified and the present made worse than it actually is. Anger becomes more and more visible as employees blame others and demand that someone else "make things all right again." They do not even think about doing something to help themselves.

At this stage, it is important to spend time sorting out problems and being clear about who has what problem, what belief or value is being violated or interfered with, and what makes managers and employees angry. Employees' feelings must be recognized and accepted as they go through this phase, but the change process must not be stopped. Rather, focus on *who* has the problem, *who* is angry, and *how* to deal with that anger. Managers and employees alike should be taught (1) how to recognize the symptoms of anger; (2) how to legitimatize the feelings associated with anger; and (3) how to deal with and resolve the causes of anger.

Blaming others is a highly stressful dead-end street. Confront their anger: ask people what they are angry about, why they are angry and what they think should be done to solve the problems. Listen to them. Use active listening and assertiveness skills such as talking to one another *openly, listening* to one another in an empathetic way, and expressing *candidly* what the *real* needs are.

This is a tough time for managers because most of the employees' anger is directed at them. It is unrealistic to expect managers to forge ahead, unaffected by sarcasm or abusive language. They are human, too. Therefore, administration must provide a special forum for the managers to vent their own frustration and anger. Managers need reinforcement and support in order to handle the change process and to deal with their own employees.

Robert E. Alberti and Michael L. Emmons point out that we many times work out our anger indirectly.[4] Problem-solving skills are very important at this stage. Employees must "own" their anger. They have to work through it, identify its causes and resolve it through negotiations, confrontation or attitudinal change. As Alberti and Emmons point out, it is not enough to say, "I'm mad as hell!" It must be followed through with ". . . and here's what I think we can do about it. . . ."[5]

PHASE FOUR—BARGAINING

As described by Kuebler-Ross, phase four in dealing with grief is the Bargaining stage.[6] *In this phase, employees try to enter into an agreement with others to prevent the inevitable from happening.* Talk focuses on the "if only's." To put it into more businesslike terms, the bargaining phase consists of negotiation: "I will give up this much, or go this far in helping you institute the change, if you in turn will do this for me." When this occurs, managers are lulled into believing that things are progressing. Perhaps they are, but most of the time, the proffered "negotiations" will compromise the change right out of existence. If enough people in the organization engage in this behavior, the result will be a reinforcement of the *status quo.*

Power and authority can move the organization through the first two phases. However, they are of little help in the third phase because anger is something which is felt but usually not discussed or dealt with in organizations. Thus, anger fuels the bargaining process in the fourth phase. Although this phase appears to be rational, logical, and professional (the bargainers may even use data, graphs, and charts), these quasi-negotiations are just a mask for the feelings behind them. Energy is channeled to stop or limit the change, not to achieve it. If some sort of compromise is reached, both parties usually comply ("To get along, you have to go along") although they know that the agreement will not work. And it almost never does. When you hear the phrase, "We decided that the way we are working now is the best way after all," it signifies that the resisters have successfully used the negotiation process to bring the change to a halt.

In the bargaining phase, conflict management skills and win-win negotiation skills are very helpful. One useful resource is Fisher and Ury's *Getting to Yes: Negotiating Agreement Without Giving In.*[7] This book provides excellent methods for developing objective criteria which can be used as measuring sticks in the negotiation stage. Rosabeth Moss Kanter's *The Change Masters* is also very helpful.[8] She describes several interesting "institutionalized" ways of negotiating: "tin-cupping," "buying-in," and "loading the rifle" are among them. Those who have engaged in such processes know full well their positive and negative aspects.

Focus on those needs threatened by the proposed change. Once they are identified openly, both sides can explore how the needs can be met without damaging the desired change. For example, one organization the authors worked with was attempting to install a computer-based, information management system. Progress was so slow and problematical that there was a danger that the system would never become operational. In all good faith, management decided to hold a "team building" session so as to bring all the players together and work on the problems of installing the new system. The design of the team building session was very rational and logical. However, the employees slated to attend the team building retreat resisted. The consultants, sensing the resistance in the group, prevailed upon management to change the design of the retreat but even then problems arose. At the retreat site, the design team and the managers began to discuss the problems in a logical and rational way. It didn't work. Frustration ran high. However, the consultants, using the fishbowl technique, finally enabled both sides to listen to each other's anger and pain regarding the change. There was a real fear in the organization that this new system would cost people their jobs. Once this fear, anger and pain were identified openly, real progress was made. The team even stayed over the weekend, on their own time, to finish addressing the real issues. When the team members returned to the workplace, progress on the implementation of the system moved very quickly.

PHASE FIVE—CHAOS

Diffused energy is *the* characteristic of phase five. Nothing seems to be working anymore. Up until this time the employees have been expending energy in avoidance, resistance and denial. Now there is a feeling of powerlessness. Former patterns and defenses lead nowhere. Employees in the organization are full of questions and insecurity; they do not seem to be sure of anything. Very little makes sense. The organization begins to lose its identity and direction. A general sense of disorientation spreads and intensifies. This state is evident in such questions and statements as "Does anyone know where we're going?" and "What *is* going on around here?" There is no anchor and, as a result, people feel as if they are living in chaos.

There are no mechanical, technical fixes available to repair matters in this phase. Both employees and managers begin to wonder if *any* of their previous efforts were worthwhile. They feel as if they have no option except to accept the reality of chaos. Administrators should be available to listen to the employees vent their frustration about a lack of direction while "giving the employees permission to be wherever they are" with the change. The search for order turns inward as both the organization and its employees accept accountability for their actions. They need time to reflect on the chaos. To process the chaos, discussions between managers and employees should be held, but *no outcomes* from those discussions should be expected. What should be conveyed is that this chaos is a necessary stage that will pass. Not knowing the direction in which the future will take them, *not* knowing the current structure is OK right now.

PHASE SIX—DEPRESSION

As employees and organizations move through the Chaos phase, they soon realize that they do not have enough energy left to produce results. Time is spent remembering "the good old days" when things made sense and people were happy. Resources are depleted and a terrible sense of nothingness prevails: people wallow in self-pity.

They are depressed, but the type of depression they are experiencing determines the intervention. Kuebler-Ross makes a distinction between reactive depression and preparatory depression.[9] Each one is different and dealt with differently.

Fear of loss causes *reactive* depression. It is alleviated by receiving help to meet a specific need or information to deal with the issues raised. In one instance a group of executives resisted change because they thought the change would cause them to lose

pay or even their positions. When the CEO addressed these fears by promising that there would be no loss of pay or job, the group solved the problem in six months.

Reactive depression is alleviated by telling employees as much as possible about the organizational change as soon as possible. Despite protestations to the contrary, our experience suggests that this is more an exception than a rule. The reason for this is the main point of this article: management waits until the last minute so to avoid the human problems associated with change. Administrators may feel very uncomfortable themselves because there is no "quick fix" available or checklist of guidelines to follow to solve the emotional problems associated with change. Therefore, they find it hard to help their employees deal with this aspect of the change. So, they delay the inevitable—and usually end up intensifying and lengthening their employees' reactive depression. Preparatory depression "is a tool to prepare for the impending loss . . ., in order to facilitate the state of acceptance."[10] At this stage, the employees must express their sorrow over the passing of the old way of doing things. Their expression must be taken as truthful and honest. No response from management is necessary: the expression of sorrow needs only to be accepted and heard.

Many executives may respond to employees' self-pity impatiently: they are not running social welfare agencies! While this is true, the fact remains that the organization is going to be spending money one way or another. If it does not give the employees time to deal with their depression, the organization will experience an increase in sick days, low morale, high turnover, and low productivity. When the depression is deepest, both the organization and the employees have the least tolerance and run the risk of taking actions which both may regret later. The organization needs task completion, goal accomplishment and profits to survive. The employees need to deal with their depression and they need patience in dealing with the demands of the organization. The organization needs patience in dealing with employees wallowing in self-pity. However, employees have a responsibility to continue to produce for the organization. While the organization must help its employees move one step at a time and concentrate on the long view, the organization also must insist on productivity. Day-to-day survival is what is important at this point.

In short, the choice is not whether money is going to be spent, but rather *how* money is going to be spent. According to William Bridges, "To achieve even half of the change a company attempts, it must spend an amount equivalent to between five and 10 percent of its annual budget for the personnel whose behavior is supposed to be changed."[11] The real trouble with self-pity is that it keeps people from talking when others are ready to listen. When the employees are ready to talk, no one is ready to listen. Consequently, employees may inadvertently be pushed to move prematurely into the next phase. To move through preparatory depression people need to surrender to reality, develop faith/hope that there is an answer, believe that one's experience is normal, wipe the slate of expectations clean, and *let go*.

PHASE SEVEN — RESIGNATION

As people work through the depression, they finally come to resignation: they accept the reality of the change and no longer resist it. If employees have had enough time and have been given some help in working through each of the previous stages, they will reach a stage during which they are neither depressed nor angry about the change.[12] However, do not make the mistake of thinking that they will actively, cheerfully support the change. Employees still need to deal with the emotional residue of anger and depression. Until it is fully processed, the employees simply won't have the extra energy necessary to actively support the change. There is some commitment to the effort, even though employees do not fully agree to it. In a sense, you could say that consensus has been reached.

Once the employees have accepted the change, continued prodding will be counter productive. Critical or cynical comments about the lack of enthusiasm may push employees away from acceptance and back into a subtle form of resistance. From a functional point of view, employees are now operating as if they have let go of the past and are accepting the change,

even though the memories are still there. Employees are ready to perform the tasks necessary to move on, even though they still have a strong wish that it didn't have to be this way.

PHASE EIGHT — OPENNESS

Once changes are accepted at the personal level and values rearranged, employees can then proceed with growth in a new direction. In the "openness" phase people finally are able to be OK with "I don't know." They are beginning to expend their energies on what others recommend, but not focused enough to initiate a project on their own. That is, they have become available to follow directions from their managers and they will be open to learning about the change itself. Now that the employees are more receptive to hearing it, the organization must repeat what the desired change is. It will mean explaining the procedures, policies, regulations, etc., one more time for the employees. The repetition may seem unnecessary, but it will produce results. However, it is still too soon to expect enthusiasm for the change(s).

PHASE NINE — READINESS

In the "readiness" phase employees are willing to explore new events and expend energy in that exploration. During this phase, the "emotional letting go" begins to be noticeable. The employees are willing to do what is asked of them with more energy than before, but still not willing to figure out on their own what to do. In this phase, management needs to be more directive in style and assign specific tasks to individuals. Managers should monitor tasks and results and thus obtain insight about what and how the employees are doing. This monitoring is intended to enable managers to help employees better understand and to provide immediate feedback and direction to the employees. This also provides both the atmosphere and the opportunity for employees to ask questions about either the tasks or their own internal feelings. It is not a means of "checking" for mistakes. In this way, managers can give employees a sense of their support and interest.

PHASE TEN — RE-EMERGENCE

In the "re-emergence" phase, the change becomes fully operational as employees "let go" emotionally and intellectually of the old ways. Employees begin to test out ideas on their own. Little by little they start once again to make an investment in themselves and in the organization. They are again willing to risk exposing themselves to the organization. They become more pro-active in their work environment, newly empowered and helpful. The employees have redefined their role and meaning in the organization. They have rebuilt what was torn apart in the chaos phase. Both the employees and the organization have developed new identities and meaning. The answers to employees' career questions become clearer. They now are more certain why they are doing what they are doing — so is the organization. This reestablishment of role and identity reenergizes both parties and gives them a sense of direction which is stronger now than it has been at any time during the change process.

Both parties also are more realistic about what they can control, both begin to initiate more active steps, both have re-prioritized, and both have weighed the different possibilities open to them and have begun to take action on their decisions.

One result is that the employees may choose new career paths. Another may be that the organization may have to redefine its culture, mission, objectives and goals. If the organization can make it possible for the employees' new career paths to be congruent with its own redefinition, then both parties benefit. However, some employees may have to look elsewhere to pursue their new careers. As much as possible, both parties should make this separation a "no-fault" event.

In summary, the generators of change in an organization and the recipients of that change must work through various stages to deal effectively with the emotional dimensions of change. By addressing, dealing with, and working through the intellectual and emotional issues involved in each phase, the organization and its employees become stronger and the change more likely to be successful and to lead to success.

REFERENCES

1. Peck, M. Scott, MD, *The Different Drum: Community Making and Peace,* (New York, NY: Simon and Schuster, 1987), p. 222.
2. Kuebler-Ross, Elizabeth, *On Death and Dying,* (New York, NY: MacMillan Publishing Co., 1969).
3. *Ibid.,* p. 50.
4. Alberti, Robert E. and Michael L. Emmons, *Your Perfect Right,* (San Luis Obispo, CA: Impact Publishers, 1986), pp. 125–138.
5. *Ibid.,* p. 131.
6. Kuebler-Ross, *op cit.,* p. 82.
7. Fisher, Roger and William Ury, *Getting to Yes,* (New York, NY: Penguin Books, 1985).
8. Kanter, Rosabeth Moss, *The Change Masters,* (New York, NY: Simon and Schuster, 1983), p. 158.
9. Kuebler-Ross, *op cit.,* p. 86.
10. *Ibid.,* p. 87.
11. Bridges, William, "How to Manage Organizational Transition," *Training,* September, 1985, p. 30.
12. Kuebler-Ross, *op cit.,* p. 112.

SUGGESTED READINGS

UNIT THREE. ORGANIZATIONAL CONCEPTS, THEORIES, AND VALUES

Ethics and Values

Andrews K: Ethics in practice, HBR 67(5):100-104, 1989.

Fry S: The ethics of caring: Can it survive in nursing? NO 36(1):48, 1988.

Huckabay L: Ethical-moral issues in nursing practice and decision making, NAQ 10(3):61-67, 1986.

Reilly D: Ethics and values in nursing: are we opening a pandora's box? Nursing & Health Care 10(2):90-95, 1989.

Organizational Culture

del Bueno D and Vincent P: Organizational culture: How important is it? JONA 16(10):15-20, 1986.

Reynierse J. and Harker J: Measuring and managing organizational culture, Human Resource Planning 9(1):1-8, 1986.

Schein E: Coming to a new awareness of organizational culture. Sloan Management Review 3-16, 1984.

Communication

Hansen M and Avadian B: Improving your written communications, JONA 19(12):18-21, 1989.

Lamar E: Communicating personal power through nonverbal behavior, JONA 15(1):41-44, 1985.

McHugh M: Information access: A basis for strategic planning and control of operations, NAQ 10(2):10-20, 1986.

Power and Influence

Bartolome F and Laurent A: The manager: Master and servant of power, HBR 64(6):77-86, 1986.

Gorman S and Clark N: Power and effective nursing practice, NO 34(3):129-134, 1986.

Kanter R: Power failure in management circuits, HBR 57(4): 65-75, 1979.

Decision Making

Dowd R: Participative decision-making in strategic management of resources, NAQ 13(1):11-18, 1988.

Drucker P: The effective decision, HBR 45(1):92-98, 1967.

Etzioni A: Humble decision-making, HBR 67(4):122-126, 1989.

Fralic MF: Decision support systems: Essential for quality administrative decisions, NAQ 14(1):1-8, 1989.

Poteet G: Nursing administrators and delegation, NAQ 13(3):23-32, 1989.

Taylor A: The decision-making process and the nursing administrator, Nursing Clinics of North America 18(3): 439-447, 1983.

Varricchio C: The process of influencing decisions, NAQ 6(4):8-15, 1982.

Innovation and Change

Haffer A: Facilitating change, JONA 16(4):18-23, 1986.

Kanter RB: The new managerial work, HBR 67(6):85-92, 1989.

Pointer D and Pointer T: Building innovative nursing departments: Thriving in turbulent times, Nursing Economics 3:73-77, 1985.

Ward M and Moran S: Resistance to change: Recognize, respond, overcome, Nursing Management 15(1):30-33, 1984.

PART II

THE NURSE ADMINISTRATOR

The role of the nurse in an executive position implies a set of activities or expectations that are likely to be exhibited by a person occupying that position. This set of expectations or activities influences the role to be performed by that individual assuming the role. The content of that role is influenced by organizational needs, as well as the expectations and interpersonal, administrative, and clinical skills of the incumbent. Various processes and nursing resources that the nurse administrator is responsible and accountable for within the health care setting include strategic planning, marketing, financial management, the organization and delivery of nursing care, recruitment, retention, and staff development, productivity and staffing, performance appraisal and evaluation, quality management, and negotiation and conflict management.

Part II includes selections of readings focusing on the nurse administrator. Unit Four focuses on the roles, functions, and responsibilities of the nurse administrator. Poulin's 1980 study replicates a 1971 study and her 1984 article describes the nurse executive role. Focused interviews are used to describe the role, identify competencies required, provide a basis for planning educational programs, and identify areas for research. Changes in the role from 1971 to 1980 are summarized, and conclusions from the data are presented. Simms, Price, and Pfoutz (1985) also used interviews to define the role of the nurse executive in various settings. Results are described according to characteristics of the respondents, perceptions of the administrative role in terms of leadership and management activities, clinical practice activities, education and research activities, and nursing administration trends. Hefferin, Horsley, and Ventura state that as research increasingly becomes a part of the nursing profession, nurses must develop their ability to evaluate and utilize research findings. Problems in understanding, accepting, and incorporating research findings were identified through survey research. Price, Simms, and Pfoutz (1987) identify factors that influence career advancement opportunities for nurse executives. Key variables related to career advancement patterns of top-level nurse administrators in health-related organizations and academic settings are highlighted. Respondent characteristics, career choice motivations, career advancement patterns, mentoring influences, and job satisfaction elements are presented.

Unit Five focuses on the processes and resources that the nurse executive manages. Strategic planning is a management task in which resources are allocated to programmed activities in order to achieve goals in a dynamic environment. Jones describes the basis for strategic planning in a health care organization, the phases of the planning process, and the external and internal environmental elements that need to be considered. Reider and Norton state that the benefits of computer technology to nursing are predicated on the profession's ability to define its requirements in the areas of practice, education, and research. The process of defining requirements for an automated nursing system is described and illustrated. A model automated nursing system identifying five major processes and the inputs, outputs, and data elements involved is proposed.

Marketing enables organizations to identify wants and needs in order to achieve organizational goals and objectives. Chaney asserts that the success of a nurse executive in the area of marketing depends on appropriate application of marketing principles (including assessment and/or awareness of needs), development of new services, promotion of services, and target-market development. In their inspiring selection, Nelson et al propose a fiduciary model of health care marketing that emphasizes honesty and public accountability, considering the patient's best interests, and avoiding unnecessary services, all of which can keep marketing consistent with the ethical tradition of medicine.

Several articles address financial management, which is a major responsibility of nurse executives. Edwardson and Giovannetti review cost-accounting methods for nursing services. Four distinctive approaches for identifying nursing costs are outlined and the methodological problems discussed. Sovie and Smith emphasize that variable billing for nursing care is critical to nurses' economic and professional accountability. They assert that identifying the costs of nursing care in hospitals helps destroy multiple myths about nurses' economic contribution and responsibility. A nursing patient classification system as the basis for variable billing for nursing care is discussed. McCloskey asserts that identification of costs for nursing interventions will permit accurate evaluation of cost-effectiveness of nursing care. Two models to determine costs of nursing care are analyzed. Stillwagon questions how costs of nursing care are affected when professional nurses practice nursing based on patient's needs as opposed to institutional policy. A different nursing care delivery system that builds on primary nursing but frees the nurse from institutional constraints is described.

In the next section the readings present innovative approaches to the organization and delivery of nursing care. Capers suggests that when nursing departments consider using a conceptual model as a guide for clinical nursing practice certain questions need to be answered before adopting a model. Answers to these questions will better facilitate the use of nursing models in hospital settings. Porter-O'Grady proposes a shared governance model for professional practice, which is an accountability-based governance system for professional workers, and analyzes three operating models that are currently in use in nursing service settings. Deremo describes the components of a proposed innovative model for change in a department of nursing that incorporates values, practice, performance, productivity, behavior, and reimbursement into one structure. Halloran, Patterson, and Kiley describe a nursing information system that provides nurses with a case-specific computerized measure of the demand for nursing services, as well as a measure of the capability to meet the demand and the resultant cost of nursing care. Primm explains the differentiated nursing case management (DCM) nursing care delivery system. She asserts that the system has been developed to promote consumer satisfaction and nurse retention through development of high quality, cost-effective nursing care. Zander explains that components of nursing case management have shown positive resolutions for some of the complex issues facing health care administrators, managers, and clinicians. The model, its practical and philosophical origins, application, and early results are described. Yano-Fong analyzes the advantages and disadvantages of Product-Line Management (PLM) in an acute care setting. Four major areas of PLM are discussed.

The readings in the next section focus on recruitment, retention, and staff development. In her provocative article, Friss states that the rapidly worsening nursing shortage is likely to continue in the absence of fundamental changes in nursing education and salaries. A long-range solution is proposed. Jones emphasizes that turnover is a major concern for the chief nurse executive. A conceptual model describing nursing turnover and a methodology for measuring the direct and indirect costs of nursing turnover is presented. Larson et al assert that it has long been assumed that job satisfaction relates to employee turnover and quality of care. The difficulties of measuring job satisfaction and the results from an assessment tool administered to nurse employees in an acute care hospital are discussed. Bailey et al describe a consortium framework in which four teaching hospitals developed a curriculum for nursing staff development. The results are compelling and would serve as a useful model for interested agencies.

The next selection of readings focuses on productivity and staffing. Because of the nursing shortage and financial constraints, productivity and staffing are challenging and often frustrating areas for nursing administrators. In his classic, yet contemporary article, Herzberg asserts that KITA — the attempt by management to "install a generator" in the employee — has been demonstrated to be a total failure. He reviews his motivation-hygiene theory of job attitudes and concludes with 10 steps to job enrichment. McHugh implies that nurse managers want simple, effective measures of productivity with which to discover productivity levels and evaluate empirically the effects of specific management decisions on this productivity. The author analyzes productivity measurement techniques and discusses ways to increase efficiency in nursing. The questions posed in the Helmer and Olson article offer a managerial guideline for reducing inefficiency. Giovannetti and Johnson state that maintaining the reliability and validity of a patient classification system for nurse staffing is a continuing challenge for nurse managers. The authors present a second-generation patient classification system that employs a built-in reliability and validity monitoring system.

The three readings in the next section deal with nursing performance and the development of a performance appraisal and evaluation system. Bushardt and Fowler describe and critique several performance appraisal methods. Sudela and Landureth report on the implementation of a criterion referenced performance appraisal system. Employee participation at all levels is seen as the key to successful implementation of that system. McCloskey and McCain studied four sets of performance data from two studies of nurses in which the same instrument was used. Findings are in remarkable agreement regarding skills performed well and those needing improvement.

The readings in the following section focus on quality management. The nurse executive must be committed to the principles of quality management to promote high-quality, client-centered care. The purpose of Alexander and Bauerschmidt's study was to investigate whether the fit between the technology of an organization and structure can be linked to organizational effectiveness. Their findings suggest that technology and structure in nursing units have implications for nursing administration. Sovie emphasizes that all nursing practices must be critically examined in terms of their contribution to quality patient care and their effects on nurses' time and morale. Five basic guidelines that could reduce time spent in documentation are proposed. Schemele and Foss discuss Crosby's principles of quality management and his quality management maturity grid (QMMG). The authors describe its use in the health care setting.

The final section in Part II contains readings on negotiation and conflict management. This area is of increasing concern to nurse executives because of their active involvement in the negotiation process. Kelley describes three interacting elements that occur in negotiations and presents a tautological model of a systems theory of negotiation. Strategies used in the negotiation process are presented. The purpose of the Johnson and Bergmann article is to encourage nurse executives to develop the brokering skills of their managers. The development of effective brokering skills rests on the acquisition of power equity, political savvy, and knowledge of the organization's culture. Booth discusses philosophies of conflict and the causes of conflict. Six solutions for ending the crises of misunderstanding, lack of cooperation, loss of power, or infringement on territory are presented.

Unit Four

ROLES, FUNCTIONS, AND RESPONSIBILITIES

CHAPTER 23

The Nurse Executive Role
A structural and functional analysis

Muriel A. Poulin, RN, EdD, FAAN

There is a body of knowledge that is basic to functioning as an administrator and that must be incorporated into programs to prepare the nurse executive. A variety of forces are creating continual demands on increasingly complex jobs and forcing educators to reassess program offerings in graduate schools of nursing. The author did a study in 1971 to determine how nurse executives viewed their positions in an increasingly complex and changing situation.[1] This paper reports on a 1980 replication of that study. The question investigated was: "What are the structural and functional components of the nurse executive's position as perceived by selected incumbents?"

CONCEPTUAL FRAMEWORK

Human action was the conceptual framework for exploring the role of the nurse executive. According to Robert K. Merton, every human act comprises five components: the actor, ends, means, conditions, and norms. The *actor* is the one who is acting; the *ends* are the goals, purposes, or objectives of the act; the *means* are the "devices" adopted to achieve adjustment between the self and the environment; *conditions* refer to the objective content of the act, the circumstances that the actor must take into account; and the *norms*

Reprinted from *The Journal of Nursing Administration,* Vol. 14, No. 2, with permission of J. B. Lippincott Company © 1984.

are the socially shared standards of rights and obligations.[2] For the purpose of this study, the *actor* is the nurse executive; the *ends* are the objectives of the job or the categories of the position holder's responsibilities; the *means* are the functions, processes, and methods utilized in carrying out the job; the *conditions,* the factors in the setting that serve as facilitators or obstacles to job performance; and the *norms,* the standards of behavior acceptable in the position. They are studied as they are perceived by the position's incumbent, the actor.

THE INSTRUMENT

The conceptual framework was the basis for identifying three broad questions from which the interview guide was developed:
1. What does the nurse executive do?
2. What means are utilized in doing the job?
3. What conditions affect performance?

In the original study, these questions were the departure points for interviews with several graduate students in nursing administration and practicing directors of nursing. From these, an interview guide was developed and pilot tested, refined, and tested again. The final tool for both studies includes demographic data and questions in the following broad categories:
1. Persons most influential
2. Nursing care
3. Personnel

4. Education
5. Overall Nursing Department responsibilities
6. Overall responsibilities in agency administration
7. Community
8. Personal assessment

THE SAMPLE

The primary consideration in selecting the sample was recognition by peers of administrative competence and/or reputation for the progressive nature of organization for delivery of nursing care. Three leaders in nursing administration participated in the selection and were not included in the sample. The nonrandomized and restricted nature of the sample is a recognized limitation in the study.

THE PROCEDURE

All nurse executives who were asked agreed to participate in the study. Both written correspondence and telephone conversations were utilized for specific arrangements. All were provided with the investigator's sabbatical proposal, which included an overview of the study to be carried out. All interviews were taped and lasted for 2 or more hours. Notes were taken by the investigator.

Standardization was assured by using the same introduction and asking the major questions in the same way. Probing questions were asked depending upon responses to the main questions. Participants answered in their own way, within their own frame of reference, and were not limited in any way. The investigator's background along with the level of competency of the participants and their interest in the study resulted in an abundance of data.

ANALYSIS OF DATA

The original classification scheme of categories was used to analyze manifest content in a systematic and objective manner. The category set was based on the substantive areas of the interview. Each major category represents a main section of the interview and each subcategory represents one of the questions in the section. Further division of subcategories was used as indicators of detailed information in each subcategory.

The category set has face validity. It evolved from the interview scheme, which was based on findings from the literature, the professional organization's official statement on the role of the director of nursing, and interviews with many qualified administrators of nursing services.

Face validity was checked and validity determined for the category set by two coders who independently applied the classification scheme to two randomly selected interviews. They were given the same transcriptions, a copy of the classification scheme, written instructions, and a copy of the interview guide.

The investigator's categorization of data was used as a base for comparing the results of the coding. The percentage of agreement among coders was high (95%) and justified the category set as developed. In the original study, a 96.6 percent agreement had been obtained in coding three interviews.

THE NURSE EXECUTIVE: A PROFILE

From the 11 women and 1 man who participated in the study, the following profile of the nurse executive in this study emerges: a single woman between the ages of 50 and 59 years. A graduate of a diploma program, she has supplemented her education, holds a master's degree, and has been in her present position for 5.3 years. She has been in nursing for 25 years, is obviously career oriented, and belongs to the American Nurses Association, the National League for Nursing, the American Society for Nursing Service Administrators, Sigma Theta Tau, and various civic organizations.

She is employed in a general hospital of from 400 to 599 beds and is assisted by 11 employees reporting directly to her. In her position, she reports directly to the chief executive officer of the agency and holds a corporate title that conveys her position at the top level of the organizational hierarchy.

Most Influential Persons

To obtain a sense of how the participants operate, the first question asked was which person(s) most influenced them in their present job. Although the majority (eight) perceived the chief executive officer as being most influential, five see the associate directors in nursing as also influencing them. One person perceives only her associates as the primary influencers and sees her role as a facilitator of operations through them. Although eight hold faculty appointments, only two people see the dean or vice-president of the university as influencing them in their jobs.

Nursing Care

Perceived as their primary role in nursing care are (1) the setting and implementation of standards and goals, (2) ensuring control mechanisms, (3) provision of personnel, and (4) the facilitation of staff functioning. The facilitation and promotion of research rather than actual research involvement is considered an important responsibility. Contacts with patients and families are limited and generally related to problems. Although four make rounds for review of the environment and for visibility, two others definitely view regular contact with patients as external to the realm of the nurse executive. As one stated, "It is unrealistic to expect the nurse executive to maintain clinical competency; the main responsibility is as an administrator at the executive level of the organization."

Personnel

Among personnel functions, respondents perceive their main role as the development and dissemination of policy, especially the development of budget and salary scales. Although much of the details of personnel management is delegated to assistants and personnel officers, a variety of specific activities receive their personal attention. This may reflect the individual's concern, interests, background, or the nature of problems. At one extreme, the executive director of the one home health agency maintains complete control over the recruiting, screening, and hiring of personnel. At the other, the nurse executive recruits, screens, and hires only her immediate assistants. Five executives are involved in developing the master staffing plan with seven delegating staffing functions to others. Although regulations of civil service and

university systems tend to limit freedom, nurse executives perceive that more effective recruiting and screening emerges from active nursing department direction. In one situation, key positions are filled within the university system with the nurse executive functioning as one of a group in the selection process.

It is evident that, contrary to the 1971 study, there is greater involvement of a greater number of people in personnel management. This appears to be a function of a decentralization and participatory management in which people are involved at appropriate points in the process. *Self-governance committees, task forces, individualized career development, leadership development* and *head nurse decisions* are terms used that denote a change in structure and climate from the previous study.

Another factor influencing a more active role on the part of nursing personnel seems to be a degree of dissatisfaction with the services provided by the personnel office. Comments such as "Interpretation of our philosophy of nursing—we can do it better" and "I have to keep reminding the personnel director that he is support to nursing and not the other way around" may indicate feelings of greater competency on the part of the nurse executive.

Educational Responsibilities

It is obvious from the data that educational responsibilities are an integral part of the nurse executive role. Opinions were stated about the need to develop competent people and the importance of staff education for quality care prior to the interview section on education. The question specific to education provided evidence of a role in education of students as well as employees.

Data clearly show that a diversity of educational activities is a large part of the nurse executive's role. Although delegation of some of these is common, all respondents retain varying degrees of personal involvement. All have staff education programs in their departments; and, as well, all are responsible for some aspect of education of students. Participants not only serve as preceptors for students but also teach classes, serve on advisory councils to schools, and regularly serve as guest lecturers. Comments about their leadership responsibility for promoting higher education, provision of tuition reimbursement, and desire for increased involvement in teaching substantiate education as a major category of functioning for the nurse executive. This finding is in keeping with a trend to greater educational involvement predicted in the earlier study.

One significant change is seen from the previous study where four of nine respondents had dual roles. In the current sample of 12, 1 respondent has responsibility for both education and delivery of care. The other seven who hold academic positions have joint appointments with direct responsibility to the executive officer of the agency for the delivery of care.

Nursing Responsibilities Other Than Inpatient Services

Nurse executive functions are not limited to inpatient care settings. All of the respondents are directing nursing activities in other settings and/or types of facilities.

Three participants as well as the one director of the home health agency are responsible for home care programs. One nursing department includes discharge planning, family practice clinic, alcoholic rehabilitation, an outreach program for unwed mothers, and neonatal home care. Another executive directs the nursing departments of two hospitals and is on the management team on a contractual arrangement for a third. In another similar arrangement, the director of nursing participates in management of a "sister" institution and serves as a consultant to three other hospital nursing departments. Three agencies were investigating the feasibility of home care programs with a major role being played by the nurse executive.

It is obvious that the responsibility of the nurse executive extends beyond nursing care in acute care settings. Extension of services into the community has expanded the role of nursing and hence the role of the nurse executive. Multi-unit agencies and services have added to the scope and complexity of the position as well as to the demands for a broader leadership role in meeting health needs on a community-wide basis.

There is geographic expansion of responsibility as well as complexity of role.

Hospital Administration Responsibilities

Over and above provision of nursing care, nurse executives function within an overall organizational structure. Perceptions of their role were studied as they involve, (1) other than nursing responsibilities, (2) policy and budget development, and (3) interdepartmental relations.

A sharp departure from the previous study arises in these areas of functioning. Originally, respondents emphatically agreed that their sphere of responsibility should be limited to nursing matters and opposed expansion of their role to other administrative functions. Data show an expanded role for the current participants. Only four have the nursing department as their sole area of responsibility. Titles do not denote the scope of the role. Of the four responsible for only nursing, two are vice-presidents, one is an associate hospital administrator for nursing, and one is executive director for nursing. On the other hand, the associate hospital director and the director of nursing have responsibility for six services as well as the nursing department. Another vice-president for nursing has Anesthesia (Certified Registered Nurse Anesthetists only), Central Supply, and Escort Services as well as Unit Management.

The expanding role is an interesting finding in view of various comments made of the inequities in responsibility at the executive level. As one participant states in response to a later question about desired change and the need for equity, "I have more F.T.E.s under my direction than any other administrator. I am responsible for a bigger budget than any other administrator. My responsibilities include operations as well as policy development at the executive level. My scope of responsibility is far greater than any of my associates at the executive level." Another points out, "The hospital director and assistant directors delegate to a cadre of people, whereas the director of nursing has daily and future problem-solving responsibilities practically every hour on the hour." The director of nursing experiences "constant response to change." The comment that hospital administrators have "fewer stresses" is interesting. As an example, one respondent explained that because "they do not identify with a particular profession, they are not involved in enhancing a profession." Moreover, they use a host of legal and management consultants not available to the director of nursing and "can be more leisurely in their approach."

It appears that directors, with their staff, see nursing as identifying gaps in care and assuming responsibility for coordination of patient care. As one participant states, because "nursing holds coordinating responsibility for care," the director of nursing can "manage other patient care departments." One respondent summarizes, "As nurses assume the role of corporate officer, they will assume other departments and all of the fiscal power that goes with it." A question that must be studied is "As job expands . . . what is relinquished?" What are the implications for organizational structure?

Community Responsibilities

There is little uniformity in the type of community activities among the respondents. However, all acknowledge a responsibility for contributing to meeting the health needs of the community outside of their own agency. The focus of involvement varies but activities attest to the participant's broad involvement in the health scene and are testimony to the recognition of their leadership responsibilities.

Personal Assessment

The personal reflections of the participants represent a broad and varied picture of the role of the nurse executive and the competencies considered essential to job performance. They all see themselves as leaders in nursing and recognize barriers to their maximum effectiveness. There is little uniformity in what they would change or eliminate from the role. Three of the 12 perceive cost constraints and overregulation as obstacles to effective performance and would eliminate them if within their power to do so. Personal strengths were acquired mainly through education and experience, and all but one express satisfaction and confidence with their competencies and role.

SUMMARY OF CHANGES 1971 TO 1980

1. *Titles* in 1980 reflect corporate responsibilities. Only one respondent held the title of director of nursing. The remaining executives held titles such as associate administrator for patient care services, vice-president for nursing, executive director for nursing and adjunct professor of nursing, and associate hospital administrator for nursing. It is interesting to note that the word *service* is not used in titles. In the previous study, all nine were directors or chairpersons of nursing with four also carrying an assistant/associate hospital administrator title.
2. *Authority* was not commensurate with responsibility. Among the present respondents, it is limited only by skill in utilization. Positions of authority are evident.
3. *Power potential* was not clear to earlier respondents. There is definite recognition and utilization among current respondents.
4. *Budget* development involved three of nine for review and approval of the total agency budget. Of the present 12 participants, 11 are involved in the total process. Greater awareness of the implications for budgetary control is obvious.
5. *Scope* of responsibility was on nursing care and efforts were directed toward shedding non-nursing responsibilities. Current data demonstrate increasing awareness of limited effectiveness of staff services and beliefs that greater efficiency can result from control over related service departments.
6. *Control* was centralized in the earlier study. Decentralization to various degrees and attempts to decentralize to operational levels are obvious in the current study.
7. *Dual roles* were held by four of the earlier nine respondents. In this study, only one held responsibility for both education and practice. Two others who hold assistant dean titles have very limited time commitments to the educational programs.
8. *Unions* were mentioned as a force influencing the functioning of the directors of nursing. In the current group, several function within

civil service, university, and union restrictions. Overregulation is the factor cited today.

9. *Open-door policy* (availability of management) was general in the first study. It was not mentioned in these data.

CONCLUSIONS AND IMPLICATIONS

Perceptions of 12 nursing administrators about what their jobs entail, the means for carrying out functions, and the conditions affecting performance were explored in this study. Data demonstrate the scope and complexities of the positions and indicate a set of functions similar to normative expectations as presented in literature and professional statements. However, data also indicate a highly dynamic situation as well as a complex, varied, and expanding role.

The skill and competencies of the respondents represent a qualified group of nurse executives and provides a microcosmic view of a larger population of similarly qualified nurse executives. Certain conclusions can be drawn from the interview data.

Functions

1. The nurse executive increasingly has a coordinating role with greater decentralization of control of practice to the operational levels. This is in keeping with a prediction in the previous study.
2. The nurse executive actively participates in the education of nursing students as well as personnel and other health-discipline students.
3. Demands on the nurse executive are mainly administrative, requiring a high degree of administrative sophistication and managerial competence.
4. The role of the nurse executive encompasses a broad spectrum of responsibility including related patient-care departments and influencing total institutional programming.
5. The role is that of a corporate officer in the organization and this role of corporate officer is as a nurse.

Structure

1. The scope and responsibility of the nurse executive includes both direction of nursing within the agency as well as a role in meeting the nursing needs of the broader community. This finding is in keeping with a trend identified in the earlier study.
2. The position of the nurse executive is at the top level of the power structure in the organization. This position accommodates itself to a broader spectrum of health services in keeping with consumer demands. This finding is also in keeping with a prediction in the earlier study.
3. Joint appointments with related educational settings indicate the active involvement of nurse executives in a variety of educational programs.

Implications

Multiple forces are influencing the role incumbents and all have implications for curriculum development. Changing professional work values with less commitment to 24-hour service to patients coupled with cost containment and pressures to increase productivity will lead to greater stress and greater need for social support systems for nurse executives.

More involvement in programming and negotiating with the chief executive officer and other vice-presidents as well as with boards of directors and consumers will follow. The need to interpret nursing to these individuals and groups and to bargain for the available dollar will require knowledge of the health care system and a strong commitment to nursing's potential role in the system as well as skill in innovating and sophistication in negotiations. The nurse executive will be a catalyst for patient care in the midst of a balanced budget orientation. The focus on cost is bringing with it a focus on quality control. As evaluation becomes more productive, we can anticipate restructuring of delivery systems for greater efficiency.

Contingency approaches to management are developing. Contractual arrangements for professional nursing care by independently practicing nurses are mentioned. Multi-unit corporations are evident. And reimbursement based on diagnoses is discussed.

The trend to multiple patient-service departments as the realm for nurse executive functioning is evident in this study. Although a few nurse executives express the desire to focus their efforts on delivery of nursing care, most see the acquisition of other patient services as a necessary development toward this goal. With the ability to ensure responsiveness to needs of patients and to needs of the nursing department, they believe they can more effectively manage some of the related departments and in doing so make this work life a bit simpler, while improving the quality of patient care.

This is an area that offers great potential for future study. If indeed certain departments are not effective, organizational behaviors should be studied. Several questions should be considered: To what extent are organizational goals actually accepted as a basis for operation? What is the decision-making process? How much do department heads collaborate for goal achievement? In essence, to what extent does the system permit implementation of standards of care?

Because all patient services converge on nursing, it, in effect, integrates many diverse elements on behalf of patients. These divergent elements may result in divergent goals. The nurse executive must cope with the disparate goals while maintaining the integrity of nursing as a service to patients. One must ask if the nurse executive is destined for an ever-increasing breadth of responsibility as a means to this end.

The nurse executive's educational role is another area that deserves study. There is definite evidence of active educational involvement. The role is seen as influencing nursing education rather than carrying responsibility for both education and practice. No longer content merely with providing settings for experience, the nurse executive *will* take more initiative in influencing the preparation necessary for competence in nursing practice.

Implications for educational preparation of future nurse executives are obvious. It seems imperative that both master's and doctoral programs be geared to development of the nurse executive for today's as well as tomorrow's health care demands.

REFERENCES

1. Poulin MA. A study of the structure and functions of the position of the nursing service administrator [Doctoral Dissertation]. New York: Teacher's College, 1971.
2. These components are based on Talcott Parson's early theory of action and have been found in Davis K. Human society, New York: Macmillian, 1949. They were further developed in a lecture course given by Dr. Robert K. Merton, October 1970.

CHAPTER 24

Nurse Executives
Functions and priorities

Lillian M. Simms, RN, PhD
Sylvia A. Price, RN, PhD
Susan K. Pfoutz, RN, PhD

Reams of information have been presented about nurse executives (Blair, 1976; Erickson, 1975; Moloney, 1979; Poulin, 1984; Stevens, 1981), but very little written about their actual functions and priorities. Drucker (1980) believes managers do many things that are not managing, and they may spend most of their time doing other things than planning, organizing, directing, and evaluating. Today's nurse executive is required to effectively combine clinical practice and research knowledge with managerial and leadership skills.

PURPOSES OF THE STUDY

The purpose of ongoing research at The University of Michigan is to define the role of the nurse administrator and the emerging role of the nurse executive through on-site interviews. The nurse executive is the top nurse administrator in any health-related organization who reports to the chief executive officer.

Professional practice disciplines such as nursing are defined by the application of knowledge in relation to the biopsychosocial influences affecting the health care of clients. Although clinical practice is a major

Reprinted from *Nursing Economics,* Vol. 3, No. 4, with permission of Anthony J. Jannetti, Inc. © 1985.

component of professional nursing, other essential components include research, education, and administration. These components must be articulated and coordinated in professional practice (Simms, Price, & Ervin, 1985). Clinical knowledge is recognized as the common denominator for general nursing practice and most nursing leadership roles; however, in the executive role, the leadership component is fully developed.

The research study addressed the following questions: (a) What demographic characteristics do nurse administrators possess? (b) How do nurse administrators perceive their roles? (c) Is there a difference in the nursing administrator role according to setting? (d) What are the clinical activities in which the administrator is involved? and (e) What are the trends in nursing administration?

OVERVIEW OF THE NURSE EXECUTIVE ROLE

Katz and Kahn (1978) conceptualized the role of the executive or manager as a subsystem of the organization. The subsystems work together to meet organizational needs and accomplish necessary tasks. The managerial system cuts across all operating structures. Three basic management functions can be distinguished: (a) coordination of substructures, (b) resolution of conflicts among levels, and (c) coordination of external requirements with organizational resources and needs.

Mintzberg (1973) used an observational approach to investigate the administrator's role. The work of five executives was documented in detail for 1-week periods. In addition to direct observation, executives' mail and calendars were monitored to determine lines of communication. Interviews also provided data on managers' perceptions of their work. Each written or personal contact was also described. From the data, role categories were developed: (a) three interpersonal roles, (b) three informational roles, and (c) three decisional roles. Informational roles included monitor, disseminator, and spokesperson. Interpersonal roles included figurehead, liaison, and leader. Decisional roles included entrepreneur, resource allocator, and negotiator.

Stevens (1981) described three components of nursing administration roles. The sociologic aspect is concerned with societal expectations; the rational component comprises the specific job functions and responsibilities assigned in the job description; and the personal component concerns the individual's choice of which role aspect to perform. McClure (1979) described four major characteristics of the nurse administrator's role: (a) The role involves highly labor-intensive work; (b) the role requires 24-hour service; (c) the nurse administrator is unable to predict and control work flow; and (d) the role is physically demanding.

Poulin (1984) repeated her own 1971 study and used focused interviews to analyze the structure and function of the executive role. She hypothesized that administrative demands could conflict with the clinical practice focus. Using the framework developed in her earlier work, Poulin studied the nurse executive's activities, means to complete jobs, and conditions affecting performance. Between 1972 and 1980, the role was noted to have expanded with more financial and community responsibility. The findings suggested the need for future-oriented, executive-level nurse administrators.

The literature has predominantly focused on administration in acute-care settings and provided little information about differences among settings. The general tasks of hospital care include physical care, medical care, curing, and expediting discharge (Stryker-Gordon, 1975).

In contrast, long-term care requires psychosocial care in a residential setting. In this setting, staff must understand long-term care, gerontology, and rehabilitation concerns as well as perform with minimal medical support (Barney, 1974; Ringland, 1981; Stryker-Gordon, 1975, 1982).

Home care involves providing nursing care (with a focus on prevention and health education) to clients in their own homes. Long-term care and community health nursing skills may receive less coverage in formal education than acute-care skills.

METHODOLOGY

This research used the constant comparative method of Glaser and Strauss (1967) as an inductive approach to develop grounded theory. Data sources included: (a) literature review, (b) taped interviews, (c) biographic forms completed by subjects, (d) monthly calendars, (e) organizational charts, and (f) detailed observations of two nurse administrators for a period of 1 month by graduate students in The University of Michigan nursing administration practicum. Data were categorized according to known and emerging conceptual categories and related properties. The categories and related properties were studied in terms of interrelationships and assumptions about nursing administration in acute-care, long-term care, and home-care settings.

SAMPLE

A convenience sample of thirty nurse administrators was selected from 10 acute-care institutions (5 from 200- to 500-bed institutions, 5 from institutions with over 500 beds); 10 home-care agencies (serving approximately 100,000 people); and 10 long-term care facilities (over 100 beds). These settings were selected because they were representative of various care settings, both locally and nationally. Nurse administrators who were registered nurses serving in top nursing roles were selected for interviews.

INSTRUMENTATION

An interview schedule using questions from the Poulin (1980) and Price (1984) instruments was administered by the researchers in tape-recorded interviews. Notes were also taken during the interviews. Forms adapted from the techniques of Mintzberg (1973) were developed to document contacts and time allocation of the nurse executives. An extensive card file was developed for categorizing information.

DATA ANALYSIS

After data collection, tapes were transcribed, and data were converted to responses on the interview forms. The responses were then coded and converted to cards for each identified category and question. Coded data were analyzed according to the research questions.

RESULTS

Data results are described according to characteristics of the participants, perceptions of the administrative role in terms of leadership and management activities, clinical practice activities, education and research activities, and nursing administration trends.

CHARACTERISTICS OF THE PARTICIPANTS

Table 24-1 summarizes characteristics of the study participants. The 30 nurse administrators were female and between the ages of 30 and 65. Long-term care administrators tended to be older, with five over 50. Acute-care nurse administrators were generally younger, with five in their 30s. Home-care administrators were more evenly distributed across age categories. Future studies are needed to determine if these characteristics are representative of a national sample.

Educational level was represented by the highest degree earned. Education categories included diploma in nursing, associate degree in nursing, baccalaureate degree, master's degree, and doctorate. The majority (55.5%) of long-term care nurse administrators held diplomas or associate degrees, while all of the acute-care and home-care nurse administrators held master's degrees. One home-care nurse administrator was doctorally prepared.

Job titles varied according to setting. Director of nursing titles were common in long-term care settings. Acute-care nursing administrators had vice president, executive director, or director of nursing titles with some administrative titles. Home-care nurse administrators were almost equally distributed among the three levels of titles. Director of nursing titles reflect responsibility for nursing services only. Administrator and health service titles suggest a broader responsibility for patient care or total personal health services. The vice president and executive director titles represent organizational or corporate-level positions.

TABLE 24-1
Characteristics of nurse administrators according to setting (N = 30)

CHARACTERISTICS	LONG-TERM CARE % (N = 10)	ACUTE CARE % (N = 10)	HOME CARE % (N = 10)
Age			
30s	22.2	55.6	33.3
40s	22.2	11.1	33.3
50s	33.3	22.2	22.2
60+	22.2	11.1	11.1
Marital Status			
Single	66.7	66.7	88.9
Married	33.3	33.3	11.1
Educational Level			
Diploma/Associate Degree	55.5	0	0
Bachelor's Degree	22.2	0	0
Master's Degree	22.2	100	90
Doctorate	0	0	10
Nurse Administrator Title			
Director of Nursing	80	40	30
Administrator, Health Service	20	10	40
Vice President/ Executive Director	0	50	30

PERCEPTIONS OF ADMINISTRATIVE ROLES AMONG SETTINGS

In all settings, nurse administrators were found to have major responsibility for patient care quality. Their direct patient care was limited except in long-term care settings where some administrators noted the need to provide 24-hour availability of their clinical expertise. Administrators in acute-care and home-care settings had major corporate responsibilities involving long-range planning, financial management, and policy-making. Personnel management varied across settings, but nurse recruitment and staffing remained major responsibilities in long-term care settings. The majority of acute-care administrators cited a dramatic increase in bargaining and union-related activities. Table 24-2 depicts responsibilities in long-term, acute-care, and home-care settings. Leadership and management activities were mentioned in response to questions about administrative responsibilities and the role's central focus (see Table 24-3).

Leadership. In descriptions of activities and responsibilities, several leadership behaviors were

identified. In the larger organization, acting as image setter and spokesperson for nursing was viewed as crucial. Nurse administrators participated in predicting organizational trends and planning at various organizational levels.

Acute-care nurse administrators uniquely described the need for developing a management team to share nursing management responsibilities. Developing leadership potential in others was noted to include offering continuing education, increasing subordinates' levels of responsibility, and decentralizing decision making in some cases. The administrator served as role model, teacher, facilitator, and change agent. Several acute-care administrators remarked that their own activities changed when other managers participated in organizational activities. This function of "people developer" was identified as important to staff satisfaction and retention as well as department operation.

When describing administrative style, few administrators described themselves as authoritarian. Most described themselves as open-door or participative managers. Several administrators believed responding

TABLE 24-2
Responsibilities of nurse administrators according to setting (N = 30)

RESPONSIBILITIES	LONG-TERM CARE (N = 10)	ACUTE CARE (N = 10)	HOME CARE (N = 10)
Budget Development	Limited	Major	Moderate-Major
Staff Development	Moderate	Major	Moderate
Long-Range Planning	Limited	Major	Moderate
Recruitment	Major	Moderate	Major
Staffing	Major	Moderate*	Moderate*
Direct Patient Care	Major	Limited	Limited
Indirect Patient Care	Limited	Major	Moderate
Quality Assurance	Major	Major	Major
Policy/Standards	Limited	Major	Major
Bargaining and Union-Related Activities	Limited	Major	Moderate
Wage and Salary Determination	Limited	Moderate	Moderate
Supervision	Major	Moderate	Major

*Includes delegated activities
Note:
Limited = Up to 20% of respondents
Moderate = 21% to 40% of respondents
Major = 50% or more of respondents

TABLE 24-3
Administrative activities considered important

LEADERSHIP	CREATIVE MANAGEMENT
Personal Activities as an:	Coordination
Image Setter	Supervision
Spokesperson for Nursing	Direction
Change Agent	Special Projects
People Developer	Fiscal Management
Trouble-Shooter	Planning
	Instruction
Other Directed Activities:	Implementation
Creating Professional Practice Environment	Coordination With Other Departments
Upgrading Division	
Developing Humane Work Environment	
Improving Staff Relationships	
Supporting Organizational Mission and Goals	
Ensuring Quality of Patient Care	
Interacting with Colleagues	

Note: The Creative Management category reflects activities related to the content of administration. The leadership category reflects the individual's personal influence in the role.

to the needs of the situation was the most effective approach. The nurse administrators were generally found to combine philosophical approaches with personal style to influence others inside and outside the organization. Some personal characteristics identified as helpful were creativity, high energy, optimism, and enthusiasm.

Management. Management responsibilities were categorized as limited, moderate, or major. Some activities were entirely delegated with the nursing administrator retaining responsibility for the activity. Other activities required administrators to act as liaisons coordinating activities of other departments with nursing.

Human and capital resource management were identified as major responsibilities of all nurse administrators. Recruitment and staff assignment were mentioned as important elements of human resource management. Staffing was frequently a delegated responsibility in acute-care and home-care settings. Many administrators were interested in acquiring and using computers to determine staff requirements and staff assignments.

Human resource management also included supervising staff. In smaller agencies, administrators served as mediators in interpersonal relationships among staff as well as clients. This activity was perceived as time-consuming and energy-draining. In larger organizations, mediation was a delegated activity that reached the nurse administrator only after unsuccessful resolution of the personnel problem by subordinates.

Fiscal concerns were recognized as essential to the survival of health-care organizations by all study participants. Nurse administrators had varied responsibility for the development and monitoring of their department budgets. Acute-care and home-care nurse administrators who participated in overall planning and policy development were more frequently involved in the development of budget proposals for their departments. Budget monitoring was another major concern. Acute-care administrators described sharing their responsibilities with other nurse managers at the departmental level. Solving fiscal problems was a common concern in all settings.

Many nurse administrators actively participated in collective bargaining and salary negotiations. Others maintained liaison relationships with other departments, such as personnel, to survey market conditions and set wage scales. In many settings, a fixed proportion of the personnel budget was allocated for discretionary merit salary increases. This proportion of the budget frequently was managed at the unit level by the nurse manager.

CLINICAL PRACTICE-RELATED ACTIVITIES

The major focus of nursing departments in all settings was the delivery of nursing services to various client populations. Table 24-4 summarizes the nurse administrators' clinical activities and categorizes them as either direct or indirect.

Direct care was limited in acute-care and home-care settings. In long-term care, administrators often covered staff positions when necessary. They also participated in client-care conferences, family interviews, and clinical consultations. These administrators valued knowing the names of all clients and their families.

Indirect care included provision and maintenance of qualified staff, development of policies and procedures, establishment and maintenance of a quality assurance program, development of standards of care, and staff supervision. In addition to formal quality of care mechanisms, incident reports and contact with physicians, clients, and families provided useful information on client care and aided in decision making about client services.

TABLE 24-4
Clinical activities according to setting ($N = 30$)

ACTIVITIES	LONG-TERM CARE ($N = 10$)	ACUTE CARE ($N = 10$)	HOME CARE ($N = 10$)
Direct Care			
Own Practice	Moderate	Limited	Limited
Family Interviews/Care Conferences	Major	Limited	Limited
Rounds	Major	Moderate	Limited
Indirect Care			
Providing Qualified Staff	Moderate	Moderate*	Moderate
Developing Policies/Procedures	Limited	Major*	Major*
Quality Assurance	Major	Major*	Major*
Setting Clinical Standards	Major	Major*	Major*
Interacting with Physicians	Limited	Limited	Limited
Supervising Staff	Moderate	Limited	Moderate
Acquisition of Appropriate Equipment	Moderate	Moderate	None
Problem Solving: Incidents, Complaints	Moderate	Major	Moderate

*Includes delegated activities
Note:
Limited = Up to 20% of respondents
Moderate = 21% to 40% of respondents
Major = 50% or more of respondents

Nurse administrators viewed their clinical practice role as a facilitative one. They offered the human and capital resources needed to provide the desired level of care as well as mechanisms for evaluation. In addition to enhancing the administrator's visibility, attending nursing rounds allowed the administrator to demonstrate personal leadership in clinical care. These administrators believed their clinical practice background was important in establishing credibility with their staff, directing nursing services, and speaking effectively for nursing in the organization.

EDUCATION-RELATED ACTIVITIES

Another important component of the professional practice model is education. The educational role of the nurse administrator includes self-development, and staff and client/community education.

Self-development included several activities. Pursuing additional formal education was reported by several acute-care administrators. Continuing education was a primary source of development for administrators in all settings. Serving as consultants and review board members also were reported as learning experiences. Reading was also mentioned in addition to peer support groups and professional organizations in which nurses share knowledge and experience.

Staff development involved the nurse administrators teaching and/or directing continuing education programs within and without the organization. Some long-term care administrators and a few acute-care and home-care administrators teach in their organizations. Other administrators teach outside the organization or affiliate with local educational institutions.

Continuing education was common to all settings with the administrator maintaining responsibility by assisting in program planning, resource allocation, and program evaluation. If other departments or organizations offer continuing education, the administrator serves as a liaison to communicate identified nursing needs.

Involvement in client/community education varied widely. Acute-care and long-term care institutions often reported limited community education, generally focusing on their own client population. In contrast, home-care agencies identified community education as an integral part of their role that was frequently shared with another department. The potential for health promotion and disease prevention through community education was recognized in all settings.

RESEARCH ACTIVITIES

As nursing seeks to develop and implement research-based practice, the leadership role of nurse administrators in research is extremely important. The study participants identified several issues relevant to research in their organizations. Administrators in acute and long-term care identified a lack of qualified staff to conduct research. Some administrators did not clearly understand clinical research.

Many administrators believed their role was to develop an atmosphere conducive to inquiry and to provide resources for research development. Two acute-care administrators had hired nurse researchers to direct research in their facilities. Others described research collaboration with other departments or institutions. Many agencies participated in research by granting access to client or staff populations, thereby participating in others' research.

While research activities in many agencies were limited, the need for more research was recognized. Research was of particular interest to nurse administrators in acute-care settings. They believed research findings were important to the development of science-based nursing practice, standards of care, and quality assurance.

TRENDS IN NURSING ADMINISTRATION

During the study, several nursing administration trends became evident. A trend toward graduate preparation of nurse administrators is notable. Nurse administrators need advanced education for their expanded responsibilities. Multifacility corporations are increasing in number and offering opportunities for nurse administrators to assume corporate-level responsibilities. Many functions of the nurse administrator are delegated with the administrator retaining accountability. The nurse administrator functions as a planner, image setter, and resource allocator who facilitates rather than performs direct services.

Health care is changing, and consumers are more actively involved in self-care and development of new care approaches such as hospices and home health. Administrators in all settings are becoming more aware of various consumer groups, assessing their needs and planning for service. For example, as America greys, nurse administrators must prepare their staff and facilities to meet the elderly's special health-care needs.

Cost consciousness was evident in all settings with prospective reimbursement altering traditional methods of delivering services. Continuity of client care among the three health-care settings is crucial as acute-care institutions attempt to provide quality care and appropriate discharge planning associated with decreased lengths of stay.

Many institutions are also seeking to provide a wider range of services. Additional services include day care, long-term care, home-health services, and increased educational programs. Long-term care settings want to offer an acceptable quality of residential care within limited budgets. Some administrators believe lobbying for changes in the mandated requirements for long-term care is the best way to increase the quality of care they provide. Home-care agencies are also interested in obtaining funding and/or reimbursement for services they would like to provide.

Related to cost consciousness is information management and an increased concern for data-based decision making. This may involve computers that can provide a data base for decision making in such areas as staffing, productivity analysis, and caseload analysis. These changes in health care reaffirm the need for collaboration between administration and education and ongoing nursing research.

Nurse administrators balance interpersonal, administrative, and clinical skills in a variety of settings. Education and research activities vary across settings.

EXECUTIVE EXPERTISE

The results of this study support Poulin's findings and yield additional evidence to indicate that a new administrative role, the nurse executive role, is emerging in acute-care and home-care settings. This dynamic role requires advanced education and a high degree of leadership and managerial acumen in addition to clinical nursing knowledge and research. The nurse executive role in long-term care settings appears to be changing less rapidly and not keeping pace with the current changes in health-care delivery. However, this setting has the greatest potential for development and could provide the greatest challenges for leadership in nursing.

REFERENCES

Barney, J.L. (1974). Nursing directors in nursing homes. *Nursing Outlook, 22*(7), 436-440.

Blair, E. (1976). Needed: Nursing administration leaders. *Nursing Outlook, 24*(9), 550-558.

Drucker, P.F. (1980). *Managing in turbulent times.* New York: Harper & Row.

Erickson, E.H. (1975, March). *Characteristics, enrollments, graduations — Graduate study in nursing administration.* Iowa City, IA: University of Iowa College of Nursing.

Glaser, B.G., & Strauss, A.L. (1967). *The discovery of grounded theory.* Chicago: Aldine Press.

Howarth, V.H. (1981). Managing community health nurse managers. *Nursing and Health Care, 2*(7), 372-375.

Katz, D., & Kahn, R. (1978). *The social psychology of organizations.* New York: John Wiley & Sons.

McClure, M. (1979). The administrative component of the nurse administrator role. *Nursing Administration Quarterly, 3*(4), 1-17.

Mintzberg, H. (1973). *The nature of managerial work.* New York: Harper & Row.

Moloney, M.M. (1979). *Leadership in nursing.* St. Louis: C.V. Mosby.

Poulin, M.A. (1980, April 20-21). *A structural and functional analysis of the role of the nurse executive.* Paper presented at the National Conference on Nursing Administration Research, Seattle, WA.

Poulin, M.A. (1984). The nurse executive role: A structural and functional analysis. *The Journal of Nursing Administration, 14*(2), 9-14.

Price, S.A. (1984). Master's programs preparing nursing administrators. *Journal of Nursing Administration, 14*(1), 11-17.

Ringland, E. (1981). I am proud to work in a nursing home. *Geriatric Nursing, 2*(5), 359-361.

Simms, L., Price, S., & Ervin, N. (1985). *The professional practice of nursing administration.* New York: John Wiley & Sons.

Stevens, B. (1981). The role of the nurse executive. *Journal of Nursing Administration, 11*(2), 19-23.

Stryker-Gordon, R. (1975). How does nursing home administration differ from hospital administration? *Journal of Nursing Administration, 5*(5), 16-17.

Stryker-Gordon, R. (1982). Leadership in care of the elderly: Assessing needs and challenges. *The Journal of Nursing Administration, 12*(10), 41-43.

CHAPTER 25

Promoting Research-Based Nursing
The nurse administrator's role

Elizabeth A. Hefferin, RN, DrPH, FAAN
Jo Anne Horsley, RN, PhD, FAAN
Marlene R. Ventura, RN, PhD, FAAN

Nursing administrators report that they and their staffs have difficulties both in evaluating the quality of available reports of nursing research and in making appropriate use of their findings to validate or improve their respective areas of practice. Ways to evaluate the soundness of the knowledge gained through research need clarification so that we can readily interpret, accept, and incorporate research-based knowledge into practice [1-3].

In this article we report on a survey conducted among hospital-based nurse administrators and researchers to determine the research-related issues existing among professional nursing staffs in their respective health care settings. Based on the data, we present implications and conclusions for nursing administrators.

PROBLEMS AND APPROACHES IN RESEARCH USE

The problems associated with the poor use of research findings are many and complex. Publishing research reports and presenting and discussing study results at conferences are not sufficient means for

Reprinted from *The Journal of Nursing Administration*, Vol. 12, No. 5, with permission of J. B. Lippincott Company © 1982.

stimulating translation of research findings into practice. Disseminating research reports does not ensure that the report will be read and the results used [4]. Nurses wishing to use research findings often find it difficult to evaluate the quality of a particular research report and may often fail to see the applicability of the findings to their own areas of practice. Some of the major contributing factors that limit the use of research findings are presented in the box on p. 216.

Certainly, there is no dearth of researchable problems or questions for study [16], and there is increasing acceptance of the notion that the essence of research is to question, not to problem solve for single or finite answers [17]. Our guiding philosophy and mission is to provide nursing services to our many clients whose problems also provide the rationale for many of our practice theories, research directions, and methodologies [18-20].

Nursing administrators are becoming acutely aware that their support is crucial in promoting innovative work and risk taking among their staffs [21,22], and many nursing administrators now openly encourage staff to understand and participate in activities that embody at least the rudiments of research: the nursing process, nursing audit, and various quality-assurance mechanisms [23,24]. Staff are encouraged and sometimes requested to carry out

Factors that limit use of research

1. Researchers frequently do not interpret or present their findings in terms that are understandable and useful for implementation. Researchers also tend to limit communications by publishing in research journals, meeting, and presenting their results to each other at research conferences that are rarely attended by practitioners. Relatively few publish research reports in nursing practice journals [5,6].
2. Much that has been done is small-scale research, with few if any replications. Validity, reliability, and generalizability of such findings are therefore open issues. Part of this replication problem arises from limited funding for such work. Also, having students replicate previous research is rarely acceptable in the academic community. A related problem is that much of the required "original" work done by students rarely gets published in either research or practice journals; replication of this original research is not done because of its unavailability to other researchers. This problem is critical [7,8].
3. Even when studies have been replicated a number of times and the findings are found to be valid, reliable, and generalizable, publication of findings does not ensure that the results will be implemented. The real problem often lies in the fact that practitioners and/or supervisors are reluctant even to try out, let alone establish new routines and procedures in the workplace [9].
4. Nurses in patient care practice are often insufficiently prepared to evaluate the quality of research; this problem can be traced to their basic nursing educational program. Two-year and three-year programs may emphasize the technical aspects of nursing rather than offer a professional or decision-making focus, a matter of value-system differences. All nurses need criteria they can use to evaluate the applicability of research findings [10].
5. Many nurses tend to see research as irrelevant to their practices. They provide care to patients according to approaches and procedures learned in their basic nursing programs and/or encountered as 'established practice' in the workplace [11,12].
6. There has as yet been no systematic attempt by the nursing profession to review all of its research and to extract the knowledge that has validity and relevance for practice. This review and evaluation of the knowledge base is critical to the development of professionalism and is the responsibility of the nursing profession as a whole [13].
7. Nursing lacks people who have expertise in both research and practice, and whose roles are designed to relate or blend the two nursing worlds. Nursing needs its own leaders to help change the profession and open new vistas for the future [14,15].

evaluations of nursing practices and programs on single and multiple-unit bases. Additionally, a number of nursing administrators have developed or are laying the groundwork for nursing research programs either on an in-hospital basis or in collaboration with their affiliated universities. These programs should provide the means by which the staff can explore nursing problems and should produce data useful for administrative and clinical practice decisions [25-28].

Setting up Programs

Nursing administrators who attempt to develop nursing research programs must make some major decisions. How inclusive should the scope of the program be? What is feasible for one organization may be impossible for another because of the many resources required for the implementation and maintenance of such a program. If we desire a combined clinician-researcher role, should and can the role be expanded to include the responsibility for implementing and publishing the findings? How best can an effective research program be organized and supported? How should it be staffed and funded?

As yet, despite the numerous efforts to develop and maintain productive nursing research programs, an important question remains unanswered: Are the findings of research actually used to change or modify nursing practice? Although several approaches have been suggested for introducing practice changes, there is little documentation concerning either the types of changes that have been introduced or the duration and longer-term reassessment of the changes.

The most notable large-scale efforts to introduce research findings into practice and to evaluate the results have been those conducted by the Western Interstate Commission for Higher Education in Nursing (WCHEN) Regional Program for Nursing Research Development [29,30], and the cooperative venture by the Michigan School of Nursing known as "Conduct and Utilization of Research in Nursing" (CURN) [31,32].

The WCHEN model for use of nursing research was tested with three successive groups of nurses in the western United States. Dyads of nurses were assisted in selecting, planning, implementing and evaluating research findings that were applicable in their facilities. Although almost two-thirds of the dyads were successful in implementing the selected research findings into clinical practice, most (68 percent) of the participants filling out the long-term outcome questionnaire described the impact on their agency as minor [33]. The nurses' general inabilities to locate, review, analyze and collate findings that were usable in their practice was a major problem.

THE RESEARCH UTILIZATION SURVEY

We started our work on the assumption that nurse involvement in the selection and adoption of new or innovative nursing practices and in research-related activities was the most probable means for promoting the implementation of nursing research findings in practice. Therefore, we developed a questionnaire to explore the views of nursing administrators and nurse researchers across the country concerning nurse involvement in such activities in their hospitals. In general, we wanted to find out:

1. How involved are nurses in the processes of selecting and adopting new nursing practices or innovations?
2. What are the probable barriers or deterrents to nurse involvement in research-related activities?
3. What criteria are used by nurses to evaluate the quality and applicability of nursing research findings for their own areas of practice?

4. What kinds of nursing practice innovations actually have been introduced in their respective hospital settings in the past year?

The Survey Methodology

Our survey sample included nursing administrators from 56 of the largest hospitals in the United States, selected on a random basis; 28 VA medical centers and 28 non-VA hospitals were included in the sample. Also included in the survey sample were 25 nurse researchers (10 VA and 15 non-VA) identified as hospital-based but not included in the original random hospital sample. Because the first six of the ten items in the questionnaire were taken from the CURN project instrument currently in use in the state of Michigan, nursing administrators and researchers in Michigan were excluded from the present survey sample. The sample responses were unevenly distributed: 20 VA nursing administrators and 10 VA researchers completed the questionnaire as compared with 9 non-VA nursing administrators and 7 non-VA nurse researchers.

VA and non-VA respondents generally agreed that nursing directors, supervisors, and head nurses were the most likely individuals to promote the use of innovative practices. Respondents also saw head nurses, nursing directors, assistant directors, and staff nurses (in that order) as the persons most involved in implementing practice changes. VA administrative and educative positions were perceived as having a high degree of responsibility (70 and 93 percent of respondents) for knowing about innovative practices and sharing this information with others, while 88 percent of non-VA respondents saw this function as important primarily for administrators.

VA nursing administrators, clinical specialists, and supervisors were identified as those most likely to evaluate the value of innovative practices and select those that are to be implemented (by 83, 80, and 77 percent of VA respondents, respectively); 81 percent of non-VA respondents saw this responsibility as part of the administrator's role. Neither the VA nor the non-VA respondents believed that evaluating and selecting innovative practices was actually carried out to its expected degree for any of the listed nursing positions.

Not unexpectedly, VA and non-VA respondents (97 and 88 percent) perceived that both securing necessary resources to implement innovative nursing practices and influencing significant persons or groups to secure permission to use the new practices are primarily administrative responsibilities. Approximately the same proportions of respondents felt that these two functions were being carried out by nursing administrators. The responsibility for assisting nursing units to incorporate the innovations into daily practice was attributed most strongly to the supervisors, head nurses, clinical specialists, and instructors by VA respondents (70 to 80 percent range). Non-VA respondents (88 percent) felt this function to be primarily the role of the head nurse. While this responsibility was perceived as actually carried out by the expected role-related individuals, their levels of performance were judged to be less than respondents had anticipated (VA, 53 to 63 percent; non-VA, 63 percent).

VA respondents saw evaluating the effectiveness of current and new nursing practices as the responsibility of the supervisor (90 percent), educative and administrative personnel (77 percent each), and the head nurse (73 percent). In non-VA hospitals, this function was seen largely as the role responsibility of head nurses and of administrators (88 and 75 percent, respectively). In judging actual role performance, however, VA respondents perceived that administrators most often carried out the function (70 percent), with other roles falling far short of expectations (supervisors, 57 percent; educative staff, 50 percent; head nurses, 47 percent). Non-VA head nurses also appeared to carry out this function at lower levels of performance than was expected by the respondents (69 percent), as did the non-VA nursing administrators (50 percent).

We also asked our administrator and researcher respondents to estimate the degree of importance that was being given to clinical nursing research by themselves and by the nurses in their respective work settings. Most respondents (93 percent VA and 81 percent non-VA) believed that it was "important" to "extremely important" that their nurse staff be familiar with current clinical nursing research. Most respondents (90 percent VA and 81 percent non-VA)

also believed that the research they personally knew about was important for nursing practice in their hospitals. However, considerably fewer respondents (47 percent VA and 25 percent non-VA) felt that their nurses also perceived clinical nursing research as an important basis for practice. Finally, 97 percent of the VA and 94 percent of the non-VA administrator and researcher respondents believe that it will be very important for nursing departments to be able to use the findings from clinical nursing research studies that will be conducted in the coming years.

We asked respondents for an estimate of the number of nurses in their hospitals who had become involved in selected types of research-related activity in the preceding twelve-month period. At least four or more nurses at many facilities had engaged in such activities as attending research conferences; reviewing the research literature to identify new knowledge; evaluating studies for possible transfer of research-based knowledge into practice; rejecting a practice due to research results; helping graduate nursing students, physicians, and non-hospital personnel in the collection of data; and conducting their own studies. Most respondents reporting nurse attendance at research conferences were from the VA (77 percent as compared with the non-VA 56 percent).

We also attempted to identify the types of problems perceived most often by nurses as barriers or deterrents to their becoming involved in research-related activities. Table 25-1 shows VA and non-VA respondents differed in their perceptions.

We asked our administrators and researchers to estimate which methods probably would be most effective for communicating or sharing research reports and study findings to their nursing staff and which methods they currently were using in their respective hospitals for this purpose. As Table 25-2 shows, although all of the suggested methods were ranked as having moderate to high potential utility for communicating research reports and findings by relatively high proportions of VA and non-VA respondents, most of the hospitals were not currently using these methods. Of those currently in use, "referring specific articles to the staff" was judged by both VA and non-VA respondents to be the most effective means of dissemination.

TABLE 25-1
Factors acting as probable barriers or deterrents to nurse involvement in research-related activities by percentage of respondent judgments

FACTORS	NONE TO LITTLE EXTENT		MODERATE TO VERY GREAT EXTENT	
	VA	NON-VA	VA	NON-VA
Research language not understood	10	31	90	69
Findings not transferable to practice	7	25	93	75
Workload too heavy to pursue research activity	7	12	93	88
Research not seen as relevant to patient care	20	37	80	63
Research participation not valued by nursing administration	80	100	20	0
Statistical analysis not understood	10	25	90	75
Patients would not cooperate	97	87	3	13
Lack of funds to support research activities	37	50	63	50
Physicians would not cooperate	67	44	33	56
Research participation not rewarded (time, dollars)	27	50	73	50
Nurses unwilling to change or try new ideas	30	31	70	69
Nurses not interested in research activity	23	31	77	69
Lack of contact with outside resources, consultants, etc.	53	50	47	50
Researchers with expertise not available to staff	57	31	43	69
Research activity not seen as beneficial to staff growth	27	44	73	56
Nurses' inability to identify researchable problems/areas	20	37	80	63
Insufficient research yet available for current problems	27	31	73	69
Insufficient research articles in practice journals	23	31	77	69
Can't judge value of research for use in clinical areas	23	12	77	88
No systematic means for sharing research with units	23	31	77	69

We asked the nursing administrators and researchers to list new ideas or approaches for modifying nursing practice that either they or their nurses had suggested during the preceding twelve months. Four respondents left this section blank and two stated that they would have to survey their staffs to determine which of the many suggested modifications had been implemented. The remaining respondents listed a total of 216 ideas or approaches for change. They were of three general types; those currently being studied or evaluated in the practice setting (VA list, 28 percent; non-VA list, 11 percent), those serving as problem areas for investigative research (VA list, 19 percent; non-VA list, 5 percent) and those already accepted into practice (VA list, 53 percent; non-VA list, 84 percent).

TABLE 25-2

Probable and current usefulness of methods for communicating or sharing research reports and findings with hospital nursing staff by percentage of respondent estimates

METHODS	METHODS HAVING MODERATE TO HIGH PROBABLE EFFECT		MODERATE TO HIGH-EFFECTIVENESS METHODS CURRENTLY IN USE	
	VA	NON-VA	VA	NON-VA
Nursing research Hot-Line index on clinical research	87	63	3	0
Index Nursicus (like the *Index Medicus*)	90	56	20	6
Med-Line Nursing Index (through Library Service)	90	69	47	25
Research conferences on all types of completed research	90	75	47	31
Research conferences on selected clinical topics	93	88	47	38
Research newsletters on selected/requested topics	87	75	27	13
Outside agencies to provide any of the above	77	63	33	13
Referring specific research-related articles to staff	90	75	70	69
Use of research-reporting types of journal clubs	70	56	17	25
Integrate research results into inservice classes	87	75	37	63

Many of the studies listed were related to the testing or evaluation of various types of equipment or products having potential benefit for patient care (such as fluid-filled beds for patients with decubiti, a bed-check alarm system to reduce patient falls, electronic thermometers and IV flow-meters, urinary drainage systems, and unit dose systems). Administrative studies included the testing of staffing patterns, flexible work-hour programs, use of administrative head nurses and operating room managers, patient and unit safety surveys, and evaluation of staff orientation programs. Clinical studies included the evaluation of music therapy and psychosocial support programs for patient groups, use of the nursing process, nursing audits and peer review models, modifications of the primary nursing concept, a host of patient teaching approaches, and nursing care plan and charting studies. Research projects were mostly exploratory and looked into such subjects as effects of family visits on confused patients, sensory deprivation among isolation and non-isolation patients, self-image and dietary compliance among hemodialysis patients and patients with other illnesses and use of

timing clocks to remind staff to turn patients for the prevention of decubiti. A few research studies were comparative or experimental. They covered topics such as patient perceptions of nursing care under three types of flexible nurse work-hour programs, accuracy of rectal versus oral temperatures among patients receiving nasal oxygen, effects of primary versus team nursing with confused patients, and comparison of bran and laxative approaches with various patient groups. From these selected study examples, it was clear that VA and non-VA nurses alike encountered many types of practice problems and used imaginative approaches to seek solutions.

Changes in Practice

As noted earlier, it was apparent that our respondents had already incorporated into practice a majority of the ideas and approaches they listed. Changes related to clinical practice included modifications of specific nursing procedures (decubiti care protocols, intravenous and hyperalimentation management and tracheal suctioning) and reflected attempts to promote a more accurate documentation of nursing services to patients (use of new patient assessment and care planning devices and protocols, special flow sheets and charting formats, and chart audits).

Changes associated with administrative practice included decisions to expand head nurses' responsibilities, establish nurse-run clinics and nursing rounds, decentralize intensive-care unit staffing, establish and define specific nurse roles (clinical specialists, nurse practitioners, charge nurses), adjust staffing patterns according to revised patient classification systems, implement primary nursing, and establish functionally responsible committees.

Educative practice changes included not only the modification of general and special unit orientation programs but also the intent to promote the professional growth of staff through the provision of special training in such activities as psychosocial interventions, patient teaching methodologies, and physical assessment techniques. Approximately 10 percent of the listed practice changes were identified specifically by our respondents as having been developed on the basis of research findings.

In anticipation of the variety of nursing practice innovations and modifications, we sought an estimate of the extent to which the nurses in their hospitals probably used certain selective criteria or processes in developing their suggestions and plans for making practice changes (see Table 25-3). The majority of respondents felt that nurses for the most part did not tend to be very systematic in their approaches to suggesting or planning changes in practice. Relatively large proportions of nurses were judged not at all concerned with determining how much work had already been done to find solutions to a practice problem, with exploring the feasibility of implementing their suggested changes, or with ways that they or others might evaluate the effect (pre- and post-measurements) of changing a practice. Nevertheless, the majority of both VA and non-VA respondents believed that their nurses sometimes applied at least some of the listed criteria.

IMPLICATIONS FOR RESEARCH USE

From the data obtained in this survey it is immediately apparent that knowing about, selecting, and making decisions to adopt new nursing practices or innovative changes in practice are most often seen as falling within the purview of nursing service administration. Once the administrative decision has been made, many individuals become involved in the actual implementation of the new or modified practice. The relevant information is passed through the supervisors and inservice staff to the head nurses, who in turn work with their staffs to implement the new practice or innovation at the unit level. Nurse administrators and researchers alike seemed to recognize that the administrator is primary in effecting both the dissemination and the utilization of research findings [34].

Although there were variations in the perceptions that the VA and non-VA respondents expressed concerning research utilization responsibilities and the actual functioning of the several identified nursing roles, there was general agreement that the actual carrying out of these responsibilities was less than maximum. If the general assumption can be made that the nursing staffs' attitudes and behaviors relating to the conduct of research and the use of research findings in practice reflect the attitudes and behaviors of their nursing service administrators about these concerns, the administrators themselves must demonstrate their commitment. This requires (1) personal self-development with respect to learning about research process, change theory, and the practical application of research findings; (2) facilitation of staff development toward familiarity with research methods and appreciation of research-based practice; and (3) hiring of staff members who can demonstrate both the commitment and the ability to apply research-based knowledge to practice [35].

VA respondents tended to place a higher value than non-VA respondents on the use of research findings as a basis for practice. Additionally, despite the larger proportions of factors perceived as barriers or deterrents to VA nurse involvement in research-related activities as compared with non-VA nurses, the data suggest that VA nurses reportedly make more frequent use of libraries, conferences and newsletters to search out research-related information. Non-VA nurses reportedly make more frequent use of journal clubs and receive more research-related information through inservice sessions. The positive attitude

TABLE 25-3
Extent to which nurses probably applied selected criteria or processes in developing suggestions for nursing practice changes by percentage of respondent estimates.

	Never		Sometimes		Usually/Always	
	VA	Non-VA	VA	Non-VA	VA	Non-VA
Assessed patient care situations to identify practice problems	0	6	60	44	37	31
Documented the extent of each problem	7	6	70	50	20	25
Ranked problems in terms of priority (degree of seriousness or need for change)	10	13	73	69	10	0
Carried out a library search for research-based solutions to problems	10	19	63	50	17	13
Selected research findings from a single small study	27	13	50	50	7	6
Selected research findings from a single large study	30	25	47	44	3	6
Selected research findings from replicated studies (findings confirmed in same manner by other investigators)	23	13	43	38	13	6
Selected research findings from related studies (findings expanded or confirmed in related studies)	20	19	57	25	10	6
Assessed degree of change required in setting and organization to adopt new practice	10	6	67	56	20	19
Determined feasibility (cost, space, convenience, staff, type of patients, etc). for making change to adopt new practice	27	13	50	31	20	31
Assessed administrative and staff willingness to accept trial-run of new practice	3	0	67	50	23	31
Assessed degree of nursing control of events and variables related to the new practice or innovation	10	6	63	31	17	38
Selected pilot unit for testing utility of new practice	10	6	67	50	20	25
Developed objectives to be met by the new practice	10	0	60	50	27	31
Developed measurement tools to evaluate effect (pre- and post-testing) of new practice	30	13	47	50	17	13
Developed specific plan or protocol for introducing proposed new change in practice	20	6	47	44	30	25

EXTENT TO WHICH PROBABLY APPLIED

among VA nurses about the feasibility of making practice changes and the willingness of the other staff to participate in such activities probably stems from the nursing service policy for all health care facilities in the VA system. This policy includes the expectation that nurses will participate and collaborate actively in research-related activities and initiate and conduct their own systematic nursing studies. VA nursing administrators are expected to encourage and provide practical support for such activities [36,37].

Perhaps the most revealing and valuable information related to the issue of research use was in the respondents' judgments of how frequently the nurses used criteria that would carry them from the reading and critiquing of research to the application of the findings. As Stetler and Marram point out, before nurses decide to modify a particular nursing practice, they must progress through three essential steps or phases. These phases are (1) Evaluating the strength of the research design used in the study or studies under consideration; (2) Evaluating the feasibility and desirability of making the practice change in the particular health care setting and (3) Planning the most appropriate and efficient means for introducing and implementing the change [38]. An essential fourth step or phase also should be included, that of evaluating the effect of the proposed practice change in the respective setting on a pre-test/post-test basis and relating both the degree and direction of this effect to the appropriate theoretical basis for the change.

The preceding phases must involve a careful evaluation of the practice problem, the setting, the available research, and the plan for implementing the selected change or innovation. A number of criteria or factors may be used. These include the following: replication of work done in the area; scientific merit of the research; degree of risk to clients/patients; clinical value or benefit of the proposed change; degree of control over the practice setting (assessing the possible intervening factors as well as how the effects of the innovation can be measured); feasibility of implementing the practice change in the setting; and estimation of the financial costs of introducing, implementing, and evaluating the planned change or innovation. Information relating to these factors can then be organized into what Haller, Reynolds, and Horsley describe as an "innovation protocol" that

becomes, in effect, a complete and viable plan for incorporating research-based knowledge into a nursing practice and for evaluating the impact of the innovated practice in relation to the client/patient, the clinical practitioner, and the setting [39].

CONCLUSION

In attempting to incorporate research-based knowledge into nursing practice, the guiding rule seems to be: "Do your homework!" To be effective, strategies for introducing change must be well-grounded scientifically as well as clinically. Nursing administrators, clinicians, researchers, and educators are all responsible for making nursing truly professional.

Clinicians often begin the process by identifying problem areas, and they are the ultimate users of research-based-knowledge. Administrators must facilitate various types of research activities in a number of ways, ranging from providing open encouragement of staff interest to securing the necessary support and resources. Researchers should include implications for nursing practice in their reports, and make concrete and practical suggestions for formatting their findings for use in the clinical setting. Educators should assist nurses through the systematic review of research, both to help extract research-based knowledge that has validity and relevance for practice and to translate the criteria for evaluating research findings into terms that clinicians can use. Through the collaborative efforts of educators, researchers, and service personnel, nursing research can and should be developed and expanded appropriately to provide the scientifically sound basis that nursing must have for its current and future practice.

REFERENCES

1. M.K. Aydelotte, "Nursing Research in Clinical Settings: Problems and Issues," *Sigma Theta Tau Reflections* 2:3-6, 1976.
2. D. Ketefian, "Application of Selected Nursing Research Findings into Nursing Practice," *Nurs. Res.* 24(2):89-92, 1975a.
3. J.C. Krueger, "Utilization of Nursing Research: The Planning Process," *J. Nurs. Admin.* 8(1):6-9, 1978.
4. M.R. Ventura, Utilization of Research Findings into Practice. Unpublished communication. Buffalo, N.Y.:

Veterans' Administration Medical Center, November, 1979.

5. H. Halpert, "Communications as a Basic Tool in Promoting Utilization of Research Findings." In H. Schulberg, A. Shelton, and F. Baker, eds., *Program Evaluation in the Health Fields* (New York: Human Sciences Press, 1969), pp. 497-505.

6. S. Ketefian, "Problems in the Dissemination and Utilization of Scientific Knowledge: How Can the Gap Be Bridged?" In S. Ketefian, ed., *Translation of Theory into Nursing Practice and Education, Proceedings of the Seventh Annual Clinical Sessions* (New York: Division of Nursing, School of Education, Health, Nursing and Arts Professions, New York University, 1975b), p. 13.

7. P.J. Wooldridge, R.C. Leonard, and J.K. Skipper, *Methods of Clinical Experimentation to Improve Patient Care* (St. Louis: C.V. Mosby, 1978), pp. 163-172.

8. S. Kim, "Pain: Theory, Research and Nursing Practice," *Advances in Nurs. Sci.* 2(2):43-59, 1980.

9. S. Ketefian, "Application of Selected Nursing Research Findings."

10. C.B. Stetler, and G. Marram, "Evaluating Research Findings for Applicability in Practice," *Nurs. Outlook* 24(9): 559-563, 1978.

11. M.E. Conway, "Clinical Research: Instrument for Change," *J. Nurs. Admin.* 8(12):27-32, 1978.

12. Ketefian, "Problems in the Dissemination," pp. 25-26.

13. J.C. Krueger, A.H. Nelson, and M.O. Wolanin, *Nursing Research: Development, Collaboration, and Utilization* (Germantown, Md.: Aspen Systems Corp., 1978), p. 335.

14. Ketefian, "Problems in the Dissemination," pp. 22-23.

15. A. Levenstein, "Effective Change Requires Change Agent." *J. Nurs. Admin.* 9(6):12-15, 1979.

16. D. Diers, "Finding Clinical Problems for Study," *J. Nurs. Admin.* (6):15-18, 1971.

17. R.S. Ludeman, "The Paradoxical Nature of Nursing Research." In M.V. Batey, ed., *Communicating Nursing Research* 2:111-122, September, 1978.

18. J. Beckstrand, "The Notion of a Practice Theory and the Relationship of Scientific and Ethical Knowledge to Practice," *Res. in Nurs. and Health* 1(3):131-136, 1978.

19. E.D. Baer, "Philosophy Provides the Rationale for Nursing's Multiple Research Directions," *Image* 11(3):72-74, 1979.

20. J.M. Kilty, "Can Nursing Research Learn from Educational Research," *Int. J. Nurs. Stud.* 13(2):97-102, 1976.

21. B.J. Ruano, "Response to Revolution — Innovation or Tropism?" In *Continuity of Care — Can or Should the Nurse Innovate Change,* National League for Nursing Publ. No. 45 1407 (New York: National League for Nursing, 1970), pp. 13-20.

22. V.E. Baker, "Nursing Administration and Research," *Nurs. Leadership* 1(1):5-9, 1978.

23. J.C. Schmadl, "Quality Assurance: Examination of the Concept," *Nurs. Outlook* 27(7):462-465, 1979.

24. B.W. Gallant and A.M. McLane, "Outcome Criteria: A Process for Validation at the Unit Level, *J. Nurs. Admin.* 9(1):14-21, 1979.

25. G.V. Padilla, "Incorporating Research in a Service Setting." *J Nurs. Admin.* 9(1):44-49, 1979.

26. J.S. Stevenson, "Developing Staff Research Potential, Part 2: Planning and Implementation of Studies," *J. Nurs. Admin.* 8(6):8-12, 1978.

27. H.C. Chance, and A.S. Hinshaw, "Strategies for Initiating a Research Program." *J. Nurs. Admin.* 10(3):32-39, 1980.

28. Wooldridge, Leonard, and Skipper, "Methods of Clinical Experimentation," p. 194.

29. J.C. Krueger, "Utilizing Clinical Nursing Research Findings in Practice: A Structured Approach," *Communicating Nursing Research* 9:381-394, April, 1977.

30. Krueger, Nelson, and Wolanin, *Nursing Research,* pp. 259-337.

31. J.A. Horsley, J. Crane, and J.D. Bingle, "Research Utilization as an Organizational Process," *J. Nurs. Admin.* 8(7):4-6, 1978.

32. K.B. Haller, M.A. Reynolds, and J.A. Horsley, "Developing Research-Based Innovation Protocols: Process, Criteria and Issues," *Res. in Nurs. and Health* 2(2):45-51, 1979.

33. Krueger, Nelson, and Wolanin, *Nursing Research,* pp. 262, 288.

34. M.L. McClure, "A Nursing Service Director's View of Her Role in Implementing Scientific Knowledge into Practice." In S. Ketefian, ed., *Translation of Theory into Nursing Practice and Education, Proceedings of the Seventh Annual Clinical Sessions* (New York: Division of Nursing, School of Education, Health, Nursing and Arts Professions, New York University, 1975), pp. 48-49.

35. J. Fawcett, "A Declaration of Nursing Independence: The Relation of Theory and Research to Nursing Practice," *J. Nurs. Admin.* 10(6):36-39, 1980.

36. G. Abraham, "Promoting Nursing Research in an Organized Nursing Service," *Am. J. Nurs.* 68(4):818-821, 1968.

37. Veterans' Administration, *Professional Services, Part Five, Nursing Service.* Department of Medicine and Surgery Manual, M-2, Part V, Revised. Washington, D.C.: Veterans' Administration, April 21, 1975.

38. Stetler and Marram, "Evaluating Research Findings," p. 559.

39. Haller, Reynolds, and Horsley, "Developing Research-Based Innovation Protocols."

CHAPTER **26**

Career Advancement of Nurse Executives
Planned or accidental?

Sylvia A. Price, RN, PhD

Lillian M. Simms, RN, PhD

Susan K. Pfoutz, RN, PhD

How do some nurses attain leadership positions? After their initial career choice, what factors influence opportunities for career advancement? Ongoing research at the University of Michigan is exploring the relationship of key variables to career advancement patterns of top-level nurse administrators in health-related organizations or academic settings reporting to a chief executive officer. The phase of the study reported here examined career paths of nurse executives. Instead of the traditional structured questionnaire, this study used a semistructured interview and a review of relevant materials to gain a richer description of factors that influence career development.

LITERATURE REVIEW

Hennig and Jardim's study of women executives in business and industry identified key elements that affect women's advancement in the corporate environment. The women in their study tended to make their career decisions in their early thirties, when they had realized that they would probably work for the

rest of their lives after child bearing and rearing were complete. They tended to concentrate on short-range planning, focusing on their current position rather than on long-term career implications.[1] Their most important priority was on-the-job competence. Because the women in their study had generally left the labor force when they married and returned at some later time, women holding administrative positions were often older than their male counterparts.

Although marriage has been advantageous to many male managers' careers because of the supportive roles taken on by their wives, marital and parenting roles have no demonstrated relationship to success for women. Brown and Harlan found that women managers were only a third to half as likely as male managers to be married and were less likely to have children.[2,3]

The career paths of educators generally progress through a series of administrative roles (committee chair, department head, etc.) toward the deanship. In their 1980 replication of a 1970 study, Hall, Mitsunaga, and deTornyay found that: nearly two-thirds of current deans had planned to become deans, whereas 10 years earlier, two-thirds had not considered the possibility until they were offered the position; almost one-third of the later group had

Reprinted from *Nursing Outlook,* Vol. 35, No. 5, with permission of the American Journal of Nursing Co. © 1987.

planned for years to become deans, compared to 11 percent in the earlier group; 65 percent of the later group, as compared to 43 percent of the earlier group, stated that the best career route to the deanship was slow progression in a top-ranked school; and the dean's salary, qualifications of the faculty, and other variables such as geographic location, budget, and potential to bring about organizational change were factors of more importance for the later deans than for the earlier ones. Because only 40 percent of the deans recommended a doctorate in educational administration, formal preparation in administration was not associated with a career route to a deanship.[4] Fine has warned that there are not enough nurse administrators with graduate degrees to keep up with the increasing demand for them. Educational support, individual preference for and availability of various clinical positions, and work conditions are thought to be contributing factors.[5]

Mentors.   The importance of influence of others, or mentoring, has been linked to an individual's professional progress and career satisfaction. The term mentor and sponsor are often used interchangeably to indicate older, more experienced persons in an organization who identify younger talent and support their career advancement. Kanter described a sponsor or mentor as a teacher or coach whose functions are primarily to train a young person to move through the organization. Sponsors often are in a position to fight for their protégés and promote them for promising career opportunities, often providing a means for neophytes to bypass the hierarchy. Kanter found that most mentors and mentees were male, because business organizations are predominantly male, and she hypothesized that mentors prefer mentees who are similar to them. She noted that women who moved up through the efforts of a male sponsor were readily accepted in the inner circles of management. However, she also found that it was both more important and more difficult for women to get this sponsored mobility.[6]

In Vance's study of the mentor experiences of contemporary nursing leaders, the respondents attested to the importance of mentorship and the support of others in their career development.[7] Eighty-three percent reported the presence of mentors in their career development and 93 percent were mentors to others. Of their mentors, 79 percent were female and 21 percent were male. The respondents in Vance's study reported that their mentors assisted them through such aspects as career promotion, intellectual and scholarly stimulation and inspiration.

METHODOLOGY

This research used the constant comparative method of Glaser and Strauss as an inductive approach to discover grounded theory.[8] Data sources included: literature review, taped interviews, biographical forms completed by subjects, organizational charts, and monthly activity calendars.

Sample.   Twelve registered nurses in top-level executive positions in service and education in selected settings in the midwestern and southern United States were chosen as a convenience sample for interviews. These settings were selected because they are prototypes of care and education in their geographic area and around the nation.

Instrumentation.   An interview schedule using questions from Poulin's and Price's instruments were administered by the researchers in tape-recorded interviews, supplemented by notes.[9,10]

RESULTS

Data results are described by key variables related to the career development patterns of nurse executives. These include: characteristics of respondents, reasons for career choice, progression of positions held, influence of others on career advancement, and elements of job satisfaction.

Characteristics of respondents.   Six nurse executives from acute and home care settings and six nurse executives from academic settings participated in the study. Eleven of them were women between the ages of 30 and 65. Those from nursing service tended to be older, with five over age 50, and single (67%). The educators tended to be younger, with three in their thirties and forties, and were more likely to be married (83%).

Educational level was determined by highest earned degree. None had less than a master's. The educators either held doctorates or were doctoral candidates. One of the acute and home care administrators held a doctorate; the rest were master's prepared.

Job titles varied according to type of setting. Eighty-three percent of the nursing service administrators were vice presidents or executive directors. The majority of the nurse educators (67%) were both professors and deans. Others were associate deans for allied health and department directors.

Career choice.   Career choice was a major indicator of career advancement patterns. Multiple reasons were given by the respondents for their choices. Eighty-three percent of the respondents reported that they were in nursing administrative positions because the opportunity had arisen. Other reasons given were the attractive benefits, a chance to affect nursing practice or to influence nursing in the broadest perspective.

Sixty-seven percent of the nursing service administrators had been in nursing education prior to their nursing service position. They indicated that often their options for career advancement were limited to education and administration. These respondents stressed that their background in education had helped prepare them for their administrative role. Only one respondent indicated that she had made a deliberate choice to move to a head nurse position early in her career.

The majority of the nurse educators (67%) stated that they had not planned to become deans, but had simply taken the opportunity when it arose. One dean said it had seemed a natural progression; she had not sought her position, but had been recruited for it. Another, who had felt thwarted because her former employers (deans) did not understand the demands of clinical nursing practice, accepted a deanship to create a model of what nursing could be.

Progression of positions held.   The nursing service administrators had progressed from staff nurse to head nurse or similar middle management positions and had moved through various administrative positions. As mentioned previously, 67 percent of the nursing service administrators had nursing education experience. Eighty-eight percent of the nurse educators had progressed through faculty ranks from instructor to professor, with con-

Characteristics of nurse administrators, by setting		
	Acute and home care (N = 6) (%)	Education (N = 6) (%)
Age		
30-39	16.7	16.7
40-49	0.0	33.3
50-59	50.0	33.3
60 +	33.3	16.7
Marital Status		
Single	66.7	16.7
Married	33.3	83.3
Highest Education Level		
Diploma/associate degree	0.0	0.0
Bachelor's degree	0.0	0.0
Master's degree	83.3	0.0
Doctorate	16.7	83.3
Doctoral candidate	0.0	16.7
Nurse Administrator Title		
Director of nursing	0.0	0.0
Administrator, health service	16.7	0.0
Vice president/ executive director	83.3	0.0
Professor and dean*	0.0	66.7
Associate dean of allied health	0.0	16.7
Professor and department director	0.0	16.7

*One dean is also the director of nursing services

comitant titles (department chair, assistant and associate dean). Some respondents noted that when they had reached the executive level, they chose positions to develop specific career-enhancing skills.

Influence of others.   Most of the respondents (83%) reported that others were influential in their career advancement. Fifty percent of the nursing service administrators chose their former teachers or deans as mentors, while 33 percent of the educators selected former nursing service directors or supervisors as being most important.

Many of the respondents indicated specifically who was helpful to them in the development of their administrative style. Nurse educators emphasized that their former deans and nurse faculty colleagues were most helpful, while nursing service administrators mentioned a combination of colleagues, non-nurse administrators, nursing faculty, and family as being most important. Two respondents said that they could not identify any specific person responsible for helping them develop their administrative style, but had developed it from their own personality and style of living.

The majority of the respondents said they are now considered mentors themselves. Fifty percent have mentored in-house staff such as associate and assistant directors and faculty chairs.

Several of the nurse executives mentioned that involvement in professional networks (collegial support groups, professional organizations) was a significant factor in their career advancement.

Satisfaction with role.   Another significant factor in career advancement was satisfaction with the nurse executive role. Sixty-seven percent of the nursing service administrators and educators reported that helping staff achieve their own potential through professional development, assisting staff to assume more responsibility, and helping individuals use their talent were the most satisfying aspects of their role.

Other satisfiers related to quality of client care, client/family satisfaction, or interactions with clients. The importance of creating an environment that fostered creative thinking supportive of the goals of the organization was also mentioned. One educator emphasized that the most satisfying aspect of her role was creating an image of nursing as an equal, but somewhat different, partner to the rest of the health professions on campus.

SUMMARY

This exploratory study has examined the effect of selected characteristics on the career advancement patterns of nurse executives in service and educational settings. The findings are not consistently in agreement with those of other researchers. For example, Hall et al. found that nearly two-thirds of nursing deans had planned their careers to attain that position. In this study, however, eighty-three percent of the respondents indicated that they had not planned their career advancement, but had simply taken opportunities that had come their way.

The influence of others was important in the career advancement of these administrators. Many individuals, including faculty and nursing service colleagues, nursing directors, deans, and non-nursing administrators supported the respondents' personal and professional development through role modeling, teaching skills, and encouragement. Deliberate career planning and education in administration were, for the most part, lacking. Although the sample is too small to generate general conclusions about the universe of nurse executives, this does suggest that it is not uncommon for deans and service administrators to learn necessary skills on the job.

REFERENCES

1. Hennig, Margaret, and Jardim, Anne. Women executives in the old-boy network, excerpt from The Managerial Woman. *Psychol. Today* 10:76–81, Jan. 1977.
2. Brown, L. Women and business management. *Signs* 6(2):266–288, 1979.
3. Harlan, A. *A comparison of careers for male and female MBAs.* Wellesley, MA, Center for Research on Women, 1978. (Unpublished manuscript)
4. Hall, B. A., and others. Deans of nursing: changing socialization patterns. *Nurs. Outlook* 29:92–95, Feb. 1981.
5. Fine, R. B. The supply and demand of nursing administrators. *Nurs. Health Care* 4:10–15, Jan. 1983.
6. Kanter, R. M. *Men and Women of the Corporation.* New York,: Basic Books, 1979, pp. 181–184.
7. Vance, C. N. The mentor connection. *J. Nurs Adm.* 12:7–13, Apr. 1982.
8. Glaser, B. G., and Strauss, A. L. *The Discovery of Grounded Theory: Strategies for Qualitative Research.* Hawthorne, NY, De Gruyter/Aldine Press, 1967.
9. Poulin, M. A. The nurse executive role: a structural and functional analysis. *J. Nurs. Adm.* 14:9–14, Feb. 1984.
10. Price, S.A. Master's programs preparing nursing administrators. What are the essential components? *J. Nurs. Adm.* 14:11–17, Jan, 1984.

SUGGESTED READINGS

UNIT FOUR. ROLES, FUNCTIONS, AND
RESPONSIBILITIES

Anderson R: A theory development role for nurse administrators, JONA 19(5):23–29, 1989.

Cutler M: Nursing leadership and management: An historical
perspective, NAQ 1(1):7–19, 1976.

Erickson E: The nursing service director, 1880–1980, JONA
6–13, 1980.

McClure M: The administrative component of the nurse
administrator's role, NAQ 3(4):1–12, 1979.

Mintzberg H: The manager's job: Folklore and fact, HRB
68(2):163–176, 1990.

Simms L, Price S and Pfoutz S: Creating the research climate:
A key responsibility for nurse executives, Nursing Economics 5(4):174–178, 1987.

Stevens B: The role of the nurse executive, JONA 19–23,
1981.

Unit Five

Managing Processes and Resources

CHAPTER **27**

Strategic Planning in Hospitals
Applications to nursing administration

Katherine R. Jones, RN, PhD

Dramatic changes that are taking place today in health care delivery and financing are requiring health care providers to sharpen their awareness of environmental influences and to incorporate effective management strategies into their clinical practices. Turmoil within the health care sector is a result of powerful forces operating on the demand for and supply of health care services.[1]

Factors affecting demand include the Medicare program's change from cost-based retrospective reimbursement to prospective reimbursement based on diagnosis related groups (DRGs), the growing resistance of employers to paying ever-increasing health care costs, the declining population growth, and the changing needs of an aging population. The factors affecting supply include decreased demand for traditional inpatient services leading to excess hospital capacity, growing physician surplus, continuing advances in costly biomedical technology, and new organizational forms of health care delivery.[2]

Hospital management must be proactive rather than reactive in this new and changing environment, or risk losing market share and jeopardizing financial stability. Nursing management, representing a major hospital resource as well as a substantial budget item, must participate actively in the planning process.

Reprinted from *Nursing Administration Quarterly*, Vol. 13, No. 1, with permission of Aspen Publishers, Inc. © 1988.

The new environment requires that health care organizations use a businesslike approach to operations. Although top management staff is responsible for developing strategies and tactics to resolve the challenges of these new constraints, the actual methods for altering daily operations will come from the operational level. Nursing administrators will ultimately be responsible for translating the constraints of prospective payment, competition, and other similar external pressures into workable solutions.[3]

Nursing administrators must therefore develop new management strategies to respond to the multiple external pressures. These new responses need to be consistent with overall organizational strategies, as well as with improvement of nursing program performance.[4] More specifically, nursing service needs to develop management responses that prevent the pressures (prospective payment, competition, retrenchment, changing public attitudes about health care) from adversely influencing the financial and operational performance of nursing units, programs, and departments.[5]

STRATEGIC PLANNING

Given that the health care field is in a time of transition, there is a need for dispassionate and efficient strategic planning.[6] The restrictions and complexities of the health care environment require

233

today's hospital to have a clear sense of direction, an understanding of its strengths and weaknesses, and the creativity and ability to maximize its strengths.[7] The process of strategic planning is designed to provide these in the context of a game plan. In the past, planning was for the short term and emphasized individual programs or pieces of equipment. The focus was the individual facility.[8] This focus is no longer appropriate as the marketplace becomes increasingly restrictive and competitive.[9]

Long-term planning is also an issue facing members of the nursing community who accept an active role in the new environment. The nursing department's long-range plan, developed in the context of the needs of the total institution, describes its newly defined missions, including minimizing costs, increasing revenue, improving productivity, enhancing quality, and decreasing the length of time that patients must be hospitalized.[10]

Strategic planning includes facility and program planning and incorporates them within a business plan and implementation strategy.[11] It is focused on the future of the entire hospital organization. The strategic planning process directs attention to resource allocation decisions and priorities. When done objectively and thoroughly, the strategic plan provides the institution with the knowledge and creativity to capitalize on its strengths and minimize its weaknesses.[12] The basis for strategic planning for a health care organization is knowledge of its internal characteristics and its external environment and willingness to identify, acknowledge, and deal with its weaknesses.[13]

The planning process involves the following steps.[14]

Phase 1. Assessing the risks, opportunities, and markets. The outcome of this assessment should be a baseline forecast of business activity, which will highlight how much planning is needed, and how fast, to address the relevant risks and opportunities.

Phase 2. Designing alternative strategies. Two or three alternatives will be generated in response to baseline scenario assumptions. These will include combinations of programs, services, policies, and operating activities to improve the hospital's success in its market. For example, alternatives may establish the relative attractiveness of various programs, services, or markets, based on estimated resource consumption or return on investment.

Phase 3. Completing the strategic assessment. A single, preferred alternative should be selected; then the reasonableness of each strategy for implementing the alternative should be tested by examining the sensitivity of various financial measures to implementation of each strategy.

Phase 4. Finalizing the implementation plan. It is necessary to identify programs, policies, services to be implemented, timing of implementation, responsible parties, and target or expected results.

External Environmental Assessment

Facility and program planning efforts must use an open systems approach. Examining only the internal environment overlooks a very important aspect of strategic planning. The external environmental assessment includes information about the area the hospital serves and its population trends; the other health care providers in the service area; and the regulatory, reimbursement, and technological trends that are occurring.[15] Much of the specific information, such as patient origin studies and service demography, is also essential for marketing activities.[16]

Three segments of the external environment need to be considered: general economic and political trends, national health care market trends, and local conditions. A detailed analysis and interpretation of current and projected data for each of these segments should inform the strategic planning process.

General Economy

Nine of the nation's leading independent economic forecasters are predicting real growth rates that average slightly more than 3% over the next few years.[17] Unemployment will remain somewhat stable, but the percentage of persons below the poverty line is expected to increase, as it has increased over the past five years. The paramount consideration in economic policy continues to be the federal budget deficit. In the health care sector, deficits will perpetuate the pressure to reduce funding through limits on payments for patient care, grants for education and research, and indirect subsidies.

National Health Care Market Conditions

Despite public and private efforts to contain health care costs, they continue to consume an ever-greater share of the nation's economic resources. A conservative estimate is that health care will account for 12% of the gross national product in 1995.[18] The aging of the population ensures that Medicare will lead the expansion, increasing perhaps from the current 16% to 19% of the total.[19]

The government continues to attempt to limit the growth of Medicare expenses, especially for inpatient care. It will probably require more cost sharing for beneficiaries and will further tighten the payments to hospitals. By 1995, the prospective payment system (PPS) will either be more comprehensive in nature or will be abandoned in favor of a more competitive approach. The replacement of the PPS might be a voucher system, competitive bidding for specific services, or a comprehensive plan based on capitation payments. Whichever evolves, the health care system will be much more price sensitive than it has been. Financial management for hospitals will shift from emphasis on the maximization of revenue to concern for efficiency and minimization of costs.[20]

If the PPS does survive, it will evolve into a more complex form that includes all hospital inpatient and outpatient care and perhaps physician services. The DRG payment rates might be further refined to differentiate severity variations within DRGs.

Payments from private sources have been affected by an emerging cost consciousness among large employers and their coalitions. This concern is manifested in the redesign of benefits to exclude some services, the shift in coverage to outpatient services, and the increase in employee out-of-pocket expenditures. Business coalitions are attempting to exert leverage to elicit discounts from providers. Some employers are getting directly involved as sponsors of health maintenance organizations and preferred provider organizations. All of these changes suggest a less benign, more price-sensitive environment with reduced demand for inpatient care.

Hospital management must monitor all reimbursement trends and attain a critical awareness of future directions, as well as identify the implications of these trends for future opportunities and constraints. Only with this information will it be possible to adjust current strategic and tactical plans. Nursing management must advocate financial excellence through a performance orientation, by motivating personnel and creating cost awareness in delivery of patient care.[21] Nursing management must be a part of, or work with, top management, and must successfully communicate the specific needs and accomplishments of the nursing department. The nursing director functions as an advocate for nursing services — arranging sufficient resources and validating claims for further investment because such investments pay off in terms of improved performance. Nursing management must analyze the financial implications of resource investments or changes in service components and must be able to predict the financial impact of such changes on nursing and nursing programs.[22]

Technological change is continuing to have profound effects on health care. Some new technologies permit more efficient, less expensive care; but more commonly, new technologies add to rather than substitute for existing technologies, adding to health care cost increases. In addition, they require more highly trained staff.

The most important effect of the financial-economic conditions on hospitals is increasing pressure to reduce inpatient care. One of the outcomes is the expansion of outpatient care, in both traditional and innovative patterns. The long-term trend of outpatient clinic visits will continue, but hospitals are also developing new services such as satellite centers, urgent care centers, ambulatory surgery centers, mobile support and ancillary services, and dialysis facilities. Some of these are necessary responses to competition from free-standing organizations; others are efforts to expand the hospital inpatient markets under the assumption that particular non-acute services complement inpatient business.

Hospitals are also developing services and activities that stretch their current definitions and missions. Some participate in or fully own facilities that have a relatively small health care component, such as life care centers. Others are using their current resources and expertise to develop businesses — hotels or eating establishments — that are related to health care. Hospitals engage in many of these ventures through more complex organizational forms that include both for-profit and not-for-profit units.

Local External Environmental Assessment

Assessing the local environment requires an analysis of the state regulatory environment, local price sensitivity, local health services markets, and competitors' positions. A crucial concern is the current and future state regulatory environment. Strategic planners need to know whether the state will move toward tighter controls or toward encouraging price competition. Possible changes in rate setting and certificates of need are most important in states that rely on regulatory strategies. It is also important to be informed about specific regulations that apply to any services the hospital wants to consider as new ventures.

Local price sensitivity has a strong influence on strategies for protecting or increasing market share. Most markets are becoming more price sensitive, but changes can be more rapid in some areas than in others. Competition occurs primarily among four groups — insurers, hospitals, physicians, and alternative delivery systems — and may be on the basis of price or level of amenities and perceived quality.

The major task in a local environmental assessment is the analysis of health service markets. Markets must be defined on at least four dimensions — consumers, physicians, needs, and technologies. The analysis should determine whether patients and physicians need services and technologies that the hospital does or can provide. By examining the market on all four dimensions, the hospital defines very specific markets that it may serve through strategic business units.[23]

Among consumers, the most important variables are geographic, economic, and demographic. An economic profile will indicate how national conditions have been manifested in the local market. Recent trends and projections showing labor force and unemployment rates must be studied, as must the local business climate. Trends in the sources of payment and especially in amounts of uncompensated care are of special concern. Demographic data, especially age, indicate the types of services that will be needed in the future. This category of information should include recent trends and projections of population distribution by age and sex.

Physician variables that must be considered are age, specialty, location, type of practice, and frequency of referrals to the hospital. Data on the trends in disease incidence and in types of services provided indicate which services can and should be expanded. Disease incidence information can help generate trend projections for different medical diagnoses and surgical procedures. Data may also be available from planning agencies and organizations to help produce demand projections. The analysis of biomedical technologies is also important and must involve both managerial and clinical personnel. The crucial questions are which technologies will be available in the future and what effects each of these technologies will have on the hospital's market.

The last component of the local assessment is a competitor profile. In addition to current data on competitors' services, utilization, charges, and so on, the profile should present available information on future goals, strategies, and capabilities. Competitors include both hospitals and less comprehensive providers, existing and potential. By studying the hospital's market share relative to that of competitor institutions, one can view the service area from the perspective of the relative importance of the hospital to the people in geographical subareas. This analysis involves calculating market shares for current and prior time periods, for the hospital itself, and for other hospitals in the service area.[24]

The above factors can be reviewed and summarized as a list of threats and opportunities facing the hospital. The next step involves conducting an internal assessment to determine the hospital's capacity for handling the threats and exploiting the opportunities.

INTERNAL ENVIRONMENTAL ASSESSMENT

The internal environment of the health care organization is the total sets of relationships — financial, political, social, legal, and professional — among those people who make up the internal constituency. One assesses the internal environment to identify the strengths and weaknesses of the major areas of hospital activity. Areas of focus include organizational design, product-line identification and development, case mix management, financial stability, operational characteristics, and human resources development.

Organizational Design

Broader definitions of management in terms of the roles of the hospital and nursing services administrators and in the level of trustee and medical staff involvement are now required. The hospital administrator must assume managerial responsibility for the overall business performance of the institution.[25] Political and environmental forces have made hospital management an even more complex and strategic task. The hospital medical staff now has to consider the impact of its medical service decisions on the hospital's financial performance. Membership on the board of trustees has evolved from symbolic community service to active corporate decision making. Nursing administrators are now responsible for budgetary and cost control, and they often have responsibility for several patient services areas.

Definition of Business

Hospital information systems are increasingly necessary as administration defines its lines of business. These information systems aid in making operational decisions, such as optimizing supply inventories and generating information needed at the managerial level to monitor and control expenditures, revenues, and cash flow. Hospital information systems are also necessary in the construction of demographic and resource consumption profiles that guide hospital product definition.

An analysis of the environment's impact on the hospital's ability to achieve its goals is required. Both internal and external factors affect the ability to reach business goals. The external factors include governmental regulations, actions of competitors, social norms and values, and personnel availability. Internal factors include communication programs to detect changes in employee needs and values. The organization needs to anticipate obstacles to gain competitive advantage. Management success or effectiveness depends on the organizational climate, which may lead to productive collaboration or problems and conflicts.

Nursing leaders must adopt a business-oriented approach to management — one in which calculated risks are encouraged and growth is stimulated within the organization.[26] Nursing leaders must be aware of their existing market, potential growth areas in that market, and variables affecting market change. Nurse managers must also build their organizations around clearly articulated values that can serve as the basis for decisions and systems building. Nursing decisions, in fact, must be made with strategic long-term plans in mind. Staffing and budget decisions need to be made with consideration for potential markets, such as home health care, day surgery, and so on. Staffing patterns must reflect data on length of stay and acuity levels for each nursing unit.[27]

Human Resource Profile

Human resource management should be a joint effort between human resource managers and line management. To manage the work force strategically, the human resources department should participate as a full member of the top management team.[28] It needs to be involved both in making business decisions and in developing and implementing organizational strategies. Every manager's success today and in the future depends on the effectiveness of his or her staff.[29]

One component of the strategic human resources management process is identification of the people requirements of business plans. More specifically, the manager asks how the composition of the work force affects current and future opportunities. The manager reviews organizational goals and determines what activities are required to achieve the goals. Current unmet skill needs are identified, and future skill needs are projected.[30]

Long-term strategic planning for human resource management is the key to high productivity, quality patient outcomes, and revenue growth.[31] The current focus on cost control and reduction of health care utilization puts the hospital at risk. To survive and manage well, the hospital must adopt a more business-oriented mode of operation and employ key personnel who are trained in the appropriate areas. The changing health care environment dictates the need for general management, marketing management, and financial management skills. It is particularly important for today's hospital managers to pay serious attention to marketing research. More important, managers are being called on to manage other than traditional inpatient services. With vertical integration, the responsibility for a growing and diverse set of products and services increases. Management needs to be flexible and able to span a broad range of specialty and business areas.

To define and defend nurses' therapeutic value under PPSs, every one of the nurses' activities should have a direct link to patient outcomes.[32] The care, handling, and nurturing of all employees is the key to high productivity. In turn, anticipation and satisfaction of patient needs are the key to long-term revenue growth. Globalism and interdependence will be the themes that influence the thinking of successful nurse managers.[33]

Salaries and Benefits

The growth in health care organizations and their greater complexity will increase the competition for individuals with well-developed management skills. Salaries and fringe benefit levels must be set at an appropriate level to recruit the most qualified personnel. Higher salaries are not the entire answer, however. The institution needs to assess what job benefits have the potential to reduce staff turnover. Employee retention and staff development programs require continual commitments of resources.

Product Line Profile

The internal assessment also involves determining the extent to which current utilization of the facility might be maintained and greater utilization accomplished. Instead of passive forecasting based on past utilization patterns, the current health care environ-

ment requires a more active assessment. The hospital must determine what new services are to be offered, what additional staff needs to be recruited, and what changes need to be made in operations.

Service Unit Identification

The hospital has different markets, defined by the different units and programs located within the facility. Planning and marketing must be performed for each of these units and programs. Each program represents specific functions, patient groups, physician groups, and resource needs. These various subunits must be identified and a determination made whether they should be treated auto-jnomously — given the opportunity to plan separately for the future and given the resources to implement the developed plan.[34] This process is called product line development.

Profit Center Profile

Various profit centers must also be identified, a task that is accomplished by making a complete list of the hospital's products and services and determining the outstanding characteristics of each. The goal of such an activity is to identify distinctive health center products as compared to products of peer group competitors. Development of a profit-center profile requires detailed analysis of the consumer groups, the case mix and severity of illness level, the profitability and costs per case or diagnostic group, and the technology required to deliver services.

Case Mix Profile

Hospitals must now compete for groups of health care purchasers and members of capitated health plans. These groups will be negotiating for services based on price per specific case type or of service. The hospital must therefore determine a realistic price on which to negotiate for these fixed-price contracts. To do this requires a computerized integrated clinical and financial management information system. Average resource consumption per severity-adjusted case type must be calculated for the potential consumers within the contracting groups. Economic grounds where costs as to the effectiveness of the treatment plan are reviewed should be established, both for the educational value and for the strategic need to increase awareness among all personnel in control of resource utilization.

Nursing administration also needs to develop a database of integrated financial and clinical data.[35] This database will facilitate the development of a clinical case mix, allowing analysis of volume, labor cost, supply cost, average length of stay, and procedure cost. It is also imperative that nursing develop a standard nursing-sensitive classification system to serve as the basis for cost finding of nursing services. Managerial decision making requires accurate and precise estimates of nursing costs on a per-patient as well as a per-diagnosis basis.[36]

Financial Profile

Medicare has switched to a PPS, and states are introducing rate setting or competitive bidding.[37] Such changes require diversification of the revenue base, accomplished by creating not-for-profit and for-profit enterprises such as satellite clinics and ambulatory surgery centers. Financial managers are being forced to concentrate on internal as well as external financial management and reporting. Financial assessment questions include how to divide the resources among the various products and services offered by the hospital and whether specific services should be eliminated and resources allocated elsewhere. These issues require consideration of the health care needs of the consumers, quality of care requirements, research and educational program needs, and profitability of the particular services under consideration.

One particularly challenging area of financial management is the development of a microcosting system that allows identification of the actual costs of various product lines and services offered by the hospital and therefore allows more knowledgeable pricing strategies. Microcosting accounting systems allow those with financial expertise to evaluate their pricing structures and see how they relate to the actual cost of producing particular services.

Intraorganizational Assessment

A critical component of the internal assessment is to ascertain how key individuals in the institution perceive its strengths and weaknesses. This analysis requires the collection of pertinent information from hospital top management, members of the board of trustees, and key medical and nonmedical staff. Such an activity should be targeted toward a broad array of hospital management service variables. It should uncover areas of facility operation that require specific correctional efforts and in which alteration will significantly improve hospital operations. This multidisciplinary approach also identifies valuable perceptions that can then be used to target educational programs.

OUTCOME OF THE STRATEGIC PLANNING PROCESS

Successful implementation of the strategic planning process allows the hospital to be proactive rather than reactive in the quickly changing and increasingly competitive health care marketplace. Through this process, the hospital will be able to develop the corporate structure, financial strength, human resources, and political effectiveness to maximize market opportunities and minimize environmental threats. It also should foster a work climate that provides opportunities for personal and professional growth and respects and rewards excellence. The hospital needs to nurture a positive work environment, characterized by mutual trust and active employee participation in work-related decisions. The ideal corporate culture enhances employee initiative, creativity, and personal dignity. The corporate culture is perpetuated by widely communicated institutional goals and objectives. A holistic approach to each employee is a shared managerial style of behavior that can reduce turnover within the institution.

A strategic management system will be developed and implemented. It relies on timely, accurate access to internal and external information bases. The information system supports both the operational strategic management of all products and services and the institutional strategic and financial planning for capital and human resources expenditures. A cost accounting system is developed that allows product line analysis. This capability allows the hospital to price all patient contracts with speed and accuracy. The cost accounting system also allows the hospital to be more responsive to marketplace demands.

The hospital cultivates internal and external political networks that facilitate change relative to corporate and institutional goals and objectives. Active cultivation of the internal political network will promote effective communication. External networks may result from involvement in legislative issues pertaining to reimbursement, biomedical ethics, and health planning. The hospital develops inpatient feeder systems, such as outpatient clinics, diagnostic imaging centers, and preferred provider networks, and alternative delivery systems, such as ambulatory surgery centers and urgent care centers. Such diversification may encourage economies of scale, expanded personnel development opportunities and patient referral networks, and competitive advantage.

Nurses are the main professional support group for the entire health care system. As such, they are well-positioned to address the pressures confronting health care organizations. Nurses also have the opportunity to control many of the costs associated with service delivery, as they control many operational decisions surrounding the delivery of nursing and medical care.[38] They have considerable ability to control use of supplies, equipment, and support personnel. Furthermore, nurses also know how the organization functions and understand and accept the need to work within the organizational framework. This is important since organizations will play a dominant role in attaining high quality and cost-effective health care in the future.[39]

REFERENCES

1. Tucker, S.L., and Burr, R.M. "Strategic Market Planning." *Topics in Health Care Financing* 14, no. 3 (1988): 44-55.
2. Ibid.
3. Mark, B.A., and Smith, H.L. *Essentials of Finance in Nursing.* Rockville, Md.: Aspen Publishers, 1987.
4. Ibid.
5. Ibid.
6. Mowry, M.M., and Korpman, R.A. *Managing Health Care Costs, Quality, and Technology: Product Line Strategies for Nursing.* Rockville, Md.: Aspen Publishers, 1986.
7. Katz, G., Zavodnick, L., and Markezin, E. "Strategic Planning in a Restrictive and Competitive Environment." *Health Care Management Review* p 8, no. 4 (1983): 7-12.
8. Gay, J.D. "Strategic Program Planning." *Topics in Health Care Financing,* 11, no. 4 (1985): 65-72.
9. Mowry and Korpman, *Managing Health Care Costs.*
10. Katz, Zavodnick, and Markezin, "Strategic Planning."
11. Ibid.
12. Ibid.
13. Killian, J.W., and Miller, V.A. "Process for Integrating Market Strategies and Financial Strategies." *Topics in Health Care Financing* 11, no. 4 (1985): 7-13.
14. Katz, Zavodnick, and Markezin, "Strategic Planning."
15. Ibid.
16. Kristoff, N. "Economists Predict Growth of Three Percent for the Coming Year." *Gainesville Sun,* December 23, 1984, p. 1.
17. Arthur Andersen and American College of Hospital Administrators. *Health Care in the 1990s: Trends and Strategies.* Chicago: ACHE, 1984.
18. Ibid.
19. Ibid.
20. Kropf, R., and Greenberg, J.A. *Strategic Analysis for Hospital Management.* Rockville, Md.: Aspen Publishers, 1984.
21. Mark and Smith, *Essentials of Finance in Nursing.*
22. Ibid.
23. Gannon, J.J., Roemer, D.R., and Barbato, R.J. "Strategic Financial Planning Under DRG-based Prospective Payment." *Topics in Health Care Financing* 11, no. 4 (1985): 21-32.
24. Silvers, J.B., Zelman, W.N., and Kahn, C.N. *Health Care Financial Management in the 1980s.* Ann Arbor, Mich.: AUPHA Press, 1983.
25. Mowry and Korpman, *Managing Health Care Costs.*
26. Ibid.
27. Ibid.
28. Getzendanner, C., Misa, K.F., and Stein, R.T. "Management's Involvement in the Strategic Utilization of the Human Resource." In *Perspectives on Prospective Payment,* edited by M. Beyers. Rockville, Md.: Aspen Publishers, 1985.
29. Ibid.
30. Ibid.
31. Mowry and Korpman, *Managing Health Care Costs.*

32. Ibid.

33. Ibid.

34. Kropf and Greenberg, *Strategic Analysis for Hospital Management.*

35. Mowry and Korpman, *Managing Health Care Costs.*

36. Ibid.

37. Relman, A.S. "Are Teaching Hospitals Worth the Extra Cost?" *New England Journal of Medicine* 310 (1984): 1256-57.

38. Mark and Smith, *Essentials of Finance in Nursing.*

39. Ibid.

CHAPTER **28**

An Integrated Nursing Information System
A planning model

CDR Karen A. Rieder, NC, USN
MAJ Dena A. Norton, ANC

The benefits of computer technology to nursing are predicated on the profession's ability to define its requirements in the areas of practice, education, and research. Often the information to be accepted, processed, and printed by a computer for a nursing work center has been identified and determined by technical rather than by functional experts. Since nurse users have been reluctant to commit the time and energy necessary to define their automation demands, they have been forced to fit their needs to already established systems. This has resulted in a mismatch between computer technology and nursing requirements.

Nurses, to date, have remained naive concerning the definition and design of information systems for day-to-day functioning because they assume that any automated hospital system would automatically satisfy nursing requirements. Yet, a recent analysis of the health care computer technology available from major companies indicated just the opposite. Nursing was the least-defined area in terms of computer applications. Although some strides have been made in nursing documentation and nurse care planning, little has

been developed specific to administrative reporting, patient classification, or the many facets of scheduling. The reason is simple — major efforts in automation have been made in areas where costs can be pinpointed and retrieved, such as pharmacy or laboratory. Documenting how many pills are dispensed or how long it takes to do a CBC is far easier than delineating time spent in the nursing process. Therefore, computer support for a nursing work center has been considered only in a limited context.

In September 1982, the Tri-Service Nursing Requirements Committee was appointed to explore computer support for nursing activities. Working in conjunction with the Tri-Service Medical Information Systems (TRIMIS) Program Office (TPO), the specific task identified by the Committee was the development of systems requirements and documentation in the areas of nursing management and automated inpatient nursing records. The ultimate goal was the improvement of patient care within military medical treatment facilities by identifying nursing requirements for a Composite Health Care System (CHCS). This CHCS was the third phase of a TRIMIS Program to develop standard automated systems for the three Military Medical Departments (TPO, 1983).

Reprinted from *Computers in Nursing,* Vol. 2, No. 3, with permission of J. B. Lippincott Company © 1984.

The committee's mission was formidable—to identify and define those functions in nursing that would benefit from automated support. The result was the creation of a nursing information system that delineates automated requirements for patient care, unit management, and nursing administration in the inpatient, outpatient, and operating room areas.

Although the focus of this paper is an automated nursing system, it is essential to view nursing as part of a larger hospital information system. The benefits of automation are best experienced when information is entered into the system by the department in which it originates and shared by all legitimate users. To justify cost and eliminate redundancy, nursing data must become part of a broader central data base. Otherwise, nursing emerges as a stand-alone system and duplicates data being recorded by other work centers, such as the admissions department, and, therefore, mimics existing manual systems. The integration of nursing database elements with those of other work centers is a crucial phase of any viable hospital information system. This integration is currently taking place within the CHCS.

PURPOSE

The purpose of this paper is to describe the process undertaken to define information requirements for an automated nursing system. To do this, we will explore the computer information requirements process at two levels. First, we will present an overview of the process that includes a description of the conceptual base and identification of nursing information functions. Second, we will take one example, workload management (staffing), and describe how this manual function is translated into a systems process.

Our focus for this article is narrow. We will not discuss computer hardware, software, or systems design; we will only address requirements. Requirements determine the information functions, the policy associated with the functions, and the data. This step is paramount because unless nursing determines what is required, it cannot effectively evaluate what is currently being offered in the data-processing market. The steps undertaken and the pitfalls encountered

during the requirements definition phase form the content of this paper.

Conceptual Framework

At the start of the project, it quickly became evident that information requirements had to be addressed in some context viable to nursing. Overwhelmed by the magnitude of the task, the Committee fumbled through the first few meetings just trying to get a "handle on" the project. There was no starting point until a conceptual base was identified.

What evolved was a simplified model for patient care that defined the domain of nursing as including patient care, unit management, and nursing administration (Figure 28-1). From this model, the committee was able to agree on the information functions of nursing within the military setting. These functions were conceptualized as being composed of the modules delineated in Figure 28-2.

The subdivision of the overall system into these logical information-handling functions forced the committee to focus on interdepartmental communications, thereby reducing redundancy and fragmentation. With this approach, the functional boundaries between inpatient and outpatient, or between

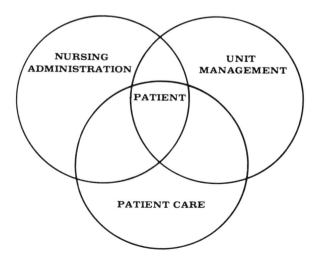

FIGURE 28-1

Nursing model for patient care.

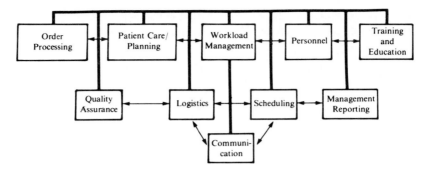

FIGURE 28-2
Nursing information functional modules.

specialty units, such as Intensive Care and Operating Room, become blurred. The scheduling subsystem is designed to ensure not only personnel coverage and to assign duty personnel, but also to schedule OR rooms, patient appointments, staff meetings or services, and to compile "to be done" lists for inpatient care. It was within this "work breakdown" framework that the following steps of the computer information requirements process took place:

1. Analyze relevance and usage of present forms and reports.
2. Analyze information flow and how data is processed.
3. Determine if and how this information process can be automated.
4. Define outputs and their format.
5. Define inputs necessary to generate outputs.
6. Define the data in terms of the data elements required for all inputs and outputs.

Analysis of Present Reports

As stated, the first step is to analyze present forms and reports. The purpose of the paperwork analysis was to detail the scope of information needed by the nursing staff in performing their professional duties. For example, in the functional module of patient care planning, each step of the patient's progress on the ward or in the clinics was chronicled with its accompanying paperwork. This paperwork could encompass patient assessment, admission note, nursing diagnosis, prob-

lem list, patient care plan, patient profile, medication record, nurses' notes, discharge instructions, and health teaching. Each piece of paper that the nursing staff created or supplemented was identified and catalogued, and samples were collected. It also was decided to include all forms that nursing accessed for information regarding patient history and status. Thus, paperwork initiated by the physician became a part of the nursing system requirements.

Once collected, these forms and reports were evaluated for relevance and usage within the nursing setting based on the following items:

Document Name: The actual name of the form or the composite name agreed upon if more than one form is being used by various specialty areas. For example, a nursing or patient assessment form will differ in Pediatrics, Med/Surg, or Coronary Care Unit.

When Used: What event initiates the use of this document? For example, an admission form is started when the patient is admitted to the ward or nursing notes may be initiated after the patient's physical or after the patient's preliminary vital signs are obtained.

Who Completes: Name the staff usually responsible for completing the form initially (ward clerk, admissions clerk, attending physician) and the location where this takes place (admitting office, adult inpatient unit, cardiac unit, nursery unit).

Who Uses: Name the staff who normally utilizes the form (if more than one staff person uses it, name the person who is the primary user, followed by the secondary users).

Purpose: What is the purpose of the information on the form? Does it fulfill its purpose and provide the information needed by the people who are the primary users? Since there may be multiple uses for a form, identify as many of them as possible.

Filed: Where is the form filed? Is it a permanent part of the patient's medical record? A part of the unit's log file? Is it destroyed? When is it filed? (Upon completion, or at the patient's discharge).

This portion of the requirements process resulted in the identification of 386 composite forms that are used by military nurses when giving patient care. Once analyzed, each form then was placed within its appropriate functional module.

Analysis of Information Flow

The second step was to identify and analyze the data that flow through each of the clinical areas. The purpose of this information flow analysis was to detail its creation and use by nursing staff in performing their professional duties. From this description of how information is processed, a physical model for nursing service emerged. This was accomplished by using a structured analysis and system specification technique that detailed every piece of data at its origin and how it is communicated within nursing service. The resulting physical model included the dimensions of patient care, unit management, and nursing administration. The model for patient care consisted of the nursing process function, namely to assess, plan patient care, implement, and reassess. Unit management consisted of teach/orient staff, schedule unit workload, interface with ancillaries, evaluate staff, maintain ward protocols, and generate unit reports. The nursing administration dimension included the following: establishing/maintaining policies and procedures, managing resources, managing education

and training, scheduling personnel, conducting quality assurance activities, and reviewing/evaluating/generating reports. It is interesting to note that the physical model of nursing information flow mirrors the conceptual model of nursing used as a framework for this project.

Determination of Appropriate Automation

The next step was to determine how this information could be automated if appropriate. Because you must decide which processing steps can be handled more efficiently by a computer, you will need the assistance of technical experts. The methodology for this step included eliminating any processes that must remain manual and combining similar computer processes to eliminate redundancy. An analysis of the physical flow resulted in the identification of five nursing information logical modules, which are the computer processes necessary to transmit the needed information. The processes identified included:

- Perform Nursing Process
- Manage Human Resources Process
- Manage Physical Resources Process
- Perform Quality Assurance Process
- Perform System Management Process

Defining Output, Input, and Data Elements

Once the processes to be automated have been identified, the data for the computer process must be developed. This consists of defining the following terms:

Outputs — screen displays or hard-copy reports that have been identified by the user as necessary. The screen displays are used either to display data stored in the system for review or to allow the user to enter and update data. Hard copy outputs are actual forms or reports generated and printed by the system, for example, patient care plans and patient assessment data. Each computer process may have several outputs with different formats specified.

Inputs — data or information that are actually placed in a computer by a user, such as a nurse, or are transmitted to nursing by another work center, such as radiology or laboratory. All the information necessary for producing output reports must be identified at this stage, but remember that most data should only be entered once.

Data elements — basic units of information having a unique meaning within a specific context, for example, "color of eyes," "date of last visit," and "patient name."

When the outputs, inputs, and data elements have been defined, the information required to enter and leave each of the nursing computer processes has been identified.

Therefore, the functional modules of nursing information have been transferred and interfaced with the logical processes of a computer system (Figure 28-3). Some nursing functions are indigenous to a unique process such as quality assurance or nursing process, while others are a common thread through-out the system, such as management reporting and message exchange. In essence, what we have done is taken the nursing model for patient care and determined the computer processes necessary to support information requirements.

In order to make this requirement process clearer, we will take one concrete example, workload management, and follow it through the steps we have just discussed, since it is a function with which all nurses are familiar and requires many hours of nursing personnel time. Historically, traditional staffing methods have been based on data related to bed occupancy. In 1980, the Joint Commission on Hospital Accreditation mandated that Nursing Services define, implement, and maintain a system by which the quantity and quality of available staff is based on identified patient needs. What is described in this example is the evolution of a current manual system for workload management into an automated process with corresponding outputs and displays.

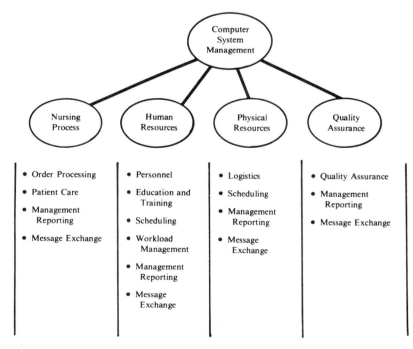

FIGURE 28-3

Logical-functional interface.

Workload Management—An Illustration

Workload Management is a methodology for allocation of staff to a nursing unit based on a classification system that defines the patient's nursing care hour requirements. The patient requirements subsequently are coupled with a staffing system that calculates the number and skill level of personnel that must be assigned to meet the identified needs. Changes to staffing levels then can be made on a daily basis to meet the delineated workload.

The first step in determining information requirements is to analyze the relevance and usage of the forms, reports, and the worksheets used manually. In this Workload Management System, six forms are used to determine and document workload:

The **Critical Indicator Guidesheet** is the basis of the patient classification system. This guidesheet lists multiple patient care activities, each with an associated point value that indicates the amount of time needed to perform the activity. Nurses use this guidesheet as a tool to classify each patient on a unit (Figure 28-4).

The **Classification Worksheet** lists each patient on a unit, the total points or time their nursing care requires, and the category of care based on the points awarded to the patient. This form also provides a summary of the number of patients in each category on that nursing unit (Figure 28-5).

The **Nursing Care Hour Requirements Charts** are used to translate the number of patients in each category into the total number

of nursing hours required for patient care. These charts are specific for each type of nursing unit (Figure 28-6).

The **Personnel Requirements Charts** convert the number of nursing hours required into full time staff equivalents. This translates into the number and level of personnel recommended to meet patient care needs.

The **Workload Management Summary Sheet** identifies on a daily basis the number of patients in each category on a nursing unit, the recommended staffing for each shift, the actual staff scheduled on each shift, and any variance

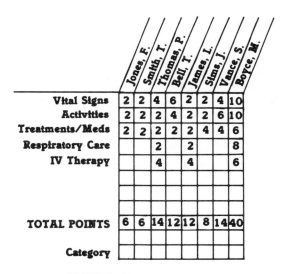

FIGURE 28-5
Patient classification worksheet.

PTS.	IV THERAPY
(4)	KVO
(4)	Herapin Lock
(4)	Chemotherapy/Blood Products
(6)	Simple (change bottle q 6-8 hours)
(8)	Complex (two or more lines)

FIGURE 28-4
Critical indicators.

PATIENTS	CATEGORY					
	I (2)	II (4)	III (9)	IV (15)	V (23)	VI (37)
1	2	4	9	15	23	37
2	4	8	18	30	46	74
3	6	12	27	45	69	111
4	8	16	36	60	92	148
5	10	20	45	75	115	185

FIGURE 28-6
Nursing care hour requirements: open unit chart.

between the recommended and the actual staffing. Any changes to the schedule are recorded on this form so that the number of personnel who actually worked on each shift is documented (Figure 28-7).

The Monthly Staffing Summary Graph is a graphic representation of the monthly data for the purpose of evaluating staffing patterns and trends (Figure 28-8).

For each of these reports or forms, the following items must be noted: its name, when it is used, what other forms are associated with it, who fills it out, who uses it, what its purpose is, and where it is filed. To simplify this process step, an Information Flow Analysis form can be created with all of the essential heading and used to analyze each piece of paperwork related to workload management. This stage of the process will provide a detailed look at the presently required paperwork.

The second step is to analyze how information is processed in the Workload Management System. This analysis is done by identifying the information flow and determining at what point the data is added to, manipulated, or processed. These processing points then must be described. In the Workload Management System, there are three processing points: classifying the patient on a given nursing unit, determining the workload for that specific unit, and managing the staffing to meet the workload.

To classify each patient, the staff nurse uses the patient's profile, patient's care plan, and medical record to identify the direct care activities ordered and compares this data to the Critical Indicator guidesheet so that the staff time necessary for this patient's care can be determined. As a result of this processing, the staff nurse completes the Classification Worksheet with each patient's name, the total number of points their nursing care requires, and the category of care based on the points awarded. This information is submitted on a daily basis to the nursing supervisor.

To determine the workload, the nursing supervisor uses the information recorded on the Classification Worksheet and the information on the Nursing Care Hour Requirements Chart for that specific type of nursing unit to determine the total number of nursing hours required for patient care. The Personnel Requirements Chart then is used to convert this number into the quantity of Registered Nurses and paraprofessionals recommended to meet this workload. This recommended staffing is recorded on a Workload Management Summary Sheet.

To manage staffing, the nurse supervisor compares the recommended staffing information on the Summary Sheet to the Master Time Schedule that has been projected for that nursing unit and records any variances on the Summary Sheet. From this Summary Sheet, nursing units that have excess staff and those that need additional staff to meet their workload can

Ward   D   Date _____

CATEGORY   HOURS

I	1	2
II	6	24
III	2	18
IV	1	23
V	0	0
Totals	10	67

	PM			NIGHT		
	RN	NRN	T	RN	NRN	T
Actual	1	1	2	1	1	2
Recommended	1	2	3	1	1	2
Variance	0	-1	-1	0	0	0
Changes	0	+1	+1	0	0	0
TOTAL	1	2	3	1	1	2

FIGURE 28-7
Summary sheet.

be identified. Any staffing changes made are noted on the Summary Sheet so that the total number of persons who actually worked on each unit for each shift is recorded. At the end of each month, the Monthly Staffing Summary Graph is created and used to evaluate staff management and to determine staffing patterns.

This description of how information presently is being processed in the manual system is termed the physical model. Nurses who have been involved with staffing know that this manual process is complex. Not only must patient requirements be considered, but a large number of variables must be evaluated each time a schedule is to be altered. Minor adjustments lead to multiple numbers of personnel changes. Therefore, the current manual workload management process has two significant weaknesses. It is time consuming and error prone due to all the calculations required.

The third step of the process involves determining how this information process can be automated. This step requires that nurses possess knowledge of computer capabilities. By looking at the physical model for workload management, they must differentiate between the information-processing steps that could be automated and those steps that must remain manual. Simultaneously, any processes that could be combined or would logically be transmitted differently by a computer need to be identified. For this phase of identifying requirements, it may be necessary to consult a technical expert.

In a composite health care system, the medical record and the patient's care plan already would have been entered into the computer; therefore, the processing step of classifying patients could be fully automated. The computer could process patient information and determine each patient's acuity category from the Critical Indicator parameters stored within the system. As orders and plans of care change, the computer also will update each patient's acuity category and display the results on demand. Lastly, it will produce a report that classifies all patients on a given unit. These classification data become the input of the workload determination process. By using the Nursing Care Hour Requirements Chart and the Personnel Requirements Charts stored in the com-

puter, the patient classification information automatically would be compared to the appropriate chart and the recommended staffing determined. The computer then will compare the recommended staffing with the current stored Master Time Schedule and identify unit deficiencies or excesses. With this information, the nursing supervisor would modify unit assignments based on the numbers of staff available.

The final process of managing staff will remain manual, since decisions made to accommodate the variances noted are predicated on the experience and skill level of available personnel. Once the decision is made to alter staffing, manual changes made in the Master Time Schedule would automatically be reflected on the Monthly Staffing Summary Graph.

The fourth step is to decide what outputs are required from the computer and in what format. In this example, the computer will provide a Classification Report, a Workload Management Summary Sheet, and a Monthly Staffing Graph. Decisions must be made as to which report can be a paper printout, which must be displayed on a screen, and if any of the reports require both formats. The Classification Report and the Staffing Summary Sheet probably need an output that is both displayed and printed, while the Monthly Staffing Summary Graph may only require a printed report.

The fifth step is simply to ensure that all the information needed to produce the required output

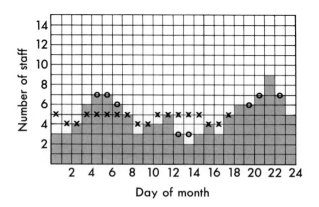

FIGURE 28-8
Monthly staffing summary.

is input to the computer. For example, if the projected Master Time Schedule is entered into the system, it should be available for determining staffing variances, since data need only be entered once into the computer. However, should the projected Master Time Schedule be excluded from the computerized system, information would have to be entered specifically for determining staffing variances or that segment of the Workload Management System would remain a manual process.

The final step is writing the detail that the technical experts must have to know exactly what the user requires from the computer. For each output identified, such as the Classification Report, a comprehensive description of the report must be written so that nonnursing personnel will understand exactly what is needed. With each description, the specific data elements required on each output report must be identified and defined. For example, on some reports, the patient name will consist of the last name, first name, and middle name. On other reports, the patient's name consists of just the last name and first initial. These would have to be defined as two separate data elements with different titles, such as "NAME-COMPLETE" and "LAST-NAME-FIRST-MIDDLE."

Two data elements listed on the Classification Report are "NAME-COMPLETE," and "POINTS-CRITICAL-GROUP-VITAL-SIGNS." Each listed data element must be defined. A data element definition does not describe the meaning of a data element in the same way a dictionary would but describes the type of information that is required on a particular report. "NAME-COMPLETE" would be defined as "last name, first name, and middle initial of known patient," rather than defined as "words or phrases by which a person is known." Likewise "POINTS-CRITICAL-GROUP-VITAL-SIGNS" is defined as "the numerical value equivalent to vital sign activities for a specific patient." This will not tell the computer expert what this element means, but will indicate that it is a number that is related to a specific type of activity. With this definition of the inputs, outputs, and data elements, a detailed description of the workload management computer process has been delineated.

CONCLUSION

A detailed methodology based on a conceptual model for defining information requirements for an automated nursing information system has been described. Using the manual process of workload management as an illustration, we have delineated the steps involved in creating a logical computerized model complete with inputs, outputs, and data elements. The resulting functional description provides a blueprint for either the design stage of a nursing system or for effectively evaluating computer hardware and software available in the data-processing market. Defining requirements is the first step toward developing the content of information to be accepted, processed, and printed by the computer for nursing.

REFERENCE

TRIMIS Program Office .(1983). *Tri-Service information systems composite health care system (CHCS) executive summary.* Washington, D.C.: Department of Defense.

BIBLIOGRAPHY

American Management Systems, Inc. (1983). *Nursing administration system — system decision paper.* (GSA Contract No. GS-00C-60084). Washington, D.C.: U.S. Navy.

Brady, F. (1967). A head nurse's viewpoint of automation. In *ANA Regional Clinical Conferences: American Nurses' Association, 1967, Philadelphia/Kansas City.* New York: Appleton-Century-Crofts.

DiMarco, T. (1978). *Structured analysis and system specifications.* New York: Yourdon, Inc.

Joint Commission on Accreditation of Hospitals. (1980). *Accreditation manual for hospitals.* Chicago, Illinois: Author.

Jotwani, P. (1981). A nursing-centered patient information system. In H. Werley, and M. Grier, (Eds.), *Nursing information systems* (pp. 179-195). New York: Springer Publishing Company.

Lee, A.E. (1982, September). What computers can do for you . . . and what they're already doing for the lucky few. *RN,* pp. 43-44, 121-127.

Reeves, T.J. (1967). Automation at the nurses' station. In *ANA Regional Clinical Conferences: American Nurses' Association, 1967, Philadelphia/Kansas City.* New York: Appleton-Century-Crofts.

Romano, C., McCormick, K., & McNeely, L. (1981). Nursing documentation: A model for a computerized data base. *Advances in Nursing Science, 4,* 43-56.

Werley, H. & Grier, M. (Eds.). (1981). *Nursing information systems.* New York: Springer Publishing Company.

Zielstorff, R. (1975). The planning and evaluation of automated systems: A nurses' point of view. *Journal of Nursing Administration, 5,* 22-25.

Zielstorff, R. (Ed.). (1980). *Computers in nursing.* Rockville, Maryland: Aspen System Corp.

MARKETING

CHAPTER **29**

Practical Approaches to Marketing

Harriett S. Chaney, RN, PhD

Increasing competition and a transition in the supply and demand function in the health care industry are forcing administrators to pursue organizational marketing programs aggressively. The nurse executive's challenge is to demonstrate the nursing department's contribution to specific organizational marketing objectives plus develop innovative programs for the promotion of the department itself. In this article, the marketing process and how a nursing executive might operationalize practical approaches to marketing and in particular the promotion process are discussed.

WHERE TO BEGIN

Developing a marketing orientation is the antecedent to successful marketing activities. A marketing orientation is a sensitivity or awareness, a vision on the part of the nurse executive of market trends, needs, and segmentation, and potential programs. The marketing oriented nurse executive views nursing as an essential, unique, and efficient health care service with current marketable programs and ideas that are worthy of systematic and aggressive development and promotion.

Many existing nursing administrative concepts and practices are consistent with marketing orientation and techniques. First, nurses recognize that the client and physician are the key constituents of health care services. Second, the nursing management team should continue to identify, through direct measure-

Reprinted from *The Journal of Nursing Administration,* Vol. 16, No. 9, with permission of J. B. Lippincott Company © 1986.

ment or observation, the wants and needs of the physician and client if the primary task of services delivery is to be marketed and delivered efficiently and economically. Finally, needs identification is not a new activity for any professional nurse. Nurses continually respond to the health needs of clients and convenience needs of physicians when we provide nursing service based on the medical plan of care and nursing diagnosis. What is different now is the scope and potential outcome of the process. In the past a nurse cared for and focused on specific clients with particular problems. Now, a market-oriented nurse needs to be more aware of groups of clients with similar problems, life-styles, and desires as well as the physician's requirements for caring for these clients. With this information, the nurse may shape the organization's future offerings so as to bring about desirable exchange relationships between the constituents and the institution.[1] Obviously, the success of this process requires the nurse executive's commitment and contribution to enhance the results for all concerned.

Research on the marketing orientation of health care administrators compared with marketing managers indicates that administrators:

— are less aggressive in their approach to marketing;
— have an underdeveloped sense of market segmentation (offering services to a market subgroup); and
— seem to focus more on clients than on physicians.[2]

These results suggest that if the nursing executive doesn't market nursing services to all the clients and physicians, no one will. The nursing activities of nurse specialists, midwives, practitioners, and experienced clinicians embody the humanitarian values, courage, talent, and expertise desirable to both constituents. Further, the marketing orientation and activities of the nurse executive should include a justification for aggressive marketing thrusts because the general administrative marketing attitude may be one of timidity. Finally, nurses already know about client market segmentation, and recognize potential client groups based on health needs, diagnosis, age, location, and life-style. This sense of market segmentation is invaluable for the development and promotion of current and future programs. Thus, knowing about the marketing process and the general marketing orientation of the health care administrator, successful marketing strategies can be initiated by the nurse executive.

PLANNING FOR THE MARKETING PROCESS

The marketing process generally is described in terms of the 4 Ps: product (service), price, placement, and promotion. These process elements undergo continual evaluation during the life-cycle of a particular product or service. Therefore, an appropriate place to begin a marketing program is with the current service activities.

Initially the nursing department manager identifies services that have one or more of the following characteristics:
— sporadic, inconsistent utilization;
— underutilization;
— impacts internal and external markets, specifically clients and/or physicians.
These characteristics indicate that a current program or activity is in need of analyses and promotion.

PROMOTING CURRENT ACTIVITIES

Examples of service activities that might be identified for initial promotion activities are: client education programs, childbirth classes, chemotherapy outpatient services, or clinic services. Ample service activities lie within the area of nursing specialization: oncology, diabetes, gerontology, pediatrics, obstetrics, etc. Once the activities are identified, several are selected and one or two objectives are developed related to the promoting of these activities.

Examples might include:
1. Developing a brochure describing childbirth classes and cost of the service,
2. Promoting childbirth classes to women's groups by sending brochures in the mail and offering speaker service to women's groups, and
3. Providing childbirth brochures to physician's offices by making a personal contact and delivering the brochures.

Initially, it is advisable to develop promotional strategies for a limited number of services then increase the marketing plan to include other services. The expansion should include nursing services that meet the needs of various market segments, i.e., differing client or physician groups.

DEVELOPING NEW SERVICES

In addition to the promotion of current service activities, the nurse executive will want to develop new profitable and marketable services. This phase of planning involves gathering data relative to internal and external markets and current national trends. The internal market of an organization are the medical staff, employees, volunteers, and the trustees. The external markets include: clients, families, the community, suppliers, regulators, professional groups, insurance companies, industrial companies, and the professional colleagues.

Alward describes several techniques for gathering information relative to markets and new services.[3] Group discussion, survey analysis, individual interviews, nominal group, and Delphi techniques are among the suggestions. These methods of market analysis require multiple resources: research methodology expertise, time, and money. This should not, however, dissuade a nurse executive from starting by selecting one of the less complicated techniques such as a simple survey or group discussion. Often suggestions for new services arise simply because someone inside or outside the organization has an idea. This idea is not the result of analyzed data but intuition. These ideas deserve analysis and feasibility consideration. Market analysis is critical to the selection of a potentially successful project as it reduces some of the risk associated with developing and investing resources on a large or even small project.

The analysis of national trends provides information regarding the future direction of the health care industry in general and organizations in particular. Current trends of interest now include: the restructuring of health organizations, establishing corporate name identity, emerging HMOs and home health agencies, and the expanding elderly population.

Following the identification of an organization's markets and a review of current trends, information must be gathered regarding the client and physician desires, competitor service activities, physician practice trends, and resource availability. Feasibility analysis will indicate if the organization has the resources, commitment, and market position to initiate a new project. The analysis will result in decisions about beginning the service when appropriate and placement of the service within the organization.

It is apparent that planning for the marketing process must be systematic and thorough. Specific objectives are developed for current and new service activities to provide direction for an orderly and complete process. With the planning process for each project complete, one can proceed with the promotion of the project.

SERVICE PROMOTION PRINCIPLES

The purposes of services and departmental promotion are twofold. First, the internal and external market elements must be informed about the current or new services being promoted. Second, promotional activities should persuade the market elements to use the service. Nurses are generally very skilled at providing information. All too often, however, nurses tend to believe that if a person is informed regarding a service, use of the service will logically follow. This is not true. Appropriate persuasion or selling skills must be combined with education if a particular market is going to be induced to use a service. Combining education

and selling for service promotion should not be viewed distainfully by a nurse executive, instead it should be seen as a golden opportunity for nurses to demonstrate creativity and boldness.

The promotion process starts by understanding the consumer demand state for the service in question. The demand states are as follows:

No Demand

This state exists when the potential market is disinterested or indifferent toward a service. No demand can occur because the service is either unknown or is considered of no value by the client. Examples of programs that might be grouped within this demand state include: safe exercise routines, well-baby clinics, nutrition education, and new surgical procedures or technology. There are two options for managing the no demand state. If it can be shown that a service is not needed or that it overlaps another for which there is already a demand, then the service should be eliminated. Conversely, if the service is simply unknown, the promotional task is to stimulate the market by connecting the service to a client need, distributing information regarding the service, and demonstrating the value of the service.

Negative Demand

This state can exist when potential clients dislike a service so much they avoid it entirely or pay a personal price to elude it. Negative demand state is widespread in health care, with clients ignoring such services as preventive dental care, outpatient clinics, annual physical examinations, stress management, and obesity treatment programs. Negative demand states can be differentiated from no demand when a client is aware of and articulates a value for managing a health care problem and chooses not to seek service. Countering a negative demand state requires an accurate identification of health problems, clear program and promotional goals, and aggressive promotional strategies. The promotional efforts provide factual information to dispel misbeliefs and indicate the consequence of avoiding necessary services. Negative demand states logically lead to health promotion programs. For example, weight control facilitates blood pressure control, latch key programs for parents and children reduce stress in the home with two working parents, exercise and nutrition programs facilitate disease prevention.

Latent Demand

When a strong client need exists but there is no service to meet this need, a latent demand state exists. Unfortunately, accompanying the latent demand state is public mistrust when the service is finally available. An example of this is the crisis rape centers. These much needed services are only now slowly being utilized as clients gain trust. So although the latent demand state is ripe for marketing and is the easiest market to define, the nurse executive will need to combine multiple resources, sensitivity, and patience in satisfying the client need.

Under Demand

Under demand occurs when a popular service is monitored and its use is found to be declining, or the utilization is sporadic. Defining causes of a decline is a difficult task. The causes, such as fluctuating seasonal demand, growing disenchantment with the physician or service director, or excessively long waiting room time, may all be intertwined. Any corrective actions must address the problem that has been identified as explicitly as possible. Re-marketing, a once-popular service, is a challenge and invites innovative promotion plans, such as swift, off-hour visits that are filled within minutes of the appointment time, discounting off-peak hours, and setting up freestanding agencies in more convenient location.

Full Demand

In an ideal world, full demand is satisfied when the service is at 100% utilization, and the client believes that the service value for their money is so good that he or she will happily suffer some minor delays in its execution. However, the full demand state is constantly under siege and needs continuous monitoring to ensure it does not overlook fundamental changes

in client needs or threats from a start-up or competing service. A famous car rental company once made inroads into a full demand market by promising that "We try harder" and went on to gain, and retain, a considerable market share for itself.

Over Demand

A service may become so popular that a state of over demand could evolve. Restless clients may vandalize property, and irritable employees and clients can grate at each other causing service deterioration. Improving service may require costly structure expansions, higher overheads with increased personnel, and a danger of an evolving hopeless bureaucracy.

A counter to over demand, if the service cannot be improved without acceptable costs, is to de-market by subtly discriminating among those who demand the service. Increased screening and selection, increased price, and increased inconvenience are all tools of this ploy, but the ethics of de-marketing are dubious. If the service is worthwhile and in great demand, a restructuring of the administration of the service is mandatory to ensure that satisfaction and value for money are maintained.

Unwholesome Demand

An unwholesome demand can exist because of a wide variety of deleterious products or "services." Tobacco, alcohol, and illegal chemical substances come to mind immediately, as do illegal abortions, medical quackery, and improperly utilized "natural" medicines. Then there are the more insidious practices, such as spiritual healing and other false promises of life-extension, which have no foundation in accepted universal medical practice. To combat these appetites, no matter how dubious these services may appear by openly condemning them runs counter to freedom of choice and challenges Constitutional protection of individual religious beliefs. A safer and better approach is to establish an alternative viewpoint through client education and then to foster and promote health care as an enviable personal and social substitution. Unselling strategies include fear, disgust, and shame as crude tools utilized by society and health care providers to inculcate a value for the pursuit of good health, spirit, robustness of body, well-being, and peer acceptance.

In summary, demand or call for a particular health care service during its life-cycle can be variable. Through utilization analysis the most appropriate marketing program and promotional strategies can be pursued.

SERVICES PROMOTION TARGET

The target for health care services promotion is generally the female.[4] It appears that women ordinarily maintain control of the family's discretionary health care dollar and are the primary purchasers of health services. It is the woman who seeks proper health care for children and facilitates appropriate care for the sick male.

The fact that women are the primary purchasers of health services is advantageous to the nursing profession, which is predominately female. A woman-to-woman communication regarding competent and humanistic health care services can be extremely potent. Physicians have long recognized this by offering nurses professional discounts. A satisfied nurse will provide credible testimony and referral of friends and acquaintances to the physician's practice. It is apparent then that a nurse executive should capitalize on the powerful woman-to-woman communication potential in seeking to penetrate the health care markets. As women, nurses can share experiential understanding, support, and trust with potential clients. Further, it is unlikely that the nurse will be viewed by the potential client as a person seeking to increase personal wealth or self-aggrandizement.

SERVICES PROMOTIONAL STRATEGIES

Promotional strategies are those activities used to encourage patronage of health care agencies or services. There are three major types of health care promotional activities: advertising, publicity, and personal promotion.[1] The objectives of all three activities are to inform, persuade, influence, and remind potential constituents, about available services.

A few basic principles need to be remembered about promotion. First, the more frequently a person encounters something the more likely they are to remember it. In other words, the more often you say hello, the better your chance is of being recalled and selected. Secondly, in general, health care services are obtained within five miles of one's home, and third, the majority of consumers expect health care agencies to advertise and report being influenced by advertising.[5] What then are the most effective, specific promotional strategies? Currently, the greatest client response is coming from direct mail, corporate advertising in newspapers, brochures, and television.[6] Publicity and personal promotion are also highly useful.

Advertising

A National Research Corporation survey indicates that the most prevalent advertising medium in health care today is direct mail.[6] An astounding 78 percent of respondents, generally female, who received direct mail recalled the name of the agency that sent it. This medium is conducive to promoting health services because it offers explanations, descriptions, and examples in a warm and personal manner. Further, direct mail can target specific market segments based upon a particular demographic parameter. Because direct mail is less expensive than other forms of advertising and it can be utilized with greater frequency, an important key to successful advertising. Direct mail to individual clients and physicians can be used or recommended by the nurse executive to promote new nursing services, programs, hours, and technologies.

Large health care corporations advertise on national network television. Thirty to sixty second commercials generally mention the locally owned hospital or services of the corporation. The local institution contributes financially to this advertising campaign often leaving little budget resource for additional local advertising. Corporations also utilize newspaper and radio advertising in the same manner. National Research Corporation's study indicated that respondents learned about a hospital because of television commercials (41%) or had read a newspaper advertisement (28%).[4]

Free public service spots are available in most forms of advertising media if one follows the procedures required and the institution is not-for-profit. Investigate taking advantage of these very useful advertising vehicles. Remember, the more you communicate with a potential client, the better your chance of being remembered.

Publicity

Publicity disseminates information by various communication media to attract public notice. Emergency helicopters and high tech vehicles are receiving a great amount of publicity on news programs. This frequent public exposure provides high agency name recognition and helps to sell the service and agency.

To obtain publicity, the nurse executive should be sensitive to potential stories that are newsworthy. Examples may include significant contributions to technology, positive clinical nursing practice, or human relations stories. Preparing the news story, a detailed outline or information sheet, makes the publicity easier and even more attractive to an editor. The real art of publicity, however, is having something to say, not just writing news releases.

Public relations activities are a fertile source of publicity. Examples include: blood pressure checking at a shopping mall, hosting meetings, volunteer response to local disasters, client educational material dissemination, and latch key program for a local parents' organization. In arranging publicity for these activities, select an articulate, poised individual with stage presence to interact with the reporter. This will facilitate the interview process and encourage photography. Brief the individual meeting the reporter on key points to be covered and suggest possible shots for photography. If the agency has the capability, it is even easier if photographs or video tapes are provided.

Many health care agencies have corporate or in-house publications. This is an important avenue of communication to all individuals associated with the organization, from the corporate board, to the physician and the client. See that each issue has information about the current activities, projects, and research of the nursing department and its personnel.

Personal Promotion

Personal promotion is contact with potential clients that serves directly, or indirectly, to promote the organization. Personal promotion is seen as a vastly more effective tool than advertising in most situations. It adds a human element to the communication, and allows a two-way dialogue between buyers and sellers.

However, personal selling or promotion is expensive, especially considering the hourly pay rate of an individual. However, when a nurse executive does not have a designated marketing budget, then personal promotion is an effective and creative opportunity to promote nursing activities. How are these opportunities created?

First, keep in mind that the chief purchaser of health care is the female. Volunteer to give talks to groups of women, for example, teachers, parent groups, networks, wive's clubs, etc. Topics of interest to women can be health, safety, parenting, organizing skills for the career wife and mother, communication, and time management. Speaking to groups meets a community need and indirectly promotes the speaker's health care agency. The agency can reap similar benefits by offering community educational programs too.

Ownership of personal promotion responsibilities does not stop with the nurse executive. Every practicing nurse promotes the profession and organization one constituent at a time when providing quality nursing care. This microscopic marketing process is paramount to reaching the 56 percent of clients who participate in the decision about which health care agency they will utilize.[7] Clients are better educated and more discriminating in making health care decisions and will be influenced by the perceptive, sensitive, and expert caring of a nurse. Selecting, training, and monitoring the personal promotion skills of every nurse is a challenging and rewarding experience for the nurse executive.

SUMMARY

In summary, marketing in health care is the process of developing, promoting, and administering health care services to a client for the benefit of both. The success of a nurse executive in the area of marketing is dependent upon the appropriate application of marketing principles. Initial marketing activities might begin with the promotion of current nursing service programs that are underutilized by either clients or physicians. Subsequent marketing activities should be directed towards developing new service programs within the nursing department. Service promotion is grounded in a particular consumer demand state and is aimed at females because they generally maintain control of the family's discretionary health care dollar. This can be an advantageous communication scenario as the female nurse can communicate with credibility to potential clients. Currently, direct mail has been highly successful at attracting client attention. Large health care corporations are using television and newspaper advertising to provide high name recognition. Personal promotion and publicity are options for the nurse executive without a discrete marketing budget.

Finally and most importantly, the relationship between a client and physician and health care agency is not robust. An individual's sense of satisfaction is so fragile that one instance of indifference can terminate the care provider and constituent relationship. This makes every individual a potential constituent for the agency with an outstanding marketing program and every professional nurse responsible for the marketing process.

REFERENCES

1. Kotler P. Marketing for nonprofit organization. 2nd ed. Englewood Cliffs, NJ: Prentice-Hall, 1982.
2. Bartlett PJ, Schewe CD, Allen CT. Marketing orientation: how do hospital administrators compare with marketing managers? Health Care Mgmt Rev 1984;9(1):77-86.
3. Alward RR. A marketing approach to nursing administration: Part one. J Nurs Adm 1983;13(3):9-12.
4. Strum AC. Who's your target? The answer will help trigger effective ads. Modern Health Care 1984;14(5): 98-102.
5. Beckham D. Some marketing moves unique; others borrowed from industry. Modern Health Care 1984; 14(5):104-106.
6. Jackson B, Jensen J. Majority of consumers support advertising of hospital services. Modern Health Care 1984;14(5):93-97.
7. Management Briefs. Nurs Mgmt 1985;16(4):10-11.

CHAPTER **30**

Taking the Train to a World of Strangers
Health care marketing and ethics

Lawrence J. Nelson
H. Westley Clark
Robert L. Goldman
Jean E. Schore

The natural limit to any person's moral universe, for Tolstoy is the distance he or she can walk, or at most ride. By taking the train, a moral agent leaves the sphere of truly moral actions for a world of strangers, toward whom he or she has few real obligations and with whom dealings can be only casual or commercial.[1]

For hospitals, physicians, and patients, the times are more than a'changing. The American health care system is undergoing an economic revolution.[2] Fewer patients, fewer occupied acute care beds, and fewer reimbursement dollars have converged to push health care providers from peaceful coexistence into outright competition. Hospitals and physicians, to remain competitive, are now marketing their services like commercial sellers.

We believe it is time to evaluate health care marketing from an ethical perspective. Health care

Reprinted from *Hastings Center Reports*, Vol. 19, No. 5, with permission of The Hastings Center © 1989.

marketing raises the fundamental questions of whether caring for the sick is actually "just" another commercial endeavor to be sold effectively and profitably to the public and whether the conduct of health care providers should be governed by the same basic ethical values that apply to any other business. Put differently, should health care providers take the train to a world where providers and patients are strangers whose obligations to each other are few and whose dealings "can be only casual or commercial?"

A MORAL EXEMPTION FOR BUSINESS?

All human activity is subject to ethical evaluation. Any human act can violate someone's rights, show disrespect for persons, or have harmful consequences for the agent or others. At a minimum, an "ethics of strangers" applies to all equally with attendant basic obligations that are "limited, anonymous, and chiefly negative: namely, not to act offensively, violently, or deceitfully."[3] Persons conducting business are subject to the same negative moral obligations as everyone else.[4] Positive ethical obligations, such as doing good by donating money to charity or maximizing shareholders' interests, may govern business activity, but their applicability is controversial. It is unarguable, however, that all persons, including those conducting business, are ethically obligated to refrain from fraud, coercion, violence, or otherwise doing harm to others.

Assuming that basic moral obligations are met, it is not unethical for business to conduct arm's-length transactions with strangers under the assumption that both parties are (more or less) independent, equally positioned, and admittedly self-interested individuals who can decide for themselves the value of the commercial transactions they make. Nor is it intrinsically unethical for a business to sell a product by intentionally associating it with a desirable extrinsic feature: for example, linking possession of a certain object (a sports car) with romantic or sexual success. (Such promotion is perhaps open to question as to whether it intentionally deceives consumers.) There is no special relationship between a business and its customers that generally obligates the former to comply with greater or higher ethical duties than those imposed by the common ethics of strangers.

HEALTH CARE PROVIDERS, PATIENTS, AND ETHICS

We will use the term "provider" to include both individual persons and corporate institutions that provide health care services to patients. The basic ethical obligations of all providers are similar because all are engaged in the special activity of caring for patients. Furthermore, the status of health care institutions as for-profit or not-for-profit entities does not affect the ethical obligations imposed upon them insofar as they all hold themselves out as caring for patients. In adddition, patients rely on institutional providers to care for them and to serve their best interests in fundamentally the same way irrespective of whether the corporate entity is nonprofit or for-profit.

While the provision of health care to patients is a business in the sense that money changes hands in return for the provision of goods and services intended to improve patient health, both the tradition of medical practice and the venerable ethical values of beneficence and loyalty to the patient's

interests on which this tradition rests clearly indicate that the provision of health care should be something *more* than a commercial transaction between strangers. In short, caring for the sick is not, and should not be, considered largely the same as commercial selling.

At the risk of oversimplification, we see patients as being fundamentally different from consumers of commercial products in three ways. First, the ill and injured are in a distinctive position of vulnerability and dependency. The vast majority of patients do not possess the knowledge or skills that would enable them to restore themselves to health in most situations. They are dependent on the special knowledge and technical skills of the provider and largely unable to judge the quality of medical care. Commercial buyers and sellers are highly independent, and consumers often can evaluate the quality of the goods offered to them.[5]

Second, a patient's own self and destiny — maybe even her very life — is at stake in an encounter with a provider. A patient frequently discloses intimate personal information to facilitate therapy. In contrast, a consumer purchasing a product lacks this highly personal and intimate stake in the transaction. The patient's very personal concern for his or her own health makes the relationship with providers substantively different than those where a consumer is dealing with a seller of products.

Third, the substance and history of the healing relationship as well as the manner in which providers present themselves to the public lead patients to trust their providers and reasonably assume that their interests receive priority in the healing encounter. Patients do not expect a physician to recommend a treatment like open heart surgery solely for the surgeon's economic self-interest. As Pellegrino and Thomasma have argued, providers are ethically obligated to put the good of the patient first.

> The good of the patient is the most fundamental norm of the physician-patient relationship. Physicians cannot interpose other priorities, such as research goals, their personal self-interests, or institutional goals, if these conflict with the good of the patient.[6]

Consequently, providers are ethically obligated to act so as to deserve and maintain the patient's trust and confidence. The special relationship that links patient and health care professional distinguishes the latter from commercial sellers:

> [T]hose who get sick or hurt have no sensible way to judge the value of medical services, let alone strike a balance of value and price, as they commonly do in the case of dresses and deodorants. So they have to trust the intentions as well as the competence of their physicians and institutions, and this trust imposes on physicians and hospitals the obligation that is the bedrock of the professional ethic. The obligation and the ethic that emerges from it measure the difference between hospitals and industry, and nowhere more obtrusively than in marketing.[7]

The obligation to maintain trust requires that providers adhere to high standards of truthfulness and disclosure. Unlike strangers who merely have to avoid deceiving others, providers should avoid even subtly misleading patients or unfairly inducing them to agree to treatment. A provider has an affirmative obligation to present accurate, fair, and honest information about health matters. The patient's responsibility to participate in his own care notwithstanding, a patient is not under an obligation to root out ambiguities, a material omissions, or confusing statements in a provider's information. A patient as patient, and especially one who is in pain, disabled, dysfunctional, or perhaps even dying, typically suffers from what Kenneth Arrow calls "informational inequality" and clearly is not in a position to cross-examine his provider about his condition or to negotiate on fair terms about obtaining appropriate health care.

In sum, providers are in a fiduciary relationship with their patients. As in law, this relationship is based on the special confidence entrusted by one party to another who, in fairness and good conscience, is bound to act in the utmost good faith and with regard to the primacy of the trusting person's interests. "[B]usiness shrewdness, hard bargaining, and astuteness to take advantage of the forgetfulness or negligence of another [is] totally prohibited" between persons standing in this relation.[8]

A FIDUCIARY MODEL FOR HEALTH CARE MARKETING ETHICS

This view of the ethics of providing health care leads us to propose a fiduciary model of ethical responsibility for health care marketing. This model assumes that it is appropriate for marketing representatives to be held to the same ethical standards that apply to the persons associated with the product, service, or profession they represent. Specifically, the means used in promoting health care services should be consistent with the ethical standards that bind providers. The main characteristics of this model concern the primacy of the patient's good, the avoidance of unnecessary services, high standards of honesty and accuracy, and public accountability.

The primacy of the patient's good.   Health care marketing should place the good of patients above other interests, especially a provider's economic interests. Marketing should be consistent with the primary goal of enhancing the health of patients as individuals and as a community. A provider's fiduciary responsibilities are not violated if rendering services to patients generates a reasonable "profit" (that is, it generates money permitting a provider to remain in operation, make a decent living, or even deliver a return on investor's capital), as long as the "profit" is created in a manner truly consistent with the best interests of patients as individuals and as a community.

Infertility clinics, for example, that use advertisements enticing persons to undergo in vitro fertilization (a procedure that costs $4,000 to $6,000 per attempt, has a success rate of perhaps 15-20%, and is not covered by most insurance) by suggesting that "the dream might still come true for you" can be seen as selling profitable services paid in cash at the expense of vulnerable people suffering the anguish and disappointment of childlessness.[9] Another infertility clinic has been criticized for allegedly using chemical rather than clinical pregnancies in calculating its publicized success rate on the basis that only one out of four chemical pregnancies results in a live birth.[10]

The avoidance of unnecessary services.   Marketing should not induce a patient to accept excessive, unneeded, or non-medically indicated health services, regardless of cost, risk, or source of payment. Although a good deal of commercial marketing is intended to create desires or needs in consumers, fostering demand for health services that are neither necessary or cost-effective is unethical.[11]

Some years ago a Nevada hospital, faced with low weekend occupancy, successfully stimulated weekend admissions by offering discount rates and a weekly drawing for a free vacation cruise.[12] One critic charged that this practice had patients spending "unnecessary days filling beds . . . often benefit[ting] no one but the hospital," given that little other than basic care was available on weekends.[13]

The promotion of cosmetic surgery with claims of complete safety or assurances of improvement in appearance and self-image can be interpreted as generating utilization of unnecessary services. One California hospital has attempted to attract cosmetic surgery patients with an advertisement implying that such surgery is performed more safely in a hospital than in less expensive settings and touting "the serenity and confidentiality" of its nonurban location.

High Standards of Honesty and Accuracy. Marketing should not merely avoid false or misleading information,[14] but also information that is unfair, incomplete, slanted, designed to take advantage of particularly vulnerable groups of patients (for example, AIDS patients who may be desperate for any respite from their uniformly fatal disease), or is otherwise inconsistent with providers' fiduciary and professional responsibilities. The burden is on the provider to meet high standards of honesty and accuracy in disclosures to patients, not on the patient to wrest the truth out of ambiguous statements or to acquire other information necessary to evaluate properly a provider's communication.

For example, one hospital promotion has called its birthing unit "more than a safe place to have your baby." This language could mislead patients into thinking that nothing can (or does) go wrong during birth there. It could also deceive patients because this hospital does not have a newborn intensive care unit, a fact making it arguably not a "safe place" at all for the birth of what might be an unexpectedly critically ill baby.

Marketing legitimately may seek to influence behavior by providing scrupulously accurate and fair information to persons utilizing health care services. For example, a university teaching hospital could properly promote the advantages of its structure (such as, continuous coverage by physicians of most specialties, the presence of sub-specialists, and access to experimental treatments) to prospective patients, but it would not be required to make "full disclosure" by describing how its physical facilities or food service are inferior to those of a competing community hospital.

If marketing makes claims about the quality of health services rendered by individual practitioners or institutional programs, reasonably objective and well-accepted evidence must be presented in support. Lay persons should be able to evaluate such claims in a meaningful manner on their own. Promotions should avoid stating or implying a guarantee of successful outcome or of patient satisfaction with the services rendered as providers cannot truthfully promise either in every case.

Despite their inability to guarantee medical results or patient satisfaction, providers do promote their services with such claims. One advertisement for an impotency clinic has stated: "*Fact:* There is no reason to suffer with impotence. No matter how old you are or how long you've been impotent, your problem can be solved" (emphasis original). A psychiatric hospital in Utah has published a promotion with the headline "She Doesn't Want To Cry All The Time. But She Does. In Two Weeks She Won't." The hospital also guaranteed patient satisfaction after two days of treatment with a money back offer. One chemical dependency program has described itself as "designed to save money as well as lives" by promising to provide two free retreatments to any patient who successfully completed its program but had a relapse within five years.[15]

Public Accountability. Providers and marketing agents should be publicly accountable for their activities. If questions are raised about the ethical propriety of their marketing activities, providers should be able to produce an explanation and justification for public comment and criticism. Marketing decisions that affect patients' health should be subjected to the rigors of public debate and ethical discussion as are so many other aspects of health care. Health care marketing is most likely to mature ethically when exposed to the light of public comment and criticism.

THE NATURE OF HEALTH CARE MARKETING

Marketing has been defined as "a social process by which individuals and groups obtain what they need and want through creating and exchanging products and value with others."[16] Traditionally, marketing has been divided into four segments denominated as place, promotion, product, and price. Marketing in health care concerns: access ("place") — the ability of a patient to get into the health care delivery system as well as the location where health care goods and services are sold; promotion — advertising, personal selling, public relations, and health education; services ("product") — in health care, services rather than products are marketed; and cost ("price") — anything of value given up by the patient in exchange for health care services such as time, money, or opportunity.[17]

Access. Here we examine one aspect of access to health care services: physician referral systems. Many hospitals offer physician referral services to prospective patients that are designed to generate more patients for a particular hospital by attracting more patients for the physicians on its medical staff. A published advertisement of one service announced:

> Now there's an easy way to find the *right* doctor with whom you'll feel comfortable *and confident.* Just call me. My name is B.W., and I'm an experienced registered nurse . . . . There is no charge for this community service. I look forward to helping you find a doctor who is just what the *patient* ordered (emphasis original).

A similar advertisement placed by a national chain of hospitals contained a picture of a nurse in uniform with the headline: "Last year, she helped 10,755 people find a doctor. One at a time." The copy noted that the service offered a "free call to a Registered Nurse who knows doctors — and understands patients . . ."; stated that the "nurse knows doctors so well . . ."; and suggested that the listed number be called "For a number of good doctors . . ."

While there is nothing wrong with helping people find a physician who can properly meet their health needs, these particular ads are ethically suspect. First, neither discloses how a physician comes to be a member of the referral panel used by the nurse. Based on our experience, only physicians who practice at the particular hospital that sponsors the referral service are placed on the panel; they are not selected from all "right," "good," or licensed doctors in a community. Second, the former ad does not disclose how the nurse determines the doctors on the panel are "right" and are persons "with whom you'll feel comfortable and confident," while the latter makes no mention of how the nurse "knows [these] doctors so well" or knows they are "good." The ads, in short, can mislead patients.

The fiduciary nature of the provider-patient relationship calls for qualitatively different disclosure than is demonstrated by these examples of marketing. Patients should not be allowed to think that the "free community service" offered gives them access to all physicians from the local community or that the nurse operating the service has personal knowledge of the professional competence of the physicians on the referral panel if she does not. Furthermore, if claims are made about the quality of the physicians on the panel, some reasonably objective evidence (something more than the opinion of some interested party) should exist to support these claims and be made available for public scrutiny. Providers could overcome these deficiencies by disclosing the compositon of the referral panel and the basis for any claims about its quality in the promotion itself.

Promotion. While all of marketing cannot be reduced to promotion, making potential buyers aware of a product and inducing them to purchase it through advertising is its most visible aspect. In the present economic climate, many providers are turning to advertising to help them compete. We do not subscribe to the view that advertising by providers (or any professional) is inherently ethically objectionable. Provider advertising that communicates accurate information useful to patients in understanding their existing health problems, identifies needed health-related services and products, and helps persons locate providers who can best satisfy their needs (by specialty, geographical location, religious affiliation, etc.) serves the best interests of patients. The timely and accurate presentation of such information increases opportunities for more autonomous decisionmaking by patients.

A hospital promotion that accurately lists its available services (such as a sports medicine program or an alternative birth center) or describes educational classes it offers to the public is not ethically objectionable. One California hospital has promoted its "affordable maternity services" by publishing a newsletter that describes the program in a factual and straightforward manner. Its statement about the program's financial aspects, for example, provides helpful information to potential patients:

> Using a sliding fee scale tailored to each family's needs and household income, families can save up to 75% of the regular cost of delivering a baby. Even families who do not qualify for the full discount can take advantage of reduced fees for hospital and physician services . . . Eligibility for the program . . . is determined in a private meeting with the . . . social worker.

This type of promotion is consistent with patients' interests and avoids omissions of material information or deception, though it does raise an issue of fairness with respect to those patients who pay the full charges and thus arguably subsidize those who do not. Unfortunately, much provider advertising falls into ethically questionable areas.

For example, a company in the United States will, for a considerable fee, provide laboratory services and experimental drugs to cancer patients whose disease has not responded to standard treatment. The company typically offers these services in conjunction with a hospital under contract. The drugs are usually administered on an inpatient basis by certain physicians on the hospital's medical staff who have no direct connection to the company. Thus, providers are intimately involved in the company's activities.

For a considerable time, this company utilized a four page promotional brochure that was given to prospective patients by providers, although its use was discontinued in June 1988. The front cover of the brochure read: "If it were your life, what would you do?" The second page contained, among other things, the following text in prominent type:

> "Think about it. If YOU had cancer, and standard treatments were known to be ineffective what would YOU do? Give up? Or fight, pursuing every reasonable option? It's a choice every cancer patient deserves."

This brochure is ethically suspect for a number of reasons. First, it presents the cancer patient with a false choice between *either* "giving up" *or* "fighting" with the resources the company provides. This language appears designed to induce the patient to think that she would be surrendering to death or yielding to despair if she did not "fight" by purchasing the company's services. However, a decision by a seriously or terminally ill cancer patient not to utilize treatment of unproven efficacy and high financial cost is not necessarily "giving up." In fact, such a decision may be both reasonable and responsible under these difficult circumstances.

Second, the brochure begs the question by implying that the company's experimental program is, in fact, a "reasonable option" for patients with advanced cancer. Perhaps it is for some, but the factual and value basis for determining reasonableness in this context will vary considerably. Nor does the brochure mention the precise nature of the benefits the experimental drugs might yield, success rates for remission or cure, or the burdens it may impose. While it is true that such disclosure is primarily the duty of the attending physician, it is ethically irresponsible to be utterly silent on whether there is any risk to the proferred service. A principal danger is that a cancer patient might obtain an initial impression that the "treatment" offered is risk-free and so have very unrealistic hopes when she learns the truth: the "treatment," interleukin-2, has harmful side effects.[18]

Third, it is both misleading and unfair to say that "every cancer patient deserves" to have the opportunity to choose between "giving up" and "fighting" by "pursuing every reasonable option." This statement asserts that these patients have a moral right to "every reasonable option" (namely, the company's experimental offerings) and implies that they are somehow wronged if denied access. The assertion is misleading in that it is far from clear that anyone "deserves" access to unproven therapy in the moral sense; it is unfair by trying to make the patient and others (most importantly, those who can influence the patient, like family members) feel guilty if they do not purchase the experimental treatment.

Advertisements by other providers have utilized similarly questionable promotional tactics. One California hospital published a newspaper ad touting its mortality rate for coronary bypass surgery as "the lowest in the country" based upon data from the Health Care Financing Administration (HCFA). The ad appeared aimed at attracting more bypass business by convincing potential surgical patients that the particular hospital is better than others: "Although coronary bypass surgery has saved many lives, there is a difference between hospitals and surgeons. It is expressed in very dramatic terms: mortality rate." Though the hospital truthfully reported HCFA data, they are difficult to interpret correctly, particularly by a vulnerable lay person. For example, the statistics may not yet be accurate enough to provide valid comparisons. Second, to be truly meaningful, mortality data must be adjusted for age, sex, intensity of patient illness, and other factors significantly affecting outcome. Such ads do not provide useful information and so do not aid patients in making informed decisions about their health care.[19]

The same critique holds true for individual providers as for institutions. An advertisement for two plastic and cosmetic surgeons noted that they are "board certified," but did not mention which specialty board (plastic surgery? dermatology? radiology?) granted the certification. The ad also stated that one doctor "has performed over 1400 liposuction operations with a *PERFECT SAFETY RECORD*" (emphasis original). The danger inherent in this claim is that it might well lead a lay person to think that liposuction is an innocuous procedure when this is not true. Reports indicate that eleven patients have died after such surgery and that the complication rate (including infection, pain, skin sloughing, bruising and lessened sensitivity to touch) is about 9 percent.[20]

Services. The choice of services providers will and will not offer the public is a key aspect of marketing. Traditionally, marketing is geared toward assessing consumer needs and wants and then determining how to meet them in a manner that will generate maximum profit. Some may believe that governmental certificate of need programs require institutional providers to offer only those services truly needed by the public, while peer review, reimbursement mechanisms, and tort law will require individual providers to do the same. However, we are not sanguine that these methods are sufficient to maintain patient good as providers' first prioriity. Even in the presence of regulatory mechanisms, providers still are ethically required to scrutinize their own behavior in the discharge of their fiduciary duties to their patients.

Provider marketing decisions pertaining to the provision of services should be made in light of four interrelated factors, all of which are linked to promoting patient welfare.

Patient outcome. If a service generates increased morbidity and mortality to which patients would not have been subjected had they received the service elsewhere or not at all, then offering the service is ethically suspect. For example, there is evidence that the success rates of established programs for cardiac transplantation (such as at Stanford Medical Center) cannot be duplicated without proper support and careful development.[21] Assuming there is an established program for heart transplantation with the resources and capacity to render the service and reasonably accessible to the patient population in need, the creation of a new heart transplant program for that population would be ethically objectionable on the ground it would likely cause unnecessary harm to some patients.

Similarly, certain services (such as microsurgery and chorionic villus sampling for prenatal diagnosis) are associated with higher morbidity and mortality rates when they are first offered than after the providers have accumulated considerable experience.[22] Consequently, a marketing decision by a hospital to add a new service must take into account its ability to properly maintain a patient load sufficient to sustain high levels of proficiency concomitant with lower morbidity and mortality rates.

Use of scarce resources. A service that utilizes a scarce resource in an inefficient manner when it demonstrably could be put to better use elsewhere is ethically highly suspect. For example, if a new heart transplant program has a significantly higher morbidity and mortality rate compared to other programs supplying the same service to the same population, not only is the individual patient at a greater risk of harm, but a scarce vital organ that might have been transplanted with success into another candidate is lost. Providers must consider the effects of their use of scarce resources on those patients who will thereby be denied access.

Provider-driven demand. Once a service is available, there is often strong economic pressure on the providers to ensure that the service is adequately utilized to make it cost-effective. Such pressures create the danger that patients will be channeled into the program in the absence of clear medical indications. For example, one study of carotid endarterectomies (the surgical scraping of fatty deposits in the arteries that supply blood to the head and neck) found that 35 percent of the procedures were done for appropriate clinical indications, 32 percent for equivocal indications, and 32 percent for inappropriate indications, with the three categories defined by a panel of nationally known medical experts.[23] Not only may patients with marginal medical indications receive a service, but patients with no medical need may receive it as well, particularly if the service seems to lack any harmful side-effects (for example, magnetic resonance imaging or ultrasound).

Increases in cost. The addition of a new service or continuation of an existing service to remain competitive may require large expenditures to purchase the latest equipment or retain highly remunerated staff. Providers must recognize that these expenditures can drive up health care costs without yielding a corresponding benefit to the patients they serve.

Marketing decisions cannot ethically be made solely on the basis of whether a service will prove profitable for the hospital, whether it will enhance the prestige of the hospital and its medical staff, or whether it will attract a surgeon who will admit many new fully insured patients. If the hospital is to remain faithful to its fiduciary responsibilities to patients, such decisions must first be consistent with patient welfare. A hospital, for example, could fulfill this responsibility by honestly evaluating whether its own economic interests or its community will be better served by the addition of another magnetic resonance imaging scanner.

Such a decision should be made quite differently than the business decision of General Motors to produce a new line of passenger cars. GM is not ethically obligated to determine whether there is consumer need for a new car or whether existing manufacturers are already producing cars that adequately meet consumer need for transportation. GM can produce a new line of cars solely because it thinks it can sell them at a profit whether or not anyone "needs" them. A hospital cannot ethically adopt this same stance.

Cost. Patient welfare should not be measured solely by whether a given health service benefits a patient more than it harms her. Patients' economic interests are important too, although balancing cost and benefit in health care is a highly inexact art. Whatever one thinks of the level of physicians' incomes or the surpluses generated by hospitals, providers bear an ethical responsibility to deliver services in a cost-efficient manner that does not line their pockets at the literal and figurative expense of patients. "Whatever the market will bear" is not the right standard to apply to the cost of health care, given the emotional, physical, and fiscal vulnerability of patients.

A physician, for example, may attempt to replace income lost through discounting fees to insurance plans by subjecting patients to additional procedures of marginal or no value. These patients may incur increased out-of-pocket expenses, waste time, and be exposed to the detrimental effects of the procedures. Such "churning" is ethically unacceptable. Other physicians consciously equate an increased level of care with high quality care. Critical self-examination and peer review are perhaps the best methods for identifying and rooting out behavior that drives up the cost of health care without generating corresponding benefit for patients.

ETHICALLY-INFORMED MARKETING

Health care marketing appears to be yet another component of our health delivery system strongly affected by the forces of expediency and economics that challenge providers' commitment to the right and the good. There is a legitimate place for marketing in health care, but it needs to be informed and shaped by the venerable and rich ethical tradition of medicine and the other healing professions. The goal of our fiduciary model is to keep the marketing of health care services consistent with this tradition.

Caring for the sick and injured should not be seen as just another commercial product to be marketed like the proverbial better mousetrap. A patient deserves much more when physicians, nurses, hospitals, and others provide services that profoundly affect her health and life.

REFERENCES

1. Stephen Toulmin, "The Tyranny of Principles," *Hastings Center Report* 11:6 (1981), 34.
2. See Thom A. Mayer, Wayne Tilson, and John Hemingway. "Marketing and Public Relations in the Emergency Department," *Emergency Medicine Clinics of North America* 5 (February 1987), 83-102.
3. Albert R. Jonsen and Stephen Toulmin, *The Abuse of Casuistry* (Berkeley: University of California Press, 1988), 291.
4. Donald P. Robin and R. Eric Reidenbach, "Social Responsibility, Ethics, and Marketing Strategy: Closing the Gap Between Concept and Application," *Journal of Marketing* 51 (January 1987), 48.
5. Roice D. Luke and Robert E. Modrow, "Marketing and Accountability in Health Care." *Hospital and Health Services Administration* (Summer 1987), 53.
6. Edmund D. Pellegrino and David C. Thomasma, *For the Patient's Good: The Restoration of Beneficence in Health Care* (New York: Oxford University Press, 1988), 71.
7. Robert B. Cunningham, "Of Snake Oil and Science," *Hospitals* 52 (April 16, 1978), 81.
8. *Black's Law Dictionary* 4th ed. (St. Paul: West Publishing, 1968), 753-54.
9. Ellen Goodman, "Selling the Sizzle," *San Francisco Chronicle* (April 11, 1989), A23.
10. Rorie Sherman, "Just Whose Embryo Is It, Anyway?" *National Law Journal* 11 (June 1989), 22-23.
11. William E. Walch and Simone Tseng, "Marketing: Handle with Care," *Trustee* (August 1984), 20.
12. Joann Lublin, "Hospitals Turning to Bold Marketing to Lure Patients and Stay in Business," *Wall Street Journal* (September 11, 1979), 34.
13. Sherman Rosen, Letter to the Editor, *Wall Street Journal* (October 1, 1979), 31.
14. Kari E. Super, "Hospital Ad Antagonizes Competitor," *Modern Healthcare* (July 18, 1986), 60; "Baptist Hospital's 'Misleading' Ad Upsets Nashville's Other Providers," *Modern Healthcare* (August 29, 1986), 82-832.
15. Cynthia Wallace, "Treatment Guarantees to Proliferate Despite Claims that Ads are Misleading," *Modern Healthcare* (July 17, 1987), 40.
16. Philip Kotler, *Marketing Management: Analysis, Planning, and Control,* 5th ed. (Englewood Cliffs: Prentice Hall, 1984), 4.
17. hPhilip D. Cooper, *Health Care Marketing: Issues and Trends,* 2nd ed. (Rockville: Aspen Publishers, 1985), 227.
18. "Interleukin-2," *The Medical Letter on Drugs and Therapeutics* 29:749 (September 1987), 88-89.
19. Linda J. Perry and Kari Super Palm, "Hospitals Unlikely to Tout Mortality Data," *Modern Healthcare* (December 4, 1987), 68.
20. *Milwaukee Journal,* 17 July 1988, G1; Erlaine F. Bello *et al.,* "Fasciitis and Abscesses Complicating Liposuction," *Western Journal of Medicine* 148 (June 1988), 703-706; for criticism of the marketing of cataract surgery and radial keratotomy as completely safe procedures, see Curtis E. Margo, "Selling Surgery," *New England Journal of Medicine* 314:24 (1986), 1575-76.
21. W. Gerald Austen and A. Benedict Cosini, "Heart Transplantation After 16 Years," *New England Journal of Medicine* 311:22 (1984), 1436-38; Department of Health and Human Services, "Medicare Program; Criteria for Medicare Coverage of Heart Transplants," *Federal Register* 51 (October 17, 1986), 37164-70.
22. Marko Godina, "Early Microsurgical Reconstruction of Complex Trauma of the Extremities," *Plastic and Reconstructive Surgery* 78 (September 1986), 285-92; Roger Khouri and William Shaw, "310 Consecutive Lower Extremity Free Flaps," *American Society for Reconstructive Microsurgery* (1988 Annual Meeting abstracts), 74; George Rhoads *et al.,* "The Safety and Efficacy of Chorionic Villus Sampling for Early Prenatal Diagnosis of Cytogenetic Abnormalities," *New England Journal of Medicine* 320:10 (1989), 609-617.
23. Constance Winslow *et al.,* "The Appropriateness of Carotid Endarterectomy," *New England Journal of Medicine* 318:12 (1988), 721-27.

CHAPTER **31**

A Review of Cost-Accounting Methods for Nursing Services

Sandra R. Edwardson, RN, PhD
Phyllis B. Giovannetti, RN, ScD

Nurse executives recognize that separate accounting for nursing services is necessary for two reasons: (a) to gain managerial control of diminishing dollars, and (b) to elevate patient care units from the status of nonrevenue-producing to revenue-producing cost centers (Covaleski, 1981; Higgerson & Van Slyck, 1982). A 1983 American Nurses' Association (ANA) survey of selected hospitals showed that 93% were attempting to isolate nursing costs either for patient groups or individual patients; 18% were itemizing charges for nursing services on the hospital bill ("Hospitals identifying," 1984).

The prospective payment system based on diagnosis related groups (DRGs) has accelerated the movement toward separating out nursing costs. Costing activity began to focus less on developing systems for rate setting and reimbursement and more on internal cost-accounting methods to enhance managerial control. This article assesses the state-of-the-art in cost accounting in nursing services and proposes areas requiring further development.

Reprinted from *Nursing Economics,* Vol. 5, No. 3, with permission of Anthony J. Jannetti, Inc. © 1987.

COST-ACCOUNTING APPROACHES

Most of the cost-accounting literature in nursing was published between 1982 and 1986. Key features of the cost-accounting methods are compared in Table 31-1.

The first step in any cost-allocation method is to select the unit of analysis for classifying patients within relevant cost categories. The most frequent units of analysis were day of service, diagnosis, timed functions, or nursing workload units (as measured by patient classification systems used for staffing). A few methods used more than one unit of analysis. In addition to the primary classification technique, some cost-allocation methods created derivative groups labeled second order categories (such as relative intensity measures).

Each report was examined to determine whether the reported method was one in use or a product of a special study. To assess the ease of data retrieval and analysis, the reports were evaluated regarding whether the raw data used were stored on a computer and were recorded for individual patients.

Several questions were raised regarding the analytic methods used. The types of calculated efficiency indicators were noted. Generated cost data were assessed in terms of the unit of analysis used for aggregating costs. The most frequently used units of analysis included costs per patient or stay, costs per patient care unit, and costs per DRG. Finally, the types of costs considered in calculating total costs were identified.

COST-ALLOCATION METHODS

Methods used for allocating hospital nursing service costs involved four major approaches: (a) costs per day of service (per diem), (b) costs per diagnosis, (c) costs per relative intensity measures (RIMs), and (d) costs per nursing workload unit (patient classification data).

Per diem methods are the oldest cost allocation methods for nursing services and have been used for both rate setting/reimbursement and internal managerial control. The allocation statistic involves average nursing care costs per patient day and is obtained by dividing the total nursing costs by the number of patient days for a selected time period. Nursing costs are usually defined as salary and fringe benefit expenses for clinical and administrative nursing personnel. Nursing costs per patient day may be reported for the entire service, major subdivisions (such as medical, surgical, and psychiatric units) or individual cost centers.

While simple to compute and understand, per diem methods are widely criticized for inadequately representing the variability in nursing care requirements for different types of patients. Patient days vary widely in terms of resource consumption (Berki, 1972; Ruchlin & Levenson, 1974; Saathoff & Kurtz, 1962).

Diagnosis-based methods attempt to reduce the variability in nursing care requirements by using information about the patient mix. Several case mix methods, including the DRG system, use medical diagnoses to develop groupings. Some have also proposed or experimented with the use of nursing diagnoses or nursing care standards for classifying patients according to their nursing care requirements (Halloran, 1983; McKibben, Brimmer, Clinton, Galliher, & Hartley, 1985; Porter-O'Grady, 1985).

The method developed by the Massachusetts Eye and Ear Infirmary (MEEI) for allocating nursing costs to patients in selected medical diagnoses emerges as a pioneer effort. It was not only among the first systems to allocate costs based on measured nursing care requirements but also among the first to assign those costs to individual medical diagnoses rather than aggregate diagnostic categories.

The MEEI has developed units of service called clinical care norms (CCNs) for all diagnoses treated at the Infirmary. Although a workload measure (the PETO patient classification system) was used, the MEEI approach is conceptually distinct from workload methods described below. Using workload data, CCNs were constructed by measuring the resources typically required to care for patients with each diagnosis at selected points during hospitalization. The system is used for rate setting and productivity evaluation (Wood, 1976, 1983). It is not known if the system has been computerized.

Several workload-based accounting methods propose that nursing care costs should be identified for units of service defined according to a nursing rather than a medical model. For example, Halloran (1983) proposed that these units of service should be nursing diagnoses.

Curtin (1983), in contrast, advocated development of 23 nursing care categories (NCCs), one for each of the 23 major diagnostic categories from which DRGs are derived. To highlight the nursing component of the care and treatment process for DRGs, Curtin proposed that a detailed nursing care plan, termed a Nursing Care Strategy (NCS), be developed for each of the 467 DRGs. Within each NCS, levels of patient care requirements would then be assessed using a patient classification system.

Others have advocated that costs be determined not on the basis of actual practice, as measured in patient classification systems for staffing, but on the basis of time required to achieve the institution's standard of care (Mason & Daugherty, 1984; Porter-O'Grady, 1985). Porter-O'Grady (1985), for example, proposed that any costing and information management system for nursing should be more highly integrated with the actual clinical practice of nursing than most patient classification systems for nurse

TABLE 31-1

Summary of key features of cost-accounting methods

AUTHOR	UNIT OF ANALYSIS	SECOND ORDER CATEGORIES	REPORT OF SYSTEM IN USE
Diagnosis-based methods			
Wood, 1976	Diagnosis, day of care	Clinical care norms	Yes
Relative intensity measures (RIMs)			
Caterinicchio & Davies, 1983	Timed functions	Relative intensity measures	Special study (N = 2,660)
Grimaldi & Micheletti, 1982b; Joel, 1983	Timed functions	Relative intensity measures	Yes
Toth, 1984	Timed functions	Relative intensity measures	Yes
Workload-based methods			
Arndt & Skydell, 1985	Workload unit	None	Special study (N = 30,000)
Ballard, Barach, & Cullen, 1985	Workload unit	None	Yes
Bargagliotti & Smith, 1985	Workload unit	None	Special study (N = 19)
Curtin, 1983	Workload unit	Nursing care category & nursing care strategy	No
Dahlen & Gregor, 1985	Workload unit	None	Special study (N = 93)
DeJoseph, Petree, & Ross, 1984	Labor & delivery risk level	Hourly charge per risk level	Yes
Ethridge, 1985	Workload unit	Relative value units	Yes
Halloran, 1983	Workload unit; nursing diagnosis	None	Special study (N = 30)
Higgerson & Van Slyck, 1982	Workload unit	Relative value units	Yes
Holbrook, 1972	Workload unit	None	Yes
Lagona & Stritzel, 1984	Workload unit	None	Special study (N = 35)
Maher & Dolan, 1982	Workload unit	None	?
Mason & Daugherty, 1984	Patient care	Units of nursing care	No
McClain & Selhat, 1984	Workload	None	Special study (N = 20)

PART OF INFORMATION SYSTEM	DATA RECORDED FOR INDIVIDUAL PATIENT	EFFICIENCY INDEX REPORTED	NATURE OF COST DATA GENERATED	COSTS CONSIDERED
?	Presumably		By care norm	Cost norms & admission charge
No	No	None	By DRG	Unclear
No	Yes	None	By DRG	Direct personnel expense
No	Presumably	Cost vs. other hospitals' costs	By DRG	Direct personnel expense
Yes	?		By day, diagnosis, surgical procedure, DRG	Direct care & a portion of all direct expenses & allocated overhead
Yes	No	None	By level of care by clinical services	Direct & indirect personnel expenses
PCS only	No	None	By patient, DRG	Direct & indirect personnel expenses
No	No, considered irrelevant	None	By stay & by severity — weighted DRG	Direct & indirect personnel expenses
No	No	None	By DRG	Direct & indirect personnel expenses
No	Yes	None	By patient	Presumably direct & indirect personnel expenses
?	?	None	By patient by clinical service	Direct & indirect, minor supply & equipment expenses
No	No	Patient days per level of staff	By unit	Direct care
Yes	Yes	None	By patient, cost center	Direct & indirect personnel expenses, supplies
No	Yes	Unclear	By patient, cost center	Unclear
No; planned	No	None	By DRG	Direct & indirect personnel expenses
No	No	None	By patient, classification, cost center	Direct & indirect personnel expenses
No; proposed	Yes	None	By case, DRG	Direct & indirect personnel expenses
No	No	None	By case & DRG; day of stay	Direct personnel expense

Continued.

TABLE 31-1

Summary of key features of cost-accounting methods (cont'd)

AUTHOR	UNIT OF ANALYSIS	SECOND ORDER CATEGORIES	REPORT OF SYSTEM IN USE
McKibben, Brimmer, Clinton, Galliher, & Hartley, 1985	Workload unit	None	Special study (N = 1,594)
Mitchell, Miller, Welches, & Walker, 1984	Workload unit	Severity of illness study underway	Special study (N = 118)
Mowry & Korpman, 1984	Workload unit	None	Special study
Nyberg & Wolff, 1984	Workload unit	None	Yes
Olsen, 1984	Workload unit	None	No
Piper, 1983	Workload unit	Daily, essential, M.D. dependent, R.N. independent	No
Porter-O'Grady, 1985	Nursing diagnosis and standards	Patient care units	No
Reschak, Biordi, Holm, & Santucci, 1985	Workload unit	None	Special study (N = 50)
Riley & Schaefers, 1983	Workload	None	Special study (N = 98)
Sovie, Tarcinale, Vanputee, & Stunden, 1985	Workload unit	None	Yes
Staley & Luciano, 1984	Workload	None	?
Trofino, 1986	Workload unit	Nursing care	Yes
Vanderzee & Glusko, 1984	Workload unit	None	No
Walker, 1983	Workload unit	None	Special study (N = 30)
Wolf, Lesic, & Leak, 1986	Workload unit	None	Special study (N = 190)

staffing. Observing that standards of practice are the basic framework for defining nursing practice, he argued that care activities selected to achieve nursing standards can be used to estimate the time required and associated nursing personnel costs.

Relative Intensity Measures (RIMs) are another example of a cost-allocation method using case mix information. RIMs are weights representing the empirically derived "cost per unit of nursing intensity." A RIM is obtained by dividing the total nursing

PART OF INFORMATION SYSTEM	DATA RECORDED FOR INDIVIDUAL PATIENT	EFFICIENCY INDEX REPORTED	NATURE OF COST DATA GENERATED	COSTS CONSIDERED
?	Yes	None	By patient, DRG	Direct & indirect personnel expenses
No	No	None	By DRG, patient, day of stay	Direct personnel expense
?	Yes	None	By patient, DRG	Direct personnel expenses
Yes	Yes	Required vs. actual vs. budgeted staff	By patient, unit, Medicare/Non-Medicare, diagnosis	Direct & indirect personnel expenses
No	No, advocated	None	By case, DRG	Direct & indirect personnel expenses, allocated hospital overhead
No	No	Current & historical cost	By unit, DRG, function & function/DRG	Nursing hours per function
No	No	None	By patient, DRG	Direct & indirect personnel expenses
No	No	None	By patient, DRG	Direct & indirect personnel expenses
PCS only	Yes	None	By DRG, patient	Direct & indirect personnel expenses
Yes	Yes	?	By patient, DRG	Direct & indirect personnel expenses
No	No	None	By case, DRG	Direct & indirect personnel expenses, allocated hospital overhead
Yes	Yes	None	By patient, DRG	Direct & indirect personnel expenses
No	?	None	By workload, unit, level of personnel	Direct & indirect personnel expenses, non-chargeable supplies
PCS only	?	None	By patient classification, diagnosis	Direct & indirect personnel expenses
Yes	Yes	None	By patient, DRG, unit	Direct & personnel expenses

costs for the hospital by the total minutes of care estimated (by the equations) necessary to provide care to all patients. The cost of care for each patient is calculated by multiplying the RIM by the minutes of care required by the patient as estimated by the appropriate equation (Caterinicchio, 1983; Caterinicchio & Davies, 1983).

RIMs are the product of a series of studies initiated by the New Jersey Department of Health in response to concerns that the DRG system inadequately represents the variability of nursing care requirements for patients. Almost from the beginning, critics have argued that the method for apportioning nursing care costs to DRGs is insensitive to differences in patient requirements for nursing care within DRGs (Caterinicchio & Davies, 1983; Grimaldi & Micheletti, 1982a).

The RIMs development studies used data from a sample of New Jersey hospitals to develop a case-mix classification system that divided patients into homogenous groups based on use of nursing resources. Unlike classification systems designed for variable staffing in which changes in nursing care requirements by shift are important, this study measured the time spent by nursing personnel in performing nursing and nonnursing activities during the entire hospitalization. Thirteen resource groups were identified by mathematical modeling of data including diagnosis, admission class, presence or absence of surgery, length of stay, nursing problems reflecting threat to life, age, discharge status, and level of care as determined by a patient classification system. Equations were then derived for predicting nursing resource use for each of the 13 resource clusters. Length of stay proved to be the single best predictor of nursing time required after patients had been classified within the 13 groups.

Reports of the RIMs method published during the development phase were based on data from 2,660 patients. Because data used were collected specifically for the study, they are presumably not part of a computerized information system. The developers do not specify what costs were used in calculating total costs, but others describing the system name direct personnel expenses (Grimaldi & Micheletti, 1982b; Joel, 1983; Toth, 1984).

Nursing workload-based methods were primarily developed for nurse staffing. Before the implementation of DRG-based reimbursement, several centers around the country used nursing workload data to determine the cost of the nursing component of the room rate (Higgerson & Van Slyck, 1982; Holbrook, 1972). While cost-accounting methods had long permitted such calculations for an entire patient care unit, these workload-based methods demonstrated the possibility of accounting for the varying nursing care costs incurred by individual

patients and generating a separate charge for nursing services. At least two recently published papers describe similar approaches for generating charges (Ballard, Barach, & Cullen, 1985; Ethridge, 1985).

Since 1983, increasing numbers of publications have proposed or reported the use of methods for allocating nursing costs to DRGs or cost centers. All of the reported approaches have been either newly implemented or in the conceptual or trial phases of development. Each proposed the following similar procedure for using workload data: (a) The patient classification system used for nurse staffing is applied as usual, (b) classification statistics are converted into required hours of care for the course of the hospitalization, (c) patient care hours are converted to dollar costs (all methods used direct nursing care costs, but differed in how they defined costs and whether they included indirect expenses) (see Table 31-1), (d) patients are classified into DRGs, and (e) nursing care costs for patients in selected DRGs are aggregated and analyzed in a variety of ways.

Both prototype and factor patient classification systems for measuring workload have been used. Several investigators have developed second order groupings such as relative value units (Ethridge, 1985; Higgerson & Van Slyck, 1982; Trofino, 1986) or various types of care measurement units (Curtin, 1983; Mason & Daugherty, 1984; Piper, 1983; Porter-O'Grady, 1985). A number of the methods reported were being developed at publication and may be in use at this time. Many investigators did not computerize the workload data nor routinely record individual patient data. Most did not calculate an efficiency index and used numerous cost definitions. Most reported costs by patient and aggregated patient data by patient care units or cost centers and/or DRGs. A few investigators reported costs per patient workload category or diagnosis.

A final variation on the use of workload data was proposed by Piper (1983). She advocated assigning nursing functions for patients in each DRG into three groups: daily essential functions (services common to all patients), physician dependent functions, and nursing independent functions. Cost analysis could then be performed for each of these functions as well as for patient care units and specific DRGs. This would permit a more detailed analysis of cost behavior but at the expense of considerable additional data collection.

CRITIQUE OF THE METHODS

Four basic methods of accounting for nursing care costs have been identified. All use some form of workload measurement, but the uses of the data vary.

Per Diem Methods

Per diem methods take the least refined approach. The total cost of providing nursing care for patients is simply divided by the total patient days for the same period. This method assumes that patient days are essentially identical, a notion long since rejected in both economic and nursing literature.

If the purpose of cost accounting is to attribute the true cost of production to each "product," per diem-based methods hold little promise. They would be valid when used to describe and compare homogenous groups created by a valid case mix classification system.

Diagnosis-based Methods

Diagnosis-based cost-accounting methods hold much more promise because they define costs for a product or output that is more homogeneous than the patient day. The dilemma with using diagnoses is how to resolve the problem of reducing the set of all possible diagnoses to a workable number. The DRG system, for example, is an attempt to reduce the 10,171 medical diagnoses identified in the International Classification of Diseases — 9th Revision (ICD-9) to 468 homogeneous resource use groupings. Similar compromises between descriptive completeness and practical usefulness may be needed when using nursing diagnoses for cost-accounting purposes.

Using Medical Diagnoses

The best example of the use of medical diagnoses for estimating nursing costs is the MEEI approach. The success of this system based on diagnoses treated at

the Infirmary probably related to the clientele's homogeneity and treatment methods. A general hospital treating patients with hundreds of diagnoses would soon become overwhelmed with the number of clinical care norms. However, the approach could be expected to work well when nursing services are provided for a limited number of conditions — each with a well defined and homogeneous course and treatment plan. The strategy may be applicable to selected units within a general hospital.

Arndt and Skydell (1985) argued that the MEEI method can be applied to general hospitals. To support their claim, they reported data that were collected with what they define as modifications to the MEEI method from a study of five Massachusetts general hospitals. However, careful examination of the method used reveals that the measurement of nursing care costs was similar to the workload-based approaches. For example, nursing care requirements were expressed as hours needed for direct and indirect care rather than as units of care (CCNs). Unlike most of the other workload-based methods, however, Arndt and Skydell's cost definition included all direct expense (personnel, supplies and equipment) as well as allocated costs of capital and other overhead expenses.

Using Nursing Standards and Diagnoses

Cost accounting based on nursing care standards withstands two common criticisms of nursing workload measurement: (a) that it perpetuates current levels of quality whether or not they are adequate, and (b) that staff nurses do not trust patient classification systems. Using standards of care as a basis for determining nursing care needs and staffing requirements appears ideal. But how closely does actual practice adhere to standards?

These criticisms raise basic questions about the validity of patient classification strategies for measuring nursing workload. Current development methods for patient classification systems measure nursing activities that are actually given during the development period to estimate future care requirements for patients. Development of patient classification systems begins with the assumption that current levels of care are at least acceptable to the institution. As measurement tools, therefore, patient classification systems are valid to the extent that quantification reflects the care actually given. Whether this level of care is consistent with nursing care standards is a separate issue.

As a result, estimating nursing costs based on standards of care constitutes cost accounting only to the extent that standards of care are consistently met. If standards represent an ideal to be achieved rather than a goal consistently met, the nursing care costs identified would either represent an overestimation of the actual cost of providing care or mask inefficiency and misuse of scarce resources.

There is also a question about how politically realistic it is to advocate for cost accounting on the basis of standards rather than measured practice. Current economic pressures on the health-care industry are forcing all health-care providers to recognize that policymakers are willing to support the ideal level of care only to the extent that services can be provided within a very modest annual overall cost increase. Cost pressures are forcing providers to address adequate rather than optimum care.

Quality of care questions might best be considered apart from the workload measurement system. Then the validity of the patient classification system must be established. Presenting empirical evidence that care provided according to a given set of process standards results in a given set of outcomes (such as readmission rates, level of patient satisfaction, length of stay, and health status) would be more persuasive for nonnurse policymakers.

The proposal to account for nursing costs on the basis of practice standards also appears to ameliorate staff nurses' suspicion of patient classification systems. Many staff nurses believe that the limited number of indicators used to classify patients for staffing purposes does not adequately describe nursing functions. Indeed, patient classification systems were never intended to describe practice. Instead, they were developed to predict anticipated nursing care requirements through a few easily measured, but statistically powerful, predictors of care requirements.

Yet lack of face validity is a serious problem. If, against their better judgment, staff nurses capitulate and apply the system as instructed, they may harbor resentment and feel frustrated when staffing appears to be inadequate. If, in contrast, staff nurses decide to beat the system by manipulating the classification process or by informally redefining the classification indicators, the system's validity is undermined for both staffing and cost-accounting purposes.

Cost-accounting approaches based on nursing models deserve further investigation because they are likely to give specific information useful to nurses in evaluating and pricing alternative intervention strategies. Yet considerable scientific work remains to be done in order for these approaches to achieve their full potential. At the least, continued research is needed to demonstrate that commonly accepted process standards are related to maximal patient outcomes. Similarly, for nursing diagnoses to be a useful basis for costing out nursing resources, additional work is needed to refine the method of classifying patients and describing the phenomena that nurses address. Until the usefulness of nursing diagnoses and nursing care standards is evident to the practicing nurse, neither method is likely to be widely adopted in cost-accounting practices.

Relative Intensity Measures

RIMs were developed in response to the charge that DRGs do not accurately reflect differences of patient acuity within diagnostic groupings. Although designed specifically for reimbursement purposes, considerable controversy exists about whether RIMs are ready for implementation as a reimbursement or rate setting method. Some have criticized RIMs and claim that: (a) the methods used to construct them were flawed, (b) they produce categories that are imprecise estimates of resource requirements, and (c) the equations become outdated quickly due to changes in practice and average lengths of stay (Grimaldi & Micheletti, 1983; Trofino, 1986). New Jersey hospitals involved in evaluating RIMs have reported that large losses would have resulted had they been reimbursed under RIM-adjusted DRGs because of major cost shifts from relatively short to relatively long stays within DRGs (Trofino, 1986).

Nursing Workload-based Methods

The most widely reported methods are those that compute costs from patient classification data gathered for staffing purposes. That so many authors working more or less independently nationwide have proposed similar methods for costing out nursing per DRGs shows unusual professional consensus. Despite widespread agreement on a general approach, however, a number of questions and concerns remain to be addressed.

Retention of workload data

Relatively few hospitals record patient classification data for individual patients in the patient record or data base, although a number advocate the practice for the future (see Table 31-1). Daily recording of the nursing care requirements of individual patients is essential if these data are to be used for cost accounting on an ongoing basis. In the absence of such records, each cost study must be designed as a special project. Samples of patients must be identified upon admission, and workload data must be gathered prospectively. The special project approach not only entails considerable data collection costs but also decreases the likelihood that data would be available on a timely basis.

Limited retrievability of data

Computerization has just begun. Few of the cost-allocation methods (such as Nyberg & Wolff, 1984; Sovie, Tarcinale, Vanputee, & Stunden, 1985; Trofino, 1986) were reported to have been computerized, although many institutions had computerized patient classification systems. Ideally, daily nursing workload values would be part of a fully automated patient record. Workload data could then be used to compute total nursing care hours and costs for each patient and used in conjunction with other patient specific information (such as DRG classification, nursing diagnosis, primary nurse, and severity of illness) to address a variety of cost and outcome questions. Halloran and Kiley (1984) have proposed a nursing information system model based on nursing diagnoses that would permit sophisticated analysis of nursing performance and would adapt to changes in payment and treatment methods.

Until fully automated systems are available, some interim steps are worth pursuing. To reduce the cost of data collection and analysis, selected DRGs can be sampled for evaluation. Because approximately 25 to 30 DRGs account for 80% of the patients seen at most hospitals, sampling these DRGs would reasonably describe hospital performance. In addition to sampling on the basis of DRGs' relative frequencies in a hospital's case load, DRGs could also be sampled because of the relative financial burden they present and the changes in services anticipated for specific DRGs. After the DRGs are selected, nursing workload units and other relevant data can be gathered manually for each patient in the sample. Finally, the cost of care for each can be computed manually or by special computer software. Although computer systems dedicated to calculation of nursing costs per DRG may be an important developmental step, the ultimate goal is to have a system capable of integrating all relevant clinical and financial information (Study Group on Nursing Information Systems, 1983).

Multiple definitions of cost

A third potential difficulty encountered in the studies is that many definitions of direct and indirect nursing care costs are used. Some confusion relates to the different definitions given to the terms "direct" and "indirect" in nursing workload measurement and financial accounting. In measuring nursing workload, direct care hours generally refer to the time spent giving care in the patient's presence, whereas indirect (or nondirect) care hours refer to that time spent by nursing personnel not in contact with a patient (Giovannetti, 1978). In some nursing workload measurement systems, indirect hours are segmented into three groups with indirect care hours referring only to those spent on behalf of a patient but not in the patient's presence (such as charting or preparing medications). The nurse's personal time (breaks or "down time") and unit-related activities (narcotic counts or hospital reports) are treated separately.

In contrast, for financial accounting purposes, direct expense refers to all costs attributable to providing care for patients and thus includes the costs of both direct and indirect care hours, staff breaks, and down time as well as some unit maintenance costs. Indirect expenses refer to those costs necessary for the operation of a unit but which cannot be traced to an individual patient or service. Examples include allocated administrative, physical plant, debt service, and equipment expenses.

In the studies reviewed, operational definitions of direct and indirect cost (expense) are frequently omitted. Most seem to define direct costs as the salary expense incurred for direct and indirect nursing care as well as unit-related and the staff's personal activities. Higgerson and Van Slyck (1982) included nonchargeable supplies. Vanderzee and Glusko (1984) also included nonchargeable supplies and may have included administrative and staff development expenses. Walker (1983) included unit management and clerical support in direct expense.

Indirect expenses were frequently not addressed. When addressed, indirect expenses included nursing administration (Mason & Daugherty, 1984; Olsen, 1984; Riley & Shaefers, 1983; Walker, 1983) and/or orientation and inservice education costs (Curtin, 1983; Olsen, 1984; Staley & Luciano, 1984; Walker, 1983). In some studies, indirect costs were defined as "overhead" or "allocated overhead" that probably included the unit's share of nursing and hospital administration, physical plant, and nonrevenue-producing departmental expenses (DeJoseph, Petree, & Ross, 1984; Lagona & Stritzel, 1984; Sovie et al., 1985; Staley & Luciano, 1984). Mason and Daugherty (1984) also named clinical support services (such as IV teams) as indirect expenses.

Such inconsistencies in definition make cross-institutional comparisons problematic. Assuming that administrators can learn from the experiences of peer institutions, nurses should begin to identify performance measures that can serve as norms or standards for institutions. Current information services such as Hospital Administrative Services (HAS) of the American Hospital Association and the Professional Activity Study of the Commission on Professional and Hospital Activities provide a limited number of indicators of nursing performance (Commission on Professional and Hospital Activities, 1979; Dalton, 1979).

The Nursing Minimum Data Set project is an effort to establish comparability of nursing data. By identifying key data elements and developing uniform definitions for these elements, the developers hope to produce a mechanism for comparing nursing data within and among care settings and client populations. One data element recommended for inclusion in the Nursing Minimum Data Set is intensity of nursing care (Werley, Lang, & Westlake, 1986). Whether current patient classification systems for nurse staffing will or should be used to measure intensity of nursing care is open to debate (Giovannetti, in press).

Unit of analysis

Cost statistics were reported in several ways in the studies reviewed. Nursing care costs were described by: (a) DRGs, (b) medical diagnoses, (c) nursing workload (patient classification) categories, (d) levels of nursing personnel, (e) patient care units, and (f) DRGs weighted by the severity of illness index.

Each statistic provides valid information for identifying and controlling costs. However, given the rapidity with which reimbursement schemes come and go, each institution should also store cost data in a generic form. Many predict, for example, that the DRG will soon be replaced or substantially modified. If an organization stores nursing cost data only as costs per DRG, future analysis of historical data could prove cumbersome, if not impossible. The most generic form in which nursing cost information could be stored would include a combination of hours of care consumed per day or shift and costs per hour of care for each patient. When historical data are needed in the future, information about patients within the relevant categories would be available.

ADDRESSING METHODOLOGICAL PROBLEMS

The large volume of literature on cost accounting that has emerged in a relatively short time indicates that nurse executives are feeling pressure to identify and understand the costs of providing nursing care. Four distinct approaches for identifying costs were uncovered among the methods surveyed. Three key problem areas became apparent: (a) lack of comparability of the information used, (b) lack of uniform definitions of cost, and (c) neglect of variables that affect nursing care in addition to patient care requirements and staff mix.

Most methods used patient classification data to measure workload and allocate costs. While patient classification data gathered to assist in staffing are the most readily available workload information, there is little comparability in systems across institutions. Each institution uses slightly different indicators and weights for measuring and quantifying workloads. This institutional customizing is necessary in order to account for the combination of patient, staff mix, support services, and physical environment characteristics unique to each hospital.

While this uniqueness is important for determining staffing requirements, patient classification data are a compromised source of information about nursing care requirements independent of organizational considerations. Although the correlation between objective patient care requirements and the output of patient classification systems for staffing could be expected to be high, it would not be perfect. Added to the lack of cross-institutional comparability is the temptation to neglect ongoing maintenance of the validity and reliability of patient classification systems that can further compromise the quality of the information.

Therefore, if the objective is to measure nursing care requirements independent of organizational idiosyncrasies, patient classification data used for nurse staffing have serious weaknesses. But, if the objective is to measure what it costs to provide nursing care in each setting given the unique combination of patient, staff mix, support services, and physical environment characteristics, patient classification data should be excellent sources of information if they are valid and reliable.

The second major problem was the lack of uniformity in defining costs. In some cases, definitions of cost were neglected altogether. When defined, most estimates of cost focused on personnel costs but varied in which costs were to be considered direct and indirect. A few investigators broadened the definition to include certain supplies and equipment, while others also included allocated overhead expenses from ancillary and support services, capital investments, and overall hospital operations. Obvious disagreement exists about whether nursing costs should include only the professional services of nurses or all of the costs of providing nursing care to patients in an institutional setting.

Finally, there was a general neglect of variables other than patient care requirements and level of staff that can affect care. Variables of particular interest include the philosophy, mission, and standards of the institution; physician practice patterns; nature and extent of support services; and adequacy of the physical plant.

RECOMMENDATIONS

These observations lead to a number of recommendations. At a minimum, those publishing cost figures would be well advised to define their terms and carefully describe the context of their studies. More attention must also be given to providing evidence of the validity and reliability of all measures used. Such information would add to the scientific credibility of the reports as well as build consensus regarding the important variables to be considered.

Finally, as a profession, nursing urgently needs a minimum data set of the type being developed by Werley and associates (1986). For cost-accounting purposes, there is a special need for data elements that could be used to identify standards of resource requirements for the delivery of optimal care. When nursing services around the country begin to gather compatible, high quality data, the profession will be in a much better position to define and defend minimum and optimal nursing care requirements for patients of various types.

REFERENCES

Arndt, M., & Skydell, B. (1985). Inpatient nursing services: Productivity and cost. Pp. 135-153 in F.A. Shaffer (Ed.), *Costing out nursing: Pricing our product.* New York: National League for Nursing.

Ballard, D.; Barach, K.B.; & Cullen, J.J. (1985). The variable nursing charge system at the hospital of Saint Raphael. Pp. 101-111 in F.A. Shaffer (Ed.), *Costing out nursing: Pricing our product.* New York: National League for Nursing.

Bargagliotti, L.A., & Smith, H. (1985). Patterns of nursing costs with capitated reimbursement. *Nursing Economics, 3,* 270-275.

Berki, S.E. (1972). *Hospital economics.* Lexington, MA: Lexington Books.

Caterinicchio, R.P. (1983). A defense of the RIMs study. *Nursing Management, 14*(5), 36-39.

Caterinicchio, R.P., & Davies, R.H. (1983). Developing a client-focused allocation statistic of inpatient nursing resource use: An alternative to the patient day. *Social Science and Medicine, 17,* 259-272.

Commission on Professional and Hospital Activities. (1979). *PAS: Meeting your changing needs.* Ann Arbor, MI: Author.

Covaleski, M.A. (1981). The economic and professional legitimacy of nursing services. *Hospital and Health Services Administration, 26,* 75-91.

Curtin, L. (1983). Determining costs of nursing services per DRG. *Nursing Management, 14*(4), 16-20.

Dahlen, A.L., & Gregor, J.R. (1985). Nursing costs by DRG with an all-RN staff. Pp. 113-122 in F.A. Shaffer (Ed.), *Costing out nursing: Pricing our product.* New York: National League for Nursing.

Dalton, J.J. (1979). Uniform-reporting systems for billing and discharge data. *Topics in Health Care Financing, 6,* 59-78.

DeJoseph, J.F., Petree, B.J., & Ross, W. (1984). Costing and charging: Pricing care in OB. *Nursing Management, 15*(12), 36-37.

Ethridge, P. (1985). The case for billing by patient acuity. *Nursing Management, 16*(8), 38-41.

Giovannetti, P. (1978). *Patient classification systems in nursing: A description and analysis.* Hyattsville, MD: U.S. Department of Health, Education, and Welfare (DHEW Publication No. (HRA) 78-22).

Giovannetti, P. (in press). Compatibility among existing patient classification systems with a minimum data set.

Grimaldi, P.L., & Micheletti, J.A. (1982a). DRGs and nursing administration. *Nursing Management, 13*(1), 30-34.

Grimaldi, P.L., & Micheletti, J.A. (1982b). RIMs and the cost of nursing care. *Nursing Management, 13*(12), 12-22.

Grimaldi, P.L., & Micheletti, J.A. (1983). A defense of the RIMs critique — RIMs reliability and validity. *Nursing Management, 14*(5), 40-41.

Halloran, E.J. (1983). RN staffing: More care — less cost. *Nursing Management, 14*(9), 18-22.

Halloran, E.J., & Kiley, M. (1984). Case mix management. *Nursing Management, 15*(2), 39-45.

Higgerson, N.J., & Van Slyck, A. (1982). Variable billing for services: New fiscal direction for nursing. *The Journal of Nursing Administration, 12*(6), 20-27.

Holbrook, F.K. (1972). Charging by level of nursing care. *Hospitals, 46*(16), 80, 84, 86, 88.

Hospitals identifying nursing care costs, ANA study reveals. (1984). *The American Nurse,* pp. 1, 16.

Joel, L.A. (1983). DRGs: The state of the art of reimbursement for nursing services. *Nursing & Health Care, 5,* 560-563.

Lagona, T.G., & Stritzel, M.M. (1984). Nursing care requirements as measured by DRG. *Journal of Nursing Administration, 14*(5), 15-18.

Maher, A.B., & Dolan, B. (1982). Determining cost of nursing services. *Nursing Management, 13*(9), 17-21.

Mason, E.J., & Daugherty, J.K. (1984). Nursing standards should determine nursing's price. *Nursing Management, 15*(9), 34-38.

McClain, J.R., & Selhat, M.S. (1984). Twenty cases: What nursing costs per DRG. *Nursing Management, 15*(10), 26-34.

McKibben, R.C.; Brimmer, P.F.; Clinton, J.F.; Galliher, J.M.; & Hartley, S.S. (1985). *DRGs and nursing care.* Kansas City, MO: American Nurses' Association.

Mitchell, M., Miller, J., Welches, L., & Walker, D.D. (1984). Determining cost of direct nursing care by DRGs. *Nursing Management, 15*(4), 29-32.

Mowry, M.M., & Korpman, R.A. (1985). Do DRG reimbursement rates reflect nursing costs? *Journal of Nursing Administration, 15*(7 & 8), 29-35.

Nyberg, J., & Wolff, N. (1984). DRG panic. *The Journal of Nursing Administration, 14*(4), 17-21.

Olsen, S.M. (1984). The challenge of prospective pricing: Work smarter. *The Journal of Nursing Administration, 14*(4), 22-26.

Piper, L.R. (1983). Accounting for nursing functions in DRGs. *Nursing Management, 14*(11), 46-48.

Porter-O'Grady, T. (1985). Strategic planning: Nursing practice in PPS. *Nursing Management, 16*(10), 53-56.

Reschak, G.L.C., Biordi, D., Holm, K., & Santucci, N. (1985). Accounting for nursing costs by DRG. *Journal of Nursing Administration, 15*(9), 15-20.

Riley, W. & Schaefers, V. (1983). Costing nursing services. *Nursing Management, 14*(12), 40-43.

Ruchlin, H.S., & Levenson, I. (1974). Measuring hospital productivity. *Health Services Research, 9,* 308-323.

Saathoff, D., & Kurtz, R. (1962). Cost per day comparisons don't do the job. *Modern Hospital, 99*(10), 14, 16, 162.

Soliman, S.Y., & Hughes, W.L. (1983). DRG payments and net contribution variance analysis. *Hospital Financial Management, 13*(10), 78-86.

Sovie, M.D., Tarcinale, M.A., Vanputee, A.W., & Stunden, A.E. (1985). Amalgam of nursing acuity, DRGs and costs. *Nursing Management, 16*(3), 22-42.

Staley, M., & Luciano, K. (1984). Eight steps to costing nursing services. *Nursing Management, 15*(10), 35-38.

Study Group on Nursing Information Systems. (1983). Computerized nursing information systems: An urgent need. *Research in Nursing and Health, 6,* 101-105.

Toth, R.B. (1984). DRGs: Imperative strategies for nursing service administration. *Nursing and Health Care, 5*(4), 197-203.

Trofino, J. (1986). A reality based system for pricing nursing service. *Nursing Management, 17*(1), 19-24.

Vanderzee, H., & Glusko, G. (1984). DRGs, variable pricing, and budgeting for nursing services. *Journal of Nursing Administration, 14*(5), 11-14.

Walker, D.D. (1983). The cost of nursing care in hospitals. *Journal of Nursing Administration, 13*(3), 13-18.

Werley, H.H., Lang, N.M., & Westlake, S.K. (1986). Brief summary of the nursing minimum data set conference. *Nursing Management, 17*(7), 42-45.

Wolf, G.A., Lesic, L.K., & Leak, A.G. (1986). Primary nursing: The impact on nursing costs within DRGs. *Journal of Nursing Administration, 16*(1), 9-11.

Wood, C.T. (1976). Split-cost accounting: A more precise and equitable way to assign patient costs. *Health Services Manager, 9*(9), 8-10.

Wood, C.T. (1983). Nursing should be a revenue-producing center. *Computers in Healthcare, 4*(11), 33-34.

CHAPTER **32**

Implications of Costing Out Nursing Services for Reimbursement

Joanne Comi McCloskey, RN, PhD, FAAN

Currently, there is much discussion in the nursing management community about "costing out nursing." In somewhat different circles, debate continues about third-party reimbursement for nurses. Considered together, these two movements benefit each other and provide important implications for cost models and politics.

COSTING OUT NURSING

The phrase, "costing out nursing services," new jargon in nursing, means simply determination of costs of services provided by nurses. However, its use refers almost exclusively to efforts to determine cost of nursing care in hospitals. Attempts to separate nursing costs from room rates have been underway for at least 10 years, although it has not been until the last three to five years, coinciding with the implementation of DRGs, that the concern is evident on a large scale in the nursing literature.[1,2] For the present, the goal is to identify the cost of nursing for a particular patient in a particular DRG category so that nursing costs can be reflected as a separate charge on the patient's bill. This goal prompts the following questions:

1. What is the cost of nursing time per DRG per acuity level in a particular institution?

Reprinted from *Nursing Management,* Vol. 20, No. 1, with permission of S-N Publications, Inc. © 1989.

2. What are the direct (hands on) and indirect (other) costs of nursing?
3. How does nursing cost compare with total hospital cost?
4. How does nursing cost compare to costs of other departments?
5. How do nursing costs at one institution compare with nursing costs at other institutions?

Ultimately, identification of costs for specific nursing interventions or services will allow evaluation of the cost effectiveness of nursing care. That is, knowing the cost and the effectiveness of specific interventions allows the reduction of costs through elimination or substitution of services and helps in the determination of whether present costs will prevent or reduce future costs. To this end, answers to the following questions are needed:

1. What nursing diagnoses are associated with what medical diagnoses (DRGs)?
2. What nursing interventions provide the best outcomes for specific nursing diagnoses?
3. What are the costs of different nursing interventions?
4. What conditions are there a) which nurses are inadequately prepared to diagnose and treat and, thus, need more educational preparation or b) for which the knowledge base is inadequate?

5. What is the cost of achieving a specific outcome for a particular nursing diagnosis?

While there has been an explosion of articles in the nursing literature on "costing out," little research has been done. Many of the studies had small sample sizes, were conducted in one institution and used patient classification systems without much regard for their reliability and validity.[2] Reports frequently do not explain the methodology used to arrive at the conclusions. Despite their limitations, the findings of these studies are cited frequently, perhaps because the information is needed so urgently. Most of the studies have addressed the question, "What is the nursing cost compared with the total hospital cost?" That nursing costs equal around 20-25 percent of hospital costs is consistent and, despite methodological concerns, these studies are beginning to demonstrate that nursing care is not responsible for the high costs of healthcare.[3-5] However, more research with larger samples, using valid and reliable measures, is needed to validate and expand upon the early findings. Future efforts in costing out need to measure the costs of specific nursing services and the effectiveness of nursing care.

THIRD-PARTY REIMBURSEMENT

Third-party reimbursement seeks payment to nurses from the government and private insurers for the cost of nursing care to individual clients. While third-party reimbursement has been sought by nurses in independent practice, there is the potential for reimbursement of nursing care delivered in hospitals. Reimbursement of nurse-run units, wherein the main treatments are nursing rather than medical, is a practical reality when nurses can identify the services provided for particular patients, with the associated benefits and costs.

Nurses in private practice and in nurse-owned clinics, who are seeking reimbursement, also must be able to communicate the services they offer and the related costs, and many of them can. To date, most third-party reimbursement for nursing provides payment to advanced nurse practitioners (e.g., nurse midwives, nurse anesthetists). These nurses must approach the providers individually and seek approval for reimbursement. In some states, this requires a change of state insurance laws.

Third-party reimbursement has been instituted without knowing the actual cost of care. Reimbursement fees to nurses are set at some percentage rate of existing physician fees. The percentage rate is variable, with little sound basis for its determination, and in some instances no predetermined level has been set. For example, in 1979 Oregon passed a third-party reimbursement bill for nurse practitioner services. Because the law did not include any basic levels of reimbursement, nurse practitioners in Oregon have had trouble getting reimbursed for more than 50 percent of physician fees.[6] To insure adequate reimbursement for nurses, data are needed for the actual cost of specific nursing services which: 1) compete with physician services and 2) are uniquely "nursing."

Community nursing agencies have kept cost records for a number of years, based on nursing cost per visit. Unfortunately, this usually is not cost per nursing diagnosis or per type of nursing treatment. Since DRGs have not yet been implemented in the community, nursing costs per DRG in the community also are unknown. Some states have defined a list of nursing services provided in nursing homes based on an assumed provider (often an LPN or aide) and the average amount of time needed (determined by the state government on the basis of time and motion studies and expert opinion).[7] Thus, there are some notable efforts to determine costs in nursing homes and community agencies. For the most part, however, the situation in these settings is the same as in hospitals; costs are determined by nursing time and little has been done to determine the costs of various nursing services.

Third-party reimbursement to nurses holds appeal for legislators who are looking for cost-effective substitutes to expensive physician and hospital services.[8-9] Legislators will adopt bills that pay nurses for services of the same or higher quality provided at a lower cost. However, to interest legislators and obtain adequate third-party reimbursement, the costs of specific services must be known. Answers to the following questions are needed:

1. What services provided by physicians can nurses provide and at what comparative cost?
2. What services currently delegated to nurses by physicians and reimbursed to physicians can be reimbursed directly to nurses at a lower cost?
3. What nursing services are not offered by other providers and what are the benefits and the costs of these services?

If unique nursing services are demonstrated to benefit clients and are cost effective, the current system that reimburses for mostly curative (medical) services will have to be revised. Revision must include charges for nursing services that are based on cost, plus a margin of profit. Nurses will have to decide what profit margin will provide enough income for continued modification of services and sufficient reward in the prevailing market.

IMPLICATIONS

Two important implications arise from efforts to determine costs of nursing services and attempts to gain reimbursement for services provided. The first relates to models to determine costs and the second to political considerations.

Costing Models: A review of studies to determine nursing costs demonstrates that the work to date is atheoretical. To guide future research and to help individual nurse administrators implement a system to determine costs and gain reimbursement, models for costing out are needed, with advantages and disadvantages clearly identified. For example, while no article reports a specific model that is guiding the

work, most of the mechanisms that have been reported in the literature can be illustrated by Model I, shown in Figure 32-1.

In this model the amount of nursing time per intensity level related to a specific DRG is multiplied by the nurse's average hourly salary (and benefits) and added to some amount for indirect costs (e.g., administration, overhead) to determine nursing cost per DRG. The model is conceptually easy to implement in hospitals. DRGs are in place and any nursing model for determining costs in the present system will have to relate costs to DRGs. To implement this model a nursing intensity instrument with associated amounts of nursing time for each level or category of care is needed. Many hospitals have adopted patient classification systems that were developed to measure nursing intensity for staffing purposes. This usually leads to *projected* levels of needs of a group of patients rather than to measures of *actual* nursing care given to individual patients.

An associated problem is the time component. Sovie has stressed repeatedly that each institution must determine its own hours of care per category on each unit.[4] While this increases the validity of the instrument, it is expensive in terms of nursing time and resources needed to conduct the workload measurements. The wide variety and nonstandardization of nursing intensity/patient acuity measures is a key reason for the difficulty in obtaining large data sets for comparison of nursing costs. Another area that lacks standardization is the determination of direct and indirect costs. Direct (hands on) cost is usually defined as the nurse's average salary, sometimes with benefits added. Average salary and benefits differ by type and qualifications of nurses and by area of the country. Some researchers have combined the salaries

FIGURE 32-1
Determination of nursing costs based on nursing intensity.

of several types of nursing personnel to determine the average cost per care giver. Also, definitions of nursing care giver are not standardized; for example, some researchers include the head nurse, while others do not. When indirect costs are added on, usually as a set lump sum for all patients, there is no agreed-upon definition of what or who to include in the calculation. There is some danger that existing studies have underestimated nursing costs by not including enough of the indirect costs.

While all these concerns are important, the major handicap of Model I is its lack of ability to define what nursing activities are provided. The model yields only nursing cost per DRG or per intensity level. Some nursing intensity rating scales require the nurse to identify the activities performed, but usually this is a "laundry list" and many items are not nursing activities. That is, not all of what nurses do is nursing. Thus, the system for documenting what nurses do must be sensitive enough to capture unique nursing functions, physician-delegated functions, and functions that nurses perform for other ancillary services (e.g., dietary, housekeeping). Further, the nursing functions that are unique from other disciplines—those that make a difference for the welfare of clients and *must* be performed by a nurse—must be measured explicitly, as illustrated in Model II, shown in Figure 32-2.

Implementation of Model II would yield nursing cost per nursing intervention or per nursing diagnosis. Also, it would allow these costs to be aggregated for specific DRG categories, and would not be medically dependent. It would allow costs to be determined for specific nursing services provided and would detail information on why certain costs are high or low. Implementation of this model would greatly benefit further development of the nursing knowledge base because it provides for the collection of data which may be used for testing of specific nursing interventions. Model II has advantages over Model I because it provides data to answer both sets of the questions listed in the costing out section of this article, while use of Model I can provide answers only to the first set. Also, Model II would provide data to begin to answer the third set of questions posed in the section on third-party reimbursement.

Model II has not been used much, probably because nursing diagnoses and interventions are not standardized nor widely used, and because it is more expensive to implement. A question that Model II raises is whether nursing diagnoses and interventions predict nursing resource consumption better than medical diagnoses. Beginning evidence indicates that they do. For example, Halloran found that nursing diagnoses accounted for 52 percent of the variance in

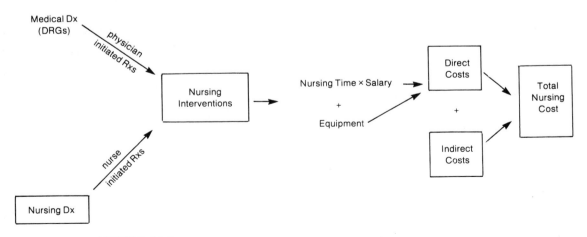

FIGURE 32-2

Model II. Determination of nursing costs based on nursing diagnoses and interventions.

nursing workload while DRGs accounted for only 26 percent.[10]

There have been remarkable accomplishments in the area of nursing diagnosis in the past decade and many institutions have implemented some form of the North American Nursing Diagnosis Association's (NANDA) approved list. However, there is no accepted standardized format readily available in computer form. The problem related to interventions is even more serious. Few lists of interventions exist and those being computerized by vendors and hospitals consist more of nursing activities than interventions. Further, lists of interventions usually confuse nursing assessment activities with intervention activities and often are written at too discrete a level.

Model II indicates that nursing interventions are of two types: 1) physician-initiated activities, based mostly on medical diagnoses and 2) nurse-initiated activities, based mostly on nursing diagnoses. The issue about collaborative interventions is moot here — both physician-initiated and nurse-initiated interventions often are done after collaboration. The point is that nurses do some things that are mostly physician-initiated (the physician wants them done related to the medical diagnoses and asks the nurse to do them as an assistant) and other things that are mostly nurse-initiated (the nurse wants them done related to the nursing diagnoses and so, does them). In practice, sometimes things are not as clear as this, but the conceptualization of different types of interventions is important as nurses seek to clarify their roles.

Models I and II represent two possible ways to determine costs. Other models related to cost per day, per standard of care, and per unit are discussed in Edwardson and Giovannetti's review of the cost literature.[11] Researchers and administrators involved in determining costs must develop models that others can understand clearly, implement and test. Reimbursement can be achieved more easily when we can explain how the figures are determined on which we are basing our charges.

Political Considerations: Efforts to cost out nursing services and seek third-party reimbursement raise two fears. First there is the fear of those currently in power that they will lose power if nursing succeeds. Some hospital administrators and physicians fear that nursing departments that are identified as revenue-generating will become too independent and thus, "non-controllable." Also, there is the fear that nurses in private practice will take away business, money, and prestige from practicing physicians. There is a general anxiety that such efforts will upset the healthcare "apple cart" of power, which is already in precarious balance.

Second, there is the fear that knowing accurately the cost of nursing services will raise, rather than lower, the cost of healthcare, especially if nursing is reimbursed according to cost, and reimbursement for other services is not adjusted. This fear relates partially to whether the addition of another provider will increase the use of healthcare services by consumers, thereby driving up costs. Further, if knowing actual costs of nursing care reveals that nursing is cost effective and thus subsidizing other providers, there could well be a request by nurses to increase their salaries. Such an action could raise costs or take money away from other providers.

As nursing increases efforts to cost out nursing services and be reimbursed for services, nurses need to engage others in discussion about the fears mentioned above. Fears motivate others to oppose efforts and nurses must be able to address tactfully these fears, even when they are unspoken. Reasons why nursing efforts to determine costs will benefit others, particularly patients, must be presented. For example, in the box on p. 287 are reasons why hospital administrators should support nursing efforts to cost out services. This list is useful for encountering questions and resistance from administrators.

Determining costs of nursing care and seeking efforts to be reimbursed by third parties for these costs brings nursing squarely into the financial arena of healthcare where money, power and influence control most of the decisions. Nurses who aspire to be effective in this arena have to be assertive and tough, with political savvy and determination. Knowledge of the issues is important, but alone, it is not sufficient for success.

Reasons why hospital directors would support efforts to determine the costs of nursing services

1. Efforts will result in knowledge about cost of nursing care now hidden in room cost.
2. Nursing care is the largest product of any hospital. While costs of other products are known, nursing costs remain obscure.
3. Knowing the cost of nursing will allow for accurate billing of nursing services, contracting with HMOs and PPOs for nursing services and better determination of cost of providing a new service.
4. Knowledge of nursing cost does *not* mean higher healthcare costs. It opens the door to cost reduction in nursing, through design of more effective delivery methods.
5. If costing out nursing services should lead to the conclusion that nursing is being unfairly compenstated or that nursing is subsidizing other services, the hospital administrator should be the first to have this information in order to promote a more equitable allocation of reimbursement among providers.
6. Knowing the type, quality, and cost of services of all healthcare providers allows consumers and managers a safe substitution of cheaper alternatives. Increased competition in the healthcare arena will reduce costs for the consumer.
7. Efforts to cost out nursing services are consistent with the values of hospital directors to promote quality care in a cost-effective manner.
8. Local efforts to cost out nursing services are in line with the national trend. Hospital and nurse directors either can take a proactive role in defining and collecting their own data or can wait passively until it is done by others, who may not collect or use the data appropriately.

As nursing struggles for provider equity in healthcare, I am reminded of a similar struggle which occurred in the 1970s between baseball players and team owners. Before 1975, an exemption to the antitrust law allowed baseball owners to keep players on low salaries and take most of the profits. Team owners argued that the old system was best because higher salaries for players would mean that prices of admission for consumers to baseball games would have to increase. As a result of organized efforts to allocate benefits more fairly, baseball players now keep a much larger percentage of the profits that they generate. As baseball fans demonstrate, ticket prices are still very affordable.

This analogy points out that nursing efforts to determine costs, and to be reimbursed adequately for services, are not going to be accomplished without resistance from the team "owners" of the current healthcare delivery system. It will take organized and consistent efforts by nursing to accomplish provider equity in healthcare. Organized efforts will be effective only when nursing has complete data about nursing costs and benefits. Nurses must document the services they provide in a systematic way and use this documentation to gain adequate reimbursement. Costing out of nursing services is a necessary task not only for cost containment and reimbursement purposes. If it is done with the documentation of nursing diagnoses and interventions, it reflects the essence of nursing.

REFERENCES

1. Trofino, J., "A Reality Based System for Pricing Nursing," *Nursing Management,* 1986, 17(1):19-24.
2. McCloskey, J.C., D.L. Gardner and M.R. Johnson, "Costing Out Nursing Services: An Annotated Bibliography," *Nursing Economics,* 1987, 5(5):245-253.
3. Walker, D.D., "The Cost of Nursing Care in Hospitals," *Journal of Nursing Administration,* 1983, 13(3):13-18.
4. Sovie, M.D., M.A. Tarcinale, A. VanPutte and A. Stunden, "Amalgam of Nursing Acuity, DRGs, and Costs," *Nursing Management,* 1985, 16(3):22-42.
5. McKibbin, R.C., P.F. Brimmer, J.M. Galliher, S.S. Hartley and J. Clinton, "Nursing Costs and DRG Payments," *American Journal of Nursing,* 1985, 85(12):1353-1356.
6. Council of Primary Health Care Nurse Practitioners, *Obtaining Third-Party Reimbursement: A Nurse's Guide to Methods and Strategies,* (Kansas City: ANA, 1984), p. 27.
7. Adams, E.K. and R.E. Schlenker, "Case-Mix Reimbursement for Nursing Home Services: Simulation Approach," *Health Care Financing Review,* 1986, 8(1):35-45.

8. Griffith, H.M., "Strategies for Direct Third-Party Reimbursement for Nurses," *American Journal of Nursing,* 1982, 82(3):408-414.

9. Posell, P.J., "Fee-For-Service," *Nursing Management,* 1983, 14(3):13-15.

10. Halloran, E.J., "Nursing Workload, Medical Diagnosis Related Groups, and Nursing Diagnosis," *Research in Nursing and Health,* 1985, 8(4):421-433.

11. Edwardson, S.R. and P.B. Giovannetti, "A Review of Cost-Accounting Methods for Nursing Services," *Nursing Economics,* 1987, 5(3):107-117.

CHAPTER 33

Pricing the Nursing Product
Charging for nursing care

Margaret D. Sovie, RN, PhD, FAAN
Toni C. Smith, RN, MS

Charging a variable amount for nursing care according to the amount of care provided is essential if we are committed to pricing our products. No other industry could survive or, more importantly, thrive by assigning fixed charges for its major product lines when the amount of materials and work hours involved in producing those products vary significantly.

Furthermore, informed customers will no longer tolerate being charged "all inclusive room rates" when it is obvious that some customers get more for the same price. Wood (1982) challenged us to imagine Hertz averaging the costs of 18-wheel, 14-wheel, and 10-wheel trucks in addition to luxury and economy cars and then charging all customers the same cost per vehicle day. Although that may seem absurd, that is how the product of nursing care has been sold in hospitals. Traditionally, two room rates are used: one for routine floor care, and one for intensive care. All patients are billed equivalent daily room charges determined by the type of assigned facility (private or semiprivate room) and the type of assigned unit (regular or intensive care), independent of the level of nursing care they need and receive.

Reprinted from *Nursing Economics*, Vol. 4, No. 5, with permission of Anthony J. Jannetti, Inc. © 1986.

UNBUNDLING NURSING CHARGES FROM ROOM CHARGES: PRICING OUR PRODUCTS

Pricing our products requires unbundling nursing charges from room charges, that is, separating nursing care charges from room, board, and other charges. The concept of variable charges for nursing care recognizes through financial accounting and billing services that patients have unique needs for nursing care that vary across their hospital lengths of stay. Their charges should accurately reflect these nursing care services.

Identifying the costs of nursing care in hospitals helps destroy multiple myths and set the record straight.

Myth 1: Nursing costs consume the majority of a hospital's room costs.

False. At Strong Memorial Hospital (SMH) in Rochester, NY, unbundling nursing charges from routine charges required approximately a 30% reduction in daily room charges in the first year.

Myth 2: Nursing care is one of the most expensive services and is responsible for high hospital costs.

False. Sandrick (1985) noted that direct nursing care accounted for only 11% of the hospital bill at Stanford and that nursing care and administration accounted for only 18.5% of total hospital charges at St. Paul-Ramsey Medical Center in St. Paul, Minnesota.

Myth 3: A predominantly registered nurse (RN) staff is too costly.

False. Wolf, Lesic, and Leak (1986) studied the costs of nursing care on two structurally identical 28-bed medical-surgical units—one using primary nursing, and the other using team nursing. Because of acuity differences, the staff mix on the primary nursing unit was 82% RN as compared to 76% RNs on the team nursing unit. The primary nursing unit's daily average costs were $1.30 less per patient day than the team nursing unit.

Myth 4: All patients receive the same amount of care each day.

False. Sovie, Tarcinale, VanPutte, and Stunden (1984) compared reported average hours of nursing care for two diagnosis related groups (DRGs) from studies completed at SMH and a Rochester community hospital (see Table 33-1). At the time of the SMH study, this 741-bed teaching hospital owned by the University of Rochester had a staff mix of 92% RNs and 8% licensed practical nurses (LPNs), nursing assistants, and technicians. Primary nursing was practiced in all inpatient units. In Lagona and Stritzel's

(1984) study of a 547-bed Rochester community teaching hospital, the nursing staff mix was 58.7% RNs, 14.6% LPNs, 17.7% nursing assistants, and 9% nursing support personnel.

Caution must be exercised in evaluating the comparative data because the staff members included in the "nursing support personnel" were not specified. However, even after conservative analysis, Table 33-1 data indicate that the SMH average direct nursing costs, with predominantly RN staff, were lower for DRGs 121 and 122 than those of the community hospital with a 58.7% RN staff. Furthermore, these data illustrate that patients with different problems in different diagnostic categories generally receive differing amounts of nursing care.

REPLACING FANTASY WITH FACTS

By pricing nursing care and by charging individual patients for the nursing care they need and receive, facts replace fantasy and myths disappear. More importantly, the individual or group consumer receives a more accurate accounting of the amount of services rendered and how these services contribute to the total bill. Charging for nursing care allows us to view the individual patient rather than the occupied

TABLE 33-1

Comparison of selected Strong Memorial Hospital (SMH) and Rochester Community Hospital data for DRGs 121 and 122

DRG	SMH (SOVIE ET AL., 1984)			ROCHESTER COMMUNITY HOSPITAL (LAGONA & STRITZEL, 1984)		
	Number of patients	Average nursing hours	Average direct nursing costs	Number of patients	Average nursing hours	Average direct nursing costs
121 AMI w CV Compl Disch Alive[a]	91	69.59	$752	16	125	$1,065
122 AMI w/o CV Compl Disch Alive[b]	211	56.58	$611	19	90	$766.80

[a]121 = Acute myocardial infarction with cardiovascular complications; discharged alive.
[b]122 = Acute myocardial infarction without cardiovascular complications; discharged alive.

bed as the consumer of nursing resources. The occupied bed concept equates all patients. Yet we know the wide variation of needs experienced by patients with different diagnoses.

A patient-specific system of charging for consumed nursing resources allows management to be aware of the varying costs of its multiple services and product lines; and when appropriate, to use such knowledge in negotiating contracts with preferred provider organizations, business, and industry. Finally, product line management requires cost accounting practices that permit analysis of component costs.

The prospective payment system uses DRGs as the products for which it pays predetermined amounts. Responsible management in such a system requires that the costs of caring for patients assigned to the various DRGs be identified and that these data are available for use in strategic planning and corporate decision making.

Charging for nursing care moves nursing from a cost center to a revenue center. Higgerson and Van Slyck (1982) define a cost center as an organizational unit, such as a patient care unit, that performs a function and uses specific resources to do so. A revenue center is a cost center that provides services for which charges are generated.

By unbundling nursing from the room rate and charging patients for the nursing care they receive, nursing becomes a revenue center. Nurses become economically as well as professionally accountable for the care they provide. This economic accountability is essential if nurses expect to provide quality care at controlled costs. We cannot control costs if we do not know what they are; and to know our costs, we must price our product or charge for nursing care.

HISTORY OF VARIABLE BILLING FOR NURSING CARE

Variable billing for nursing care was introduced about 15 years ago and is now used in hospitals in the District of Columbia and the following 14 states: Arizona, California, Connecticut, Florida, Illinois, Maine, Massachusetts, Minnesota, New York, North Dakota, Oregon, Virginia, Washington, and Wisconsin.

LaViolette (1979) described three variable billing systems operational in the early '70s. Montana Deaconess Medical Center, a 370-bed hospital in Great Falls, implemented a patient classification billing procedure in 1971 with hourly charges specified for each classification. The hourly charges for nursing care at Montana Deaconess ranged from 75¢ per hour for routine nursing care to $2.55 per hour for intensive care unit (ICU) services (Holbrook, 1972). St. Luke's Hospital Medical Center, a 420-bed hospital in Phoenix, AZ, began its billing system in 1974; the system had seven acuity levels with each classification level charge including required nursing care hours and supplies (Higgerson & Van Slyck, 1982). The Massachusetts Eye and Ear Infirmary, a 174-bed specialty hospital, began using a productivity-based accounting system in 1976. The system has four components with the nursing care charge component based on clinical care units (CCUs) which were developed from extensive case studies (Wood, 1982). These CCUs represent the amount of nursing care delivered to patients based on diagnosis and days of stay.

DeJoseph, Petree, and Ross (1984) described Stanford's program for stratified charges for obstetrical care, a system in which each woman is charged only for the care she receives. Ethridge (1985) described the patient acuity billing system in operation at St. Mary's Hospital and Health Center in Phoenix, AZ. The system is built on a patient classification system with eight acuity levels: I through V on the general units, and VI through VIII on the ICUs. Ethridge emphasizes that the actual costs of nursing care must be known and that a patient acuity billing system is the most effective way to accumulate these data by case mix.

In 1985, policymakers in Maine mandated that the costs of nursing care for each patient be specified. Maine was the first state to require all hospitals to provide to any requesting patient an itemized bill that specifies the costs of nursing care and other services provided. In addition, an amendment was added to Maine's prospective payment law mandating that reports be submitted by hospitals on nursing costs in terms of "patient classification" ("Maine's DONs Adopt," 1985; "Maine's 42 Hospitals," 1985).

NURSING PATIENT CLASSIFICATION SYSTEM AS THE BASIS OF CHARGING

A nursing patient classification system (NPCS) that is valid and reliable and based on patient needs and the care delivered to meet those needs provides a sound basis for variable billing for nursing care. Validity means that the system used accurately reflects nursing needs. Reliability means that the system consistently measures those nursing care needs. Giovannetti and Mayer (1984) emphasized the importance of quarterly reliability monitoring and even more frequent monitoring if a high degree of reliability is not obtained.

SMH has been using a NPCS since 1977. This NPCS measures the relative amount of nursing care required by a patient by assigning the patient, through the sum of selected indicator weights, to one of four categories of nursing acuity — 1 representing the lowest need category, and 4 representing the highest. The system is comprised of two instruments — one specifically designed for psychiatric patients and one general instrument for all other patients.

Because the Strong Memorial Hospital NPCS has been described in previous publications, details will not be repeated here (Sovie, Tarcinale, VanPutte, & Stunden, 1985). Since February 1, 1985, the system

TABLE 33-2

Nursing care hours assigned per category of acuity

UNIT NUMBER	UNIT DESCRIPTION	CATEGORY				UNIT CHARGE FOR NONCLASSIFIED PATIENT DAY
		1	2	3	4	
Pediatrics						
3-3400	Neonatal ICU	—	7.9	10.2	16.7	10.2
4-1600	Infants/toddlers	4.0	4.6	5.7	7.7	4.6
4-3600	School-age	3.2	4.8	5.8	6.7	4.8
4-1400	Adolescent	3.2	4.8	5.8	6.7	4.8
4-1600l	Pediatric ICU	—	16.5	18.2	20.5	18.2
Obstetrics/ Gynecology						
3-1200	Normal postpartum	3.5	4.3	4.8	5.6	4.3
3-2300	Newborn nursery	—	3.0	3.5	4.2	3.5
3-1400	High-risk maternal	4.2	5.2	6.2	7.2	5.2
3-1600	Gynecology	3.3	4.1	5.1	6.4	4.1
3-3600	Mixed unit	3.3	4.1	5.1	6.4	4.1
Surgery						
5-1400	Orthopedics	3.4	3.8	4.7	6.2	3.8
5-3400	Orthopedics	3.4	3.8	4.7	6.2	3.8
5-3600	Neurosurgery	3.2	3.6	5.0	7.4	3.6
6-1400	General surgery	3.4	3.6	4.8	6.2	3.6
6-1600	Genitourinary	3.2	4.2	5.0	6.2	4.2
6-3400	Cardiothoracic	4.0	4.4	5.2	7.0	4.4
6-3600	Ear/Nose/Throat/Eye	3.2	3.4	4.6	5.6	3.4
8-1400P	Plastic	4.0	4.4	5.2	6.8	4.4
8-1400B	Burn ICU	—	11.0	16.0	19.0	16.0
8-3600	Surgical ICU	—	13.0	16.0	20.2	16.0

has been used to charge patients variable daily rates for nursing care based on the assigned category of nursing acuity and unit assignment.

Each category of nursing acuity on each patient care unit has assigned average hours of nursing care. These hours are derived from time studies on each patient care unit (VanPutte, Sovie, Tarcinale, & Stunden, 1985). Table 33-2 notes the specific nursing care at SMH. The last column is a "fixed charge," that is, a unit charge to be applied if a patient is not classified on a particular day. This fixed charge is for the second lowest category of nursing acuity on each unit. The concept of a fixed charge is essential after nursing charges have been unbundled from routine room rates. The hospital or patient care unit cannot

afford to give away its nursing care, and a fail-safe system must be implemented to ensure that each patient in the institution has a daily nursing charge.

The concept of relative value units (RVUs) has not been used by nursing at SMH. The preference has been to stay with hours per category by unit as illustrated in Table 33-2. However, RVUs could be used. An RVU of 1 equals the hours required by the lowest acuity category. Table 33-3 shows the conversion of the hours on the general medical units to RVUs.

When a NPCS is used as the basis for charging, an audit trail must be clearly established. Documentation in the patient record should confirm that the nursing care warranted by the selected indicators was provided to the patient. Periodic audits must be

TABLE 33-2

Nursing care hours assigned per category of acuity—cont'd

UNIT NUMBER	UNIT DESCRIPTION	CATEGORY				UNIT CHARGE FOR NONCLASSIFIED PATIENT DAY
		1	2	3	4	
Psychiatry						
1-9200	Community mental health clinic high-risk	—	4.0	4.6	6.0	4.6
2-9200	Affective disorder	—	3.9	4.6	6.4	4.6
3-9000	General psychiatry	—	3.3	4.4	6.0	4.4
4-9000E	Neuropsychiatry	—	3.7	4.4	6.2	4.4
4-9000W	Behavioral therapy	—	3.5	4.6	6.9	4.6
Medicine						
5-1200	Rehabilitation	3.7	4.7	6.4	8.6	4.7
5-1600	Neurology	3.4	4.0	5.9	7.7	4.0
7-1200	General medicine	3.1	3.6	5.2	6.9	3.6
7-1400	General medicine	3.1	3.6	5.2	6.9	3.6
7-1600	General medicine	3.1	3.6	5.2	6.9	3.6
7-3400	General medicine	3.1	3.6	5.2	6.9	3.6
7-3600	General medicine	3.1	3.6	5.2	6.9	3.6
8-1600	Medical ICU	—	8.6	12.7	16.2	12.7
8-3400	Telemetry & medicine	3.1	3.8	5.6	7.3	3.8

Emergency Department

Boarded patients to be charged 13 minutes per hour.

TABLE 33-3
Conversion of hours on general medical units to relative value units (RVUs)

UNIT OF MEASUREMENT	CATEGORY OF NURSING ACUITY				FIXED CHARGE
	1	2	3	4	
Hours to be charged	3.1	3.6	5.2	6.9	3.6
Minutes of nursing care	186	216	312	414	216
RVUs	1	1.2	1.7	2.2	1.2

conducted to verify that patients have received services for which they were billed.

To ensure the existence of an audit trail at SMH, the patient care flowsheet was revised to accommodate all NPCS indicators (see Figure 33-1). Nurses indicate the care given on the flowsheet and also document pertinent observations in the patient's progress notes as needed. Because we use the category of nursing acuity as well as the unit assignment to determine our daily nursing care charge, documented evidence is critical to confirm the accuracy of category assignments and patient charges.

Although the selected indicators help ensure that the patient is assigned to the appropriate category of nursing acuity, they do not represent the total nursing care needed or received by the patient. The hours assignment per category of acuity represents the average amount of time required to meet the total care needs of this type of patient and is based on the total nursing care hours required by patients in each 24-hour period in each acuity category (VanPutte et al., 1985).

When the patient is discharged from the hospital, a summary data record from the daily nursing patient classification is printed and placed in the permanent record (see Table 33-4). This requirement ensures that these data are retrievable for future inquiries and clinical studies.

Other uses of a NPCS include: (a) productivity monitoring (Dale & Mable, 1983; Evans, Laundon, & Yamamoto, 1980; Grant, Bellinger, & Sweda, 1982);

(b) budgetary planning, monitoring, and control (Finkler, 1982; Maher & Dolan, 1982); (c) patient assignments because acuity levels reflect nursing intensity of patients; and (d) unit staffing (Alward, 1983).

THE BILLING SYSTEM

With a valid and reliable NPCS in place and nursing care hours assigned to each acuity category on each patient unit, the institution is ready to proceed to the next step—determination of the hourly rate and separation of nursing care costs from hotel costs. The type of hourly rate to be charged must be determined. For example, will a unit-specific hourly rate be charged, or will an hourly rate be applied across all hospital units? Because SMH has a predominantly RN staff (93%) with primary nursing practiced in all settings, we decided to have a hospital-wide hourly rate for nursing care.

Developing the hourly rate.   Working in collaboration with staff members from financial services, the hourly rates for nursing care in 1985 and 1986 were determined. Direct patient care costs were defined as salary and benefits for clinician I's (head nurses), assistant clinicians, RNs, LPNs, technicians, and nursing assistants. Indirect care costs were divided into two categories: indirect administrative costs and indirect overhead costs. Indirect administrative costs included salary and benefits for clinical nursing chiefs; nurse clinician IIs (clinical specialists); all central nursing administrative personnel; and all central and service clerical office personnel. Also included were nonsalary expenses related to unit staff such as conference registration fees, travel, or books. Indirect overhead costs included administrative office space costs, building and equipment depreciation, plant operation and maintenance, housekeeping, and cafeteria costs.

The following nursing accounts were excluded from the cost base used to calculate the hospital-wide hourly rate because they were currently charging separate rates for these services and had not been bundled in the routine room rate: outpatient department, labor and delivery, operating room, postanesthesia room, psychiatric emergency/ambulatory, long-term care, ambulatory surgery, cancer center;

PATIENT CARE FLOWSHEET

Directions:
The nurse completing the intervention must place a check mark (✓) in the appropriate slot and write her initials at the bottom of each column. Full signature and title should be documented in the space provided. Document all pertinent observations/interactions in the Progress Notes and/or appropriate record.

INTERVENTION/ACTIVITY	DATE N	D	E	DATE N	D	E
Complete (Total) Bath						
Bath with Assistance						
Self Care						
Oral Care						
Perineal Care						
Simple Skin Care						
Prone						
Supine						
Left Side						
Right Side						
Turn: (spec.)*						
Assist with Oral/Tube Feed						
Total Oral/Tube Feed						
Bedrest						
Bathroom Privileges						
OOB within Chair						
Ambulate with Assist.						
Ad Lib						
Sleep						
Transfer: (spec.)*						
Prep. for test/proc. (spec.)						
Specimen Coll: (spec.)						
IV Insertion Site Check						
IV Delivery Sys and						
Dressing Change						
Date IV Inserted						
IV Insertion Site Check						
IV Delivery Sys and						
Dressing Change						
Date IV Inserted						
Other Interventions						
(Specify)						
Patient Teaching (Document)						
Discharge Planning (Document)						
Emotional Support (Document)						
Referral/Consult. (Document)						
Stool (describe)						
Weight						
Initials						

INITIALS	SIGNATURE/TITLE	INITIALS	SIGNATURE/TITLE

SUGGESTIONS FOR RECORDING

Turn/Transfer*
Self
1 assist.
2 assist. (Difficult)

List the following under "Other Interventions."

I. **Hygiene:**
   a. Shampoo
   b. Shave
   c. Eye Care

II. **Functional:**
   a. ROM (Passive or Active)
   b. Exercises (spec.)

III. **Pulmonary Rx**
   a. Suction
   b. Turn, cough, deep breathe
   c. Postural drainage/cupping
   d. Incentive Spirometer
   e. Oxygen Therapy (specify)
   f. Respirator
   g. Vital Capacity

IV. **Wound Care:**
   a. Simple
   b. Extensive
   c. Heat Lamp

V. **Girths**

VI. **Traction Check**

VII. **Circulation, motion, sensation checks**

VIII. **Anti-embolism stockings**

IX. **Tube Care (specify N/G, foley, etc.)**

X. **Special Needs**
   Isolation/Isolette (specify)
   Assistive Devices
   Protective Devices

XI. **Electrode Care**

XII. **Monitor** (specify mechanical, visual)

XIII. **24 hour Attendance**

XIV. **Assist Patient Off Unit** (spec.)

KEY
proc. = procedure
spec. = specify
coll. = collection
sys. = system
assist. = assistance

FIGURE 33-1

Patient care flowsheet.

and emergency department (exclusive of the budget needed for boarders). Consequently, in determining the nursing hourly rate allocation, costs such as those for indirect administrative and indirect overhead functions had to be allocated between the unbundled nursing accounts and other nursing accounts.

Nursing managers are responsible and accountable for patient unit secretaries and patient care supplies. However, the decision was made that these expenses belonged in the room rate as a part of the hotel and board charges and did not qualify as nursing care costs.

Using these decision rules, the hourly rate of $18 was determined for 1986. The components of the hourly rates for the first 2 years (1985 and 1986) are found in Table 33-5. A separate nursing charge structure is used for patients boarded in our emergency department for clinical observation and monitoring. In this area, patients are charged for 13 minutes of nursing care, that is $3.90 for each hour of stay in the boarding area. Thus a patient in the

boarding unit with a stay of 18 hours would have a nursing charge of $70. Stays in the boarding unit are limited to a maximum of 24 hours. Patients who cannot be discharged within that period of time must be admitted.

Because of New York's charge control law, SMH's financial officers determined that there would be no operating margin added to the nursing care hourly charge. This is an individual decision to be made by each institution. Most institutions probably would choose to add profit margins and move from the hourly costs depicted in Table 33-5 to charges that are higher than costs (Van Slyck, 1985).

Reducing the room rate is the final step in unbundling nursing charges from the all-inclusive room rate. Table 33-6 reports the room rate reductions in our first 2 years. In 1985 (the first year of charging for nursing care), the room rates were reduced on the average of 30%. In 1986, room rates were reduced approximately 5.6%. In 1986, the nursing and finance office projections are built on a total of 233,170 patient days with projected nursing charges of $26,837,334.

With variable billing for nursing care, patients receiving more care are charged higher rates. On the general patient care units, daily charges have ranged from $56 to $155; while on the intensive care units, they have ranged from $142 to $369.

Developing the billing system. Collaboration among nurse administrators and information systems and financial management staff is essential for

TABLE 33-4
Sample nursing patient classification summary sheet

Name: John Doe		ID#: 577809386144	
Date	Class[a]	SOW/Day[b]	Care Unit[c]
3/08/86	3	29	834
3/09/86	3	30	834
3/10/86	3	28	834
3/11/86	3	27	834
3/12/86	3	28	834
3/12/86	3	28	934
3/13/86	3	28	834
3/14/86	3	30	834
3/15/86	2	23	834
3/16/86	2	24	834
3/17/86	2	18	834

[a]Class = Acuity category or the relative amount of nursing care required by a patient
[b]SOW/Day = Daily sum of weights
[c]Care Unit = Telemetry & Medicine (see Table 33-2)

TABLE 33-5
Components of 1985 and 1986 nursing hourly rates

COMPONENT	1985	1986
Direct salary and benefits	$14.71	$15.91
Indirect administrative costs	1.34	1.98
Indirect overhead costs	.06	.08
TOTAL	$16.11	$17.97
Hourly rate for nursing care	$16.11	$18

establishing a reliable billing system. In a 741-bed hospital with an occupancy rate averaging 90%, an automated system was critical. However, because SMH does not yet have a fully automated patient information system, we had to develop a billing system based on the NPCS instruments that were being optically scanned.

A computer program reads the scanned data and calculates the category of nursing acuity to be assigned to each patient by summing the weights of each checked indicator. Each patient is classified once daily on the day shift, and that classification is completed by 3 p.m. Arrangements must be made to prevent a dual charge in case a patient is transferred to another unit and the nurses on both units classify the patient. If this problem occurs, the classification with the

higher sum of weights is used to determine category assignment and daily charge. This rule seems to be the fairest to all patients.

For those patients who become more acutely ill in the evening and are transferred to an ICU after classification forms have been completed, they are billed the lower unit charge for that hospital day. When they are released from the ICU, they will probably be billed the higher charge for that day.

To enter the charge on the patient's bill, the nursing acuity daily file is matched against the running midnight census files. Another guideline is that every patient in the hospital at midnight is charged for nursing care for the previous day. This is similar to the Hospital of Saint Raphael's variable billing system in New Haven, CT (Ballard, Barach, & Cullen, 1985). The guideline also follows the industry standard of charging for the day of admission and not charging for the day of discharge. Any patient who has not been classified is assigned the fixed charge designated for the respective unit.

Other computer programs have been designed to produce the required management information reports. These include programs to prepare monthly, quarterly, and annual NPCS summary reports providing summary data by unit per category. Table 33-7 illustrates the reporting format of the NPCS data for the orthopedic units.

The monthly, quarterly, and annual revenue reports are additional management data provided by the billing system. Table 33-8 is an example of the fourth

TABLE 33-6
Room rates before and after unbundling nursing care

ALL INCLUSIVE 1984 ROOM RATE		1985 ROOM RATE (NURSING UN-BUNDLED)	1986 ROOM RATE (NURSING UN-BUNDLED)
Private	$310	$230	$220
Semipri-			
vate	280	200	190
ICU	750	500	460
Nursery	120	75	70

TABLE 33-7
NPCS data for orthopedics between 1/1/86 and 3/31/86

UNIT		FIXED	CATEGORY				TOTAL
			1	2	3	4	
514	Patient Days	21	278	757	841	208	2105
	% per Unit	1	13.21	35.96	39.95	9.88	100
534	Patient Days	15	311	742	848	215	2131
	% per Unit	0.7	14.59	34.82	39.79	10.09	100
Total Patient Days		36	589	1499	1689	423	4236
% per Service		0.85	13.9	35.39	39.87	9.9	100

TABLE 33-8
1985 Fourth quarter orthopedics nursing revenue report

	OCTOBER		NOVEMBER		DECEMBER		
UNIT	NUMBER OF CHARGES	REVENUE ($)	NUMBER OF CHARGES	REVENUE ($)	NUMBER OF CHARGES	REVENUE ($)	TOTAL QUARTERLY REVENUE ($)
Ortho 512	664	46,695	631	46,004	685	49,249	141,948
Ortho 534	667	45,790	624	44,136	679	48,775	138,701
TOTAL	1,331	92,485	1,255	90,140	1,364	98,024	280,649

quarter nursing revenue report for the orthopedic units. The nurse administrators realize that charges do not equal revenue. However, because all other services at SMH use the terms "charges" and "revenues" interchangeably in their reports, the nursing report is intended to be consistent.

Variance analysis is an important management control function (Finkler, 1985). Nurse administrators are responsible for identifying and explaining unexpected variances. Nursing patient classification data when combined with worked hours can be used to monitor productivity with explanations of significant variances (Dale & Mable, 1983; Evans et al., 1980).

Variances must also be explained in terms of monthly charge and expense reports. Each patient care unit is expected to generate charges that exceed staff expenses because indirect administrative and overhead costs as well as direct nursing care costs are factored into the hourly nursing care rates. When negative variances appear, the causes must be determined, and corrective action taken when possible. Variance analysis coupled with expert judgment determines when adjustments should be made to patient charges for nursing care.

Midyear charge corrections. Whenever significant changes occur in unit patient care technology, services provided by other departments that affect nursing care, case mix of patients, or staff mix of staff numbers, the hours assigned to patient classification categories must be adjusted. Daily monitoring of acuity reports and analyses along with the observations of clinical leaders will provide the data

required for deciding whether to revalidate the hours assignments. Depending on the perceived variance, revalidation may be done by a panel of experts or by repeat time studies (Giovannetti & Mayer, 1984).

The entry on the patient bill for nursing care. Another important decision that must be made involves how the patient bill entry should appear. At SMH, the nurse administrators wanted the entry to state "nursing care." Figure 33-2 is a sample summary portion of a patient's bill.

BILLING INQUIRIES ABOUT NURSING CARE CHARGES

At the time of preparation, variable billing for nursing care at SMH was 15 months old. The patient billing and account offices have explained nursing charges to many patients, insurers, and interested parties while explaining charges for multiple services provided by other departments. Usually their explanations suffice.

With an average of 60 patients discharged daily and conservatively considering 450 days in the 15 months of variable billing, we have discharged approximately 27,000 patients. The nurse administrators have been involved directly in resolving only 17 billing inquiries. The Office of Methods, Procedures, and Quality Control is assigned the responsibility of managing the patient classification and billing systems as well as preparing and disseminating all management information reports related to the systems. This office also receives inquiry referrals and tracks responses. The 17 billing inquiries received to date can be grouped in three major areas: (a) lack of clarity or understanding

THE UNIVERSITY OF ROCHESTER STRONG MEMORIAL HOSPITAL
601 ELMWOOD AVENUE, ROCHESTER, NEW YORK 14642
PATIENT ACCOUNTS OFFICE — OFFICE HOURS 9:30 AM-4:00 PM
Area Code — 716-275-3351

PLEASE REFER TO
BILLING NUMBER
WHEN CONTACTING

THE PATIENT
ACCOUNTS OFFICE

BILLING NUMBER	ADMITTED	DISCHARGED	DAYS IN HOSPITAL	BILLING DATE	F.C.	PAGE
053158941327	06/04/86	06/12/86	8	06/19/86	20	1

PATIENT DOE, JOHN

BILL TO DOE, JOHN
25 SIMPSON AVE.
ROCHESTER, NY 14618

INSURANCE	POLICY NUMBER
ROCH BLUE CROSS	V 316729-10

DATE OF SERVICE	PROCEDURE CODE	DESCRIPTION	NO. OF SERVICES RENDERED	TOTAL CHARGES	INSURANCE NO. 1	INSURANCE NO. 2	PATIENT AMOUNT
		SUMMARY BY SERVICE					
		ROOM-PRIVATE	6	1326.00			
		ROOM-ICU	2	920.00			
		010 DIAGNOSTIC RADIOLOG	8	344.00			
		012 OPERATING ROOM	30	3189.94			
		014 ANESTHESIOLOGY	46	905.10			
		015 RESP. THERAPY	12	580.30			
		020 PHARMACY	08	436.45			
		022 BLOOD BANK	8	153.00			
		025 SOLUTIONS	2	28.10			
		026 SPECIAL EQUIP	1	8.00			
		027 MICROBIOLOGY	1	13.00			
		030 HEMATOLOGY LAB	16	166.60			
		038 CLINICAL LABS	26	413.20			
		39/31 SPECIAL LABS	1	28.20			
		040 HEART STATION	6	216.00			
		600 NURSING CARE	8	1434.00			
		PAYMENTS	1	217.00 −			
		TOTAL DUE		10161.89			
		TOTAL RECEIPTS		217.00 −			
		NET SUMMARY TOTALS		9944.89			

THIS IS THE ONLY DETAILED BILL YOU WILL RECEIVE WITHOUT AN ADDITIONAL CHARGE
— PLEASE SAVE FOR YOUR RECORDS —

INSURANCE BENEFITS ARE ESTIMATED
AND MAY BE ADJUSTED UPON RECEIPT OF THE FINAL INSURANCE PAYMENT

TOTAL CHARGES LESS CREDITS   10161.89   9975.89   31.00 −

DETACH AND RETURN THIS PORTION WITH YOUR PAYMENT

DOE, JOHN	053158941327	06/04/86	06/12/86	06/19/86	31.00 −
PATIENT NAME	BILLING NUMBER	ADMITTED	DISCHARGED	BILLING DATE	PATIENT BALANCE

YOU MAY RECEIVE SEPARATE BILLS FROM YOUR PHYSICIANS, INCLUDING RADIOLOGIST AND ANESTHESIOLOGIST.
THE RED CROSS SUPPLIES BLOOD WITHOUT COST. HOWEVER, THERE IS A SERVICE CHARGE FOR THE PROCESSING AND ADMINISTRATION OF BLOOD.

AMOUNT DUE WITHIN 30 DAYS

MAKE CHECKS PAYABLE TO: **STRONG MEMORIAL HOSPITAL**

FIGURE 33-2
Summary portion of a patient bill.

of what constitutes nursing care charges or how such charges are determined on a daily basis; (b) suspected billing errors that included no charges, double charges, or inadequate charges for nursing care; and (c) challenges that nursing care charges were too high or unwarranted.

Each inquiry was resolved to the patient's or third party's satisfaction. Nurses must be able to describe in understandable terms exactly what nursing care encompasses and to help patients and families understand the value of nursing care. Like any valuable service, nursing care has a separate and distinct charge. For too long, nursing care has been hidden in the room rate. Coming out or being unbundled as a separate, distinct daily charge that varies with the amount of nursing care provided is essential for complete pricing of our health-care products. Variable billing also reflects nursing's "coming of age." Nursing care is a scarce health resource, and as such, must be valued and charged for.

Inquiries about hospital bills by patients, families, and third-party payers are opportunities for public education about nursing care. During our first year of variable billing, all inquiries have been handled personally by the clinical nursing chiefs on each service. These nursing directors have involved the head nurses and staff from the units where the patients received care. At general staff and management meetings, all inquiries and their resolutions have been discussed.

Collaboration with the staff in the patient billing office is essential. The managers in this area have been instrumental in helping us successfully launch a nursing care billing effort. These key individuals needed to learn about the NPCS, the hours study, and the process by which patient charges were determined. We also shared our efforts to build an audit trail through documentation in the patient record. These business office managers and their staff have successfully answered the vast majority of inquiries and forwarded only 17 inquiries for our direct responses.

PROBLEMS TO BE ANTICIPATED AND RESOLVED

Each institution must make its own decision on when and how frequently each patient will be classified. At SMH, we made the decision that a single patient classification on the day shift was satisfactory to capture the patient's acuity level. Early in the development of the system (approximately 8 years ago), we completed a study in which each patient was classified on the day shift and again on the evening shift. No significant changes in acuity categories were found, and the single classification on the day shift became the norm. In a study classifying patients on the day and evening shifts for a 2-month period, Grant et al. (1982) reported similar findings.

Each staff group must decide the time of day for classifying patients. At SMH, the majority of staff prefer to classify patients in the afternoon. If the patient is to be transferred to another unit during the day shift, sending and receiving nurses may confer and agree that patient classification will be done by the unit providing the highest amount of nursing care to the patient. Patients who transfer at other times of the day (such as evenings or nights) are not reclassified.

Ensuring a manual back-up system is imperative. One must always be prepared for scanner or computer problems. Consequently, we have devised a manual system in which staff members must manually code the patient's unit and identification data as well as classify the patient. Unfortunately, when humans transcribe numbers, there are increasing chances for error. We created a 48-hour period during which patient classification categories, identification number errors, and other potential problems can be corrected. Every effort is expended to be thorough and accurate the first time. Needless edits and corrections due to carelessness consume precious human resources and cannot be afforded.

SYSTEMS MAINTENANCE AND REVISION

The nursing billing system is expected to generate approximately $27 million in charges in 1986. Such a fiscal responsibility requires daily monitoring, periodic audits, and revisions as needs are identified. One administrative office should be designated as responsible and accountable for the billing system. This office can be charged with working with all the essential and supporting departments and assuring that the system is effective and that appropriate charges are entered and captured.

Rater reliability is critical in a system that establishes the basis for charging patients for nursing care. Quarterly rate reliability studies and periodic audits are also an assigned responsibility of the designated administrative office. Daily, weekly, monthly, quarterly, and annual reports on patient classification and charges must be generated, distributed, and analyzed. The Coordinator of Methods, Procedures, and Quality Control (who is responsible for our system) is also accountable for meetings with external auditors. System monitoring, maintenance, and revision are essential for effectiveness and efficiency.

WHAT DIFFERENCE DOES VARIABLE CHARGING FOR NURSING CARE MAKE?

Nurses have always had professional accountability for their nursing practice. With unbundling and variable charging for nursing care, nurses now have economic accountability as well. How good it feels to be regarded as a revenue center, not simply a cost center. What a difference it makes when nurses classify their patients and accurately account for relevant indicators with retrievable documentation in the record.

We have made significant progress in helping patients and families understand why nursing care has been unbundled from the room rate. There have been television interviews, newspaper features, and articles in hospital publications. During the 1986 celebration of National Nurses Week, the Staff Nurse Executive Committee offered a seminar entitled "Nursing Care—What We Charge For" to the general public and medical center staff.

Product costing is readily available when individual patients are billed for nursing care using the patient classification system. These charges are entered into the patient's record along with all other services delivered. Upon discharge, the total charges are available.

These charges can also be aggregated in whatever manner the institution decides. For example, we can provide reports with nursing charges by DRG as well as by ICD9-CM. When program management is of interest, we can aggregate and display charges by program or requested product lines. Captured nursing patient classification data facilitate clinical studies that address nursing acuity levels of particular patient groups. Program and hospital budgeting can be more accurately projected and monitored. Finally, comparative studies can be undertaken among similar institutions that relate to patients and not to the widget-like entity of an occupied bed (see Table 33-9).

TABLE 33-9
Comparison of Strong Memorial Hospital (SMH) and Stanford average nursing hours for four DRGs

DRG		SMH (SOVIE ET AL., 1984)		STANFORD (MITCHELL ET AL., 1984)	
		Number of patients	Average nursing hours	Number of patients	Average nursing hours
121	Acute myocardial infarction with cardiovascular complications; discharged alive	91	69.59	13	109
122	Acute myocardial infarction without cardiovascular complications; discharged alive	211	56.58	12	68
209	Major joint procedures	232	93.86	32	88
210	Other/hip/femur procedures; Age 70 &/or complications and comorbidities	78	143.00	32	95

Although differences in sample size exist, each study compared the average nursing care hours provided to patients in four DRGs. The availability of such data will encourage comparative studies that may help us find ways to do things differently and better for patients.

BUSINESS SENSE IN PRACTICE

The identification of nursing costs helps nurses understand the business aspects of their practice. Nurses at SMH know that direct nursing costs that were previously included in room costs ranged from 18% to 24% (Sovie et al., 1984). They know that in the first year of variable billing we reduced room rates approximately 30%. Nurses know that in 1986 they are expected to generate $27 million in revenue. This context for practice differs drastically from the prior era in which we inaccurately believed that nurses and nursing care were responsible for high costs and therefore should be the first place for reductions when the belt tightened.

Economic and professional accountability are the building blocks of successful image makers. The excellence of nursing care is recognized, and charges are generated based on the variable needs and care given to individual patients. We are no longer invisible. Coming out of the room rate and charging for nursing care feels great!

REFERENCES

Alward, R.R. (1983). Patient classification systems: The ideal vs. reality. *The Journal of Nursing Administration, 13*(2), 14-19.

Ballard, D., Barach, K.B., & Cullen, J.J. (1985). The variable nursing charge system at the Hospital of Saint Raphael. In F.A. Shaffer (Ed.), *Costing out nursing: Pricing our product* (pp. 101-111). New York: National League for Nursing.

Dale, R.L., & Mable, R.J. (1983). Nursing classification system: Foundation for personnel planning and control. *The Journal of Nursing Administration 13*(2), 10-13.

DeJoseph, J.F., Petree, B.J., & Ross, W. (1984). Costing and charging: Pricing care in OB. *Nursing Management, 15*(12), 36-37.

Ethridge, P. (1985). The case for billing by patient acuity. *Nursing Management, 16*(8), 38-41.

Evans, S.K., Laundon, T., & Yamamoto, W.G. (1980). Projecting staffing requirements for intensive care units. *Journal of Nursing Administration, 10*(7), 34-42.

Finkler, S.A. (1982). The distinction between costs and charges. *Annals of Internal Medicine, 96*(1), 102-109.

Finkler, S.A. (1985). Flexible budget variance analysis extended to patient acuity and DRGs. *Health Care Management Review, 10*(4), 21-31.

Giovannetti, P., & Mayer, G.G. (1984). Building confidence in patient classification systems. *Nursing Management, 15*(8), 31-34.

Grant, S.E., Bellinger, A.C., & Sweda, B.L. (1982). Measuring productivity through patient classification. *Nursing Administration Quarterly, 6*(3), 77-83.

Higgerson, N.J., & Van Slyck, A. (1982). Variable billing for services: New fiscal direction for nursing. *The Journal of Nursing Administration, 12*(6), 20-27.

Holbrook, F.K. (1972). Charging by level of nursing care. *Hospitals, 46*(16), 80-88.

Lagona, T.G., & Stritzel, M.M. (1984). Nursing care requirements as measured by DRG. *The Journal of Nursing Administration, 14*(5), 15-18.

LaViolette, S. (1979). Classification systems remedy billing inequity. *Modern Healthcare, 9*(9), 32-33.

Maher, A.B., & Dolan, B. (1982). Determining costs of nursing services. *Nursing Management, 13*(9), 17-21.

Maine's DONs adopt common strategy for costing. (1985). *American Journal of Nursing, 85*(10), 1166-1167.

Maine's 42 hospitals, obeying a unique new law, begin to charge their patients for nursing care. (1985). *American Journal of Nursing, 85*(10), 1166-1167, 1190, 1192.

Mitchell, M., Miller, J., Welches, L., & Walker, D. (1984). Determining costs of direct nursing care by DRGs. *Nursing Management, 15*(4), 29-32.

Sandrick, K. (1985). Pricing nursing services. *Hospitals, 59*(22), 75-78.

Sovie, M.D., Tarcinale, M.A., VanPutte, A.W., & Stunden, A.E. (1984). *A correlation study of nursing patient classification, DRGs, other significant patient variables, and cost of patient care.* Unpublished study, University of Rochester, Rochester, NY.

Sovie, M.D., Tarcinale, M.A., VanPutte, A.W., & Stunden, A.E. (1985). Amalgam of nursing acuity, DRGs and cost. *Nursing Management, 16*(3), 22-42.

VanPutte, A.W., Sovie, M.D., Tarcinale, M.A., & Stunden, A.E. (1985). Accounting for patient acuity: The nursing time dimension. *Nursing Management, 16*(10), 27-36.

Van Slyck, A. (1985). Nursing services: Costing, pricing and variable billing. In F.A. Shaffer (Ed.), *Costing out nursing: Pricing our product* (pp. 39-53). New York: National League for Nursing.

Wolf, G.A., Lesic, L.K., & Leak, A.G. (1986). Primary nursing: The impact on nursing costs within DRGs. *The Journal of Nursing Administration, 16*(3), 9-11.

Wood, C.T. (1982). Relate hospital charges to use of services. *Harvard Business Review, 60*(2), 123-130.

CHAPTER **34**

The Impact of Nurse Managed Care on the Cost of Nurse Practice and Nurse Satisfaction

Carol A. Stillwaggon, RN, EdD

Here we are in the middle of yet another nursing crisis. It is predicted that this crisis is of even greater magnitude than previous ones, due to rising patient acuity levels, an aging population and a dramatic decline in nursing school enrollments.[1] The shortage is compounded by the attractive career opportunities now available to women and by the dwindling supply of high school graduates who previously made up the pool of potential nursing students. With each crisis in this profession, the issues become increasingly complex. All of these factors, coupled with the cost containment issues on national and state levels, attest to the fact that this crisis will not be solved easily. Radical changes in our nursing care delivery system will be necessary if we are to continue meeting the nursing needs of patients while conserving our scarce nursing resources. This suggests the need for a radical departure from tradition in the analysis of the nursing shortage. We must ask whether this is a true shortage or whether we are abusing our limited nursing resource by less than appropriate use of it?

This article reports on a study carried out at Saint Francis Hospital and Medical Center in Hartford,

Reprinted from *The Journal of Nursing Administration,* Vol. 19, No. 11, with permission of J.B. Lippincott Company © 1989.

Connecticut. The study was designed to address the issues of appropriate nurse use and nurse satisfaction. The rationale underlying the study evolved from years of practice and observation in the acute Hospital setting.

How many times have nurses been heard to say, "they're telling my patient he has cancer tonight; I wish I could be here to support him," or "I have been with this patient all through the first and second stages of labor and now I have to leave when it's time for her to deliver." These statements and others like them repeated over and over again indicate that something is wrong. It was not uncommon for a nurse who had to miss a significant point in a patient's hospitalization to have spent several hours of "on duty time" carrying out non-nursing tasks.

Thus, the realization began to emerge that nurses were practicing nursing based on the demands of bureaucracy rather than on the nursing care needs of patients. For example, nurses go to lunch and dinner based on the cafeteria's established hours of service; nurses are on duty to "cover a nursing unit;" nurses work sequential hours because "it has always been done that way!" Look further and question why patients in the acute care setting always come to the nurse and not vice versa. Follow a patient from admission to discharge; the patient comes to the emergency room to one group of nurses, is admitted to CCU (another group of nurses), transferred three days later to a telemetry unit, and on and on. At each transfer point there is new or additional nursing assessment, planning, documentation, and repetitive actions consume hours and dollars. In this acute care setting we are constantly asking the patient to adjust to us and our methods and our boundaries. Most of these factors were a by-product of our nursing care delivery system and were within our power to control and change. Therefore, when faced with the dilemma of cost constraint and nursing shortage, our nursing administrative group chose the present nursing care delivery system to examine for potential system change.

Nursing care delivery systems, we discovered, were directly bound to prevalent social values and management theories in any given era. In the early 1900s, functional nursing predominated. This era reflected the scientific management beliefs of Weber, et al.[2] In that era, we were a different people, predominantly immigrants adopting to an emerging industrialized society. Thus pyramidal management, heavy supervision, rules, policies, and procedures were necessary. In the late '40s and early '50s humanistic management emerged with an emphasis on human values and Maslow's[3] work on the hierarchy of human needs. These values, coupled with a shortage of nurses, provided a basis for the emergence of team nursing. Team nursing was conceived to foster a return to professionalism, through augmentation of the professional nurses' leadership role and greater attention to the individual needs of patients.[4] At the same time, in response to Maslow's work, hospitals began to provide employees with paid leave, insurance, and differentiated wage scales. However, the bureaucratic structures remained intact.

Nursing continued to seek better methods for delivery of nursing care to patients and the next delivery model to emerge was the primary nursing system. Closely aligned with the writings of Herzberg,[5] primary nursing focused on nurse/patient satisfaction as an outcome of a trusting, goal-directed relationship. Primary nursing has been known as the most "professional" system, but it continued to be affected by a bureaucratic, pyramidal hospital structure.

Today's literature and the concepts of Ouchi,[6] Naisbitt,[7] and Toffler,[8] speak to the changing social needs of our century: the crumbling of the closed system pyramid to be replaced by open systems; the role of supervision being changed to networking through peer consultation; and the elimination of procedure books to be supplanted by individual innovation. How could we as nurse administrators change our nursing delivery system to conform to these changing social needs, and yet remain cost effective and responsive to the current nursing shortage?

The system we envisioned maintained the best attributes of primary nursing, ie, professional nurse responsibility for each patient throughout hospitalization, accountability for nursing assessment, and planning and evaluation of patient outcomes. The registered nurses' authority for delegation of tasks to support staff was already a part of our primary system but could be significantly expanded, in order to emphasize the professional nurse's role in process.

What was eliminated from our proposed system were factors that restrained our current delivery system, especially any form of hourly commitment to the institution. This embodies more than self-scheduling, in fact we did away with the work scheduling. Scheduling, according to Webster,[9] implies a timetable, and patients' needs seldom conform to timetables. Time schedules also implied a set number of hours in the possible absence of patient needs. This could represent a costly misuse of nursing dollars in addition to a diversion of valuable nursing resources. Schedules, we thought, also subtly implied that nurses were unable to determine, through assessment and contracted patient agreement, when nursing care was needed or most appropriate.

In the developing system, we further proposed that the patient would maintain the same nurse throughout hospitalization. The patient would not be subjected to a new nurse at each organizational boundary. This would solidify the nurse/patient relationship and eliminate repetitive actions. Again, repetitive actions are costly and inefficient, as well as being an annoyance to the patient.

The delivery system, named Managed Nursing Care (MNC), began to take on specific characteristics as outlined in Table 34-1.

TABLE 34-1
Distinctions between the traditional and investigative systems

	TRADITIONAL SYSTEM	INVESTIGATIONAL MODEL (MANAGED NURSING CARE)
Communication	Generally downward Isolation from peers	Collegial relationships Networking with peers
Initiation	Inhibited by routines of care and multiple procedures	Innovation and experimentation encouraged
Practice		
Control of Hours worked	40/hours/week Scheduled meals Scheduled break Control of non-nursing tasks	Freedom to move in and out of the system based on patient need. Non-nursing tasks eliminated.
Freedom in Practice	Freedom to practice dictated by procedure	Guided by standard care

In addition to professional responsibility for process and time management, the major changes in Managed Nursing Care related to; communications, initiative and practice.

Communications

In the present hierarchial system communication is generally downward. Although primary nursing has fostered some change in this direction, it has not become a focus of change. The registered nurse still tends to look upward for direction and is therefore usually more or less isolated from peers. The Managed Nursing Care system encourages and is partially dependent on peer professionals for purposes of consultative networking. This action of networking with peers ought to foster a stronger collegial relationship and collaborate interaction among professional nurses.

Initiative

Another focus of Managed Nursing Care was to foster initiative and innovation in nursing practice and eliminate routine as much as possible. Routines implied an hourly progression through a set of traditional activities which had little to do with individual patient assessment or need. These "traditional activities" were primarily the tasks associated with nursing practice that could be labeled as hygienic in nature or "physician comfort" measures.

If the nursing action or adaption of care was better for the patient, or determined by patient need, it was encouraged. In this arena, we hoped to break down the argument that "we've always done it that way."

Practice

Practice, or the application of the art and science of nursing, was broken down into two categories:

Control of Hours Worked. There was no preconceived institutional expectation of required hours, ie, 40/week, 8/per day, etc. The professional nurse would come to the hospital as necessary to provide necessary nursing care for a patient population.

Whether that activity required one hour a day or 15 hours a day, was a discretionary judgment made by nurse/patient contract. The only requirements the professional nurse would have to fulfill would be to maintain the stipulated standard of care; and to reach an agreement with the patient as to when nursing care would be most appropriately rendered.

Thus, the nurse would be given the freedom to cross artificial institutional barriers, such as unit barriers, and move in and out of the system based on the needs of the patient and the nurse.

Control of practice would also embody the removal of non-nursing task expectations from the professional nurses' responsibilities. These tasks would be delegated to non-professional staff or back to the department of origin. Included in this subsection would be nursing-related tasks that did not require professional management such as; vital signs, ambulation, body weights, feeding, etc.

STUDY PARAMETERS

Once the administrative group had defined the nursing delivery system, we discussed potential sites for implementation. Because Managed Nursing Care represented a dramatic departure from tradition, it was decided that a critical care area would not be selected for initial study. We also wanted our study to include cases that required a high degree of nursing care similarities so that we could more easily draw conclusions regarding required hours of care. The area of women/child health was suggested and agreed upon for the following reasons:

1) it was a low risk area, 2) multiple similar cases could be isolated and studied for nursing care costs; and 3) due to the high delivery rate two studies could be run simultaneously; studying costs in both the Primary system and the managed nursing care system.

To rule out as many variables as possible, the patient population was defined as follows:

- 100 cases* (50 in the traditional system and 50 in the pilot study) were to be included in the parallel study.
- Cases for inclusion would be limited to anticipated normal spontaneous deliveries without anti-partum or post-partum pathophysiology.

---

* 100 cases of normal spontaneous delivery represented 10% of all normal deliveries without co-morbidity, in 1987.

- Normal infant without comorbidity (100 cases of normal spontaneous delivery represented 10% of all normal delivery without anti and post-partum pathophysiology on an annual basis).

With the system defined, the study site selected, we restated our research questions:

1. Could nursing care be delivered in a more cost effective manner when freed from bureaucratic constraints?
2. Could nurse satisfaction be maintained or increased in the Managed Nursing Care System?

The entire proposal was presented to administration and received approval for a pilot study. It's hard to be against a study which could possibly identify the need for *fewer* hours of professional nursing care.

Since a representative group of nursing staff members has been involved in the planning stages, it was now appropriate to further discuss the proposal with the entire staff and to seek volunteers for implementation. At this stage, we received a wide divergence of reactions. Almost in replication of the bell curve, a small percentage of staff said "it would never work," a few were eager and willing to try, and the vast majority took a "wait and see" attitude.

The only requirements for volunteering for the study were a minimum of six months of practice in women and children's division, specifically, labor and delivery and/or family centered care; and satisfactory evaluations in the women/child health division.

Since the nurses working in the women and child health division already took mother and baby assignments, the prime area for reeducation was in the labor and delivery units. This experience had been provided in an original orientation and in episodic assignments but needed to be repeated to facilitate the project. Likewise the nurse from labor and delivery needed to be refreshed regarding mother/baby care.

The expected case load for the project was anticipated to be the same as the case load in labor and delivery or family centered care:

1. Labor and Delivery: two normal, uncomplicated patients. Case load decreasing dependent on the stage of labor.

2. Mother/Baby: Usual assignment — 3 mothers, 3 babies.

DATA COLLECTION
Costs

To measure true costs of nursing care, weekly tabulation of nursing hours worked was collected from actual time cards. If patients in the investigational model required care after the assigned nurse has left the hospital, these hours were tabulated and included in the weekly computations.

Nurse Satisfaction

A Likert-type rating scale was developed by the investigator to measure the degree of nurse satisfaction with the two systems, especially in relation to:

1. Freedom to decide what nursing actions were required by patients;
2. Control over who would perform the work to be done and the nurses' freedom to move in and out of the system.

IMPLEMENTATION

The registered professional nurse was responsible for the process of nursing according to the defined standards of practice. The registered professional nurse had the authority to either delegate the tasks of nursing to an alternate care giver or carry out the task if this would facilitate implementation of the care plan.

Another aspect emphasized was the nurses' freedom to leave the hospital upon completion of nursing care. The actual time for the nurses' presence or absence was decided verbally by concensus between patient and nurse.

Nurses practicing in the investigational model received their patients upon the patient's admission to the hospital's labor room. They stayed with the patient throughout labor and delivery. This process minimized the time spent in nursing assessment, reassessment, formulating care plans, documentation, and additional care planning. As the patient moved from one area to another, ie, labor room, delivery room, recovery room and finally the postpartum unit, the nurse went with her. This practice also fostered continuity of care and the identification of "my patient," and "my nurse."

The nurses could also use periods of patient quiescence to go to alternate units to care for the other patients in their case load. Ultimately, the nurse provided care when it was more needed and most acceptable to the patients.

The nurses decided how long they would be at the hospital to meet the nursing needs of their patients. When these needs were met, they had the freedom to leave, whether they had been there for 12 hours or only two hours.

When the professional nurse prepared to leave the hospital she informed the head nurse and gave a report of care to the nurse who would assume her patient responsibilities in her absence. This was a crucial juncture. It was anticipated that the professional nurse would absent herself from the hospital when all required care had been completed. Should an unexpected crisis occur with a patient in the absence of her nurse, the covering nurse would intervene as usual according to hospital protocols and in addition notify the patient's project nurse. The project would then have various choices:

1. Ascertain that the problem had been satisfactorily resolved, (ie, call patient for her interpretation).
2. If unresolved, the nurse would initiate active follow-up, such as coming to the hospital to assess and intervene, calling an MD and receiving further prescriptions if necessary, or documenting plan, action and outcome.

OUTCOMES OF THE STUDY
Costs

Based on the hours of care, the collected data supported the hypothesis that nursing care costs were lower when based on the actual needs of patients versus the conformity to a pre-scheduled wage and hour system.

Table 34-2 indicates that the mean cost in the investigational model was $61.71 less per case. On the

TABLE 34-2

Mean hours of care and cost per case: Traditional model vs. investigational model (P > .0001)

	TRADITIONAL	INVESTIGATIONAL
Hours of Care per Case	20 hours	14 hours 44 minutes
Cost of care per Case	$222.60	$160.89

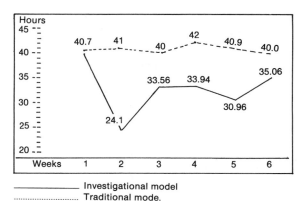

———— Investigational model
.... Traditional mode.

FIGURE 34-1

Average hours worked per week by Registered Nurses in the investigational model and in the traditional model of nursing practice.

two-tailed T-test this was significant at the 5% level of confidence. Table 34-2 also shows the mean cost of care per case for both the investigational and the traditional model.

The cost factors in Table 34-2 were calculated by multiplying the total hours of care by the average registered nurse salary. The difference in the mean hours of care per case is noted to be five hours and 56 minutes less in the investigational model.

Figure 34-1 presents the difference in the hours of care worked per week by nurses in the two models. There is little room for variation in the traditional model since 40 hours is the norm for full-time employees. When nurses had options regarding time use, the hours spent at the hospital decreased. However, the patient's satisfaction with care received remained high.

Nurse Satisfaction

The Likert-type scale measuring nurse satisfaction was filled out by the nurses at the completion of the study; the same nurses completed the scale four weeks after their return to traditional practice. Table 34-3 indicates the nurses' high degree of dissatisfaction with the Traditional Model of care.

The same scale was completed by the nurses in the new delivery model. All of these nurses indicated a high (5) degree of satisfaction with the delivery system as it related to defined parameters. The only item that scored below 5 was item No. 3 under Freedom "to decide who will perform nursing actions."

The mean score in this cateogry was a 3 with a range of 2-4. (1 = low, 5 = high). The nurses explained that although they "had the freedom to delegate technical tasks to an alternate care giver they were at times reluctant to do so." This could have been related to co-worker resistance; or a carry-over from a tradition that dictated "the completion of all tasks."

The nurses' comments on conferences after completing the rating scales were, "The patient becomes 'my' patient" and "I got so into this that I didn't want to break for coffee or lunch."

Given accountability for time management, the nurses managed their time to the benefit of the patient, themselves, and the organization. Time management, patient management, and self-management; it was motivational theory in action.

Upon return to the traditional (40 hours/week) delivery system, the nurses comments were equally revealing. "Now we're back to the same old routines, pills, baths and babies"; "In this system you don't have to think you just follow routines"; and "You don't know what freedom is until it is taken from you."

Patient satisfaction or response to care was not studied directly in this project because we had alternative systems for measuring this response, ie, daily interviews with the Head Nurse and patients' written

TABLE 34-3
Nurse satisfaction: Traditional model mean scores*

Freedom	To decide what nursing care must be done	3
	To decide when nursing care will be done	2
	To decide who will perform nursing actions	2
Control	Hours off	1
	Time off	3
	Elimination of non-nursing tasks from practice	1

*On a scale of 1 to 5; 1 = least satisfaction; 5 = greatest satisfaction

comments on the standardized Hospital evaluation tool following discharge. But this study would not be complete without the mention of the patients' response to their care. Patients were told that they were part of a study group and the study was explained to them. However, because the standard of care would not be altered, the patients were not considered subjects. The patients' positive reactions to this system were phenomenal. They expressed their high level of satisfaction in letters to the president of the hospital, the investigator, the hospital's public relations department, and most importantly, to the nurses themselves. The patients' positive comments and tangible expressions of warmth and affection for "their nurse" did much to augment the nurses' self image and pride in their accomplishments and their profession.

SUMMARY

Our study indicates that there is an alternative to the present Primary Nursing Care Delivery System. The alternative care system was less costly than the traditional system, in the initial test area. Empowering the nurse to make pivotal decisions about nursing care and about their own time schedule elicited increased professionalism, self-pride and satisfaction in the work to be done.

The alternative system, Nurse Managed Care, may not fit all situations or in each nurse's life style, but it does offer an option that is cost effective and extremely sensitive to the appropriate use of the scarce nursing resource. It offers hospitals and nurses the opportunity to break with worn out traditions and move into the 21st Century with a purer focus; namely, nurses working with patients for the sole purpose of providing nursing care.

REFERENCES

1. Davis C. Secretary's Commission on Nursing. Final Report, Volume 1, December 1988, Washington, DC.
2. Weber M. Theory of Social and Economic Organization. 4th Edition Translation 1947. New York: Free Press, 1964.
3. Maslow A. Motivation and Personality. New York, Harper and Row, 1954.
4. Lambersten EC. Nursing Team Organization and Functioning. New York, Bureau of Publications, Teachers College, Columbia University, 1953.
5. Herzberg, F. Work and Nature of Man. New York: World Publishing, 1966.
6. Ouchi W. Theory Z. Massachusetts: Addison Wesley, 1981.
7. Naisbitt J. Megatrends. New York: Warner Books, 1982.
8. Toffler A. Future Shock. New York: Random House, 1970.
9. Webster's New Collegiate Dictionary (9th Edition). Springfield, Mass: Merriam Webster; 1987;1050.

CHAPTER **35**

Using Nursing Models to Guide Nursing Practice: Key Questions

Cynthia Flynn Capers, RN, PhD

Many nursing departments are considering use of a nursing conceptual model as a guide for clinical nursing practice.[1-4] Having served as Project Coordinator for implementation of the Neuman Systems Model as the conceptual base for nursing practice at Fitzgerald Mercy Division of Mercy Catholic Medical Center, I found that some preplanning issues must first be addressed. Consider each of the following questions in relation to your hospital setting (Table 35-1). Seek pertinent answers prior to initiating the nursing model project. This preplanning step can identify factors which facilitate, and possibly hinder, the use of a model in clinical practice. Decisions about having a conceptually guided nursing practice can then be made in light of the specific characteristics of the nursing department. If a model is to be adopted for nursing practice, more definitive plans can then be initiated.

IS THE NURSING PRACTICE ENVIRONMENT CONDUCIVE TO USING A NURSING CONCEPTUAL MODEL?

Nursing departments and units within hospitals are making strides in becoming autonomous. No matter how autonomous nurses are, however, it must be remembered that nurses do *not* practice in isolation

Reprinted from *The Journal of Nursing Administration*, Vol. 16, No. 1, with permission of J.B. Lippincott Company © 1986.

from other health care disciplines. The opposite is actually true; nurses interface with *more* health care professionals than any other hospital professional group. Thus, it is suggested that other health professionals know about plans to have a conceptually guided practice. Sharing information is important, but seeking permission is discouraged. As a strategic move, nurses may find it necessary to gain support of power groups, such as hospital administrators and physicians. The main point is that nurses must be politically astute as to how to facilitate change within the context of their specific health care environment.

A subquestion related to having a conducive environment is: What is the method of delivering nursing care to patients? Is it primary nursing? team nursing? functional nursing? Is the method of delivering care congruent with the method of thinking about and "conceptualizing" your nursing practice? For example, a holistic nursing conceptual model is more congruent with primary rather than functional nursing because the primary nurse is responsible for total care, which is not necessarily true in functional and team nursing.

Another subquestion is: What other changes are taking place within the hospital? Will these changes affect the nurses in such a way that use of conceptually guided nursing practice will be impeded? For example, many nursing departments are decentralizing nursing units. With decentralization, some units could choose *not* to implement the conceptual model

TABLE 35-1
Preplanning questions

Is the nursing practice environment conductive to using a nursing conceptual model?

Which nursing conceptual model will serve as the guide for nursing practice?

What outcomes are anticipated from using the nursing conceptual model?

Who uses the model?

How will nurses be prepared for using the model?

How and when will goal attainment be evaluated?

What financial resources are available to support the project?

---

while others could choose to do so. Is this acceptable? Would the care given still reflect the philosophical beliefs and values of the nursing department? Also, with the advent of diagnosis-related groups (DRGs) and rising costs of health care, nursing administrators face cost reductions measures such as budgetary constraints and staffing decreases. How will these factors impact with implementation of a conceptually guided nursing practice within hospital setting?

For example, having a nursing conceptual model to guide practice may enable nurses to gather a detailed data base that identifies actual and potential health care problems. Primary, secondary, and tertiary preventions as nursing interventions can be directed to the identified health care problems.[5] Consequently, nurses can be more focused and goal-directed, and ultimately, make better use of their time. This is of particular importance when nursing departments are faced with decreased staffing. I speculate that use of a nursing conceptual model to guide nursing practice is one way that quality care can be enhanced in light of staffing decreases.

WHICH NURSING CONCEPTUAL MODEL WILL SERVE AS THE GUIDE FOR NURSING PRACTICE?

The chosen nursing practice model should be congruent with the nursing philosophy. Since this phi-losophy articulates beliefs and tenets about nursing, the model should promote nursing behaviors that operationalize the philosophy. Further, the nursing model chosen should be similar to the nursing process in place prior to use of the model. If the nursing behaviors prescribed by the nursing conceptual model differ greatly from the behaviors in place, more resistance to change is likely. Likewise, if the language of the nursing model is esoteric and unfamiliar to nurses, resistance is also likely.

WHAT OUTCOMES ARE ANTICIPATED FROM USING THE NURSING CONCEPTUAL MODEL?

At the beginning of the project articulate, in measureable terms, the goals you expect to accomplish by using a nursing conceptual model in practice. Doing this forces you to be more realistic about what can be accomplished. Further, specify a projected time schedule for attaining the goals. Although a revision of the schedule will probably be necessary, a time line offers further direction to activities associated with the planning, implementation, and evaluation of the nursing project.

WHO USES THE MODEL?

Identify persons who will be directly and indirectly involved in the model's use. For example, the professional nurses (RNs) on the units are responsible for doing the initial assessment and then establishing the plan of care based on the conceptual model. The practical nurses (LPNs) may be responsible for the care of selected patients and provide input for the plan of care. The head nurses or nurse managers plan nursing activities on the unit to facilitate implementation and follow through with the project. The nursing coordinators or assistant directors of nursing have administrative responsibility for several nursing units and thus may coordinate use of the model in clinical practice.

Indirectly, the staff development nurses and clinical specialists may be responsible for the educational preparation of nurses for use of the model. The project coordinator may oversee of the planning, implementing, and evaluating of the project. Finally, the director of nursing or associate vice president of nursing has responsibility for decision making and interdisciplinary communications that make the environment conducive to having a conceptually guided nursing practice.

Each person's level of involvement must be made explicit to minimize role confusion. Further, job descriptions for each nursing position should include statements about responsibility for the conceptually guided practice.

HOW WILL NURSES BE PREPARED FOR USING THE MODEL?

This question involves a number of factors. Educational programs must be developed to prepare nurses to use the nursing conceptual model. Other subquestions must be answered: Will the educational program offer information about the model and then its use in the hospital setting, or will emphasis be placed on changes in nursing approaches and documentation process and then information on the conceptualization? That is, will an inductive or deductive approach to learning be developed? When will the educational programs be offered? What will the length of the program be? Will the educational program be required for all nurses? If so, does this mean that the nursing department will absorb class time as work time for each nurse?

Currently, nurses learn about nursing models primarily in graduate level courses. However, it is nurses from associate degree, diploma, and baccalaureate programs who provide most direct patient care in hospital settings. Since most articles and books are directed to the advanced learner, your educational program must focus on providing basic information.[6]

HOW AND WHEN WILL GOAL ATTAINMENT BE EVALUATED?

Specifying the manner that goal attainment will be measured and developing a timetable for implemen-

tation and evaluation are integral to answering this question. These concerns were initially raised in question #3, however, further elaboration about goal attainment is appropriate. First, the design of a project for using a conceptual model to guide nursing practice fits that of evaluation research. Three phases of evaluation research are

> planning . . . the goals are established and strategies for realizing and evaluating these goals are put into place.
> implementing . . . movement is made towards actual use of the model on nursing units. It may be initiated with a pilot study to refine the mode of implementation on other units.
> evaluating . . . activities are directed toward determining the extent to which the project objectives have been met.

The planning, implementation, and evaluation phases often overlap, with revisions frequently made in the implementation phase. Also, goal attainment will be influenced by intervening variables, such as resistance to change, differing educational background of nurses, vacillating interdisciplinary support, and strained communication patterns. Each of these factors may undermine the intent of the nursing project and require specific strategies to overcome. Thus, when evaluating goal attainment, it is important to look at the specifics related to the particular goal as well as the contextual factors influencing goal attainment.

A subquestion related to evaluation is: who will evaluate? I advise involving all levels of nursing. In doing so, several perspectives about goal attainment will be obtained. In the ideal situation, an outside evaluator would be used to increase the objectivity associated with the evaluation process.

Methods of evaluation need to be assessed at a preplanning phase so that appropriate preparatory steps can be taken. For example, you may need consultants to offer suggestions for evaluation designs, data retrieval, and if appropriate, statistical analysis. Too often, nursing professionals initiate innovative projects and then fall short on evaluating outcomes. As a result, the actual significance of the innovation can be lost.

WHAT FINANCIAL RESOURCES ARE AVAILABLE TO SUPPORT THE PROJECT?

Both hidden and obvious cost factors are associated with using a conceptual model. The hidden costs are often 'time' related, such as

- time needed to prepare nurses;
- preparation and teaching time for instructors;
- time needed in transition from "old" to "new";
- time associated with meetings.

The more obvious cost factors are

- salary of project coordinator;
- consultants' fees;
- cost of new forms;
- cost of teaching aids;
- secretarial hour.

I suggest using a retrospective and prospective cost/time analysis for approximating the financial outlay associated with using a nursing model as a guide for nursing practice.

SUMMARY

After considering the questions posed the more specific steps associated with using a nursing model to guide clinical practice are started. The planning, implementation, and evaluation approaches can now be tailored to your nursing department's unique situation.

REFERENCES

1. Capers CF, O'Brien C, Quinn R, et al. The Neuman systems model in practice: planning phase. J Nurs Admin 1985;15(5):29-38.
2. Anna DT, Christensen DG, Hahon SA, et al. Implementing Orem's conceptual framework. J Nurs Admin 1978;8(9):8-11.
3. Auger TA, Dee V. A patient classification system based on the behavioral systems model of nursing: Part 1. J Nurs Admin 1983;13(4):38-43.
4. Mastal MD, Hammond H, Roberts MP. Theory into hospital practice: a pilot implementation. J Nurs Admin 1982;12(6):9-15.
5. Neuman B. The Neuman Systems Model: Application to Nursing Education and Practice 1982; Norwalk: Appleton-Century-Crofts, 8-29.
6. Capers CF. Some basic facts about models, nursing conceptualizations, and nursing theories. J Cont Ed Nurs 1986; Sept/Oct 17(5):149-54.

CHAPTER **36**

Shared Governance and New Organizational Models

Tim Porter-O'Grady, RN, EdM

Nursing executives are struggling to keep up with the rapid pace of organizational change in health care. Many are trying to jockey their nursing departments into the power arena as the organization develops along corporate business lines. One major aim of these leaders is to ensure nursing's place at the policymaking table.

All of these efforts are commendable and deserve unrestrained support from the nursing profession. One question, however, arises as we witness these transitions: Where is the bedside nurse who provides direct patient care in the midst of this political and organizational maneuvering?

CALL FOR CHANGE WITHIN NURSING ORGANIZATIONS

Some nurses wonder if all of this restructuring at the top administrative level has any basis in value for nursing practice or if it simply enhances the power of the nurse administrator without altering the working conditions of the staff nurses. Much of the work of the National Commission on Nursing (1983) and the National Commission On Nursing Implementation Project (1986) has indicated that the important changes for the professional practice of nursing must

Reprinted from *Nursing Economics,* Vol. 5, No. 6, with permission of Anthony J. Jannetti, Inc. © 1987.

occur *within* the nursing organization — primarily in the practice setting itself. Here is where the greatest degree of change is needed and where it is often least in evidence.

Concomitant with the policy and organizational changes occurring at the administrative level is a real need to address structural changes at the practice level directly influencing the work of nursing. Unless the work place is directly addressed, much power may be concentrated at the top of the organization with no one left to do the work at the front lines of nursing practice. This is especially true now when nurses have many other career options and when the value of a service is becoming a major consideration in health care. Those who can offer the best service for the best price will be the future providers regardless of current and past expectations and roles. This means that nurses and the nursing profession must effectively translate the service provided into economic and product terms. Otherwise, nursing's value and ability to succeed may be seriously questioned.

Newer production strategies such as product line management are not the answer. This strategy of organizing the institution around its products and services in order to create a more manageable and direct market relationship may be efficient at its best but begs the question for nurses. An organization can have an effective product line approach and still be narrow, autocratic, sexist, controlling, and devaluing of nurses and nursing practice. Nurses can face the same working relationships, attitudes, and conditions that originally created resource problems (Mocci, 1987).

Models of participative management are not the solution either to nursing staff concerns about their profession and their work place. If professional practice means accountability with control, authority, and autonomy over factors related to the professional's work, then management benevolence will not address the issue. Participative management by its very definition means allowing others to participate in decisions over which someone else has control—in this case, the nurse manager, supervisor, and/or administrator. The act of allowing participation identifies for the "participant" the real and final authority figure. The nurse also comes to realize that such benevolence can be withdrawn at any time.

The true professionals exhibit an inherent ownership of the role manifested in the work of the profession. This ownership cannot be given or taken away from those individuals by anyone except their peers and then only when they have clearly compromised the standards of the work or public trust engendered in the role. For the professional, this accountability does not transfer to the institution or its management simply because the institution provides the service. The organization certainly has some legitimate responsibility in assuring that it fulfills its responsibility to provide services effectively and safely. Yet the institution does so through the trust established between the professional nurse as provider of the service and the institution.

PROBLEMATIC FEATURES OF MANY ORGANIZATIONAL STRUCTURES

In order to "hedge its trust," the traditional organization through its managers has constructed a whole range of strategies that limit the risk inherent in its trust of the nurse. Strong hierarchies, clear authority structures, solid approval formats, extensive policies and procedures (often to limit the risk created by independent judgment), and task list job descriptions (even though criterion referenced) are excellent

examples. All are designed to constrain those very behaviors inherent to professional practice. These behaviors include: lateral relationships and dialogue, clinical judgment reflecting the unique nature of every problem, control of the practice environment, validation of care, peer-based quality determination and assurance, a defined role in governance, and a consensus-based decisional model (Porter-O'Grady & Finnigan, 1984).

If one examines the organizational structures of the majority of nursing services, these practitioner-based professional characteristics are either not present or reside in the management track only. A detailed examination of these organizations reveals a close approximation to the organizational models of blue-collar institutions that provide primarily vocational or technical services. Nurses will either have to stop claiming that they are truly professional or will have to redefine the structures that support the nurses' work in a manner that assures a professional practice environment. Clearly, in many institutions, this calls for tremendous organizational transformation.

Fortunately, we are entering a health-care delivery system that will demand the fullest expression of professional nursing practice and organizational structures and systems to support it. The symptoms calling for change are clear:

1. Illness costs too much money, and funding sources are shrinking.
2. Services are moving outside the institutions and into the home and community.
3. Technology is shortening the "acute" phase of a person's illness experience.
4. Consumers have more tools to take care of themselves, and more will be available.
5. The system is becoming a health system where clients will not have to access physicians first before obtaining health-based services designed to keep them well.
6. The population is aging and is committed to staying independent longer.
7. Small community-based entrepreneurial services will affiliate with more complex systems

to integrate a whole range of health-related services.

8. Nurses have a broad base of health knowledge and are therefore well positioned to provide a wide latitude of creative health services.

While these are a small portion of the changes occurring in health care, they make a clear statement regarding the many opportunities available to nurses and their organizations in the exercise of their professional work. Critical responses will involve the internal systems in the nursing organization that make these opportunities attractive options for practicing nurses. The fundamental question asks if the nursing organization is structured and operating in such a manner that its nurses can identify and design a response to the marketplace and perform with the accountability and independence such a marketplace will demand. Can nurses assume these responsibilities with ease because the organizational structure has facilitated their accountability as professional practitioners rather than stripping them of this control?

CREATING AN EFFECTIVE NURSING ORGANIZATIONAL STRUCTURE

The nurses of tomorrow will be confronted with a new range of options for providing service. Behaviorally, nurses must fit their skills to the frameworks within which they will be used. Nurses must be able to exercise accountability within a supportive organizational structure.

For what is the nurse accountable? Is it nursing practice; and if so, what specifically does this mean? The nursing organization must clearly define its service and the value of that service. The entire nursing organization must step back from the daily routine to ask what it is doing and what is being accomplished. What difference does nursing practice make? The nurse needs a conceptual framework that guides individual and group actions, thinking, and values. Without this common set of values or practice beliefs, the nurse cannot answer questions about outcomes of care. Without an adequate conceptual framework, the nursing service is deprived of mission and direction.

Logically conceived practice standards, quality assurance plans, and performance evaluations have no basis upon which to validate content without a conceptual or practice model that expresses the basic values of nursing practice.

DETERMINING A CONCEPTUAL FRAMEWORK

Conceptual framework determination is an important first step in the professional organization's conception. Rather than structuring the nursing organization on old bureaucratic values of industrial organizations, we must follow the values of the profession that the organization aims to organize and support. Structural mechanisms should evidence both the validity of the professional practice model and the work of the professional group.

Clearly, this calls for a leap of commitment from the organization's nursing and general administrative leadership. Structuring such an organization means questioning some of the basic values of traditional management and the traditional rewards of that role. In a professional practice model, the location of power will depend on its use and may be centered within the nursing organization in ways the manager may have no authority to alter or change.

FEATURES OF PROFESSIONAL PRACTICE MODELS

Professional practice models such as shared governance, therefore, are not participatory management models. Instead, they are an accountability-based governance system for professional workers. Authority, control, and autonomy exist in the organization based on specifically defined areas of accountability. Specified accountability arises according to need and location for best expression. For example, all issues related to practice are dealt with by the practitioner solely and specifically with the manager playing no legitimate role in that specified clinical decisional framework.

In order to function in any work place, a context for formalizing an organizational structure must be provided. However, in a professional governance framework, that structure reflects a decisional base and design different from traditional organizations.

Structure is constructed from the center of the shared governance work place rather than from the hierarchical periphery. Authority is established in specified processes rather than in identified individuals. From these functions and placements of accountability, the professional organization takes form. In nursing, the major service components generally involve practice, quality, education, peer process, or governance. Within these five functional characteristics, most operational processes unfold. The goal in a shared or professional governance model is to determine the base of accountability for each functional service component and build appropriate structures based on the following guidelines:

1. Authority is assigned based on appropriate location, and a defined mechanism is established for determining such assignment.
2. The manager's role is to facilitate, integrate, and coordinate the system and resources required for the system's maintenance and growth.
3. The professional nurse has an obligation not only to do the work of nursing care but also to undertake those activities that ensure the ongoing operation of the nursing service.
4. The nursing care system must be self-supporting and self-directed while integrating with other systems that collectively offer care services to a highly variable consumer community.
5. The operative mechanics of the nursing service must be structured so that the expected standards of services are met and assured within the clinical practice framework.

The structural design of a nursing service or agency must look and function differently when the above guidelines are applied. When the organization must assume responsibility for defining, measuring, delivering, and evaluating practice in the clinical milieu, new methodologies for structuring and organizing must be provided.

The work setting changes design formats and begins to structure the organization from the center

outward. At the heart of the organization is the practicing nurse. The next levels of the organization contain the functional processes that collectively address the elements supporting the nurse's practice: standards, quality assurance, peer processes (such as competence definitions, role descriptions, and evaluation formats) continuing education, and governance (including management). The outermost level of the organization comprises the management and administrative functions that service to coordinate, integrate, and facilitate the internal operating system and articulate it with the external institutional and/or consumer system (see Figure 36-1).

PROFESSIONAL GOVERNANCE APPROACHES

Three operating methods are currently in use in nursing service settings that exemplify professional governance approaches. They can generally be classified as councilar, congressional, or administrative models.

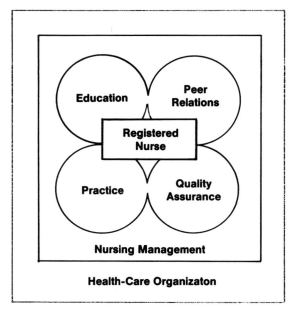

FIGURE 36-1
Professional governance framework.

The councilar model uses council formats to structure staff and management governance processes. The councils are usually elected and have authority vested in them for defined functions. The control variable is moderated by the appropriate delineation of management or clinical accountability. Usually, practice, quality assurance, and education are the primary clinical or staff formats. They are often comprised of a majority of practicing nurses who maintain the controlling majority on the councils. Issues and structures as well as processes related to the defined areas of accountability are described and developed under the authority and approval of these councils.

While management has representation on these groups, they generally do not hold the majority in these forums and are therefore in the dependent position in decision making related to issues of clinical practice. The management team has a management council that focuses its deliberations on facilitating system operations and resources. The majority of members on this council are managers with the clinical staff having some minority representation.

Collectively, the chairs of these councils with the chief nursing officer compose the service's executive group or council that has responsibility for coordinating and integrating the work of the councils and addressing issues of the service as a whole. Usually, a bylaw or rule structure describes the functional components of the process and delineates the appointment of the councils, officers, and staff controls in the organization (see Figure 36-2).

The congressional format operates similarly to the constitutionally empowered representative system of government. Usually, a president and a cabinet of officers are elected from the staff of the organization in order to fulfill serveral operating or control functions in the nursing organization. This official group oversees the operation of the service. Specific processes are undertaken by various committees often chaired by the cabinet officers. These committees are variously empowered or assigned specific accountabilities for which they must report through a formal format to the cabinet of the nursing organization. Cabinet members are a mix of management and clinical representatives. Some organizations equilibrate the cabinet between the management and clinical representatives; others weight it toward the clinical practitioner consistent with the belief that the organization is a clinical service.

Control and power issues in the governance mechanism are defined between the executive (nurse administrator and the management team) and the cabinet (staff representatives). The role of the staff in "congress" is also defined with specified powers for review, report, and approval of the cabinet's work and its various appointed committees (see Figure 36-3).

The administrative model follows more conservative lines with the alignment of authority for specified roles, functions, and processes delineated between the management and clinical tracks. The authority level of the organization is divided between the administrative management and clinical staff in varying degrees of numerical parity.

Clinical accountability and authority structures are usually associated with specific practice issues. The staff elects a representative group mandated to represent staff interests in issues of clncal practice. The management team also is represented on the forums and participates in group decisions. Sometimes the

FIGURE 36-2

Shared governance organization model.

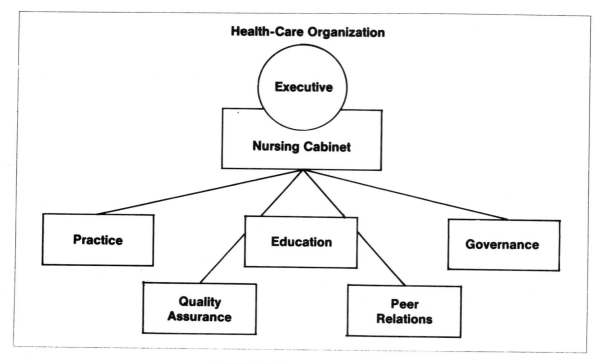

FIGURE 36-3
Congressional governance model.

representation is evenly divided between management and the staff; in other settings, representation is weighted in favor of management or staff depending on the model's design and the degree of trust in the setting. Because the nurse executive frequently has a mechanism for vetoing considerations of the various decision-making groups, this model may be considered the least accountability-based or professionally structured (see Figure 36-4).

While these models are currently the most prevalent, many variations of the professional governance or shared governance approach can be developed. Regardless of specific design, the following characteristics are key to any professional governance model:

1. Authority is defined by the allocation of accountability within the appropriate decision-making body.

2. The traditional management role moves from leading, organizing, planning, and controlling to the more cohesive roles of integrating, facilitating, and coordinating.

3. The defined forums for specified decision making are points of final authority for their assigned accountabilities and are not subject to another source for approval and mandated performance.

4. The executive function is not solely management by role or membership. The decisional bodies (councils, cabinets, or commissions) hold defined representation at the executive level in nursing service.

5. Mechanisms exist outside exclusive management function for organizationally addressing nursing practice, quality of care, professional development, and peer processes

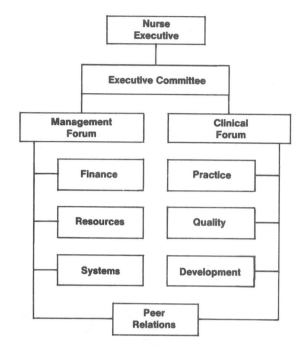

FIGURE 36-4

Administrative shared governance model.

(credentialing, privileging, performance, and evaluation).

6. Approved and supportable bylaws, rules and regulations or policy frameworks exist that prohibit the unilateral dismantling of the governance system once support and broad-based approval have been obtained from the members of the professional organization and the institution's governing body.

MAINTAINING LONG-TERM CHANGES

Clearly, a professional governance system is not achieved easily or quickly. Movement to such systems requires an organizational transformation—not just a transition to newer approaches. Behavioral changes of a significant nature are required from clinical and management staff. Roles are considerably redefined and restructured. Dialogue from all constituencies within and without the nursing organization must occur during the deliberations for these structural changes.

A major advantage of these professional governance models is their timeliness for helping nursing services adapt to the many demands of the current marketplace. Positioning will be key to the success of health services. Internal continuity and professional structuring that can allow corporate service entities to function maximally will be the rule.

Nursing has long been positioned in dependent employee roles. In professional structures, relationships and roles are redescribed and constructed, thus positioning the professional organization and its members in a more direct relationship with accountability for determining policy, goals, service responses to consumer demand, interdisciplinary roles, and health services to be offered by nurses.

The challenging environment in health care today calls for creative and dramatic responses to a new set of variables influencing health services delivery. Many of the opportunities appear ready made for nurses. To access these opportunities, nurses must act in a concerted and deliberative manner. Creating organizational structures that demand the highest responsibilities from professional nurses will be the vehicle that moves us into a new age of health care.

REFERENCES

Moccia, P. (1987). The nature of the nursing shortage: Will crisis become structure? *Nursing And Health Care,* 8(6), 321-322.

National Commission On Nursing (1983). *Summary report and recommendations.* Chicago: American Hospital Association.

National Commission on Nursing Implementation Project. (1986, November 7). *Report of the invitational conference.* Milwaukee, WI.

Porter-O'Grady, T. & Finnigan, S. (1984). *Shared governance for nursing: A creative approach to professional accountability.* Rockville, MD: Aspen Systems, Inc.

CHAPTER **37**

Integrating Professional Values, Quality Practice, Productivity, and Reimbursement for Nursing

Dorothy E. Deremo, RN, MSN, CNAA

This country is in the midst of a health care revolution: prospective payment systems are replacing cost-based models of reimbursement; outpatient services are on the increase, leaving sicker patients in hospitals; length of hospital stays continues to decrease; the population grows older; the incidence of acquired immunodeficiency syndrome (AIDS) as an endemic disease continues to increase; and the evolution of corporate health care systems is increasingly evident. Add the largest nursing shortage in recent history, and there emerges a crisis of major proportions. It is evident that something must be done, but what? Nursing care delivery must be restructured and redesigned, but how? Nurse executives across the country are asking themselves these questions. How can they use the Chinese definition of crisis, that is, "danger and opportunity," to change a dangerous situation into a constructive opportunity for the advancement of nursing? Do we use as a model the path of the magnet hospitals?

At Henry Ford Hospital (HFH) in Detroit, the Department of Nursing has already implemented many strategies that the magnet hospital literature has highlighted as successful ways to develop excellence in

hospital nursing practice. These strategies should have a positive impact on R.N. recruitment and retention. The strategies include decentralized nursing administration, shared governance, a preceptor program, an onsite B.S.N. completion program for R.N.s and Associate Degree in Nursing (A.D.N.) completion program for L.P.N.s, creative work schedules, a career ladder system, the beginning of a nurse case management system, and a forgiveness education loan program for nursing students. The forgiveness education loan program covers nursing student tuition and book expenses with a contractual agreement that requires the student to work at HFH upon graduation for a specified period of time. With each month of work, a percentage of the loan is forgiven and does not need to be paid back.

These strategies are important aspects of any progressive nursing service. However, implementation of magnet hospital strategies is not enough. Despite all good intentions, most hospital staff nurses still have a professional fantasy in a blue collar reality. A revolution needs to take place at the nursing unit level to develop a professional nursing model that ties values, practice, quality, performance, productivity, behavior, and reimbursement together.

The purpose of this article is to present a model for change that incorporates these components into a

Reprinted from *Nursing Administration Quarterly,* Vol. 14, No. 1, with permission of Aspen Publishers, Inc. © 1989.

structure for redesigning hospital nursing into a professional nursing model. First, pertinent literature on the nursing shortage and structure of nursing organizations will be explored. Second, a description of the process by which the model has evolved will be presented. Finally, the model and its various components will be explained.

THE CURRENT ENVIRONMENT

Analyses of the nursing shortage and its implications occur regularly in both the health care literature and the media. Frequently mentioned reasons for the shortage include lack of autonomy in practice, low pay, low prestige, poor working conditions, increased opportunities for women in traditionally nonfemale occupations, and an improved economy that offers female workers the option to stay home. Proposed solutions to the nursing shortage focus on increased recruitment of high school students into nursing programs, government subsidy of nursing education, and improved wages and benefits for nurses. Such specific solutions are proposed as ways to enhance recruitment to nursing and improve the retention of nurses once they have entered the profession.[1-5]

These solutions may not be successful as long-term solutions to the nursing shortage, particularly for hospitals. Many nurses leave the profession for other careers; nurses who choose to stay in nursing frequently leave hospitals for the greener pastures of home care, entrepreneurships, and affiliated careers that allow more autonomy and prestige. Focusing efforts on increasing hourly wages and benefits will only neutralize some factors that are unsatisfactory. They will not provide solutions to the deeply rooted problems of low prestige, lack of autonomy in practice, and poor working conditions.[6]

A major factor related to the nursing shortage may be the highly bureaucratic structures of hospitals that deny nurses the professional autonomy and remuneration that is commensurate with professional nursing service.[1,6,7]

Although nursing is often described as a profession, nurses in hospitals typically are *not* able to function as professionals. The hierarchical chain of command common to most hospitals, the hourly wage structure, and the ways nurses are assigned to tasks are incompatible with a concept of the professional that includes (1) authority based on knowledge, (2) independent judgment, and (3) adherence to a professional code of ethics that extends beyond the organizational structure. In the typical hospital nursing structure, there is a failure to use the classic precepts of management: greater knowledge of day-to-day practice does not reside higher up in the hierarchy, and persons with authority often have less relevant information in conflict situations.[8]

The nursing shortage has become severe enough that many hospitals, in Detroit and elsewhere in the nation, have closed beds and curtailed admissions because of short staffing. Coupled with the staffing crisis in nursing is an increased demand for more intense and skilled nursing care needed by the current population of seriously ill hospitalized patients. It is, therefore, imperative that new models of nursing delivery and reimbursement be tested to deal with the staff nurse dissatisfiers of lack of autonomy in practice, low prestige, poor working conditions, and economics. To accomplish this, the current parent–child relationship that exists between hospital institutions and nursing employees must be restructured to provide a more professional relationship that would benefit all concerned.

MODEL EVOLUTION

The seeds for this model started almost a decade ago. In the late seventies, the author assisted in the development of a nursing faculty group practice through Wayne State University College of Nursing. The Primary Care Nursing Service (PCNS) was born with a great deal of enthusiasm and limited structure. All providers in the PCNS had been clinical nurse specialists, certified as adult or family nurse practitioners, and had joint faculty appointments with the college of nursing. Within three years, the PCNS went from a practice that had no clients, no record-keeping system, no filing system, no receptionist, two phones, and two exam rooms to a busy practice with 2,700 clients, 9 support staff members, and 12 examination rooms.

The experience was a hallmark in the author's career because for the first time she was functioning as a professional and practicing nursing as taught. The quality and productivity of performance was directly tied to reimbursement and professional survival. The clinical nurse specialists wrestled with providing continuity and access to clients, 24 hours per day, 7 days per week, 365 days per year. How would clients be covered when their nurse went on vacation or was ill? The nurse specialists had to learn how to collaborate, consult, and refer in a way that they had never been exposed to as staff nurses. The nurse specialists were truly accountable for their own practice for the first time in their career.

The author left hospital nursing because it was too restricting. Why was nursing faculty group practice so radically different from other nursing positions? The nurse specialists were responsible not only for the clinical health of their practices but also for the financial health of their practices. They had no one to blame for problems but themselves in group practice.

This "Camelot" experience was a far cry from what the majority of hospital staff nurses experience. What would happen if this type of nursing group practice model was inculcated into a rigid hospital system at the nursing unit level? This is the evolution of the idea that forms the foundation of this model for change.

In the last seven years, this idea has grown and modified as the author has been reacquainted with the realities of hospital nursing. The blue collar reality of hospital staff nurses is a major hurdle to be overcome. Attempts to deal with this issue have resulted in Porter-O'Grady's work with shared governance;[9] Manthey's development of primary nursing;[10] Clifford's work with professional roles and salarying registered nurses;[11] Zander's development of Nurse Case Management;[12] and Davidson's work with nursing units as business franchises.[11] All have focused on varying aspects of professionalism in nursing. However, nursing needs a model that integrates these various approaches to facilitate professional practice of the staff nurse.

In architecture, form follows function, but function can also follow form. It may be necessary to develop a structure that fosters rather than impedes professional behavior for professional behavior to manifest itself. Therefore, the structure of professional nursing values, delivery of service, and reimbursement systems must be addressed in order to create an institutional environment that facilitates professional nursing behavior. Professional nursing behavior will be essential to improve quality, to efficiently and effectively use resources, and to provide coordinated services that satisfy patients, nurses, and others in this changing health care climate. The Department of Nursing at Henry Ford Hospital has begun to explore these issues.

In spring 1988, the Department of Nursing started to revise its career advancement program (which included a clinical ladder); develop a shared governance system; and revise its quality assurance program, documentation system, and policy and procedure system. This plan came about as a result of a departmental strategic planning process that began in January 1988. The planning committee was composed of a cross-section of participants and included staff nurses, nurse managers, clinical nurse specialists, and directors. Through the remainder of 1988, many of these changes were implemented.

These changes had been tracked and fine-tuned by the Nurse Executive Council (NEC) in its quarterly strategic planning meetings. The NEC is a committee chaired by the vice president of nursing and includes chairpersons of the nurse manager group and three divisional practice committees (staff nurses), as well as the associate administrators (directors) of each nursing division. The NEC meeting in the first quarter of 1989 was very troubling. The group unanimously agreed that many changes had occurred, but many nursing employees at all levels continued to be confused about the overall direction and plan. This confusion had transpired despite the setting of detailed goals and objectives that contained time frames and responsibility charting. It became clear that a visual model was needed to provide clarity and to serve as a vehicle to communicate how the many changes within the department fit into an overall framework.

A rough draft of the model was completed within two days. After discussion with NEC members, it was modified and improved. Since that time, the model has been presented to the nursing staff on all three shifts during Nurses Week. It has also been used as a vehicle for discussion with physicians and administrative colleagues. Thoughtful suggestions have been given that have strengthened the model presented below.

MODEL COMPONENTS

The proposed model for change has four major components that are equivalent to the parts of a three-legged stool (Figure 37-1). The first component is a conceptual platform (or seat) that contains the mission, goals, values, and conceptual framework of the model. The other three components equate with the legs of the stool: each is necessary to balance and support the platform. These three legs include a professional value system, a professional nursing care delivery system, and a professional reimbursement system. Although the components are pictured as separate, they actually are interrelated and complement one another. If one component is weak, the

stool becomes unbalanced. The experience of model implementation at HFH will be described in order to explain its utility.

Conceptual Platform

The first component, or conceptual platform, contains five elements. The fundamental element starts with the ultimate vision for the department, to develop the hospital into a center of excellence for nursing. This visionary outcome is supported and clarified by four concepts: (1) that nursing care will be high quality, client-focused, efficient, effective, professional, caring, and responsive; (2) that nursing staff should follow the behavioral values of the "3 Cs and 3 Ps" (communication, collaboration, cooperation, participation, professional growth, and personal growth); (3) an acknowledgement that the nursing process is the organizing framework for the entire department; and (4) that nursing units are to be characterized as unit practice franchises. All of these concepts interact.

The conceptual platform is essential to focus energy and direction. Excellence needs to be explicitly stated. To reinforce the values in care delivery, the hospital developed a 15-second television commercial in which nurses at HFH are described as being professional, caring, and responsive. The vice president of nursing speaks for nursing in the commercial. (This was one of five commercials; the other four featured physicians talking about various aspects of medical care.) This consistency in message and theme was designed to reinforce culture change. The behavioral values of staff have been articulated in a pamphlet that all nursing staff members have received. This pamphlet has also been given to all new staff members and is discussed during orientation. Finally, the behavioral values have been incorporated into the design of the shared governance system, career advancement program (including a clinical ladder), and nursing development programs.

These three parts of the conceptual platform provide the "affective glue" for the entire model. The last two parts dealing with the nursing process and unit franchise system provide the "cognitive glue" of the platform. The nursing process is what nurses do.

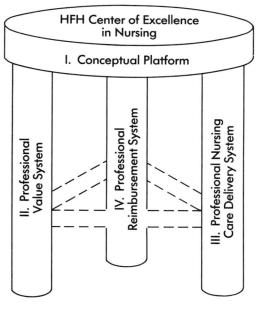

FIGURE 37-1
Model for change.

Often, however, the systems that are designed for staff nurses do not facilitate — and sometimes actually impede — the use of the nursing process. Therefore, a conscious decision must be made to use the nursing process as the organizing framework in clinical systems design.

Even less thought has been given to the financial design of nursing units. Many hospitals still identify nursing units as cost centers rather than as revenue centers. In addition, many unit nurse managers, let alone staff nurses, have no idea what their unit budgets contain. It is difficult to increase quality and improve cost effectiveness when nursing unit caregivers are ignorant of the financial realities of their behavior. The parent–child relationship between nursing administration and staff is perpetuated in this type of environment. Staff expect nursing administration to "fix" all the problems, but remain unhappy about the solutions that are imposed upon them. In addition, professional accountability and responsibility are not fostered.

To change the dynamics of this blue collar reality, it is essential that the financial environment of the nursing unit change. Davidson has coined the phrase, "unit franchise."[11] The term is a good one because it implies a balance between centralization and de-centralization of accountability and authority. Most people understand that owning a McDonald's franchise means that owners have their own businesses, but are also partners with the McDonald's Corporation. To maintain the franchise, owners must abide by certain quality and product standards. (They cannot buy their hamburger patties from Burger King.) Thus, this concept of a partnership can be readily applied to nursing units.

A nursing practice unit franchise describes the financial vision of having staff nurses as partners with the hospital. The nursing unit becomes a business in which the staff are concerned with both the clinical health and the financial health of the unit. It is in the staff's best interest to do the right thing the first time. They are partners with the hospital; however, a unit cannot be an island unto itself. It must at least meet hospital standards of quality, product, and cooperation. Therefore, in this model, quality and cost-effectiveness can be linked in a way that is a win for the patients, the nursing staff, the physicians, and the hospital.

Professional Value System

The first component that supports the conceptual framework is the professional value system. HFH has chosen to put into operation the behavioral values of the staff ("The 3 Cs and 3 Ps") through the use of a shared governance structure and career advancement program. The values of communication, collaboration, cooperation, participation, professional growth, and personal growth are built into both of these two structures. The process taken in developing the shared governance system and career advancement program can be seen in the Box, "Professional Value System."

The Department of Nursing decided to utilize shared governance committees to gain some experience with the concept. Concurrently, the first year was spent in educating committee chairs and members to assist them in being more effective in their new roles. It was thought that it would take one year to sort through the problems that existed in the governance structure, to collect data, and to refine the shared governance system in order to implement it fully.

The initial shared governance committee structure can be seen in Figure 37-2. It should be noted that the foundation for the shared governance structure resides in the unit practice committee, or UPC. Staff who are elected to the UPC elect a UPC chairperson. The nursing manager is a nonvoting, permanent member of the UPC. Each UPC chairperson sits on a divisional practice committee, and they in turn elect a chairperson. The vicechairperson of the divisional practice committee is a clinical nurse specialist who is agreed upon by the chairperson and the associate administrator for that clinical division. The associate administrator is a nonvoting member of the divisional practice committee. In addition, a nurse manager representative also sits on the divisional practice committee, as do representatives from nursing quality assurance and nursing development and research. Divisional practice committee chairpersons sit on the operations committee that is chaired by the vice president of nursing. Members of the operations

---

Professional value system

A. Shared governance
  1. Develop shared governance structure
  2. Define committee purposes, membership, officers, and bylaws
  3. Implement structure (see Figure 2)
  4. Define roles, skills, and abilities needed to facilitate the shared governance process
     Examples:
       Setting an agenda
       How to run a meeting
       Win/win negotiation
       Conflict management
       Team building
       Professional ethics
  5. Provide education to committee chairpersons and members*
  6. Clarify purposes, roles, and responsibil-
     ities of committees after six months of experience
  7. Refine structure and roles after one year
  8. Fully implement shared governance

B. Career advancement program (CAP)
  1. Expand CAP to include education and management track with clinical track (see Figure 3)
  2. Define roles and job descriptions
  3. Utilize nursing process as a framework for developing behavioral criteria in clinical track
  4. Develop evaluation instruments
  5. Refine peer review process for credentialing and promotion
  6. Fully implement revised CAP*

---

*Step of process HFH currently holds.

committee include not only the divisional practice committee chairpersons, but also the associate administrators of each clinical division, the associate administrator of nursing development and research, the nursing administrative manager of nursing finance, the director of special projects, and an administrative assistant. Members of the operations committee also chair the practice, development and research, quality assurance, finance, and resources subcommittees. The nursing administrative forum contains all of the unit nurse managers, the associate administrators, and the clinical nurse specialists within the department. Finally, the NEC is composed of a smaller group from the operations committee and one divisional chairperson. This council meets quarterly to do strategic and long-term planning and evaluate the progress of the department in relation to its quality assurance program. Thus, there is staff nurse representation at the unit, division, and departmental level in the governing structure.

Like the shared governance committee structure, the career advancement program also facilitates incorporation of professional values by the nursing staff. A clinical ladder existed when the vice president first came to the hospital. It was decided to expand the career advancement program to include an education and management track (See Figure 37-3). Because of the values of the department in promoting and rewarding bedside nursing, the clinical track allows the bedside nurse to achieve four levels of promotion. The clinical nurse III is at a higher level in the career advancement program than an education coordinator or assistant nurse manager, and has a higher salary range. Therefore, it is possible to stay at the bedside and be rewarded without having to go into an education or management position.

Professional Nursing Care Delivery System

The second leg supporting the conceptual platform is the professional nursing care delivery system. Many frameworks were considered in restructuring nursing care delivery. It was decided that nurse case management would provide the best conceptual framework for restructuring nursing practice into a professional model that would allow full utilization, not only of registered nurses, but of nurse extenders. Nurse extenders will be a reality in the future because

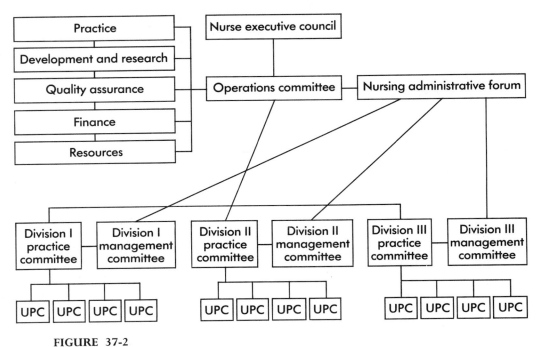

FIGURE 37-2

Shared governance committee structure. From Henry Ford Hospital, Detroit, Mich, 1989.

of the nursing shortage, and need to be addressed and incorporated into a professional delivery model. Three subcomponents were identified (see Box, "Professional Nursing Care Delivery System"). These three subcomponents included a nursing staff recruitment system to deliberately build for the future, an integrated nursing information system (NIS) to support nursing practice, and, finally, the nursing care delivery system itself.

The nursing staff recruitment programs are essential to provide the needed registered nurses and nurse extenders to support a nursing care delivery system. Many programs have been developed, implemented, and are now "bearing fruit." The nurse assistant program for workers over the age of 55 has been very successful and well received. The nursing specialty technician (NST) is a position that has been developed by a task force of registered nurses who defined the tasks, job description, and curriculum. The NST must either be certified as a paramedic, or be a student nurse who has completed a critical care extern program. Although the NST position met with

some resistance, it is now very well received and is requested in all of the intensive care units and specialty areas.

Other unusual and successful programs have been developed with Wayne State University College of Nursing. These include the second career-second degree B.S.N. program and the coop workstudy program. The second career-second degree program is designed for individuals who have a bachelor's degree in another field and wish to take thirteen months of concentrated nursing courses. Upon completion, they receive a second major and bachelor of science degree in nursing. The program has been flooded with applicants and was unable to accommodate all of them for the first class that started in September 1989. There has been a similar response to the coop generic B.S.N. program. This program is designed to combine course work (three or four days a week) with hospital employment (one or two days a week) during the ten consecutive semester program, which lasts slightly longer than three years. In both programs, the hospital pays for the tuition, books, and

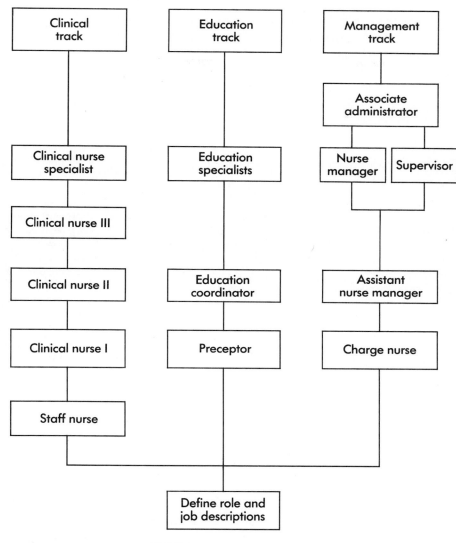

FIGURE 37-3

Career advancement program.

some expenses for the students, using a forgiveness loan format that is worked off over a period of 20 to 40 months after the student graduates. To round out the staff recruitment programs, HFH still has a diploma school of nursing. The hospital is actively exploring ways to convert this diploma program into a Two-Plus-Two A.D.N./B.S.N. Program.

The second piece that supports professional nursing care delivery is a nursing information system (see Box, "Nursing Information System"). If nursing is to achieve quality, efficiency, and effectiveness, it must have better information for clinical and financial decision making. Many systems have been developed for patient acuity, nursing staffing, documentation,

---

Professional nursing care delivery system

Conceptual framework: Nurse case management

A. Nursing staff recruitment system

1. Develop nurse extender programs
2. Implement nurse extender programs
3. Develop onsite degree completion programs
4. Develop collaborative degree programs with Wayne State College of Nursing
5. Explore conversion of current HFH Diploma School of Nursing to Two-Plus-Two A.D.N. and B.S.N. program*

B. Nursing information system. See Box, "Nursing information system"

C. Nursing care delivery system

1. Write grant to fund model development
2. Define roles of staff*
3. Define knowledge, skills, and abilities of staff
4. Do needs assessment of staff for nurse case management roles
5. Develop education program to teach necessary skills
6. Identify pilot units to educate staff
7. Implement nurse case management on pilot units
8. Revise program, based on pilot experience
9. Implement nurse case management throughout the department

---

*Step of process HFH currently holds.

policies and procedures, and quality assurance. However, few nursing information systems (NIS) have been developed that integrate these components. At HFH, the decision has been made to design a quality assurance program, documentation system, policies and procedures, and a nurse staffing and finance system that is based on the nursing process, standards of practice, and standards of care. Content of forms has been purposely organized in a way that can be easily adapted to computer screens. Finally, a request for information (RFI) was sent to various computer vendors in the spring of 1989. After reviewing vendor proposals, vendor selection will be made, the plan will be finalized, and implementation of the system is expected to occur within one to two years.

Nursing staff recruitment and a nursing information system are necessary to support the actual professional nursing care delivery system itself. The Department of Nursing had already decided to use nurse case management as its model for practice. Concurrent with this decision, an announcement by Robert Wood Johnson and Pew Charitable Trusts had been made regarding grant money to "strengthen hospital nursing." The vice president of nursing had already made a commitment to implementing the model for change. However, it was obvious that grant funding would support more immediate design and implementation of the model. Therefore, a grant application was written and submitted early in 1989. HFH was selected as one of the grant recipients.

Nursing information system (NIS)

1. Develop an integrated unit-based nursing information system
2. Utilize the nursing process, standards of practice, and standards of care as a framework for system design
3. Develop four integrated system components

a. Quality assurance (QA)
  1. Develop QA program using marker model
  2. Develop generic standards of practice and standards of care
  3. Implement QA program
  4. Develop area specific standards of practice and standards of care*
	b. Documentation
	  1. Use Gordon's functional health patterns and nursing diagnosis as conceptual framework
	  2. Develop forms that facilitate the nursing process
	  3. Use "check off" system to facilitate easy translation to computer screen design*
	  4. Use standards of practice and standards of care for care planning and evaluation
		c. Policies and procedures (P and Ps)
		  1. Revise P and Ps using standards of care and practice
		  2. Implement revised P and Ps*
		  3. Design NIS to highlight appropriate P and Ps for staff when developing care plan
			d. Nurse staffing and finance
			  1. Validate and streamline current patient classification system (PCS)
			  2. Design new PCS, nurse staffing, and cost of nursing care, based on standards of practice and standards of care*

*Step of process HFH currently holds.

The next step was the development of a nurse case management task force, whose charge is to define the roles of various members of the Department of Nursing in relation to nurse case management. They will then be involved in defining the knowledge, skills, and abilities necessary for nurse case management to be successful. A needs assessment of the staff will be done to identify strengths and areas for improvement in relation to the nurse case management roles as defined by the task force.

An education program will also be developed to teach the necessary skills for these roles. Staff education and implementation of nurse case management will begin on selected pilot units. The program will be revised and refined using the data collected during the pilot experience. The department will then be ready to implement nurse case management throughout the hospital.

Professional Reimbursement System

The final leg that supports the conceptual platform is the professional reimbursement system. The process for implementing the system is shown in the Box, "Professional Reimbursement System." The vice president of nursing identified the need for the unit nurse manager to become more sophisticated in utilizing business skills as an essential foundation to

---

Professional reimbursement system

A. Teach nurse managers (NAM) business skills
B. Develop nursing unit as a business with a revenue and expense budget managed by the NAM*
C. Develop unit charges for nursing administrative or educational functions
D. Develop a relative value system for each nursing unit
E. Develop business curriculum for nursing staff
F. Teach staff business skills
G. Develop nursing staff salary structure
H. Assign salaries to staff
I. Develop nursing unit as business franchise that is jointly managed by staff and NAM
J. Develop gain-sharing system, based on unit quality, efficiency, and effectiveness
K. Implement nursing unit practice franchise gain-sharing system

---

*Step of process HFH currently holds.

make the radical transition to a nursing unit practice franchise system. Nursing managers will need to be role models, mentors, and coaches if this part of the model is to be successful. Therefore, the department reviewed various educational approaches for the nurse managers. It decided on using a self-paced computer interactive education program specifically designed for unit nurse managers by Hamilton KSA. The advantage of this program is that the content is consistent with departmental aims and includes practical application exercises that can be used to manage the nursing unit. Group meetings seem to validate self-acquired computer assisted instruction.

Although the nurse managers have been receiving monthly revenue and expense reports for the last two years, they have only been actively involved in the budgeting process for the last year. The education process has been most helpful in improving levels of confidence in the personnel and financial management of the nursing unit.

The next step will be to develop unit charges for nursing administrative functions and nursing development and research functions. Cost of nursing orientation and incident reporting are examples of these types of charges. Currently, if a unit has a turnover problem because the nursing staff are not getting along, there is no real financial impact to the unit. The same is true for quality problems. Nursing staff have little understanding of the cost of problems involving the quality of care. It is very expensive to report incidents, have them investigated by risk management, and to schedule patient and family follow-up meetings. If the concept of a franchise is to be effective, the costs of services that support the nursing unit and the cost of quality problems need to be charged to the unit. In addition, other types of measures will need to be used to evaluate quality and effectiveness. These may include patient satisfaction surveys, physician satisfaction surveys, nursing satisfaction surveys, and a relative value system for each nursing unit.

A relative value system will be necessary to level out the playing field. Each nursing unit has a different ability to make a profit, based on the major types of diagnosis related groups (DRG) and case mix usually found on that particular unit. For example, a medical unit will have greater difficulty in generating a profit than a cardiothoracic unit. However, both contribute to the overall mission of the hospital. Therefore, a system needs to be developed that will allow each to benefit equally if they are delivering the same level of quality and cost-effective nursing care.

Once the nursing managers become expert at running their units as clinical businesses, they will then be in a position to act as mentors and coaches for their staffs. It is planned that a business curriculum will be developed for the nursing staff to teach business skills. In addition, a nursing staff salary structure will be developed, and registered nurses will become exempt employees. These changes will set the groundwork for the development of the nursing unit as a business franchise that is jointly managed by the nursing staff and the nurse manager.

As part of the nursing unit franchise system, it will be necessary to develop a gain sharing system that is based on unit quality, efficiency, and effectiveness. The relative value system, unit charges, and audits of quality and satisfaction will be used to decide the level of gain sharing each unit will receive. It is expected that gain sharing will be based on unit performance, rather than individual performance. This is to promote the unit's functioning as a team to produce quality nursing care in an efficient and effective manner.

The nursing unit will also have to cooperate with other areas in the hospital and other units to provide quality service. Units that try to function as an island unto themselves will not be effective, and this should be reflected in their revenue and expense report. For example, if a nursing unit is not cooperating with social services, there may be difficulty discharging patients in a timely fashion. This increase in length of stay will increase the expenses of the unit and decrease its net revenue. Another example is that of problems between an intensive care unit and a general practice unit. If the units are not proactive in resolving their problems, the total length of stay of the patient may suffer and the revenues of both units will suffer. A final example is in the area of coverage. It will no longer be the responsibility of nursing administrations to provide coverage to the unit. Each unit will have to identify creative ways to cover their practice, improve quality, and decrease cost. This is the ultimate empowerment of staff nurses at the unit level. This allows bedside nurses not only to practice in a professional environment but to be reimbursed as professionals.

The model for change presented incorporates values, practice, quality, performance, productivity, behavior, and reimbursement into one structure. This integration is essential if nursing is to come into its own as a profession and change its professional fantasy to a professional reality based on values, nursing care delivery, and reimbursement. The description of the evolution of the model and how it has been put into practice at HFH has been presented as one way to tie these components together. This is an ongoing process and there is yet much to do in order to achieve this new vision.

Basil S. Walsh once said, "We don't need more strength or more ability or greater opportunity. What we need is to use what we have."[13(p57)] The opportunity for nursing to become a true profession exists. Nurses have the ability and the strength to achieve that goal. What nurses need is to pursue new, creative ways of building and reinforcing a professional environment. The model for change that has been presented is one way of achieving that goal.

REFERENCES

1. Scherer, P. "When Every Day Is Saturday: The Shortage." *American Journal of Nurses* 87, no. 10 (1987): 1284–90.
2. "Fed Up, Fearful and Frazzled." *Time,* 14 March 1988, pp. 77–78.
3. Will, G. "The Dignity of Nursing." *Newsweek,* 23 May 1988, p. 80.
4. American Hospital Association. *The Nursing Shortage: Facts, Figures, and Feelings.* Chicago: American Hospital Association, 1987.
5. Fagin, C.M. "The Shortage of Nurses in the United States." *Journal of Public Health Policy* 1, no. 4 (1980):293–311.
6. Herzberg, F., Mausner, B., and Synderman, B. *Motivation to Work.* New York: Wiley, 1959.
7. Ringold, E.S. "The Crisis in Nursing." *Working Mother* 8, no. 10 (1985):36–40.
8. Strauss, A. "Interorganizational Negotiation." *Urban Life* (October 1982):267–79.
9. Porter-O'Grady, T. "Shared Governance and New Organizational Models." *Nursing Economic$* 5, no. 6 (1988):281–86.
10. Manthey, M. "Answering the Primary Questions, Delivery System of Primary Nursing." *American Journal of Nurses* 88, no. 5 (1988):646–47.
11. Scherer, P. "Hospitals That Attract (And Keep) Nurses." *American Journal of Nurses* 88, no. 1 (1988):34–40.
12. Zander, K. "Nursing Case Management: Strategic Management of Cost and Quality Outcomes." *Journal of Nursing Administration* 27, no. 5 (1988):23–30.
13. Davis, W. *The Best of Success.* Lombard, Ill: Great Quotations, 1984.

CHAPTER **38**

Case-Mix: Matching Patient Need with Nursing Resource

Edward J. Halloran, RN, PhD, FAAN
Cheryl Patterson, RN, MSN
Marylou Kiley, RN, PhD

The degree of patients' dependence on nursing care is as important to the management of nursing department resources as it is in their clinical management. The nursing dependence must be ascertained to ensure effective patient management, and to more efficiently utilize nurses — the costs for whom make up 20-30 percent of total hospital expense. The contributions nurses make in patient care management are not well understood because nursing is often blurred together with medicine and the outcome of nurses' activity sometimes is attributed to physicians.

To insure the care is delivered in an efficient manner, the nursing care delivered must be related to some valid notion of what nursing is, and be measured against this standard. Efficient care is the method of achieving the stated and measurable objectives of providing nursing care at the lowest cost. Of value to nurses are data describing patient demand and nurse allocation — data which can be used to make informed decisions about nursing care effectiveness and its cost. This paper describes a nursing information system which provides nurses a case-specific computerized measure of the demand for nursing services, as well

Reprinted from *Nursing Management*, Vol. 18, No. 3, with permission of S-N Publications, Inc. © 1987.

as a measure of the capability to meet the demand and the resultant cost of nursing care. The measures employed are standardized to facilitate comparison of demand and allocation in the variety of settings where nursing is practiced. A comprehensive patient classification tool and a description of the nurses assigned to give care are the elements which offer considerable promise for insuring patients get what nursing care they need — no more and no less.

CASE-MIX MANAGEMENT

The development of the diagnosis related group (DRG) concept facilitated the melding of two seemingly unrelated hospital activities: medical care and financial management. In addition, the DRG concept helped explain the considerable variation in treatment costs from one hospital to another by citing differences in the medical diagnoses and treatments provided for hospitalized patients. All hospitals now can be differentiated by their medical case-mix; some hospitals treat more medically complex (and therefore, more expensive) patients than others.

Medical case-mix alone, however, does not explain all variability in the costs of treating hospitalized patients, nor do physicians direct all of the clinical services that a patient receives in the hospital. Clinical attributes of patients, including demand for nursing care and social services, have been associated with variations in the case cost and length of hospital stay. Nurses individualize the care provided their patients, and this, too, may vary according to the nurse's experience and education. The momentum of the diagnosis related group and prospective payment have caused hospitals to examine case costs, for which the nursing provided is a substantial part. Case-specific examinations of the nursing care patients received have shown a high degree of association between length of hospital stay and the amount of nursing care provided patients.

To optimally manage a patient's hospital course, data explanatory of patient nursing care dependency are required. A nurse management information system, based on patient case-mix and nurse capability, enables those responsible for allocating nursing resources to manage patient care more effectively and efficiently. This nursing case-mix management system complements the DRG medical data system and the social service data system: together these three disciplined-related data sources provide information highly predictive and explanatory of patient resource use, cost and length of stay.

THE HOSPITAL COURSE

The hospital length of stay has been employed as a surrogate measure of the use of hospital resources. Berki, *et al.*, have shown that there is considerable variation in LOS that is not explained by medical diagnosis.[1] This is not surprising since provision of medical care (or nursing care for that matter) does not depend on hospital status. The complexity of the patient's medical problem (as defined by DRG), the degree of the patient's functional incapacity (nursing dependency), as well as the patient's social and economic resources actually determine the setting for patient care (hospital, nursing home or home) and the amount of nursing care provided.

Nurses contribute to the management of a hospital patient's care by diagnosing and treating human responses to actual or potential health problems. When nursing diagnoses (present or absent anytime during hospital stay) were introduced into a regression equation, over 50 percent of the variability in hospital days for 2,552 patients from one hospital was explained ($R^2[36,2515] = .508$, $p > .001$) by the model.[2] When registered nurses diagnose and treat nursing conditions, they act in synergy with patients, physicians, and social workers to insure the patient's hospital course is optimum in length, in resources consumed, and in placement for aftercare consistent with functional and social independence.

Wennberg, McPherson, and Caper observed differences in admission rates for various illnesses and attributed the variability to physician behavior.[3] Yet, the decision to admit or not admit a patient is in part due to the patients' dependence on services that they would ordinarily perform for themselves if they had the necessary strength, will or knowledge. The latter phrase was drawn from Henderson's definition of nursing, which reads:

> Nursing is primarily helping people (sick or well) in the performance of those activities contributing to health, or its recovery (or to a peaceful death) that they would perform unaided when they have the necessary strength, will, or knowledge. It is likewise the unique contribution of nursing to help people to be independent of such assistance as soon as possible.[4]

The dependence of patients on nurses constitutes a rationale for hospital admission, the effect of which was not measured by Wennberg, yet is an alternative explanation for variability in admission rates to hospitals for patients with particular medical conditions.

Nursing dependency has implications for hospital length of stay that are as direct as medical diagnosis. When a patient lacks the capacity to provide the monitoring or care essential to recover (or to die peacefully), nurses assist patients and families until they can be independent of this assistance. Thus, the need for nursing care is an integral component and contributes to variation in length of hospital stay.

ACCOUNTING FOR PATIENTS AND NURSES

Developing a data base for managing resources in a nursing service depends upon a number of considerations about patients and nurses. *First,* nursing work is temporal: it goes on 24 hours a day, every day the patient is in the hospital. *Second,* patient conditions may change drastically and change often during hospital stays. *Third,* the services which nurses allocate for patients are integrated within themselves and conveyed to the patient by their presence: thus, the amount of time nurses spend with the patient represents the various amounts and levels of consumption (and, therefore cost) of nursing services. *Fourth,* nurses consider each patient unique: the likelihood that any given patient is like any other one is remote. Even though each patient is unique, the study of many patients over time reveals patterns of their need for care which are comparable between wards, within patient groups like DRGs, and among hospitals.

In addition, the size of nursing staffs in American hospitals varies considerably according to system constraints, such as hospital organization (support received from hospital departments; i.e., housekeeping, supply, clerical, food service, linen, and pharmacy), tradition, and economics.[5] Accounting for these patient, nurse, and hospital conditions is essential to constructing a data-based nursing information and patient management system.

DEVELOPMENT OF A COMPREHENSIVE PATIENT CLASSIFICATION

Only recently has retrievable information about nursing care become available. While patient classification schemes, indicative of nursing dependency, have been employed in American hospitals for many years, such information about patients has either been discarded, stored separately from the patients' hospital records, or been in a form that is neither retrievable nor possible to relate to other patient information.

Patient classification schemes traditionally conceptualize nursing as the completion of some standard work complex or task pattern (defined in time intervals) associated with selected patient demand attributes. Assumed in these staffing methodologies is the existence of a standard value which defines the nurse-patient ratio applicable to all situations. Acceptance of the assumption underlying these methods means the considerable variability observed

from one hospital to another in size of nursing staff is related to the staff-patient interaction alone. Differences among nurses, in organizational support systems, tradition (past practices) and economics, play no part in determining staff size and composition in these methodologies. While these task-time methods may be used by nurse managers to support staffing decisions, the results so obtained are often incongruent with the decision-making processes employed by bedside nurses. Further, the current methods do not distinguish nurses from non-nurses. When patient demand attributes are identified, staff allocations, often in full-time equivalent (FTE) units, are made with little distinction between registered nurse, LPN, or aides as caregivers. Such distinctions are not made because there is no standard minimum competence required for performing any nursing task or procedure. The illogical extreme in using a time and task-oriented nurse staffing system can be observed in the efficiency-driven American nursing home industry. All of the care procedures are done for patients primarily by aides, but the quality of living conditions and the forced dependence are a national scandal.[6]

Nursing is as much an intellectual endeavor as it is a physical one. To decide what to do for a person requires considerable knowledge applied in some orderly manner. A nurse assesses a person's need for nursing care, plans the care, implements the planned care and evaluates its result in resolving the patient's problem. Patient assessment is a most crucial step because all care flows from assessed patient need.

Nursing diagnosis terminology can summarize the nurse's assessment. The diagnoses describe patient conditions and situations that are amenable to nursing intervention. In this manner, nursing care, in one sense, is being defined by specifying problems in patients which nurses have the knowledge, skill and experience to treat. The methods used by nurses to treat these maladies are best summarized in Henderson and Nite (1978), *Principles and Practice of Nursing.* The nursing diagnosis is a sound method of operationally summarizing patient problems in terms that are meaningful to nurses.

PATIENT INFORMATION AND USE

A nursing diagnosis-based patient classification system is used to describe all patients on a daily basis to capture information about nursing dependency. The data is used to help clinicians optimize where patients receive nursing care both during and after the hospital episode. The options for care include movement within the hospital (transfers from one unit to another, particularly to and from ICUs) and after discharge (self care, family care, visiting nurse, assisted living or extended-care facility).

Data used to support the nurse's resource allocation decision at the bedside include a comprehensive view of patient conditions at specified time intervals. Because of the dynamic nature of a hospitalized patient's requirement for nursing, a snapshot is obtained every 24 hours.

Information is gathered once daily on day shift by the nurses caring for the patients. The data collection technology includes use of a portable hand-held computer terminal with wand scanners (light pens) used with a bar code system. All 61 of the diagnoses and each of the nurses' social security numbers are converted to bar codes. First, the patient's hospital number is entered. The nurse then enters the nursing personnel bar codes of those nurses who cared for the patient for the past 24 hours. By this method, an accounting is made of all nurses who were involved in the care of every patient from admission to discharge. The nurse then enters any of the 61 patient descriptors (conditions or diagnoses) felt to apply to that patient on that particular day. By 1:00 p.m., all data entered in the portable hand-held terminals are transmitted by telephone line to the hospital mainframe computer (see Figure 38-1). At 1:30 p.m., the processing is completed and reports containing hard copy of the data are distributed to each ward by 2:30 p.m. each day. These are used by subsequent shift nurses to assign patients and to speak with selected patients and their physicians about care alternatives (see Figure 38-2).

After approximately two weeks of familiarization with the nursing diagnosis definitions and the use of the technology, a nurse requires approximately two minutes to rate each patient in his or her assignment and to enter the data in the terminal. It requires approximately 60 seconds to transmit the data from one terminal to the mainframe computer. Each ward has two terminals so that it generally requires two minutes to transmit data over the telephone line. The technology facilitates the collection and storage of a considerable amount of data regarding each individual patient. Thirty-three inpatient wards are now involved in the daily data collection.

The nursing diagnosis patient measurement device employs standardized terminology to define relative need for nursing care. The tool has been pilot-tested in a psychiatric hospital, a children's hospital, and a women's hospital.[7] Further trials are underway or planned for an emergency service, recovery room, operating room, home care program and nursing home.

The conditions are not weighted with time values as it has not been determined that the treatment for grieving is more or less time consuming than that for incontinence. Further, society depends upon the nurses to establish priorities (treat impaired airway before treating body image disturbance), and allocate self (care time) in the most effective and efficient manner possible. The nurse involves the patient, and often the patient's physician, in establishing short- and long-term treatment regimens. The nurses also may combine treatment methods, and give a bed bath to support good hygiene, provide comfort, manage immobility, and treat grieving, all at the same time. The measurement device is used to help allocate nursing resources and supports the judgments bedside nurses are required to make. The nursing diagnosis-based patient classification scheme supports the resource allocation decisions made by bedside nurses.

THREE EXAMPLES

Tables 38-1, 38-2, and 38-3 represent data derived from three actual patients discharged from a university-affiliated teaching hospital in Cleveland. Examination of these specific cases illustrates the use of the nursing component of the patient information system to manage patient care and allocate nursing care.

UNIVERSITY HOSPITALS OF CLEVELAND
NURSE / PATIENT SUMMARY

	RN Code Number	Other Code Number	Consultant Code Number
TODAY			
LAST NIGHT			
LAST EVENING			

Primary Nurse Code Number _____

NAME

HOSP. NO.   DATE

SERVICE

SEX   AGE

DIVISION   ROOM NO.

Date Today _____

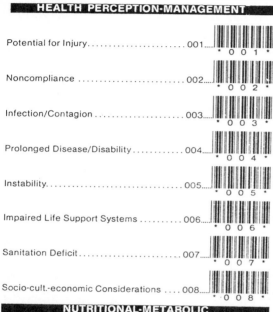

HEALTH PERCEPTION-MANAGEMENT

Potential for Injury..................... 001   *001*

Noncompliance 002   *002*

Infection/Contagion 003   *003*

Prolonged Disease/Disability 004   *004*

Instability.............................. 005   *005*

Impaired Life Support Systems 006   *006*

Sanitation Deficit...................... 007   *007*

Socio-cult.-economic Considerations 008   *008*

NUTRITIONAL-METABOLIC

FLUID

Excess Volume....................... 009   *009*

Volume Deficit....................... 010   *010*

Potential Volume Deficit 011   *011*

Bleeding 012   *012*

NUTRITION

Less Nutrition than Required 013   *013*

More Nutrition than Required......... 014   *014*

Potential for Excess 015   *015*

SKIN INTEGRITY

Actual Skin Impairment 016   *016*

Potential Skin Impairment 017   *017*

Alterations in Oral Mucous Membrane.... 018   *018*

Altered Body Temperature 019   *019*

ELIMINATION

URINARY

Incontinence 020   *020*

Other Altered Urinary Elim. Pattern....... 021   *021*

BOWEL

Constipation.......................... 022   *022*

Diarrhea.............................. 023   *023*

Incontinence 024   *024*

ACTIVITY-EXERCISE

Activity Intolerance 025   *025*

Ineffective Airway Clearance.............. 026   *026*

Altered Breathing Pattern................. 027   *027*

Impaired Gas Exchange.................. 028   *028*

Altered Tissue Perfusion 029   *029*

SP-3530(9/85)

FIGURE 38-1

University Hospitals of Cleveland nurse/patient summary.

Decreased Cardiac Output .... 030 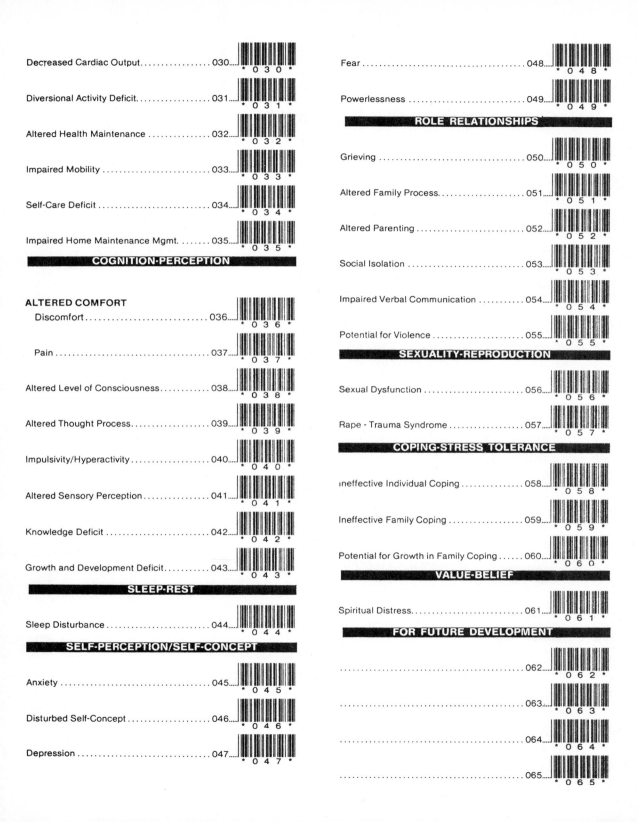 *030*

Diversional Activity Deficit 031 *031*

Altered Health Maintenance 032 *032*

Impaired Mobility 033 *033*

Self-Care Deficit 034 *034*

Impaired Home Maintenance Mgmt. 035 *035*

COGNITION-PERCEPTION

ALTERED COMFORT

Discomfort 036 *036*

Pain 037 *037*

Altered Level of Consciousness 038 *038*

Altered Thought Process 039 *039*

Impulsivity/Hyperactivity 040 *040*

Altered Sensory Perception 041 *041*

Knowledge Deficit 042 *042*

Growth and Development Deficit 043 *043*

SLEEP-REST

Sleep Disturbance 044 *044*

SELF-PERCEPTION/SELF-CONCEPT

Anxiety 045 *045*

Disturbed Self-Concept 046 *046*

Depression 047 *047*

Fear 048 *048*

Powerlessness 049 *049*

ROLE RELATIONSHIPS

Grieving 050 *050*

Altered Family Process 051 *051*

Altered Parenting 052 *052*

Social Isolation 053 *053*

Impaired Verbal Communication 054 *054*

Potential for Violence 055 *055*

SEXUALITY-REPRODUCTION

Sexual Dysfunction 056 *056*

Rape - Trauma Syndrome 057 *057*

COPING-STRESS TOLERANCE

Ineffective Individual Coping 058 *058*

Ineffective Family Coping 059 *059*

Potential for Growth in Family Coping 060 *060*

VALUE-BELIEF

Spiritual Distress 061 *061*

FOR FUTURE DEVELOPMENT

.... 062 *062*

.... 063 *063*

.... 064 *064*

.... 065 *065*

Hospital 1 — Division 30 for Report Date 07/02/86

	JSMITH	RWILLINS	HBROWN	CDAVIES	DJONES	ECLARKE	LJOHNSOE	JSTEPHES	SPETERS	ROBRIEN	Total Number Conditions
Room	3000	3017	3023	3024	3026	3027	3030	3031	3032	2033	
HEALTH PERCEPTION — MGMT.											
001 Potential for Injury					1						1 001
002 Noncompliance											002
003 Infection/Contagion	1	1	1		1	1	1			1	7 003
004 Prolong Disease/Disab.	1	1	1	1	1	1	1	1	1		9 004
005 Instability									1		1 005
006 Impaired Life Support Sys.									1		1 006
007 Sanitation Deficit											007
008 Soc-Cult-Econ Consid.											008
NUTRITIONAL — METABOLIC											
009 Excess Fluid Volume					1				1		2 009
010 Fluid Volume Deficit											010
011 Pot. Fluid Vol. Deficit		1		1			1				3 011
012 Bleeding	1	1		1	1	1				1	6 012
013 Less Nutrition Than Required		1	1	1	1	1	1	1	1		8 013
014 More Nutrition Than Required											014
015 Pot. For Excess Nutrition											015
016 Actual Skin Impairment		1		1	1				1		4 016
017 Potential Skin Impairment	1	1	1		1	1	1	1	1		8 017
018 Alt. in Oral Mucous Memb.	1	1	1		1	1			1	1	7 018
019 Altered Body Temp.		1		1	1	1					4 019
ELIMINATION											
020 Urinary Incontinence			1						1		2 020
021 Other Alt Urin. Elim. Patterns						1	1				2 021
022 Constipation				1	1						2 022
023 Diarrhea						1			1		2 023
024 Bowel Incontinence						1			1		2 024
ACTIVITY — EXERCISE											
025 Activity Intolerence		1			1	1			1		4 025
026 Impaired Airway						1			1		2 026
027 Altered Breathing Pattern						1			1		2 027
028 Impaired Gas Exchange									1		1 028
029 Altered Tissue Perfusion						1			1		2 029
030 Decreased Cardiac Output						1					1 030
031 Diversional Activity Def.		1		1	1	1		1			5 031
032 Alt. Health Maintenance						1					1 032
033 Impaired Mobility						1			1		2 033
034 Self-Care Deficit					1	1			1		3 034
035 Impaired Home Maint. Mgmt.						1					1 035
COGNITION — PERCEPTION											
036 Discomfort	1	1		1	1	1	1		1		7 036
037 Pain									1		1 037
038 Alt. Level of Consciousness						1			1		2 038
039 Altered Thought Process						1					1 039
040 Impulsivity/Hyperactivity											040
041 Altered Sensory Perception		1			1	1			1		4 041
042 Knowledge Deficit	1	1	1	1	1		1	1		1	8 042
043 Growth/Development Def.											043

FIGURE 38-2

University Hospitals of Cleveland nursing conditions profile.

		J	R	H	C	D	E	L	J	S	R	Total Number Conditions
SLEEP — REST												
044	Sleep Disturbance		1			1	1					3 044
045	Anxiety		1		1	1	1					4 045
046	Disturbed Self-Concept						1					1 046
047	Depression							1				1 047
048	Fear		1			1	1	1			1	5 048
049	Powerlessness		1		1	1	1	1			1	6 049
ROLE RELATIONSHIPS												
050	Grieving			1	1	1				1		4 050
051	Altered Family Process	1	1		1	1	1					5 051
052	Altered Parenting	1	1			1						3 052
053	Social Isolation		1			1						2 053
054	Impaired Verbal Comm.						1					1 054
055	Potential For Violence											055
SEXUALITY — REPRODUCTION												
056	Sexual Dysfunction											056
057	Rape — Trauma Syndrome											057
COPING — STRESS TOLERANCE												
058	Ineffective Indiv. Coping											058
059	Ineffective Family Coping											059
060	Pot. For Growth in Fam. Cop.	1	1	1	1	1	1	1		1	1	9 060
VALUE — BELIEF												
060	Spiritual Distress		1									1 061
		3	3	2	3	3	3	3	3	3	2	
		5	7	9	1	3	2	3	6	5	9	
		4	3	8	7	7	8	9	4	7	9	
		9	9	4	3	3	8	3	3	7	2	Total
		2	3	3	9	3	5	6	9	3	6	Number
		1	2	7	8	0	4	1	9	2	3	Conditions
		0	3	6	8	4	4	0	1	7	4	
CONDITIONS/PATIENT:		10	23	8	14	24	35	11	7	24	7	163

TOTAL NUMBER OF PATIENTS   10
AVERAGE NUMBER OF COND/PATIENT   16

• The first patient was admitted primarily for wound care. Condition 16, "Actual Skin Impairment," refers to a skin ulcer and the needed dressing regimen. On the last hospital day this was the only active nursing problem. Other conditions attended to during the hospital stay included "Anxiety" the first two days, "Discomfort" the first four days, "Potential for Growth in Family Coping," and "Potential Skin Impairment" toward the end of the hospital stay.

It could be argued from the outset that this hospitalization was not necessary. Perhaps this wound could have been managed more cost effectively on an outpatient basis or with a home care nurse. Or perhaps after a brief hospital stay of two or three days, the patient might have been discharged with knowledge and supplies equipping the patient and/or family to perform the dressing regimen at home. A home team nurse could monitor the wound status during periodic visits. Many of these hospital days could have been saved. The DRG number is 278, Cellulitis — Age 18-60, without complications and DRG payment weight is .8096 (See Table 38-1).

• The second patient experienced a variety of conditions during the hospital stay. "Knowledge deficit about self-care" and "physiologic instability" were resolved after the first few days. "Potential for excess nutrition" and "altered urinary elimination pattern" were conditions that existed throughout the hospital stay. There was a sudden decrease in the number of conditions from day six to days seven and eight. Most of the conditions on day six were in the area of individual and family coping.

TABLE 38-1

PATIENT'S NURSING CONDITIONS BY DAY							
Day of stay	1	2	3	4	5	6	7
Patient	16	16	16	16	16	16	16
Conditions	34	36	36	36	60	17	
	36	45	37				
	45						

DRG 278 Cellulitis   Age 18-60 without complications

DRG weight .8096

TABLE 38-2

PATIENT'S NURSING CONDITIONS BY DAY								
Day of stay	1	2	3	4	5	6	7	8
Patient	4	4	4	10	4	4	21	21
Conditions	5	5	5	19	14	15		
	15	9	10	21	21	21		
	21	15	15	31	22	22		
	42	21	21	32	37	36		
		35	22			37		
		42	35			51		
		60	60			59		

DRG 294 Diabetes, age greater than or equal to 16
DRG weight .8087

TABLE 38-3

PATIENT'S NURSING CONDITIONS BY DAY							
Day of Stay	1	2	3	4	5	6	7
Patient	12	1	1	1	10	2	10
Conditions	33	12	9	2	15	12	12
	34	20	10	9	20	23	13
	37	25	13	10	23	24	16
	41	29	20	12	24	34	24
	45	33	24	13	25	39	25
		46	34	25	20	33	33
		41	32	23	36		34
			33	24			35
			34	25			41
			36	32			42
			60	33			45
				34			48
				35			
				36			
				39			
				60			

DRG 174 G.I. hemorrhage,   age greater than or
DRG weight .9185   equal to 69 and/or
                           complications and
                           comorbidity.

How do family characteristics influence the preparation for discharge? How is the problem of altered urinary elimination addressed in preparation for discharge? Could some strategy have been implemented for this problem that would have allowed this patient an earlier discharge? For DRG 294, Diabetes, DRG weight is .8087. While the DRG weight for both these patients is nearly equal, the nursing dependency varies significantly (See Table 38-2).

● The third patient experienced a higher number of conditions and had the most conditions still being addressed on the last hospital day. Should the patient have been discharged before these conditions were resolved? Where did this patient go after discharge? To a skilled rehabilitation facility? To a nursing home? If the patient was sent home, what kind of referrals, equipment, or assistance were obtained for the patient? The assigned DRG was 174, G.I. hemorrhage, age greater than 69 and/or complications and comorbidity, and the DRG payment weight was .9185 (See Table 38-3).

In all cases the concern is whether the decisions made resulted in the most effective and efficient patient care. Could the care have been provided as well, but more cost-effectively, in another setting? In addition to concerns about placement and referral, optimizing length of stay—either increasing or decreasing—is another aspect of patient management to be assessed.

Patient management is central to the purpose of this information system. As clinical decisions are made in the interest of more effective and efficient patient care, ramifications for management of nurses will become apparent. That is, decisions about patient care are of the first order with implications for nurse management being of the second order and, therefore, generated by the first order decisions.

LEVELS OF DECISION AND MANAGEMENT REPORTS

Decisions affecting patient care management and resource allocation are made within a nursing service at three levels of the organization. These decisions are sequenced by the distance from the patient at which they are made.

The first level involves the nurse's allocation of effort to care for a patient. This apportionment has two stages: 1) the assignment of this nurse to that patient; and 2) the nurse's allocation of her/his time to particular needs of the patient, based on some prioritization process. For example, a nurse is assigned one patient: is the nurse's first priority the patient's sensoria or respiratory status or immobilized state or shock? The demands on a nurse for resource allocation are great. Similarly, a nurse who has been assigned four patients must determine whether her or his time will be equally distributed, or whether one patient will receive 50 percent of the nurse's time while each of the others requires a lesser percentage.

The second stratum of resource allocation also occurs at the ward level. The head nurse measures the patient needs and estimates staff capacity to meet them in the aggregate by nurses across shifts. This assignment decision is based on the head nurse's knowledge of patients' demands and of nurse ability to meet observed patient needs.

More removed from patients are the third level of nurse decision makers: normally director and assistant directors, they are responsible for all wards. They need data for each ward that describes its patient characteristics (number and complexity) and nurses (number, competence, and productivity) for control purposes. From this aggregate data, staff, and perhaps patients, are allocated to the various wards.

Resource allocation can then be taken a further step in which interhospital comparisons of patient nursing needs and nurse characteristics are made. The information which directors from independent institutions share from each other's data benefits each one's decision processes and influences the future

allocations of them all. Setting patient care priorities, assigning of nurses to patients, and nurse staffing constitute the full spectrum of nursing resource allocation decisions. To be of value, and, therefore, used by nurses and nurse managers, a data-based information system must be seen as supportive of decision making in setting priorities at the bedside, in making nurse-patient assignments, and in programming nurse staffing for the various wards.

OPTIMIZING THE MATCH

In the past, the management tools of a hospital nursing department were aggregated measures of the cost of nursing care and nursing hours per patient day. Nurse executives were involved in patient care only in a tangential way through policy and procedure or quality assurance committees. Measures were crude and so, too, were decisions based on them. Today's nurse administrator has to bring the nursing service into the mainstream of case-mix management. Physicians, nurses, and social workers must know the cost implications of the decisions they make in treating patients. Nurses and physicians need assistance in deciding the most cost-effective manner for treating patients. Management reports derived from clinical data supplied by the nurse will reduce the dissonance between nurse and nurse manager. The overly averaged, aggregated nature of currently existing nursing information available to nurse managers invariably leads them to different conclusions than a bedside nurse would make. The information system must be carefully designed to enable the mutual responsibility of nurses and nurse managers alike to achieve positive patient care results, and to manage nursing resources efficiently.

Nursing diagnosis terminology and descriptors of the nurse are the measures taken to represent the resource and demand elements of what should be an equation. Management reports incorporating information about both patients and nurses are under development. Of particular interest is a measure of the productivity of nurses. For example, are the correlates of productivity a nurse's education, experience, rated performance, or salary? The answer to these questions will affect strategic decisions on

TABLE 38-4

University Hospitals of Cleveland patient discharge summary

PATIENT NAME: Schmidt, F.   Hospital Number: 000894394   Marital Status: Widowed

ADMIT DATE: 04/04/86   DISCH. DATE: 04/17/86   DISCH. DIVISION: 60

PHONE NUMBER: (216) 555-1901   ZIP CODE: 44097   PAYOR: 900 Medicare DRG
                                                                              900 Medicaid/AFA

SEX: Female   DISCH. DISPOSITION: Home/Home Health Care

	Date	5	6	7	8	9	10	11	12	13	14	15	16	17	Total	
	Room	2		2	2	2	2	2	2	2	2	2	2	2		
		0		0	0	0	0	0	0	0	0	0	0	0		
		7		7	7	7	7	7	7	7	7	7	7	7		
		0		0	0	0	0	0	0	0	0	0	0	0		
	CONDITION															
001	Potential for Injury	1	1	1	1	1	1	1	1	1	1	1	1	1	13	001
003	Infection/Contagion		1	1	1	1	1	1	1	1	1	1	1	1	12	003
004	Prolonged Disease/Disab.	1	1	1	1	1	1	1	1	1	1	1	1	1	13	004
011	Pot. Fluid Vol. Deficit				1										1	011
012	Bleeding		1	1	1	1									4	012
016	Actual Skin Impairment		1	1	1	1	1	1	1	1	1	1			11	016
017	Potential Skin Impairment				1	1	1	1	1	1	1	1	1	1	10	017
021	Other Alt. Urin. Elim. Pat.			1	1										2	021
022	Constipation		1	1	1	1	1		1	1	1	1	1	1	11	022
025	Activity Intolerance	1	1	1	1	1	1	1	1	1	1	1	1	1	13	025
027	Altered Breathing Pattern				1										1	027
028	Impaired Gas Exchange				1										1	028
029	Altered Tissue Perfusion				1										1	029
031	Diversional Activity Def.					1	1	1				1	1		5	031
033	Impaired Mobility	1	1	1	1	1	1	1	1	1	1	1	1	1	13	033
034	Self-Care Deficit	1	1	1	1	1	1	1	1	1	1	1	1	1	13	034
035	Impaired Home Maint. Mgmt.					1				1		1	1	1	6	035
036	Discomfort		1	1	1			1	1					1	6	036
037	Pain	1	1	1	1	1	1	1	1	1	1	1	1	1	13	037
041	Alt. Sensory Perception					1									1	041
042	Knowledge Deficit	1	1	1	1	1	1	1	1	1	1	1	1	1	13	042
044	Sleep Disturbance	1	1	1											3	044
045	Anxiety	1	1	1		1			1	1	1	1	1		9	045
046	Disturbed Self-Concept												1		1	046
048	Fear	1	1	1		1	1	1	1	1	1		1		10	048
049	Powerlessness	1	1	1	1	1	1	1	1	1	1	1	1	1	13	049
060	Pot. for Growth in Fam. Cop.		1										1		2	060
	CONDITIONS/DAY:	11	17	17	20	17	15	13	15	16	14	15	16	15	201	27

TABLE 38-4
University Hospitals of Cleveland patient discharge summary — cont'd

ICD9 Codes and Diseases
    Code   Disease
    715.8   Osteoarthrosis, more than one site
    736.42   Genu Varum (Acquired)

ICD9 Codes and Procedures
    Code   Procedure
        Total Knee Arthroplasty

DRG Number	DRG Weight	DRG Name
209	2.2674	Major Joint & Limb Reattachment Procedures

Numbers of Associates: 40
Primary Nurses   Consultants:
Robb, I.H.   Caritas, L.

---

nurse recruitment, retention, promotion, and transfer practices.

Information about the available nursing staff is required to be matched with the patient demand factors to produce an assignment. Nurse factors of education, experience, capability to perform physical and psychological aspects of care, and salary rate are used to make assignments and are essential to cost out nursing care and examine the productivity of nurses. The staff assigned to the next three shifts are matched with the ward patients using the ward report as a tool to optimize the match. Preliminary results of an investigation of nurse-patient assignments using the Nurse-Patient Assignment Users Manual indicate that considerable improvement in effectiveness is achievable when assignments are better managed.[5] Great efficiency can be achieved by attending to this level of resource allocation. These efficiency and effectiveness dimensions of the nurse-patient assignment relate to both the clinical management of patients and the management of scarce nurse resources. Finally, there will be capacity to facilitate comparisons of patient and nurse parameters across nursing services from different institutions.

The individual Patient Discharge Summary report is currently being produced (See Table 38-4). This patient-centered report merges medical diagnosis and procedure data as well as demographic data with that of the nursing information system. The hospital stay is profiled by listing the patient's daily ratings. With this information, the patient's flow through the system can be reviewed. As costs associated with patient movement are great (especially into intensive care units), it would seem beneficial to question the placement of patients throughout their hospital stay.

The number of different caregivers, noted on the report, indicates the extent of continuity of care provided the patient. This report, which merges elements from various data bases, will enable examination of a patient's hospitalization.

By paying more attention to nurses' work, complications to illness will be prevented or detected early, and patients (and families) enabled to assume knowledgeable care of themselves. As expenditures for nurses are large and their impact on patients great, hospital management systems (clinical and financial) must account for them. The charge-based financial and data processing systems are fast becoming obsolete. Clinical case-mix systems will replace them and the nurses' role in patient care management must surface as central to the hospital mission to provide good care at less cost. A sound model is one built on the base of decisions a nurse makes to allocate time to one or more patients. Similarly, the measurement of nurse-patient assignments is the foundation for costing out nursing care.

THE COST OF NURSING CARE

The cost implications are derived from applying a cost algorithm to the patient classification and nurse assignment process. A direct cost algorithm for one eight-hour shift is shown in Table 38-5. Here, in this idealized assignment, complex patient demands were met with a more highly paid nurse with more time to allocate to the patient's needs. Using the algorithm, cost for nursing care is a function of both patient demand and nurse capability. The cost of nursing care for the two patients with 26 nursing conditions differed because of dissimilarities in the salaries (and presumably the capability) of the two nurses assigned and the number of patients in, as well as the complexity of, the nurses' caseloads. On the other and, where

the rehabilitation potential exists, the patient may be managed in the hospital (on skilled nursing rates) for 2-3 weeks in preparation for returning home.

Cost information is vital for the successful management of a nursing department. Once known, one can seek changes that are intended to reduce cost without negatively impacting on care. For example, patients with certain nursing conditions may be associated with substantial physical care and eventual nursing home placement for aftercare. Were such conditions known to clinicians early, screening and detection could lead to earlier post-hospital care.

Per-patient cost information can be cumulated by DRG or by nursing diagnosis for the purpose of setting prices for care. Such decision-support

TABLE 38-5
Cost algorithm using nurse-patient assignment

NURSE	HOURLY RATE*	NURSE RATE PER SHIFT	NUMBER OF CONDITIONS OF PATIENTS ASSIGNED	PATIENT COST WEIGHT	DISTRIBUTION OF NURSE COST BY PATIENT
1	$12.30	$98.40	28	28/54	$51.00
			26	26/54	47.40
2	11.25	90.00	26	26/70	33.50
			22	22/70	28.25
			22	22/70	28.25
3	11.25	90.00	19	19/53	33.00
			17	17/53	28.50
			17	17/53	28.50
4	11.25	90.00	14	14/51	24.70
			13	13/51	22.90
			12	12/51	21.20
			12	12/51	21.20
5	5.45	43.60	12	12/56	9.50
			12	12/56	9.50
			11	11/56	8.60
			11	11/56	8.60
			10	10/56	7.40
6	5.45	43.60	10	10/39	11.20
			9	9/39	10.00
			9	9/39	10.00
			8	8/39	8.90
			3	3/39	3.50

Total Cost $455.60
Fringe benefit costs not included.

capability would be invaluable were a hospital to negotiate with a Health Maintenance Organization (HMO) to provide care for patients on a per capita or per-patient basis.

Describing patient medical condition, nursing dependency, social and economic circumstances (currently available demographic and payor information), provides clinicians, health service researchers, and economists with a comprehensive set of patient variables upon which the health care system can be more accurately modeled. Those seeking control of hospital costs would do well to more fully describe patients' circumstances that contribute to health and health-related expenditures.

Clinical and managerial resource allocation decisions are best made when there is a climate of understanding and trust regarding the basis for making decisions. For nurses, those decisions are derived ideally from what is going on at the patient's bedside.

REFERENCES

1. Berki, S.E., Ashcraft, M.L.F., and Newbrander, W.C. (1984), "Length of stay variations within ICDA-8 diagnosis related groups," *Medical Care,* 22:2:126-142.
2. Halloran, E.J., & Halloran, D.C. (1985), "Exploring the DRG/nursing equation," American Journal of Nursing, 85:10:1093-95.
3. Wennberg, J.E., McPherson, K., & Caper, P., "Will payment based on diagnosis related groups control hospital costs?", *New England Journal of Medicine,* 311:5: 295-300.
4. Henderson, V., & Nite, G., *Principles and Practice of Nursing,* 6th edition (New York: Macmillan Publishing Co. 1978).
5. Halloran, E.J., *Nurse Staffing Issues and an Analysis of a Task Oriented Nurse Staffing Methodology.* Unpublished master's essay, Yale University, New Haven, 1975.

6. Vladek, B.C., *Unloving Care: The Nursing Home Tragedy* (New York: Basic Books, 1980).
7. Kiley, M.L., & Halloran, E.J. [Nursing assignment project, University Hospitals of Cleveland] unpublished raw data, 1983; Miller, A., "Nurse-patient dependency — is it iatrogenic?", *Journal of Advanced Nursing,* 10:63-69; and Munson, F., Beckman, J., Clinton, J., Kever, C., & Simms, L., *Nursing Assignment Patterns User's Manual* (Ann Arbor: AUPHA Press, 1980).

BIBLIOGRAPHY

American Nurses' Association. *Nursing: A Social Policy Statement.* Kansas City, Missouri: American Nurses' Association. 1980.

Caterinicchio, R. & Davies, R. "Developing a Client-focused Allocation Statistic of Inpatient Nursing Resource Use: An Alternative to the Patient Day." *Social Science and Medicine.* 17:259-272.

Giovanetti, P. *Patient Classification Systems in Nursing: A Description and Analysis.* Washington, D.C.: U.S. Department of Health, Education, and Welfare. 1978.

Halloran, E.J. "Nursing Workload, Medical Diagnosis Related Groups, and Nursing Diagnoses." *Research in Nursing and Health.* 8:4:421-433.

Halloran, E.J., Kiley, M.L., Nadzam, D., & Nosek, L. [Pilot test of a nursing diagnosis based patient classification instrument]. Unpublished raw data. 1984.

Horn, S.D., Sharkey, P.O., & Bertram, D.A. "Measuring Severity of Illness: Homogeneous Case Mix Groups." *Medical Care.* 21:14-25.

Nadzam, D. "The Comparison of Nursing Diagnoses with Patient Problem Titles in Nursing Care Plans in an Acute Psychiatric Setting." Manuscript submitted for publication. 1984.

Shin, Y. *Variation of hospital cost and product heterogeneity.* Health insurance studies contract research series (77-11722). Washington: U.S. Department of Health, Education and Welfare. 1977.

CHAPTER **39**

Implementation of Differentiated Practice Through Differentiated Case Management

Peggy L. Primm, RN, PhD

Differentiated Nursing Case Management (DCM) is a nursing service delivery system encompassing the best intentions of Primary Nursing and Total Patient Care while building on aspects of nursing practice known to be valued by current nurses and other health professionals. The system has been developed to result in consumer satisfaction and nurse retention through delivery of high quality, cost effective nursing care. DCM is designed to provide differentiated levels of nursing practice:

1. with a minimum of the current RN practice,
2. consistent with the minimal expectations for ADN and BSN prepared decision making of the future,
3. providing for continuity of care without interchangeable substitution of ADN and BSN levels of practice,
4. incorporating all currently employed staff nurses within the unit/agency into differentiated job descriptions for Nursing Assistants, LPN's, Case Associates, Case Managers, Targeted Population Case Managers (may be Clinical Specialists), and

Reprinted from *Michigan Nurse*, Vol. 61, No. 8, with permission of *Michigan Nurse* © 1988.

5. locating accountability and authority for planning and provision of high quality, cost effective nursing care at the staff nurse level.

The delivery system is effective across organizational structures and patient populations in Acute Care, Long Term Care, and Home Health Care agencies.

Job descriptions for Nursing Case Managers and Nursing Case Associates reflect the competencies expected of future graduates from registered nurse level nursing education programs. LPN job descriptions represent competencies of LPN current legal licensure and education. This provides an environment in which students can have positive experiences in role transition from education to the nursing service setting. In each setting, new graduates will practice in jobs recognizing the full potential of their education.

In today's health care system, the retention of currently employed nurses is very important. The Differentiated Nursing Case Management system incorporates all currently employed registered nurses into the job descriptions for Nursing Case Managers or Nursing Case Associates. Other members of the nursing staff, including LPN's and Nurse Assistants (if already employed) continue to practice within their current legal scope of practice. Each nurse, along with the nurse manager, considers his/her current practice patterns and interests, along with the unit patient population, length of stay, staffing resources and acuity levels to identify the job description that will be most satisfying for the nurse. Across the year of implementation, adjustments in the staffing pattern, staffing mix, and assignment methods result in maximum continuity of care for patients. Indicators of the quality and cost of nursing care and patient satisfaction continue to be monitored.

Differentiated Nursing Case Management places accountability for planning, provision and evaluation of effectiveness of nursing practice at the staff nurse level. The system encompasses the philosophy that all patients benefit from the full scope of nursing practice, but that the Case Manager does not need to be present every shift. Case Managers plan and implement nursing care directly and provide for continuity of care through delegation to other nurses (Case Associates) around the clock and throughout the patient's stay. Nursing care provided within each shift is consistent with the Case Manager's documented comprehensive nursing plan of care. Physician's orders are incorporated into the nursing plan of care and continue to be implemented in a timely manner. Each unit will determine the most effective staffing pattern needed to provide patients with continuous, high quality, cost effective nursing care.

This system is designed to facilitate nurses' management of nursing care. Multi-disciplinary planning and minimum standards of practice address cost effective utilization of resources and continuity of care. Patients, physicians, and administrators find increased nursing accountability and continuity of patient care from admission to discharge from the agency. Patients are admitted to a Case Manager's load within 24 hours of admission to the hospital. Each patient's Case Manager will collaborate with appropriate members of the health care team, the patient, family, and/or significant others, to meet the overall goals of nursing care while the patient is in the hospital and plan to meet needs for further care after discharge.

CHAPTER **40**

Nursing Case Management
Strategic management of cost and quality outcomes

Karen Zander, RN, MS, CS

The profound changes in reimbursement practices have created a much-needed catalyst for an equally profound restructuring of traditional care delivery systems and practice patterns at every level of acute care institutions. The shift in concern from "hi-tech" to "hi-speed" care must be addressed with specific organizational solutions which start from a detailed knowledge of the production process at the care provider level. Nursing Care Management, a model and set of technologies for the strategic management of cost and quality outcomes by the clinicians who give the care throughout an entire episode of illness, provides these solutions.

In the case management model at New England Medical Center Hospitals, designated patients are admitted to a formally-prepared group practice composed of an attending physician and a specific group of staff nurses from each of the units and clinics likely to receive these patients. Although all the nurses in the group practice will give direct care as the patient's primary or associate nurse while the patient is on his/her unit, the group practice designates one of the nurses to be the case manager. The case manager's authority extends across all units for the episode of care, as does the authority of the attending physician.

Reprinted from *The Journal of Nursing Administration*, Vol. 18, No. 5, with permission of J. B. Lippincott Company © 1988.

The group uses a Case Management Plan (CMP) and Critical Path to map, track, evaluate, and adjust the patient's course and achievement of outcomes. Convincing data from the first year of implementation validates the model and stimulates its continued development.

FINDINGS

The initial findings from use of case management are both qualitative and quantitative. Although the complete model has not been in place long enough to evaluate, even the components have yielded exciting results.

Case 1: Ischemic Stroke Patients

In September, 1986 the clinicians involved in treating ischemic stroke patients set a number of goals for more efficient care. Using CMPs and Critical Paths to study and revise current practice, the clinicians were able to make dramatic changes in just 6 months: a 29% drop in the average length of stay and a 47% drop in the average number of Intensive Care Unit (ICU) days.[1] The decreased ICU stay increased quality by minimizing the sensory deprivation experienced by patients in those settings. In addition, the patients on the general unit were able to have more access to their families and were able to transfer to rehabilitation services 7 to 10 days sooner.

It is essential to note that these changes were not made by "slicing off" days in a vacuum from quality standards, but rather through a truly collaborative change in clinical management agreed upon by nurses, physicians, and administrators. Similarly, the average ICU days for subarachnoid patients dropped by 10%. As in ischemic stroke patients, cost was decreased while quality remained high.[2]

Case 2: Induction and Consolidation, Adult Leukemia Patients

This example describes how clinicians will welcome case management if they are given control and perceive that quality does not have to be sacrificed. In fact, in this case, quality was drastically improved![3] In addition, average consolidation charges were dramatically cut when that phase of treatment was given in the home rather than the hospital.

- In developing a critical pathway for patients undergoing induction therapy for leukemia, we discovered that the usual practice was to admit the patient 2 to 4 days before putting in a Cooks catheter. Chemotherapy was then started, followed by antibiotic therapy and/or antifungal therapy that continued for 3 to 4 weeks. A complete fever work-up was done at least once a day. Electrolytes and CBC (complete blood count) were also drawn daily. Reviewing subsequent readmission patterns showed that the patient was hospitalized four more times for consolidation treatment with chemotherapy.
- After examining current practice, the following changes were made: (1) The Cooks catheter is placed on Day 2 of hospitalization; (2) When the patient is no longer neutropenic and is afebrile, antibiotic therapy and antifungal therapy are completed at home; (3) Mouth care for thrush is begun on day 1 before symptoms are evident; (4) If no new organism is identified, a fever work-up is done every 48 hours; and (5) Only essential electrolytes and blood counts are drawn on a daily basis.

- These changes have reduced the patient's length of stay from 6 to 8 weeks (42 to 56 days) to approximately 32 days. The number of unnecessary diagnostic tests has also been reduced. We are now giving low dose consolidation chemotherapy at home thus eliminating 14 additional days of hospitalization. By implementing these changes, we found that quality outcomes were not only maintained, but were improved. Infection rates decreased with home chemotherapy, patients slept through the night when a complete fever workup was not done, much more time is spent at home with families, and finally, patients reported increased satisfaction with care and a feeling that they were in better control of what happened to them.

Case 3: Abdominal Aortic Aneurysm Repair Patients

In this example of an individual patient who was treated by a physician–nurse group practice, quality outcomes were met although the patient stayed 2 days longer because of major complications. In the past, similar patients would have possibly experienced longer, more fragmented care and far more insecurity in the hospital.

The patient was a 76-year-old man with a history of coronary artery disease who had been followed by the vascular physicians and outpatient nurse for several years before his surgery. He was admitted to the group practice associated with the specific vascular physician and outpatient nurse, i.e. a senior primary nurse on the vascular floor, the vascular operating room nurse, and the senior primary nurse in the Surgical Intensive Care Unit (SICU). Each of the nurses became the patient's primary nurse during his stay on her unit, and the vascular floor primary nurse assumed the case manager role for the smooth coordination of his care throughout all phases. His critical pathway went according to plan until he had a retroperitoneal bleed in the SICU and had to return to surgery, during which he also had a myocardial infarction. Because of these complications he was transferred on Day 10 (instead of Day 7) from the SICU but only required two additional days of total hospitalization. The 10 to 13 day length of stay allotted for DRG 110–Major Vascular Surgery was only increased to 16 for this patient, attributable both to his prior health and to the technical, interpersonal, and management skills of the group practice. The nurses enlisted the caring of his wife at every phase of his treatment, and his follow-up visits in ambulatory were well used to support his recovery.[4]

Perhaps this case would have had the same results before case management. The challenge, however, is that all patients will be clinically managed as well as this patient was, and that realistic outcomes will be actualized.

MODEL DESCRIPTION

The Nursing Case Management Model was developed from our 13-year history of primary nursing along with a 2-year investigation of nursing and physician practice as they relate to clinical outcomes of care. It differs from other more commonly-known case management models[5,6] because:

1. The "product line" is managed by the actual care givers who are accountable clinically and financially for each patient's outcomes,
2. It is built on case-type specific protocols framed by reimbursement-allotted lengths of stay,
3. "Quality" is prescribed in written detail, managed concurrently, and evaluated collaboratively, and
4. The patient and family are actively engaged as members of the health care team and given specific responsibilities and control.

The model (Figure 40-1) links structure, process, and outcome along three dimensions: work *design,* clinical management *roles,* and concurrent monitoring as *feedback.*[7]

In the model, "Design" entails Case Management Plans and Critical Paths. A Case Management Plan is a comprehensive protocol for an entire episode of care which shows the relationships between (1) a DRG or subset, its related patient problems, with each of their intermediate and length of stay outcomes, and the nursing and physician processes (tasks) necessary to achieve them; (2) the clinical work in relation to time for every case-type for asthma in the emergency room over 4 hours to schizophrenia over 3 years; and potentially (3) nursing acuity (tasks) with the cost of the product (Figure 40-2).[8]

A Critical Path is an abbreviated, one-page version of a CMP which shows the critical, or key incidents that must occur in a predictable and timely order to achieve an appropriate length of stay (Figure 40-3). Critical Paths are tools that, once individualized by the primary nurse and physician within the first 24 hours of admission, are used on every shift on each consecutive unit to plan and monitor the flow of care. Variances are either justified or actions are taken immediately to rectify the variance. They are used to organize change-of-shift report, identify patient problems for consultation, and as a management tool for RN–MD collaboration.[9]

The second dimension of the model, "Role," is the way the work design is converted into actual outcomes. Managed care must be more than a philosophy and protocol — it must include professionals skilled as

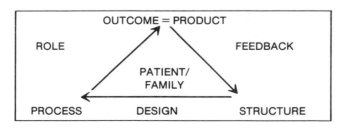

FIGURE 40-1

Case management model.

both clinicians and managers who are committed to the welfare of both patients and the institution. The case manager is responsible for revising the CMP in accordance with an assessment of the individual patient's needs combined with the knowledge of attainable outcomes gleaned from experience and research. The case manager, working in a group practice, is accountable for meeting outcomes within an appropriate length of stay, the effective use of resources, and established standards (clinical processes and outcomes).

The third dimension of the model is "Feedback," or the set of methods used to evaluate care concurrently and in aggregates and trends retrospectively.

Because the most important evaluation is that which can be done while the patient is still undergoing care, concurrent tools and systems are crucial. In nursing case management, these are:

- Accurate assessments of problem and goal identification which include the patient's and family's perception and concerns,
- Use of the CMP and Critical Path *every day* and/or *shift* or visit,
- Regular case consultations by both the group practices and the immediate care unit,
- Collaborative monitoring by physicians, nurses, and other key professionals,

---

NEW ENGLAND MEDICAL CENTER HOSPITALS
DEPARTMENT OF NURSING

EXCERPT CASE MANAGEMENT PLAN

DIAGNOSIS: **Idiopathic Pediatric Scoliosis, with surgery, without complications**   UNIT: **Floating 7 South**   DRG: **215**
MDC: **8**   LENGTH OF STAY: **14 days**   USUAL OR DAY (from admission day = 1): **3**

HEALTH OUTCOMES

DIAGNOSIS	OUTCOME (The patient...)	DAY VISIT	INTERMEDIATE GOAL (The patient...)	DAY VISIT	PROCESS (The nurse...)	DAY VISIT	PROCESS (The physician...)
Fluid/electrolyte imbalance; third space shifting secondary to large volume loss and replacement	Vital signs are stable and consistent with admission baseline.	5-6 4-14	• Is afebrile. • Maintains VS within the following range: P____BP____R____T____	4 5-9 10-14 1-14	• Takes vital signs q2h for 8h post op then q4h if patient afebrile and vital signs stable, then q shift. • Notifies MD if P>____, BP>____, R>____, T>____, or if P<____, BP<____, R<____, T<____.	PTA 1	• Upon family's request arranges for self blood donation by patient over a 3-4 month period. • On admission assesses the patient's cardiac status. Orders an EKG. Reviews cardiac landmarks on scoli scoli series. If there is evidence or history of abnormality or compromise an echocardiogram and/or cardiology consult may be ordered.
	Voiding pattern is at baseline normal.	4-6 6-7 4-14	• Maintains urine output over 1cc/KG/hr while foley catheter in. • Voids 8 hours after foley is discontinued. • Maintains Specific Gravity under .1020.	4 5-6 7-14 4-6 5-6 7-14 4-14 4	• Measures and records I/O q1h for 24h, then q4h if stable (while foley in), then every shift. • Notifies MD if output under ____cc/hr while foley in. • Monitors specific gravity q2h for 8h, q4h for 48 h if stable, then every shift. • Notifies MD if SG over .1020. • Calculates 24h I/O for OR day on return to unit.	1	• Orders the following lab studies CBC with differential PT, PTT, Platelet Count, BUN, Creatinine, Urinalysis with Sediment.
	Has no edema.	8-9	• Returns to baseline skin turgor.	4-8 9-14 4-10 4-7	• Balances IV and oral intake to achieve maintenance fluid requirements, then forces oral fluids to maintenance. • Observes dressing when patient turned and notifies MD of new or increased bloody staining. • Empties and records hemovac drainage q4-8h. Notifies MD of drainage over 100cc in 4h.	PRN 24h Prior to OR	• Orders a bleeding time if there is a suggestive history and/or abnormal coagulation studies. • Types and crossmatches the patient for appropriate volume of blood based on weight and exact procedure to be done (usually 6-8 units in adolescent patients).

FIGURE 40-2

Excerpt case management plan.

Patient _____

MD _____

Case Manager _____

Date Critical Path _____

    Reviewed by MD _____

        Date

Case Type Myocardial _____

           Infarction _____

DRG _____ 122 _____

Expected LOS   7 Days

**MYOCARDIAL INFARCTION
CRITICAL PATH**

	Day 1	Day 2	Day 3	Day 4	Day 5	Day 6	Day 7
ICU	—————————————————————— 6S ———————————————————————————						
Consults		Cardiac Rehab. Dietician				Copy of Low Chol. No Added Salt Diet	
Tests	EKG	EKG	EKG Receive MBs R/I or R/O MI		Holter ETT Cath.		
		ETT if nec. for Day 6 Echo, Muga, if nec.	Holter if nec. on Day 5		if nec.		
Activity	BRP w/ Commode		OOB Chair		Amb in Rm/Hall w/Asst	Up Ad————→ Lib Stairs	
Treatments	O$_2$ —————————————————————————————→ D/C O$_2$						
	Cardiac —————————————————————————————→ Monitor					D/C Monitor p negative Holter	
	I & O qd —————————————————————————————→					D/C I & O qd wt, unless CHF	
	IV ————————————— Heparin ———————————————————→ D/C Heparin		Lock				Lock
Diet	No Added Salt, Low Chol. Diet ——————————————————————————————→						
Discharge Planning			VNA		Check w/ Attending RE:D/C Date	Discharge Orders	Discharge before 12 Noon
Teaching	Angina, MI, PN., Med, Teaching Plan in Chart	Begin MI Teaching Plan	3 discharge classes Formal Med tx				Amb Classes Re:Risk Factors Diet & smoking

Admission Date _____   Discharge Date _____   Discharge Time _____

    Days in ICU _____   Stress test date _____   Cardiac cath. date _____

    Days in Routine bed _____   Thalium _____

                         Routine _____

            Holter date _____

Copyright: New England Medical Center Hospitals 1987, Department of Nursing

	VARIATION	CAUSE	ACTION TAKEN
DATE			

FIGURE 40-3

Critical path.

- The use of planned telephone appointments for initial assessments, follow-up calls, etc., and
- Patient education in groups.

Retrospectively, a Management Information System (MIS) audit for primary nursing which includes charts, patients, families, staff nurses, and the 24-hour nursing leadership team is conducted every 4 months to evaluate the structures and processes of professional practice.[10] Problem-focused quality assurance programs, similar to those used in most hospitals, are also conducted. As the clinical management of patients becomes better understood, feedback can be used to transform structures in regard to variables affecting length of stay, the appropriate timing of interventions such as patient education, the influence of individual practice patterns on outcomes, the role of hospital management, the effects of other department's policies and procedures on nursing, and the most effective ways to give patients and families more confidence and participation in their care.

In summary, the three dimensions of the model become reality when a set of "Ground Rules" (listed in the box on this page) is activated.[11] Currently, patients in six broad diagnostic categories are being case managed (cardiac, stroke, neonates, pediatric and adult leukemia, vascular, and orthopedic).

EVOLUTION TO CASE MANAGEMENT

The Nursing Case Management Model developed as staff nurses, managers, and administrators asked hard questions about their practice in relation to increased acuity, shortened lengths of stay, and the many issues of concern to the nursing profession (see box on page 56.)[12] This intensely ambiguous and pressured environment presents nursing's best and possibly last opportunity to produce gains for all constituencies: the patients and families, the care providers, their institutions, and payors (our new clients).

Several strong beliefs drive the continuous evolution of the model and build on the strengths of primary nursing while rectifying some of its weaknesses. These beliefs are:

1. Nurses have always been managers of care, but have labored with outdated management tools

---

New England Medical Center Hospitals Department of Nursing

Ground rules: case management

- Every designated patient will be assigned to a nursing group practice on or before entry to the NEMCH.
- Every group practice will assign a nursing care manager who works with an attending physician in evaluating an individualized Case Management Plan (CMP) and Critical Path for each patient.
- A Critical Path is used to facilitate the care for every patient.
- Report will be based on Critical Paths.
- Negative variances from Critical Paths and/or CMP require discussion with the attending physician, and a case management consultation when necessary.
- Every case manager must be a primary nurse or an associate when the patient is in his/her geographic area.
- The nursing case manager and physician case manager must communicate on a regular basis.
- Case managers will evolve/negotiate a flexible schedule that accommodates the needs of their patients and group practice as well as the needs of their units.
- Responsibility of the case manager begins at notification of patient's entry into the system and ends with a formal transfer of accountability to the patient, family, another health care provider, or another institution.
- Group practices will meet on a regular basis.

(such as nursing care plans) and shift-centered management systems.
2. Quality is not a vague ideal, but rather is defineable using specific clinical process and outcome standards that are the resolution of patient problems. Quality in health care is thus a product, not a service.
3. The true cost of producing a range of expected outcomes can be understood and revised on a case-type basis. Diagnostic Related Groups (DRGs) are not in themselves, descriptive of

Management seminar series
The nursing production process

Questions

1. What is the Production Process as it related to the Nursing Product?
2. How should we help primary nurses define long- and short-term goals (ie, outcomes) for their patients?
3. How should we help primary nurses determine approaches and interventions for their patients?
4. How should we help primary nurses (1) "move" the patient from admission to discharge and (2) achieve maximum continuity of care?
5. Besides patient and family condition, what variables most strongly affect length of stay and how can those variables be improved?
6. How can we improve the production process by changing staffing mix, scheduling patterns, use of associates, flextime, etc.?
7. How should Primary Nursing Consultation be improved to better assist nurses as case managers?
8. What management tools (computer, documentation, use of charts, and schedules) should be used by primary nurses, senior staff nurses, charge nurses, and nurse managers to improve decision-making for cases?
9. How should we achieve better congruence and collaboration with (1) other New England Medical Center nurses and (2) other departments?
10. How should the nursing management staff and vertical teams be supported and educated in the year to come?
11. How can primary nurses be held accountable for getting their patients to outcome?
12. What is your vertical team's DRG/length of stay project and what is your analysis of it?

immobility, etc.) that can often be prevented through astute management.

4. Nursing makes a major contribution to clinical outcomes through powerful interventions based on a diagnostic reasoning process, and by making the system work for the physicians and patients. Because of nursing's 24-hour access, nursing allocates much of a hospital's resources.
5. Nurses and physicians have always worked interdependently, but in parallel structures rather than in formal collaborative practice groups with protocols. Also, clinicians tend to assume that high technical know-how indicates high case management skills, which is not necessarily true. Therefore, even highly-skilled clinicians can benefit from learning updated management strategies.

GENERIC STEPS: THE TRANSITION FROM PLANNED CARE TO MANAGED CARE

There is nothing easy or magical about building a model for case management, except perhaps the energy that is rechanneled from struggling with chronic bureaucratic situations to real solutions for patient-centered care. It requires administration's relentless focus, openness, and risk-taking, all difficult approaches to keep while maintaining the usual operations of a department.

It is often impossible for busy hospital administrators, nurses, and physicians to spend hours in meetings to plan case management. However, nursing can take the lead, working one-to-one and in small groups to effect change. It is most advantageous to begin with a group of experienced nurses from the units to which a certain case-type is admitted, help them design a tentative model and Case Management Plan, and then support them in collaborating with physicians and hospital administration. The steps below can be used for guidelines.

1. *Define the Business*
   a. What are your high-volume case-types?
   b. What is their average length of stay (including operating room time, visits, days in the system)?

costs because they are based on a biomedical model. On the other hand, the more (potentially) controllable costs of an episode of care are in the nursing realm of self-care deficits and physical complications (respiratory,

c. What are the usual patient problems (nursing diagnoses) related to specific DRGs or their subsets?

d. What are realistic clinical outcomes attainable (75% to 100% of the time) at the end of the entire expected episode of care related to each problem?

e. What are the intermediate outcomes; benchmarks?

f. What tasks do physicians and nurses do to get an "average" patient to the intermediate outcomes?

g. If you have physicians who have individual preferences for the standard treatment of certain design case-types, design a different CMP and Critical Path for each physician.

h. For case-types with high dependency on support services such as social service, form additional columns on the CMP to indicate their expected processes. However, most support services will be adequately addressed through the coordinating processes of the nurse.

2. *Design Critical Paths*
   a. Lay out care the way it currently is organized.
   b. Revise the timing of key events in collaboration with the institution.
   c. Start tracking variances from the norm.
   d. Use Critical Paths as a basis for shift reports thereby ensuring managed care.

3. *Form Group Practices*
   a. Identify attending-level physicians who are interested.
   b. Identify a primary nurse and associate on each unit to which that attending physician's patients are admitted.
   c. Collaboratively design and use CMPs and Critical Paths.
   d. Begin monitoring and evaluating.

4. *Provide Advanced Skills and Knowledge*
   a. Expose (and test if possible) all nurses, physicians, and others regarding background knowledge about current trends in health care.[13]
   b. Teach nurses management skills. NEMCH has three mandatory days for management training for all nurses in the first year and three mandatory classroom days for newly-appointed group practice members.

c. Provide specific curriculum that emphasizes:
   i. The need for clinicians to manage toward both clinical and cost outcomes,
   ii. Group practice responsibilities,
   iii. Collaboration skills,
   iv. Increased physical and family assessment skills,
   v. Use of the telephone in assessment, support, and follow-up,
   vi. Methods for including patients and families in the setting and evaluation of outcomes,
   vii. The timing and content for more effective patient teaching,
   viii. Use of resources in discharge planning,
   ix. Concurrent review through case consultation and live audits of patients, and
   x. Time management techniques.

Begin to Evaluate the Model
   a. What variables most effect length of stay? Are they due to patient, provider, or institution problems?
   b. What are the role changes for the nurse, especially in relation to authority and satisfaction?

SURPRISING DISCOVERIES

By establishing case management, accountability — that great diviner of professional status — is clarified and assigned to a specific staff primary nurse as case manager. In this transformation from task to outcome-based practice, the staff nurses, their managers, and administrators have made important discoveries:

• Even the best nurses are task-oriented (which is the core of their effectiveness), but they view the tasks as a means to an end, not the end. They do not define themselves or their worth by tasks, but rather by making a difference in patient outcomes. In fact, they perceive each shift as a chance to work on intermediate goals.

• Standards of excellence must be integrated into one's everyday practice to strategically manage cost/quality outcomes. For the most part, progress notes and care plans have not accomplished this mission.

Nurses do what they do because of what they hear in the report and see in the patient. Perhaps as a group, nurses are visual, auditory learners rather than readers and writers. If this is true, then nurses need to improve and develop "audiovisual" mechanisms such as report, rounds, and voice-activated computers rather than base a fast-paced applied science on slow information systems!

- Nurses become less territorial and more creative as they focus on outcomes and their management for an entire episode of care. Thus, formerly "intuitive knowledge" is raised to a formal operational level. As this occurs, nursing can join and eventually lead the industry in effecting episode-based rather than unit-based care.
- Stetler and DeZell, in collaboration with an expert panel of nursing staff and managers, have outlined four new nursing diagnoses that inherently acknowledge nursing's powerful interventions in the context of outcomes. They are: (1) potential for extension of the disease process, (2) potential for complications related to treatment, (3) potential for complications unrelated to treatment, and (4) potential for complications/self-care.[14]
- The best way to empower staff nurses is through roles which increase their authority. Authority is the foundation of accountability and has several sources. In case management, the nurse's three greatest sources of authority are: (1) the patient and family, (2) the group practice (peers and physicians), and (3) the nurse manager.
- The most supportive, effective, fast-responding nursing departments have a balance of centralized and decentralized functions. Case management is the decentralization of the accountability for clinical and case-cost outcomes to the staff nurse level. Paradoxically, centralized structures enable this fundamental decentralization.

SUMMARY

The case management model was initiated by nursing administration and is supported by hospital administration because it clearly outlines and activates the strategic management of cost and quality outcomes. It is patient-centered in assessment, plan, and delivery because it is collaborative in goal-setting and evaluation. When patients and families perceive that the clinicians know their business and have confidence that their fellow-providers can give quality care in shorter time, so will they.

Case management goes a long way towards lessening the potential credibility gap between institutions and consumers, and clearly establishes that the control of health care lies at the provider–patient juncture. Projects to better involve patients in their care, such as increasing knowledge of their critical paths, and self-medication programs, have been implemented.

Everyone in health care knows how much effort it takes for plans to go smoothly. The key to the success of case management is clinician involvement at every phase. If clinicians do not proactively develop systems and become case managers, there will be new layers of nonclinical people who begin to direct our business. Are nurses ready for case management? Can we justify standing still? However difficult and futuristic case management appears, the alternatives are worse — lost control, lost authority, lost confidence, lost enthusiasm, and lost pride.

Nursing case management will not be a panacea, but it does provide a new direction for professional nursing.[15] It is highly adaptive to the current climate and highly applicable to most settings. Nursing case management "ups the ante" on professional practice as it continues to yield exciting, tangible results.

REFERENCES

1. Caplan L, et al. Managed care for stroke patients. Boston: New England Medical Center Hospitals, July 9, 1987;1.
2. *Ibid.*
3. Woldum K. Critical paths: marking the course. Definition 1987; Summer 2(3):1–2.
4. Hayes J, Isaacson L, Wilson L. A nursing group practice. Unpublished video. Boston: New England Medical Center Hospitals, 1987.
5. Evashwick C, Ney J, Siemon J. Case management: issues for hospitals. Chicago: The Hospital Research and Educational Trust, 1985.
6. Merrill J. Defining case management. Business and Health July/August 1985;5–9.

7. Zander K, Etheredge ML, Bower K. Nursing case management: blueprints for transformation. Boston: New England Medical Center Hospitals, 1987;3..

8. *Ibid,* p. 24.

9. Woldum, 3.

10. Zander K, Bower K, Etheredge ML. Evaluation — Management information system (MIS): primary nursing. In Handbook of professional practice. Boston: New England Medical Center Hospitals, 1985;156–179.

11. Twyon S. Ground rules: case management. Boston: New England Medical Center Hospitals, July 1, 1987.

12. Zander K, Etheredge ML, Bower K., 114.

13. Guy S, Comeau E. DRGs: a programmed instruction. Boston: New England Medical Center Hospitals, 1986.

14. Stetler C, DeZell AD. Case management plans: designs for transformation. Boston: New England Medical Center Hospitals, 1987;26–32.

15. National Commission on Nursing Implementation Project: Report. Milwaukee, WI: NCNIP, November 1986;3–6.

CHAPTER **41**

Advantages and Disadvantages of Product-Line Management

Deborah Yano-Fong, RN, MSN

The purpose of this paper is to analyze the advantages and disadvantages of implementing Product-Line Management (PLM) in an acute care setting, with particular emphasis on how PLM responds to the current economic environment facing these settings. Four major areas will be discussed: 1) a general overview of what PLM is and how it is implemented in an acute care setting, 2) an analysis of how PLM responds to the competitive environment and to DRGs and prospective payment, 3) the disadvantages PLM has on the organizational structure, and the ethical issues raised and 4) a summary of how the advantages and disadvantages are evaluated.

The reference articles were selected from the Business Index from 1978 to 1986. In the literature, the term product-line management (PLM) and product management (PM) are synonymous, as are the terms marketing manager and product manager.

OVERVIEW OF PRODUCT-LINE MANAGEMENT

Historically, PLM was first introduced in 1928 by Procter and Gamble to market their new product, Lava soap.[1] During the 1960s, approximately 84

Reprinted from *Nursing Management*, Vol. 19, No. 5, with permission of S-N Publications, Inc. © 1988.

percent of the large manufacturing companies adopted this business technique to compete successfully in their rapidly changing environments.[2] The product manager emerged as the integrator and coordinator of production, distribution, and sales of consumer products.[3] The goal of management was to produce a quality product in the most cost-effective manner; this required timely decisions to respond quickly to the changing needs of consumers and remain competitive.[1]

Acute care settings/hospitals historically have been organized and managed along functional lines. There was not a focus on costs of production or the elements of production.[4] The recent trend in the hospital industry toward competition in response to changes in reimbursement regulations has changed this industry. These changes suggest the need for a comprehensive organizational system, which analyzes the environmental pressures and develops strategies to meet these challenges.[5]

PLM is a new and progressive organizational approach which has been borrowed from the business world to develop, manage, and market healthcare programs in the hospital setting.[4] According to Bruhn and Howes, "The PLM approach is based on the premise that the hospital is a business enterprise with multiple service lines." Therefore, PLM is a planning and management system which coordinates and facilitates the services within a product line to provide comprehensive and cost-effective care to each patient.[4]

Increasingly, hospital services are defined as products and product lines, which indicates a shift in healthcare from services to products.[1] MacStravic defines a product in health services as, "A set of activities and experiences that are offered and consumed by an identifiable set of people in ways that are different from other sets . . . or a set of products that when planned, managed, or marketed as a group yields some advantage over being treated as isolated individuals."[6] With the application of PLM to the acute care setting, the following three characteristics are necessary for its implementation: 1) planning in relation to defining the hospital's activities in terms of product lines and services, target markets, and costs associated with production of each service, 2) management as it relates to organizing, directing, and controlling operations of the hospital product lines and 3) marketing approaches which treat specific services as different in that they serve different needs and represent distinct marketing challenges.[4,6,7,8] These characteristics will help the product manager to: 1) develop an understanding of the relationship between service mix and the market place; 2) develop competitive pricing strategies, and 3) understand the relationship between service mix and medical/nursing staff.[4]

These characteristics of PLM will be analyzed to determine the advantages or disadvantages they present for a hospital in today's economic environment.

ADVANTAGES OF PLM

Response to competition. Since recent legislative initiatives are indicators of the dramatically altered healthcare environment, they reinforce the competitive influences in today's healthcare market. Gregory and Klegon state the supply side factors as: "Surpluses of physicians and beds, improvements in outpatient, medical, diagnostic, and surgical capabilities, and changes in inpatient practice (as reflected in decreasing lengths of stay). . . . On the demand side, business, third-party payors, and other charge-paying groups are approaching hospitals for discounts and preferred provider arrangements."[9]

In order to respond to this environment, hospitals are identifying a need for the development of a system to look at the financial, marketing, and strategic planning of an institution concurrently.[9] This need fits well with the major emphasis of PLM, which is to focus on the strategic and operational definitions regarding which products to offer or where costs are to be controlled.[6]

Traditional management efforts in the hospital setting to control costs were done by controlling functional departments, but with the development of DRGs, PLM works to control costs by influencing how physicians manage their patients. MacStravic states, "the challenge of influencing physicians to use hospital resources more prudently and efficiently is a totally new one for more institutions." Because physicians are becoming highly specialized and there is an increase in competition among them, a product-line approach may prove effective, because the product manager can reason with the physician from the perspective of how his practice influences the overall outcome of the product line.[6]

Another focus of PLM is on "identifying, achieving, and maintaining a specific market position for each product line. . . . By focusing on specific programs or products, the hospital may be able to develop 'centers of excellence' that attract patients and referrals from a wide area."[6] This focus is accomplished through marketing a product line. The concept of marketing in hospitals has become more prevalent over the last ten years, because of the changes from regulation to competition.[10,11] Weil states, "The procompetition theory is proposed most frequently by President Reagan and other advocates of supply-side economics. It makes price a supreme consideration in the purchase of medical care, places providers at financial risk for their actions, and has the goal of slowing the rate of increase in federal healthcare expenditures."[11]

Marketing has been a major factor in successful business ventures, and its application to the hospital setting in response to increased competition is evidenced through such systems as PLM.[12,13] Bartlett *et al.* state that in the hospital context, "the marketing concept can be defined as a management understanding that the key task of the hospital is to identify the wants and needs of key constituents (notably patients and physicians)," and then shape the organization's products to bring about the desired exchange between the customers and the hospital.[12] In other words, marketing a program brings about the voluntary exchange of products with specific target markets for the purpose of achieving organizational objectives.[14] Targeting a particular market and developing a successful marketing plan are two components of marketing which are essential to its effectiveness. Targeting a particular market means: 1) identifying a service/product that the community needs on a regular basis; 2) performing a service better than your competitor, or 3) matching the services to the socioeconomic character of the community.[12] This concept is seen in the strategic value of product-line marketing, which specifically identifies the decision-makers who constitute the market for a specific product, and then focuses on capturing as many members of the intended market as possible.[4,6]

Marketing plans enable the hospital to make optimal use of all their resources in the planning and delivery of healthcare programs which are needed and desired by their clients.[12] This pursuit of excellence and the goal of meeting the needs of clients in conjunction with the strong marketing plan are seen as the key to surviving in an environment where inpatient utilization is decreasing.[10,15] The challenge for the product manager is to be able to maintain enough, but not too many, product lines for maximum success in regard to marketing, and to be able to identify when not to market a product line.[6]

PLM response to diagnosis related groups (DRGs)/ prospective payment systems (PPS). PLM allows hospital products to be organized in a variety of ways: DRGs, patient demographics, physician specialty groups, or specific procedures. The hospital product line also can be redefined to a specific category such as an individual diagnosis or patient case.[1] PLM can utilize the DRGs effectively to define product lines for the hospital because DRGs provide the hospital administrators and physicians with a "mechanism to control costs through a more precise understanding of the hospital's production process."[16]

Block and Press present one way in which DRGs are used by a marketing manager in a PLM setting.

DRGs describe "a diagnosis for which the patient will be treated and for which the hospital will be paid. They have shape, form, and product qualities;" this means the marketing manager can determine which DRGs are profitable, which DRGs have only potential profit, or which DRGs will incur losses.[17]

Benz and Burnham describe how one hospital implemented product lines based on the International Classification of Diseases — 9th Revision — Clinical Modification (ICD-9-CM) codes.[18] These product lines were specific to that hospital. The ICD-9-CM codes were used as the basic elements of the product line, because each code represents a single, discrete diagnosis. This code described the consumer, not just the product itself. Then the ICD-9-CM codes were grouped according to clinical areas to comprise the product lines. An example is the musculoskeletal product line, which includes the following patient groupings: arthritis/rheumatism, sports medicine, joint replacement, and fractures/injuries. However, this developmental process was important, "because it promoted a greater understanding of both the hospital and its clientele and provided new perspectives on how market needs could be satisfied." These two examples show how DRGs fit into the PLM concept. They also show how "DRGs will lead to product definition on the part of the medical care industry for the first time."[19]

An effect of PPS based on DRGs is the change in focus from the traditional cost-based reimbursement, which focused on inputs, to the focus of payment based on the case, which is an output measure.[20,21] The "case" is considered to be the final product of a healthcare institution. It represents all the traditional services needed for a specific diagnosis or treatment. The goal of efficient and effective case management is achieved, when the blending of inputs ensures a maximum production of outputs of an acceptable quality.[21]

PPS will result in price competition between hospitals.[19,22] Hospitals will need to analyze their case mix in order to position their services according to market attractiveness. These factors are easily evaluated with a PLM system. For example, a product manager in a hospital in the East Bay identified a need for transportation to and from outpatient visits. After analyzing the case mix and market attractiveness of this service, transportation was provided, because the clientele were older and their resources for transportation were limited. An increase in outpatient visits was observed as transportation needs were met.

Marketing is another tool that hospitals can employ to ensure their financial well-being under prospective payment, by helping them to take advantage of opportunities created by PPS.[23] Meyer states that the following changes will occur in healthcare marketing due to PPS: "1) Marketing will become more aggressive as hospitals move to protect present market positions and to create new ones in their search for revenues . . . 2) Marketing will become more segmented as hospitals realize the diversity of the markets . . . 3) Marketing will become integrated into the hospital's organization."[23]

The changes in the marketing focus due to PPS have the best opportunity of being implemented within a PLM hospital, because of the philosophy and flexible structure of PLM to make quick decisions.[7] Decisions are made more quickly, because there is a less hierarchical structure in PLM. An advantage of PLM is that it can adjust effectively to the economic environment. For instance, with increased competition, marketing becomes an important aspect of PLM. PPS/DRGs have been shown to be quite adaptable to PLM.

DISADVANTAGES OF PLM

Many of the changes discussed earlier in acute care settings are in response to increasing competition, which would lead to the need for more intensive marketing. The proposal made by many was that competition would help to reduce charges and costs among hospitals. Thomas Weil presents four flaws in this thinking as it relates to healthcare:

1. Proliferation of many small units may increase the nation's healthcare marketplace, because hospitals have high fixed and low variable and marginal costs;
2. In a capital- and labor-intensive industry it takes a considerable length of time to shift effectively toward a procompetition model;

3. The free marketplace assumes that buyers and sellers are well-informed, which may not be true in healthcare; and
4. The outcome of procompetition may result in rationing of healthcare.[11]

Thomas Weil's flaws 1, 3, and 4 can be addressed together from a PLM perspective. The product manager under ideal situations would analyze the various product lines in relationship to cost effectiveness, considering the particular line not only in itself, but also in relation to the organization's overall goal. In other words, the product manager must analyze the effects of discontinuing a product line, which is essential to community needs or which could create a two-tiered system of healthcare, or which may cost the organization more money because of overhead costs which are no longer shared.[6] If the product manager does not do an adequate job of analyzing a product line, then certainly there is the potential for ethical issues to arise, such as lack of information to the client and limited access to healthcare.

Marketing strategies utilized in PLM raise ethical concerns in healthcare, because marketing is said to be the process by which people are convinced to buy products that they do not want or may not need.[14] When this concept is related to healthcare services, ethical issues are raised, because of the lack of information consumers have in order to make appropriate choices.

Although more emphasis is being placed on ascertaining the consumer's health needs with PLM, there still remains a gap between need as perceived by the consumer and the products that hospitals offer. A gap can also exist if a hospital discontinues a service and no other organization provides it. Such situations raise the ethical question of whether healthcare is a right or a privilege. Barbara Norkett states that, "Healthcare providers must be sensitive to these ethical concerns and be prepared to defend the cost-benefit ratio of marketing activities. . . . The sign of a true professional is having a service to offer the public, being sensitive to the wants and needs of clients, and meeting those needs."[14]

This is certainly possible under a PLM system. The organization can move "profits" from successful product lines to help support socially necessary programs, which may not be as successful. The organization can weigh the pros and cons of both choices in a cost-effective as well as a needs-assessment manner. A PM of the Medical/Surgical product line in an acute care setting in the East Bay was faced with a similar problem. A nursing unit within this product-line had only five patients a day. The unit was closed because of this low census, for obvious economic reasons. However, instead of eliminating this service entirely, the patients were placed on another unit which then had an additional service and an increased census.

Another potential disadvantage of PLM is the need to restructure the organization. Most organizations change to a matrix structure.[1,4] (See Figure 41-1 for

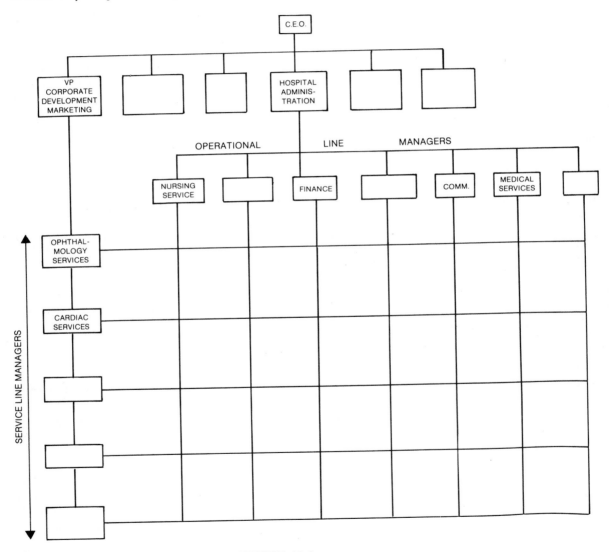

FIGURE 41-1

Example of Matrix structure.

an example). Since PLM cuts across traditional departmental lines, the traditional functional structure is replaced by a matrix system, which is project-oriented. This matrix organization makes sense in relation to PLM, because budgeting, cost control, planning, and quality control are identified in relation to the final product or project.[1,6,16] A formal definition of a matrix organization is one with both hierarchical (vertical coordination) and lateral (horizontal coordination) structure.[16]

The disadvantage of a matrix organization for PLM is that such a drastic change does not occur rapidly.[4] During this transition period, lines of authority could become hazy.[24] In addition to this transition where roles are hazy, a particular characteristic of a matrix organization is dual lines of responsibility and authority.[16] Potentially this could have a dramatic impact on nursing's role in the hospital setting, because there would no longer be one centralized nursing department. Nursing would be distributed according to how it interfaced with the various product lines. Nursing either could lose power in how it effects patient care or perhaps gain an important voice *if* within each product line nursing had a significant impact on the product line.

PLM has some potential disadvantages if not implemented effectively because many ethical issues will be raised and some of its advantages could be negated. The issue of whether or not a matrix organization is in the best interest of the nursing profession is raised, because PLM is only implemented with a matrix system.

CONCLUSION

Although there are distinct disadvantages to PLM, these aspects can be adjusted for or the deleterious effects minimized if the organization maintains an increased awareness. The application of PLM in its ideal form certainly has advantages in terms of dealing with the economic pressures affecting healthcare today. PLM can combat increased competition effectively by employing marketing strategies. The PPS/DRGs can be incorporated into PLM to help define product lines. However, PLM is complex and dynamic like the environment and organization it should be used in. This makes it "all the more capable of dealing with that environment, however, and all the more appropriate for use for hospitals."[6]

The strength of the PLM concept lies in the fact that it provides for a managerial focus on products as profit-generating systems as well as looking at all aspects concerned with the final product. Due to this perspective, the patients can benefit from a higher level of accountability required of persons responsible for their care. PLM also allows for flexibility in the role of the product manager. Since this is a relatively new and popular management technique in the healthcare industry, further studies on its effectiveness and ethical impact are warranted, especially in relation to nurse product managers, and in relation to some of the longer term effects on institutions which have implemented PLM.

REFERENCES

1. Anderson, R.A., "Products and Product-Line Management in Nursing," *Nursing Administration Quarterly,* 1985, 10:65-72.
2. Lyonski, S., "A Boundary Theory Investigation of the Product Manager's Role," *Journal of Marketing,* 1985, 49:26-39.
3. McDaniel, C. and D.P. Gray, "Product Manager," *California Management Review,* 1980, 23:87-94.
4. Bruhn, P.S. and D.H. Howes, "Service Line Management: New Opportunities for Nursing Executives," *Journal of Nursing Administration,* 1986, 16:13-18.
5. Autrey, P. and D. Thomas, "Competitive Strategy in the Hospital Industry," *Health Care Management Review,* 1986, 11:7-14.
6. MacStravic, R.S., "Product-Line Administration in Hospitals," *Health Care Management Review,* 1986, 11:35-43.
7. Gregory, D. and K. Kaufman, "New Ventures, Products, Services: Managing the Diversification Risk," *Healthcare Financial Management,* 1983, 37:30-34.
8. Hise, R.T. and J.P. Kelly, "Product Management on Trial," *Journal of Marketing,* 1978, 42:28-33.
9. Gregory, D. and D. Klegon, "The Value of Strategic Marketing to the Hospital," *Healthcare Financial Management,* 1983, 37:16-22.
10. Doody, M.F., "The Financial Manager as Marketer," *Healthcare Financial Management,* 1985, 39:12.
11. Weil, T.P., "Procompetition or More Regulation?" *Health Care Management Review,* 1985, 10:27-35.

12. Bartlett, P.J., C.D. Sheve, and C.T. Allen, "Marketing Orientation: How Do Hospital Administrators Compare with Marketing Managers?" *Health Care Management Review,* 1984, 9:77-86.

13. Gannon, K.R., "Nursing's Impact on a Business Venture," *Nursing Administration Quarterly,* 1985, 10:90-96.

14. Norkett, B., "The Role of Nursing in Marketing Health Care," *Nursing Administration Quarterly,* 1985, 10:85-89.

15. Peters, J.P. and S. Tseng, "Ten Hospitals Forge New Directors and Strategies," *Healthcare Financial Management,* 1984, 38:24-29.

16. Fetter, R.B. and J.L. Freeman, "DRGs: Product Line Management Within Hospitals," *Academic Management Review,* 1986, 11:41-54.

17. Block, L.F. and C.E. Press, "Product Line Development by DRGs Builds Market Strength," *Healthcare Financial Management,* 1985, 34:50-52.

18. Benz, P.D. and J. Burnham, "Case Study: Developing Product Lines Using ICD-9-CM Codes," *Healthcare Financial Management,* 1985, 39:38-41.

19. Crawford, M. and M.D. Fottler, "The Impact of DRGs and Prospective Pricing Systems on Health Care Management," *Health Care Management Review,* 1985, 10:73-84.

20. Finkler, S.A., "Flexible Budget Variance Analysis Extended to Patient Acuity and DRGs," *Health Care Management Review,* 1985, 10:21-34.

21. Orefice, J.J. and M.C. Jennings, "Productivity — A Key to Managing Cost-per-Case," *Healthcare Financial Management* 1983, 37:18-24.

22. Forbush, D., "Hospital Sales and Market Communications: More Than Just Promotion," *Healthcare Financial Management,* 1983, 37:40-44,.

23. Meyer, M.F., "How Will PPS Affect Hospital Marketing Techniques?" *Healthcare Financial Management,* 1983, 37:42.

24. Mischek, M.G., "Ten Reasons Not to Reorganize," *Healthcare Financial Management,* 1983, 37:110-116.

CHAPTER **42**

The Nursing Shortage
Do we dislike it enough to cure it?

Lois Friss, DrPH

Employers of hospital nurses are letting the public know via journals, newspapers, television, and recruiting ads that they are having difficulty filling budgeted vacancies. Just as in the 1960s and the early 1980s, when employers had the same problem, the proposed remedies are the traditional ones geared for a quick fix without changing the underlying employment system.

The remedies focus on recruiting, lobbying for expansion of educational programs, recruiting abroad, providing free housing, and paying bonuses to current employees who recruit new nurses. Refresher programs to encourage inactive nurses to return to hospitals are not advocated yet, but they soon will be despite a history of failure of such endeavors. Other prescriptions, such as the provision of flexible worker hours and daycare centers for children, stem from the assumption that nurses have home-career conflicts.

Nurses are being urged to solve the problem. They are told that they should "get their own house in order," they "need to organize," and they "should become more assertive."

Investigators with a sociological orientation argue that physician-nurse and nurse-administrator

Reprinted from *Inquiry*, Vol. 25, No. 2, with the permission of Blue Cross and Blue Shield Association © 1988.

relationships must change so that nurses will have more autonomy and respect. Economists and others argue that the pay range needs to be lengthened to make career nursing worthwhile. Articulate nursing leaders propose that nurses be educated in mainstream university baccalaureate programs.[1]

Too few voices emphasize the necessity for implementing several mutually reinforcing practices. Indeed, if nurses' pay were related to education at the entry level and improved for continuing performance, baccalaureate education would become more attractive and increased respect and autonomy would follow. This in turn would greatly promote recruitment of career-oriented nurses and full-time work among all levels of nurses.

The current system of nursing education and compensation is not perceived by all nurses and administrators as flawed. One seemingly logical assumption is that an employment system so pervasive exists because the advantages offset the disadvantages. In this article I first explore the current education and compensation system to explain the reasons for the continuation of the system. I then look at nursing from a broader perspective to demonstrate that there is a larger public policy problem. After offering reasons why policy makers need to address the problem, I conclude with suggestions for remedying the problem.

MANAGEMENT AND NURSES SEEM TO LIKE THE SYSTEM

Hospital administration has much to gain from the current employment system. First, there is a staffing advantage. Managers have unusual flexibility over nursing work assignments. For example, in the late 1970s and early 1980s, when revenue could be optimized by, for example, giving nursing tasks to respiratory technicians, this was easily done. When prospective reimbursement created incentives to bundle tasks, these duties were simply reassigned to nurses because of the work flexibility nurses are willing to accept. The large pool of part-time workers makes it easy to adjust staffing to occupancy. Indeed, the use of flexible staffing is perceived as an indicator of a well-managed hospital.

No firm line exists between the tasks and judgments expected from graduates of two-, three-, and four-year education programs — associate degree in nursing (A.D.N.), R.N. diploma, and bachelor's of science in nursing (B.S.N.), respectively. Because nurses from each of these programs all hold the same license, and certification is not required, the hospital has a pool of generalist workers to assign among departments, shifts, weekends, and specialty units.

Another advantage of the present system is that employers do not have to pay more for education, experience, and performance.[2] The career ladders in existence are modest. A survey by the American Hospital Association indicated that almost half of all community hospitals had only one nursing position level.[3] Six years of experience in intensive care led to a beginning salary differential of 11.4% to 12.6% depending on education. This is far from the amount necessary if nursing is to remain attractive. The recommended salary differential would allow a nurse with 15 to 20 years of experience and demonstrated competence to have the opportunity to earn at least twice the salary of a new graduate.[4] Besides the small pay differential given to experienced nurses, shift differentials remain low and fringe benefits are less than those in other industries.[5]

The traditional system has enabled hospitals to have technologically expert workers readily available at minimal cost. A generous education system has produced new graduates for more than two decades

to meet increased demand, replace experienced nurses, and compensate for the large number working part-time.[6] Hospital managers, therefore, assume that their preservice training costs and in-service career development costs should be low.

Many individual nurses also benefit from the employment system. There is no other occupation that allows those with an interest in science and service to complete their basic education in two years, work for a competitive entry-level salary, and study and advance, if they so choose, through the bachelor's, master's, and doctoral level while working desired hours. The employment system with its many options for part-time work and flexible hours is also compatible with combining home and family life. Indeed, nurses probably need day-care centers less than other workers do, because many arrange to work evenings, nights, and weekends when other family members are available.

The very lack of the requirement for a bachelor's degree as a condition of practice (an anomaly for a professional occupation) along with minimal professional certification means that there are few artificial barriers to employment. Most nurses can find a job wherever they move. The low unemployment rate that characterizes nursing provides income security that is treasured as much by many nurses as the lack of potential for higher income frustrates other nurses.[7]

SO WHAT'S THE PROBLEM?

Despite the advantages of this education-employment system to some nurses and managers, it is costly to other systems and individuals. Career-oriented bedside nurses reach a salary ceiling within a few years. With an average annual salary of $22,394 for staff nurses in November 1984 and salary increases averaging 3.5% to 4% in 1986 (when health care inflation was 7.1%), it is not hard to see why college freshmen are preparing for other careers.[8] In addition, because less than half of nurses have more than five years of tenure in a single hospital, there is a shortage of "mentors" to train and motivate nurses during the critical early career period. Thus, the lack of enthusiastic mentors combined with the stagnant salary structure and emphasis on flexible staffing encourages career-oriented incumbents to leave[9] and high-potential practitioners to choose other careers. These, and other, factors combine to reinforce a downward cycle of occupational attractiveness (see Figure 42-1).

Although the traditional pay system for nurses appears advantageous for hospitals, the aggregate cost of health care is not necessarily lower. Eventually hospitals will be forced to award above-average salary increases in response to delayed competitive pressures, to incur extraordinary recruiting expenses, and to experience lower productivity from part-time or casual workers. Furthermore, public policies based on the faulty assumption that wages of core workers should be suppressed so that every hospital, regardless of occupancy or quality, can survive will be counterproductive. Such policies will lead either to survival of marginal hospitals or to a shortage of expert workers or both.

Besides the direct cost for nurses, such as salaries and benefits, educational costs have been high.[10] Since 1967, the federal government has spent $1.6 billion in support of basic nursing education. The federal expenditure yielded 1,000-2,000 nurses per year between 1974 and 1983 at an estimated cost of $35,000-$43,000 per nurse.[11] (There has been a steady increase in the ratio of nurses to the total population.) Based on consistent federal reports that there was not likely to be an aggregate shortage of registered nurses during the next decade, federal support of entry-level nursing education was discontinued.[12]

Ironically, this federal support may have harmed the long-term supply more than it helped. Because employers relied on new graduates, they moderated wage increases for older workers, thus discouraging full-time work and career commitment. Over time, the profession has become less attractive to new recruits, as shown by the decline in applications to all types of nursing schools and acceptance of students with lower Scholastic Aptitude Test scores.[13]

Graduates from basic baccalaureate programs have been declining since 1979.[14] This is ominous for two reasons. Nurses with higher education have higher lifelong labor force participation than other nurses. Projections are that although the aggregate supply of nurses will be adequate through the 1990s, there will

be half as many baccalaureate degree nurses as will be needed and one-third as many graduate degree nurses as will be needed.[15] These projections of adequate numbers but inadequate quality have been made consistently by the Department of Health and Human Services. They were affirmed in the prestigious report on nursing and nursing education done by the Institute of Medicine under the auspices of the National Research Council.[16]

The present education system for nurses is not as good as it should be, characterized as it is by too many programs (i.e., 1,477 of them), declining enrollments, and faculties without adequate preparation.[17] Graduate nursing education is so unattractive as a personal career investment that the federal government must subsidize the education of nurse clinicians and faculty members to attract a marginally sufficient number.

Nursing labor is often perceived as being less expensive than the alternatives. For instance, managers often substitute nurses for technological investments, such as bedside computer terminals, information systems, or better support services because nurses are less costly in the short run. Yet the truism that cheap or undervalued goods are not treated with respect or with an eye to the long term holds true in hospitals as in life generally. Technological innovations, such as labor-saving monitoring incubators for adults in critical care, will occur only when manufacturers and industry leaders find it worthwhile to invest in them.

Managers seldom consider policies to alter the hospital wide delivery system instead of only the nursing system. Examples of such alternatives might be to: 1) change admission policies to ensure a more predictable work load on nursing units, 2) transfer tasks to physicians in critical care units, 3) set up an appointment system for other professionals who will be visiting on nursing units, 4) involve patients' families in providing care, 5) give nurses authority over housekeepers on nursing units, 6) allow nurses to reschedule surgeries, x-rays, and other tests, and 7) standardize physician orders.

These ideas are not necessarily the universal or right answers. The point is that managers must also look for innovative solutions in the systems

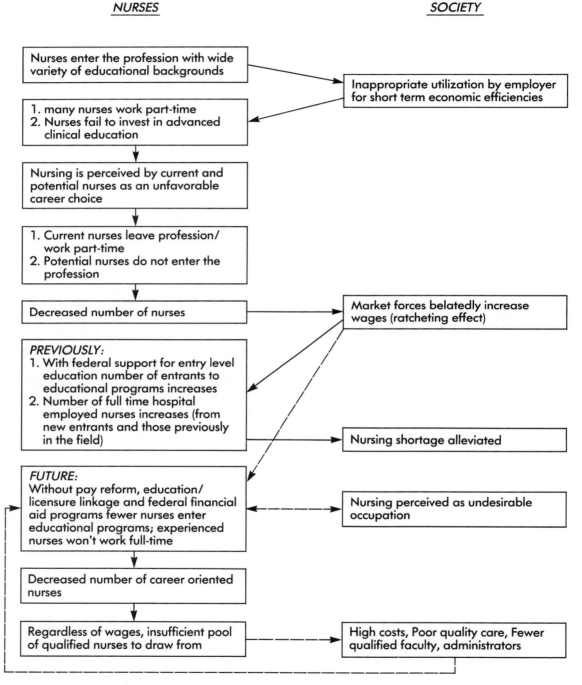

FIGURE 42-1

Self-reinforcing downward cycle of occupational attractiveness.

surrounding the nursing department and accept the need for pay and education reform.[18] We do health care managers a disservice if we assume that they will be unable to rise to the challenge of strategically managing a professional service work force.

Another critical, but unmeasured, effect is on the quality of care owing to the large number of part-time nurses and those who come from supplemental agencies or who are educated abroad. Common sense tells us that workers who are unfamiliar with organizational routines or are unable to communicate or participate in organization-specific training will not be able to carry as heavy a workload and perform as safely as long-term workers. Employers will, of necessity, lighten their load or run a higher risk of error. In either case, the productivity and morale of permanent nurses decline.[19]

WHY INSIST THAT THE INDUSTRY "FIX" IT?

At the height of the popularity of nursing as a career, there were large high school graduation classes, limited career options for bright women, a large reservoir of mature women looking for jobs, and a federally funded educational system. These circumstances were the underpinnings for the continuation of long periods between pay adjustments that occurred only after pressures to change became intense and publicized.

Now, however, the pool from which nurses are drawn has dried up. If hospital executives respond with their usual reactions, they will give above-average pay adjustments to all nurses, able or not, and nursing schools will have fewer qualified faculty but will educate all levels of nurses. Eventually, there will be pressures to relax immigration and licensing requirements for nurses, which are already lax.[20] Prospective students at all levels will be less qualified than in the past, and baccalaureate graduations will plummet. The public will receive poor value for its nursing education and nursing service money. Fortunately, there is an alternative scenario that can be instituted.

Physician and policy analysts have been informed that it is illogical to consider the current crisis in nursing as simply a supply problem.[21] The evidence is that the nursing supply increased 55% between 1977 and 1984 compared with an 8% growth in the population. During this period inpatient days and occupancy rates also declined. Rather than a supply problem, there is a demand problem as hospitals increasingly substitute R.N.s for other workers: the ratio of full-time equivalent R.N.s to patients increased 82% between 1972 and 1986. Some of this is surely justified by the increase in the severity of illness of hospitalized patients and the increasingly sophisticated technology used.[22] But would anyone believe that all of this substitution would have occurred if nursing salaries for experienced nurses had increased as recommended?[23]

In some states, educational budgets are encouraging hospitals to reexamine their use of available licensed personnel and to subsidize technical education as other employers have traditionally done. State educational planners and politicians are reluctant to budget money for high-cost nursing education programs when the enrollment demand is soft, one-third of employed nurses are working part-time, and only 25% of nurses over age 55 are working. They reasonably ask why employers don't change salaries and working conditions for those already educated.[24]

As the proportion of the gross national product devoted to health increases and the medical care portion of the Consumer Price Index increases faster than the index as a whole, the public, through its elected representatives, can also reasonably be expected to question the value received for its investment. Stories in the press and on television of overworked nurses, nurses unfamiliar with hospital routines, nurses unable to speak English, and patient care errors will eventually erode public confidence in nursing care in hospitals. This loss of confidence combined with higher costs and more copayments can lead ultimately to an unwillingness to pay medical care costs through insurance, taxes, or direct payments.

Besides wanting nursing care at a reasonable cost, patients obviously want good care provided by competent nurses. Recent research also suggests that improved communication between nurses and doctors is imperative for quality patient care. For instance, one study shows that when nurses have the authority to cancel elective surgery in critical care units whenever there is inadequate staffing, mortality rates are lower.[25] Another study on nurses and patients suggests that the satisfaction of the nursing staff is the strongest determinant of aggregate client satisfaction. Client satisfaction, in turn, predicts the rate of subsequent compliance with medical regimens.[26] Such data indicate the high stakes the public has in changing how hospitals pay and manage nurses.

Long-term trend projections suggest that a hospital employment system geared to young and part-time workers is inappropriate. The nurse population will be aging throughout the 1990s, and as a result the overall high activity rate (i.e., the proportion of the nurse population working as nurses) is expected to decline to 72% from the current 76.6%.[27] It is not too early (and may almost be too late) to design strategies appropriate for a mature work force if we are to moderate the effects of this prediction. Again, the greatest concern is with baccalaureate nurses, because this group is aging faster than the other groups. This results from the decline in the numbers of younger new recruits to nursing and the increasing proportion who are second-step nurses—those who are upgrading their education after receiving a diploma or A.D.N. degree.

Much of hospital care is paid by publicly funded programs, primarily Medicare and Medicaid. Many policy analysts contend that it is morally wrong for public agencies to perpetuate an inequitable compensation system in an industry dominated by women. (Comparable-worth experts estimate that nursing wages would be 18.8% higher if it were a male-dominated occupation.)[28] Because 97% of nurses are women, it can be argued that the public is paying for a system that discriminates against women. Tight employer networks fix entry-level wages, use common job descriptions, establish few pay steps and short ranges, and do not compete with each other for experienced nurses. These practices are perpetuated through industry-sponsored salary surveys and through lobbying activities.[29]

WHAT ARE WE GOING TO DO ABOUT IT?

Changes in the nursing work force will not come from nurses or hospitals, because the current system is functional for hospitals and the majority of nurses. Because nursing is free from serious wage competition and extensive professional credentialing, hospitals can control hourly wages and staffing, a very desirable management prerogative. Nurses also benefit from the dysfunctional system by having the freedom to negotiate interesting careers with little risk of unemployment wherever they move. As this paper has indicated, however, the public welfare demands that the system be changed. Therefore, as neither nurses nor hospitals will make the needed changes, those outside the professions must do so.

Accepting this premise means acknowledging that employment reform depends on outsiders with a long-term view. The challenge is to develop a policy consensus among payers, legislators, and professional associations, in addition to major hospitals and nurses.

A basic premise that requires reexamination is the notion that paying nurses with more education, experience, and responsibility would substantially increase aggregate costs. It is likely that having a significant proportion of higher-paid workers in a well-managed organization with necessary support services would be more productive than having many more nurses with lesser ability getting paid the same regardless of performance and responsibility. Payroll costs depend on hourly wages, number of hours, patient load, and fringe benefits, not hourly wages alone.[30]

Criteria for Change

Before an alternative scenario can be proposed, the criteria for change must be established. Multiple strategies should:

- be compatible with the educational expectations of contemporary career-oriented professionals;
- clarify the upward-mobility channels for aides, practical nurses, and registered nurses with diplomas and A.D.N. degrees;
- ensure an adequate supply of applicants for master's and doctoral programs so that advanced positions can be competitively filled, as other professions do;
- encourage hospitals to invest in retention of available nurses;

- promote equitable pay and fringe benefits by freeing the market from employer domination wherever it exists; and
- be technically feasible.

Alternative Scenario

I propose an alternative scenario with three components: 1) develop two levels of nursing practice with education linked to licensure, 2) increase the number of pay steps while extending the range of each step, and 3) assign nurses based on education and licenses as well as competence. Together these actions will clarify career paths and encourage needed reforms without disrupting the system or requiring large continuing federal subsidies.

Part 1. Hospitals need nursing personnel with all levels of talent and educational preparation. They also need a core group of full-time nurses investing in their own skill development. We cannot avert future shortages if we disregard qualified individuals who aspire to a bachelor's degree. Nor would it be wise to eliminate nursing education in community colleges, because A.D.N.-level nurses perform well in many hospital positions. Furthermore, preserving community college education enables many nurses to enter the profession who cannot afford a four-year college education or who are not academically inclined at the moment to enter a baccalaureate program.

A similar case cannot be made for R.N. diploma education, which is terminal education because the student does not get academic credit equivalent to the amount of time invested. But having two rather than three entry-level nursing education programs by itself is not enough. Graduates of A.D.N. and B.S.N. programs should take separate exams related to entry-level competency and should be paid differently and be given different responsibilities.

The advantage of linking education to licensure is that high school counselors, parents, and prospective students could see the trade-offs between time and money invested in various levels of nursing education and the income deferred in pursuing that education. Similarly, different examinations and licenses would clarify entry-level competencies for employers and encourage pay differentiation on a basis accepted elsewhere in society.

With clearly differentiated nursing education, what would happen to existing R.N. diploma schools? Gradually, these programs would choose to affiliate either with community or four-year colleges, thus completing the trend begun in 1952 for nursing to enter the mainstream of education.[31] Although many diploma R.N. training programs, as well as some physicians and administrators, resist such a step, community colleges have been in an untenable position for several years trying to cram licensed practical nursing (L.P.N.) education into one year and A.D.N. education into two years. In truth, A.D.N. graduates often attend the equivalent of three years of college to meet the R.N. requirements. A restructured two-year program is long overdue.

Another question is, "What will become of existing R.N. and A.D.N. nurses?" All existing nurses would be "grandfathered in." The new differential testing and certification requirements would affect new graduates only. Nurses have been expecting a change for some time; the growth in baccalaureate enrollments among already licensed nurses has been impressive — 267% since 1975.[32] The American Hospital Association reports that a survey of participants of a teleconference on nurse titling and licensure found a high degree of consensus on the need for change, the inevitability of change, and the appropriateness of two different exams for two levels of nursing practice.[33]

Linking education with licensure meets the first three criteria in the previous section and is feasible. Nursing has competency-based models, so that even nurses unable to commute to an accredited program can obtain a bachelor's degree. The Association of State Boards of Nurse Examiners already writes exams for two levels of nursing — licensed practical nurses and registered nurses. With consensus, new nursing examinations for A.D.N. and B.S.N. graduates can readily be developed by the National Council of State Boards of Nursing, Inc., which already has a task force addressing the issue.

The American Nurses Association and the American Student Nurses Association endorse two levels of nursing practice based on the two- and four-year academic programs. Pilot projects are under way in several states. The National League for Nursing, the accrediting organization for R.N. programs, has taken a position that professional nursing practice should require, as a minimum, the baccalaureate degree. The baccalaureate representatives, however, do not have a plurality of votes in the league, and the league therefore has been unable to take an advocacy position.

What is not feasible is to expect that nursing can achieve these changes without the active support of physicians and hospital administrators, and especially their professional associations. Progress requires that licensing requirements and nurse practice acts be changed, which in turn requires joint lobbying with employers and physicians. Nursing has laid the groundwork; the technical components are in place. Nursing, however, lacks the power to overcome dissension in its own ranks while neutralizing the opposition of those employers who have not accepted the need to realign nursing education and licensure to be compatible with modern education and work expectations. The apprentice era with its "convent" student culture and antiintellectual stance has ended. The responsibility for effecting change may fall on those who need the services, who can support fundamental social changes. If hospital leaders fail to exercise their responsibility, they will continue to lose market share among career-oriented men and women to other employers who meet the expectations of professional workers.

The Kellogg Foundation has funded a multidisciplinary group, the National Commission on Nursing Implementation Project, to identify emerging trends and implement the recommendations set forth by the National Commission on Nursing and by the Institute of Medicine in 1983. Regional, state, and local activities will focus on five implementation projects. One of them is a process to move the nursing education system toward preparing two categories of nurses — technical and professional.

Part 2. Addressing the other root cause of the recurring cycle of nurse shortages, the compacted salary structure, requires refocusing industry attention on retention rather than recruitment. If policies concentrate only on entry-level strategies and programs based on the home-career conflict assumption, the core group will not be individuals who are interested in full-time work over a lifetime. Instead, industry's proclivity to overemphasize part-time work

and encourage early retirement will be reinforced. Public policies are needed to overcome this suboptimizing tendency.

First, the theory (reinforced by practice) that nurse wages must be kept low enough so that every hospital can hire the number of nurses it deems desirable to survive is untenable and needs to be challenged. Certainly, the country faces serious questions about the quality, cost, and rationing of health care. But it is unrealistic to expect one group of professional workers to accept low wages and unfavorable working conditions in the futile hope that fundamental decisions can be avoided. Timely, constructive adjustments require that true costs be felt rather than artificially moderated.

Next, oligopolistic forces (hospital control of labor markets) should be moderated. Hospitals should be encouraged to compete for experienced nurses rather than continue past practices of establishing entry-level wages and perpetuating a flat pay structure. To ensure that nursing wages are influenced by a competitive market, on the up side as well as the down side, several initiatives are available:

- Recruiting foreign or domestic nurses from low-wage areas blunts pressures for wage increases for nurses already working. Therefore, employers should not be reimbursed for national and international recruiting expenses. Any further attempts to loosen immigration policies, such as extending temporary work visas (H-1 visas) beyond the legally permissible five years, should also be resisted.[34]
- Employer or industry attempts to co-opt supplemental employment agencies through exclusive contracts or negotiated rates should be prohibited, since these agencies are often the only timely source of wage competition in a community. Moreover, employers should not be able to use their own "pools" to blunt the competition of supplemental agencies.
- Industry-sponsored salary surveys should be examined for antitrust violations. Individual employers should be expected to follow comparable-worth guidelines recommended for business generally.[35]
- Nurses should not be exempt from wage and hour laws that affect most other workers. Such

exemptions are frequently a thinly disguised method of avoiding overtime pay. Although this may be a desirable financial objective for employers in the short term, the commonly accepted business practice is to create salaried positions with enough differential (in pay and involvement) to offset the loss of overtime pay.

- Pay policies should give priority to increasing pay for skills, longevity, responsibility, and career development rather than emphasizing entry-level pay. The term "career ladder" should be reserved for programs with long ranges and many steps. Career ladder is a misnomer if only a few steps with a limited range can be identified and educational differences are modest.
- Fringe benefits should be redesigned to meet the needs of mature workers: tax-reducing options (403-b and 401(k) benefit accounts), pensions, and activity programs for elderly dependents, for example.
- Finally, the research thrust on nursing productivity needs to be expanded to include organizationwide determinants of turnover, such as hospital personnel policies, general management involvement, physician practices, and local employment markets. It is unlikely, given current findings, that answers to productivity (and quality) issues will be found in the nursing department separate from organizational culture, strategies, support, and career systems as well as the community wage-setting system.

All of these suggestions are technically feasible. Many well-managed hospitals encourage the career involvement of their nurses. As a result, they seldom rely on supplemental agency nurses and have a waiting list for positions in good times and bad. What is required is an enlightened industry approach in which many hospitals will have to make marginal adjustments, which will cumulatively yield much and convey a positive message to potential and current nurses.

Part 3. If the above two strategies are adopted, a synergistic effect will occur. Because of the linked education and licensing requirements, it will be easier for employers to assign nurses appropriately upon graduation. Paying for responsibility, education, and performance will lead to better utilization of nurses.

Nursing will have an image as a mainstream career rather than one for submissive women willing to work for inadequate lifetime wages. And educational curriculum development will be enhanced as well.

With the proper placement of differently educated and licensed nurses, nursing curriculums will reflect and enhance employment practices. Educational differences are difficult, if not impossible, to sustain when not reinforced at work.

Another synergistic effect will stem from giving older nurses career incentives. When young nurses do not see nurses with long tenure being rewarded for commitment and performance, they look elsewhere or adopt the same part-time, disengaged expectations. Thus, the cutbacks in the mid-1980s in nurse staffing to achieve higher operating margins sowed the seeds for worse shortages. Not only was part-time work and early retirement encouraged for experienced nurses, but also young nurses learned that dedication does not pay off. The relevant lesson from business is that productivity gains should be shared with the workers—that any cutback should be accompanied by investment in career-oriented, valuable workers.

CONCLUSION

Although there may not now be an aggregate shortage of registered nurses, there are regional and specialty shortages. Furthermore, the supply of basic baccalaureate graduates is declining, suggesting that nursing is losing its career attractiveness among talented women, those most likely to work full-time throughout their working lifetimes. This is especially serious given the projections that there will be a much greater demand for B.S.N. and graduate-prepared nurses in the next decade as faculty, administrators, researchers, as well as clinicians. Aside from quantity, quality is a serious issue, because there is reason to believe that the academic quality of applicants is declining at all levels.

Nursing could be a very desirable occupation for career women and men if the linkages among education, work, and pay were more logical. Society needs a nursing work force that encourages the best utilization of all levels of nurses while assuring access to both entry-level and advanced-level nursing careers. Hospitals and society can ill afford to lose nursing candidates among college-bound women by continuing to pay all nurses the same regardless of education, experience, and competence.

The difficulty lies in seeing the nursing "shortage" as a social and organizational dilemma that the participants have no real need to solve. The problem must be addressed as a public policy issue. Once this is done, the political consensus and tactical strategies needed to address the problem become paramount. Until then, the downward cycle of occupational attractiveness will require expensive recruiting strategies and continuing subsidization of graduate nurse education. The end result of such inaction will be nursing care provided by a melange of nurses paid irrespective of competence and education. There is no reason to believe that aggregate costs would be lower under such a system, although the quality of nursing care and education might well be.

REFERENCES

1. C. Fagin, "The Visible Problems of an 'Invisible' Profession: The Crisis and Challenge for Nursing," *Inquiry* 24 (Summer 1987): 119.
2. Institute of Medicine, *Nursing and Nursing Education: Public Policies and Private Actions* (Washington, DC:National Academy Press, 1983).
3. M. Beyers, R. Mullner, C. Byre, and S. Whitehead, "Results of the Nursing Personnel Survey, pt. 1: RN Recruitment and Orientation," *Journal of Nursing Administration* 13 (April 1983): 34-37.
4. E. Ginzberg, J. Patray, M. Ostrow, and E. Brann, "Nurse Discontent: The Search for Realistic Solutions," *Journal of Nursing Administration* 12 (November 1982): 7-11.
5. *American Nurse* 15 (February 1983): 3, 16. In 1982 hospitals spent 31% of payroll for fringe benefits compared with 37% for all industries; see R. McKibbin, "Economic and Employment Issues in Health Care: The Nursing Perspective," in *Health Care: An International Perspective,* ed. John Virgo (Edwardsville, IL: Southern Illinois University Press, 1984), p. 247.

   Hospitals spent a smaller percentage than industry as a whole did on legally required benefits (other than Social Security) and tax-deferred items—pensions, profit-sharing plans, thrift plans, and tax-exempt life insurance—but substantially more on vacation, holidays, and sick leave; see W. Cleverley, "From the Editor," *Topics in Health Care Financing* 12 (Summer 1986): vi-vii.
6. Of the registered nurses employed in nursing in 1984, 33.8% were employed part-time. This is much higher than in other occupations and has increased from 32% in 1980. See U.S. Department of Health and Human Services, *National Sample Survey of Registered Nurse, 1984: Summary of Results* (Washington, DC: Bureau of Health Professions, April 1986), p. 29; and U.S. Department of Health and Human Services, *The Registered Nurse Population: An Overview* (Washington, DC: Bureau of Health Professions, 1982), p. 17.
7. U.S. Department of Health and Human Resources, *Report on Nursing: Fifth Report to the President and Congress on the Status of Health Personnel in the United States* (Washington, DC: Bureau of Health Professions, March 1986), pp. 10-14. In May 1985, when occupancy rates, admissions, and length of stay were down and hospital employment was also down, the R.N. unemployment rate was 2%. This contrasts with 7.5% in the rest of the economy, 3.5% for practical nurses, and 3.5% for hospitals overall; see *Hospitals* 59 (May 1, 1985): 30.
8. U.S. Department of Health and Human Services, *The Registered Nurse Population* (Washington, DC: Public Health Service, 1986), p. 36; American Nurses Association, *The Nursing Shortage: A Briefing Paper* (Kansas City, MO: ANA, 1987).
9. Contrary to common belief, nurses are not leaving either the profession or hospital nursing. The concern is that nursing is failing to attract and retain those who expect to invest in their own education and work full-time over a lifetime.
10. Federal support for nursing education has been an anomaly. No other undergraduate occupation receives direct educational support.
11. S. Eastaugh, "The Impact of the Nurse Training Act on the Supply of Nurses, 1974-1983," *Inquiry* 2 (Winter 1985): 404-417.
12. *Nursing and Nursing Education* (note 2).
13. Educational Testing Service (Princeton, NJ, 1987).
14. P. Rosenfeld, "Nursing Education: Statistics You Can Use," *Nursing and Health Care* 7 (June 1986): 327-329. In 1984, there was an overall 4% decline in fall admissions and a 5.3% drop in enrollments. The number of graduates from generic baccalaureate programs has declined continuously for the past five years, just the opposite of the trend for women in all other areas of education.
15. *Report on Nursing* (note 7), pp. 10-67.
16. *Nursing and Nursing Education* (note 2).

17. In 1980, of the 20,000 full-time nursing faculty, only 7% held a doctoral degree and 68% had a master's degree; see ibid., p. 136.

18. Nurses themselves have documented the characteristics of nursing service in well-managed hospitals; see *Task Force on Nursing Practice in Hospitals: Attraction and Retention of Professional Nurses* (Kansas City, MO: American Academy of Nursing, 1983).

19. Part-time workers appear to be as motivated by job challenge and complexity as full-time workers are. Supplemental agency nurses were found not to be different from staff nurses on measures of job involvement and satisfaction, and they were at least as well qualified and experienced. See P. Prescott and T. Langford, "Supplemental Agency Nurses and Hospital Staff Nurses: What Are the Differences?" *Nursing and Health Care* 2 (April 1981): 200-206; and B. Kehrer, P. Deiman, and N. Szapiro, "The Temporary Nursing Service R.N.," *Nursing Outlook* 32 (July-August 1984): 212-217.

20. A record 8,000 nurses applied to take the April 1, 1987, certification exam given by the Commission on Graduates of Foreign Nursing Schools. Passing this exam leads to an H-1 visa and other documents needed to work in U.S. hospitals. H-1 status is good for a two-year stay as a non-resident alien, with extensions possible. Nursing is one occupational category that encounters few obstacles from the Immigration and Naturalization Service; see the "Perspectives" section in McGraw-Hill's *Medicine and Health,* May 11, 1987.

21. L. Aiken and C. Mullinix, "The Nursing Shortage: Myth or Reality?" *New England Journal of Medicine* 317 (September 1987): 641.

22. Of the respondents to the AHA 1987 Hospital Nursing Personnel Survey, 81.3% said that patient severity of illness had increased between April 1986 and April 1987. Interestingly, although the shortage was reported to be a major problem for more than 50% of all responding hospitals, nursing expenditures increased only 3.2% over 1986. The mean average hourly expense was $12.70, a 4% increase over 1985. Although this average and this increase are not trivial, they do not indicate wage competition.

23. The evidence concerning pay compaction and the arguments for a steepened pay line are presented in L. Friss, "Simultaneous Strategies for Solving the Nursing Shortage," *Health Care Management Review* (in press 1988). Economic theory and prevailing management practice agree that if workers become expensive, management will be stimulated to substitute less expensive workers or make the expensive workers more productive with technological innovations.

24. Recent federal legislation — S. 1402 — perpetuates the dysfunctional approach by establishing model professional nurse recruitment centers rather than employer/nurse career centers.

25. W. Knaus et al., "An Evaluation of Outcome From Intensive Care in Major Medical Centers," *Annals of Internal Medicine* 104 (March 1986): 410-418.

26. C. Weisman and C. Nathanson, "Professional Satisfaction and Client Outcomes," *Medical Care* 23 (October 1985): 1179-1192.

27. *Report on Nursing* (note 7), pp. 10-55.

28. M. Aldrich and R. Buchele, *The Economics of Comparable Worth* (Cambridge, MA: Ballinger Publishing Co., 1986), p. 138.

29. See L. Friss, "External Equity and the Free Market Myth," *Review of Public Personnel Administration* 7 (Fall 1987): 74-91, for a case study of the Los Angeles nurse employment system. Nursing constitutes 17% of the female professional-technical work force. Furthermore, salaries of many other, primarily female occupations are pegged to hospital nursing salaries, including practical nurses, nurses' aides, laboratory technicians, physical therapists, and occupational therapists.

30. Nursing constitutes 30% of all hospital costs. Increases in nursing costs are attributed to changes in staffing levels rather than hourly wages and are not the cause of the inflation in hospital costs; see D. Abernathy and E. Pearson, *Regulating Hospital Costs: The Development of Public Policy* (Ann Arbor, MI: Health Administration Press, 1979), p. 32.

31. The 273 diploma programs represent only 18% of all basic R.N. programs and have been steadily declining since 1965 (National League for Nursing, *Nursing Student Census* [New York: NLN, 1985], pp. 1, 35). These schools are concentrated in the North Atlantic and Midwestern states. During the past 10 years, diploma graduates have declined by 43%. This decline is attributed to the lack of resources for maintaining quality programs and student preference for coeducational education.

32. *Nursing Student Census* (note 31), p. 32.

33. American Hospital Association, *An Executive Summary: Building Momentum for the 90's: Nurse Titling and Licensure* (Chicago: AHA, Mar. 19, 1987).

34. See "U.S. Limits Stays of Foreign Nurses: Immigration Law Increases Severe National Shortage," *New York Times,* April 10, 1988, pp. 1, 15.

35. G. Sape, "Coping With Comparable Worth," *Harvard Business Review* 85 (March 1985): 145-152.

RECRUITMENT, RETENTION, AND STAFF
DEVELOPMENT

CHAPTER 43

Staff Nurse Turnover Costs
Part I, a conceptual model

Cheryl Bland Jones, RN, MS

A major concern for the chief nurse executive (CNE) in dealing with the nursing shortage is turnover, particularly the turnover of registered nurse (RN) employees. The CNE is now faced with replacing significant numbers of RN employees who leave, while balancing complex patient care demands with limited departmental resources. Furthermore, the competitive hospital environment places the CNE in direct competition with other health care administrators for funding and personnel. The CNE can articulate a stronger position for the allocation of resources aimed at RN retention if quantitative nursing turnover cost data are available.

Health care administrators must weigh the costs of turnover with those of retention measures. Turnover not only impacts the costs associated with hiring and orienting new staff members, but can also lead to staff instability and a decrease in the quality of patient care.

The purpose of this study was twofold: (1) to develop a conceptual model describing nursing turnover in relation to the overall health care delivery system; and (2) to develop and test a methodology for measuring the direct and indirect costs of nursing turnover. The study also identified methods used by hospitals to calculate nursing turnover costs.

Reprinted from *Journal of Nursing Administration*, Vol. 20, No. 4, and Vol. 20, No. 5, with permission of J. B. Lippincott Company © 1990.

SIGNIFICANCE OF RN TURNOVER COSTS

To date, there has been little documentation in the literature, identifying and describing the actual costs associated with nursing turnover. The turnover cost information reported has not been calculated in a consistent fashion. The possibility also exists that some hospitals may not even maintain nursing turnover or turnover cost information.

The information obtained from this study provides a foundation upon which CNEs can evaluate RN turnover and retention. The results can be useful in weighing the cost of turnover against the cost of retention measures and can allow CNEs to determine if turnover costs do, in fact, outweigh the costs of retention strategies. Further, by knowing the costs of turnover, the CNE will be able to demonstrate potential organizational savings if retention investments are made.

CONCEPTUAL FRAMEWORK FOR NURSING TURNOVER COSTS

In business and nursing, several models describe various causes of employee turnover.[1-4] These models demonstrate the impact of departmental, unit, and individual factors such as job stress, autonomy, and job satisfaction on employee turnover in general, and more specifically, on nursing turnover. The information available on the causes of employee/nursing turnover was used as an impetus for the investigation of nursing turnover costs in this study.

From a broad perspective, this study used a conceptual framework which integrated important concepts from both the nursing and business literature. The conceptual model (Figure 43-1) shows that nursing turnover is affected by many factors. The overall health care environment affects the hospital environment which, in turn, directly impacts the nursing department environment. Costs and benefits of turnover can be analyzed and evaluated, and the results can be used to alter hospital and nursing departmental policies and practices in an effort to reduce nursing turnover and turnover costs. Major

components of the conceptual framework will be discussed.

The health care environment consists of all factors outside the hospital setting that affect and are affected by the hospital setting. There are four primary means by which this external environment affects the hospital setting: regulatory factors, such as those for accreditation; political factors, such as the prevailing climate for elder and indigent care reimbursement; economic factors, such as the current nursing shortage; and social factors, such as competitiveness between health care organizations.

The hospital environment consists of factors within the hospital setting which are unique to its

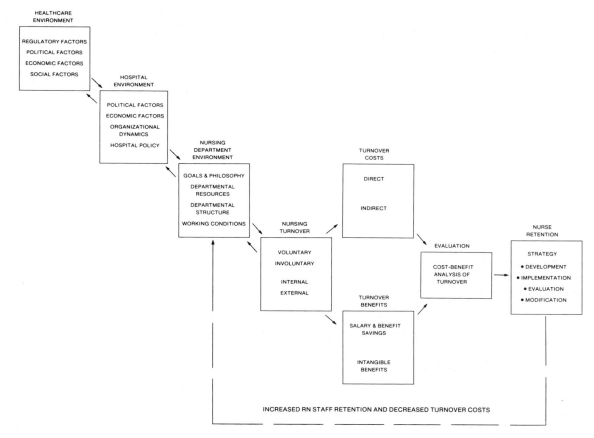

FIGURE 43-1
Conceptual framework for nursing turnover.

internal interaction. The internal environment continuously responds to external environmental changes. Factors which comprise the hospital environment and influence the nursing department environment include political factors, such as internal resource allocation; economic factors, such as the hospital's profit margin; hospital policy; and organizational dynamics, such as departmental structures, interaction, and competition.

The nursing department environment is the aspect of the internal hospital environment comprised of nursing personnel working toward common nursing service goals. More specifically, the nursing department encompasses those elements which influence nursing turnover behavior including: goals and philosophy, such as formalized departmental objectives; departmental resources, such as financial and personnel components available within the department; departmental structure, such as the articulation of nursing divisions and units within the nursing department; and working conditions, such as scheduling, employee job satisfaction, and leaders' management style. The nursing department's overall operation is influenced by units and individuals that are contained therein.

Nursing turnover is the process whereby nursing staff leave or transfer within the hospital environment. This definition of turnover, encompasses voluntary and involuntary turnover,[1] as well as internal and external turnover.[5] Voluntary and involuntary nursing turnover were not differentiated in this study because costs are incurred whether RNs are requested to leave or resign. Only external turnover was examined in this study, because these costs may have a greater financial impact on the hospital than internal turnover.

Turnover costs are those direct and indirect costs incurred by the hospital due to nursing termination. Direct costs are defined as those costs that are directly associated with staff nurse recruitment. Indirect costs are defined as those costs incurred after the new RN has been hired to fill a vacancy left by an RN turnover.

Turnover benefits encompass those salary and benefit savings realized by the hospital, such as decreased new employee salaries. There are also intangible benefits that result from RN turnover, such as

the infusion of new knowledge and ideas when employees enter the environment. Turnover benefits were not analyzed in the current study, but are a potentially valuable aspect of the overall model and deserve investigation.

Turnover costs and benefits are linked through evaluation. Evaluation can include both formal and informal methods of turnover cost and benefit comparison. One financial management process, cost-benefit analysis, is incorporated into the study's conceptual framework to provide an appropriate mechanism for evaluation.

Nurse retention is the process of retaining RN employees. Nurse retention consists of the development and implementation of strategies and activities by a nursing department and hospital with the stated purpose of retaining RN employees. Examples of retention strategies are financial incentives and rewards, flexible scheduling, and the use of a participative management style by nursing leaders. Equally essential in the nurse retention process is the analysis and evaluation of the cost-effectiveness of the retention strategies employed. After analysis and evaluation of retention strategies, modifications can be made to adapt and change strategies so that the most cost-effective strategies are employed. Nurse retention would serve as a feedback mechanism to the nursing department environment, whereby RN staff retention would be increased and turnover costs would be decreased. Nurse retention would also have a potential, albeit indirect, effect on the hospital environment by reducing overall turnover and turnover costs, and on the health care environment by improving the overall quality of care delivery.

REVIEW OF NURSING RESEARCH LITERATURE

A review of the nursing literature reveals no evidence of turnover cost research; rather, the literature has typically focused on causes of nursing turnover.[6-10] Despite the fact that specific turnover cost research has not been conducted, the number of articles related to other aspects of turnover indicates that there is considerable interest in the problem and that such research would be valuable.

The costs associated with nursing turnover have been estimated in the literature to range from as little as \$1,280 to as high as \$50,000 per RN turnover.[2,11-18] However, these figures may not be completely accurate since the costs of advertising, travel, public relations, and nurse recruiter fees are frequently excluded in nursing turnover cost estimates.[11] Additionally, these figures often do not include the indirect costs of nursing turnover.[18] Indirect costs could be of financial significance because of the decreased initial productivity of new employees and the decrease in staff morale and group productivity that nursing turnover imposes.

Hoffman[19,20] presented methods which could be used to determine the costs associated with recruiting, hiring, and training new RNs. She advocated separating the costs per RN hired into five cost categories: advertising and recruiting, hiring, costs of unfilled positions, orientation/training, and turnover. Hoffman noted that identification of overall turnover costs allows the nurse administrator to analyze each cost component for specific items that may be targeted for further investigation and cost reduction.

Published reports in the nursing literature rarely include a breakdown of nursing turnover costs. The wide range in turnover costs reported suggests that the processes for calculating these nursing turnover costs is not consistent, or perhaps that these costs are crude and unsubstantiated estimates. The present inconsistency in the nursing literature regarding calculating and reporting of turnover costs makes direct comparison of turnover cost estimates both difficult and confusing.

REVIEW OF BUSINESS LITERATURE

Hall[21] presented a turnover cost estimation model to facilitate easy retrieval of turnover cost information in the business arena. Direct and indirect costs are distinguished in this model for the purpose of determining the ratio of these costs. Hall considered direct costs to be those costs normally incurred in the employment function that are easily identifiable and directly associated with recruitment. Indirect costs are less visible and are those incurred after the new employee has been hired. Hall introduced a method

of estimating learning curve productivity losses for new hires, based on the belief that new employees are not as productive as seasoned employees. This method of estimating productivity losses allows an organization to estimate losses incurred during the new employee training period. Hall suggested that the use of this model would allow human resource managers to propose solutions for employee turnover and to compare the cost of implementing a turnover-reduction program with savings. He also pointed out that this model would allow substantiation of funds allocated to reduce employee turnover, thereby protecting the organization's productivity and profitability. Rousseau[22] supported the use of Hall's model of turnover cost calculation, noting that this method was more appropriate for calculating employee turnover costs than more traditional methods, which make less accurate estimates of decreased new employee performance.

While turnover has typically been depicted as having negative consequences, both nursing and business literature identify many positive outcomes associated with employee turnover.[23-25] Financially speaking, opportunities exist for cost reduction and consolidation when an employee terminates. Specifically, positive outcomes of turnover can be appreciated financially by the organization in the form of decreased salaries for new employees, decreased employee benefit costs, decreased sick leave pay, decreased vacation pay, and a return on recovered capital. Furthermore, there are positive outcomes of turnover that are much more difficult to quantify, such as organizational gains due to the infusion of knowledge and ideas by replacements, the stimulation of policy changes, and the decreased exhibition of withdrawal behaviors.

NURSING TURNOVER COST CALCULATION METHODOLOGY

The Nursing Turnover Cost Calculation Methodology (NTCCM) was developed using an adaptation of Hall's turnover costs estimation model[21] and Hoffman's nursing turnover costs calculation methods.[19,20] The NTCCM divides costs into two principal groups, direct and indirect (Figure 43-2).

DIRECT COSTS

Advertising/recruiting
Unfilled positions
Hiring

INDIRECT COSTS

Termination
Orientation/training
Decreased productivity

FIGURE 43-2

Nursing turnover cost
categories.

Direct costs are those costs incurred during the new RN hiring process. Specifically, direct costs include advertising and recruiting costs, costs of unfilled RN positions, and hiring costs. Indirect costs are those incurred after a new RN has been hired. Indirect costs include RN termination costs, orientation and training costs, and costs of decreased RN productivity.

SUMMARY

While the literature review provided some estimates of nursing turnover costs, the emphasis was primarily on the causes of nursing turnover. Given the nursing shortage and the general milieu of cost-containment in today's health care delivery system, the importance of quantifying nursing turnover costs is evident. Documentation of nursing turnover costs provides one piece of information needed to make a comparison of the costs of nursing turnover with the benefits of turnover. Inconsistencies in the nursing literature regarding the actual costs of nursing turnover lead to a review of the business literature to provide direction for calculating nursing turnover costs. Both the nursing and business literature were used to develop the conceptual framework and to formulate a Nursing Turnover Cost Calculation Methodology (NTCCM).

This study examined one portion of the overall conceptual framework, namely that of nursing turnover costs. Nursing turnover costs were opera-

tionalized and measured during the second phase of the study through the application of the cost calculation methodology. The NTCCM was employed to measure nursing turnover costs at four hospitals in a southeast metropolitan area. Part II (May 1990) will provide a detailed breakdown of nursing turnover costs at the hospitals studied.

REFERENCES

1. Price JL, Mueller CW. Causal model of turnover for nurses. Acad Mg J 1981:24(3):543-565.
2. Hinshaw AS, Smeltzer CH, Atwood JR. Innovative retention strategies for nursing staff. J Nurs Adm 1987;17(6):8-16.
3. Martin TN. A contextual model of employee turnover intentions. Acad Mgmt J 1979;22(2):313-324.
4. Taunton RL, Krampitz SD, Woods CQ. Manager impact on retention of hospital staff: Parts I & II. J Nurs Adm 1989;19(3):14-18 & 19(4):15-19.
5. Globerson S, Malki N. Estimating the expenses resulting from labor turnover: an Israelian study. Mgt Intl Rev 1980;20(3):111-117.
6. Hinshaw AS, Atwood JR. Nursing staff turnover, stress, and satisfaction: models, measures, and management. In: Werley H, Fitzpatrick J, eds. Annual Review of Nursing Research. Vol. 1. New York: Springer Publishing, 1983.
7. Landstrom GL, Biordi DL, Gilles DA. The emotional and behavioral process of staff nurse turnover. J Nurs Adm 1989;19(9):23-29.
8. Prescott PA. Vacancy, stability, and turnover of registered nurses in hospitals. Res Nurs Health 1986;9(1):51-60.
9. Price JL, Mueller CW. Professional turnover: the case of nurses. New York: SP Medical and Scientific Books (1981b).
10. Weisman CS, Alexander C, Chase G. Determinants of hospital staff nurse turnover. Med Care 1981;19: 431-443.
11. Droste T. High price tag on nursing recruitment. Hospitals 1987;61(19):150.
12. Jolma DJ, Weller DE. An evaluation of nurse recruitment methods. J Nurs Adm 1989;19(4):20-24.
13. Kerfoot K. Retention: What's it all about? Nurs Econ 1988;6(1):42-43.
14. Loveridge CE. Contingency theory: Explaining staff nurse retention. J Nurs Adm 1988;18(6):22-25.
15. Mann EE, Jefferson KJ. Retaining staff: using turnover indices and surveys. J Nurs Adm 1988;18(7&8):17-23.

16. Marquis B. Attrition: the effectiveness of retention activities. J Nurs Adm 1988;18(3):25-29.

17. Prescott PA, Bowen SA. Controlling nursing turnover. Nurs Mgmt 1987;18(6):60-66.

18. Wolf GA. Nursing turnover: some causes and solutions. Nurs Outlook 1981;29(4):233-236.

19. Hoffman FM. Financial Management for Nurse Managers. Norwalk, CT: Appleton-Century-Crofts, 1984.

20. Hoffman FM. Cost per RN hired. J Nurs Adm 1985; 15(2):27-29.

21. Hall TE. How to estimate employee turnover costs. Personnel 1981;58(4):43-52.

22. Rousseau L. What are the real costs of employee turnover? CA Magazine 1984;117(12):48-55.

23. Dalton DR, Todor WD. Turnover: a lucrative hard dollar phenomenon. Acad Mgmt Rev 1982;7(2):212-218.

24. Kesner IF, Dalton DR. Turnover benefits: the other side of the "costs" coin. Personnel 1982;59(5):69-76.

25. Lowery BJ, Jacobsen BS. On the consequences of overturning turnover: a study of performance and turnover. Nurs Res 1984;33(6):363-367.

Part II, measurements and results

This is the second in a two-part series which discusses the measurement of nursing turnover costs at four acute care hospitals in a southeast metropolitan area. The conceptual framework and Nursing Turnover Cost Calculation Methodology (NTCCM) developed during this study were presented in Part I (JONA, April 1990). This article discusses the application of the NTCCM, the study's findings, implications for nurse administrators, and recommendations for future research.

Four acute care hospitals in a southeast metropolitan area, ranging in size from 239 to 611 beds with an average of 355 beds, participated in this study to examine nursing turnover costs. On average, the hospitals employed 341 RNs for 335 FTE positions, had 88 RNs leave, and hired 133 new RNs during the 1988 FY. The hospitals had a mean of 49 RN positions open throughout the study year, with approximately 45 preexisting vacancies from FY 1987.

The average salary for incumbent staff RNs at the hospitals ranged from $26,440 to $27,250, excluding shift differentials and fringe benefits. The average starting salary for staff RNs ranged from $23,100 to $24,100, excluding shift differentials and fringe benefits. The average incumbent salary was only $3,317, or 14%, higher than the average new RN salary. The mean annual RN salaries of the nursing departments totaled $8.3 million with a range of $6.0 million to $11.0 million.

Availability of RN Turnover Cost Data

Hospital sources consistently reported that specific, detailed nursing turnover costs were not calculated at the hospitals. Nevertheless, all sources validated the importance of possessing this information. Categories of data were maintained differently at each hospital and differently between departments within the hospitals, with some duplication among the departments. The hospitals generally made limited but broad attempts to calculate some nursing turnover costs; however the NTCCM called for much greater detail than was maintained by the hospitals.

Results

Turnover and turnover cost data were collected from various departments within the hospitals during semistructured interviews. Data were then grouped according to the NTCCM classification: direct costs included advertising/recruiting costs, costs of unfilled positions, and hiring costs; indirect costs included termination costs, orientation/training costs, and costs of decreased new RN productivity. Descriptive statistical analyses were performed on the turnover data and on each cost category.

NURSING TURNOVER RATES

The nursing turnover data collected from each hospital were analyzed in aggregate for turnover rate measures. While the methods for calculating nursing turnover rates were similar at the four hospitals, there were some differences. This necessitated the calculation of a standardized RN turnover rate[1] for the hospitals during the 1988 FY, using the following formula:

$$\text{Turnover rate} = \frac{\text{Number of RN terminations/fiscal year}}{\text{Average RN workforce/ fiscal year}} \times 100$$

Rate calculation by this method revealed a mean turnover rate of 26.8%, with a range of 18.5% to 36.2%.

NURSING TURNOVER COSTS

Nursing turnover costs were calculated for FY 1988 and were adjusted, whenever appropriate, to account for preexisting vacancies. Table 43-1 illustrates the six turnover cost category means, medians, standard deviations, and ranges. Summing the costs from the six categories reveals that the mean total cost of nursing turnover reported was $902,590, with a range of $604,402 to $1,651,601. The total nursing turnover cost equalled approximately 11% of the mean total annual RN salaries paid by the hospitals. Each of the cost categories will be discussed in more detail below.

Advertising and recruiting costs

These costs are associated with attracting new RN employees to fill vacancies caused by staff RN turnover. Advertising and recruiting costs include personnel department costs; supply costs; school and job fair visit costs; advertising costs for professional journals, conventions, newspapers, etc.; agency and search fees; student visitation day costs; student nurse program costs; and seminars for recruitment training. This study found the total mean advertising/recruiting cost to be $169,615 with a range of $99,168 to $292,962. The mean avertising/recruiting cost per RN turnover was $1,887 and ranged from $1,181 to $2,688.

Costs of unfilled positions

These are organizational costs incurred due to temporarily filling vacancies, and decreased operations caused by staff shortages resulting from RN turnover. Costs attributable to unfilled positions include the costs of hiring replacement and temporary nurses which were above the normal funding level of the unfilled position; overtime expenses paid to RN employees above the position funding; and the organizational revenues lost due to closed beds. The total mean cost for unfilled positions was $355,428 with a range of $115,374 to $849,578. The mean cost per RN turnover for unfilled positions was $4,101 with a range of $1,358 to $7,794.

Hiring costs

Costs are incurred by a hospital once a prospective RN staff employee enters the interview process. These costs include activities associated with the interviewing and hiring of new employees, such as management time, salaries, and fringe benefits; processing costs and supplies; pre-employment physical examinations; moving and travel expenses; internal referral bonuses; and recruitment bonuses. Hiring costs due to RN terminations were calculated by determining a unit hiring cost per RN and multipyling that figure by the number of RN turnovers during FY 1988. This study found a total mean hiring cost of $58,889 with a range of $35,603 to $109,621. The mean hiring cost per RN turnover was $655 and ranged from $448 to $1,006.

Termination costs

Organizational costs are also incurred due to RN terminations. These costs include the payment of unused vacation to terminating staff RNs, the costs of conducting exit interviews, and the costs of processing the necessary termination paperwork. The hospitals reported paying only unused vacation time; they did not pay unused sick time to employees who terminated. The cost of unused vacation pay was

TABLE 43-1

RN turnover dollar costs during study year* (n = 4)

SUBCATEGORY	MEAN	MEDIAN	SD	RANGE	SUBCATEGORY	MEAN	MEDIAN	SD	RANGE
Advertising/recruiting					**Hiring, continued**				
Recruiter personnel salaries	28,247	31,365	11,545	10,352-39,906	Employment processing	53,621	39,478	29,404	31,800-103,726
Supplies	8,471	8,823	3,499	3,639 12,598	SUBTOTAL	58,889	45,166	30,022	35,603-109,621
School and job fair visits (n = 1)	915	1,829	1,584	0-3,658	SUBTOTAL, DIRECT	583,932	415,684	392,407	252,199-1,252,161
Advertising	47,823	33,094	29,748	26,512-98,593	**Termination**				
Student visitation days†	0	0	0	0	Unused vacation/sick pay§	12,595	12,760	4,699	7,420-17,440
Student nurse hiring program	44,447	36,311	20,653	26,291-78,874	Exit interviews	1,624	1,579	811	525-2,812
Seminars (n = 1)	156	312	270	0-624	SUBTOTAL	14,219	13,938	4,186	9,899-19,098
Misc. recruitment (n = 3)	39,556	43,502	28,974	0-71,220	**Orientation/training**				
SUBTOTAL	169,615	143,165	78,099	99,168-292,962	Staff time/salaries	123,118	118,923	71,160	27,039-227,587
Unfilled positions					Supply/equipment	1,694	800	1,976	106-5,069
Temporary RNs (n = 2)	23,955	23,955	36,940	0-87,678	Preceptor system	63,071	59,933	12,517	50,399-82,017
Overtime	58,143	53,151	32,022	19,036-107,233	SUBTOTAL	187,882	196,260	71,419	80,463-278,546
Lost revenue from closed beds (n = 3)	273,331	188,534	276,984	0-716,256	**Decreased new RN productivity**				
SUBTOTAL	355,428	228,381	294,921	115,374-849,578	Period 1	72,664	73,136	27,828	41,585-102,799
Hiring					Period 2	33,234	34,753	15,276	13,862-49,568
Interviews	2,738	2,532	1,375	1,047-4,840	Period 3	10,660	9,202	15,466	5,544-18,690
Secretarial processing	1,305	1,352	718	369-2,148	SUBTOTAL	116,557	118,511	48,037	60,991-168,216
Payroll processing‡	1,225	1,227	288	918-1,526	SUBTOTAL, INDIRECT	318,658	361,753	97,654	151,686-399,440
					TOTAL	902,590	677,179	435,509	604,402-1,651,601

*Excluding costs attributable to preexisting vacancies.
†Not reported.
‡Estimated at two hospitals.
§Estimated at all four hospitals.

calculated by taking the difference between the average RN salary at hire and upon termination (estimated at $2 per hour) and multiplying by the amount of unused vacation hours. The mean termination cost was $14,219 with a range of $9,899 to $19,098. The mean termination cost per RN turnover was $163 and ranged from $118 to $193.

Orientation and training costs

These are costs incurred by hospitals to train and familiarize new RNs with hospital and nursing policies and procedures. These costs include: salaries and benefits of the training staff (clinical specialists, staff development employees, head nurses, and secretaries); supply costs (audiovisual costs, books, etc.); classroom costs; and preceptor system costs, including the reduced efficiency of the preceptor while training new employees. Orientation and training costs were calculated per new RN hire during FY 1988. This unit cost was then multiplied by the number of RN terminations to reflect orientation and training costs due to RN turnovers. This study found a mean orientation and training cost of $187,882 with a range of $80,463 to $278,546. The mean orientation and training cost per RN turnover was $2,117 and ranged from $1,518 to $3,316.

Costs of decreased new RN productivity

Productivity losses are incurred during the employee training and orientation period when new employee productivity is low. More specifically, the costs of decreased new RN productivity include losses during the period of time required by new RNs to become 90% as productive as seasoned employees. These costs were measured by determining: 1) the average weekly pay rate for new RNs; 2) the average number of weeks for a new RN to reach 90% productivity; and 3) the level of productivity achieved by the typical new hire during each third of the learning period. Hall's learning curve productivity losses formula[2] was adapted and applied to calculate the cost of decreased new RN productivity. Decreased productivity costs were calculated per new RN hire during FY 1988. This unit cost was then multiplied by the total number of RN terminations to reflect decreased productivity due to RN turnover. The hospitals reported the

average number of weeks taken by an RN to reach 90% productivity was 6.7. At the end of the three periods, the typical new RN was reported as being 27%, 68%, and 90% productive, respectively. The total mean decreased productivity cost was $116,557 with a range of $60,991 to $168,216. The mean decreased new RN productivity cost per RN turnover was $1,276 and ranged from $915 to $1,543.

Direct and indirect costs

Grouping the cost categories into direct and indirect costs reveals that direct costs equaled $583,932 of the total cost of nursing turnover during FY 1988, while indirect costs equaled $318,658. Table 43-2 indicates that direct nursing turnover costs constituted the largest proportion, 61%, of total nursing turnover costs, with a range of 41% to 76%. Indirect costs of nursing turnover were found to be 39% of total turnover costs, ranging from 24% to 59%. Relative proportions of the six individual cost categories are also shown in Table 43-2. On average, the unfilled position costs, orientation and training costs, advertising, and recruiting costs, and the costs of decreased new RN productivity were responsible for over 90% of nursing turnover costs. Hiring costs and termination costs constituted less than 10% of the total costs.

The total nursing turnover costs were divided by the number of nurses reported as turning over at each

TABLE 43-2
Category percentages of total costs (n = 4)

CATEGORY	MEAN	MEDIAN	SD	RANGE
Advertising/ Recruiting	19	18	3	16-25
Unfilled positions	35	36	16	19-52
Hiring	6	7	0	6-7
SUBTOTAL, DIRECT	61	63	15	41-76
Termination	2	2	0	1-2
Orientation/ training	24	19	13	13-45
Decreased new RN productivity	14	11	5	10-22
SUBTOTAL, INDIRECT	39	37	15	24-59

of the hospitals to calculate the average turnover cost per RN. Table 43-3 shows that the mean cost per RN turnover for the sample was $10,198. The turnover cost per RN ranged from $6,886 to $15,152.

Discussion

Earlier estimates of nursing turnover costs[3,4] are less than those costs documented by this study. Furthermore, the results of this study demonstrate that the range of nursing turnover costs is one and one-half to four times greater than some more recent estimates.[5-8] It should be pointed out, however, that the range of turnover costs reported in this study ($6,886 to $15,152 per RN) is substantially less than some estimates made by others.[9,10] A large-scale study would help determine accurate turnover costs at the national level and would alleviate the confusion caused by the current wide range in cost estimates.

TABLE 43-3

Dollar cost per RN turnover by category during study year (n = 4)

CATEGORY	MEAN	MEDIAN	SD	RANGE
Advertising/ Recruiting	1,887	1,841	546	1,181- 2,688
Unfilled positions	4,101	3,626	2,818	1,358- 7,794
Hiring	655	582	219	488- 1,006
SUBTOTAL DIRECT	6,643	6,040	3,534	3,002- 11,488
Termination	163	170	28	118- 193
Orientation/ training	2,117	1,816	709	1,518- 3,316
Decreased new RN productivity	1,276	1,324	258	915- 1,543
SUBTOTAL, INDIRECT	3,556	3,506	540	2,862- 4,349
TOTAL	10,198	9,378	3,357	6,886- 15,152

Although the sample size of the present study was small, and definite conclusions cannot be drawn, there appears to be no correlation between turnover rates, turnover costs, and hospital size. Future studies could refute or confirm this conclusion.

LIMITATIONS OF THE STUDY

The accuracy of this study's results are limited by several factors. The sensitive nature of the data and the competitive hospital milieu made data collection challenging. Turnover cost calculations were limited by the availability and accuracy of retrospective hospital records; therefore, some turnover costs had to be estimated in cases when exact cost records were unavailable. However, estimated costs accounted for less than 5% of the total turnover costs.

The costs of nursing turnover reported in this study represent the costs associated with hiring and training an "average" nurse, and may not be indicative of instances where nurses with specialized training must be hired. The present study is also limited in its generalizability to the larger hospital population because of its small sample size and because the results reflect the cost of staff RN turnover in only one geographic region.

Despite these limitations, the turnover costs reported represent the best estimates of costs attributable to RN turnover at the hospitals studied. If anything, the reported costs are probably conservative, since estimates of lost revenues due to closed beds were based largely on room charges alone and did not take into consideration profits on supplies and ancillary services. Furthermore, overhead costs were not included in any of the cost categories because the hospitals did not charge overhead to their departments.

IMPLICATIONS FOR NURSE ADMINISTRATORS

Nursing turnover has several implications for the CNE. First, this study found that the hospitals studied, on average, lost over $900,000 due to nursing turnover during FY 1988. That loss may be passed on to the healthcare consumer in the form of increased room and ancillary charges. Second, the tangible loss from nursing turnover that constituted the greatest proportion (35%) of overall nursing turnover costs was the cost of unfilled positions. Aside from the monetary significance, there are important patient care implications as well. Quality patient care is potentially compromised when severe staff shortages force high patient-nurse ratios.

Next, results of the study suggest that some cost categories contribute relatively little to the total cost of nursing turnover. Attempts to measure these small costs on a periodic basis may not prove cost-efficient. Instead, the CNE should consider an initial study to determine the relative impact of each cost category using the NTCCM. Thereafter, attention could be focused on the more important cost categories.

One of the CNE's major responsibilities is to make efficient use of hospital resources. This goal becomes difficult to achieve when a hospital loses the equivalent of 11% of annual nursing salaries in nursing turnover costs. The CNE can use the NTCCM developed during this study to analyze hospital losses caused by nursing turnover, to evaluate more cost-effective methods of dealing with resultant nursing turnover activities and to examine reallocation of resources lost through nursing turnover to activities that would promote nurse retention.

RECOMMENDATIONS FOR FUTURE RESEARCH

This study should be replicated using a larger sample to provide support for its findings and to examine regional and national nursing turnover cost variations. Furthermore, replication of this study using a concurrent, longitudinal study design would identify trends in nursing turnover and the associated turnover costs. Nursing turnover costs could also be examined on a unit basis to determine whether there are significant variations within a hospital. This type of examination would allow comparison of similar units in different hospitals.

Finally, further investigation of the present study's conceptual framework to examine the benefits of turnover and the costs and benefits of nurse retention will allow nurse administrators to compare the costs and benefits of nurse turnover and retention activities.

This comparison could facilitate the allocation of resources that would most efficiently maximize hospital revenues.

SUMMARY

This study demonstrated that the costs of nursing turnover can be high (over $10,000 per RN turnover), and that the potential for adverse impact on the nursing department, the hospital environment, and the healthcare environment exists. The results of this study are important, particularly in the midst of a national nursing shortage, for several reasons. CNEs are responsible for obtaining, allocating, and managing nursing department resources; knowledge of nursing turnover costs will allow them to make more informed decisions about how best to allocate scarce resources. The findings of this study are also important to hospital administrators because they demonstrate the financial impact of high rates of nursing turnover on healthcare delivery. Finally, these findings provide nurse researchers direction for future research into the costs and benefits of nursing turnover and retention activities, so that cost-effective methods of minimizing organizational costs can be determined.

REFERENCES

1. Hoffman FM. Financial management for nurse managers. Norwalk, CT: Appleton-Century-Crofts, 1984.
2. Hall TE. How to estimate employee turnover costs. Personnel 1981; 58(4):43-52.
3. Donovan L. The shortage. RN 1980;8:21-27.
4. Wolf GA. Nursing turnover: Some causes and solutions. Nurs Outlook 1981;29(4):233-236.
5. Mann EE, Jefferson KJ. Retaining staff: Using turnover indices and surveys. J Nurs Admin 1988(7&8):17-23.
6. Marquis B. Attrition: The effectiveness of retention activities. J Nurs Admin 1988;18(3):25-29.
7. Hinshaw AS, Smeltzer CH, Atwood JR. Innovative retention strategies for nursing staff. J Nurs Admin 1987;17(6):8-16.
8. Prescott PA, Bowen SA. Controlling nursing turnover. Nurs Mgm 1987;18(6):60-66.
9. Droste T. High price tag on nursing recruitment. Hospitals 1987;61(19):150.
10. Kerfoot K. Retention: What's it all about? Nurs Econ 1988;6(1):42-43.

CHAPTER **44**

Job Satisfaction
Assumptions and complexities

Elaine Larson, RN, PhD, FAAN,
Pat Chikamoto Lee, RN, MN,
Marie Annette Brown, RN, PhD,
Judy Shorr, RN, MS

It is a personal as well as a management goal in every profession to maximize job satisfaction; the nursing literature is replete with articles on the subject.[1-5]

> Because health care organizations are concerned with the quality of life in general, they should have a profound interest in the quality of an employee's work life quite aside from their primary concern for productivity in patient care.[6]

It is assumed that enhancement of job satisfaction is desirable. Yet our assumptions about why, what, and how we actually measure job satisfaction need examination. In this article we will discuss some of these assumptions and complexities and will present the results of a study in which the evaluation of job satisfaction was more comprehensive than that of previous studies. The results of the study are congruent with our proposed model.

WHY MEASURE JOB SATISFACTION?

Improving job satisfaction is often mistakenly looked upon as the panacea for the ailments of the or-

Reprinted from *The Journal of Nursing Administration,* Vol. 14, No. 1, with permission of J. B. Lippincott Company © 1984.

ganization. For example, staff nurses may focus on a single issue, either personal (such as child care arrangements) or professional (such as frequent weekend scheduling), and perceive that if it were resolved they would be more satisfied and less stressed. If, in response, nurse managers attribute all levels of organizational problems to the issue staff is most vocally unhappy about, costly intervention that deals with it may not yield the expected overall improvement.

More formally stated organizational reasons for obtaining overall measures of job satisfaction relate either to using the results to reduce staff turnover and absenteeism or to improve the quality of the product rendered—in this case, patient care. An underlying assumption exists that, given adequate measuring tools, we would find a direct correlation between productivity and job satisfaction: The satisfied employee is a productive employee.

Job Satisfaction and Turnover

It makes intuitive sense that increasing job satisfaction should increase job retention and improve performance. We assume that people tend to leave situations where they are dissatisfied. A happy professional is more likely to remain on the job and to help create a work environment more pleasant for colleagues and clients. Much data substantiate the belief that job satisfaction and employment longevity are correlated.[7-11] A relationship between turnover and dissatisfaction with content or type of work has been demonstrated in student nurses.[12]

These relationships, however, can be quite complex. It is clear that a very unhappy employee working under the most difficult conditions is likely, if at all possible, to leave the job if personal circumstances permit. But under ordinary circumstances, the measurable aspects of job satisfaction only partially explain why individuals stay in a particular job. Jones et al. found that only 30 percent of the nurses working in a burn unit changed jobs because of job-related dissatisfaction.[13] Clearly, other factors such as family situation, educational opportunities, mobility, or social values strongly affect the decision to retain a job.[14] We can conclude that job satisfaction is only one of several factors that contribute to turnover and absenteeism.[15]

As a further complexity, any one factor has varying effects on employee satisfaction, the effects depending upon the employee's expectations and the importance he or she places on that factor. For example, a raise in pay may bring satisfaction primarily as a result of factors such as the perceived equity of the increase rather than the amount itself (expectations); it will bring little satisfaction if the additional money is of little value to the individual (importance).[11]

However, there is evidence that information regarding job satisfaction can make a difference. Nurse managers can focus intervention/change strategies in areas more likely to result in a decrease in staff turnover. Redfern reported that nurses who stayed in their jobs were more satisfied with certain extrinsic satisfiers such as hospital policies, working conditions, pay, and advancement opportunities than were their counterparts who left.[16] Interestingly, she also found, among nurses who quit or remained, no differences in certain intrinsic factors such as autonomy, security, use of ability, achievement, and responsibility—factors that have been identified by others as important job satisfiers.[17-19] Thus, it behooves the manager to conduct a cost-benefit analysis

of any change in administrative structure or policy that is designed solely to decrease turnover. On the other hand, managers should also recognize that it is appropriate to enhance employees' job satisfaction purely for humane reasons, even if the results are not directly or immediately measurable in turnover rates.

The question remains: Does increasing job satisfaction increase employee retention? The evidence points to a strong correlation, but other factors such as one's potential mobility are equally important.[14] Furthermore, the degree and direction of change in job satisfaction are heavily influenced by the individual's expectation as well as the level of importance attached to particular factors.

Job Satisfaction and Quality of Care

Clearly, job autonomy and ability to participate in decision making are important for maximizing satisfaction. It seems reasonable to assume that a happier nurse will deliver better patient care. Nevertheless, job satisfaction is, at best, an indirect measure of the quality of care delivered: quality and satisfaction may well be independent of each other.[20,21] As quality assurance programs become more sophisticated and as it becomes more important to document adequate care, to identify and solve problems, and to demonstrate cost benefits of programs, more information on this subject may emerge.

Reasons why job satisfaction and quality of work do not correlate more directly are poorly understood. The problem may be related to the high demands placed on the nurse, a concept currently popularized by the term "burnout." Some have found, however, that nurses in high-stress jobs are not necessarily less content.[2] In fact, these units often seem to attract highly motivated and enthusiastic professionals whose satisfaction is enhanced by the high-demand situation. It may be that the propensity to deliver quality care is more an ethical decision or personality characteristic. It would be interesting to know if nurses who give high-quality patient care are also likely to be more competent and thoughtful parents, spouses, friends, community members, and so on. This subject certainly deserves further study.

MODEL OF RELATIONSHIPS BETWEEN JOB SATISFACTION AND PERFORMANCE

When considering job satisfaction, it is tempting to conclude that, from the clinical perspective, increased satisfaction will increase performance or output and that, from the management viewpoint, increased satisfaction will improve staff retention. This simplistic model is inadequate to explain the relationships involved in job satisfaction. We here propose a more comprehensive model (Figure 44-1).

In the following sections, we will discuss some of the difficulties in measuring job satisfaction and will describe a study that tested the correlation between previous job expectations and the importance placed on certain aspects of the job, with the resultant measurable levels of job satisfaction.

DIFFICULTIES IN MEASURING JOB SATISFACTION
Timing

Retrospective evaluation of changes in job satisfaction, even after only a short period, correlate poorly with changes measured concurrently.[22] In addition, the mere decision to terminate a job will result in some attitude changes that would be reflected in job satisfaction measurements. In their study, Porter and Steers noted that "it is quite probable that the act of withdrawal significantly altered the attitudinal predisposition under study."[11] It is likely that factors that influence an individual's decision to terminate employment also affect the entire gestalt of the work situation, as well as how the individual continues to relate to certain aspects of his or her job. Thus, it is risky to determine attitudes and their relation to turnover retrospectively.

Validity/Reliability of Information Obtained

Discrepancies have been found between what nurses say are satisfiers and how satisfied they actually feel.[23] There is also the difficulty of eliciting valid information regarding job problems if the nurse is unsure how the information will be used.[24] Practicing nurses may be more accustomed to performance evaluations

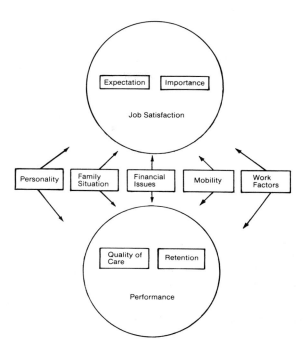

FIGURE 44-1

Relationships between job satisfaction and performance.

than to research, where the confidentiality issues are quite different. That is, information in a performance evaluation is provided for the specific purpose of appraising an individual. In contrast, job satisfaction information is gathered for the purpose of identifying potential problems or issues that would influence the satisfaction of nurses as a group. The identity of the individual is unimportant. To feel safe in providing honest answers about job satisfaction, nurses must be sure that the information they supply will not be associated with them as individuals.

Lack of Sensitivity of Instruments

Job satisfaction is often used as an outcome measure of the success of various program changes or interventions (i.e., day care centers, career ladders, primary nursing, changes in work hours, increased salary) to enhance the environment for employees or clients.[25-27] If one attempts to evaluate the influence of a particular intervention, the separate and combined influences of other factors may mask any effect, or the evaluation tools themselves may be too insensitive to detect change. Hence, there is a problem in evaluating the effects of specific interventions on job satisfaction. In a study of 3500 nurses in Texas, for example, the job dissatisfiers identified by nurses rank ordered as follows: poor salary; inadequate regulatory laws; lack of administrative support; inadequate continuing education; lack of support of nursing administration and available child care, inservice, and fringe benefits.[28] An improvement in only one of these factors might not produce enough change in job satisfaction to be statistically significant even though the factor might be extremely important to a number of nurses.

Even more subtly, the stress of interventions or changes in the work setting, which may eventually lead to increased job satisfaction, will for a time create increased stress and perhaps subsequent dissatisfaction. Thus, the timing of evaluation of such interventions will greatly affect the results obtained.[29]

Complexity

All job factors have varying impact on employee satisfaction, an impact that is based on that individual's *expectations* for the job and the value or *importance* of that factor to the individual. Satisfied employees cannot be obtained with a "shopping list" of job factors that can be maximized. Satisfaction occurs when an individual's needs and job characteristics are compatible and discrepancy between expectations and reality is minimized.[30]

Investigators have found that when the expectations of prospective new employees were modified to reflect the realities of the organization, job longevity was increased.[31-33] Thus, it is important to identify perceptions (expectations) on *entering* a job in order to avoid unrealistic expectations and the resultant dissatisfaction. Seybolt et al. have gone an additional step beyond entry assessment and have attempted to evaluate the direction of changes from the perspective of nurse employees over time in an effort to identify where management changes might be useful for increasing job satisfaction and longevity. They did find

significant differences in satisfaction between nurses who left and those who stayed. Primarily, the differences were in intrinsic factors dealing with professional issues such as autonomy and the chance to make full use of one's abilities.[7] The investigators did not, however, consider the possible discrepancy between the expectations of these nurses and what they actually encountered in their jobs.

Individuals' relationships with their jobs are similar to other relationships in their lives, such as marriage. The expectations one brings into a job or marriage and the subjective evaluation of how well those expectations are met strongly influence that individual's satisfaction, regardless of the "realities" of the situation. For example, women with high *unmet* expectations of husband participation in child care may be less satisfied with their marriage than women with lower expectations, even though the absolute levels of husband participation may be higher in the high-expectation group. An evaluation of the absolute levels of husband participation in child care by an outside observer would miss the underlying dynamic accounting for a woman's satisfaction unless expectations were considered.

In addition to fulfilling expectations, another important issue must be considered. People order their needs and wants in each different area of life. Usually these priorities differ among various subgroups in the profession and fluctuate over time. For example, a university medical center may attract predominantly young, baccalaureate, single, or recently married nurses. These young professionals may be committed to a feminist ideology of child care and have high expectations that the university medical center will be a forerunner in providing quality, on-site day care/ early education programs. Though they may express strong dissatisfaction if absolutely nothing on the worksite is available for women needing this service, most have delayed childbearing and are not parents. The importance of this dissatisfaction is low compared with their need for more administrative support in attending continuing education and personal growth seminars. The nurse manager must carefully assess such priorities in order to decide what combination of changes might maximize improved job satisfaction.

Even though no relationship or job setting could possibly be ideal for all persons, several general areas need the attention of managers. Porter has identified four major factors related to job satisfaction and withdrawal.[11]

1. Organization-wide factors (pay, promotion, management)
2. Work environment (relations with co-workers)
3. Job content (the work to be done)
4. Personal factors (age, tenure, family, personality)

When the innumerable factors that could possibly affect job satisfaction are multiplied by the individual employee's expectations and the value placed on each factor, it is easy to see that a single nondimensional measure of job satisfaction is at best superficial; at worst, meaningless or misleading.

EXPECTATIONS AND VALUE IN JOB SATISFACTION

Some investigations, using Vroom's expectancy theory,[34] have attempted to measure the extent to which an employee's expectations are met in a job. Because a clear understanding of the functions and tasks of a job has been shown to significantly increase job satisfaction and decrease one's propensity to leave a job and because others have recognized that individuals vary in the importance they place on various facets of the job,[30] we have attempted to correlate the level of job satisfaction expressed by nurses after 6 months of employment with both the extent to which their expectations were being met and the importance levels of various job factors.

Methods

A New Employee Assessment tool was conceived and developed for this study. It was based on the recognition that the initial 6 months of employment constitute a critical time period. Items in the tool were based on a review of salient issues of job satisfaction in both nursing and psychology. It was pretested for clarity, consistency, and validity, using an interview format. For 1 year the instrument was

then mailed to all RN employees after 6 months of employment. After qualitative assessment of these data, the questionnaire was revised into its present format with fixed-alternative responses. Responses generated were standardized to enable measurement of 35 quality of work-life factors (Figure 44-2). A copy of the entire tool is available from the authors upon request.

New employees were informed during orientation that they could participate in an evaluation of their job after 6 months of employment. At the end of the 6-month probationary period, the questionnaire was mailed to them with a cover letter and return envelope. A follow-up letter was mailed within 1 month if the questionnaire had not been returned. During the first 6 months of 1982, 87 questionnaires were mailed and 60 were returned, a 69 percent response rate.

Multiple regression techniques were applied to evaluate the extent to which job expectations and importance of work conditions predicted current levels of job satisfaction. Analysis of covariance (controlling for expectations and importance of work conditions) was used to assess whether there were significant differences in job satisfaction by educational background, entry level into the job, and shift worked.

Results

Respondents were employees at a 336-bed, acute care, university-affiliated hospital. Our sample consisted of the 60 nurses from 17 clinical units who completed the 6-month assessment. Most respondents (44, 73.3%) were experienced nurses. Only four were assistant head nurses or above; the others were hired as staff nurses. The majority (46, 76.7%) had a baccalaureate or higher degree, with only 14 (23.3%) educated in associate arts or diploma programs. Most nurses had heard about their position through advertising (16, 26.7%), employee referral (9, 15.0%), or because they worked as student nurses in the study institution (8, 13.3%). Other sources of information about their positions included listings in the telephone book, correspondence, or working as temporary nurses in the study hospital.

	Never Met 1	2	3	4	5	Consistently Met 6
1. The chance to learn new things						
2. Primary care nursing						
3. Working relations among health care professionals						
4. Your scheduling pattern						
5. Your salary						
6. Promotional opportunities						
7. Unit orientation						
8. All RN staff						
9. The opportunity for growth through unit/department participation						
10. Utilization of your abilities						
11. Your interactions with other departments						
12. Your shift assignment						
13. Your fringe benefits						
14. Career opportunities						
15. Hospital orientation						
16. Research/teaching atmosphere						
17. The variety of clinical cases						
18. Independent/expanded function of the nurse						
19. Feedback from your supervisor						
20. Weekend coverage						
21. Your educational benefits						
22. Job security						
23. Adequacy of inservices provided						
24. Demands of the job						
25. Feedback from your co-workers						
26. Weekend compensation agreement						
27. Your input is considered in the patient's care						
28. Assistance and support from your supervisor						
29. Adequacy of staffing						
30. Your input is considered in unit activities						
31. Assistance and support from your co-workers						
32. Use of contractual staffing pattern						
33. Your work in general						
34. Accessibility/availability of resource people						
35. Relations among medical staff and nursing staff						

FIGURE 44-2

An excerpt from the new employee assessment tool listing 35 quality of life factors evaluated. The respondents were asked to place a check mark in the column that indicated the degree to which the job expectations were being met.

Factors of importance in selecting employment at the study institution are listed in Table 44-1. Major factors related to professional issues, although the hospital's affiliation with a school of nursing was rated as the least important factor.

Areas of satisfaction and dissatisfaction polarized around different issues. High levels of job satisfaction were related to professional issues such as learning, whereas factors with which employees were least satisfied were related to employment issues such as salary and staffing (Table 44-2).

The most striking result of our study was that all 35 satisfaction variables were significantly predicted by respondents' job expectations and the importance they placed on working conditions. For the whole group, 55.9 percent of variance in satisfaction scores was explained by nurses' expectations and by the value they placed on each variable ($p = 0.001$). On the other hand, mean satisfaction scores were not significantly different according to educational preparation

TABLE 44-1
Factors in order of importance in considering employment at study institution

FACTOR	SCORE (MAXIMUM = 4)
Opportunities for growth	3.37
Teaching environment	3.32
Relationships among health professionals	3.17
Professional atmosphere	3.15
Primary care nursing*	3.08
Geographical location	3.08
Benefits	2.95
University-affiliated hospital	2.91
Acuity level/type of clients	2.80
All RN staff†	2.80
Scheduling	2.69
Salary	2.59
Affiliation with school of nursing	1.95

*More important to nurses with baccalaureate or masters degree (3.19) than to those with diploma or associate arts degree (2.29)
†More important to nurses with masters degree (3.75) than to others (2.73)

($p = 0.23$), shift worked ($p = 0.42$), or entry level into the job ($p = 0.78$). This may be explained in part by the homogeneity of the study group.

Discussion

Because of the complexity of the issue, a multifaceted approach to increasing and measuring job satisfaction is needed. Such isolated innovations as providing day care, giving merit raises in salary, and offering recognition through "Nurse of the Week" awards often have little overall effect in reducing dissatisfaction. Intervention strategies must be considered in light of the expectations and importance values of individuals.

Enhanced job satisfaction requires a concerted effort in a variety of areas. Initially, a realistic staff orientation is important to assure that new employees have an accurate idea of the intrinsic as well as the extrinsic characteristics of the organization. Interviews with staff after a period of employment and upon termination can alert managers to problems that should be addressed.[35] Furthermore, managers can analyze and emphasize motivational needs that relate to personal growth and self-actualization[6] and can carefully place individuals in roles that are as congruent as possible with their abilities, interests, and expectations.

It is critically important to identify people's perceptions on entering a job and to provide sufficient information to avoid unrealistic expectations. Otherwise, the result is dissatisfaction.

A major focus should be placed on differential expectation levels at the time of entry into the organization and the extent to which these expectations are met or altered over the course of employment. This strongly suggests the need for as much attention to expectations as to reactions to the work situation.[11]

Expressed intent has been shown to be a more sensitive predictor of turnover than satisfaction scores.[11] Therefore, questions that elicit employees' future plans should be included in any tool designed to help plan and anticipate staffing. Such questions might include, "Do you plan to be in this same job

TABLE 44-2
Areas of high and low job satisfaction (Out of 35 possible factors)

HIGH SATISFACTION		LOW SATISFACTION	
FACTOR	SCORE (MAXIMUM = 6)	FACTOR	SCORE (MAXIMUM = 6)
Chance to learn new things	5.29	Salary	3.85
Variety of clinical cases	5.22	Weekend coverage	4.17
All-RN staff	5.17	Interaction with other departments	4.26
Assistance and support of co-workers	5.15	Promotional opportunities	4.29
Independent/expanded function of the nurse	5.15	Unit orientation	4.27
Accessibility/availability of resource people	5.07	Adequacy of staff	4.29

a year from now?" or "If you could, would you get a new job?"[7]

Because remembered changes in job satisfaction correlate poorly with measured changes, even after 6 months or less, and because the very act of withdrawing from a position alters attitudes and satisfiers, assessment of job satisfaction should not be done retrospectively or by exit interview alone. A realistic perception of the job can be obtained from employees after 6 to 12 months of employment.[31]

We conclude from our work that the measurement of job satisfaction is more reliable and valid when it includes both the expectations of the individual and the importance of particular factors. For example, a nurse may expect to work the day shift, but if those hours are not very important to her there will be little effect on her job satisfaction if her expectations are not met. Likewise, even if working the day shift is very important to a nurse, a realistic expectation that this will not be possible will allow her to adjust to the fact, and job dissatisfaction will not necessarily result if she has some idea what to expect. Thus, expectations regarding a job variable and the perceived importance of that factor are separate entities contributing separately and jointly to job satisfaction. If the nurse both expects and highly values the day shift, she will be unhappy indeed with any variation in her hours. If she neither expects nor cares, this job variable will not enter at all into her feelings about her job.

We have only begun to understand , measure, and enhance job satisfaction. As nurse managers we must share more than our intervention strategies; we also need to discuss topics such as selection procedures and the data we use as a basis for our management decisions. Through a multifaceted approach we can start dealing creatively with the issue of job satisfaction for the benefit of both nurse employees and patient care.

REFERENCES

1. Walker DD, Bronstein JE. Job satisfaction survey: a tool for organizational change. Nursing Administration Quarterly 1981;5:14-7.
2. Nichols KA, Springford V, Searle J. An investigation of distress and discontent in various types of nursing. J Adv Nurs 1981:311-31.
3. Slavitt D, Stamps P, Piedmont E, House AM. Measuring nurses' job satisfaction. Hospital and Health Services Administration 1979;24:62-76.
4. Stubbs DC. Job satisfaction and dissatisfaction. J Nurs Adm 1977;7:44-9.
5. Stember ML, Ferguson J, Conway K, Yingling M. Job satisfaction research — An aid in decision making. Nursing Administration Quarterly 1978;2:95-105.
6. Timmreck TC, Randall PJ. Motivation, management and the supervisory nurse. Supervisor Nurse 1981;12:28-31.
7. Seybolt JW, Pavett C, Walker DD. Turnover among nurses: it can be managed. J Nurs Adm 1978;8:4-9.

8. Araujo M. Creative nursing administration sets climate for retention. Hospitals 1980;54:72-6.

9. Bayley EW. Breaking a turnover cycle — A successful approach . . . on burn units. Supervisor Nurse 1981;12:19-21.

10. Sutermeister RA. People and productivity. New York: McGraw-Hill, 1976.

11. Porter LW, Steers RM. Organizational, work and personal factors in employee turnover and absenteeism. Psychol Bull 1973;80:151-76.

12. Saleh SD, Lee RJ, Prien EP. Why nurses leave their jobs — An analysis of female turnover. Personnel Administration 1965;28:25-8.

13. Jones CA, Tholen D, Feller I, Dunlap K. Nurse retention in burn care: a report of 14 years' experience. Heart Lung 1981;10:295-308.

14. March JG, Simon HA. Organizations. New York: John Wiley, 1958.

15. Myrtle RC, Robertson JP. Factors influencing health care workers' satisfaction with supervisor. Journal of Health and Human Resources Administration 1979;1:364-78.

16. Redfern SJ. Hospital sisters: work attitudes, perceptions and wastage. J Adv Nurs 1980;5:451-66.

17. Allen RF, Kraft C. From burn-out to turn-on: improving the quality of hospital work life. Hospital Forum 1981;24:18-20 + .

18. Alexander CS, Weisman CS, Chase GA. Determinants of staff nurse perceptions of autonomy within different clinical contexts. Nurs Res 1982;31:48-52.

19. Sorensen JL, Sorensen TL. The conflict of professionals in bureaucratic organizations. Administrative Science Quarterly 1974;19:98-106.

20. Joiner C, Johnson V, Corkrean M. Is primary nursing the answer? Nursing Administration Quarterly 1981; 5:69-76.

21. Kent L, Larson E. An assessment of current practice of primary nursing when measured against previously established standards. J Nurs Adm 1983;13:34-41.

22. Hardin E. Perceived and actual change in job satisfaction. J Appl Psychol. 1965;49:363-7.

23. Donovan L. What nurses want (and what they're getting). RN 1980;43:22-30.

24. Watson LA. Keeping qualified nurses. Supervisor Nurse 1979;10:29 + .

25. Crump CK, Newson EFP. Implementing the 12-hour shift — A case study. Hospital Administration (Canada) 1975;17:20-4.

26. Munson FC, Heda SS. Service unit management and nurses' satisfaction. Health Serv Res 1976;11:128-36.

27. Fairbanks JE. Primary nursing: more data. Nursing Administration Quarterly 1981;5:51-62.

28. Wandelt MA, Pierce PM, Widdowson RR. Why nurses leave nursing and what can be done about it . . . a landmark study recently conducted in Texas. Am J Nurs 1981;81:72-7.

29. Bronson J, Johnston M. Stressed but satisfied: organizational change in ambulatory care. J Nurse Adm 1980; 10:43-6.

30. Herzberg F, Mausner B, Snyderman B. Motivation to work. New York: John Wiley, 1955.

31. Wanous JP. Organizational, entry: from naive expectations to realistic beliefs. J Appl Psychol 1976;61:22-9.

32. Lyons T. Role clarity, need for clarity, satisfaction, tension and withdrawal. Organizational Behavior and Human Performance 1971;6:99-110.

33. Wanous JP, Lawler EE III. Measurement and meaning of job satisfaction. J Appl Psychol 1972;56:95-105.

34. Vroom VH. Work and motivation. New York: John Wiley, 1964.

35. Tinney TR, Wright WN. Minimizing the turnover problem: a behavioral approach. Supervisor Nurse 1973; 4:47-9.

CHAPTER **45**

A Consortium Approach to Nursing Staff Development

Katherine Pam Bailey, RN, MS
Mary Hoeppner, RN, MS
Susan Brakke Jeska, RN, BAN, MBA
Sharon Schneller, RN, MS, CCRN
Judith Szalapski, RN, MS

Rapid advancement in healthcare technology and research, the current nursing shortage, and the increased patient acuity level in medical centers require a sophisticated, responsive program of nursing staff development to assure that patients receive high quality care. While medical centers have found that excellent educational programming has a positive effect on the quality of care, this programming is expensive to provide. Minnesota's four tertiary care public teaching hospitals — Hennepin County Medical Center, Minneapolis Veterans Administration Medical Center, St. Paul-Ramsey Medical Center, and the University of Minnesota Hospital and Clinic — have found that high-quality nursing staff development can be provided efficiently and effectively through a consortium effort. This article highlights the results of such an effort as a model to encourage other collaborative ventures.

BACKGROUND

Spurred by the nursing shortage of the late 1970s and increasing concern over health-care costs, each of the four major public teaching hospitals in

Minnesota sought cost-effective ways to educate nursing staff, especially in the critical care areas. Each facility placed a high priority on nursing staff development to assure quality care for high acuity patients, promote professional nursing practice in an environment of rapid technological advancements, and facilitate staff retention. Each facility was already expending considerable resources in the area of nursing staff development, but there was a need to do more.

In joint discussions, the nursing directors of the four facilities recognized their crucial mutual problems of recruitment, retention, and preparation of staff for critical care units. Based upon these concerns, the nursing staff development groups from the four medical centers joined the directors to brainstorm ideas and potential solutions and later were asked to develop recommendations on how to proceed. The staff development representatives considered alternative collaborative approaches, including program sharing and joint programming. After weighing the costs and benefits of various approaches, they recommended to the nursing directors that the four facilities participate in joint programming. This discussion provided the genesis of a consortium approach to nursing staff development across the four facilities.

Reprinted from *Nursing Economics,* Vol. 7, No. 4, with permission of Anthony J. Jannetti, Inc © 1989.

The collaborative effort in nursing staff development was further facilitated by the long history of cooperation among the four facilities. Since 1967, the four facilities had interacted through an organization of all hospitals affiliated with the University of Minnesota Medical School. In 1975, in recognition of the similarities of their missions, the four facilities began meeting informally to share information and discuss issues of mutual concern. In 1980, this joint forum was formalized as the Minnesota Association of Public Teaching Hospitals (MAPTH). The collaborative program for nursing staff development is now one of MAPTH's most successful, ongoing ventures.

THE APPROACH

The administrative model and philosophy. The MAPTH Staff Development Committee, which consists of nursing education representatives from each facility, develops the budget and administers the program. In approaching the development of a common core curriculum, the MAPTH Staff Development Committee adopted a consensus-based, collaborative approach rather than one based on equity and "score-keeping." Each hospital contributes equally to the MAPTH budget for joint educational offerings: For the current budget year, this contribution per institution is $22,500. This annual contribution funds salaries for the nursing education coordinator and secretary, office supplies, printing, duplication, travel, capital equipment, postage costs, and the fee paid to the independent administrative agency. In-kind contributions (such as faculty time and facilities) are made by each facility without regard to "rotation" or "turn-taking" protocols. To assure maximum flexibility and independence from the administrative structures of the four institutions, MAPTH education funds are administered by an independent agency that provides fiscal management for a variety of other groups.

MAPTH program offerings are available to nurses on staff at MAPTH facilities at no charge, and eligibility for attendance is determined by each hospital's policy. MAPTH faculty (who are exclusively nurses) are selected based on expertise rather than on their institutional affiliation. The course schedule is set annually based on the needs, activities, and work calendars of each facility. Course site assignments are made on a space-available basis.

During its initial 2 years, the consortium operated without staff support as a project of nursing education representatives of the four facilities. Since 1982, a nursing education coordinator and part-time secretary have been used. The nursing education coordinator reports directly to the chair of the MAPTH Staff Development Committee with input from each of the institutions coming through that committee. As the program has matured, the skills required of the nursing education coordinator have evolved from a strong emphasis on curriculum development to a greater focus on coordination and management skills.

The education model. The education model for critical care education follows curriculum development principles based on the nursing process: (a) assessment, (b) planning, (c) implementation, and (d) evaluation. Fourteen 1- or 2-day modules compose the adult critical care course; the course is presented in its entirety four times annually (see Table 45-1). By using the same framework across all modules, development and revision of courses are simplified. Courses for pediatric/neonatal critical care, operating room, and psychiatric care follow a similar framework with some modifications consistent with the requirements of the subject matter and target audiences. All modules and courses meet the standards for nursing continuing education endorsement.

THE RESULTS

Efficiency. Because of the shared approach, the MAPTH consortium has proven to be cost-effective in many ways. For example, each facility realizes a significant savings in nursing faculty FTEs by participating in a joint program. In 1987, the MAPTH programs accounted for 681 faculty teaching hours. Assuming a conservative preparation time of 3 hours for each teaching hour plus indirect salary expenses of .20/FTE (a total of 3,269 hours), total teaching hours provided through MAPTH accounted for 1.57 FTEs. If each hospital had to provide this staff development program separately, each would expend 1.57 FTEs for nursing faculty. However, since

TABLE 45-1
Adult critical care course 6-month schedule

MODULE	DATES	TIME	LOCATION
Renal	July 5-6	7:30 a.m.-4:00 p.m.	HCMC[b]
	October 4-5	7:30 a.m.-4:00 p.m.	HCMC
GI/Hepatic	July 19-20	7:30 a.m.-4:00 p.m.	HCMC
	November 8-9	7:30 a.m.-4:00 p.m.	HCMC
Pulmonary I	August 2-3	7:30 a.m.-4:00 p.m.	HCMC
	November 1-2	7:30 a.m.-4:00 p.m.	HCMC
Pulmonary II[a]	November 4	7:30 a.m.-4:00 p.m.	HCMC
Hematology/			
Immunology[a]	August 16	7:30 a.m.-4:00 p.m.	UMHC[c]
Stress	August 24	7:30 a.m.-4:00 p.m.	HCMC
Cardiovascular	September 6-7	7:30 a.m.-4:00 p.m.	HCMC
	December 6-7	7:30 a.m.-4:00 p.m.	HCMC
Hemodynamics[a]	September 9	7:30 a.m.-4:00 p.m.	HCMC
	December 9	7:30 a.m.-4:00 p.m.	HCMC
Neurology	September 20-21	7:30 a.m.-4:00 p.m.	HCMC
	December 20-21	7:30 a.m.-4:00 p.m.	HCMC
Ethics	October 12	7:30 a.m.-4:00 p.m.	UMHC
Intra-aortic balloon	October 14	7:30 a.m.-4:00 p.m.	UMHC
pumps[a]			
Endocrine	October 19	7:30 a.m.-4:00 p.m.	UMHC
Pacemakers[a]	October 25	7:45 a.m.-3:15 p.m.	SPRMC[d]
Multisystem failure[a]	November 15	7:30 a.m.-4:00 p.m.	UMHC

[a]Denotes Advanced/Level II module
[b]HCMC = Hennepin County Medical Center
[c]UMHC = University of Minnesota Hospital and Clinic
[d]SPRMC = St. Paul-Ramsey Medical Center

each facility contributes only about one-fourth of the teaching time, each facility "saves" 1.18 FTEs.

Other savings accrue for facility use, cost of audiovisual aids, instructional materials, and equipment. These savings allow each institution to expand supplemental offerings or reallocate resources to other uses.

MAPTH's program statistics are impressive. From 1981 to 1987, overall program costs declined 55% from $73,747 to $33,157 while the number of modules offered increased substantially from 4 to 63 (see Figure 45-1). Program costs include instructional and administrative costs. Instructional costs are defined as expenses related to planning, faculty preparation, presentation, and coordinator time. Printing, duplicating, program materials, and secretarial time are the constituents of administrative costs. During

this same period, the average program cost per module has decreased from $1,873 to $526 (see Figure 45-2). For example, the per-learner cost for the basic adult critical care modules presented in 1987 was $90, down from $114 in 1986 and $120 in 1985. Based on preliminary data, similar declines in costs are anticipated in the other courses as well.

The number of MAPTH participants has increased 178%, from 1,133 in 1982 to 3,152 in 1987. Average attendance per program has remained fairly stable over the last 5 years at about 50 participants per session (see Figure 45-3). Program attendance is monitored quarterly, and schedules are adjusted accordingly to maximize cost-effectiveness. Since the program's inception, the pool of qualified nurse faculty has grown from 18 to approximately 100. A

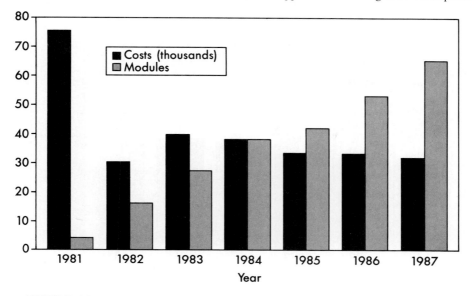

FIGURE 45-1

Program costs (in thousands of dollars) and number of modules presented by year.

qualified nurse faculty member is defined as a nurse who has attained clinical and/or educational expertise in a specific field of practice.

The dramatic decline in program costs is attributable in part to these factors:

- A flexible curriculum framework that provides the foundation for basic courses and supports development of secondary-level MAPTH curriculum and supplementary programming within each institution.
- Shared costs for coordination, course facilities, and development of course content, audiovisuals, and instructional materials.
- Centralization of coordinating and clerical support services which promotes efficiency and effectiveness.
- Reductions in duplication across courses and offerings among institutions.
- Reduction of initial development time through the use of faculty who are specialty experts in each area.
- Increased efficiency in curriculum changes through the use of faculty who are familiar with the course framework and have established working relationships with each other.

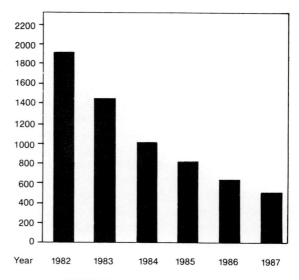

FIGURE 45-2

Average program cost per module.

- Economies of scale realized by presenting courses to larger groups, drawing from a larger pool of faculty, and offering courses in centralized locations.

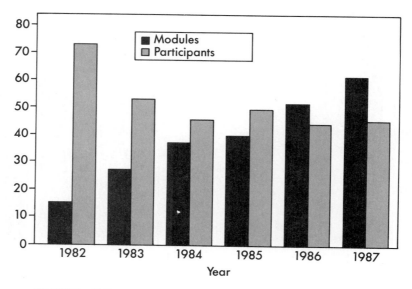

FIGURE 45-3
Number of modules presented and average number of participants.

In addition, revenue can be generated by opening programs to community participants who attend on a "fee-for-service" basis.

The benefits of the collaborative venture extend beyond economics. The pool of approximately 100 nursing faculty experts provides a driving force within the hospitals for improving patient care, facilitating change, and establishing professional standards. The large faculty pool and the flexibility of the curriculum framework have made it easier to respond to critical issues and medical advances through content revision and development of new courses. The teaching role provides faculty with opportunities for job enrichment and recognition.

The evaluation forms from participants indicate that the nursing staff of the four hospitals respond positively to the course content. The content of the jointly developed courses was matched with the performance competencies established by the individual participating agencies for the clinical setting. The courses provide opportunities for networking across facilities, allow for rapid integration of new research, and facilitate technology transfer.

ENCOURAGEMENT TOWARD COLLABORATION

The idea of a consortium approach to nursing staff development is not unique to this Twin Cities venture (Meade, Burger, & Nicksic, 1985; Meyers, 1984; Slate, Doucet, May, & Stark, 1985; Stetler, McGrath, Everson, Foster, & Diffley-Holloran, 1983; Thompson et al., 1987). But operating collaboratively without regard to parity adds a distinctive approach. The results of the MAPTH nursing staff development consortium are compelling and serve as a useful model for interested agencies.

While joint educational programs are the end-product of such a consortium, MAPTH institutions have found that process should guide outcome. MAPTH facilities found it valuable to devote considerable initial attention to the development of: (a) a shared vision and philosophy, (b) common goals, and (c) a good working process and uncomplicated operating structure. With a strong, shared guiding vision, program development goes much more smoothly. Consulting efforts MAPTH has undertaken with newer consortia have demonstrated that attempts to focus on joint program development before giving the necessary attention to the philosophical underpinnings tend to be self-defeating.

Even in today's competitive environment, cooperative ventures can succeed. Participation in a collaborative programming venture requires facilities to relinquish some of their autonomy; the MAPTH facilities have found, however, that the benefits exceed the risks. The economies realized from shared course development and centralized course offerings can be significant. And beyond the cost savings lie the less tangible but very real benefits of developing nursing faculty expertise, sharing ideas across institutions, and improving patient care and staff morale.

REFERENCES

Meade, M.E., Burger, S., & Nicksic, E. (1985). Contracts for continuing nursing education. *Journal of Continuing Education in Nursing,* 16(4), 121-126.

Meyers, R. (1984). Meeting continuing education needs and cost containment. *Journal of Continuing Education in Nursing,* 15(2), 50-52.

Slate, E., Doucet, M., May, L., & Stark, J. (1985). An urban consortium: A low cost quality approach to critical care education. *Journal of Continuing Education in Nursing,* 16(6), 193-196.

Stetler, C.B., McGrath, S.P., Everson, S., Foster, S.B., & Diffley-Holloran, S. (1983, October). A staff education consortium: One model for collaboration. *Journal of Nursing Administration,* 13(10), 2328.

Thompson, R., Pitotti, R., Philip, J., Beard, J., Sanger, N., & Arnott, G. (1987, November). A cost-effective method for increasing nursing staff expertise. *Nursing Management,* 18(11), 67-68.

CHAPTER 46

One More Time: How do you Motivate Employees?

Frederick Herzberg, PhD

How many articles, books, speeches, and workshops have pleaded plaintively, "How do I get an employee to do what I want him to do?"

The psychology of motivation is tremendously complex, and what has been unraveled with any degree of assurance is small indeed. But the dismal ratio of knowledge to speculation has not dampened the enthusiasm for new forms of snake oil that are constantly coming on the market, many of them with academic testimonials. Doubtless this article will have no depressing impact on the market for snake oil, but since the ideas expressed in it have been tested in many corporations and other organizations, it will help — I hope — to redress the imbalance in the aforementioned ratio.

"MOTIVATING" WITH KITA

In lectures to industry on the problem, I have found that the audiences are anxious for quick and practical answers, so I will begin with a straightforward, practical formula for moving people.

What is the simplest, surest, and most direct way

of getting someone to do something? Ask him? But if he responds that he does not want to do it, then that calls for a psychological consultation to determine the reason for his obstinancy. Tell him? His response shows that he does not understand you, and now an expert in communication methods has to be brought in to show you how to get through to him. Give him a monetary incentive? I do not need to remind the reader of the complexity and difficulty involved in setting up and administering an incentive system. Show him? This means a costly training program. We need a simple way.

Every audience contains the "direct action" manager who shouts, "Kick him!" And this type of manager is right. The surest and least circumlocuted way of getting someone to do something is to kick him in the pants — give him what might be called the KITA.

There are various forms of KITA, and here are some of them:

Negative physical KITA. This is a literal application of the term and was frequently used in the past. It has, however, three major drawbacks: (1) it is inelegant; (2) it contradicts the precious image of benevolence that most organizations cherish; and (3) since it is a physical attack, it directly stimulates the autonomic nervous system, and this often results in negative feedback — the employee may just kick you in return. These factors give rise to certain taboos against negative physical KITA.

The psychologist has come to the rescue of those who are no longer permitted to use negative physical KITA. He has uncovered infinite sources of psychological vulnerabilities and the appropriate methods to play tunes on them. "He took my rug away"; "I wonder what he meant by that"; "The boss is always going around me" — these symptomatic expressions of ego sores that have been rubbed raw are the result of application of:

Negative Psychological KITA. This has several advantages over negative physical KITA. First, the cruelty is not visible; the bleeding is internal and comes much later. Second, since it affects the higher cortical centers of the brain with its inhibitory powers, it reduces the possibility of physical backlash. Third, since the number of psychological pains that a person can feel is almost infinite, the direction and site possibilities of the KITA are increased many times. Fourth, the person administering the kick can manage to be above it all and let the system accomplish the dirty work. Fifth, those who practice it receive some ego satisfaction (one-upmanship), whereas they would find drawing blood abhorrent. Finally, if the employee does complain, he can always be accused of being paranoid, since there is no tangible evidence of an actual attack.

Now, what does negative KITA accomplish? If I kick you in the rear (physically or psychologically), who is motivated? I am motivated; you move! Negative KITA does not lead to motivation, but to movement. So:

Positive KITA. Let us consider motivation. If I say to you, "Do this for me or the company, and in return I will give you a reward, an incentive, more status, a promotion, all the quid pro quos that exist in the industrial organization," am I motivating you? The overwhelming opinion I receive from management people is, "Yes, this is motivation."

I have a year-old Schnauzer. When it was a small puppy and I wanted it to move, I kicked it in the rear and it moved. Now that I have finished its obedience training, I hold up a dog biscuit when I want the Schnauzer to move. In this instance, who is motivated — I or the dog? The dog wants the biscuit, but it is I who want it to move. Again, I am the one who is motivated, and the dog is the one who moves. In

this instance all I did was apply KITA frontally; I exerted a pull instead of a push. When industry wishes to use such positive KITAs, it has available an incredible number and variety of dog biscuits (jelly beans for humans) to wave in front of the employee to get him to jump.

Why is it that managerial audiences are quick to see that negative KITA is *not* motivation, while they are almost unanimous in their judgment that positive KITA *is* motivation? It is because negative KITA is rape, and positive KITA is seduction. But it is infinitely worse to be seduced than to be raped; the latter is an unfortunate occurrence, while the former signifies that you were a party to your own downfall. This is why positive KITA is so popular: it is a tradition; it is in the American way. The organization does not have to kick you; you kick yourself.

Myths About Motivation

Why is KITA not motivation? If I kick my dog (from the front or the back), he will move. And when I want him to move again, what must I do? I must kick him again. Similarly, I can charge a man's battery, and then recharge it, and recharge it again. But it is only when he has his own generator that we can talk about motivation. He then needs no outside stimulation. He *wants* to do it.

With this in mind, we can review some positive KITA personnel practices that were developed as attempts to instill "motivation":

Reducing time spent at work. This represents a marvelous way of motivating people to work — getting them off the job! We have reduced (formally and informally) the time spent on the job over the last 50 or 60 years until we are finally on the way to the "6½-day weekend." An interesting variant of this approach is the development of off-hour recreation programs. The philosophy here seems to be that those who play together, work together. The fact is that motivated people seek more hours of work, not fewer.

Spiraling wages. Have these motivated people? Yes, to seek the next wage increase. Some medievalists still can be heard to say that a good depression will get employees moving. They feel that if rising wages don't or won't do the job, perhaps reducing them will.

Fringe benefits. Industry has outdone the most welfare-minded of welfare states in dispensing cradle-to-the-grave succor. One company I know of had an informal "fringe benefit of the month club" going for a while. The cost of fringe benefits in this country has reached approximately 25% of the wage dollar, and we still cry for motivation.

People spend less time working for more money and more security than ever before, and the trend cannot be reversed. These benefits are no longer rewards; they are rights. A 6-day week is inhuman, a 10-hour day is exploitation, extended medical coverage is a basic decency, and stock options are the salvation of American initiative. Unless the ante is continuously raised, the psychological reaction of employees is that the company is turning back the clock.

When industry began to realize that both the economic nerve and the lazy nerve of their employees had insatiable appetites, it started to listen to the behavioral scientists who, more out of a humanist tradition than from scientific study, criticized management for not knowing how to deal with people. The next KITA easily followed.

Human relations training. Over 30 years of teaching and, in many instances, of practicing psychological approaches to handling people have resulted in costly human relations programs and, in the end, the same question: How do you motivate workers? Here, too, escalations have taken place. Thirty years ago it was necessary to request, "Please don't spit on the floor." Today the same admonition requires three "please"'s before the employee feels that his superior has demonstrated the psychologically proper attitudes toward him.

The failure of human relations training to produce motivation led to the conclusion that the supervisor or manager himself was not psychologically true to himself in his practice of interpersonal decency. So an advanced form of human relations KITA, sensitivity training, was unfolded.

Sensitivity training. Do you really, really understand yourself? Do you really, really, really trust the other man? Do you really, really, really, really cooperate? The failure of sensitivity training is now being explained, by those who have become opportunistic exploiters of the technique, as a failure to really (five

times) conduct proper sensitivity training courses.

With the realization that there are only temporary gains from comfort and economic and interpersonal KITA, personnel managers concluded that the fault lay not in what they were doing, but in the employee's failure to appreciate what they were doing. This opened up the field of communications, a whole new area of "scientifically" sanctioned KITA.

Communications. The professor of communications was invited to join the faculty of management training programs and help in making employees understand what management was doing for them. House organs, briefing sessions, supervisory instruction on the importance of communication, and all sorts of propaganda have proliferated until today there is even an International Council of Industrial Editors. But no motivation resulted, and the obvious thought occurred that perhaps management was not hearing what the employees were saying. That led to the next KITA.

Two-way communication. Management ordered morale surveys, suggestion plans, and group participation programs. Then both employees and management were communicating and listening to each other more than ever, but without much improvement in motivation.

The behavioral scientists began to take another look at their conceptions and their data, and they took human relations one step further. A glimmer of truth was beginning to show through in the writings of the so-called higher-order-need psychologists. People, so they said, want to actualize themselves. Unfortunately, the "actualizing" psychologists got mixed up with the human relations psychologists, and a new KITA emerged.

Job participation. Though it may not have been the theoretical intention, job participation often became a "give them the big picture" approach. For example, if a man is tightening 10,000 nuts a day on an assembly line with a torque wrench, tell him he is building a Chevrolet. Another approach had the goal of giving the employee a *feeling* that he is determining, in some measure, what he does on his job. The goal was to provide a *sense* of achievement rather than a substantive achievement in his task. Real achievement, of course, requires a task that makes it possible.

But still there was no motivation. This led to the inevitable conclusion that the employees must be sick, and therefore to the next KITA.

Employee counseling. The initial use of this form of KITA in a systematic fashion can be credited to the Hawthorne experiment of the Western Electric Company during the early 1930's. At that time, it was found that the employees harbored irrational feelings that were interfering with the rational operation of the factory. Counseling in this instance was a means of letting the employees unburden themselves by talking to someone about their problems. Although the counseling techniques were primitive, the program was large indeed.

The counseling approach suffered as a result of experiences during World War II, when the programs themselves were found to be interfering with the operation of the organizations; the counselors had forgotten their role of benevolent listeners and were attempting to do something about the problems that they heard about. Psychological counseling, however, has managed to survive the negative impact of World War II experiences and today is beginning to flourish with renewed sophistication. But, alas, many of these programs, like all the others, do not seem to have lessened the pressure of demands to find out how to motivate workers.

Since KITA results only in short-term movement, it is safe to predict that the cost of these programs will increase steadily and new varieties will be developed as old positive KITAs reach their satiation points.

HYGIENE VS. MOTIVATORS

Let me rephrase the perennial question this way: How do you install a generator in an employee? A brief review of my motivation-hygiene theory of job attitudes is required before theoretical and practical suggestions can be offered. The theory was first drawn from an examination of events in the lives of engineers and accountants. At least 16 other investigations, using a wide variety of populations (including some in the Communist countries), have since been completed, making the original research one of the most replicated studies in the field of job attitudes.

The findings of these studies, along with corroboration from many other investigations using different procedures, suggest that the factors involved in producing job satisfaction (and motivation) are separate and distinct from the factors that lead to job dissatisfaction. Since separate factors need to be considered, depending on whether job satisfaction or job dissatisfaction is being examined, it follows that these two feelings are not opposites of each other. The opposite of job satisfaction is not job dissatisfaction but, rather, *no* job satisfaction; and, similarly, the opposite of job dissatisfaction is not job satisfaction, but *no* job dissatisfaction.

Stating the concept presents a problem in semantics, for we normally think of satisfaction and dissatisfaction as opposites-i.e., what is not satisfying must be dissatisfying, and vice versa. But when it comes to understanding the behavior of people in their jobs, more than a play on words is involved.

Two different needs of man are involved here. One set of needs can be thought of as stemming from his animal nature — the built-in drive to avoid pain from the environment, plus all the learned drives which become conditioned to the basic biological needs. For example, hunger, a basic biological drive, makes it necessary to earn money, and then money becomes a specific drive. The other set of needs relates to that unique human characteristic, the ability to achieve and, through achievement, to experience psychological growth. The stimuli for the growth needs are tasks that induce growth; in the industrial setting, they are the *job content.* Contrariwise, the stimuli inducing pain-avoidance behavior are found in the *job environment.*

The growth or *motivator* factors that are intrinsic to the job are: achievement, recognition for achievement, the work itself, responsibility, and growth or advancement. The dissatisfaction-avoidance or *hygiene* (KITA) factors that are extrinsic to the job include: company policy and administration, supervision, interpersonal relationships, working conditions, salary, status, and security.

A composite of the factors that are involved in causing job satisfaction and job dissatisfaction, drawn from samples of 1,685 employees, is shown in Figure 46-1. The results indicate that motivators were the

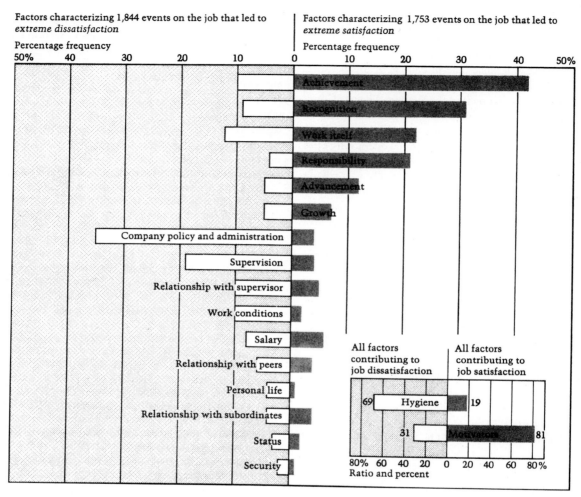

FIGURE 46-1

Factors affecting job attitudes, as reported in 12 investigations.

primary cause of satisfaction, and hygiene factors the primary cause of unhappiness on the job. The employees, studied in 12 different investigations, included lower-level supervisors, professional women, agricultural administrators, men about to retire from management positions, hospital maintenance personnel, manufacturing supervisors, nurses, food handlers, military officers, engineers, scientists, housekeepers, teachers, technicians, female assemblers, accountants, Finnish foremen, and Hungarian engineers.

They were asked what job events had occurred in their work that had led to extreme satisfaction or extreme dissatisfaction on their part. Their responses are broken down in the exhibit into percentages of total "positive" job events and of total "negative" job events. (The figures total more than 100% on both the "hygiene" and "motivators" sides because often at least two factors can be attributed to a single event; advancement, for instance, often accompanies assumption of responsibility.)

To illustrate, a typical response involving achievement that had a negative effect for the employee was, "I was unhappy because I didn't do the job successfully." A typical response in the small number of positive job events in the Company Policy and Administration grouping was, "I was happy because the company reorganized the section so that I didn't report any longer to the guy I didn't get along with."

As the lower right-hand part of the exhibit shows, of all the factors contributing to job satisfaction, 81% were motivators. And of all the factors contributing to the employees' dissatisfaction over their work, 69% involved hygiene elements.

Eternal Triangle

There are three general philosophies of personnel management. The first is based on organizational theory, the second on industrial engineering, and the third on behavioral science.

The organizational theorist believes that human needs are either so irrational or so varied and adjustable to specific situations that the major function of personnel management is to be as pragmatic as the occasion demands. If jobs are organized in a proper manner, he reasons, the result will be the most efficient job structure, and the most favorable job attitudes will follow as a matter of course.

The industrial engineer holds that man is mechanistically oriented and economically motivated and his needs are best met by attuning the individual to the most efficient work process. The goal of personnel management therefore should be to concoct the most appropriate incentive system and to design the specific working conditions in a way that facilitates the most efficient use of the human machine. By structuring jobs in a manner that leads to the most efficient operation, the engineer believes that he can obtain the optimal organization of work and the proper work attitudes.

The behavioral scientist focuses on group sentiments, attitudes of individual employees, and the organization's social and psychological climate. According to his persuasion, he emphasizes one or more of the various hygiene and motivator needs. His approach to personnel management generally emphasizes some form of human relations education, in the hope of instilling healthy employee attitudes and an organizational climate which he considers to be felicitous to human values. He believes that proper attitudes will lead to efficient job and organizational structure.

There is always a lively debate as to the overall effectiveness of the approaches of the organizational theorist and the industrial engineer. Manifestly they have achieved much. But the nagging question for the behavioral scientist has been: What is the cost in human problems that eventually cause more expense to the organization — for instance, turnover, absenteeism, errors, violation of safety rules, strikes, restriction of output, higher wages, and greater fringe benefits? On the other hand, the behavioral scientist is hard put to document much manifest improvement in personnel management, using his approach.

The three philosophies can be depicted as a triangle, as is done in Figure 46-2, with each persuasion claiming the apex angle. The motivation-hygiene theory claims the same angle as industrial engineering, but for opposite goals. Rather than rationalizing the work to increase efficiency, the theory suggests that work be *enriched* to bring about effective utilization of personnel. Such a systematic attempt to motivate employees by manipulating the motivator factors is just beginning.

The term *job enrichment* describes this embryonic movement. An older term, job enlargement, should be avoided because it is associated with past failures stemming from a misunderstanding of the problem. Job enrichment provides the opportunity for the employee's psychological growth, while job enlargement merely makes a job structurally bigger. Since scientific job enrichment is very new, this article only

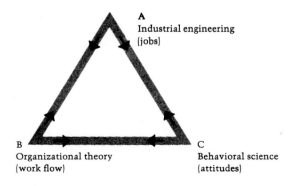

FIGURE 46-2

"Triangle" of philosophies of personnel management.

suggests the principles and practical steps that have recently emerged from several successful experiments in industry.

Job Loading

In attempting to enrich an employee's job, management often succeeds in reducing the man's personal contribution, rather than giving him an opportunity for growth in his accustomed job. Such an endeavor, which I shall call horizontal job loading (as opposed to vertical loading, or providing motivator factors), has been the problem of earlier job enlargement programs. This activity merely enlarges the meaninglessness of the job. Some examples of this approach, and their effect, are:

- Challenging the employee by increasing the amount of production expected of him. If he tightens 10,000 bolts a day, see if he can tighten

TABLE 46-1
Principles of vertical job loading

PRINCIPLE	MOTIVATORS INVOLVED
A. Removing some controls while retaining accountability	Responsibility and personal achievement
B. Increasing the accountability of individuals for own work	Responsibility and recognition
C. Giving a person a complete natural unit of work (module, division, area, and so on)	Responsibility, achievement, and recognition
D. Granting additional authority to an employee in his activity; job freedom	Responsibility, achievement, and recognition
E. Making periodic reports directly available to the worker himself rather than to the supervisor	Internal recognition
F. Introducing new and more difficult tasks not previously handled	Growth and learning
G. Assigning individuals specific or specialized tasks, enabling them to become experts	Responsibility, growth, and achievement

20,000 bolts a day. The arithmetic involved shows that multiplying zero by zero still equals zero.
- Adding another meaningless task to the existing one, usually some routine clerical activity. The arithmetic here is adding zero to zero.
- Rotating the assignments of a number of jobs that need to be enriched. This means washing dishes for a while, then washing silverware. The arithmetic is substituting one zero for another zero.
- Removing the most difficult parts of the assignment in order to free the worker to accomplish more of the less challenging assignments. This traditional industrial engineering approach amounts to subtraction in the hope of accomplishing addition.

These are common forms of horizontal loading that frequently come up in preliminary brainstorming sessions on job enrichment. The principles of vertical loading have not all been worked out as yet, and they remain rather general, but I have furnished seven useful starting points for consideration in Table 46-1.

A Successful Application

An example from a highly successful job enrichment experiment can illustrate the distinction between horizontal and vertical loading of a job. The subjects of this study were the stockholder correspondents employed by a very large corporation. Seemingly, the task required of these carefully selected and highly trained correspondents was quite complex and challenging. But almost all indexes of performance and job attitudes were low, and exit interviewing confirmed that the challenge of the job existed merely as words.

A job enrichment project was initiated in the form of an experiment with one group, designated as an achieving unit, having its job enriched by the principles described in Table 46-1. A control group continued to do its job in the traditional way. (There were also two "uncommitted" groups of correspondents formed to measure the so-called Hawthorne Effect—that is, to gauge whether productivity and attitudes toward the job changed artificially merely because employees sensed that the company was paying more attention to them in doing something different or novel. The results for these groups were substantially the same as for the control group, and for the sake of simplicity I do not deal with them in this summary.) No changes in hygiene were introduced for either group other than those that would have been made anyway, such as normal pay increases.

The changes for the achieving unit were introduced in the first two months, averaging one per week of the seven motivators listed in Table 46-1. At the end of six months the members of the achieving unit were found to be outperforming their counterparts in the control group, and in addition indicated a marked increase in their liking for their jobs. Other results showed that the achieving group had lower absenteeism and, subsequently, a much higher rate of promotion.

Figure 46-3 illustrates the changes in performance, measured in February and March, before the study period began, and at the end of each month of the study period. The shareholder service index represents quality of letters, including accuracy of information, and speed of response to stockholders' letters of inquiry. The index of a current month was averaged into the average of the two prior months, which means that improvement was harder to obtain if the indexes of the previous months were low. The "achievers" were performing less well before the six-month period started, and their performance service index continued to decline after the introduction of the motivators, evidently because of uncertainty over their newly granted responsibilities. In the third month, however, performance improved, and soon the members of this group had reached a high level of accomplishment.

Figure 46-4 shows the two groups' attitudes toward their job, measured at the end of March, just before the first motivator was introduced, and again at the end of September. The correspondents were asked 16 questions, all involving motivation. A typical one was, "As you see it, how many opportunities do you feel that you have in your job for making worthwhile contributions?" The answers were scaled from 1 to 5, with 80 as the maximum possiblescore. The achievers became much more positive about their job, while the attitude of the control unit remained about the same (the drop is not statistically significant).

How was the job of these correspondents restructured? Table 46-2 lists the suggestions made that were deemed to be horizontal loading, and the actual vertical loading changes that were incorporated in the job of the achieving unit. The capital letters under "Principle" after "Vertical loading" refer to the corresponding letters in Table 46-1. The reader will note that the rejected forms of horizontal loading correspond closely to the list of common manifestations of the phenomenon on page 60, left column.

STEPS TO JOB ENRICHMENT

Now that the motivator idea has been described in practice, here are the steps that managers should take in instituting the principle with their employees:

1. Select those jobs in which (a) the investment in industrial engineering does not make

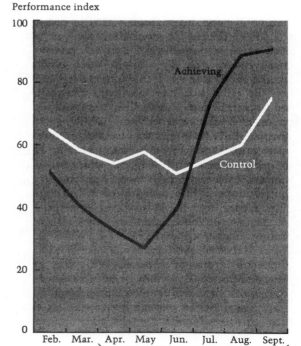

Performance index

FIGURE 46-3

Shareholder service index in company experiment (3-month cumulative average).

Job reaction mean score

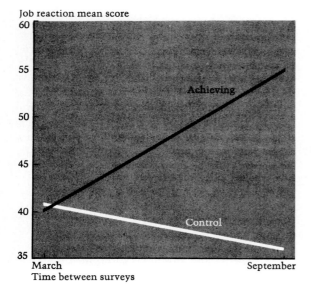

FIGURE 46-4

Changes in attitudes toward tasks in company experiment (changes in mean scores over 6-month period).

changes too costly, (b) attitudes are poor, (c) hygiene is becoming very costly, and (d) motivation will make a difference in performance.

2. Approach these jobs with the conviction that they can be changed. Years of tradition have led managers to believe that the content of the jobs is sacrosanct and the only scope of action that they have is in ways of stimulating people.

3. Brainstorm a list of changes that may enrich the jobs, without concern for their practicality.

4. Screen the list to eliminate suggestions that involve hygiene, rather than actual motivation.

5. Screen the list for generalities, such as "give them more responsibility," that are rarely followed in practice. This might seem obvious, but the motivator words have never left industry; the substance has just been rationalized and organized out. Words like "responsibility," "growth," "achievement," and "challenge," for example, have been elevated

to the lyrics of the patriotic anthem for all organizations. It is the old problem typified by the pledge of allegiance to the flag being more important than contributions to the country — of following the form, rather than the substance.

6. Screen the list to eliminate any *horizontal* loading suggestions.

7. Avoid direct participation by the employees whose jobs are to be enriched. Ideas they have expressed previously certainly constitute a valuable source for recommended changes, but their direct involvement contaminates the process with human relations *hygiene* and, more specifically, gives them only a *sense* of making a contribution. The job is to be changed, and it is the content that will produce the motivation, not attitudes about being involved or the challenge inherent in setting up a job. That process will be over shortly, and it is what the employees will be doing from then on that will determine their motivation. A sense of participation will result only in short-term movement.

8. In the initial attempts at job enrichment, set up a controlled experiment. At least two equivalent groups should be chosen, one an experimental unit in which the motivators are systematically introduced over a period of time, and the other one a control group in which no changes are made. For both groups, hygiene should be allowed to follow its natural course for the duration of the experiment. Pre- and post-installation tests of performance and job attitudes are necessary to evaluate the effectiveness of the job enrichment program. The attitude test must be limited to motivator items in order to divorce the employee's view of the job he is given from all the surrounding hygiene feelings that he might have.

9. Be prepared for a drop in performance in the experimental group the first few weeks. The changeover to a new job may lead to a temporary reduction in efficiency.

TABLE 46-2

Enlargement vs. enrichment of correspondents' tasks in company experiment

HORIZONTAL LOADING SUGGESTIONS (REJECTED)	VERTICAL LOADING SUGGESTIONS (ADOPTED)	PRINCIPLE
Firm quotas could be set for letters to be answered each day, using a rate which would be hard to reach.	Subject matter experts were appointed within each unit for other members of the unit to consult with before seeking supervisory help. (The supervisor had been answering all specialized and difficult questions.)	G
The women could type the letters themselves, as well as compose them, or take on any other clerical functions.	Correspondents signed their own names on letters. (The supervisor had been signing all letters.)	B
All difficult or complex inquiries could be channeled to a few women so that the remainder could achieve high rates of output. These jobs could be exchanged from time to time.	The work of the more experienced correspondents was proofread less frequently by supervisors and was done at the correspondents' desks, dropping verification from 100% to 10%. (Previously, all correspondents' letters had been checked by the supervisor.)	A
The women could be rotated through units handling different customers, and then sent back to their own units.	Production was discussed, but only in terms such as "a full day's work is expected." As time went on, this was no longer mentioned. (Before, the group had been constantly reminded of the number of letters that needed to be answered.)	D
	Outgoing mail went directly to the mailroom without going over supervisors' desks. (The letters had always been routed through the supervisors.)	A
	Correspondents were encouraged to answer letters in a more personalized way. (Reliance on the form-letter approach had been standard practice.)	C
	Each correspondent was held personally responsible for the quality and accuracy of letters. (This responsibility had been the province of the supervisor and the verifier.)	B, E

10. Expect your first-line supervisors to experience some anxiety and hostility over the changes you are making. The anxiety comes from their fear that the changes will result in poorer performance for their unit. Hostility will arise when the employees start assuming what the supervisors regard as their own responsibility for performance. The supervisor without checking duties to perform may then be left with little to do.

After a successful experiment, however, the supervisor usually discovers the supervisory and managerial functions he has neglected, or which were never his because all his time was given over to checking the work of his subordinates. For example, in the R&D division of one large chemical company I know of, the supervisors of the laboratory assistants were theoretically responsible for their training and evaluation. These functions, however, had come to be performed in a routine, unsubstantial fashion. After the job enrichment program, during which the supervisors were not merely passive observers of the assistants' performance, the supervisors actually were devoting their time to reviewing performance and administering thorough training.

What has been called an employee-centered style of supervision will come about not through education of supervisors, but by changing the jobs that they do.

CONCLUDING NOTE

Job enrichment will not be a one-time proposition, but a continuous management function. The initial changes, however, should last for a very long period of time. There are a number of reasons for this:

- The changes should bring the job up to the level of challenge commensurate with the skill that was hired.
- Those who have still more ability eventually will be able to demonstrate it better and win promotion to higher-level jobs.
- The very nature of motivators, as opposed to

hygiene factors, is that they have a much longer-term effect on employees' attitudes. Perhaps the job will have to be enriched again, but this will not occur as frequently as the need for hygiene.

Not all jobs can be enriched, nor do all jobs need to be enriched. If only a small percentage of the time and money that is now devoted to hygiene, however, were given to job enrichment efforts, the return in human satisfaction and economic gain would be one of the largest dividends that industry and society have ever reaped through their efforts at better personnel management.

The argument for job enrichment can be summed up quite simply: If you have someone on a job, use him. If you can't use him on the job, get rid of him, either via automation or by selecting someone with lesser ability. If you can't use him and you can't get rid of him, you will have a motivation problem.

CHAPTER **47**

Productivity Measurement in Nursing

Mary L. McHugh, RN, PhD

The twin constraints of a nursing shortage and tight budgets have made nursing productivity a high priority among nursing service managers. Nurse managers want simple, effective measures of productivity with which to discover productivity levels and evaluate empirically the effects of specific management decisions on this productivity. Obviously, control of nursing department operations is in large part dependent on achieving optimal productivity levels. There is, however, some confusion about what "nursing productivity" is and how to measure it.

PRODUCTIVITY, EFFICIENCY, AND EFFECTIVENESS

Productivity is the ratio between input and output. The more input one must invest to produce output, the lower the productivity. Conversely, if one finds a way to produce the same amount and quality of output with less input, productivity is increased. Thus, productivity is a *ratio,* not a constant.

The terms *good* and *poor* are somewhat misleading when applied to productivity. There is no inherent standard for what constitutes acceptable productivity. It is a management responsibility to define what constitutes a minimum acceptable level of productivity in each work setting.

Reprinted from *Applied Nursing Research,* Vol. 2, No. 2, with permission of W. B. Saunders Co. © 1989.

There is considerable confusion about the relationships among the concepts *productivity, efficiency,* and *effectiveness.* The term *efficient* often is used incorrectly as a synonym for the term *productive* (Channon, 1983). *Efficiency* refers to an economy of input and generally translates into the speed with which a task gets done; this may or may not be a function of finding a way to minimize the physical motions/effort expended on the task. *Effectiveness* refers to success. That is, *effective* nursing interventions produce the desired patient outcome. Increasing *efficiency* and/or *effectiveness* will not necessarily increase *productivity,* yet reducing them will almost certainly impair *productivity.* Even the combination of *efficient* plus *effective* does not equal *productive.*

Efficiency improvements do not become productivity improvements until the conserved resources are reinvested to increase the amount or quality of the output. This will become clearer from this scenario: A nurse completes her work faster (improves efficiency) and still produces successful patient outcomes (maintains or improves effectiveness) — and then spends the time saved making out her grocery list. Clearly this nurse's improved efficiency did not improve nursing department productivity. On the other hand, decreases in efficiency will almost certainly lower productivity.

Effectiveness improvements are often signs of improved productivity: if one increases effectiveness without increasing input or decreasing output, one has improved productivity. In health care, however, effectiveness improvements often are achieved by changing inputs that have little or nothing to do with nursing activities. For example, prior to the introduction of antibiotic therapy for pneumonia, patient survival rates were strongly affected by the amount and quality of the nursing care. After antibiotics were introduced, many patients survived regardless of the quality of nursing care, as long as the patient received the prescribed medication. In this case, effectiveness, in terms of improved survival rates, was improved by changing the type of input. A drug was substituted for nursing care and institutional productivity was increased. Evaluating a change in nursing productivity in this situation is more complex since the effectiveness improvement was a function of a nonnursing input. In order to accurately determine if changes in efficiency or effectiveness are related to changes in productivity, one must be able to measure productivity. That is not a trivial task in nursing.

PRODUCTIVITY MEASUREMENT

Productivity measurement in industry is a relatively straightforward process. Inputs are usually measured by calculating the dollar cost of all materials and labor invested in production of the company's products. Output measurement is slightly more complex because it accounts for both the number and quality of items produced. Industrial quality-control engineers define minimum standards appropriate to the product and employ inspectors to discard units that fail to meet the standard. Therefore, output measurement consists of a count of the product units that passed quality-control inspection.

Unlike the situation in manufacturing, obtaining a satisfactory measure of productivity in nursing is extremely difficult (Young & Hayne, 1988). Inputs consist of the dollar cost of nursing hours, which can be calculated fairly easily. One can use nursing hours or total nursing payroll plus the cost of benefits as a measure of inputs. The payroll measure will allow more costly hours such as overtime, registered nurse (RN) versus Licensed Practical Nurse (LPN) or aide, and clinical nurse specialist hours to be appropriately weighted. However, no satisfactory measure of nursing output has yet been devised.

A traditional measure of nursing productivity, "nursing hours per patient day," has never been satisfactory because "patient day" as a measure of nursing output takes account of neither patient acuity nor quality of nursing care. Furthermore, nursing hours per patient day is a dangerous measure of productivity because a decrease in nursing hours per patient day could involve a decrease in productivity as easily as it might reflect an increase or no change in productivity. For example, a reduction in nursing hours might cause nurses to eliminate patient teaching. Then, out of the habit of teaching, nurses are unlikely to teach even when they do have time. Thus, a reduction in nursing hours per patient day can produce an even larger reduction in productivity. A "patient day" is really not a nursing output; it is an institutional output and relatively insensitive to nursing productivity.

There is now some suggestion that using average acuity levels in a nursing unit might be a useful measure of nursing output because average acuity is a function of both census and acuity. Productivity would then be a measure of the ratio of nursing hours to average unit acuity. This measure is slightly better than nursing hours per patient day, because acuity measures are normally based on measures of nursing care requirements. Theoretically, acuity could be used to measure units of patient service just as hours are units of nursing input. However, this approach assumes that nurses do indeed deliver all of the care items called for by the patient acuity levels; patient classification systems tend to measure what patients need rather than what care was delivered.

Conceptually, there is another problem. Nursing hours are *inputs,* and nursing actions are *throughputs.* The acuity measures just described come dangerously close to defining inputs and throughputs as outputs. This would be analogous in manufacturing to defining an assembly line worker's output as the number of calories he or she must burn in an hour rather than the amount of acceptable product produced in an hour.

Patient classification systems were designed to measure the number of nursing hours needed. The ratio of nursing hours available (actual nursing hours) to average acuity is nothing more than a measure of available hours to needed hours. That is more a measure of the appropriateness of management staffing strategy than of the productivity of the nurses who worked. Using average acuity as a measure, productivity gains that lead to a reduced need for staff will appear as an understaffed condition rather than an increase in productivity.

The reality is that an ideal measure of nursing productivity does not exist — and will not exist until the nursing profession is better able to define and agree on just what constitutes nursing output. What are nursing's products? How are they to be measured?

Nursing's true product has to do with protecting, maintaining, and improving the health status of our patients. That is, patient outcomes are our true product. Measuring nurses' contributions to patients' health status is very difficult, however, and it will be a long time before we can measure that concept directly.

It seems likely that a measure of nursing output will need to combine quality of care measures with patient days, mean acuity levels, and at least some measure of patient outcome (e.g., mortality rates, iatrogenic complication rates) to create a nursing output index. In the meantime, what can nurse managers do to improve productivity?

HOW TO IMPROVE PRODUCTIVITY

Productivity is generally improved when operations become more efficient and the time saved is used to accomplish more work or reduce staffing costs. There are two ways to increase efficiency: (a) eliminate inefficiencies and (b) obtain tools that allow people to do their work faster and/or better. The first action nursing service managers should take is to scrutinize their operations for inefficiency. The Helmer and Olson questions (see next article) offer an excellent managerial guideline for reducing inefficiency.

Once efficiency is increased, the manager is responsible for ensuring that staff members use the time they save to reduce overtime, decrease nursing errors and omissions, and increase the overall quality of care; a smart manager will not assume that staff will naturally convert efficiency into productivity. In other words, the time gained from increased operational efficiency must be reinvested in activity that benefits patients or reduces the nursing salary budget if productivity gains are to be realized.

After concerted efforts have produced a lean and efficient yet effective nursing service, the manager's job is still not done. As a general rule, productivity increases when people are provided with tools that enable them to do their job better and faster. Managers should be ever vigilant for new and old technology that can be used to reduce human effort; obviously, however, the cost of the technology must be evaluated in terms of the money it will save in nursing time.

For example, if you have a surgical unit in which nurses spend much time starting, restarting, and regulating intravenous (IV) lines, you might analyze the cost of using a volumetric pump for every IV. Will the pumps actually reduce the amount of time nurses spend restarting and regulating IVs? Will the pumps reduce iatrogenic complications by reducing the incidence of too fast or too slow infusion of prescribed medications and fluids? If the answers are yes, the manager would then need to calculate the full cost of the pumps, including staff training and machine maintenance costs, and the cost of the nursing hours saved (or the value of the reduction in complications). Using these two figures, the manager can then project the length of time the machine must operate before it begins to save more money than it cost. This is called the breakeven point. Any usable pump life after that breakeven point will represent an increase in productivity provided that nurses reinvest the time saved on manual IV care in other productive activities.

CONCLUSION

Productivity control is an important part of a nurse manager's responsibility, especially now that patient acuity is rising, the supply of nurses is declining, and budgets are tight. Nurse managers have a particularly challenging task because of difficulty documenting productivity changes. Direct measures of nursing productivity are not yet available; indirect measures only estimate changes in productivity and are controversial. It is important that managers understand the relationship between the productivity, efficiency, and effectiveness of nursing care. Efficiency is easier to measure then productivity, but a measure of efficiency is *not* a measure of productivity. The manager must understand that efficiency improvements do not automatically translate into productivity improvements. Productivity only occurs with good management of the time saved through greater efficiency.

The manager can improve productivity by searching out and eliminating sources of inefficiency and insuring that increases in efficiency are matched with reductions in staffing costs and/or improvements in care quality. Another important way to increase productivity is to use technology to make work more efficient or to improve the quality of the output. In today's environment of increasing acuity, nursing shortage, and tight budgets, nurse managers must use every means to improve productivity in nursing departments to stay competitive and to maintain an acceptable quality of nursing care.

REFERENCES

Channon, B. (1983). Dispelling productivity myths. *Hospitals, 57*(19), 103-119.

Young, L., & Hayne, A. (1988). *Nursing administration From concepts to practice.* Philadelphia: Saunders.

CHAPTER **48**

Sources of Inefficiency
Questions

F. Theodore Helmer, PhD
Shirley F. Olson, DBA

Some of the keys to increased efficiency come from the following questions:

- Can some of the nursing tasks accomplished during the day and evening shifts be switched to the night shifts? Is there a balance between shifts? Are the proper number of nurses scheduled?
- Can the unit increase the number or skill levels of the clerical staff to relieve the more expensive RNs of routine tasks?
- Is the cost of a higher skill mix cost-effective when unit objectives and the efficiencies of the nursing unit are reviewed?
- Are nurses spending too much time in housekeeping duties that might be done less expensively by increasing the housekeeping staff?
- Are the nurses running too many errands?

- Can paperwork be streamlined or not completed at all?
- Are all meetings cost-effective?
- Why is the shift report so long?
- Can greater use be made of volunteers?
- Can any established policies or procedures be changed to influence efficiency?
- Can the layout of the unit be modified to save steps and time?
- Is the cost of additional training supported by increased efficiency of the nurses? Are inservices given during slow periods on slow days?
- Are the staff spending their time properly?
- Are the patient assignments made with efficiency in mind?

Reprinted from *Applied Nursing Research,* Vol. 2, No. 2, with permission of W. B. Saunders Co., © 1989.

CHAPTER **49**

A New Generation Patient Classification System

Phyllis B. Giovannetti, RN, ScD
Judith Moore Johnson, RN, BA

Monitoring and maintaining the reliability and validity of a patient classification system for nurse staffing is a continuing challenge for nurse managers. The traditional methods employed involve extensive manual efforts, which lead to infrequent and often inaccurate testing. The value of patient classification data is therefore limited. The authors describe a new second-generation patient classification system that employs a built-in reliability and validity monitoring system.

The expanded use of information from patient classification systems has placed new demands on their capacity to yield reliable and valid data in a timely fashion. A second-generation patient classification system, ARIC (Allocation, Resource Identification and Costing), incorporating innovative design features made possible with recent software advances, provides unit-specific classification information and ongoing reliability and validity monitoring capabilities.

The primary objective of the first generation patient classification systems initially developed in the early 1960s at Johns Hopkins University and other sites was to predict nurse staffing levels from shift to shift.[1] Today, the objectives have greatly expanded.

Information related to productivity monitoring, long range planning, budgeted staff tracking, trend analysis, costing, charging, and the linking of patient classification information to a wide variety of pertinent data such as quality criteria, length of stay, nursing diagnoses and medical care data are among the frequent demands. Nursing executives now use work load information for negotiating contracts with HMOs, evaluating trends in patient care demands and generally minimizing economic risks.[2,3,10]

With these and other expanded requirements of patient classification data comes the added pressure to repeatedly demonstrate the accuracy of the information. The methods traditionally employed for maintaining and monitoring the reliability and validity of patient classification systems involve extensive manual efforts.[4-8] While these methods have proven accurate they are labor intensive, which leads to infrequent and often inadequate testing. In short, the traditional methods are increasingly being recognized as inadequate for the complexity and sophistication of the expanded objectives.

THE ARIC SYSTEM

The ARIC patient classification system (Copyright James Bahr Associates, 1988) is a computerized patient classification approach employing a patient-,

Reprinted from *The Journal of Nursing Administration*, Vol. 20, No. 5, with permission of J.B. Lippincott Company, © 1990 and James Bahr Associates © 1988.

personnel-, unit-, and shift-specific relational data base that operates on a personal or mainframe computer. Unlike most other classification instruments, the critical indicators used to group or categorize patients are totally site-developed for each specialty area, such as medical-surgical, rehabilitation, nephrology, pediatrics, ICU and mental health. Critical indicators refer to the descriptions used to identify the appropriate category of care. They represent those care activities or patient characteristics that have the greatest impact on nursing care time.[1,7,8] Comparability of categorical information within and between nursing units, and indeed, between hospitals and clinics, is maintained through the establishment of universal categories with distinct care time ranges. Work sampling studies are required on site to validate the mean care hours per patient class (category) and shift of the unit-specific instruments and to establish the percentages of variable care times (direct and indirect) and fixed care times (unit-related and personal). The ARIC system was originally developed by James Bahr Associates in 1981 and has been implemented in a variety of inpatient and ambulatory care settings.[3,11,12]

The ARIC patient classification instrument employs a combination of steps that provide the care giver with multiple pathways for determining the appropriate class or category for each patient. Figure 49-1 is an example of a site specific patient classification instrument for a medical unit. To establish the class or category of the patient, the care giver first identifies the dependent care description which best represents the patient's therapeutic regime. In the example provided (Figure 49-1), five dependent care options are available: Type A through Type E. Each type is composed of a set of critical indicators representing the current therapeutic regimen of the patients on the unit. Associated with each type is the average and the range of direct nursing care time required to carry out the patient's dependent care requirement. The care giver then selects the independent care description which best describes the patient's/family's need for psychosocial support and education. The independent care description also includes consideration of the critical analysis of the patient's support system and need for nursing

intervention as well as the extent of coordination and referral activity involved. Again, five options are available, ranging from very low (Code V) to extremely high (Code X). The range of time required to provide each level of independent care is also indicated. The combined dependent and independent care assessments lead to a unique class or category of care, depending upon their individual levels. For example, if the medical patient's dependent care requirements are best described as Type B and his independent care needs best described as moderate (M), his class or category of care will be 3.

The dependent care indicators selected for each unit-specific instrument are developed from chart data using optical scan forms. Patient medical records from each unit or specialty area are systematically reviewed for the type and frequency of physicians' orders. Those orders most frequently occurring in that unit are printed on the scan forms. Further, each specialty area-dependent care indicator has a standard time associated with it, thereby creating a time range for each patient type. For example, the Type A category range is 0.0 to 0.99 hours and the Type B range is 1.00 to 1.99 hours (Figure 49-1). The dependent orders most frequently selected for each time range are used to describe the patient type unique to each unit. This process greatly enhances the face validity of the system which in turn is known to affect its reliability.[5,6,9] Further, this process allows for comparison of patient categories across units and participating hospitals and clinics even though the dependent care descriptions may be vastly different. The optical scan forms may be updated and rerun to revise the dependent care indicators whenever therapeutic regimes are thought to differ from those existing at the time of implementation. The expected ranges of independent care times were originally developed through observational sampling studies conducted during the system's development, and are repeatedly updated with data from participating hospitals.

The distinction between dependent and independent care assessments is a useful approach in the separation of nursing functions derived from the physician-directed therapeutic regime (dependent) and the nurse-initiated care (independent). The distinction between dependent and independent is

Medicine

STEP 1		STEP 2		STEP 3
DEPENDENT DESCRIPTION	RANGE	**INDEPENDENT NEEDS**	CODE	CLASS
Type A .75 Hrs. (Avg.)	0.0 - .99 Hrs.			
Intake/Output Q 8 Hrs.		Very Low (0-15 mins)	V	1
Vital Signs Q Shift		Low (16-30 mins)	L	2
Routine Meds 1-3 Doses		Mod (31-60 mins)	M	3
		High (1-2 hours)	H	3
		Extremely High (> 2 hours)	X	4
Type B 1.5 Hrs. (Avg.)	1.0 - 1.99 Hrs.			
Intake/Output Q 8 Hrs		Very Low (0-15 mins)	V	3
Vital Signs Q Shift		Low (16-30 mins)	L	3
Routine Meds 4-8 Doses		Mod (31-60 mins)	M	3
Mouth Care		High (1-2 hours)	H	4
Chair W/Assistance/Dangle		Extremely High (> 2 hours)	X	4
Type C 2.5 Hrs. (Avg.)	2.0 - 2.99 Hrs.			
Vital Signs Q 2 Hrs		Very Low (0-15 mins)	V	4
Intake & Output Q Shift		Low (16-30 mins)	L	4
Routine Meds 4-8 Doses		Mod (31-60 mins)	M	4
Mouth Care		High (1-2 hours)	H	4
Walk in Hall w/1-2 Assistants		Extremely High (> 2 hours)	X	4
Type D 3.5 Hrs. (Avg.)	3.0 - 3.99 Hrs.			
Vital Signs Q 2 Hrs		Very Low (0-15 mins)	V	4
Intake & Output Q Shift		Low (16-30 mins)	L	4
Routine Meds 4-8 Doses		Mod (31-60 mins)	M	4
Mouth Care		High (1-2 hours)	H	5
Flat in Bed/Log Roll		Extremely High (> 2 hours)	X	5
Type E 4.5 Hrs. (Avg.)	4.0 - 4.99 Hrs.			
Vital Signs Q 1 H x 8/Shift		Very Low (0-15 mins)	V	5
Intake & Output Q Shift		Low (16-30 mins)	L	5
Transfuse Blood (1-2 Units)		Mod (31-60 mins)	M	5
Routine Meds 4-8 Doses		High (1-2 hours)	H	5
Mouth Care		Extremely High (> hours)	X	5
O₂ per Cannula/Mask				
Flat in Bed/Log Roll				

FIGURE 49-1

ARIC Patient Classification Instrument. Copyright James Bahr Associates, 1988. ARIC is a trademark of JBA. The ARIC system software and documentation are protected under US copyright laws and trade secret laws. Patents covering many of ARIC's unique features are pending.

important and can form the basis for determining nursing costs related to nursing diagnoses and interventions.[2]

Patients are classified at the end of each shift for the care required on the shift that is just ending.

These data serve several functions: 1) they provide workload data for required staffing; 2) they are compared with the prediction for staffing requirements for the past shift to determine how well the system predicted the need for staff; 3) they are linked

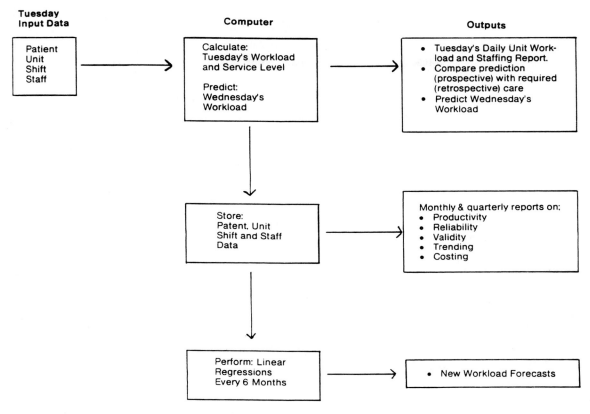

FIGURE 49-2

Functions of patient, unit, and shift-specific data.

to current stored values to provide staffing predictions for upcoming shifts; 4) they are stored as patient-, unit-, and shift-specific data for costing and trend analysis; and 5) they are added to predictive staffing requirements to form the basis of linear regressions. Figure 49-2 displays the flow of data input and output.

RELIABILITY MONITORING

The reliability of the ARIC patient classification information is measured in two ways. First, by comparing the care giver's assessment of the patient's *dependent* care requirements with an "expert rater's" assessment using a different form and second, by comparing the care giver's assessment of the patient's *independent* care requirements with the expected independent care requirements for that class as generated by computer analyses.

To test the reliability of the dependent care requirements, the optical scan forms are employed once per week on each unit by an expert rater. At the same time, the care giver classifies the patient in the usual way, using the instrument as a guide. Both sets of data are entered into the computer: the dependent care workload calculated from the scan form and the dependent care workload calculated from the instrument. The data are linked with individual patient record data to generate the Dependent Reliability Testing Report (Figure 49-3). As the scan form data only deals with the dependent nursing care requirements, the software uses the independent care assessment of the nurse classifier in calculating the "expert" classification.

Wellcare General Hospital

Care Code Reliability Testing

Unit: 4000N   Date: 07/08/89   Shift: Afternoon

Room Bed	Independent Care Needs (1)	Dependent Care Type (2)	Classification Scantron Expert Classification (3)	Care Provider Classification (4)
401A	M	E	5	4
402A	L	C	4	5
403A	M	A	3	4
404A	M	C	4	5
405A	M	C	4	5
406A	M	C	4	5
407A	L	B	3	3
408A	L	B	3	3
409A	M	B	3	5
410A	H	A	3	4
410B	V	B	3	5
411B	M	D	4	4
412A	M	E	5	4
413A	M	B	3	3
415A	M	A	3	3
416A	V	B	3	3
417A	H	A	3	3
418A	M	B	3	3
419A	L	B	3	5
420A	H	B	4	4
420B	M	B	3	4

Total Unit Workload (hours)   48.70   **56.00**

Acceptable Range is 0.90-1.10. Ratio from test = 1.15

*** Care Code Reliability not within Acceptable Range ***

FIGURE 49-3

Dependent reliability testing.

Traditionally, the approach used to measure reliability has been to calculate the percentage of agreement of the categories selected between two raters. The ARIC approach focuses instead on the actual work load calculations. The difference between the two work loads provides a more meaningful analysis because it relates directly to the cost or magnitude of any discrepancy. For example, in Figure 49-3 the overall work loads calculated for the afternoon shift on Unit 4000N are quite different. As illustrated in Figure 49-3, the total work load calculated by the Scantron expert rater using the scan form is 48.70 hours while the total work load calculated by the care providers is 56.00 hours. The difference amounts to approximately one care provider and, as evident from the report, suggests that the reliability is not within an

acceptable range. Such discrepancies could have a significant impact on staffing and costs. The report also displays the discrepancies in work load on a patient-specific basis so that the source of difference can be identified.

Guidelines are provided to assist in identifying plausible causes for any decrease in reliability. Should the dependent care indicators no longer represent current therapeutic regimes, new scan forms can be developed and the unit may rescan for a period of four to six weeks to develop more representative indicators.

The assessment of the reliable use of the independent care component of the classification instrument is made by comparing the amount of independent care, as assessed by the care giver, with the expected amount, as determined historically for that category or class of patient. The stored database of expected independent values is unit-specific. The comparison of the nurse's estimate with the historical database appears on a separate computer-generated report, the Patient Class Average Assessment Report. The computer stores the combinations of dependent and independent values used to calculate the overall patient class. All patients are displayed on the report by class and age group. The amount of independent care time for each class is compared with the expected amount of independent care time for the class to reveal the reliability or estimate of agreement. Independent times outside of the expected range are identified and a listing of individual patients' records by care givers may be produced to aid in investigating the plausible cause of unreliability.

VALIDITY MONITORING

Following implementation and initial validation, ongoing validity monitoring begins. As previously described, stored data are combined with retrospective classification data to predict staffing requirements for upcoming shifts. The stored data include unit-specific class weights for anticipated admissions, discharges and surgical days. The system also takes into account the "recuperative rates" for patients on each unit. For example, on admission a patient on an oncology unit may be classified as a Class Two (low requirements for nursing care). At the beginning of the next shift the patient receives intravenous chemotherapy requiring frequent monitoring, medication and support for nausea and vomiting and emotional support for anxiety. The patient is now assessed as a Class Five (high requirements for nursing care). The computer program stores this progression from Class Two to Class Five and builds this information into the prediction formula for that unit.

The ARIC system also stores the activity of patients who are not on the unit for the entire twenty-four hour period. This includes outpatients receiving unit based diagnostic tests or treatments, patients who are admitted and expire on the same shift and patients who are transferred or discharged during a shift. Every six months, more frequently if necessary,

linear regressions are run against the patient, unit, day of week and shift-specific information to provide a new set of predictive standards.

Each month a detailed comparison between the required and the predicted work load is provided on a Monthly Forecast Monitor Report. The differences between the required and forecasted work load are calculated and reported as the percent absolute error. Guidelines are provided for determining the acceptable ranges of the percent absolute error for each unit. A unit which has a very homogeneous patient population would be expected to have a percent absolute error of less than five percent. A unit with a diverse patient population may have a percent absolute error as high as ten or fifteen percent. In the case of a unit with a diverse patient population a major shift in the percent absolute error will indicate a need for investigation of validity. For example, if the monthly percent absolute error increases from ten percent to sixteen percent, investigative action is required. Possible causes need to be assessed and appropriate corrective actions taken.

CORRECTIVE ACTION

Three flow charts have been developed to assist in the analysis of the reliability and validity monitoring reports: Figure 49-4, Dependent Reliability Monitoring Flow Chart; Figure 49-5, Independent Reliability Monitoring Flow Chart; and Figure 49-6, Validity Monitoring Flow Chart. Should action be required to improve the validity or reliability of the system, several mechanisms are available to assist in the process. If the instruments are being inappropriately used, the involved care givers can be identified by printing a report that lists patients classified by care giver. Inappropriate use may stem from misunderstanding or inappropriate orientation. If it is determined that the care givers are, in fact, classifying appropriately, the validity of the instrument should be questioned. If care activities have changed, the unit may need to rescan to develop new profile statements of dependent care. The software provides the mechanism for revising the factors and associated values as well as for producing a new set of unit-specific critical indicators. Alternatively, if the dependent care profile

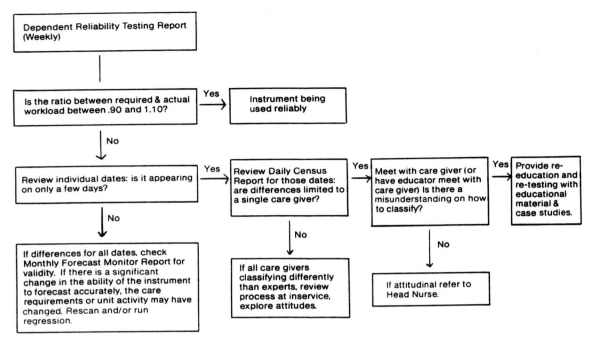

FIGURE 49-4

Dependent reliability monitoring flow chart.

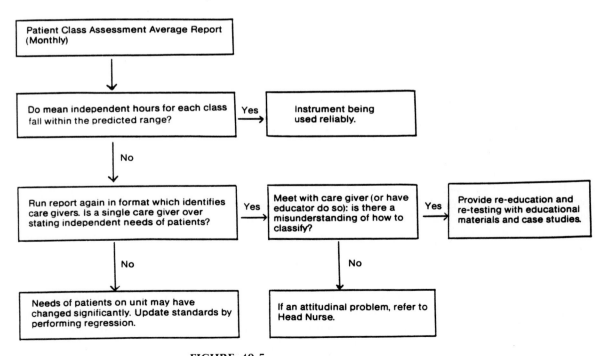

FIGURE 49-5

Independent reliability monitoring flow chart.

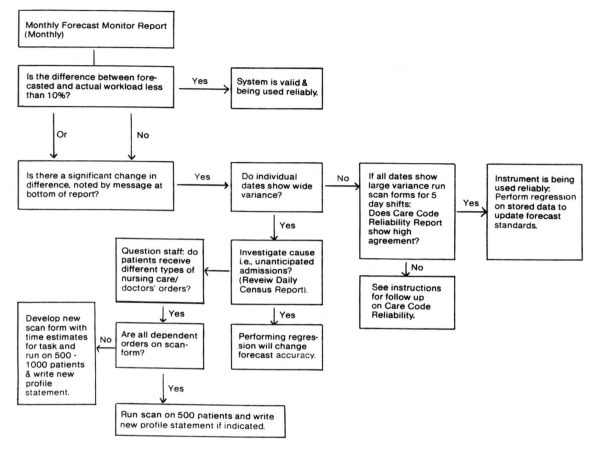

FIGURE 49-6

Validity monitoring flow chart.

statements have not changed but the pattern of patient care has changed (shorter stays, different doctors, new treatment modalities, or an altered staff mix) the predictive software may be updated by running the regression function against the stored data for the unit. This function would normally be performed every six months but more frequent updates might be necessary if the care delivery measurement is continually changing.

As previously noted, the ARIC system operates on a personal, mini, or main frame computer, using the Unify Relational Database under the Xenix, Unix, or AIX operating systems. These operating systems, like all operating systems (such as DOS), determine the basic capabilities of the hardware and software

and permit the application software (in this example, ARIC) to be a multi-tasking, multi-user system. Simply put, more than one person can use the software at a time, and several functions can occur simultaneously.

SUMMARY

The traditional approaches to monitoring reliability and validity are time consuming and costly and frequently lead to the abandonment of reasonable classification instruments. With the advent of micro computers and relational database software, nursing executives are now able to track reliability and validity on an ongoing basis. Because patient classification data are retained, they can be used to provide more accurate work load predictions and descriptions. Further, the ability to identify the source of problems with unit-specific instruments or nurse classifiers leads to the required corrective mechanism. Increased confidence in the reliability and validity of the work load data provides the staff nurse with direct evidence of the accuracy of the patient classification instrument and the nursing executive with a significantly stronger tool in budget planning and tracking, contract negotiations and financial risk reduction.

REFERENCES

1. Giovannetti P. Understanding patient classification systems. J Nurs Admin 1979;9(2):4-9
2. McCloskey JC. Implications of costing out nursing services for reimbursement. Nurs Mgmt 1989;20(1):4-46, 48, 49.
3. Edwardson S, Bahr J, Serote M. Patient classification and management information systems as adjuncts to patient care delivery. In: Mayer G, Madden MJ, Lawrenz E, eds. *Patient Care Delivery Models*. Rockville, MD: Aspen, 1990;pp. 293-313.
4. Edwardson S, Giovannetti P. A review of cost accounting methods for services. J Nurs Economics 1987;5(3):107-117.
5. Giovannetti P, Mayer G. Building confidence in patient classification systems. Nurs Mgmt 1984;15(8):31-34.
6. Williams MA. When you don't develop your own: Validation methods for patient classification systems. Nurs Mgmt 1985;19(3):90-96.
7. DeGroot HA. Patient classification system evaluation Part 1: Essential system elements. J Nurs Admin 1989;19(6):30-35.
8. DeGroot HA. Patient classification system evaluation Part 2: System selection & implementation. J Nurs Admin 1989;19(7):24-30.
9. Poulson E. A method for training and checking interrater agreement for a patient classification study. Nurs Mgmt 1987;18(9):72-80.
10. Sovie M, Tarcinale MA, VanPutte A, Stunder A. Amalgam of nursing acuity, DRGs and costs. Nurs Mgmt 1985;16(3):22-24.
11. Giovannetti P, Burkhalter B. Final report: Test and monitor patient classification systems. National Institutes of Health 1988, Contract NO1-C1-7-2101.
12. Johnson JM. Quantifying an ambulatory care patient classification instrument. J Nurs Admin 1989;19(11):36-42.

CHAPTER **50**

Performance Evaluation Alternatives

Stephen C. Bushardt, DBA
Aubrey R. Fowler Jr, PhD

PERFORMANCE EVALUATION ALTERNATIVES

The primary purpose of any health care facility is to provide the best possible patient care. At the same time the facility must maintain a reasonable control on costs. Many cost and care factors are directly attributable to the explosive growth of medical technology in recent years. The basic quality of the care given and the efficiency with which the facility operates are ultimately a reflection of personnel performance. With differing levels of impact physicians, nurses, administrators, clerical staff, janitors, and other health care workers combine their talents and efforts to provide patients with the care and treatment they need.

With this reliance on employees performance it is necessary for the administrators to make every effort to ensure that their employees perform as effectively and efficiently as possible. The benefits of such performance are extensive. Foremost among those benefits are improvements in the quality of nursing, improvements in providing suitable food services, and improvements in maintaining a clean facility. Also, the primary purpose of the facility will be more effectively met in any other of the facilities functions relating to patients. In addition, as employee performance improves, the likelihood of negligent or incompetent

Reprinted from *The Journal of Nursing Administration,* Vol. 18, No. 10, with permission of J. B. Lippincott Company, © 1988.

care will decrease, offering the facility protection against malpractice litigation. Finally, as employee performance improves, productivity will be expected to increase, thereby lowering the labor-cost component of health care. This latter benefit is of additional value in markets suffering from shortages, such as nurses, since greater productivity will allow for the maintenance of service levels with fewer employees.

Performance Appraisal Methods

Most performance appraisals use a series of rating scales. These evaluation instruments can be divided based on what they are measuring. In the traditional approach, the basis for evaluation is traits associated with the individual such as attitude, commitment, and dedication. An increasingly common approach is to base the evaluation on job-related behavior such as punctuality and quality of care.

Trait approach

The trait approach evaluates traits associated with the employee's character under the assumption of a relationship between an individual's characteristics and job performance. The employees are usually evaluated on a series of scales often ranging from one to five, where each scale measures a different trait. The popularity of this technique stems in large part from the ease of development and the belief in our ability to judge a person's character.

Unfortunately these instruments are notoriously unreliable with few raters agreeing on what the meaning of point 4 on the attitude scale is. Furthermore, performance appraisal, while often being used for judgment decisions such as merit pay, promotions, transfers, and discharge, is also used for employee development. The instrument let the employees know how to improve their ratings. Due to the ambiguous nature of traits and their relative permanence the feedback value to the employee is useless to nonexistent.[1]

The courts have been even less kind to the trait approach to evaluation as a result of poor reliability and potential discrimination effects. The courts require objectivity and demonstrable relation to the job, which are both difficult to achieve with the trait approach.

Behavioral approach

The behavioral approaches use a series of scales where each scale measures some job related behavior. The shift from employee characteristic to job-related behavior is an important one, but, as currently used, has not proven to be appreciatively more effective than the trait approach. These failures stem from the common practice of using the same instrument for different jobs, where the behaviors are not relevant.

A second major shortcoming has been a lack of reliability. The raters, when evaluating punctuality on a behavioral scale of 1 to 5, seldom agree on the meaning of 3 or average punctuality. The solution that is often called for is rater training, though studies indicate little long-term effect associated with this training.[2] Closely associated with the issue of reliability is the failure to develop independent scales. Research studies using factor analysis strongly indicates when using multiple rating scales, the rater is in reality evaluating a single characteristic as the scale scores tend to have strong co-variance.[3,4]

In attempting to overcome the apparent shortcomings of the earlier behavioral approaches, two adaptations have been set forth: Behavior Anchored Rating Scales (BARS) and Task Oriented Performance Evaluation System (TOPES). The superiority of these specific behavioral approaches is derived in part from the use of descriptors associated with major points on

each scale. BARS uses job related behavioral examples for each point on the scale. TOPES uses behavioral descriptions of task accomplishments. Another superiority of these two methods in large part is derived from their method of development. Each is outlined briefly, and the specific advantages, disadvantages, and applicability are discussed. In addition, references will be given so that those interested in considering either technique can obtain a more complete description of how to develop and use it.

Behaviorally Anchored Rating Scales — BARS

Behaviorally Anchored Rating Scales is the older and more complex of the two techniques. In essence, BARS relies on the descriptions of particular jobs as a basis for identifying key job elements and then uses descriptive statements of good and bad behavior from the job. The individual being evaluated is next rated in accordance with how closely his or her behavior is described by the behavioral descriptors associated with a particular job dimension. For instance, if we treat patient relations as an important dimension of nurses' jobs, we might develop the following range of behavioral descriptions as illustrated in Table 50-1.

With these descriptors each nurse can be evaluated and his or her performance ranked by choosing the most appropriate descriptor. Obviously the closer to descriptor #1 one is ranked, the better the performance. In addition, the nature of the ranking gives an indication of the behavior changes needed to improve performance. Therefore, the BARS format is superior as a tool for inducing performance improvements to a scale that simply asks an evaluator to rank a nurse's patient relations on a 1 to 10 scale, or worse yet, asks about the nurse's attitude toward patients.

The above example is intended as just that. It does not pretend to be an appropriate or accurate reflection of how to rank nurse's patient relations. To develop such an appropriate descriptor list is an extensive process involving those who will do the evaluations and those who will be evaluated. This involvement of the ultimate subjects of the evaluation system has several benefits: it creates a greater understanding of and willingness to accept the evaluation

TABLE 50-1
BARS performance dimension: Patient relations

Excellent	1. Employee always treats patients with dignity and cheerfulness, respecting their individual needs while performing professional duties. Employee receives frequent favorable comments from patients under his or her care.
Good	2. Employee treats patients with dignity and respect without becoming involved in their individual problems. Employees receives occasional favorable comments from patients.
Average	3. Employee is impersonal with patients, tending their medical needs but avoiding personal interaction. Employee is the subject of few comments by patients.
Poor	4. Employee becomes impatient with patients and is concerned more about performing his or her tasks than being of assistance to patient's nonmedical needs. Employee generates some complaints from patients.
Unacceptable	5. Employee is antagonistic toward patients, treating them as obstacles or annoyances rather than individuals. Employee generates frequent complaints from patients and causes them considerable upset.

instrument; it is more likely to generate accurate descriptions of good, bad, and indifferent behavior; and it helps to ensure that the behavior being evaluated is actually related to effective job performance. It suffers, however, from increased time and cost requirements of developing a BARS system. Time and cost requirement are also increased since each job being evaluated must have a separate rating scale. BARS, therefore, finds its greatest use in larger organizations with many employees in most job categories so the developmental costs can be spread over many evaluation subjects. Detailed explanations of the development and use of BARS can be found in the performance appraisal literature.[5,6,7,8,9]

There are a number of specific benefits that an organization can receive from the use of BARS. Because it is based on job descriptions and observed behaviors, it is more defensible in court than most other performance evaluation systems.[10,11] The use of BARS is more likely to lead to favorable employee response and improvements in performance since it gives clear indications of acceptable behavior[12] and is not as threatening as characteristic based systems.[13] The effective use of BARS can help to alleviate the problems of staff shortages attributable to employee burnout and turnover[14] by giving a clearer measure of acceptable performance and objective goals to strive for. This should reduce frustration in the employee and create greater job satisfaction.[15] Finally, a BARS system can serve to better acquaint employees and managers with the actual requirements of a given job[16] leading to more realistic performance expectations and less opportunity for misunderstanding between superiors and subordinates.

Task Oriented Performance Evaluation System—TOPES

A more recent development in performance appraisal that offers many of the advantages of BARS while avoiding excessive costs is the Task Oriented Performance Evaluation System.[17] Unlike BARS, TOPES concentrates directly on the various tasks that comprise a job rather than the specific behaviors related to those tasks. It is behaviorally based since it measures task accomplishment but does not directly measure or compare behavioral activities. Because specific job behaviors need not be described, the development of a TOPES instrument is much simpler and much less complex since a single basic evaluation scale can be used for each job in the organization, varying only in the task elements of the job instead of the behavioral descriptors. TOPES, therefore, retains the direct job relationship needed for legal defensibility but in a considerably simplified format.

An additional feature of TOPES is that it allows for varying importance of different job tasks to be reflected in a weighting system that leads to a composite performance score unavailable from BARS. This composite score makes it easier to compare employees on the same job and, if properly developed, allows for comparisons of employees across jobs. These comparisons are not possible with BARS and might be highly critical in using performance evaluation results as a basis for merit pay or other benefit allocation decisions.[18] Finally, TOPES is suitable for measuring performance in areas that are quantifiable, allowing for objective evaluations, or nonquantifiable, requiring a subjective scale. The basic TOPES evaluation scale is illustrated in Table 50-2.

The employee is evaluated with the above scale on each of the several task elements of his or her job. Those task elements are given weights that are decimal values adding up to one, i.e. four tasks with weights .4, .3, .2, and .1. The more important the task, the higher the weight assigned. The score on each task is multiplied by its weight, i.e. an employee rated as good on task 1 has a score of 4 × 0.4, or 1.6. The scores for each task are then added and a composite score is created that may be evaluated on a total job basis by comparing it back to the rating scale. Obviously, the higher the composite score, the better the evaluation.

A prime criterion for measurement of a performance evaluation technique's effectiveness is acceptance by the employees being evaluated. They must view the appraisal instrument and the appraisal process as fair. This can be best achieved by employee participation in the development of the instrument. The task elements, as well as the weights, should be developed with employees in the job category for which the instrument will be used. The job description can be used to start the discussion of weights and elements. The discussion should not be limited to the job description, as many times these are inaccurate. It is imperative for organizational effectiveness that supervisors and employees hold a common agreement concerning what task should be done, as well as which tasks are most important. On those occasions when employees develop weights and/or identify limited or inappropriate task elements in the

TABLE 50-2
Task scale: Generic

Excellent	5. Performance of this task is superior in nature leaving little or no room for improvement. An individual performing at this level is eligible for the maximum individual rewards.
Good	4. Performance is better than that of the average employee but does allow for improvement. An employee performing at this level is eligible for moderate individual rewards.
Average	3. Performance is acceptable meeting the basic requirement of the task involved but leaving substantial room for improvement. An average employee is eligible for system but not individual rewards.
Weak	2. Performance is barely adequate to meet task requirements. It needs substantial improvement in quality and/or efficiency. An employee performing at this level is not eligible for any rewards.
Unacceptable	1. Performance fails to meet minimum standards and must be immediately improved. Failure to improve will subject the employee to disciplinary action and eventual dismissal.

eyes of administrators, this does not represent a failure of the process but the uncovering of unclear policies and/or procedures.[19] In essence, the failure of past communication is being identified and hence can be clarified. The impact of TOPES development extends beyond a limited appraisal process.[20]

For example, the nurse's aides working on the med-surgical floor of a large county hospital identified the following task elements in their jobs: assisting the nurses, responding to patient calls, and a series of task elements associated with routine duties. The nurse's aides assigned equal weights to each task element. The nursing supervisor in charge was shocked, as assisting the nurses was clearly most important since the quality of health care is directly involved. If employees disagree on task elements and weights, is it any wonder that conflict is high and productivity is low?

As a recent development, TOPES offers few examples of practical application. It does, however, offer promise as an easy to use, effective method of performance evaluation. It is simple in its development and application; its results are easily interpreted and used; and it offers a clear indication to employees of the quality of their overall performance and of performance areas that can or should be improved. Finally, it serves effectively as the basis for reward systems based on individual merit.

SUMMARY

The two behaviorally oriented evaluation systems have as their major disadvantage the cost and difficulty of devising appropriate instruments. Their development can be time consuming and their use may require a separate instrument for each job category or subcategory being evaluated. Obviously there are different behaviors required of admitting clerks versus food service workers, hence requiring different evaluative tools. Furthermore, the required behaviors of surgical nurses and pediatric nurses will differ, requiring specially designed instruments. However, once the instrument is developed, the use of the behaviorally oriented evaluations will give a superior result. Since the instrument is specifically job related and less subjective in its scoring, the results of the evaluation better reflect the employees' actual performance and are more likely to stand up in court. Furthermore, since the orientation is toward behaviors rather than characteristics, the evaluation is less likely to be perceived as a personal attack by the individual receiving a substandard evaluation. Therefore, it serves as a better basis for improving performance since it identifies specific activities that need correction rather than personal characteristics that must change. Finally, the behaviorally oriented instrument may be seen as a much fairer evaluative tool by employees since they frequently have input into its development and can see that the behaviors measured are directly related to the accomplishment of job objectives. Likewise, employees will view the tool as fairer since it is much easier to challenge adverse scores based on objective evaluations than on those subjectively based.

Health care facilities are dependent on the quality of their employees' performance for the accomplishment of their goals. Therefore, an effective measure of performance is necessary as a basis for establishing and enforcing performance standards. The two evaluation systems described above meet that need. They both avoid the problems associated with trait based systems, are less subject to bias or misunderstanding than most other systems, and with proper development and rater training, will effectively meet all of the evaluation needs of the employer. The two systems are sufficiently different in nature as to offer real choice but are both based on the actual performance of job related activities, thereby offering greater reliability, improved employee acceptance of the result, and greater applicability in making decisions regarding personnel actions.

REFERENCES

1. Glueck WF. Personnel: a diagnostic approach. 2d ed. Dallas: Business Publications, Inc., 1978.
2. Glueck WF. Personnel: A diagnostic approach. 2d ed. Dallas: Business Publications, Inc., 1978.
3. Cascio WF. Applied psychology in personnel management. Englewood Cliff, NJ: Prentice Hall, Inc., 1987;85.
4. Bernardin H, Bealty RW. Performance appraisal: assessing human behavior at work. Boston, MA: Kent Publishing Co., 1984.
5. Bushardt SC, Fowler A, Sukumar D. Behaviorally anchored rating scales: a valuable aid to the personnel function. Akron Business and Economic Review. Summer 1985;16:26-32.
6. Schwab, Heneman, DeCotiis. Behaviorally anchored rating scales: a review of the literature. Personnel Psychology 1975;28:552-6.
7. Kearney WJ. The value of behaviorally based performance appraisals. Business Horizons. June 1976;19:75.
8. Campbell JP, Dunnette MD, Arvey RD, Hellervik LV. The development and evaluation of behaviorally anchored rating scales. J Appl Psychol 1973;57:19-22.
9. Rosinger G, Myers LB, Levy, GW, Loar M, Mohrman SN, Stock JR. Development of a behaviorally based

performance appraisal system. Personnel Psychology. Spring 1982;39:75-88.

10. Klassen CR, Thompson DE, Luben GL. How defensible is your performance appraisal system. Personnel Administrator 1980;25(12):80.

11. Holley WH, Field HS. Performance appraisal and the law. Labor Law Journal 1975;26(7):423.

12. Kearney WJ. The Value of behaviorally based performance appraisals. Business Horizons. June 1976; 19(3):75.

13. Bushardt SC, Schnake ME. Employee evaluation: Measure performance not attitude. Management World. February 1981;41-42.

14. Potter B. Avoiding burnout: Joint employer-employee responsibility. Hospital Progress, 1981;62(6):52.

15. Burton GE, Kundtz R, Martin A, Pathak DS. The impact of role clarity on job satisfaction for hospital managers. Hospital Topics, 1981;58(1):17.

16. Blood MR. Spin-offs from behavioral expectation scale procedures. J Appl Psychol August 1984;59(4):513-515.

17. Fowler AR, Bushardt SC. TOPES: Task oriented performance evaluation system. SAM-Advanced Management Journal Fall 1986.

18. Bushardt SC, Fowler AR. Compensation and benefits: today's dilemma in motivation. Personnel Administrator 1984;29(11):83.

19. Blood MR. Spin-offs from behavioral expectation scale procedures. J Appl Psychol. August 1984;59(4): 513-515.

20. Fowler AR, Bushardt SC. TOPES: Task oriented performance evaluation system. SAM-Advanced Management Journal. Fall 1986.

CHAPTER **51**

Criterion Referenced Performance Appraisal System: A Blueprint

Katherin D. Sudela, RN, MSN,
Libbie Landureth, RN, MSN

Administration's decision to institute a salary system based on merit stimulated the development of our criterion reference performance evaluation system. Designed specifically to measure the performance of all our registered, professional nurses, it covers a variety of positions in the organization.

The potential negative effect of a formal performance evaluation system can easily be underestimated. Disadvantages to the evaluator probably greatly outnumber those to the evaluatee. As the term "system" implies, there is a strong hint of order. In practical terms this means someone will have to look after the program — i.e., administer it. Formality also suggests that documentation will be required and it is well known how easy it is to unleash a blizzard of paper. "System" also suggests a requirement for conformity, a need for standardization, neither one of which is usually warmly received by effective headstrong managers."[1] Operationally, this means taking from managers their traditional methods of rewarding employees. The implementation of a system of performance appraisal may be resisted for a variety of other reasons. Nurse managers, often suffering from a poor professional self-image, are uncomfortable in

Reprinted from *Nursing Management,* Vol. 18, No. 3, with permission of S-N Publications, Inc. © 1987.

passing judgment on others. They fear reprisal in various forms, often rightly so. Poorly developed management skills and a failure to communicate assertively with subordinates also contribute to this poor professional self-image. As noted by Yura and Walsh:

> Unless she has a clear idea of who she is evaluating, why she is evaluating, what she is evaluating, when she should evaluate, where she should evaluate and how she should evaluate, she could be less than effective and perhaps unfair in her evaluation.[2]

The authors believe, as suggested by del Bueno, that:

> Performance evaluation should be a continuous process based on an articulated set of elements. Those elements inherent in a good performance appraisal system are content, tools/forms, training, a reward system and an accountability system.[3]

Development of the performance evaluation system was done through committee work. The committee had five subcommittees based on the various levels of nursing service personnel. The subcommittees were responsible for identifying expected behaviors for that particular level of personnel based on the job description and the role as it was then implemented. All areas within the Hospital District were represented. An education department staff member worked with each of the subcommittees through individual meetings and was responsible for arranging meeting times and places, circulating meeting notices, and gathering and distributing paperwork and media. Primarily, she was responsible for facillitating group work and recording the proceedings of the meetings.

The overall scheme is depicted in Figure 51-1, for the assessment, planning, implementation and evaluation activities involved in the change.

The goals of the performance evaluation committee were formulated by the committee chairpersons. They were: 1) the development of a system of performance appraisal for salary administration to be used in evaluating Nursing Supervisors, Nursing Instructors, Head Nurses, Staff Nurses, and Expanded Role Nurses; 2) the implementation of the performance appraisal system; 3) the evaluation and revision of the system after the initial six months; and 4) annual evaluation and revision of the performance appraisal system.

Samples of various performance appraisal tools were collected and a variety of systems examined for possible use and applicability to our setting. Sample tools and descriptions of systems representing management by objectives, graphic rating scales, forced distribution systems, ranking systems, and behaviorally anchored rating systems were presented to the committee members. After extensive discussion, a decision was made in accordance with Joint Commission guidelines for a criteria-based evaluation tool related to the standards of performance specified in the individual's job description.[4] The tool was organized into "competency categories" arrived at in a manner described later in this article.

The subcommittees were intended to represent nurses from a variety of classifications, rather than to be a homogeneous group from the classification itself. Each group was asked to list the major categories of criteria upon which a professional nurse of the classification should be evaluated. These lists were then combined, and similar items were fused into single categories with more global titles. The resulting "competency categories" were Job Knowledge, Professionalism, Teaching/Learning Skills, and Management/Organization/Administration. The Expanded

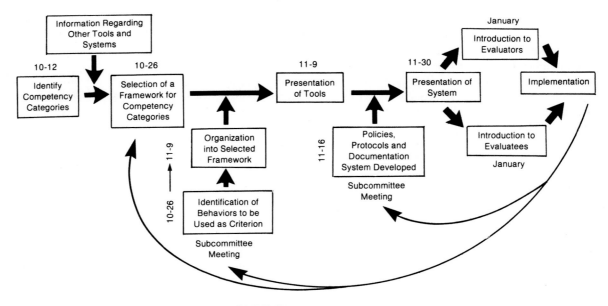

FIGURE 51-1

Evaluation committee flow chart.

Role Nurse subcommittee elected to have an additional category entitled "Character Traits." Each subcommittee met six to ten times, usually once every one to two weeks, reporting back to the general committee at approximately monthly intervals.

The subcommittee work was the most difficult and time-consuming. Each committee began by considering the job description for their classification. Any items that were behaviorally stated were used as a starting point and were organized under the appropriate competency category. Then the group brainstormed for additional behaviorally stated items that were of *equal weight* and *not contained explicitly* in the job description. Non-behaviorally stated items contained in the job description were restated behaviorally and included. A sample from the staff nurse tool is shown in Figure 51-2.

GENERATION OF POLICIES AND PROCEDURES

Subcommittee members were presented with information about various systems and asked to make recommendations for policies and procedures to guide the performance appraisal system. From this data, policies and procedures for evaluation for employees, scoring the tool, storage of the completed tool, confidentiality of the evaluation results, review of disputed evaluation results, follow-up for improvement, revision of tools, and salary distribution were drafted. These were reviewed by the Performance Evaluation Committee, the Personnel Department staff, a group of consultants, the Hospital District Administrative Staff, and the Nursing Service Directors.

To implement a pilot study of the performance appraisal tools, a program was presented to teach the use of the tools to all persons who had responsibilities for evaluating registered professional nurses in the Hospital District and to orient all registered nurses who would be evaluated. For the evaluators, a two-day workshop was offered on two separate occasions. The workshop program covered the following topic areas:

1. Introduction to Evaluation;
2. History of the Performance Evaluation Committee;
3. Goals of the Evaluation Process;
4. Pitfalls of the Evaluation Process;
5. Techniques for Conducting an Evaluation Interview;
6. Values Clarification;
7. Assertiveness Training;
8. Performance Appraisal Tools; and
9. Performance Appraisal Policies and Procedures.

In addition, the workshop provided active involvement for the participants in the areas of values clarification, evaluating the performance of a subordinate, and presentation of the evaluation to the subordinate in an evaluation interview. Videotaping with playback and discussion was used to analyze several of the evaluation interviews.

Those registered nurses who were to be evaluated with the new performance appraisal tools were introduced to the tools in meetings which were held in both hospitals on all three shifts. The history of the Performance Evaluation Committee and the evolution of the appraisal tools was explained to the participants. The new tools were distributed and reviewed, and feedback was solicited. The procedure for the pilot study of the tools was explained, and the policies and procedures for the appraisal system were reviewed.

Following the educational activities, we started to use the appraisal tools. Evaluators were instructed to evaluate the registered nurses in their area of responsibility following these steps: 1) evaluator completes an evaluation; 2) evaluatee completes a self-evaluation; 3) evaluatee and evaluator discuss the two evaluations; 4) evaluatee and evaluator together complete one final copy of the evaluation; 5) evaluatee and evaluator together complete a copy of the goal-setting form; and 6) evaluator forwards the completed forms to the Department Head.

At the end of 45 days, the appraisal tools were collected for scoring. Arrangements had been made with a faculty member of the University of Texas School of Public Health for the use of their computer in scoring the tools and in doing some comparative statistics on the score data. Scores were calculated by adding all the individual item scores for the group of

Classification:
Staff Nurse (RN)

	1	2	3	4	5	Not Applicable	No Knowledge	SCORE
I. Nursing Knowledge A. Clinical Competency 1. *Assessment:* Assesses actual or potential patient problems a. Makes accurate multiple systems assessments of patients 1) Nurse's notes and verbal reports point out present physical and emotional condition of the patient.								
2) Utilizes *physical assessment skills* with patients to determine appropriate nursing interventions as evidenced by written and verbal communication regarding patient.								
b. Recognizes and records signs and symptoms of disease process as demonstrated in nurse's notes, verbal reports, etc.								
c. Reports significant physiologic and psychosocial changes to the appropriate person (as applicable per unit)								
d. Acts as a resource person for coworkers and student nurses regarding patient diagnosis and treatment, by sharing ideas and knowledge at activities such as patient assessment conferences, during nursing and medical rounds and during shift report, etc.								
2. *Planning:* Provides options for solutions to actual or potential patient problems. a. Acts as a resource person for coworkers and student nurses regarding appropriate nursing intervention for individual patient needs, by sharing ideas and knowledge at patient assessment conferences, during nursing and medical rounds, during shift report, etc.								

FIGURE 51-2

Sample of performance appraisal tool for staff nurses (partial tool).

IDENTIFICATION INFORMATION

NURSE	100000
EVALUATOR	200000
HOSPITAL	1
UNIT	Obstetrics
SHIFT	Day
TENURE	121 Months
DATE OF EVALUATION	April 1, 1986

PERFORMANCE INFORMATION

ITEMS	RAW SCORE	NUMBER OF ITEMS	ADJUSTED SCORE
NURSING KNOWLEDGE VSN1-VSN58	169	40	4.225
PROFESSIONAL BEHAVIOR VSN59-VSN86	80	19	4.211
TEACHING VSN87-VSN96	38	9	4.222
MANAGEMENT VSN97-VSN126	114	28	4.071
STAFF NURSE VSN1-VSN126	401	96	4.177

STANDARD SCORE = .411

FIGURE 51-3

Nursing performance reports for staff registered nurses.

items to obtain the "raw score." The raw score was then divided by the number of items in the group on which a score of from 1 to 5 was marked. The resulting figure was reported as the "adjusted score." This scoring method allowed items which had been marked as "Not Applicable" or "No Knowledge," or items which had not been marked, to be left out of the scoring. An example of the individual score report is displayed in Figure 51-3. The "standard score" as reported at the bottom of the individual score report was calculated by computing the mean and standard deviation for all the nurses evaluated with this appraisal form and comparing the individual's final adjusted score with this mean and standard deviation. The resulting standard score is the number of standard deviations the individual's score is above or below the mean for their group.

The final adjusted scores for the nurses in the study population were analyzed by units, unit groups, shift, self versus other as evaluator, hospital, and evaluator using the condescriptive and analysis of variance procedures in Statistical Package for the Social Sciences (SPSS). An evaluator report was generated for each nurse who participated in the study by evaluating at least one other nurse. This report compared the individual's statistics with those for all other evaluators using the same form. These reports were distributed and the evaluators were asked to review their own scoring statistics for indications of harshness, leniency, excessive use of "Not Applicable," "No Knowledge," or blank responses.

Following the pilot study, the tools were revised through further subcommittee work. These subcommittees generally were made up of the original members, although in some cases new members were added. The committee members were asked to consider form revisions based on the available statistical data from the pilot study. It was assumed that items receiving a high percentage of "Not Applicable" or "No Knowledge" ratings were either not relevant to the job description of the classification, not able to be monitored by the evaluator, or not stated clearly enough to allow use of the item.

During this meeting, items that received a high percentage of the ratings in the "Not Applicable" or "No Knowledge" category were considered one at a time. Items were either revised, deleted or left unchanged, according to the consensus of the subcommittee. Final drafts were prepared from these revisions. Subcommittee members also were invited to provide feedback on system policies and procedures. The climate of the subcommittees was relaxed and effective responses to the system were encouraged.

RECOMMENDATIONS FOR IMPLEMENTATION

The person responsible for the planning, implementing, evaluating and monitoring of the system should be from the group for which the system is designed. The committees should represent a broad slice of the target group, with active participation from members at all levels in the organization. Depending on the size of the target population, the individual responsible for the overall project should be released from other organizational responsibilities. Due to the amount of time, effort and money expended in the development of such a system, the potentially negative aspects of such a system must be examined on the front end of the project and weighed carefully against the positive outcomes.

Performance appraisal provides a method for recognition of exceptional performance and distribution of rewards based on merit. A criterion referenced tool is one way to provide for planning for professional growth that is directly related to the job description. Training of both the *evaluator* and the *evaluatee* is essential to successful implementation of any such system. Computer services are indispensible in obtaining a comprehensive analysis of scores if the pool of data is large. Probably most important is the participation of employees at all levels of the organization in the development of the tool and system.

REFERENCES

1. Lloyd, William F., "Performance Appraisal: A Short-sighted Approach for Installing a Workable Program," *Personnel Journal,* September 1977, p. 446.
2. Yura, Helen and Mary Walsh, "Guidelines for Evaluation: Who, What, Where, When, How," *Supervisor Nurse,* February 1972, p. 33.
3. del Bueno, Dorothy, "Implementing a Performance Evaluation System," *Supervisor Nurse,* February 1979, p. 48.
4. *Accreditation Manual for Hospitals* — AMH '87 Joint Commission on Accreditation of Hospitals, Chicago, Illinois, 1987, p. 142.

CHAPTER **52**

Nurse Performance
Strengths and weaknesses

Joanne Comi McCloskey, RN, PhD, FAAN
Bruce McCain, PhD

Fueled by the continuing debate concerning entry into practice and the growing concerns for cost effective use of resources, nursing has become increasingly concerned with defining and measuring the performance of its practitioners. Few studies have been done that measure the performance of individual practicing nurses, and fewer yet that point out the specific areas of strengths and weaknesses. This article presents a comparison of results of performance skill rankings obtained from two studies in which individual nurse performance was measured using the same instrument.

REVIEW OF THE LITERATURE

Recent interest in nursing performance has resulted in the formation of several national groups concerned with defining competencies for different types of nurses. For example, the National Commission on Nursing Implementation Project (NCNIP) is an ongoing 3-year project funded by the W. K. Kellogg Foundation to coordinate implementation of the recommendations of the National Commission on Nursing. The first work group identified the characteristics of professional and technical nurses of the future (DeBack, 1987).

Reprinted from *Nursing Research,* Vol. 37, No. 5, with permission of The American Journal of Nursing Company © 1988.

This project and five others concerned with nursing competence were reviewed in the 1987 July-August issue of the *Journal of Professional Nursing.* The work of these groups is helpful, but they have not documented the actual performance of nurses. The typical methodology used was a consensus of a group of identified leaders. Only one of these projects has used a measurement approach. Under a commission from the National Council of State Boards of Nursing, the American College Testing Program (ACT) conducted a large national study to examine the content validity of the registered nurse licensure test plan in June 1984 (Kane, Kingsbury, Colton, & Estes, 1986; Yocum, 1987). Several groups of nurses were asked how often newly licensed RNs performed 222 activities. In general, although all types of graduates were performing the same activities, the data were not sensitive to differences in how well the activities were performed.

The debate over entry into practice has fostered some performance research concerned with the effectiveness of a nursing education. Reviews of this research are reported elsewhere (Dennis & Janken, 1979; McCloskey, 1981). In addition, Schwirian (1978b) and associates did a critical review of all research conducted during the period 1965-1975 related to the identification and use of predictors of nursing success. Of the 398 studies reviewed, only 25 were concerned with on-the-job performance. One feature of previous studies is that groups of nurses have been compared on their overall performance rather than comparing individual nurses' performance of some skills with their performance of other skills. A second feature is that the researchers have generally assessed people's general impressions or biases about the performance of different groups of nurses rather than measuring actual performance of individual nurses.

One way to measure individual performance is to compare ratings by different persons. Comparisons of self-rated performance with head nurse ratings has been done in a number of studies (McCloskey, 1983a, 1983b; Nelson, 1978; Schwirian, 1978a, 1979; Welches, Dixon, & Stanford, 1974). Most of these found a significant, though not high, correlation between self and supervisor rating. Two more recent studies on the performance of the new graduate (Stull & Katz, 1986; Williams & Scott-Warner, 1985) compared the expectations held by faculty members with those held by nursing service personnel. In one of the few studies to compare skill type, Stull and Katz found that both educators and service agency administrators expected the baccalaureate nurse to be most proficient at interpersonal relationship and planning evaluation skills and less proficient at leadership and critical care skills. Results of both studies indicated that those in service and education held similar expectations and that neither group was satisfied with the actual performance of new graduates.

To provide more direction for administrators and educators who need to know where to put efforts and resources to improve performance, studies are needed that measure actual performance of practicing nurses and analyze performance strengths and weaknesses. The purpose of this investigation was to address the following research question: What are the specific behaviors that nurses are best at and what are those for which more preparation is needed?

METHOD

Four sets of performance data from two previous studies in which self and head nurse performance ratings were measured with the same instrument were extracted and rank ordered individually. They were then compared to determine the specific skills nurses performed best and worst. Both studies used the Schwirian (1978a, 1979) Six-Dimension Scale of Nursing Performance to measure performance. Both studies are briefly explained here as they are presented in detail elsewhere.

Description of the Studies: McCloskey and McCain (1984, 1987) (referred to in this paper as the 1987 study) tested a model of commitment and determined how several variables affected performance, turnover, and absenteeism. All newly employed nurses at a large university midwestern hospital over a 16-month period were followed for 1 year after they began work. The initial sample of 320 nurses included 22% associate degree nurses, 16% diploma nurses, 59% baccalaureate nurses, and 3% master's degree nurses. Ninety-five percent of the sample were female, 96% were white. The mean age was 27 years, with 59% between 20 and 25 years old. The nurses averaged 3 years of experience as a registered nurse and 5 years in health care. The performance data from this longitudinal study consisted of 142 self-ratings obtained at the end of 1 year of employment and 193 head nurse ratings obtained at the end of 1 year of employment for the same staff nurses or when the nurse left during the first year of work.

In an earlier study, McCloskey (1983a, 1983b) (referred to in this paper as the 1983 study) studied whether nurses with different levels of educational preparation differed in job effectiveness. The sample consisted of all nurses located on 52 units in 12 randomly selected hospitals in the Chicago area. The sample of 299 nurses included 18% practical nurses, 21% associate degree nurses, 45% diploma nurses, and 16% baccalaureate nurses. Ninety-eight percent of the sample were female, 76% white, and 40% were aged 26-35 with another 34% aged 36-55. The nurses averaged 8 years of experience in nursing; 5% of the sample had 1 year or less of experience. The performance data for this cross-sectional study were self-ratings of the 299 nurses and head nurse ratings for 106 of the same nurses.

Instrument: The Six Dimension (6-D) Scale of Nursing Performance (Schwirian, 1978a, 1979) consists of 52 items grouped into six subscales: Leadership, Critical Care, Teaching/Collaboration,

Planning/Evaluation, Interpersonal Relations/Communications, and Professional Development. The 6-D Scale is appropriate for use in a variety of settings. It consists of items that tap observable nurse behaviors which apply to both recent graduates and experienced nurses.

Schwirian reported alpha reliability coefficients from .84 to .98 for the subscales; alpha reliability coefficients for the 1987 study data ranged from .79 to .95. For the 1983 study, test-retest reliability coefficients were .77 (self-rating) and .97 (head nurse rating) overall with coefficients for the subscales ranging from .75 to .98. Interrater reliability, determined in the 1983 study by comparing the ratings of 10 head nurses with their assistant head nurses, was .89 for the total scale and ranged from .72 to .94 for the six subscales.

Content and construct validity for the 6-D Scale were determined by Schwirian using typical scale development procedures. An initial pool of 76 items was reduced to 52 after factor analysis. Nursing graduates who had been identified by nursing school faculty as having the most promise for successful nursing performance scored higher than other graduates. In the 1983 study construct validity was further validated by distinguishing groups classified on another scale as high, moderate, and low performers. Finally, in the 1987 study, a factor analysis provided support for the scale's conceptual dimensions, although leadership and professional development skills tended to load with the other factors.

For both studies reported here, each item was rated on a scale of 1, *not performed very well,* to 4, *performed very well.* For each behavior the nurse also had the option of indicating that this skill was not performed at all (not a part of the job). Scoring of the scale for both data sets was identical: mean scores for each item, subscale, and the overall scale were determined. Behaviors that were not performed were not included in the mean scores, thereby allowing comparison of all types of nurses on the work that they did.

Data Analysis: This data analysis compared the rankings of skills done by four groups: in 1987, rankings done by 142 staff nurses and 193 head nurses and, in 1983, rankings done by 299 staff nurses and

106 head nurses. For each of the head nurse and self-ratings in both studies the rank ordering of items was determined according to mean ratings. Using these four lists of item rankings, Spearman rank correlations were calculated comparing (a) the self 1983 ranking with the head nurse 1983 ranking and the self 1987 ranking with the head nurse 1987 ranking, (b) the head nurse rankings in the 1983 and 1987 studies, and (c) the staff nurse rankings in the 1983 and 1987 studies. The 10 items ranked by staff nurses in 1987 as those they performed best were compared with (a) rankings by head nurses and (b) staff and head nurse rankings for these items in 1983. The same comparisons were made for the 10 items the staff nurses in 1987 rated as those they performed poorest. Finally, subscale rankings for both studies were compared, including an analysis by educational level, experience, and type of unit on which the nurses worked.

RESULTS

Comparison of Self and Head Nurse Rankings: Spearman rank correlation coefficients calculated between the self and head nurse measures of performance were: $r = .823$ for 1983 data and $r = .787$ for 1987 data. Standard deviations for staff nurse item means were somewhat smaller (e.g., see 1987 range of .431-.726 in Table 52-1) than those of the head nurses (1987 range of .777-.887, see Table 52-1), indicating more agreement among staff nurses on the overall ranking. Standard deviations were smaller on both lists for skills rated highest compared with skills rated lowest indicating more agreement on the skills rated highest (see Tables 52-1 and 52-2).

Although head nurses generally gave lower ratings, their rankings of the skills performed best and worst by the staff nurses agreed, for the most part, with the staff nurses' own rankings. Skills identified as professional development were at the top of both lists whereas teaching/collaboration skills were concentrated at the bottom of both lists.

Both staff and head nurses said that the same two skills were performed best: accept responsibility for own action and maintain high standards of self-performance (see 1987 data in Table 52-1). Both staff and head nurses also agreed on the three skills

TABLE 52-1
Self and head nurse ratings on Schwirian scale compared for two studies: Top 10 items

| BEHAVIOR | SUB-SCALE[a] | MCCLOSKEY & MCCAIN, 1987 | | | | | | MCCLOSKEY, 1983 | | | | | |
| | | SELF | | | HEAD NURSE | | | SELF | | | HEAD NURSE | | |
		RANK	M	SD	RANK	M	SD	RANK	M	SD	RANK	M	SD
Accept responsibility for own actions	PD	1.0	3.76	.431	1.0	3.33	.777	1.0	3.73	.522	2.0	3.18	.943
Maintain high standards of self-performance	PD	2.5	3.52	.515	2.0	3.24	.824	2.0	3.64	.547	3.0	3.09	.893
Seek assistance when necessary	IPR	2.5	3.52	.603	12.0	3.05	.825	3.0	3.59	.591	1.0	3.25	.969
Communicate a feeling of acceptance of each patient and a concern for the patient's welfare	IPR	4.0	3.43	.676	8.0	3.08	.858	11.0	3.36	.675	11.5	2.98	.915
Display a generally positive attitude	PD	5.0	3.39	.556	3.0	3.18	.866	8.0	3.41	.615	13.5	2.96	.944
Assume new responsibilities within the limits of capabilities	PD	6.0	3.35	.674	6.0	3.11	.884	5.0	3.49	.653	13.5	2.96	.965
Perform technical procedures (e.g., oral suctioning, tracheotomy care, intravenous therapy, catheter care, dressing changes)	CC	7.0	3.32	.747	7.0	3.09	.796	6.0	3.45	.751	8.0	3.03	.957
Explain nursing procedures to a patient prior to performing them	IPR	8.0	3.30	.661	17.0	2.93	.770	4.0	3.51	.626	9.5	3.02	.870
Identify and include immediate patient needs in the plan of nursing care	PE	9.0	3.26	.627	22.5	2.85	.870	23.5	3.14	.721	24.0	2.77	1.031
Verbally communicate facts, ideas, and feelings to other health team members	IPR	10.0	3.25	.726	20.0	2.86	.887	14.0	3.24	.744	11.5	2.98	.951

[a]Key: PD = Professional Development, IPR = Interpersonal Relations/Communications; CC = Critical Care, PE = Planning/Evaluation.

TABLE 52-2
Self and head nurse ratings on Schwirian scale compared for two studies: Bottom 10 items

| BEHAVIOR | SUB-SCALE[a] | MCCLOSKEY & MCCAIN, 1987 | | | | | | MCCLOSKEY, 1983 | | | | | |
| | | SELF | | | HEAD NURSE | | | SELF | | | HEAD NURSE | | |
		RANK	M	SD	RANK	M	SD	RANK	M	SD	RANK	M	SD
Identify and use community resources in developing a plan of care for a patient and his family	TC	52.0	2.29	.830	50.0	2.39	.910	52.0	2.08	.948	50.0	2.17	1.028
Communicate facts, ideas, and professional opinions in writing to patients and their families	TC	51.0	2.31	.839	51.0	2.25	1.007	51.0	2.21	1.131	51.0	2.12	1.234
Develop innovative methods and materials for teaching patients	TC	50.0	2.36	.884	52.0	2.18	.975	50.0	2.46	.917	52.0	1.88	1.195
Identify and use resources within your health care agency in developing a plan of care for a patient and his family	TC	49.0	2.61	.806	45.0	2.52	.832	48.0	2.57	.887	49.0	2.23	1.141
Plan for the integration of patient needs with family needs	TC	48.0	2.71	.777	43.0	2.54	.863	49.0	2.54	.851	45.0	2.35	1.046
Identify and include in nursing care plans anticipated changes in patient's condition	PE	47.0	2.76	.769	41.5	2.58	.897	45.0	2.81	.834	41.5	2.40	1.019
Use teaching aids and resource materials in teaching patients and their families	TC	46.0	2.77	.759	41.5	2.58	.901	46.0	2.80	.886	46.0	2.33	1.115
Guide other health team members in planning for nursing care	L	45.0	2.78	.718	49.0	2.41	.896	43.0	2.88	.829	41.5	2.40	1.137
Promote the use of interdisciplinary persons	TC	44.0	2.80	.783	48.0	2.48	.874	47.0	2.71	.844	47.0	2.31	1.048
Use mechanical devices (e.g., suction machine, Gomco, cardiac monitor, respirator)	CC	43.0	2.81	1.117	14.0	2.99	.829	32.0	3.03	1.033	7.0	3.04	.909

[a]Key: TC = Teaching/Collaboration, PE = Planning/Evaluation, L = Leadership, CC = Critical Care.

performed worst: develop innovative methods and materials for teaching patients; communicate facts, ideas, and professional opinions in writing to patients and their families; and identify and use community resources in developing a plan of care for a patient and the family (see 1987 data in Table 52-2).

The Spearman rank correlation procedure compared *ranks* of individual item means. To compare means of subscale self-ratings with means of subscale head nurse ratings, Pearson correlation coefficients were calculated. The head nurse ratings for each of the subscales, except Leadership, were significantly correlated, $p < .05$, with the staff nurse self-ratings on the same subscales. However, the correlations were modest with the highest being $r = .24$ for critical care. Thus, although head nurses did not necessarily agree with individual staff nurses on how well they performed a particular skill or a set of skills (most particularly, they disagreed on the performance of leadership skills), the two did agree on the ranking of skills. That is, there was strong agreement on which skills and which set of skills were performed best and worst by staff nurses.

Comparison of the Two Studies: Spearman rank correlations were calculated comparing the head nurse rankings in 1987 with those in 1983 and the staff nurse rankings in 1987 with those in 1983. The correlation coefficient between head nurse rankings obtained in the two studies was $r = .896$; between staff nurse rankings, $r = .889$. Thus, the two samples of staff and head nurses ranked the various skills that nurses perform in similar orders. The 10 top-performed items identified by staff nurses in the 1987 study are compared with the head nurse ratings and with the ratings from the 1983 study in Table 52-1. Table 52-2 shows the comparisons for the 10 items ranked as those performed poorest.

The top three best-performed items as rated by staff nurses in the 1987 study were also rated as the top three items by both staff and head nurses in the 1983 study. All four groups (staff and head nurses in 1983 and 1987) rated three items on the list as being in the top 10, and at least three groups rated four more items in the top 10.

All four groups rated virtually 9 out of 10 items (bottom 10 are items ranked 43-52; 41.5 is close to 43) in the bottom 10 (Table 52-2). The only disagreement was with the item "use mechanical devices: e.g., suction machine, Gomco, cardiac monitor, respirator." In both studies, staff nurses gave themselves poorer ratings in this area than the head nurses, although the higher standard deviations for the staff nurse ratings indicated that staff nurses had less agreement than head nurses on how well they performed this skill. Analysis by unit type indicated that critical care nurses performed this skill better than nurses from other types of units.

Comparison of Subscales by Educational Level, Experience, and Type of Unit: For both the 1983 and the 1987 studies, the skills identified by both staff and head nurses as those performed best were professional development skills; those that were performed worst were teaching/collaboration skills. Table 52-3 compares the rankings of the six subscales by staff nurses and head nurses for the 1987 data. Although there was strong agreement on the excellent performance of professional development and poor performance of teaching/collaboration skills, the two groups agreed less on skills in the other categories. To examine this further, skill performance rankings for the 1987 data were compared by the nurse's educational preparation, amount of job experience, and type of unit worked on. These analyses were done to determine whether the general findings of skills performed best and worst held up for all groups.

To determine whether the findings were true for all *educational groups,* the subscale rankings of diploma, associate degree, and baccalaureate nurses (master's degree nurses were insufficient in numbers to include as a group) were compared using the 1987 data. There were few differences. The largest difference was in the performance of critical care skills. Critical care was ranked third by diploma nurses, fourth by associate degree nurses, and fifth by baccalaureate degree nurses, but was ranked second or third by head nurses for all groups. Diploma nurses generally rated themselves higher and were rated higher by head nurses on performance of critical care skills. Because diploma nurses were older and

TABLE 52-3
Self and head nurse comparison for ranking of subscales: McCloskey & McCain 1987 data

RANKING	SCALE	SELF MEAN RATING ($N = 142$)	RANK	HEAD NURSE MEAN RATING ($N = 193$)	RANK	COMBINED RANK
Highest	Professional development	3.29	1	3.11	1	1
	Interpersonal relations/Communications	3.17	2	2.88	3	2.5
	Critical care	2.93	5	2.89	2	3.5
	Leadership	3.03	3	2.60	5	4
	Planning/Evaluation	3.02	4	2.71	4	4
Lowest	Teaching/Collaboration	2.73	6	2.54	6	6

had more experience, this finding may reflect experience more than educational preparation. Associate degree nurses generally rated themselves lower on teaching/collaboration and interpersonal relations/communications skills, and head nurses rated them lower on planning/evaluation skills and professional development skills.

To determine whether the general findings held up for nurses with different levels of *experience,* three groups were created: those in their first job as a registered nurse, those in their second job, and those whose current job was their third or more. Again, the rankings were similar to the previous findings. In all three groups, both staff and head nurses ranked professional development skills highest and teaching/collaboration skills lowest. Staff nurses in all three experience groups ranked interpersonal relations/communications the second highest; their head nurses ranked this either second or third. Planning/evaluation was generally ranked fourth by all three groups of staff nurses and their head nurses. For all experience groups, head nurses rated leadership skills lower than the nurses themselves rated them, but the head nurses rated staff nurses higher in critical care skills than the nurses rated themselves. Those in their second job were generally rated lower on leadership, teaching/collaboration, and planning/evaluation. Also, those with the most experience rated themselves

higher on leadership and interpersonal relations/communications whereas their head nurses rated them higher on critical care skills.

Type of unit was also examined for its effect on skill ranking. Nurses were categorized as working on one of six types of units: general medical, general surgical, intensive care, obstetrics/pediatrics, specialty medical (e.g., psychiatry, hemodialysis), and specialty surgical (e.g., orthopedics, neurosurgical). The findings for all units were essentially the same as those already reported. The only exception was that both staff and head nurses in the intensive care units ranked critical care skills in first place, equal with professional development skills.

To examine the possible bias of head nurse characteristics, three variables related to the head nurse — *age, educational level,* and *job tenure* — were correlated with their own ratings. The analyses revealed that head nurses with associate degrees gave significantly higher, $p < .05$, scores on teaching/collaboration than head nurses with baccalaureate or master's degrees. On the other performance subscales, there were no differences among head nurses with different educational preparation. As only 4% of the sample had head nurses with associate degrees, this does not have a large impact on the findings. Head nurse age and tenure were significantly correlated, $r = .391$, $p < .000$. Head nurses who had held their job longer gave higher scores on teaching/collaboration and lower scores on critical care, $p < .05$. Older head nurses gave somewhat higher scores than younger head nurses across the board in all categories.

DISCUSSION

The comparison of performance data from two studies indicates that nurses, irrespective of educational level or experience or unit type, share some of the same perceived strengths and weaknesses. Specifically, the findings suggest that nurse educators and in-service directors should seek to improve the teaching/collaboration, planning/evaluation, and leadership skills of their students and practicing nurses. Staff nurses perceived that they were better at leadership than their head nurses thought they were. This may indicate overconfidence on the part of staff nurses or it may indicate that head nurses undervalue the abilities of staff nurses in this area. On the other hand, most staff nurses ranked their performance in critical care skills rather low, whereas head nurses ranked them higher in this area. This may indicate that staff nurses lack confidence in their critical care skills. In particular, it appears that staff nurses lack confidence in the critical ability to work with mechanical devices. Publications by Kieffer (1984) and Sweeney and Regan (1982) indicated that students do not receive much instruction about cardiac monitors, resuscitation equipment, and respirators in basic nursing programs. The increasingly widespread use of such high technology equipment may necessitate more continuing education in this area.

The specific skills nurses perform well are used daily in the hospital routine. This routine includes the performance of technical procedures such as suctioning, intravenous therapy, and dressing changes. Staff nurses rated themselves highly on these technical skills and head nurses agreed. These technical procedures and the top-ranked professional development skills are also the backbone of nursing curricula. From the first day in the first nursing course, stress is placed on the importance of seeking assistance when necessary, of maintaining high standards and assuming responsibility for one's own action.

On the other hand, the bottom-ranked skills are neither the routine of the hospital nor the nursing school curriculum. Teaching/collaboration and planning/evaluation skills which involve the family, the community, and innovation are difficult skills to learn. Consequently, staff nurses may require additional education at the graduate level before they can achieve high levels of competence. It also may be that these skills were rated lower because they are not valued by the practice institution as much as skills in other areas. For example, does a nurse who plans and writes a good care plan, who routinely teaches the family and patient, who knows the community resources and makes needed referrals earn more salary or social recognition for these actions? More discussion needs to take place on the proper role of the educational and service agency regarding the learning of specific skills. As it stands now, it seems that both emphasize, for the most part, the learning of the same kind of skills.

Findings also indicate that more research needs to be done on the relationship of head nurse age and staff nurse performance. In both the 1987 and the 1983 studies, older head nurses who had more head nurse experience (and also less formal education) gave higher performance ratings. What exactly does this mean? A manager's perceived similarity to a subordinate is believed to increase performance ratings (Pulakos & Wexley, 1983), but the older head nurses in the 1987 study were not similar to the typical nurse in the sample, who tended to be under 25 years and a recent graduate of a baccalaureate program. Do older head nurses, in fact, know their job better and elicit better performance from their staff nurses or, with age, do their standards for evaluation become more tempered?

There are few other studies to which the findings of this study can be compared. Stull and Katz (1986), who studied perceptions rather than actual performance, reported that both educators and nurse executives *believe* that new baccalaureate nurses perform teaching/collaboration and planning/evaluation and interpersonal skills better than critical care and leadership skills. Our results show that baccalaureate nurses like other nurses, in fact, perform teaching/collaboration and planning/evaluation skills less well than critical care and leadership skills. These results agree with recent findings from the American Association of Critical-Care Nurses Demonstration Project in which the Schwirian 6-D Scale was also used. In that study 46 critical care nurses reported they performed teaching/collaboration and planning/evaluation skills less well than the other types of skills (Pamela Mitchell, MS, FAAN, personal communication, January 5, 1988).

In conclusion, the national effort to define competencies and the research to date have focused on comparing the performance of new graduates of different types of basic educational programs. In the future these efforts need to be expanded to include the nurse with a graduate degree, the experienced nurse, the role of the employment setting and supervisor in facilitating performance, and the study of excellence as well as competence.

REFERENCES

DeBack, V. (1987). The National Commission on Nursing Implementation Project: Report to the participants of nurses in agreement conference. *Journal of Professional Nursing, 3,* 226-229.

Dennis, L. D., & Janken, J. K. (1979). *The relationship between nursing education and performance: A critical review.* (DHEW Pub. No. HRA 79-38). Washington, DC: US Government Printing Office.

Kane, M., Kingsbury, C., Colton, D., & Estes, C. (1986). *A study of nursing practice and role delineation and job analysis of entry-level performance of registered nurses.* Chicago: National Council of State Boards of Nursing, Inc.

Kieffer, J. S. (1984). Selecting technical skills to teach for competency. *Journal of Nursing Education, 23,* 198-203.

McCloskey, J. C. (1981). The effects of nursing education on job effectiveness: An overview of the literature. *Research in Nursing and Health, 4,* 355-373.

McCloskey, J. C. (1983a). Nursing education and job effectiveness. *Nursing Research, 32,* 53-58.

McCloskey, J. C. (1983b). *Toward an educational model of nursing effectiveness.* Ann Arbor, MI: UMI Research Press.

McCloskey, J. C., & McCain, B. E. (1984). *Commitment, satisfaction, performance of hospital nurses.* (DHHS Publication No. NU 01050). Washington, DC: US Government Printing Office.

McCloskey, J. C., & McCain, B. E. (1987). Commitment, satisfaction, performance of newly employed hospital nurses. *Image: The Journal of Nursing Scholarship, 19,* 20-24.

Nelson, L. F. (1978). Competencies of nursing graduates in technical, communicative, and administrative skills. *Nursing Research 27,* 121-125.

Pulakos, E. D., & Wexley, K. N. (1983). The relationship among perceptual similarity, sex and performance ratings in manager-subordinate dyads. *Academy of Management Journal, 26,* 129-139.

Schwirian, P. M. (1978a). Evaluating the performance of nurses: A multidimensional approach,. *Nursing Research, 27,* 347-351.

Schwirian, P. M. (1978b). *Prediction of successful nursing performance,* Parts I and II. (DHEW Publication No. HRA 77-27). Washington, DC: US Government Printing Office.

Schwirian, P. M. (1978b). *Prediction of successful nursing performance,* Parts III and IV. (DHEW Publication No. HRA 79-15). Washington, DC: US Government Printing Office.

Sweeney, M. A., & Regan, P. A. (1982). Educators, employees, and new graduates define essential skills for baccalaureate graduates. *Journal of Nursing Administration, 12*(9), 36-42.

Stull, M. K., & Katz, B. M. (1986). Service and education: Similar perspectives of the performance of the new baccalaureate graduate. *Journal of Professional Nursing, 2,* 160-165.

Welches, L. J., Dixon, F. A., & Stanford, E. D. (1974). Typological prediction of staff nurse performance rating, *Nursing Research, 23,* 402-409.

Williams, E. M., & Scott-Warner, M. (Eds.) (1985). *The preparation and utilization of new nursing graduates.* Boulder, CO: Western Interstate Commission for Higher Education.

Yocum, C. J. (1987). Practice patterns of newly licensed registered nurses: Results of a job analysis study. *Journal of Professional Nursing, 3,* 199-206.

CHAPTER **53**

Implications for Nursing Administration of the Relationship of Technology and Structure to Quality of Care

Judith W. Alexander, RN, PhD
Alan D. Bauerschmidt, PhD

Theorists have proposed that the fit between the technology of an organization and its structure can be linked to organizational effectiveness.[1-5] The purpose of the study presented in this article was to investigate this proposition by examining the fit between technology and structure on nursing units and the effectiveness of these units as indicated by quality of nursing care delivered.

CONCEPTUAL FRAMEWORK

The concepts of technology, structure, and quality of nursing care as they relate to quality of care provided are presented in Figure 53-1.

Technology

Technology was defined as the acts employed by nursing personnel to change the status of an individual from hospitalized patient to discharged person. Using

Reprinted from *Nursing Administration Quarterly*, Vol. 11, No. 4, with permission of Aspen Publishers, Inc. © 1987.

Perrow's framework,[6] Overton, Schneck, and Hazlett reported that technology on nursing units had the dimensions of instability, variability, and uncertainty.[7]

Instability refers to the unpredictable fluctuations in patients and techniques as indicated by the number of patients susceptible to emergencies, the frequency of nursing observations required, and the amount of specialized technical monitoring needed. *Variability* represents differences among patients and is measured by the degree to which patients exhibit different problems that lead to the application of many nursing techniques. *Uncertainty* expresses the degree to which patients are not well understood. Uncertainty is made operational as the number of patients who have more than one diagnosis, who have complex nursing problems, and who need complex nursing techniques based on intuition and feedback from the patients.

The routine-nonroutine continuum has been used to describe technology.[8] Dimensions of technology vary independently, but organizations with lower instability, variability, and uncertainty are characterized as routine. Nonroutine organizations have greater instability, variability, and uncertainty. In this study,

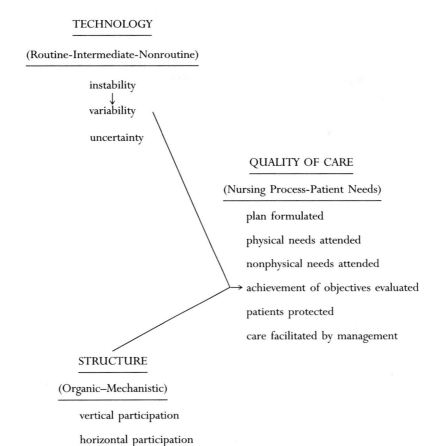

TECHNOLOGY

(Routine-Intermediate-Nonroutine)

instability
↓
variability

uncertainty

QUALITY OF CARE

(Nursing Process-Patient Needs)

plan formulated

physical needs attended

nonphysical needs attended

achievement of objectives evaluated

patients protected

care facilitated by management

STRUCTURE

(Organic–Mechanistic)

vertical participation

horizontal participation

formalization

FIGURE 53-1

Diagrammatic representation of conceptual relationship between technology and structure and the quality of care provided.

technology is considered nonroutine if a high score on the technology instrument is obtained, intermediate if a medium score is obtained, and routine if a low score is obtained.

Structure

Structure was defined as the allocation of work roles and administrative mechanisms to control and integrate work activities. The dimensions of organizational structure continue to be troublesome for re-searchers. Early work by Pugh et al. defined the five primary dimensions of organizational structure as specialization, standardization, formalization, centralization, and configuration.[9] Based on the research of Pugh et al., Alexander's study on nursing units indicated that the five dimensions of organizational structure are (1) unit size, (2) teaming/vertical differentiation, (3) job specialization, (4) ward centralization, and (5) task coordination.[10] The research reported here identifies three dimensions of structure that seem to be a simple combination of those mentioned above and are labeled *vertical participation, horizontal participation,* and *formalization.*

Vertical participation describes a situation in which superiors seek input from subordinates for decision making and subordinates consult with their superiors concerning job-related tasks. This dimension includes the ideas of configuration, centralization, and vertical differentiation from the Pugh et al. and Alexander studies. *Horizontal participation* refers to participation by the individual in decision making and task definition. This second dimension incorporates the ideas of specialization and task coordination. *Formalization* is the extent to which rules, procedures, and instructions exist, a definition consistent with that from Pugh et al. The dimension of unit size from the Alexander study was not included in this study.

The mechanistic-organic continuum has been used to describe structure.[11] Mechanistic structure is characterized by a low degree of participation, highly specific task descriptions, and highly formalized procedures. *Organic structure* describes a high degree of participation, low specification of tasks, and few procedures. In this study, structure is considered organic if a high score is obtained and mechanistic if a low score is obtained.

Quality of Nursing Care

Effectiveness on nursing units was defined by the quality of care delivered. Quality was determined by evaluating the nursing process and patient needs as described by Haussmann, Hegyvary, and Newman in 1976.[12] Nursing process is defined as a comprehensive set of nursing activities performed in the delivery of a patient's care and includes assessing the problems or needs of the patient, planning for care, implementing the plan of care, and evaluating and updating the plan of care. Assessing patient care needs involves the nurse's focusing on the needs or problems of patients and comprises six dimensions of quality nursing care: (1) formulation of the nursing care plan, (2) attention to physical needs, (3) attention to nonphysical needs, (4) evaluation of care, (5) protection of patients, and (6) administration of the delivery of care.

Integral to this study was the proposal that there is no most effective structure for all organizations.

Earlier research suggested that effective organizations have nonroutine technology and an organic structure, routine technology and a mechanistic structure, or intermediate technology matched with any structure.[13-16] Thus the propositions tested in this study were:
- Nursing units with nonroutine technology produce higher quality nursing care if the structure for delivery of care is organic.
- Nursing units with routine technlogy produce higher quality nursing care if the structure for the delivery of care is mechanistic.
- Nursing units with intermediate technology produce the same quality of care irrespective of the structure for the delivery of care.

Because both technology and structure are multidimensional, the propositions are tested for the match between the technological and structural dimensions.

METHOD

This exploratory, descriptive study used 34 nursing units in 3 general hospitals ranging in size from 150 to 450 beds. Complete data were obtained on 27 units.

Five personnel on each unit were selected randomly from a list of full-time nursing personnel who had worked on the unit for at least three months. The sample was structured to provide responses from registered nurses, licensed practical nurses, and other nursing personnel in proportion to their representation on the staff of the unit. Eighty-one percent of the total number selected participated in the study, for a total of 187 nursing personnel including the head nurse and 1 to 5 nursing personnel from each unit. The patients were randomly selected from those who met the criteria for length of minimum stay established for each unit (i.e., 1 hour for a labor and delivery unit and 24 hours for general units). Seven to 20 patients participated from each unit for a total of 340 patients. All participants signed an informed consent form.

Technology was measured using the 34-item, five-point, Likert-type scale published by Overton, Schneck, and Hazlett in 1977[17] and developed from the work of Perrow.[18] The results of the study described here are consistent with those of the

Overton group and of a repeat study published in 1981.[19] The reliability and validity of this instrument were established by Overton and her colleagues. Reliabilitycoefficients for the dimensions in this study were .86 for instability, .77 for variability, and .81 for uncertainty.

Structure was measured by a 21-item, five-point, Likert-type scale developed by Leifer and Huber and employed in 1977 to measure organicity of structure.[20] This instrument was developed from the empirical findings of Duncan[21] and of Burns and Stalker[22] and has not been subject to extensive testing for validity and reliability. In the present study, reliability was determined to be .74 for vertical participation, .63 for horizontal participation, and .60 for formalization.

Quality of care delivered on nursing units was measured using the Rush-Medicus Nursing Process Monitoring Methodology published in 1979.[23] Extensive testing of this instrument for reliability and validity was done by the developing group. In the current study, four RN observers collected data on the quality of care provided on the 27 nursing units by gathering information from patients' records, observing and interviewing patients and nursing personnel, observing the environments of units, making inferences, and observing unit management. Data collection took place on different days of the week and at different hours of the day. The units studied repre-

sented all major acute nursing areas except psychiatry and the operating room. In training, the pairs of observers reached interrater reliabilities of .88 and .92. Data collection followed the Rush group procedure except that the principal investigator was not a hospital employee. Because consent to approach patients after their random selection was obtained from the charge nurse and because patients gave written informed consent, a convenience sample resulted on some units.

Table 53-1 gives the types of units studied and the mean, range, and standard deviation of the quality scores for each unit. Quality scores ranged from 66 to 90 with a possible range of 0 to 100; the mean was 79.08, and the standard deviation was 5.48. Thus the quality of care was relatively high on these units.

RESULTS

Data were analyzed by calculating for the independent variables "fit" variables that were the absolute values of the differences between the technology and structure scores. This technique assumes that for each dimension of technology there is a "best" match with a dimension of structure in terms of organizational effectiveness. Thus the concept of fit combines two variables into a new variable that is the underlying proposition of this study that a proper match be

TABLE 53-1
Quality scores by type of unit

TYPE OF UNIT	N	RANGE	MEAN	STANDARD DEVIATION
Emergency	1		80.16	
Surgery*	8	66.16–83.50	74.64	11.36
Medical†	7	72.00–80.33	75.80	3.63
Pediatrics	2	70.50–77.66	74.08	5.15
Obstetrics	2	83.60–84.66	84.13	0.74
Labor and delivery	2	86.66–80.60	83.60	5.32
Intensive care	3	83.66–90.66	87.99	3.90
Nursery	2	87.66–88.00	87.83	0.24
Total	27	66.16–90.66	79.08	5.48

*Includes the gynecology unit
†Includes the medical-surgical unit

achieved. Additionally, the use of fit variables reduces the number of independent variables. A complete regression model would have resulted in 6 independent dimensions and the possibility of 9 two-way interaction variables for a total of 15 independent variables, rather than the 9 fit variables. A complete discussion of fit variables as used in the present study can be found in a study by Alexander and Randolph.[24]

To further reduce the number of independent variables, this study reports regression analysis using only the three most significant differences as independent variables. The result is a significant model that explains 52 percent of the variance in quality of care. Table 53-2 presents this equation and associated results.

A positive regression coefficient indicates that a large difference between values for technology and structure will lead to greater quality, whereas a negative coefficient indicates that a smaller difference is important in *not* reducing the quality of care. The data

were coded so that small differences between values for technology and structure matched nonroutine technology with organic structure or routine technology with mechanistic structure, while large differences matched nonroutine technology with mechanistic structure and routine technology with organic structure. Interpretation is complicated by the fact that both technology and structure have three dimensions, so that each fit variable represents one aspect of fit between technology and structure. Negative regression coefficients support the hypothesized direction of the match between technology and structure.

Significant regression coefficients occurred for the differences between the technological factor of variability and the structural factor of horizontal participation with $F = 8.40$ at $p = .009$ and between the technological factor of uncertainty and the structural factor of formalization with $F = 17.64$ at $p = .0003$. Figure 53-2 diagrams the resulting relationships between structural and technology

TABLE 53-2

Multiple regression results of significant technology-structure difference scores related to quality of care (n = 27)*

Model:
$$Q_1 = 77.72\dagger + 1.92 \left| I_i - VP_i \right| - 3.03\ddagger \left| V_i - HP_i \right| + 3.71\S \left| U_1 - F_i \right|$$
$$(1.09) \quad (1.37) \quad (1.04) \quad (0.88)$$

Source	Degrees of freedom	Sum of squares	Mean square	F	R^2
Model	3	337.49	112.49	8.28§	.52
Error	23	312.508	13.58		
Total	26	649.999			

ANOVA

Source	Degrees of freedom	Sum of squares	F
$\left| I_i - VP_i \right|$	1	26.64	1.96
$\left| V_i - HP_i \right|$	1	114.06	8.40‡
$\left| V_i - F_1 \right|$	1	239.62	17.64†

*Key: Q = quality, I = instability, VP = vertical participation, V = variability, HP = horizontal participation, U = uncertainty, F = formalization. Standard error of the estimates are given in the parentheses under the regression coefficients.
†*p* < .0001
‡*p* < .01
§*p* < .001

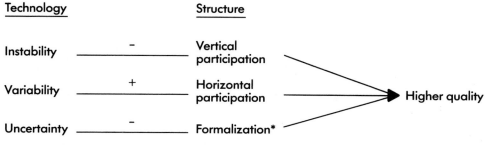

FIGURE 53-2

Proposed combinations of technological and structural dimensions that support delivery of quality care. *A high formalization score means few rules and procedures.

dimensions as they relate to quality of care and is illustrative of the following discussion.

Technological Instability/Vertical Participation

The positive regression coefficient for the difference between the technological dimension of instability and the structural dimension of vertical participation suggests that the larger that difference, the greater the quality of nursing care. This relationship suggests that as instability increases because more emergencies occur or more frequent nursing observations and more technical monitoring are required on a unit, the nursing superiors on that unit will seek less input from their subordinates for decision making and will require greater consultation from subordinates concerning job-related tasks. On the other hand, if technological instability is low, then vertical participation should be high to improve quality of care.

Technological Variability/Horizontal Participation

The negative regression coefficient for the difference between technological variability and horizontal participation suggests that the larger the difference between these two dimensions, the lower the quality of nursing care. To minimize a decrease in quality of care, high technological variability—indicated, for instance, by variation in the diagnoses of patients in the unit—should be matched with greater horizontal participation that calls for positive attitudes toward

the involvement of individuals in decision making and task definition. Conversely, little technological variability in the patients on the unit should require less horizontal participation in order to produce quality nursing care.

Technological Uncertainty/Structural Formalization

Finally, the match between technological uncertainty and structural formalization has a positive regression coefficient, which suggests that a larger difference between these two factors will produce higher quality nursing care. The implication is that units with greater uncertainty as indicated by more complex nursing problems require higher degrees of formalization to provide quality care; units with less uncertainty require lower degrees of formalization to produce quality nursing care.

The intercept for the model is also significant at the .05 level. The value of the intercept is 75.27, again suggesting that, as measured on a range from 0 to 100, the quality of care on the nursing units in this study was generally high.

DISCUSSION

Results of this study suggest that the fit between variability and horizontal participation and the fit between uncertainty and formalization are significant. But only one of these differences between the technological and structural dimensions supports the idea that nonroutine technology should be matched with organic structure (proposition 1) or that routine technology should be matched with mechanistic structure (proposition 2) to produce higher quality nursing care. This difference is between the technological dimension of variability and the structural dimension of horizontal participation. The differences between technological instability and structural vertical participation (though insignificant) and between technological uncertainty and structural formalization matched nonroutine technology with mechanistic structure or routine technology with organic structure to produce scores indicating higher quality. Consequently, propositions 1 and 2 are supported only by the difference between technological variability and structural horizontal participation.

The lack of support for propositions 1 and 2 could be due to a lack of variance on the technological dimension that would put all the nursing units in an intermediate technology category and would support proposition 3 that the same quality of care is produced irrespective of the structure for delivery of care when intermediate technology is used. In other words, if all the units were characterized by intermediate technology, then no significant finding would emerge concerning structure. However, the lack of variance on the technology variable seems unlikely given the replication of the results of the Overton study.[25] The suggestion is that perhaps technology and structure interact differently on nursing units than has been hypothesized in the literature based on research in other settings.

In the 1981 National Commission on Nursing Report, nursing leaders stated, "The traditional image (of Nursing) included a bureaucratic, hierarchical governance structure that regards nurses as low level employees rather than professional practitioners who along with physicians are central to the provision of unique health care services to patients."[26] Given this view of nursing units, it is likely to suppose that the interrelationships between technology and structure suggested by this study do exist.

The relationship found in this study between uncertainty and formalization is also supported by the research of Argote[27] and of Sheridan, Vredenbrugh, and Abelson.[28] Argote, in a study of 30 emergency rooms, found that programmed activities (akin to formalization) have a positive, although nonsignificant, correlation with quality of nursing care in contexts of both high and low uncertainty. Sheridan et al. studied 701 nursing employees in 4 acute care hospitals and found that uncertain nursing technology had an inverse effect on nursing performance and created a need for stronger direction from head nurses.

Thus, interpretation of these results suggests that nursing units that have high technological instability and require frequent nursing observations and technical monitoring should be structured to allow low vertical participation, with superiors infrequently consulting with their subordinates in decision making. Nursing units with greater technological variability, characterized by varying patient diagnoses and problems, should develop a structure that allows more horizontal participation as reflected in positive attitudes toward the involvement of personnel in decision making and task definition. Finally, nursing units with more technological uncertainty as indicated by complex nursing problems should employ more rules and regulations to produce higher quality nursing care.

To summarize, these findings suggest that technology and structure in nursing units are constructs that consist of three dimensions whose interrelationships have implications for nursing administration. The findings support the notion that one method of organization on nursing units is not right for all nursing units. Which organizational structure is appropriate depends on the degree of technology that characterizes a particular nursing unit.

Nursing managers can affect structure by their approaches to staffing units, coordinating with other departments, and planning for the delivery of nursing care. If, on the other hand, structural characteristics are fixed because of staffing shortages, physician request, or limitations of the physical plant, then consideration should be given to changing the technological characteristics of the patient population.

Two examples may be helpful and are illustrated in Figure 53-3. In comparison with other units, orthopedics and urology units (box 2) are lowest in

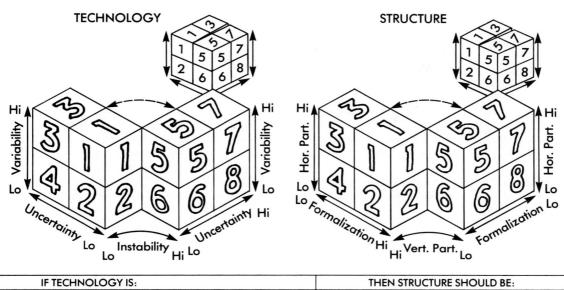

FIGURE 53-3

Summary of possible matches among dimensions of technology and structure that support delivery of quality care.

instability and uncertainty and are low in variability. These units would deliver higher quality care if they were structured to have high vertical participation, a high degree of formalization, and low horizontal participation. On the other hand, labor and delivery or cardiac intensive care units (box 8) are high in instability, intermediate in uncertainty, and low in variability, and should be structured to include low vertical participation, moderate degrees of formalization, and low horizontal participation.

This technique for deciding on an appropriate match between the technological and structural dimensions of nursing units is quite complicated. Unfortunately, this study was unable to derive a simpler method by using the nursing assignment patterns of primary, team, and functional nursing. However, it is hoped that the results presented here will give nursing administrators guidelines for making organizational changes that could lead to improved quality of patient care.

The usual disclaimers associated with research findings must also be made for this study, which should be repeated with a larger sample in different geographic locations before generalizations can be comfortably made. Replication of the instrument measuring structure, in particular, is needed because of the low reliability scores and lack of consistency with the original Leifer and Huber instrument.[29] An experimental design that would allow the researcher to make some of the manipulations suggested in the examples would indeed add credence to the ideas proposed here from the results of this study.

REFERENCES

1. Woodward, J. *Industrial Organizations: Theory and Practice.* New York: McGraw-Hill, 1965.
2. Perrow, C. "A Framework for the Comparative Analysis of Organizations." *American Sociological Review* 32, no. 2 (1967):194-208.
3. Harvey, E. "Technology and the Structure of Organizations." *American Sociological Review* 33 (1968):247-59.
4. Child, J. "Organizational Structure, Environment, and Performance: The Role of Strategic Choice." *Sociology* 6 no. 1 (1972):1-22.
5. Khandwalla, P.N. "Viable and Effective Organizational Designs of Firms." *Academy of Management Journal* 16 (1973):481-95.
6. Perrow, "A Framework for the Comparative Analysis of Organizations."
7. Overton, P., Schneck, R., and Hazlett, C.B. "An Empirical Study of Technology of Nursing Units." *Administrative Science Quarterly* 22, no. 2 (1977):203-19.
8. Perrow, "A Framework for the Comparative Analysis of Organizations."
9. Pugh, D.S., et al. "Dimensions of Organizational Structure." *Administrative Science Quarterly* 13, no. 2 (1968): 65-105.
10. Alexander, J.A. "The Organizational Foundations of Nursing Roles: An Empirical Assessment." *Journal of Social Science and Medicine* 18 (1984):1045-52.
11. Burns, T., and Stalker, G.M. *The Management of Innovation.* London: Tavistock Publications, 1961.
12. Haussmann, R.K., Hegyvary, S.T., and Newman, J. *Monitoring Quality of Nursing Care: Part 2. Assignment and Study of Correlates,* U.S. Department of Health, Education, and Welfare Pub. No. (HRA) 76-7. HEW, 1976.
13. Harvey, "Technology and the Structure of Organizations."
14. Child, "Organizational Structure, Environment, and Performance."
15. Leavitt, J.H. "Applied Organizational Change in Industry: Structural, Technological, and Humanistic Approaches." In *Handbook of Organizations,* edited by J.C. March. Chicago: Rand McNally College Publishing, 1965, pp. 1144-70.
16. Thompson, J.D. *Organizations in Action.* New York: McGraw-Hill, 1967.
17. Overton, Schneck, and Hazlett, "An Empirical Study."
18. Perrow, "A Framework for the Comparative Analysis of Organizations."
19. Leath, P., and Schneck, R. "Nursing Subunits Technology: A Replication." *Administrative Science Quarterly* 26 no. 2 (1981):225-36.
20. Leifer, R., and Huber, G.P. "Relations among Perceived Environmental Uncertainty, Organizational Structure, and Boundary Spanning Behavior." *Administrative Science Quarterly* 22, no. 2 (1977):235-47.
21. Duncan, R.G. *Multiple Decision Making Structures in Adapting to Environmental Uncertainty: The Impact of Organizational Effectiveness.* Working paper, Northwestern University Graduate School of Management, Paper No. 54-71, 1971.
22. Burns and Stalker, *The Management of Innovation.*
23. Hegyvary, S.T., et al. *User's Manual for Rush-Medicus Nursing Process Monitoring Methodology (Addendum to Monitoring Quality of Nursing Care: Part 4).* National Technical Information Service Pub. No. HRP 0900638. Springfield, Va.: NTIS, 1979.
24. Alexander, J.W., and Randolph, W.A. "The Fit between Technology and Structure as a Predictor of Performance in Nursing Subunits." *Academy of Management Journal* 28 (1985):844-59.
25. Overton, Schneck, and Hazlett, "An Empirical Study."
26. National Commission on Nursing. *Summary of Public Hearings.* Chicago: Hospital Education and Research Trust, 1981, pp. 10-11.
27. Argote, L. "Input Uncertainty and Organizational Coordination in Hospital Emergency Units." *Administrative Science Quarterly* 27 no. 3 (1982):420-34.
28. Sheridan, J.E., Vredenbrugh, D.J., and Abelson, M.A. "Contextual Model of Leadership Influence in Hospital Units." *Academy of Management Journal* 27, no. 1 (1984):57-78.
29. Leifer and Huber, "Relations among Perceived Environmental Uncertainty, Organizational Structure, and Boundary Spanning Behavior."

CHAPTER **54**

Clinical Nursing Practices and Patient Outcomes: Evaluation, Evolution, and Revolution
Legitimizing radical change to maximize nurses' time for quality care

Margaret D. Sovie, RN, PhD, FAAN

The current nursing shortage may be the best thing yet to confront the profession of nursing and the institutions that are dependent on nurses to manage as well as provide the required health care to patients and families. Some describe it as a crisis; and as Dr. John Romano (1964) reminded us, crisis when written in Chinese is done so in two characters: one meaning danger; and the other, opportunity. Nurses have to seize this opportunity and revolutionize selected structures and processes in nursing and the health-care delivery systems as well as assist consumers of nursing services to modify some of their traditional expectations of nursing services. "Revolutionize" means to bring about a radical change or to alter extensively or drastically as contrasted with "evolutionary" which means gradually changing or progressing.

Today's problems are too severe and the demands too extreme to depend on evolution or gradual change. The continuous turbulence on the

Reprinted from *Nursing Economics,* Vol. 7, No. 2, with permission of Anthony J. Jannetti, Inc. © 1988.

health-care scene, particularly in hospitals, has produced a prolonged tension with pressures that demand revolutionary change. These same tensions and pressures provide a readiness and receptiveness to change, new approaches, and revisions in structures and processes that will maximize the time nurses have to provide care for patients and families. The focus is certain—high quality patient/family care. To achieve and maintain it requires change.

Everyone in nursing must be empowered to help create new and better ways of providing nursing care to patients and families. We must critically examine what needs to be done, what difference it makes in patient outcomes, and the best way to do it to produce the desired results. There should be nothing that escapes scrutiny, examination, and evaluation. There should be no sacred cows. We should discard what does not work or what does not produce the desired results and design and implement new approaches that do. Nurse administrators and managers need to legitimize the slaughtering of sacred cows and facilitate the radical changes as well as support the continuous evolutionary changes that are required to maximize nurses' time for quality care. The doors to change need to be opened wide. Practicing nurses can lead the way in a partnership for change — a partnership with patients, physicians, other health-care providers, and the administrators, regulators and payers of the health-care organizations in which all work side by side to accomplish the mission of high quality, individualized care.

REEVALUATING NURSING CARE PLANS

If practicing nurses are to lead the way, we should begin by looking at what we as nurses do and what difference it makes in patient outcomes. I suggest that the first targets are the sacred cows called the nursing care plan and the nursing problem-oriented SOAP notes. The revolution needs to start here. More time is devoted to trying to get nurses to complete care plans and nursing problem lists as currently structured than to any other aspects of nursing. And when nurses are so little motivated to comply with JCAHO regulations as well as nursing's own standards of practice, it should tell us something is wrong. Valuable time is devoted to nursing a system's structural component and policing that component — time that could better be devoted to nursing the patient and family. Furthermore, we have little, if any, evidence that patient outcomes are affected positively or negatively when a completed nursing care plan is in the patient record and "supposedly" guiding the nursing care interventions of all nurses.

Ferguson, Hildman, and Nichols (1987) examined the effects of three types of nursing care planning systems on selected patient outcomes: length of stay; number of readmissions within 30 days; patient satisfaction; number of nosocomial infections; incident reports related to patient safety; medication or treatment errors by nurses; number of analgesics/narcotics administered to patients; and acuity level upon discharge. The three types of nursing care planning systems studied were: (a) a printed Kardex with physicians' orders and menu of nursing tasks; (b) standardized nursing care plans with provision for individualizing same on the chart; and (c) a Kardex that was a permanent part of the chart with inclusion of nursing diagnoses and nursing orders as well as

physician dependent functions. Data were collected over a 7-month period. Essentially, no significant differences were found on any of the outcome variables. In other words, the type of nursing care plan had no effect on patient outcomes. These investigators concluded that written care plans with identified nursing diagnoses and nursing outcomes are not essential to deliver individualized quality care. They urged more research and if these results are validated, a revision in JCAHO requirements.

Written care plans may be an extremely valuable way to teach undergraduate nursing students. However, they may not be an essential activity in guiding professional nursing practice or assuring quality patient outcomes. In fact, it could be that they are consuming valuable time as well as space in both the record and the computer and that they are not contributing to patient outcomes. This sacred cow needs to be targeted, if not for slaughter — for revolutionary transformation.

I believe that practicing nurses have been demonstrating with their overwhelming lack of enthusiasm for compliance to the nursing care plan standard that written care plans (as now construed) are not essential to quality patient care. I once thought that generic or standardized care plans were the answer. At least, with the latter, the nurse only had to review and individualize to the patient. Even this approach has not found acceptance. The nurses may pull the generic care plan and place it in the record, but it is not uniformly individualized and, more troubling, probably not even read. This should provide us with insights. Nurses are continuing to give individualized care, and patients are responding and getting better. De La Cuesta (1983) identified the conflict between nursing education and practice as it relates to the care plan:

> It is necessary for educational purposes to break down in detail the elements of the problem-solving method and to expect from nursing students written and formalized reports on what they are doing at each stage as a training exercise to heighten their consciousness of what is required in detail. However, once the nurse is qualified, has been educated in the approach, has mastered the skills . . ., it may not be necessary to continue the extensive obligation to record. (p. 370)

Benner (1982), in her outstanding work *From Novice to Expert,* has described how different levels of nurses function and perceive clinical situations. The five levels of proficiency in acquiring and developing skills call for different approaches to guiding and directing care.

McHugh (1986) also examined the nursing process in terms of its relevance for the novice or the expert. Using Benner's five levels of skill proficiency, McHugh concluded that the written nursing process or care plan serves the novice or advanced beginner. However, more advanced practitioners and experts may be frustrated at best by a system more suitable for beginners.

Virginia Henderson (1982) has challenged us to distinguish between nursing and the nursing process. She states that the latter is an analytical process that should be used by all health-care providers who are problem-solving. Henderson suggests that the nursing process evolved from the movements to "individualize nursing care, identify and help people with their psychosocial as well as their physical problems, emphasize the science of nursing as opposed to the art of nursing, and establish the right of the nurse to an independent, professional and unique role" (p. 104). Henderson states that the best health care is patient/family focused; and that since 1937, she has been stressing planning *with* rather than *for* the patient and family. She states:

> I question the nurse's identifying a patient's problem and making a plan to solve it, although he or she can help the patient and the family do both, just as he or she can help them implement and evaluate the programme.

She concludes her critique of the nursing process with these words:

> While the nursing process recognizes the purpose of the problem-solving aspects of the nurses' work, a habit of inquiry and the use of investigative techniques in developing the scientific basis for nursing, it ignores the subjective or intuitive aspect of nursing and the role of experience, logic and expert opinion as bases for nursing practice. In stressing a dominant and independent function for the nurse, it fails to stress the value of collaboration of health profes-

sionals and particularly the importance of developing the self-reliance of clients. (p. 109)

All of these studies should help us in leading this one revolutionary change — removing the mandate that each patient have a nursing care plan as now required by our own ANA and JCAHO standards. Let's experiment, promote, and test different approaches!!!

Zander's (1988) nursing case management is a collaborative model of strategic management by nurses and physicians of episodes of illness. Her results are exciting. In ischemic stroke patients, this case management approach resulted in a 29% reduction in length of stay and a 46% reduction in ICU days. Zander describes the "critical path" as an abbreviated, one-page version of a case management plan and states that these critical paths, once individualized by the primary nurse and physician, are used to plan and monitor patient care. Interestingly, Zander's model combines the plan and the documentation, thus eliminating redundancy and promoting efficiency in recording. Zander states:

> Nurses have always been managers of care, but have labored with outdated management tools (such as nursing care plans) and shift-centered management systems. (p. 7)

The case, in my opinion, has been made. The sacred cow of "nursing care plans" must be slaughtered and a new and better something put in its place.

NURSING PROBLEM-ORIENTED RECORDING AND SOAP NOTES

The next sacred cow on my target list is the problem-oriented recording system with a nursing problem list, SOAP notes, and SOAPIER notes. The time that nurses spend recording on patient and hospital records must be reduced. Again, this time must be freed to focus on patient care activities that will be related to desired patient outcomes. At least five basic guidelines (if fully implemented) could considerably reduce time spent in documentation:

1. **Document at the source of data collection, at the patient's side.** Flow sheets to

capture routine care and completed treatments, vital sign records, intake and output sheets, and medication administration records could all be kept in the patient's room or in the immediate area. Everything on these records can be used in the process of making the patient and family informed partners in the care process.

2. **Avoid redundancy in recording.** If the data are recorded once on a permanent record, they should not be recorded again.

3. **In the progress notes, record only significant observations and changes in the patient's condition or response** — those that are critical for evaluating the patient's progress and clinical decision making. I do not believe that it is necessary to identify the specific problem and then give the subjective and objective symptoms, followed by the assessment, and then the plan for each entry, or to compound it further with the description of the intervention, and the evaluation of the response. Treatment records and/or flow sheets can be designed to capture many of these critical data elements.

4. **Forcing the generation of a separate nursing problem list should be eliminated.** Without even going near a patient, I can predict that in 9 out of 10 patients, I will find a knowledge deficit on the problem list. I wonder how valuable this problem or diagnosis is as it relates to guiding nursing interventions and the results in patient outcomes. I suggest that the competent nurse, as well as proficient and expert level nurses, will all teach the patient as an integral aspect of their nursing care. The very essential aspects of patient teaching (including the assessment of learning needs, teaching, and response) can be documented on patient education flow sheets.

5. **Where separate nurses notes remain, discontinue their use and move rapidly to having the nurses record significant observations on the progress record integrated along with the physician and other professional care givers.**

These five guidelines will help conserve time. To capture more time-saving approaches and maximize the creative talents of the staff, create a Documentation Revision Team and charge them with the responsibility to find new and better ways to capture essential patient care data while conserving nursing time. Then establish pilot units and test the revised approaches.

New documentation methods are being tested around the country, and those that have merit will survive and deserve replication. The PIE method (Problem Identification, Intervention and Evaluation) incorporates the plan of care into the nursing progress notes, eliminating the need for a traditional care plan according to Buckley-Womack and Gidney (1987). The system includes a comprehensive flow sheet where routine interventions and assessments are documented. Siegrist, Dettor and Stocks (1985) have illustrated what they believe to be the major advantages of the PIE system with a case study. I found their Daily Patient Assessment Sheet very interesting and one that could be helpful to nurses interested in flow sheet innovations.

Matthewman (1987) and a committee of staff nurses created a combined care plan and Kardex in their efforts to streamline documentation.

Murphy, Beglinger, and Johnson (1988) eliminated problem-oriented records in their 600-bed private hospital and created a system of charting by exception that includes a nursing/physician order flow sheet, a patient teaching record along with a graphic record, and the nurses' notes. In their pilot unit, registered nurses (RNs), using the traditional charting method, averaged 44 minutes per shift in documentation activities. In the new system of charting by exception, the average dropped to 25 minutes, a decrease of 44%. There were different time savings for licensed practical nurses (LPNs) and unit secretaries. In all, the time savings in this institution with charting by exception equaled *100 hours per day,* the equivalent of *12.5 additional 8-hour shifts* each day.

These examples illustrate that a revolution has begun, and we need to help spread the change — Our patients and their families will be the central beneficiaries in addition to the nurses who will experience increased satisfaction and less stress due to standards that do not serve them or their patients. Kramer and Schmalenberg (1987) in their revisit of 16 magnet hospitals reported the stress that some forms of nursing documentation have created:

> . . . written nursing care plans. "I hate them. I hate them. I hate them. They really take time away from my patients. . . . drudgery, repetition, and time-consuming writing out of a care plan. No other professional group has to write out in such detail what they plan to do. Why do nurses have to do so?" (p. 34)

Legitimizing revolutionary changes in planning and documenting care will help maximize nurses' time for quality patient care. Virginia Henderson (1987) summarizes with these words:

> Nothing would more radically improve health care than simplifying the form and language of the health record, identifying its essential content, and making a copy of it available to the patient. To best serve the public interest, health-care providers must work with recipients and their families. They must also collaborate with each other in helping citizens prevent diseases, recover from illnesses, cope with handicaps, and die peacefully when death is inevitable. (pp. 17-18)

Let's create a patient care plan and eliminate the current nursing care plan. In this newly designed patient care plan, the patient/family and the physician as well as the nurse and other care providers will focus together on the problems to be addressed in this episode of care and the care that will follow.

PATIENT CARE PROGRAMS

The patient and family need to become central partners on the health-care team and, wherever possible, become more actively involved in the care and treatment program. Hospital systems and procedures will have to change, and nurses and other providers will have to learn new behaviors. Self-administration of medications, including patient controlled analgesics, should become a norm rather than the exception. Perhaps every bedside stand should have a medication drawer where all individual medications are maintained and dispensed.

Patient/family education programs need creative work and creative materials that will assist nurses in the teaching of critical information and skills. Media specialists and writers could be employed for a designated period, along with a librarian, to get materials prepared, catalogued, and ready for use. Volunteers could help deliver software and brochures. Closed circuit television could be used to greater advantage. Some nursing staff vacancy money may need to be used to produce technological tools to assist and complement the nurse with essential aspects of patient care.

Standard and routine care procedures must be examined. Are they necessary in the frequency and format in which they are currently administered? If not, what is essential to the desired outcome, and how do we change it to create the desired outcome? A classic example is incentive spirometry. More nursing and patient time have been wasted on a treatment with little or no value for a large number of patients. Equipment as well as time have been squandered. Making certain that treatments are appropriate to the patient's specific needs is a good beginning.

The routine taking of temperature and vital signs when there is no indication of need also needs to be questioned. Daily monitoring data may be appropriate for all patients in an acute care hospital, but more frequent measurements, without specific indicators of need, are useless rituals.

In this important area of patient care programs and procedures, the nurses who are primarily involved in delivering the care must be empowered to critically examine their routines and challenge those activities of questionable merit. Of course, where patients are directly involved, caution must be exercised as changes are evaluated. Carefully controlled demonstrations or pilot programs are warranted, and patient outcomes must be continually monitored as the changes are introduced.

Hobson and Blaney (1987) have identified three additional areas where change can cut costs and not care: inefficient use of patient care supplies; ineffective motivation and teaching of patients; and poor patient scheduling. The point I want to underscore is that it *cannot be business as usual.* Nurses have too much to do, and patients are in great need of effective and efficient services.

EXQUISITE TEAMWORK NEEDED MORE THAN EVER BEFORE

To meet the increased demands with existing staff requires exquisite team work, and that means everyone needs to work closely together.

- **Physician/nurse joint practice or collaborative practice is essential.** There is no time for parallel play. Joint planning, management, and evaluation of the patient's care and progress are essential.
- **Support services must deliver their services in a timely and responsible manner.** Medications must be there when needed as well as patient care supplies and equipment. Nurses' time cannot be squandered on the telephone chasing after required services. Nurses cannot be expected to make up for inadequate support services. If this belief exists, it too must be slaughtered.
- **Unit support services, such as housekeeping functions, may need to be restructured.** Housekeepers need to be responsive to the needs of the patient units, and head nurses must be able to establish priorities for housekeeping in order to meet patient care needs. This desired outcome may call for revolutionary structural changes with all staff who work on a unit being made responsive to the head nurse as well as to their respective department heads.
- **The time may have finally come when 24-hour, 7-day a week secretarial services are absolutely essential requirements to support the nurse's ability to care for patients.** Again, the shortage and vacant position dollars may be considered for adding the required support staff to manage the system and free the nurse to care for patients.
- **New unit services should be explored and tested.** A hospital concierge may provide many useful services that once fell within the domain of nurses. The concierge could get the newspapers, arrange for telephone or television service, order special meals for family members, arrange sleeping accommodations for the families of critically ill patients, and

the list goes on. All of these vital patient care services need to continue, but they can be done by someone other than the professional nurse.

STAFF MIX

The nursing shortage has demanded an adjustment to the nursing staff mix—Some may say that it has created a demand for revolutionary change. I disagree. This is one area where I believe evolution is indicated. Here are the facts on the shortage as summarized by the Delaware Valley Hospital Council in an August 1988 statement before a Pennsylvania Subcommittee on Health:

- The major cause of the current shortage is increased demand as opposed to a contraction of supply.
- The output of nurses increased by 55% between 1977 and 1984, compared to an 8% growth in population.
- Nurses are not leaving their profession. Almost 80% of RNs are actively employed.
- Ratios of nurses to patients in hospitals increased from 50:100 in 1972 to 91:100 in 1986.
- The proportion of RNs in the hospital nursing staff changed. In 1968, RNs were 33% of the nursing staff mix; in 1986, RNs were 58% of the nursing staff mix.
- RN employment in Medicaid and Medicare certified nursing homes increased 22% from 1981 to 1986.
- RN Medicare home health visits increased 60% between 1980 and 1987.
- The supply is at risk. Undergraduate enrollments in baccalaureate and associate degree programs have experienced a 30% decline since 1983. (pp. 2-3)

What do these facts portend for staff mix? Certainly the movement to an all-RN staff has been halted. And maybe this too will serve nursing's desired future. The supply conditions have forced hospitals and other users to examine staffing and support services and identify new approaches to maximizing nurses' time for patient care. The roles of nursing assistants and LPNs are being explored with renewed interest. How can these auxiliary personnel complement the registered professional nurse so that quality care at controlled costs is achieved? The more than 400 tasks that have been identified as being performed by nurses are being reviewed and parceled out to ancillary staff including unit secretaries and other support service staff.

Having LPNs and nursing assistants become part of a unit's staffing complement does not have to interfere with primary nursing. Yet some say primary nursing may not survive. My belief is that every patient deserves a primary nurse just as every patient has an attending physician. Primary nursing has demonstrated its worth. Marie Manthey (1988), an originator of the primary nursing model, makes the following statement in the article *Myths that Threaten:*

> The essential ingredient of the (primary nursing) delivery system is the establishment of a responsibility relationship between a nurse and a patient. . . . The primary nurse's decisions are carried out by those who care for the patient in her absence. . . . The shortage of RNs does not have to mean a loss of professional progress. (p. 55)

We will have to focus more attention on team building and ancillary staff supervision. With careful mix changes, we can identify the best assistance roles that will support primary nursing and quality patient care.

RETENTION OF STAFF

The essential element in accomplishing clinical practice analyses and evaluation is the retention of professional nurses who feel empowered to examine the relationships of clinical practices to patient outcomes and who will help us identify the critical components for potential change. Shared governance and participative management are features of a professional practice model that must be woven into the hospital fabric. Nurses need to be in control of their own practice and active participants in the management of patient care services and activities.

Hinshaw, Smeltzer, and Atwood's (1987) study of organizational and individual factors predicted to influence job satisfaction and turnover of nursing staff found that job stress buffered by satisfaction leads to reduced turnover.

> The major stressors to be buffered were lack of team respect and feelings of incompetence while the primary satisfiers were professional status and general enjoyment in one's position, which correlated significantly with the ability to deliver quality nursing care. (p. 14)

These investigators identified the following strategies that can provide the satisfiers:

- Orientation and cross-training must be provided to help nurses feel competent in the care they are expected to deliver.
- Group cohesiveness must be fostered.
- Professional growth opportunities must be provided including continuing education, research development and projects, tuition reimbursement, professional recognition for achievements, committee responsibility, and career mobility.
- Control over professional nursing practice within the institution must be achieved.
- Autonomy in the nurse's own professional practice must be felt. (pp. 14-16)

Institutions and their executives will do well to concentrate on retention of existing staff. Competent, proficient, and expert level nurses will help achieve the needed revolutionary and evolutionary changes. Their value needs to be recognized with financial differentiation for experience as well as special longevity benefits and perquisites. Furthermore, they deserve the added prestige of having their value recognized by membership and leadership in the participative management and shared governance structures that are in place or are being developed. Finally, the nurses must have strong administrative leadership and backup support, including head nurses and directors who are supportive, available, flexible, and who have excellent business skills they are willing to share. There is no doubt that nurses will continue to be excellent care givers and knowledgeable business partners as the evolutionary and revolutionary changes unfold. Yes, the shortage is real. The crisis is now. But the opportunities are many. The future is bright!

REFERENCES

Benner, P. (1982). *From novice to expert. American Journal of Nursing, 82*(3), 402-407.

Buckley-Womack, C., & Gidney, B. (1987). A new dimension in documentation: The PIE method. *Journal of Neuroscience Nursing, 19*(5), 256-260.

De La Cuesta, C. (1983). The nursing process: From development to implementation. *Journal of Advanced Nursing, 8,* 365-371.

Ferguson, G.H., Hildman, T., & Nichols, B. (1987). The effect of nursing care planning systems on patient outcomes. *Journal of Nursing Administration, 17*(9), 30-36.

Henderson, V. (1982). The nursing process. *Journal of Advanced Nursing, 7,* 103-109.

Henderson, V. (1987). Nursing process — A critique. *Holistic Nursing Practice, 1*(3), 7-18.

Hinshaw, A.S., Smeltzer, C.H., & Atwood, J.R. (1987). Innovative retention strategies for nursing staff. *Journal of Nursing Administration, 17*(6), 8-16.

Hobson, C.J., & Blaney, D.R. (1987). Techniques that cut costs, not care. *American Journal of Nursing, 87*(2), 185-187.

Kramer, M., & Schmalenberg, C. (1987). Magnet hospitals talk about the impact of DRGs on nursing care — Part II. *Nursing Management, 18*(10), 33-39.

Manthey, M. (1988). Myths that threaten. *Nursing Management, 19*(6), 54-55.

Matthewman, J. (1987). Combining care plan and kardex. *American Journal of Nursing, 87*(6), 852-854.

McHugh, M. (1986). Nursing process: Musings on the method. *Holistic Nursing Practice, 1*(1), 21-28.

Murphy, J., Beglinger, J.E., & Johnson, B. (1988). Charting by exception: Meeting the challenge of cost-containment. *Nursing Management, 19*(2), 56-72.

Romano, J. (1964). And leave for the unknown. *Journal of the American Medical Association, 190*(4), 282-284.

Siegrist, L.M., Dettor, R.E., & Stocks, B. (1985). The PIE system: Complete planning and documentation of nursing care. *Quality Review Bulletin, 11*(6), 186-189.

Zander, K. (1988). Nursing case management: Strategies management of cost and quality outcomes. *Journal of Nursing Administration, 18*(5), 23-30.

CHAPTER **55**

The Quality Management Maturity Grid
A diagnostic method

June A. Schmele, RN, PhD

Sandra J. Foss, RN, MS

Quality, or excellence, is discussed frequently in current management literature. Leaders of the corporate world clearly endorse the value of an organizational thrust toward quality in order to remain competitive and economically sound in the business world.[2-7] The health care field is just beginning to recognize the value of well-entrenched business sector approaches to quality management. One example is the work of Deming[8] who has been widely recognized for his post-World War II influence on Japanese productivity and quality. However, it is only recently that his work has been given serious consideration in the health care literature.[9] The health care sector can greatly benefit from many of these corporate insights and strategies related to quality.

In addition to Deming's work, some of the most profound and revolutionary ideas about quality in today's business sector have been advanced by Crosby[10,11] who is recognized as a "guru of excellence." His philosophy of quality management is articulated in the titles of his books, *Quality is Free*[12]

and *Quality Without Tears.*[13] Crosby is the founder of Philip Crosby Associates (PCA), a consulting firm working with more than 900 businesses. The firm assists corporations to maximize quality assurance techniques and practices. Quality College, which is the educational arm of PCA, insists that a quality improvement process must begin at the executive level, move through management levels, and eventually penetrate the entire organization. Crosby believes that his methods will work whether the product is manufacturing or service oriented. He lists four key principles of quality management: (1) Quality denotes conformance to requirements, (2) Defect prevention, rather than inspection, is the way to attain quality, (3) A standard of zero defects is the only acceptable quality standard, and (4) The cost of poor quality can amount to 40% of operating costs in a service agency.[14] Although simple in concept, Crosby's ideas about quality management are solidly grounded on philosophical principles that are foundational to effective management at all levels of the organization. The necessity of a strong commitment of top management to quality improvement is the key to quality management. Crosby states that "Quality management is a systematic way of guaranteeing that organized activities happen the way they are planned. It is

Reprinted from *The Journal of Nursing Administration,* New York: Vol. 9, No. 9, with permission of J. B. Lippincott Company © 1989.

a management discipline concerned with preventing problems from occurring by creating the attitudes and controls that make prevention possible."[15]

Further development of the idea of quality management is found in Crosby's development of the concept of quality management maturity. The concept encompasses a progressive movement through several developmental stages which an organization goes through in their quest of a fully developed program of quality management. The organization which has attained a high level of quality maturity implies the presence of an integrated climate of quality which predominates the total management of the organization. The organization which operates at a state of quality maturity "would want to make certain that everything was done exactly right — the first time."[16] To further operationalize this concept, Crosby has developed the Quality Management Maturity Grid (QMMG).

QUALITY MANAGEMENT MATURITY GRID

The QMMG was first published in *Quality is Free*.[17] The grid (Figure 55-1) assesses the organizational system through the perceptions of persons working in the organization and then identifies areas needing improvement. According to Crosby, quality maturity has five stages on a continuum from least desirable to most desirable:

1. *Uncertainty.* Problems are dealt with as they occur. No one is able to identify why there are problems.
2. *Awakening.* A quality assurance team is established. Management begins to ask why they do not have quality.
3. *Enlightenment.* Corrective action and communications are established. Management becomes committed to quality.
4. *Wisdom.* Problems are identified early through employee feedback and quality control. Everyone is open to suggestions for improvement and prevention becomes routine.
5. *Certainty.* Problems are prevented except in unusual circumstances.

Crosby suggests that the grid represents a fluid process, thus over time there may be movement in both directions.

The value of using the QMMG is mainly evaluative with the intent of improving the total organizational system. It can, of course, be used in smaller organizational subsystems, as well, for example, a specific nursing department or unit. Crosby also suggests its benefits for the new manager who is responsible for quality improvement. In all of these instances, the grid can be used as an effective diagnostic tool.

There is minimal evidence in the health care literature of use of the QMMG. Snyder reports using Crosby's five stages of organizational growth described in the Grid to establish a quality assurance program for a food service program.[18,19] Mowery and Korpman identify Crosby's principles of quality and encourage the health care profession to begin adopting some of these ideas.[20] Since the use of the QMMG is well established as a quality assessment measure in the business community, this preliminary project was undertaken to further determine the value of the tool in the health care sector.

ASSESSING QUALITY

According to Crosby, quality management maturity is defined by the managers' and the professionals' views of quality. He emphasizes that ". . . quality is too important to leave to the professionals. Professionals must guide the program, but the execution of quality is the obligation and opportunity of the people who manage the operation."[21] Through the use of the QMMG, the executive can determine precisely where the organization stands in relationship to quality. The importance of this determination is as an assessment measure upon which organizational quality improvement interventions can then be based. In view of Crosby's suggestion of the need to assess the quality maturity of managers and professionals as well, the determination was made to test the QMMG on a group consisting of both nurse managers and non-managers.

The convenience sample we used consisted of a group of 140 management and non-management registered nurses who were widely dispersed throughout a south central state. These nurses identified themselves as having an interest or role in quality assurance as evidenced by their presence at a state-wide

QUALITY MANAGEMENT MATURITY GRID

Rater _____   Unit _____

Measurement Categories	Stage I Uncertainty	Stage II Awakening	Stage III Enlightenment	Stage IV Wisdom	Stage V Certainty
Managment understanding and attitude	No comprehension of quality as a management tool. Tend to blame quality department for quality problems	Recognizing that quality management may be of value but not willing to provide money or time to make it all happen.	While going through quality improvement program learn more about quality management; becoming supportive and helpful.	Participating. Understand absolutes of quality management. Recognize their personal role in continuing emphasis.	Consider quality management an essential part of company system.
Quality organization status	Quality is hidden in manufacturing or engineering departments. Inspection probably not part of organization. Emphasis on appraisal and sorting.	A stronger quality leader is appointed but main emphasis is still on appraisal and moving the product. Still part of manufacturing or other.	Quality department reports to top management, all appraisal is incorporated and manager has role in management of company.	Quality manager is an officer of company, effective status reporting and preventive action. Involved with consumer affairs and special assignments.	Quality manager on board of directors. Prevention is main concern. Quality is a thought leader.
Problem handling	Problems are fought as they occur; no resolution; inadequate definition; lots of yelling and accusations.	Teams are set up to attack major problems. Long-range solutions are not solicited.	Corrective action communication established. Problems are faced openly and resolved in an orderly way.	Problems are identified early in their development. All functions are open to suggestion and improvement.	Except in the most unusual cases, problems are prevented.
Cost of quality as % of sales	Reported: unknown Actual: 20%	Reported: 3% Actual: 18%	Reported: 8% Actual: 12%	Reported: 6.5% Actual: 8%	Reported: 2.5% Actual: 2.5%
Quality Improvement actions	No organized activities. No understanding of such activities	Trying obvious motivational short-range efforts	Implementation of the 14-step program with thorough understanding and establishment of each step.	Continuing the 14-step program and starting Make Certain.	Quality improvement is a normal and continued activity.
Summation of company quality posture	We don't know why we have problems with quality	Is it absolutely necessary to always have problems with quality?	Through management commitment and quality improvement we are identifying and resolving our problems	Defect prevention is a routine part of our operation	We know why we do not have problems with quality.

FIGURE 55-1

Quality management maturity grid. *From Crosby, PB: Quality is free, New York, 1979, New American Library.*

continuing education conference entitled "Developing a Quality Assurance Program." The tool was administered to the conference attendees prior to the conference session.

INSTRUMENTATION

The instrument used was an adaptation of Crosby's QMMG. The adaptation consisted of minimal rewording of the Grid items to make them applicable to the health care setting and a rearrangement of the format into a scaled questionnaire for ease of administration and scoring (see box on this page). In order to avoid biasing the respondent, the names of the specific stages of quality maturity were omitted from the questionnaire. Scoring values for each of the six major questions ranged from 1 (least desirable) to 5 (most desirable). The reliability measure for internal consistency of the instrument was 0.76. Additional demographic questions included information regarding basic and present educational level, present position and length of time in this position, type of facility where employed and age of the participant. The demographic characteristics of the participants are shown in Table 55-1.

QUALITY MANAGEMENT MATURITY

The average mean grid score for the group was 3.03 with a possible range of 1 (least desirable) to 5 (most desirable). The standard deviation (SD) was 0.10. The mean score of 3.03 represented a fairly positive perception of quality maturity in the agencies which the sample represented. The score was indicative of the Enlightenment phase in which the organization decides to move ahead and begin a systematic quality improvement program, which was consistent with the fact that the sample population was already participating in a conference which dealt with the establishment of a quality assurance program. This congruence is supportive of the validity of the QMMG. Other data indicated that nearly half the respondents had an inaccurate view of the perceived cost of quality activities versus the actual cost of such activities. These data support the need for nursing personnel to be better informed regarding the cost of quality

---

Selected items from quality assurance maturity evaluation*

1. Check the one answer which you think best represents the administrator's (manager's) understanding and attitude about quality assurance.

_____ No comprehension of quality as a management tool. Tend to blame others for "quality problems."

_____ Recognizing that quality assurance may be of value but not willing to provide money or time to make it all happen.

_____ While going through quality improvement program learning more about quality assurance; becoming supportive and helpful.

_____ Participating. Understand absolutes of quality assurance. Recognize their personal role in continuing emphasis.

_____ Consider quality assurance an essential part of the agency.

6. Check the one answer which you think best sums up the agency's position on quality.

_____ "We don't know why we have problems with quality."

_____ "Is it absolutely necessary to always have problems with quality?"

_____ "Through management commitment and quality improvement we are identifying and resolving our problems."

_____ "Prevention of inadequate care is a routine part of our operation."

_____ "We know why we do not have problems with quality."

*Adapted from Quality Management Maturity Grid, Crosby, 1979.

---

assessment activities. Approximately one fourth of the respondents indicated that they perceived that the agency quality improvement activities were consistent with a continuous quality assurance program. This is in keeping with the fact that most agencies have a quality assurance program in operation.

There was no significant pattern of association shown between the respondents' perception of quality maturity and variables in present position, length of time the position had been held, education levels, types of facilities, or age groups. As the nurse

TABLE 55-1
Demographic characteristics of 140 survey participants

	FREQUENCY
Age distribution	
26-35	67 (48%)
36-45	43 (42%)
46-55	24 (17%)
Non Response	6 (4%)
Basic nursing education	
Baccalaureate	60 (43%)
Associate Degree	41 (29%)
Diploma	32 (23%)
Other	7 (5%)
Employment setting	
Acute Care	105 (75%)
Psychiatric	10 (7%)
Ambulatory Care	10 (7%)
Home Health	6 (4%)
Other	9 (7%)
Position	
Nurse Executive	8 (6%)
QA Coordinator	21 (15%)
Assistant DON	16 (11%)
Head Nurse/ Assistant	29 (21%)
Nurse Educator	36 (26%)
Staff Nurse	14 (10%)
Other	16 (11%)
Years in present position	
< 1	36 (26%)
1 to < 3	42 (30%)
3 to < 5	24 (17%)
5 to < 10	25 (18%)
> 10	13 (9%)

executive begins a quality improvement program it will be important for him or her to be aware that participants may be similar in spite of varied backgrounds in education and experience, and may have similar learning needs and abilities. It follows that quality assurance-enhancing activities such as coaching, consultation, staff development, and continuing education, ought to be based upon the quality management maturity phase of the target group.

It would also appear in this sample that most nursing service organizations are relatively neutral in regard to their quality maturity. This lack of strong commitment in either direction may require an aggressive approach to convince organizational participants that there really is a need to focus upon a serious program of quality improvement.

Data were compared between the managers and non-managers. Managers were considered those persons occupying positions as Administrators or Directors of Nursing, Assistant Directors of Nursing, Head Nurses or Charge Nurses. All other positions were placed in the non-management category. The sample consisted of 52 managers (37%) and 88 non-managers (63%).

Total mean scores were 3.04 (SD .12) for the management and 3.06 (SD .08) for the non-management groups. An analysis of variance of the mean scores between the management and non-management groups showed no significant difference. Using Chi-square analysis, no significant differences were found between the management and non-management groups in relation to their place of work, years employed at the facility, educational preparation or age. The mean scores of both groups were indicative of the early phase of Enlightenment. During this phase, management becomes committed to quality and corrective actions during the establishment of communications. According to Crosby, this phase signifies that the group is firmly committed to problem identification and resolution as well as to establishing, maintaining and improving a quality assurance program.[22] Again, the similarity of the quality maturity level of managers and non-managers alike, as well as the relatively neutral quality maturity scores, may be cause for concern, since there is a need for managers to assume the leadership role in order for a quality improvement program to flourish.

DISCUSSION AND APPLICATION

Crosby's QMMG offers an assessment tool that provides health care agencies with data upon which to develop a proactive approach to quality assurance programming.

It is the perception of the authors that there may be merit in the further modification of the QMMG instrument. For example, it may be of value to represent each of the five phases of quality maturity with several single focused items, rather than only one composite idea having multiple items. Further instrument testing in an organizational setting, including reliability and validity testing, will enhance the value of the tool. According to PCA Senior Vice President Gausz, a related "Profile" is currently being used as a quality diagnostic tool in the PCA's work with health care agencies.[23,24]

The use of this successful corporate approach in the health care field offers an exciting challenge to nurse executives. Crosby proposes a quality improvement program which consists of 14 steps that would serve as a "how to" approach to advance through the stages of the quality maturity grid.[25]

1. *Management Commitment*

It is imperative that top management espouses the program of quality improvement with emphasis on defect prevention. Crosby stresses the importance of policy formulation that states that every person will "perform exactly like the requirement or cause the requirement to be officially changed to what we and the customer really need."[26] An example of this step would be the incorporation of nursing practice standards into the performance requirements for professional nurses.

2. *Quality Improvement Team*

Team members consist of representation from various departments or units who are committed to specific actions needed for quality improvement. Whether or not the team was interdisciplinary would depend upon the organizational quality improvement goal. The higher in the total organization that the quality improvement program originated, the greater will be the likelihood of success throughout the organization. This team could consist of a reformulation of the traditional Quality Assurance Committee, provided that the team contained the leaders that

had the power and authority needed to bring about quality improvement.

3. *Quality Measurement*

Measurements must be available for the key areas of activity or service. This focus is comparable to Joint Commission requirements in which the monitoring of key aspects of nursing services are called for. The use of these measurements (standards and criteria) must be followed with appropriate evaluation and remedial action.

4. *Cost of Quality Evaluation*

It is advisable to calculate the cost of quality based upon the correct action that will benefit an agency. For instance, it is relatively simple to calculate the cost of repeated x-ray or laboratory tests due to inadequate patient preparation.

5. *Quality Awareness*

Informing employees of the cost of unquality activities may be one of the most important aspects of quality improvement. Nurses frequently indicate that they are unaware of cost implications. For example, the knowledge, in exact dollars, of the additional cost related to inadequate patient preparation for a given test may be the motivating force to remedy the unquality situation.

6. *Corrective Action*

There is much value in shared problem identification and the development of solutions by those who are closest to the problem. Various types of problem solving mechanisms, such as one-to-one conferencing, unit meetings, or quality circles may be used effectively to examine a problem and select the corrective action.

7. *Establish an Ad Hoc Committee for the Zero Defects Program*

A small committee of thought leaders is developed to instill within all employees the meaning of zero defects and the idea that "everyone should do things right the first time."[27]

8. *Supervisor Training*

This quality improvement training of key management persons is essential to the success of the program.

9. *Zero Defects Day*

The performance standard of "zero defects" for the entire organization ought to be a mutually understood and shared experience that will mount the new quality initiative. Again, the higher in the organization this plan originates from, the greater the impact of the quality improvement program. The active involvement of both managers and professional practitioners is imperative.

10. *Goal Setting*

It is vital for supervisors and employees to formulate specific measurable goals for specified time periods such as 30, 60 or 90 days. This goal-setting approach can be incorporated into ongoing management by objective programs or performance evaluation systems.

11. *Error Cause Removal*

Employees are asked to identify and describe problems that are preventing their performance of error-free work. This problem description is then sent on to the responsible functional unit for solution. A typical problem might be the lack of readiness of a patient room for occupancy and the subsequent inability of nurses to perform the admission assessment. If this is an habitual problem, it would be appropriate for the nursing department to send on the problem description to the housekeeping department for appropriate action.

12. *Recognition*

It is worthwhile to establish award programs that will provide recognition of outstanding quality per-

formance. A creative reward system will increase motivation of both managers and staff.

13. *Quality Councils*

It is important to bring together key quality professionals to provide a communication forum to continue the quality improvement program. According to Crosby, the professional sharing of concerns, feelings, and experiences is necessary and growth-producing.

14. *Do It Over Again*

The quality improvement program typically will require 12 to 18 months to get underway. The inevitable turnover and new approaches will require a new thrust at least every two years to continue the journey toward quality maturity. It would be vital to incorporate this quality improvement thrust into the orientation programs as well as continuing education efforts of the total organization. In addition, ongoing evaluation of the quality improvement program is essential.

CONCLUSION

Key principles introduced by Crosby have very strong implications for the nurse executive who ultimately holds the responsibility for the quality of nursing care. Although some of Crosby's principles sound deceptively simple, the impact of their implementation could have far reaching effects upon the quality of care. Crosby, who defines quality as a "conformance to requirements," insists that the level of quality maturity of the organization will depend upon the top management commitment to this conformance. The 14 steps of quality improvement outlined by Crosby provide the guidelines to move an organization progressively through the steps of quality management maturity. This approach is in keeping with Joint Commission requirements as well.

The QMMG, as an organizational quality assessment method, can be used at any organizational level and has two-fold implications for nurse executives: first, it is a tool to communicate the characteristics of a quality focused nursing service organization and secondly, it is a yardstick to measure progress toward the ultimate goal of quality maturity. The challenge of implementation lies in the truth that quality improvement starts at the top and involves doing jobs right the first time, thus eliminating the cost of redoing and reworking.

REFERENCES

1. Crosby PB. Quality is free. New York: New American Library, 1979:1.
2. Peters TJ, Waterman RH Jr. In search of excellence. New York: Harper & Row, 1982.
3. Peters T, Austin N. A passion for excellence. New York: Random House, 1985.
4. Peters TJ. Thriving on chaos. New York: Alfred A. Knopf, Inc., 1987.
5. Iacocca L with Novak W. Iacocca. An autobiography. New York: Bantam Books, 1984.
6. Naisbitt J, Aburdene P. Re-inventing the corporation. New York: Warner Books, 1985.
7. Ishikawa K. What is total quality control: The Japanese way. Englewood Cliffs, NJ: Prentice-Hall, 1985.
8. Deming WE. Quality, productivity, and competitive position. Cambridge: Massachusetts Institute of Technology, 1982.
9. Gillem TR. Deming's 14 points and hospital quality: Responding to the consumers demand for the best value health care. Journal of Nursing Quality Assurance 1988; 2(3):70-78.
10. In quest of quality. Time, March 26, 1984:52.
11. Fierman J. Why enrollment is up at quality college. Fortune 1985; April 29:170.
12. Crosby, 1979.
13. Crosby PB. Quality without tears. New York: New American Library, 1984.
14. Fierman J. Fortune, April 29, 1985:170.
15. Crosby, 1979, 19.
16. Crosby, 1979, 19.
17. Crosby, 1979, 32-33.
18. Snyder OP, Jr. A model food service quality assurance system. Food Technology 1981;36(2):70-76.
19. Snyder OP, Jr. A management system for food service quality assurance. Food Technology 1983;37(6):61-67.
20. Mowery MM, Korpman RA. Managing health care costs, quality, and technology. Rockville, MD: Aspen, 1986.
21. Crosby, 1979, 23.
22. Crosby, 1979, 29.
23. Gausz B. Telephone conversation. Winter Park, FL: Philip Crosby Associates, Inc., Oct. 13, 1988.
24. Crosby, 1984, 4.
25. Crosby, 1979, 108-119.
26. Crosby, 1979, 112-113.
27. Crosby, 1979, 116.

CHAPTER **56**

Negotiating Skills for the Nursing Service Administrator

Jean Ann Kelley, RN, EdD, FAAN

NATURE OF NEGOTIATION

Negotiation is an indispensable tool to the nursing service administrator. It has been rated as one of the "greatest of human inventions."[13] Yet reliable knowledge about the negotiation process and the skills needed to use this tool effectively within the health field has been limited. Exploration of the nature of negotiation may clarify why negotiation is indispensable, how the process operates, and what skills are essential in the practice of nursing service administration.

Regardless of the level of administrative involvement, every nurse negotiates. However, the person in top clinical or administrative positions in nursing service has the added responsibility of negotiating on behalf of the nursing service organization.[3] Accomplishing organizational objectives according to an established timetable with a minimum of resources while influencing resolution of conflicts is a major basis upon which nursing service administrators are evaluated and retained or released.

Although negotiation ranks as an indispensable tool, it means different things to different people. To Strauss all social interaction involves negotiation.[12] It is perceived as a dynamic, cyclic interactional process, with the goal of achieving social order. Viewed

through the eyes of this scientist, negotiation is analyzed through three interacting elements. First, there is the *process element,* which involves the tactics and strategies used, such as persuasion, tradeoffs, appeals, kickbacks, demands, compromises toward middle positions, threat and force, payoffs of deals, and mutual agreements. Some of these techniques of negotiations have a negative connotation and are avoided by nursing service executives, yet they are used in negotiations, and counterstrategies need to be planned. Next is the *structural element,* which includes the interacting parties in a negotiation, the balance of power, the environmental setting, the presence or absence of an audience, and the time setting. The last interacting element is the *negotiation situation.* It encompasses the number and complexity of issues to be resolved, the number and experiences of negotiators, and the options open to avoid discontinuation of the negotiations. While emphasizing the scientific analysis of the structure and processes of negotiation, this approach neglects the human factors in and outcome of the interaction.

Similarly, Williamson described negotiation as a mutual interaction that serves as a model for nursing practice.[14] Nurse-patient relationships are believed to change to negotiation when interdependence and sharing a trust occur. As a cyclic, explorative process, nursing negotiations go through two major interactive phases. The gathering and analysis of information

Reprinted from *Nursing Clinics of North America,* Vol. 18, No. 3, with permission of W. B. Saunders Company © 1983.

coupled with mutual goal setting and strategy divising, implementation, and evaluation constitute the first phase. The other interactive phase centers on exploration of negotiable issues with the aim of reaching agreement to proceed with the negotiations, to refer the issue to another health professional, or to terminate the interaction. Unlike that of Strauss, this approach stresses the importance of interaction between the process and the outcome of negotiations.

On the other hand, Cohen sees negotiation as a process that uses power, information, timing, and pressure to get a commitment to change behavior.[3] Power is the ability to use resources to achieve worthwhile goals. It may involve competition, legitimacy, risk taking, investment, persistence, and strategies in attitudes. Successful negotiation is based on accurate and sufficient information gathered by critical listening, questioning, and reading cues. To achieve agreement in negotiations, group tension must be reduced. Two elements aid in this reduction of stress: (1) time or the deadlines held by both parties and (2) organizational pressure on a negotiator to take or to avoid risks. The perfect approach is described as persuasive negotiation. Although no two negotiations are identical, general guidelines to effective negotiations are suggested: (1) believe in yourself as an effective negotiator; (2) personalize negotiations by seeking help from an opponent in solving a problem because collaborative settlements are commitments made to individuals, not organizations; (3) assess and validate an opponent's needs before shaping your offer; (4) encourage an exchange of information to validate your needs assessment of an opponent but do so through a slow, time-released plan; (5) establish a concession pattern in which each side gets a share of success but make concessions one at a time, not in multiples; (6) consult with your negotiations team on concessions offered or to be offered; (7) be attuned to changing circumstances in the negotiation, such as introduction of new material or negotiators; and (8) take notes during the negotiation and offer to draft a clear, accurate, and concise final agreement.[2]

Negotiation is characterized by Nierenberg as a cooperative human process when people interact for the purpose of reaching mutually agreed upon conclusions to issues as a result of need satisfaction of all parties involved.[9] Three elements are believed to interact in this process: (1) knowledge of human behavior based on Maslow's hierarchy of needs, (2) preparation for negotiation through the identification of assumptions and positions held by both parties, and (3) strategies and techniques for bringing about need satisfaction and mutual agreement on issues. Negotiation is seen as having order, relation, and structure. A framework of human needs on one side, level of interaction of the parties on another side, and level of application on a third side is proposed as a guide to improving negotiating skills. By determining the needs of interacting parties and applying purposeful strategies to meet those needs, issues are addressed and mutually resolved. While need theory is the basis for this approach to negotiations, it has a broad theoretic base in that it draws upon theories of communication, history, economics, sociology, psychology, change, systems, and decision making.

Mann and Steckel treat negotiation as a contracting process in which the nurse and the patient interact with the classic elements of a contract: an offer, genuine assent, competent parties, legal format, and mutual consideration.[7,11] The goal of this approach to negotiation is to achieve a formalized written agreement. Unlike other views of negotiation, this one centers on adherence to the terms of a contract or the outcome of the negotiations.

Negotiation is depicted as a bargaining process by Cresswell and Murphy and by Bacharach and Lawler.[1,4] Taking Strauss' lead, Cresswell and Murphy developed a systems model of negotiation with four interacting elements: (1) *negotiation input,* or the resources, expectations, standards, ethics, and environmental aspects; (2) *negotiation situations,* or the issues being bargained for; (3) *negotiation process,* or the behaviors, strategies, and tactics used by negotiators; and (4) *negotiation output,* or the outcomes of the negotiation process. Cresswell and Murphy believe the interactive nature of a bargainable issue with input from the environment is the primary influence on the developmental character and outcome of a negotiation.

According to Bacharach and Lawler, negotiation is a bargaining process in which the concept of power is central.[1] The behavior of parties in a negotiation and the settlement reached is determined by the dependence dimension of bargaining power. Parties to a negotiation compare the costs and benefits of not reaching an agreement versus reaching a settlement. Based on this comparison, bargainers assume a position, real or imagined, on a bargaining power continuum that ranges from zero sum to variable sum. The designated position of power dictates the tactical actions or concessions such as arguments, bluffs, inducements, and punitive sanctions to be used in reaching the desired bargaining settlement. Negotiation is perceived as human interaction wherein bargaining power and processes interrelate with the outcome of achieving maximal gain or minimal loss for each party.

These competing approaches to negotiation give priority to different constructs. Strauss emphasizes interaction of structure and process, whereas Williamson stresses the outcome of interaction between information and an issue. Cohen, on the other hand, holds that persuasion through the wise use of power, information, time, and pressure is most critical to the outcome of the negotiation. Nierenberg values human needs and need satisfaction as the basis for successful negotiation. Mann and Steckel accent adherence to a bargained contract. Cresswell and Murphy support a bargaining process within an interactional systems model, while Bacharach and Lawler focus on dependence of bargaining power and its potential for maximal gain and minimal loss. While differing in emphasis, these competing interpretations of the nature of negotiations do agree on the overall goal of the negotiation process. The common outcome each approach strives to achieve is an exchange of ideas over an issue that will bring about change in relationships among parties in conflict.

Three different goals with diverse outcomes occur in negotiations. First, there is the negotiation goal of gaming, or the competitive process, in which the outcome is that one party wins and the other loses. This is the winner-takes-all philosophy of negotiation. There is also the negotiation goal of revenge, or the get-even philosophy, in which both parties lose. The revenger loses respect, and the revengee loses ground over the issue. Then there is the cooperative goal of negotiation, or the concern-for-others philosophy, in which all parties leave a conflict winning something while dissimilar interests are brought to a mutual meeting of the minds on an issue. Although the competing approaches to negotiations presented earlier differ in emphasis, they do agree in that effective negotiation is not a competitive game with the winner taking total victory or revenge. Instead it is a collaborative human process designed to achieve a mutually satisfying agreement in which all parties leave feeling they have gained. As a human enterprise, negotiation involves the sharing and setting of common goals, resolution of identifiable issues, and the use of proven strategies of change.

FRAMEWORK FOR NEGOTIATION

The development and refinement of negotiation skills in nursing service administration has a basic foundation. As reflected in Figure 56-1, knowledge of the nature of the process constitutes the fundamental structure for effective negotiations. A selection of a workable framework to guide actions, homework in preparation for each negotiation, and the judicial use of proven strategies and techniques to achieve the desired outcome are built on this structure.

A tautologic model of a systems theory of negotiation provides a practical framework.[8] As shown in

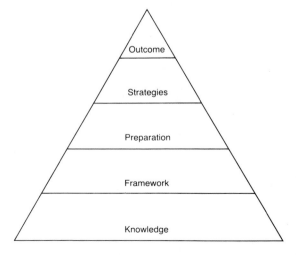

FIGURE 56-1
Structure for effective negotiation skills.

Figure 56-2, the first interacting component in this framework is the concepts in the negotiation process that are drawn on as parties interact and move toward a satisfying agreement. Six common concepts are politics, power, confrontation, contracting, conflict-resolution, and role-status. Another interacting component is the multifaceted role of the nursing service executive. It may be perceived as an educator-researcher-clinician-consultant-administrator role or as a human relations-health care systems-nursing-administrator role. These two components interact at various levels. While Nierenberg stipulates three levels of interaction, interpersonal, interorganizational, and international, this framework suggests six different levels: intrapersonal, interpersonal, intradepartmental, interdepartmental, intraagency, and interagency. Central to this interchange of concepts, roles, and level of interaction is the problems, issues, and trends component that precipitates the need for negotiation, for example, verification of credentials, labor relations, staff development and professional autonomy, and relationships between nursing education and service.

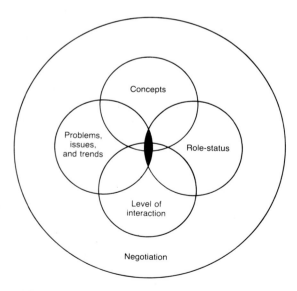

FIGURE 56-2
Tautologic model of a systems theory of negotiation.

NEGOTIATING SKILLS
Classic Skills

While a framework provides a skeleton to support the behaviors a nursing administrator chooses in a negotiation, it does not reveal the inner secrets of the skills essential for effectiveness and efficiency in negotiations. Skills are related closely to the negotiation process but differ in that they are more specific, are less complex, and are cautiously selected for each negotiation. Three familiar classes of skills exist: technical, human, and conceptual.[3,6] In general, *technical skills* are speaking, writing, listening, demonstrating, and computing abilities, but in negotiations they are the special strategies and tactics used to help parties reach a mutually satisfying settlement. Achieving strategies is the overall plan of bargainers during negotiation, while using tactics is the specific technique to reach short-range and long-range goals. *Human skills* are those abilities used to establish and maintain a negotiating climate and that contribute to bringing issues to a close. These skills of negotiation include empathy, building of trust, interviewing, communicating, sensing and anticipating human needs, as well as reflecting the relative worth of ideas. *Conceptual skills* in negotiations are those abilities that help in gathering and interpreting information that is used to shape strategies, offers, and counteroffers. Included in this classification are skills in observing, analyzing, interpreting, synthesizing, diagnosing, criticizing, planning, and organizing strategies, as well as evaluating the effectiveness of tactics.

Every nursing service administrator negotiates, regardless of the level of administrative practice. As shown in Figure 56-3, at the first level of nursing administration, be it in the functional, team, or primary method of nursing care delivery, the staff nurse is most closely involved at the intrapersonal and interpersonal level of interaction as negotiations occur between the patient and nurse, between the physician and nurse, or between nurse and nurse. This nursing administrator has need for greater competency in the technical skills of negotiations, as much time and effort is devoted to using negotiation tactics in patient care. The middle category of nursing

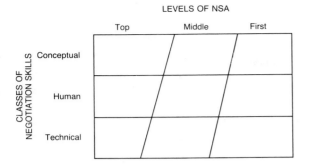

FIGURE 56-3

Relation of negotiation skills to three levels of nursing service administration (NSA).

manager at the head nurse or unit coordinator level gets involved with intrapersonal and interpersonal interaction but is more entangled with intradepartmental and interdepartmental aspects of negotiation. This involvement with interaction among nurses, other health professionals, and departments requires that the middle level nursing administrator have a balanced repertoire of competencies in all three skill areas. Meanwhile the top level nurse administrator holding a director, assistant administrator, or vice-presidential position will interact at the intrapersonal, interpersonal, intradepartmental, and interdepartmental levels but more so in intraagency and interagency negotiations. More time will be spent planning and evaluating negotiating strategies, many of which will be implemented by others. Actually, negotiation skills are the ways a nursing executive uses negotiation techniques to achieve the overall goal of negotiation. As nurses move from the first through the top level of administration in an organization, priority is placed on a different set of negotiation skills and on different levels of interaction.

Preparation Skills

Although the literature on negotiation increasingly contains information on the nature of the process, little is said about the preparation aspects, strategy selection, and evaluation. Even less is written about

potential applications of negotiations to health care phenomena.

What a negotiator needs to know and how to plan to use that knowledge most effectively in a given interaction is the essence of preparing for negotiation. The development of a map of preparations for negotiations is crucial.[9]

As shown in Figure 56-4, the map starts with a self-evaluation of your philosophy of negotiation as well as your reactions in group discussions, sensitivity to the behavior of others, and ability to see alternatives. It involves skill in acquiring knowledge about your opponent's philosophy, style, and previous negotiation experiences, for there are two distinct sides to a point of view—yours and your opponent's. While the overall objective of negotiations is to achieve a collaborative agreement, an initial preparatory step is the identification of minimal and maximal results desired from the negotiation. This is done by describing the known and hypothesizing the unknown objectives and by gathering facts to validate or disprove your assumptions about and interpretation of previous negotiations. Once objectives for a negotiation are established, they can be tested by such tactics as "releasing a trial balloon," leaking information, or changing your position in order to see an opponents reaction. Subsequently, the major and minor issues to be negotiated are specified, and those you can support and those that may be supported by the other side need to be delineated. Question your position on each issue and your opponent's. Project your negotiation needs and your opponent's. Identify strategies that might be useful to you and to your opponent and define what are you willing to concede, take, or renegotiate. Then prepare a set of strategies and counterstrategies. Decide, too, upon a single versus a team approach to negotiations. In addition, establish mechanisms for assessing verbal and nonverbal communication before, during, and after the negotiations. Moreover, identify as many ways as possible of determining the climate and barriers in a negotiation. Preset criteria for evaluation of the negotiation. Now retrace the map, but from the viewpoint of the other side. Such preparatory skills in negotiation will draw heavily on conceptual and technical abilities of a

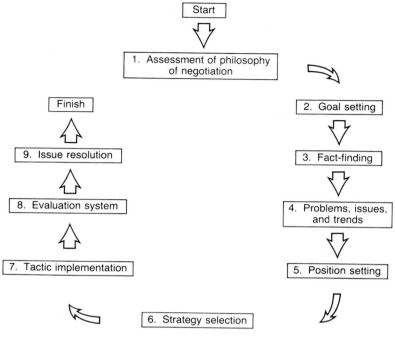

FIGURE 56-4

Map for preparation of negotiations.

nursing administrator as the collaborative resolution of an issue is reached.

Skills in Selection of Strategy

Selection of strategy in negotiation requires several skills. Initially it involves the creation of a blueprint of questions.[9] Questions posed at the right moment, with the right content, in the right way will move a group forward in the direction of conflict resolution. Clear, concise, clarifying questions that foster a co-operative relationship require forethought. Questions may be raised to achieve designated purposes, such as ones that cause attention, seek information, release information, stimulate thinking, or bring closure to discussion. Thinking through a comprehensive list of questions that needs to be asked during a negotiation helps organize a negotiator. A proposed list of questions frees a negotiator to listen more closely to the deliberations, to be more aware of the climate and

barriers, and to control the discussion by using certain questions at the appropriate moment. In framing questions prior to a negotiation, consideration needs to be given to the (1) purpose, or why it needs to be asked; (2) content, or what needs to be asked; (3) timing, or when it needs to be asked; and (4) method, or how it needs to be asked. Not only does a negotiator need to map out a strategy for questions but also needs to anticipate questions to be raised by the other side. An effective negotiator in nursing service administration is like the wise and prudent lawyer who prepares a list of all possible questions and responses that may be raised by both parties in a case.

Another major skill in selection of strategy is that of climate control. All negotiation climates have at least three basic interacting elements: the physical world, one's internal world, and other's internal world. As these worlds collide during negotiations, different climates are formed. Some are supportive and positive to the negotiations, while others are defensive and negative. For example, a climate of equality in negotiation would be characterized by trust, respect, and a free exchange of information among the negotiators, while a climate of superiority would reveal suspicion, fear, dogmatic and obstructive behaviors, as well as a rigid position on issues.

A wide variety of climates are discernible and created during a negotiation. There are problem-oriented, spontaneous, emphatic, accepting climates versus the gamemanship, neutral, controlling, evaluating climates. Six commonly encountered climates are the (1) *educative climate* in which information is exchanged that assists with understanding and resolution of issues, (2) *results-oriented climate* as opposed to prognostic, (3) *tiring climate,* (4) *attentive climate* in which both parties listen intensely, (5) *belligerent climate,* and (6) *dishonest climate.*[9]

Climate-control tactics aimed at creating, changing, or maintaining a certain climate are subtle, obvious, and numerous. Starting deliberations a few days prior to a major holiday, setting the site of the negotiations in your home territory as opposed to a neutral location, and placing an opponent in a chair with uneven legs are typical tactics. Climate-control strategies and tactics such as questions need to be projected before and assessed throughout a negotiation.

A third skill in selection of strategy involves recognizing and consciously reducing barriers. The most common communication barriers in negotiation are selective listening, hidden meaning, and loaded words.[10] Strategies for reducing these barriers have been identified as (1) doing a self-analysis of your listening conduct during discussions to determine your nonverbal responses and those events that distract or irritate you and (2) working consciously to improve your skills in understanding through purposeful listening. It has been estimated that on an average people spend 25 per cent of their time listening to others, but top executives spend more time listening in order to recall, to understand, or to evaluate issues. Tactics frequently used to remove communication barriers during a negotiation include the purposeful use of questions, the gradual introduction of new material, the use of concrete words and ideas while avoiding abstractions, diagnosing an opponent's reactions, and helping the other side examine their assumptions and position.

One of the most critical skills in selection of strategy is the understanding and choice of specific tactics. Cohen gives priority to three strategic negotiation activities: building trust, gaining commitment, and managing the opposer.[3] In negotiations, opponents most commonly encountered and requiring management are the idea type and the visceral type. The idea type can be approached on an intellectual level with tactics involving logic, facts, figures, explanations, and evidence. The visceral opponent, however, responds on an emotional level and requires different tactics. Stress, suspicion and jumping to conclusions are characteristic of the visceral negotiator. Tactics that save the public face and self-image of an opponent are needed to convert an emotional negotiator into a cooperating one. Effective negotiators avoid making visceral opponents by restraining an inclination to retaliate when the other side is provocative and by judging the actions and motives of an opponent only after careful and thorough review of information. Compromise and conciliation are the tactics of choice in dealing with the visceral type.

Nierenberg, on the other hand, offers an extensive list of tactics that are sensitive to the when, how, and where factors of negotiations so that human needs of all parties in an interaction are satisfied.[9] Some "when" tactics are (1) forbearance or waiting out a point, (2) surprise or reversal by changing or shifting positions on an issue, (3) actual or pretended withdrawal, and (4) feinting or distraction. Prevalent "how" and "where" tactics involve the use of the blanket or shotgun approach, taking a chance versus using calculated judgment, the introduction of multiple alternatives for making concessions on lesser points and taking concessions on major points, as well as use of participation, association, and disassociation techniques. A less well-known tactic is the "salami" in which a negotiator takes concessions bit by bit and eventually wins the whole log. More complex tactics are to purposefully create misunderstandings, to intentionally stretch out discussion on the final agreement to get more concessions, and to imply an offer is final and unchangeable. For each tactic, a set of countertactics should be anticipated.

Many of these tactics fall into the classification of technical skills of negotiations. They can be learned through practice and experimentation. They are indispensable tools to all levels of nursing service administrators.

Evaluation Skills

The process of determining the relative value of a negotiation is as critical a skill as is preparation and selection of strategy. A check list for evaluating the effectiveness will assist in further refinement of these skills.[9] Suggested categories for a check list are as follows:
— What is the goal of the negotiations?
— When should negotiations be started?
— What preparations were made for negotiation?
— What are the areas of initial agreement?
— What are the issues to be negotiated?
— Strategy selection:
  Change tactics
  Question blueprint
  Type of negotiating climate
  Listening conduct
  Semantic difficulties
  Sufficient time allowed for interaction
  Use of disclosure of information and its risks
  Fact-finding efficiency
  Imposition of time limits
  Use of concessions
— Closure techniques

To determine the relative worth of a negotiation requires making value judgments. Observable criteria for judging a negotiation as positive are situations in which the bargainers were open-minded, used questions purposefully, listened critically, communicated clearly, reacted to discussion calmly and with value-free responses, and proposed a number of alternative solutions. Standards for judging a negotiation as negative are situations in which the bargainers used a few proven strategies; asked questions that raised anxiety; interrupted and contradicted speakers; relied on jargon and clichés; reacted to discussion with emotional, abrasive, and value-laden responses; and proposed either-or solutions.

APPLICATION OF NEGOTIATING SKILLS TO NURSING SERVICE ADMINISTRATION

Opportunities for a nursing service administrator to use negotiation skills are multidimensional. Patient compliance, contingency contracting, job counseling, dealing with the malcontent or drug-abusing employee, recruitment of nurses, staffing and census control, stress management, financial reimbursement for nursing services, labor relations, and merger of hospitals and their nursing services are but a few situations in need of effective negotiations. What then are the essential negotiating skills for the nursing service administrator? There are three key skills: preparing an overall plan to be achieved during a negotiation, selecting a strategy and using it while taking part in a negotiation, and evaluating the conduct of negotiation. The second skill is one of the most difficult to master. It requires both knowledge and practice. Effective negotiators never plateau, they just continue to develop and refine these key skills by seizing every opportunity to enter into the art of negotiating.

REFERENCES

1. Bacharach, S., and Lawler, E.: Bargaining: Power, Tactics and Outcomes. San Francisco, Jossey-Bass, Inc., Publishers, 1981.
2. Cohen, H.: The fine art of negotiating. Educational Leadership, *38:* 27-31, 1980.
3. Cohen, H.: You Can Negotiate Anything. Secaucus, New Jersey, Kyle Stuart, 1980.
4. Cresswell, A., and Murphy, M.: Teachers, Unions and Collective Bargaining in Public Education. Berkeley, McCutchan Publishing Corp., 1980.
5. Harris B.: Supervisory Behavior in Education. Englewood Cliffs, New Jersey, Prentice-Hall, Inc., 1965.
6. Katz, R.: Skills of an effective administrator. Harvard Business Review, *1:* 33-40, 1955.
7. Mann, R.: The behavior-therapeutic use of contingency contracting to control an adult behavior problem: Weight control. J. Appl. Behav. Anal., *5:* 99-108, 1972.
8. Mantle, D.: Framework for negotiations in nursing service administration. University of Alabama in Birmingham, 1979 (unpublished).
9. Nierenberg, G.: Fundamentals of Negotiating. New York, Hawthorn Books, 1973.

10. Nierenberg, G., and Caiero, H.: Meta-talk: The Guide to Hidden Meaning in Conversation. New York, Cornerstone Library Inc., 1973.

11. Steckel, S.: Patient Contracting. East Norwalk, Connecticut, Appleton-Century-Crofts, 1982.

12. Strauss, A.: Negotiations: Varieties, Contexts, Processes and Social Orders. San Francisco, Jossey-Bass, Inc., Publishers, 1979.

13. Ways, M.: The virtues, dangers and limits of negotiation. Fortune, Jan. 15, 86-90, 1979.

14. Williamson, J.: Mutual interaction: A model of nursing practice. Nurs. Outlook, *29:* 104-107, 1981.

CHAPTER **57**

Nurse Managers at the Broker's Table
The nurse executive's role

Jo Ann Johnson, RN, DPA
Corinne L. Bergmann, RN, MS

Nurse executives have learned the value and necessity of being at the broker's table, whether the table be in the board room, cafeteria, an office, or outside the organization. The broker's table is a symbol representing full participation in organizational decisions. Nursing needs active involvement in the organizational decision-making process to attain its goals in care provision and maintenance of professional standards.

Thompson referred to brokering as coalition management. He argued that when the complexity of the technology exceeds the comprehension of an individual, resources required exceed the capacity of an individual to acquire, and the organization faces contingencies on more fronts than an individual is able to keep under surveillance, then coalition management occurs.[1] The necessity of coalition decision-making recognizes the complexity, ambiguity, and the turbulent environment within which health care services are now provided.

Brokering occurs at all levels of the organization. For this reason, nurse executives need to be proficient in it, and should develop the skills of first-line and

Reprinted from *The Journal of Nursing Administration*, Vol. 18, No. 6, with permission of J. B. Lippincott Company © 1988.

middle-level managers to be effective brokers. Nurse managers are frequently preoccupied with day-to-day operational problems. Therefore, the concept of a broker's table is often not visualized as a meaningful symbol. This is unfortunate because symbols facilitate management of chaos, confusion, and unpredictability.[2] The nurse manager must recognize that brokering occurs at the nurses' station, in the corridor, and in the coffee room, as well as around a conference table.

Brokering involves negotiation, defines success situationally, and ensures that everyone comes out a winner. The focus is less on who is right[3] than the achievement of desired changes directed toward a future goal. Brokering is a political process. "Politics is a process that results when groups of heterogeneous individuals with different goals, interests, values, and perceptions work together in organizations toward common organizational goals."[4]

Regrettably, the political process has been referred to as a game.[5,6] Although nurse executives recognize the legitimacy of the game, nurse managers (especially new first-line managers) may not. A nurse manager may need to be shown the importance of how politics can enhance his/her role as a patient advocate. Sharing past examples of where this has worked in an organization is an effective strategy to legitimize the game for the nurse manager. Another strategy is to help a manager be very clear about priorities, so that there is room for compromise or backing down on lesser issues.[7]

Del Bueno and Freund[8] provided a list of politically successful skills and tactics for the nurse executive. Many of them are also available and useful for a manager. These have been modified for the nurse manager role as follows:

1. Build Your Own Team

Use interviewing and selection of employees as a way to reduce potential conflict situations on a nursing unit/service,[9] as well as to provide skills necessary to provide quality nursing care. Loyalty of subordinates is a building block in a power base. Choose a team to provide cohesiveness and support.

2. Establish Alliances with Both Supervisors and Peers

Del Bueno and Freund warn that all alliances are not with colleagues the manager considers friends; and one needs to be able to clearly distinguish between the two. Maintenance of alliances with supervisors and peers with whom the manager does not share friendship requires ongoing positive results from the relationship. Alliances with colleagues who offer friendship can be a source for strong support. Both groups can serve as resources, and for whom the manager can be a resource.

3. Use All Possible Channels of Communication

A hard reality for new nurse managers is that the most valuable communication may be with persons who differ in their points of view. Disagreement forces managers to reexamine their own ideas. The reassessment leads to confirmation or revision of ideas and opinions and builds more confidence when presenting ideas to others. Knowledge of how to explore ideas through the informal system first, makes experiences less painful and more successful.

4. Maintain a Flexible Position and Maneuverability

Avoid taking a firm stand on positions (win-lose situations) or issues unless they are ethically and morally essential to the method of operation.[10] Sometimes managers enter into a win-lose situation not because of ethics or morals but because of failing to recognize the legitimacy of their opponent's values. In those situations, by using effort and creativity, a collaborative solution may be found to result in a winning conclusion for both parties.

Learning collaborative negotiation skills is particularly essential in working with physicians. "It is critical for nurse managers to acknowledge that physicians have significant political power in the hospital and attempt to make all confrontations with them win-win situations."[11] Time restrictions, value differences, and cognitive limitations can halt the search for collaborative solutions. Successfully managing those barriers can lead to effective communication and brokering with groups who have more political power in an organization.

5. Be Courteous

"Smiling and cheerfulness are excellent weapons to throw an enemy off guard."[12] Courtesy not only catches adversaries off guard, but also makes others feel good and invites courteous behavior in return (another win-win situation).

6. Increasing Visibility

Be at the right place at the right time. In large organizations anyone aspiring to move up the hierarchy must make themselves and their achievements visible to those higher in the chain of command.[13] Serving on committees and task forces are appropriate ways to accomplish this objective.

Strasen[14] added the following two useful strategies:

7. Networking

"It is the process of exchanging information between strategically placed individuals who have access to ideas and other people."[15]

8. *Mentoring*

The process whereby a seasoned, successful businessperson takes a young inexperienced executive "under his or her wings" and "shows him/her the ropes."[16]. This is a strategy used in field experience requirements in graduate programs in nursing administration. The authors have found it beneficial to require that the mentor be in a different organization than the student. This enables the mentor to more freely share political realities and strategies.

9. *Coopting*

Coopting was defined by Selznick in 1949 as "the process of absorbing new elements into the leadership or policy-determining structure of an organization as a means of averting threats."[17] It could involve taking a "complainer" and bringing them into the system in such a way that the problem becomes "ours" not "yours." Angry, upset physicians might be asked to serve on (chair?) a task force to solve the situation about which they are upset or blocking the solution.

In exchange for a potential long-term solution one should be prepared in the short run to deal with anger, hostility, and uncomfortable questions. By using cooptation, there is potential for a win-win situation.

Although the above strategies all relate to the process of brokering, they do not adequately address the issue of power differentials among the parties. Power has been defined by Claus and Bailey as the ability and will to affect others' performances.[18] Emerson (1962) pointed out that dependency is the obverse of power.[19] Thus, the ultimate goal of acquiring power is to gain independence or autonomy. However, in our large, complex health care organizations that require coalition management, a better operational goal is to seek more equitable power distributions among the brokers. The achievement of a collaborative solution (or even a compromise) at the broker's table is heavily dependent on the power equity among the parties. Assisting nurse managers to gain power equity will enhance their success as brokers on their units and service.

Recognizing that power is the opposite of dependency and vulnerability should legitimize the right of the nurse manager to seek power. Once legitimacy for power acquisition is established, it becomes a matter of the manager knowing what sources of power exist and how to acquire them.

Fortunately, professional nursing literature now contains many articles,[20-23] and recent books (del Bueno and Freund[2] and Strasen[3]) which identify both the sources of power, how to acquire it, and even how to teach power concepts.[24]

Power, like other resources, must be acquired (it is never given freely). Zaleznik argued that power can be capitalized just as monetary resources are capitalized.[25] This is accomplished by building multiple sources of power. These include: authority, informational, expertise, referent, reward, coercive, personal, organizational, and connectional.[26,27]

The degree of access to the different types of power varies within different levels of the organization's hierarchy. For example, authority, legitimate or positional power, increases as one moves up the hierarchy, and vice versa.

The duration of the effectiveness of different power sources also varies over time. Strasen stated that both legitimate power (authority) and coercive power were only effective in the short run; while referent power and expert power were more effective in the long run.[28]

One of the confounding variables in acquiring power and developing political skills is the organizational context within which it all occurs. Health care organizations are becoming increasingly larger and more complex; they are by definition bureaucracies.[30] The issue is not to bemoan or lament the fact that large organizations are bureaucracies, but to understand the characteristics of bureaucracy so that organizations become more functional and management of them more effective. The bureaucratic characteristics that are most pertinent to brokering are those of authority (legitimate power) and chain of command (hierarchy). In the case of authority, power is delegated by the organization (through the hierarchy) to each position. The power belongs to the position and not the person.

It is almost inevitable that when one speaks of authority, there will soon follow a reference to the concept of responsibility. Webster defines responsibility as being answerable for one's actions. Synonyms listed were: reliability and trustworthiness. It is not the definition per se that is of particular significance, but the link that is deeply embedded in our belief system i.e., that authority and responsibility should be equal. A complaint frequently heard is that one does not have the authority to carry out responsibilities. This belief or myth ignores the fact that authority is only one source of power and supports Strasen's statement that the use of authority is only effective in the short run.[30]

Wright[31] makes an argument that as one progresses down the organizational structure the concept of shrinking authority applies (Figure 57-1). In fact, there is an inverse relationship, as authority shrinks, responsibility increases (ask any nurse manager). This factor enables one to understand that the sources available for capitalizing power are dependent on where the position is located in the organizational structure. The further down the hierarchy a managers' position, the greater the necessity for emphasizing other sources of power rather than authority. This in no way negates the importance of authority. Strasen cited the difficulty that clinical specialists have when they do not have access to authority as part of their power base.[32]

Another organizational factor that is both relevant to the acquisition of power and defines the terms of the political game is the organizational culture in which the brokering occurs. Understanding the shared norms, values, and beliefs that shape expectations and behavior is critical to effective brokering. Del Bueno and Freund provide "An Organizational Checklist" which a nurse manager can use to assess the culture.[33] Such an assessment is as

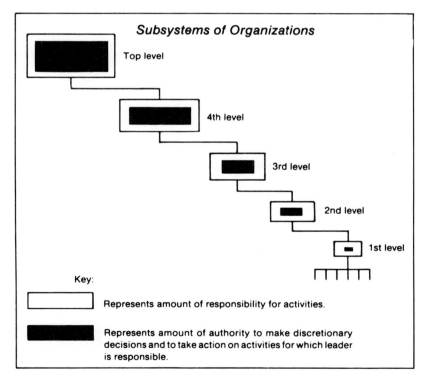

FIGURE 57-1

Wright's concept of shrinking authority. From Michigan State University, Graduate School of Business Administration, East Lansing, Mich.

essential to becoming a successful broker as the patient assessment is to the provision of quality nursing care.

When a nurse manager has acquired sufficient power equity, learned political skills, and identified the organizational culture, the resources (capital) must be "spent" at the broker's table. This expenditure must result in accomplishments that some significant others (superiors/peers/subordinates and/or physicians) perceive as significant. Such accomplishments are inevitably visible and will in turn increase one's power base and political skills (a winwin situation). To attempt to horde this capital would be to lose it. None of these resources are ends in themselves; they are only means to other ends.

In summary, the authors have used the symbol of the broker's table to encourage nurse executives to develop the brokering skills of their managers. Developing brokering skills rests upon managers' acquisition of power equity, political savy, and knowledge of the organization's culture. These resources combine to empower one for success at the broker's table.

REFERENCES

1. Thompson JD. The control of complex organizations. In: Organizations in action. New York: McGraw-Hill, 1967:133.
2. del Bueno DJ, Freund CM. Power and politics in nursing administration. Owings Mills, MD: National Health Publishing, 1986:XV.
3. Strasen L. Key business skills for nurse managers. Philadelphia: JB Lippincott, 1987:322.
4. Strasen, 313.
5. Cavanaugh DE. Gamesmanship: the art of strategizing: J Nurs Admin 1985;15(4):36-39.
6. Strasen, 314.
7. del Bueno, Freund, 12.
8. del Bueno, Freund, 11-12.
9. Strasen, 318.
10. del Bueno, Freund, 12.
11. Strasen, 322.
12. Strasen, 320.
13. del Bueno, Freund, 8.
14. Strasen, 283-299.
15. Strasen, 284.
16. Strasen, 294.
17. Selznick P. TVA and the Grass Roots. Berkeley, California. University of California Press. 1949 in J. D. Thompson Organizations in Action Chap. 3, p. 35 1967.
18. Claus K, Bailey J. Power and influence in health care. St. Louis: CV Mosby, 1977:20.
19. Emerson RM. Power-dependence relations, American Sociological Review. Vol. 27 Feb. 1962 pp. 31-40 in J. D. Thompson Organizations in Action Chap. 3, p. 30 1967.
20. Cavanaugh, 36-39.
21. Lamar E. Communicating personal power through nonverbal behavior. J Nurs Admin 1985;15(1):41-44.
22. Heineken J. Power: conflicting views. J Nurs Admin 1985;15(11):36-39.
23. Courtemanche JB. Powernomics: a concept every nurse should know. Nurs Mgmt 17(1):39-41.
24. Heineken J, McCloskey J. Teaching power concepts. J Nurs Educ 15(11):40-41.
25. Zaleznik A. Power and politics in organizational life. Harvard Business Review May 1970;48:47-60.
26. Heineken, McCloskey, 40-41.
27. Strasen, 301-331.
28. Strasen, 306.
29. Perrow C. Why bureaucracy: Complex organizations: A critical essay. Glenview, IL: Scott Forman, 1972:6.
30. Strasen, 306.
31. Wright RG. Subsystems of organizations. In: The nature of organizations. Encino, CA: Dickenson Publishing Co, 1977: 113.
32. Strasen, 307.
33. del Bueno, Freund, 27-32.

CHAPTER **58**

Conflict Resolution

Rachel Z. Booth, RN, PhD

Conflict, both the functional and dysfunctional aspects, permeates all types of relationships between individuals, groups, and organizations, and an attempt to eliminate conflict can result in a stifling situation. Because conflict is always present, there is a great urgency to seek modes of resolution in a society that has become suffused with stress, as well as being exceedingly complex. Conflict, however, needs to be meaningfully exploited in order to provide a healthy balance between stimulation and resolution.

There are varied definitions of conflict: it has been described as arising "from a lack of clarity with regard to role and task accomplishment definitions, or- . . . because of differences in values, philosophies, or perceptions." Another defines it as "all kinds of opposition or antagonistic interaction."[1-2]

Traditionally, it has been unacceptable to recognize and discuss sources or issues of conflict among professionals. Even if it was addressed, conflict was viewed as a personality problem that was so laden with emotion that one hardly could detect the true cause or source. Similarly, conflict has all too often connoted negativism and even violence between individuals and groups.

The nursing profession continues to undergo rapid change in assuming new roles and different relationships with the consumer and other health professionals. Also, nurses are assuming leadership roles that only physicians and administrators have occupied in the past. This results in an obvious shift of power and control, and increases the probability of conflict between all the individuals involved.

When one group loses territory or resources to another group, the situation becomes ripe for the generation and escalation of conflict. If the conflict is not resolved, both groups are likely to spend much more time, energy, and other resources on combat than is appropriate or justifiable.

For a long time, social scientists have proposed the conflict model as one in which divergent interests are emphasized and, as a result, individuals and groups are divided.[3] The three different philosophies of conflict have tended to follow the same theory of divergence since it was first acknowledged in the late nineteenth century.[2] Initially, conflict was viewed as negative; later it was conceived as somewhat negative but inevitable if not acceptable; and currently, it is perceived as a necessary and positive state of being.

The first view is espoused by the traditionalists who perceive all conflict as bad and destructive, and believe that the source of conflict must be removed. Therefore, if a staff or faculty member generates conflict or disagrees with the ideas of another, then that person must be dismissed as soon as possible.

Such an approach seems unfair to the person generating the conflict in that the reason for dismissal is rarely discussed, giving the individual little opportunity to alter any undesirable behavior. To take such

Reprinted from *Nursing Outlook,* Vol. 30, No. 8, with permission of the American Journal of Nursing Co. © 1982.

a drastic action also stifles motivation, creativity, and the desire to meet the goals of the unit or the organization. The traditionalists' philosophy has been instilled and inculcated in children during their early, formative years by the family, the school, and the church. We see children and adults expected to get along with others at any cost, and to comply with directions given by elders and those in authority.

After the mid 1940s, the behavioralists established their view that conflict is somewhat harmful but inevitable. Due to this inevitability, conflict needs to be managed as effectively as possible, with efforts made to minimize its presence.

When an employee or faculty member is a "problem," frequently sufficient pressure is exerted to minimize his or her power in the organization, or the person is forced to resign. A common practice is to transfer the "troublemaker" to another unit, or schedule the person to an undesirable shift. Today, we frequently see this mode of coping with conflict even though the behavioralists had their heyday in 1940s to 1960s.

The third and most recent philosophy is that of the interactionists. They believe that conflict is a creative force: it is healthy, must be present, and must be stimulated as well as resolved. If conflict is absent, individuals or groups merely maintain the status quo, view their work as simply a job to earn money, lack motivation, and suffer from decreased satisfaction and morale. Companies have gone bankrupt, in part due to an excess of agreement and a conflict free management group.[2]

Always agreeing is translated into excessive cooperation which may be just as dysfunctional as an excess of conflict. Too much cooperation results in stagnation and an absence of new ideas, thus decreasing the progress and growth of a group or an organization. Cooperation is often viewed as the opposite of conflict, and conflict as synonymous with competition.

Both views seem to be misconceptions and, as Robbins notes, conflict and cooperation exist on two separate continuums, that is, one is not the opposite of the other.[2] Cooperation exists when two or more parties are working toward mutually acceptable goals and their interests are, at some point, convergent. This is not the opposite of conflict.

In W. B. Lacy's review of prior research concerning cooperation, trust, and gender, his findings show that females are more trusting and trustworthy than men in initial interactions. Women, however, are less willing to forgive a person if that trust is violated and will react with greater vindictiveness and retaliation than men. Likewise, it was found that females expect a higher level of cooperation from their opponents than do males.[4]

These research findings are relevant to nurses. Since nursing is a female dominated profession, it can be assumed that nurses have a higher level of expected cooperation from others during initial interactions. If these expectations of trust are violated, it follows that it is more difficult to forgive the person who is guilty of the violation.

Even though competition and conflict are not synonymous, the former can very easily cause the latter. If one person gains at the other's expense, it is not surprising that the relationship becomes one of strain and mistrust. As a nurse assumes more authority and responsibility for decision-making in patient care matters, the physician's authority and responsibility decrease. The loss of control over patient matters is not easy to accept, especially for those individuals who may be threatened either in relation to economic security or their concept of self.

WHAT CAUSES CONFLICT?

Conflict arises due to both individual and organizational sources and may be intrapersonal, interpersonal, or interorganizational. Intrapersonal conflict may be inherent in a person's role; that is, there is a lack of fit between the person's goals and the expectations of their role. "Intrapersonal conflict exists in the cognitive and affective realms of an individual's mind. Thus, an individual may perceive that he or she is conflicting with the organization or other employees, but the conflict, in fact, exists only in that person's mind, not at a behavioral level."[5] As long as the conflict is intrapersonal, it is not apparent to others; yet the person may exhibit signs of stress and anxiety.

Interpersonal conflict occurs between two or more people and is most often caused by differences in communication and behavioral styles. Since a major portion of our waking time is spent in some form of communication — either listening, talking, reading, or writing — there is a high likelihood that numerous problems will emanate from these activities.

One of the most lethal ways to percipitate a conflict is to withhold information. Imagine a notice of an important meeting being distributed but the notice is purposefully withheld from a member of the group.

The converse of this can be true: when there is a communication overload. If a person is continually barraged by unnecessary letters, memos, or telephone calls from an individual, then that person starts scanning or just laying communication aside. The danger lies in missing an important communication buried among the overabundant messages received.

Semantic difficulties will be a source of conflict as long as human beings interact. It has been shown that different interpretations are placed on the same events to the point that, in some cases, the event is not recognized as the same one.

Differences in vocabularies between physicians and nurses has often been cited as one cause of conflict between the professions. Also, individuals from different geographical areas may attach different meanings to the same term; or they may have a dialect or speech pattern that is unique to a certain group or area and this may be a source of misunderstanding. To compound the matter, differing communications patterns, perceptions, misunderstandings, and filtering occur and increase as more people become involved.

BEHAVIORAL FACTORS

Another type of communication problem is an individual's lack of willingness to carry the problem to the person who has the authority to resolve or at least explore it. The problem then may fester and become a crisis.

In many instances, subordinates selectively filter messages going to a superior. As a result, only the good messages are communicated or are emphasized and the unpleasant communications may be ignored or de-emphasized. Or, the superior may discover the true communication and become distrustful of a subordinate.

Emotional and antagonistic behavior increases the likelihood of conflict, and reduces one's control and power in a relationship. In general, people find it extremely difficult to discuss differences in a direct manner. Instead the problem is often discussed with others who are not directly involved, thus, resulting in a maelstrom of discontent and rumors. This type of behavior is most prevalent in organizations where ideas have been suppressed to the extent that the only way to achieve input is to talk via the grapevine.

Other difficulties that are inevitable can be the result of differences in educational and social backgrounds. An individual who has an authoritative and dogmatic manner in dealing with others usually prefers one-way communication and has difficulty listening or eliciting input. People with low self-esteem will perceive others as a threat and this can result in antagonism between the two individuals, resulting in interpersonal conflict.[2]

A chairperson of a committee who sets the agenda without input from members or who does not allow member's contributions during the meeting is a good example of someone whose behavior is very likely to generate a lot of conflict. If a meeting is called merely to formalize a decision already made, little committee support to implement the decision can be expected, in fact, committee members, in a passive manner, can sabotage the decision.

A common source of conflict is the traditional behavioral pattern between physicians and nurses — expressed as the physician's dominance and nurse's deference.[6] As the educational level of nurses increases and more positions of power and control are assumed by nurses, the dominant-deferent type of relationship is likely to shift to a more collaborative-collegial one.

FOUR DIFFERENT LABELS FOR CONFLICT

Frequently, differing demands and expectations are made by different people. Very often there are conflicting expectations between staff nurses and hospital management or between nurses and physicians. The clinician may have one set of expectations communicated from nursing service administration and another set from the medical staff. Rosse and Rosse describe this "inter-sender" type of conflict as ". . . incompatible demands placed upon an individual by different role senders."[7]

A second type of role conflict takes place when there is a disagreement between the values and beliefs of the occupant of the role in comparison to the expectations set forth by others. For instance, disagreement can occur if one professional challenges the practice decisions of another professional. This places the persons involved in an untenable situation until there is some form of reconciliation.

Besides person-role conflict there is inter-role conflict, and also role overload conflict. The former takes place when an individual assumes multiple responsibilities in different types of roles which may be incompatible. The working mother who is a nurse must reconcile her role as a mother, wife, nurse, and community member, as well as a member of the profession. Not an easy task for anyone to manage.

Role overload, is very common in today's highly technological work environment. The work to be accomplished is far too much to be expected of one individual. Recently, much attention has been directed to this type of overload as studies are being conducted on the work stress that nurses encounter in the hospital.

Certain characteristics of organizations also predispose to conflicting situations.[2] The larger the size of the organization, the greater the potential for conflict. As the administrative levels in the hierarchy increase, the organization becomes more impersonal, communications more difficult, and labor divided more unevenly. There is an increase not only in size but in the use of rules and procedures. Since an organization tends to assume a bureaucratic form of operation when it becomes a certain size, one can safely predict that there will be a linear relationship between conflict and bureaucratic encumberances.

Even though interdependence is a positive factor in an organization, when the "activities of one group are perceived to have fairly direct consequences on the ability of another to pursue its goals," conflict can easily develop.[2] The greater the interdependence, the greater the potential for conflict.[8] Thus, the nurse practitioner or intensive care nurse who work in a more interdependent relationship with the physician

can anticipate more conflict. What may cause conflict for one person or group in an organization, however, may not for another; it is the individual, the situation, and other individuals or groups in the organization that determine the amount and type of conflict.

The important point to remember is to recognize and understand conflict and to seek the most effective mode for its resolution. Additionally, if one is aware of the causes of conflict, one may anticipate its presence, thus decrease the negative impact and excess anxiety and tension that conflict produces.

ACHIEVING A HEALTHY SOLUTION

But how should we behave in such a conflict prone society? It is common knowledge that there are the usual personality clashes, difficulties in the male/female relationships, competition between physician and nurse, and other problematic arenas. During the past decade, however, a trend toward interprofessional activities and programs has placed professionals in close, interdependent relationships where they share goals, tasks, clients, control, and power.

There are six modes of conflict resolution: confrontation, bargaining, smoothing, avoiding, forcing, and unilateral action.[9] Usually, the method of choice is confrontation. Even though this has had a negative connotation over the years, its true meaning is to openly and freely discuss the issue about which there is a disagreement.

By openly discussing both sides of an issue and freely sharing both views, the process of confrontation can provide a long-term solution. To use this mode requires a deliberative and cognitive approach.

Prior to entering into the confrontation process, three requisites are necessary in order to be successful. The first is that each party must possess an equal motivation to resolve the issue. Otherwise, either of the parties can resort to another mode of resolution which then destroys the attempt at problem-solving.

The second requisite is for each party to have an equal or near equal power base. If this requisite is absent, then it is easy to utilize another mode of resolution such as forcing or withdrawing. It is important to recognize that power may be derived from sources other than position. A staff nurse may be powerful due to expertise in a clinical area or due to the influence she or he has with others in the organization.

The third requisite is for each party to have the necessary information with which to engage in problem solving. To generate solutions without having access to the appropriate data is a waste of time and can cause frustration, not to mention its effect on the quality of the solution. Of course, in order to do this, all the data surrounding the issue must be available for the discussion. To enter into a confrontation without having the appropriate data and information is a handicap from the very beginning.

In order to engage in confrontation, attention must be paid to the process, with both sides of the issue clearly differentiated and understood. This can be accomplished by stating each party's preferred solution aloud and asking for verification of the statements. In this way, both parties may ascertain the magnitude of the differences in order to develop the appropriate strategies for continuing the process. Confrontation is of no assistance in discussing value differences, such as beliefs about morality, race, and religion; therefore, value judgments must be eliminated from the process.

It is wise to develop a strategy for engaging in the process ahead of time; think it through carefully. Role playing ahead of the confrontation is a useful strategy.

If differences are not dealt with in a timely manner and with the appropriate people, then the differences can very easily escalate into a war. In the process of a confrontation, it is important not to place the fault or guilt onto another person — a form of projection. As soon as one side is defensive — because guilt is laid at their door — any healthy resolution of the issue is precluded. It does little good to state "you are not hearing me correctly." This causes the other person to become defensive since he or she is blamed for the lack of resolution.

A more effective comment, is, "let me restate the issue so we may be clear as to the real problem." Responsibility for accurate communication is placed on both parties, and the climate is much more conducive to solving problems.

Confrontation is a technique that is very difficult for many people. It can be learned but it needs to be free of emotional overtones. Henning and Jardim note that, because of their traditional feminine experience, women may fall into the trap of being overemotional, intolerant, and painfully vulnerable to criticism.[10] These characteristics cause the attempts at resolution through confrontation to fail and lapse into forcing or withdrawing. For those groups who successfully use a healthy confrontation, it has been shown that they consistently perform at higher, more productive levels than those who do not.[11]

BARGAINING GAINS A RESOLUTION

A second mode of resolution is bargaining: each side gives something and each receives something in return. With this tactic, it may be necessary to have a third party serve as negotiator or arbitrator if the parties have difficulty moving toward resolution. Again, it is important to clearly identify the positions of both parties and to know the preferred solution of each party.

It is possible for a conflict not to be ready for negotiation, thus the process must be delayed. In this case, Bartos advises that to propose an extremely limited concession will stall the negotiations, as well as make the opponent angry. On the other hand, "an unexpectedly high concession may cause the opponent to increase his level of expectation, thus making it likely that the negotiator will have to settle for a less desirable outcome." He believes that it is fair to split the difference and then agree on a position somewhere between the two preferences.[7] It is advisable to hold the negotiation in a neutral setting; not in the offices of either party involved in the issue.

Perhaps nurses should utilize bargaining when dealing with physicians and other professionals if it is evident that confrontation will not work. Bargaining or negotiating is a time consuming process and is commonly used in labor disputes between management and staff. It has probably been underutilized by nurses in health care settings. Bargaining was most often used as the mode of conflict resolution in a study of over 200 physicians in five academic medical centers.

I had similar findings in my study of all possible paired combination of five health care professional groups in an academic health center. Bargaining was most often used between the paired professions of medicine-dentistry and medicine-pharmacy.[13]

A decision resulting from bargaining is often a short term solution. The same issue may need to be dealt with by confrontation at a later date. The important result of negotiation is that the involved parties are able to proceed with their tasks even though neither party received the optimal choice.

SMOOTHING IT OUT

A third mode of resolution is by smoothing over the conflict. It is a process whereby both parties minimize their differences and emphasize areas of common interests and agreements. In this type of situation, the differences are not acknowledged and consequently, a solution is not found. Each party resumes regular activities and in a short period of time the problem presents itself again, and in many instances, has reached a crisis.

A potential conflict may be smoothed over when either party is fearful of the other party or is afraid of the results of the expected decision. This often occurs in a superior/subordinate relationship when the subordinate wishes to convey that "all is well." The subordinate may be fearful of posing to the superior controversial issues on questionable situations for fear of being judged less than competent or not capable of handling the issue. Such a method is most likely to be used in those organizations and areas where conflict is perceived as bad.

AVOIDING CONFLICT ALTOGETHER

Another common method of resolving conflict is through avoidance. In this case, either party may withdraw from the discussion. This is a powerful technique and may be purposefully used to frustrate the other party. Withdrawal from the problem frequently is used after other methods for resolution have failed.

To avoid a conflict merely for avoidance sake does nothing but cause escalation of the problem. Yet, there may be times when a person must use avoidance in order to postpone the discussion until a more appropriate time due to hostility, lack of data, or lack of agreement on the problem or preferred solution.

Avoidance or withdrawal frequently occurs when there is a great difference in the power between the two parties. The less powerful one may have a feeling of helplessness. The director of nursing has position power so a staff nurse may very well be intimidated; unable to enter into the process of resolution with the director.

Alienation can occur if either one of the parties withdraws from the problem-solving process, for whatever reason. Alienation, B. W Duldt points out, ". . . is created when one person decides it is useless to continue trying to communicate with another and therefore refuses to interact , or leaves the scene." She further cites McClure's study involving 50 hospital nurses in which alienation was found to be one of the major reasons why nurses resigned their positions. This was due to the powerless feeling that nurses had in relation to nursing service administrators.

FORCING THE ISSUE

A fifth mode of resolution is to force a solution, no matter what or how. With this method, a person uses power to gain an optimal solution for one party. Determined to win, the person forcing the outcome thus creates a win or lose situation. Individuals occupying positions of authority can easily use this form of resolution. Forcing requires little time to resolve an issue but it may create other problems that are ultimately very time consuming. For the loser, who was forced, a sense of powerlessness and mistrust usually results. As with previous methods of resolution, this only provides a short-term solution.

UNILATERAL ACTION

The final mode of resolution is unilateral action; where an individual makes a decision and takes action without considering the views or adding input from others. Eventually, such behavior becomes extremely damaging to morale and commitment to the organization's goals. This type of resolution is very similar to forcing an issue; the difference is that unilateral action excludes a relationship between two parties.

In a study of 200 registered staff nurses who were employed in 10 different hospitals, Bartol found that nurses used collaboration most frequently in conflict situations. Compromise was the second most frequently used mode, followed by forcing, accomodating, and avoiding — in that order.[15] According to the definition of terms used in this study, collaboration is synonymous with confrontation, compromise with bargaining, and accommodation with smoothing.

In a study of 23 individuals from the professions of dentistry, medicine, nursing, pharmacy, and social work/community planning — smoothing was used most frequently when looking at all the possible combinations of pairs of professions. Bargaining was the second most frequently used mode, followed by avoidance, confrontation, and forcing the issue, in that order.[13] In contrast another study showed that confrontation is most often used in industrial organizations, followed by forcing the issue and smoothing it over in that order.[12]

It is unwise to make any judgment of the different way conflict is resolved except to say that one may be more effective than others in certain types of situations. Hall, however, has placed the modes in an ideal order, going from the most to the least ideal: confrontation (collaborating), bargaining (compromising), smoothing (accommodating), forcing, and avoidance.[15]

Nurses are very vulnerable to conflict due to the pivotal role they assume in the delivery of care, the new functions and responsibilities they are undertaking, the acquisition of more power and control in the health setting, the interdependence with other professionals, and the differentiation between professionals. Any one of these can present a major problem, not to mention their collective impact that nurses can encounter on a daily basis as a multiple source conflict. It is imperative that nurses recognize and understand this complex phenomenon, and become familiar with the varying techniques to resolve conflict. Individuals can move from one method of resolution to another as indicated by the situation. Even though they may have a preferred mode, they are not limited to any specific way and may explore and learn other modes that may be equally desirable, if not more effective.

REFERENCES

1. Tye, K. The elementary school principal: key to educational change. In *The Power to Change: Issues for the Innovative Educator,* ed. by C. M. Culver and G. J. Hoban. New York, McGraw-Hill Book Co., 1973, pp. 25-33.

2. Robbins, S. P. *Managing Organizational Conflict: A Nontraditional Approach.* Englewood Cliffs, N.J., Prentice-Hall, 1974.

3. Heller, C. Unresolved issues in stratification theory. In *Structured Social Inequality: A Reader in Social Stratification,* ed. by Celia Heller. New York, Macmillan Co., 1969, pp. 479-487.

4. Lacy, W. B. Assumptions of human nature, and initial expectations and behavior as mediators of sex effects in prisoner's dilemma research. *J. Conflict Resolu.* 22:269-281, June 1978.

5. Zey-Ferrell, Mary. *Dimensions of Organizations.* Santa Monica, Calif., Goodyear Publishing Co., 1979.

6. Kalisch, B. J., and Kalisch, P. A. An analysis of the sources of physician-nurse conflict. *J. Nurs. Adm.* 7:50-57, Jan. 1977.

7. Rosse, J., and Rosse, P. Role conflict and ambiguity: an empirical investigation of nursing personnel. *Eval. Health Prof.* 4:385-405, December 1981.

8. Schaefer, M. *Conflict Management.* Paper presented at Nurse Practitioner Symposium, Cross Keys, Maryland, October 1976.

9. Weisbord, M. R., and others. Three dilemmas of academic medical centers. *J. App. Behav. Sci.* 14:284-304, July-Aug.-Sept. 1978.

10. Henning, Margaret, and Jardim, Ann. *The Managerial Woman.* New York, Anchor Press, 1977.

11. Lawrence, P., and Lorsch, J. Differentiation and integration in complex organizations. *Adm. Sci. Q.* 12:1-47, July 1967.

12. Bartos, O.J. Simple model of negotiation: a sociological point of view. *J. Conflict Resolu.* 21:565-579, Dec. 1977.

13. Booth, R. *The Management of An Interprofessional Program in An Academic Health Center: A Case Study.* College Park, Md., University of Maryland, 1978. (Unpublished doctoral dissertation)

14. Duldt, B. W. Anger: an alienating communication hazard for nurses. *Nurs. Outlook* 29:640-644, Nov. 1981.

15. Bartol, G. *The Styles of Conflict Management Used in Co-Worker Relationships by Nurse Practitioners Employed in Hospitals.* New York, Teachers College, Columbia University, 1976. (Unpublished doctoral dissertation)

SUGGESTED READINGS

UNIT FIVE. MANAGING PROCESSES AND
RESOURCES

Strategic Planning

Fine R: Consumerism and information: Power and confusion, NAQ 12(3):66-73, 1988.

Mintzberg H: Crafting strategy, HBR 64(4):66-75, 1987.

Nelson M: Advocacy in nursing: How has it evolved and what are its implications for practice? NO 36(3):136-141, 1988.

Porter-O'Grady T: Restructuring the nursing organization for a consumer-driven marketplace, NAQ 12(3):60-65, 1988.

Romano C: Development, implementation, and utilization of a computerized information system for nursing, NAQ 10(2):1-7, 1986.

Marketing

Alward R: A marketing approach to nursing administration. I. JONA 13(3):9-12, 1983.

Alward R: A marketing approach to nursing administration. II. JONA 13(4):18-22, 1983.

Beaupre BA: An administrative marketing strategy: A different perspective on the nursing process, JONA 18(11):37-41, 1988.

Camunas C: Using public relations to market nursing service, JONA 16(10):26-30, 1986.

Norkett B: The role of nursing in marketing health care, NAQ 10(1):85-89, 1985.

Stanton M and Stanton G: Marketing nursing — a model for sciences, Nursing Management 19(9):36-38, 1988.

Financial Management

Kersey J: Increasing the nursing manager's fiscal responsibility, Nursing Management 19(10):30-32, 1988.

McGrail G: Budgets: An underused resource, JONA 18(11): 25-31, 1988.

Marks F: Refining a classification system for fiscal and staffing management, JONA 17(1):39-43, 1987.

O'Conner N: Integrating patient classification with cost accounting, Nursing Management 19(10):27-29, 1988.

Rosenbaum H, Willert T, Kelly E, Grey J and McDonald B: Costing out nursing services based on acuity, JONA 18(7):10-15, 1988.

Organization and Delivery of Nursing Care

Capers C, O'Brien C, Quinn R, Kelly R and Fenerty A: The Neuman systems model in practice, JONA 29-38, 1985.

Capers C: Using nursing models to guide nursing practice: Key questions, JONA 16(11):40-43, 1986.

Hesterly S and Robinson M: Nursing in a service line organization, JONA 18(11):32-36, 1988.

Koerner B, Bunkers L, Nelson B and Santema K: Implementing differentiated practices: The Sioux Valley experience, JONA 19(2):13-19, 1989.

Koerner B, Cohen J and Armstrong D: Professional behavior in collaborative practice, JONA 16(10):39-43, 1986.

Krenz M, Karlik B and Kiniry S: A nursing diagnosis based model: Guiding nursing practice, JONA 19(5):32-36, 1989.

Maas M: Nursing diagnosis in a professional model of nursing: Keystone for effective nursing administration, JONA 16(12):39-42, 1986.

Moore T and Simendinger E: The matrix organization: Its significance to nursing, NAQ 3(2):25-31, 1979.

Spitzer-Lehmann R: Middle management consolidation, Nursing Management 20(8):59-62, 1989.

Tonges M: Redesigning nursing practice: The professionally advanced care team (PROACT) model. I. JONA 19(8): 31-38, 1989.

Tonges M: Redesigning nursing practice: The professionally advanced care team (PROACT) model. II. JONA 19(9): 19-22, 1989.

Toohey E, Shillinger F and Baranowski S: Planning alternative delivery systems: An organizational assessment, JONA 15(12):9-15, 1985.

Townsend M: A participative approach to administrative reorganization, JONA 20(2):11-14, 1990.

Veninga R: When bad things happen to good nursing departments, JONA 17(2):35-40, 1987.

Westcot L: Nursing education and nursing service: A collaborative model, Nursing & Health Care 376-379, 1987.

Zander K: Second generation primary nursing: A new agenda, JONA 18-24, 1985.

Recruitment, Retention, and Staff Development

Balasco E and Black A: Advancing nursing practice: Description, recognition, and reward, NAQ 12(2):52-62, 1988.

Buerhaus P: Not just another nursing shortage, Nursing Economics 5(6):267-279, 1987.

Gleeson S, Nestor O and Riddell A: Helping nurses through the management threshold, NAQ 11-16, 1983.

Harrington C: A policy agenda for the nursing shortage, NO 36(3):118-119, 153-154, 1988.

Helmer F and McKnight P: One more time — solutions to the nursing shortage, JONA 18(11):7-14, 1988.

Hofmann P: Accurate measurement of nursing turnover: The first step in its reduction, JONA 37-39, 1981.

Pfoutz S, Simms L and Price S: Teaching and learning: essential components of the nurse executive role, Image 19(3):138-141, 1987.

Simms L, Erbin-Roeseman M, Darga A and Coeling H: Breaking the burnout barrier: Resurrecting work excitement in nursing, Nursing Economics 8(3):177-187, 1990.

Productivity and Staffing

Benefield L: Motivating professional staff, NAQ 12(4):57-62, 1988.

Cleland V: A nurse staffing evaluation model, Michigan Hospitals 21(2):13-17, 1985.

Giovannetti P: Understanding patient classification systems, JONA 9(2):4-9, 1979.

Hendrickson G, Doddato T and Kovner C: How do nurses spend their time? JONA 20(3):31-37, 1990.

Kirk R: Using workload analysis to facilitate quality and productivity, JONA 20(3):21-30, 1990.

Kopelman: Job redesign and productivity: A review of the evidence, National Productivity Review 10(3):237-255, 1985.

Nauert L, Leach K and Watson P: Finding the productivity standard in your acuity system, JONA 18(1):25-30, 1988.

Performance Appraisal and Evaluation

Brief A: Developing a usable performance appraisal system, JONA 9(10):7-10, 1979.

O'Loughlin E and Kaulbach D: Peer review: A perspective for performance appraisal, JONA 12(9):22-27, 1981.

Quality Management

Hinshaw A, Scofield R and Atwood J: Staff, patient, and cost outcomes of all-registered nurse staffing, JONA 30-36, 1981.

New N and New R: Quality management that works, Nursing Management 20(6):21-24, 1989.

Negotiation and Conflict Management

Adams R and Applegate C: Managing conflict — techniques managers can use, AORN 46(6):1116-1120, 1987.

Cohen A: The management rights clause in collective bargaining, Nursing Management 20(11):24-31, 1989.

Cleland V: A new model for collective bargaining, NO 36(5):228-230, 1988.

Colvin CH: Conflict and resolution: Strikes in nursing, NAQ 12(1):45-51, 1987.

Gullett CR and Kroll M: Rule making and the National Labor Relations Board: implications for the health care industry, Health Care Management Review 15(2):61-65, 1990.

Laser R: I win — you win negotiating, JONA 24-29, 1981.

Wade-Koch M: Conflict management: A generic approach for the health care worker, Caregiver 1(3):8-10, 1988.

Wilson C, Hamilton C and Murphy E: Union dynamics in nursing, JONA 20(2):35-39, 1990.

PART III

NURSING AND FUTURE HEALTH CARE DELIVERY

What is the future of nursing and health care delivery in the twenty-first century? What impact will the nursing profession have on health care policy formulation and the delivery of health care services? Will nursing still be in transition from an occupation to a profession, or will it have achieved full professional status? What information will nurse administrators need to know to function effectively in their roles? What innovative educational changes in nursing curricula will be necessary to address the tremendous growth in the knowledge base related to technology in health care? What do the futurists envision as nursing's role in the twenty-first century?

Part III includes articles pertaining to the future role of nursing and health care delivery. Christman emphasizes that rapid expansion of knowledge and technology in health care mandates changes in the educational preparation of nurses. He proposes that the clinical doctorate will become the entry-level requirement for the practice of nursing. Aydelotte, an innovative futurist, cautions that strategic vision and decisions are needed today to protect the preferred future of nursing. To make these decisions, nursing needs a vision of what is desirable, what is valued, and above all, what is most worthwhile to society. Six strategic decisions are outlined. She proposes that it is time for nurses to carve out an image and transform themselves into that image — a preferred future. Felton's article focuses on obstacles to nursing's preferred future. If the profession is to achieve its preferred future, it must address equity, excellence, threats to affirmative action, and recruitment. These issues must be addressed if the orientation of the nurse as an educated person and as a true national resource is to be maintained. Haddon asserts that the final frontier heralds a new era in which nurses finally assume their rightful place as leaders in the health care delivery industry. Nurses will assume this leading role as a result of a systematized body of knowledge, new nursing technologies, and modern management techniques. Nurses are agents of change in moving health care from a cottage industry to a full-fledged business enterprise — a business of compassion, empathy, and quality.

CHAPTER **59**

The Future of the Nursing Profession

Luther Christman, RN, PhD, FAAN

The commonly accepted belief that the past is prologue holds for forecasting the future of health care as well as for other phenomena. For example, a child born in 1982 could expect to live 74 years, an increase of 24 years over a child born in 1900.[1] This substantial increase in life span will show another large increment by the end of this century.

The lengthening of the average life span occurred in three different stages that grew out of the steady accumulation of scientific knowledge. The first stage ran from roughly the turn of the last century to the late 1930s and can be classified as an era of sanitation. Development of immunological techniques took place during this period, and the ravages of the highly contagious diseases and their concomitant secondary effects were markedly curtailed. The second stage, which lasted well into the 1960s, was the era of antibiotics. The combined advances of the two eras eliminated all the quick killers and left to be solved the slow disease processes such as cancer and cardiovascular, renal, and endocrine diseases. The third stage of technological innovation will enable the effective management of these relatively slow-killing forms of disease, a condition that appears to have given rise to attacks against the technological imperative by science writers, economists, and bureaucrats.

A brief review of the effect of each of the three stages may place them all in a perspective that permits more rational discussion and prediction. Development of immunological techniques and antibiotics had a major impact in curtailing the forces that produce ill health until the capability of each particular form of endeavor reached its limits. Each was cost-effective. The same can be said of technology except that its full capability has not yet been demonstrated. Refinement of present technology, the development of new and simpler equipment, and occasional major breakthroughs are occurring. Over time, the costs of technology decline, and its use creates additional healthy years of life as the primary disease process is further controlled. Although the loss of brain cells, nephrons, and other important cells takes place unremittingly with age and death is inevitable, various ways will be found by means of vitamins and other chemicals to retard the aging of cells. In essence, society may soon be approaching the analogue of the parson's one-horse shay.

NURSING IN TODAY'S ENVIRONMENT

When considering the possible dimensions of the future role of the nursing profession, one must first examine current social phenomena and trends. No professional role exists in a vacuum or grows in isolation. Instead, roles develop to meet the expectations of others. It might be said that professional roles are invented by society to supply the services that can be rendered only by those with specialized knowledge. Society gives certain rights and privileges to

Reprinted from *Nursing Administration Quarterly,* Vol. 11, No. 2, with permission of Aspen Publishers, Inc. © 1987.

these roles but, in turn, it exacts certain obligations. The professions that most effectively fulfill those obligations are most apt to obtain the rewards given for maintaining an adequate supply of services.

Effective Nursing Requires Advanced Training

Almost everyone is keenly aware of the rapid expansion of knowledge and the growth of technology. Both developments greatly affect all professionals. Daily confrontation with a constantly expanding stream of new and complicated information is creating uneasiness in all types of practitioners. So rapid is the creation of new knowledge that many patients probably are being treated by obsolete methods every day. What are the implications for nurses of this set of conditions? One imperative is that all nurses must form positive attitudes toward continued and advanced study. Scientists who have studied the rate at which knowledge is expanding predict that the lifetime of all knowledge will shrink so dramatically that most persons will not have current information. Thus, the knowledge that most persons possess will become outmoded almost faster than they are able to acquire new knowledge, so that many of people's actions will be based on obsolescent information.

Because of the tremendous rate at which scientific knowledge is accumulating, it is not risky to predict that the clinical doctorate will become the entry level requirement for the practice of nursing. If nurses wish to have parity on the health team, they must have equally rigorous clinical preparation.

Expert knowledge is a prime means by which power, influence, and economic rewards are secured. The laws governing the practice of nursing in all of the states will be modified greatly when this level of preparation is the common denominator. Imagine how different the milieu of care will be when every nurse, every patient, every hospital administrator, and every physician addresses all nurses as "Doctor."

The debate over requirements for entry-level practice of nursing has moved beyond the tediousness of stereotypic argumentation among nurses to one of more serious import. If one correctly reads the signs of the future of health care, the issue of entry level has

assumed a higher level of abstraction — can nursing survive and grow as a profession without university education as a mandate for the basic level of preparation? For too long a time, nurses have drawn invidious comparisons between themselves and other nurses at different entry levels. In the process, they almost seem to have been oblivious to what is happening to educational preparation in the entire health field. Nurses are the only health care practitioners who have a weak academic background at the entry level. They are the proverbial low ones on the totem pole when compared with all other health professionals. What is more, the gap in knowledge between other health professionals and nurses is increasing. The entry-level preparation of physicians and dentists aside, clinical psychologists acknowledge nothing less than the doctorate; dietitians insist on a baccalaureate degree, and growing numbers are enrolling in graduate study. Similar levels of preparation are required for beginning physical therapists, occupational therapists, medical record librarians, and medical technologists. Social workers and hospital administrators recognize master's preparation and above as the nominal education, while pharmacists are required to obtain a professional doctorate as the basic preparation. Thus, the social mandate for health care practice is preparation not at the baccalaureate level but at higher levels. Are such levels of preparation necessary for the provision of health care?

One does not need a crystal ball to foresee that unless nurses have levels of education comparable to those of other prominent health care providers, nurses will become the babysitters for the other professions. If the continuing disparity in scientific and theoretical background between nurses and other health care professionals is not corrected, nurses may find themselves in the position of making the other professions look good instead of directly serving patients and improving the practice of nursing. One cannot have a poor educational background and maintain much influence over the form and direction of the health care delivery system. A worrisome prediction under these conditions is that the nursing profession may fail to attract its share of bright young minds and thus may be doomed to mediocrity. Nurses may protest that they are being ignored because they are primarily women, but that assertion is self-deluding. Men in the nursing profession have the same general attitudes and behaviors. Most of the health care professions mentioned above include large percentages of women who have found the time and means to obtain the appropriate education.

Effective Nursing Means Training in High Tech Skills

That opportunity knocks but once is a long-surviving adage. The specifics of many new and unusual developments in the health care system are relatively unpredictable. All that can be predicted is that those who may now appear over-prepared but who are ready to manage change in the best and most efficient fashion will succeed. Time and events will not wait for nurses. Nurses either will be ready or will be passed over by those more qualified. Furthermore, much of what will become interesting and exciting in the care of patients will transfer almost unnoticed until such new practices become regular features of the health care delivery system. The only certainty is that each new spin-off from science and technology will require sophisticated knowledge. The possessors of the required expert knowledge will become the prime participants in the provision of care; those without such knowledge will have secondary status. The growth of knowledge in the basic sciences is exponential. It is on university campuses that strong links with scientific research and channels for the dissemination of new knowledge provide the possibility of developing the scholarly and professional approaches to learning so necessary to accommodating new knowledge readily.

Nurses with less than a university education are far removed from links with new knowledge and probably are being taught obsolete knowledge throughout their entire basic preparation. Thus, they begin their careers with a significantly weak, questionable base of scientific knowledge. Because most nurses involved in the direct care of patients do not have a university education, they lack the fundamental knowledge that can facilitate the discovery of new and imaginative patterns of nursing care delivery systems.

The false ideologies of technical and professional nursing have demonstrated the fallacy of thinking that

nurses can be alert users of science for the welfare of patients if they do not share a common base of scientific knowledge and understanding. Nurses will not be able to overcome the lag time in using sciences effectively until a large number are prepared at the doctoral level. A ratio of 1:5 at the master's level and 1:20 at the doctoral level is probably a basic necessity now to deal effectively with new scientific developments until the profession becomes fully prepared by means of doctoral education to pull its weight in the health care delivery system.

In all likelihood, the economic well-being of nurses has been severely hampered by the presence of so many small, local, non-baccalaureate programs. Because employers can staff their hospitals with a minimum number of registered nurses supplemented by additional, less qualified nursing personnel, they do not find it necessary to compete on the open market for nurses in the same way they do for all other types of professional staff. The climate for this kind of economic exploitation is furthered by the adamant stance of faculty members who wish to perpetuate categories of training below the baccalaureate level. If all nurses were educated in universities, the economic law of supply and demand would operate as it does for all other types of educated persons that communities need.

Launching a professional career is far different for persons who have a doctoral degree than for those who do not. The ease of moving to more advanced levels is apparent. The sheer satisfaction of having levels of knowledge similar to those of colleagues on the health team, the adequacy of that base for absorbing new knowledge, and the capability of using sophisticated methods of science are all intrinsic satisfactions that stimulate interest in the job at hand. In addition, a base is formed for pursuing employment that permits the two career family to flourish with less strain than otherwise.

This state of affairs is both stimulating and alarming. The challenge is exciting. Nurses, if properly prepared, will have the potential for treating patients in a sophisticated manner not thought possible even a few years ago. On the other hand, nurses will also have to commit a sizable portion of time to organized study. The license a nurse holds will become more a license to study than a license to practice. Adopting this style of life may be difficult for some nurses. A certain aura of antiintellectualism has always been apparent within the profession. Nurses with advanced and specialized knowledge frequently have been suspect. Such an attitude is not as ingrained or widespread in the other major health professions, where the reverse is usually the case.

Nursing students graduating today have more than 40 years of practice ahead of them because the mandatory retirement age will be eliminated. During this period, changes in the delivery of health care will be more extensive than in all of history. Just the introduction of one product of technology — the computer — will change the whole methodology of giving care. Hospitals will go on-line so as to be able to use massive computers. Central computerized laboratories will replace existing individual hospital laboratories. Many patient-monitoring devices will likewise be centralized. Consultation with expert nurses from other areas of the country will be routine. By merely putting in a request, physicians, nurses, and others will receive almost instant printouts of current information about the management of any clinical problem. Hospitals will have an entirely different staffing pattern. Only expertly trained personnel will be necessary. The intense pressure for numbers of personnel will be replaced by a search for quality and competence.

The bulk of the care will be programmed through the computer in a highly individualized and scientifically precise way based on all of the known data on the patient, including all data undergoing change through automatic monitoring, accumulated information in the national (international) databank about the patient's disease entity, and the clinical insights of the care providers. The massive numbers of people required to staff the infrastructure of support services will be markedly reduced or replaced, to a considerable degree, by robots and computer operation. Nurses' stations will not be needed. Release from such requirements will make possible a more imaginative type of architecture. Construction will be designed more appropriately around what is best for patients.

The voluminous medical charts for patients that now exist will be unnecessary. All the clerical work that encroaches on the time of nurses and physicians will be substantially reduced through computer programming. Management strategies will change considerably. Furthermore, computer-assisted managerial techniques will reduce the number of managers necessary to operate health care facilities. In addition, each manager and each health care provider of whatever profession will be monitored continuously for every error of commission and omission. A state of perfect accountability will be in place. All acts of excellence will likewise be recorded. Thus, quality assessment will be automated. This methodology may replace peer reviews. Renewal of licensure could be based on these data. National norms of performance could be established for licensure renewal based on meeting or exceeding these norms rather than on more flimsy continuing education credits.[2] It is only a matter of time until computerized means are available for measuring professional performance with a high degree of accuracy. All professional persons will be living in the proverbial fishbowl. Fortunately, all new information will be stored in knowledge banks that will be easily accessible so that all types of providers will learn how to be their own teachers.

FUTURE WORK OF NURSES
More Time for Holistic Patient Care

It is certain that the work time of nurses will undergo great revision. What will nurses be doing? For one thing, freed from ritual and routine, from the problems of coordination, and from endless paperwork, they will have much more time to devote to patients. Nurses will attend professionally to all the psychosocial problems that persons usually have when they are ill, effectively draining off the anxiety of a patient with such life-threatening illnesses as myocardial infarction, attending to the depression and other mixed emotions of a patient with terminal carcinoma, and assisting a dying patient's family through their grief. In essence, nurses will be expected to acquire the skills needed to deal very sensitively with the wide range of emotional reactions to illness that are expressed in patients' behaviors.

Nurses will spend considerably more time as health teachers. Since the entire population of the country is becoming much better educated, most patients will be able to act as intelligent collaborators in their health care instead of as passive recipients of attention. A test of the capability of nurses to facilitate this constructive movement will be how well nurses can establish the rapport necessary to ensure success in this endeavor. As leisure time increases, families, if adequately assisted, are likely to become more involved in caring for ill family members. Because of better education and mass communication, patients and their families will be capable of making fairly accurate estimates of the quality of care they are receiving.

Need for Clinical Investigative Ability

In the future all nurses will be expected to have clinical investigative ability. Relatively few nurses will be full-time researchers, but application of the scientific method to problems of practice will be commonplace. Because nursing care is an applied science, all nurses will have to obtain some research training. Consequently, the means of transforming scientific knowledge into improved nursing care will be a major concern for nurse practitioners.

The clinical management of each and every patient will take the form of a mini-research design. What is now labeled the nursing process will be replaced by the more rigorous practice of using the methods of science for each clinical act. The more generalized concepts of nursing care plans and of conditioned and restricted behavior as prescribed by procedure books will fade into oblivion. Scientific rigor will be developed to a very high order. Thinking and behavior will be integrated into complex levels of sophistication in each practitioner.

New Dimensions in Nurse-Physician Relationship

The relationship between physicians and nurses will take on new dimensions. As nurses become better educated, the knowledge gap between nurses and physicians will decrease as the knowledge overlap increases. As a result, nurses will be capable of working as close collaborators with physicians on the clinical designs of patient care. From such interaction, many novel and useful formats of care are certain to evolve. Furthermore, through collaborative research, the entire system of delivering care to patients will undergo extensive reorganization. The studies being done by behavioral scientists, industrial engineers, and economists are furnishing enough knowledge to change radically many of the organizational inefficiencies in the health care system.

New Forms of Health Care

Health care will assume new forms. Most physicians and nurses focus on the management of episodic illness or crisis. In the future, this preoccupation will be less emphasized. Nurses and physicians will collaborate in programs to prevent illness and maintain health rather than seek patients only when they are ill. The economic rewards of practice probably will be tied more closely to keeping the population healthy than to attending to the cure process. Furthermore, advanced technology will enable patients to receive much of their care in their homes. Telemetry, sensoring devices, and the richer preparation of providers will make this feasible. This development, too, will require that nurses be prepared at much higher levels because they will be working as solo practitioners in the patient's home.

None of the foregoing is highly imaginary. All of the trends commented on here have already been initiated in some form or other. New and more startling innovations certainly exist in the minds of some researchers. As studies follow on studies, the cumulative effect is dramatic. The push of science, sparked by the work of inquisitive scientists, shows no signs of abatement.

TOMORROW'S TRENDS AND TODAY'S NURSES

What does all this mean for today's young students and for nurses already in the field? To compete successfully in this technological age, many deficits in knowledge will have to be overcome. Computer-assisted nursing practice will require that nurses possess a richer base of knowledge, including more training in mathematics and statistics and in biophysical and behavioral sciences. Nurses will have to learn techniques for using computers effectively and acquire the understanding needed to translate research findings into improved care. Since nurses will have much more time to work closely and intimately with patients, they will have the opportunity to refine their practice, in all its dimensions, to a notable extent.

The direction of future progress will be controlled not by health care providers but by worldwide developments in science and technology. Providers will adapt to these changes by retraining, by constant pursuit of new knowledge, by preparation that is wider and deeper than has been the case historically, and by a greater interdependence of effort. If the concept of the past as prologue has any validity, it only exists as a highly speeded up version of events as the spectacular growth of science acts as a catalyst to heighten the momentum of the rapidity of change.

As John Naisbitt and others have documented, we are moving into a postindustrial world of knowledge.[3] The cybernetic culture will be the dominant ethos. The sophistication of the hardware and software of the computer era has barely begun. Computer technology will be a major tool enabling radical reconstruction of the health care system. As Stanley Lesse has so imaginatively described in his recent book, *The Future of the Health Sciences,* the use of this technology will reorder the system.[4] He envisions a system in which citizens will monitor their own care in precise ways. Technology, in essence, will be the primary care modality. Vast storage banks of scientific data will be available to make this new form of primary care and the lifelong monitoring of each person's health a certainty.

It is conceivable that there will be a sharp reduction in demand for health care professionals. There may be intense competition for employment both within and among professional groups. Probably only the most competent will enjoy full career patterns. Those who are complacent and do not read the signs well will pay the costs of their disregard. Others who are caught up in the excitement of change and keep pace with developments in knowledge will experience an exhilaration of accomplishment that cannot be imagined.

Regardless of the individual reaction of each nurse to the awesome developments in science, the inevitability of remarkable change confronts the profession. All of us must be aware of that reality. The best outcomes for patients and for nurses will be achieved if we are active in enriching knowledge as the basis of practice in proportion to the expansion of knowledge. Adjustments of less quality will be maladaptive and make the future of the profession problematic.

REFERENCES

1. National Association for Home Care. "Attempted Dismantling of the Medicare Home Health Benefit." Report to Congress, Washington, DC, July 21, 1986.
2. Christman, L. "The Future of Nursing is Predicted by the State of Science and Technology." In *The Nursing Profession, A Time to Speak,* edited by N.L Chaska. New York: McGraw-Hill, 1982, pp. 802-06.
3. Naisbitt, J. *Megatrends.* New York: Warner Books, 1982.
4. Lesse, S. *The Future of the Health Sciences.* New York: Irvington, 1981.

CHAPTER 60

Nursing's Preferred Future

Myrtle K. Aydelotte, RN, PhD, FAAN

In the last 25 years, that is, since 1960, many events, discoveries, and natural upheavals have changed the world, such as the increase in air travel, the launching of satellites, the women's movement, the sexual revolution, the thrust of nuclear energy, the Vietnam War, and the growth of telematics.

Several trends and issues in the world will shape what it will be 25 years from now. These trends and issues reside in our social institutions, the economy, the demography of the population of the United States, science and technology, and the health care industry. To identify the forces giving rise to these trends and issues is difficult, because their interplay is complex.

Social institutions. Our social institutions are undergoing radical modification in almost every sector. Unless some social intervention occurs, we are drifting toward a distinct two-culture society, the rich and the poor, reducing the large middle class that has been dominant in our society. However, inherent in our very social and political structure has been a value system that emphasizes opportunity for work and education, mobility from one class to another, and fairness. I predict that the current trend toward benefitting the favored will not persist and that the pendulum will swing back to a balance assuring the maintenance of the large middle class and addressing

the question of how to interrupt the culturization and socialization of the poor.

Currently, there is national concern over the quality of education provided both children and adults. The movement to improve the quality of teachers has caught the attention of legislators and political bodies, resulting in efforts to reduce large classes in elementary and secondary schools and stress basic skills. At the college and university level, the trends of corporatization and entrepreneurship are evident. Faculty members are caught up in the entrepreneur movement and many are establishing their own businesses as consultants, inventors, and designers. The collegial system, which has developed for centuries, is giving way to the formal structure of business and to hierarchical decision making.

The costs of education will continue to rise. Growth in the number of well-educated blacks and some other ethnic groups has slowed. However, these trends will change over time. In 2010, individuals will be better educated, more informed, and more highly skilled in the use of the information available to them.

Changes are also occurring today in the structure of the family, especially in the role of women. There are now 63 million families in the United States. Currently, 54 percent of all married women with children are in the labor force, and the number of single-parent families continues to grow. Further, the number of women in the work force has increased by 20 percent over the past 25 years. Since 1970, the divorce rate has risen by 80 percent, and the number

Reprinted from *Nursing Outlook,* Vol. 35, No. 3, with permission of the American Journal of Nursing Co. © 1987.

of women heading households by 84 percent. Women are marrying later or not at all. Women still face pay inequalities, sex segregation in jobs, salary discrimination, lack of advancement in positions, and a lower standard of living because of divorce. The trends in the employment of women, both in numbers and in the percent of newly created jobs now occupied by women, are such that by the end of the century women will make up most of the work force.[1]

Unless there are some social interventions and value changes, it appears that these trends will continue. Further, children will be raised in households different from those of today. Although the traditional family pattern will continue, a new definition of family is emerging. Unmarried older women are choosing to have children. Selected intimate groups not connected by marriage or by genetics are seen as families. The extended family of today consists of several sets of parents, step-parents, the consequential grandparents and great grandparents, and intimate friends. Because divorce does not incur the social stigma it carried a few years ago, an individual may marry more often and for shorter periods of time.

The changes in family structure and lifestyle have given rise to family resource coalitions and religious groups wishing to strengthen the family. Attention is being given to the need for daycare centers and agencies, preparation for being parents, sharing of family responsibilities, and public policies to support family leave for child care, especially in the early years.

By the year 2010 A.D., with the increase of women in the political arena, I predict that child care will be addressed and advancement of a number of other issues concerning women will be apparent. I must temper that statement, however, because progress has been slow. The general societal attitudes toward women, child bearing and rearing, marriage and the family are deeply rooted. Further, there is little evidence that the socialization of girls has changed markedly. The present culture continues to stress femininity, male dominance, and womanly dependence. The myth that women will be cared for persists, even among women.

Demographic changes. By the year 2010, the increase in the elderly population will be substantial. By 2020,

the baby boomer population (those born shortly after World War II) will have reached the age of sixty-five. Over the coming decades, the proportion of society over 65 years of age will nearly double. The number who are young and who provide services to these groups will be relatively small, for the number of high school graduates, which peaked in 1977, will not begin to climb until the 1990s.[2]

Although the number of individuals 75 years and older will not constitute the majority of elderly until the year 2040, 30 years later than the date we are examining, the number of frail elderly will be high. An increasing number will experience limitations in activity and chronic disability in the decade that follows. The implications for society and nursing, at the present time and in future decades, are many.

Most current programs of caring for the elderly, especially the functionally disabled, have not been satisfactory; 22 percent of those over 85 years of age today are in nursing homes, and the care in many homes is suspect.

Currently, 1.2 million elderly Americans live in the community and are cared for by family members. The "young old" are caring for the "old old," with only 10 percent using formal community services; families are caught up in the provision of care to older family members when their energies are needed for the care of children. With the increase in elderly in 2010, the matter is extremely important. Nursing must respond to meet the needs of this population.

Our society is becoming not only older, but more diverse. There is a rapid growth in both the Spanish-speaking and the Asian populations. Although currently the majority of people agree that integration of all people in our society is essential to our national development, there is not a state of real integration.[3] The caste system identified by Gunnor Myrdal continues. Within the next 25 years, we will see a pluralistic society of greater diversity and increased integration. I predict that the commitment to integration of all peoples will hold.

Information technology and biotechnology. Over the past 20 years, tremendous growth has taken place in technology, both that involving information and that concerned with living organisms. The current trend in the development of telematics and biotechnology will continue. These changes will be accompanied by both continuing and new legal and ethical concerns.

Telematics is the term applied to new information technologies. These technologies include machines and communication systems, bringing together video, computers, and satellites; networks, management systems, and artificial intelligence. There will be advances in the information technologies used in data bases, which will be clinical, epidemiological and environmental and will concern individuals and communities. Artificial intelligence will lead to highly sophisticated clinical and administrative decision making. Other systems will lead to management of complex machines. A major use in the health field will be the surveillance of clients and patients for clinical information and safety.

In the field of biotechnology, we have already seen major developments. Recombinant DNA research has led to genetic engineering, human gene therapy, and various molecular products. It has been legal to patent genetically engineered microorganisms since 1980. During the next 25 years, we will continue to see new pharmaceuticals and new chemical compounds resulting from biotechnology, and dramatic developments in gene therapy.

The risks, legality, and ethics of technology will continue to be subjects for debate. Consensus has not yet been reached on the ethics of abortion, surrogate mothers, fetal surgery, imperiled infants, maintenance of life in selected cases, elderly suicide and euthanasia. Government regulation of technology, especially biotechnology, will continue. Ethical concerns about confidentiality, mind control, gene manipulation, and ownership of genetic material remain. More attention to ethics and legal issues will be required of health professionals. Time will be required to reach consensus on ethical questions that deal with the beginning and ending of life in our pluralistic society.

Economy. Discussion of the future centers on consideration of the world economy and specifically on health care economics. Since the 1970s, the United States has lost 23 percent of its share of the world's trade market. The trade deficit is at an all-time high, as is the federal deficit. U.S. productivity has slowed down and U.S. invention has declined. I cannot

predict the world economy in 2010, but there will be fewer young to carry the cost of health care and they will be burdened by a deficit incurred by this generation. Health care spending's share of the GNP reached a new high in 1985. Spent on health care was $425 billion, equal to 10.7 percent of the GNP. It rose 8.9 percent above the 1984 level and outstripped the inflation rate (3.9%) and growth of the GNP (5.6%). One-fourth of the cost was the result of intensity of care and the length of stay of those over 65 years of age.[4] The forces that are driving costs upward are of two kinds: first, those of the cost of providing the service plus inflation and second, demand or use factors, such as the requirements of the aging population and number of individuals with increased insurance coverage.

The current administration's objectives are to redirect public responsibility, reduce controls and regulations on the health care market, and encourage competition and private enterprise. The changing federal role in health care financing has led to changes in Medicaid and the introduction of prospective payment.[5,6] But not yet addressed are questions of policy relating to chronic illness and disabilities or the social policy of health care — health as a social good — or the long-range financial impact of the lack of foresight directed toward health promotion and prevention.

Currently, the uninsured are a sizable minority. Approximately 15 percent of the population, or 35 million people, lack health insurance.[7] The impact of social and financial inequality results in distinct patterns of morbidity and mortality among different populations.[8,9]

With the changes in federal initiatives, several states have introduced strategies to restructure the state hospital payment system, using a competitive approach. The shift of the burden from federal to state to private payors and limiting choice of provider may not, however, be the answer to health financing or to the provision of care. Attempting to control the market through competition may in fact be even more costly unless regulatory controls are placed on medical technology, pharmaceuticals, and litigation, for example. The basic issue is what amount of the gross national product we should give to health care and how it should be rationed.[10] This basic issue in health care financing focuses on serious questions of social ethics and governmental responsibility for access to health care as well as what that health care will be.

The current trend is moving us toward a multiple-tiered system in which the poor and uninsured will receive support financed by federal, state, and local government. The health care for these populations will be placed on the market for competitive bidding. Other groups will receive care through group insurance plans and private pay.

In my opinion, this trend will continue into the next few decades. Particular attention needs to be given to defining the basic package that will be given to the lower tier.

HEALTH CARE IN 2010 A.D.

The current trends in health care are corporatization and privatization. The provision of health care in the United States is becoming a health-industry complex, in some respects not unlike the military industry complex. There is movement of units of service, including hospitals, into multi-institutional systems, especially those that are investor owned, but even the nonprofit systems are using the same type of institutional structure and approaches.[11,12]

Currently, there are 250 multihospital systems in the United States.[13] Some are establishing HMOs and PPOs to lock up referral patterns so that all services in the system are used. Others have developed surgicenters, nursing homes, clinics, various types of outpatient services, and emergency centers. The programs that these systems offer are highly diversified, including health education, counseling, screening, and public lectures. Some have further diversified by sponsoring insurance plans, hotel services, transportation, supply services, and management. Integration of financing, management and services has taken place. Marketing and advertising, unheard of a few years ago, are accepted practices.

Given the trend and the financial activity of the investor-owned multisystems, I predict the following future for the health care system.

- The health industry by 2010 will be controlled by a few dozen national and international companies, not unlike the airlines of today or large,

diversified producers of service goods. These health industries will be highly diversified and will operate in a variety of settings. They will offer many different services and products related to their services, such as health products or related products, insurance, hotels and management.

- The systems will reflect a blurring of delivery models. Combined to capture the market will be HMOs, PPOs, independent surgicenters, clinics, and other types of health services.
- Nonprofit health care systems may convert to profit systems or increase the number or kind of subunits that produce a profit.
- The nature of the hospital will change. It will consist of multiple intensive care units offering highly specialized scientific and technological services. The case mix of patients will represent very complex conditions requiring sophisticated medical interventions. The patients will remain in the hospital for short periods.
- To capture the market, there will be new programs for individuals who wish to maintain their health and to delay the onset of chronic disease.
- The public hospital as it is today will not exist.
- The majority of physicians will be employees of chains or in group practices associated with chains. Today, over 50 percent of physicians are employees.[14]

Slowing these trends somewhat are countercurrents that reflect concern about the momentum of corporatization and privatization and what they represent. There is a growing concern about quality of service, brought about not only by the emphasis on restructuring to capture the market and to introduce efficiency, but also the economy and reimbursement policies. The concern about quality is expressed by purchasers of the services, the third-party payors, including businesses that are negotiating contracts. Although quality of services may be the most frequently verbalized concern, there are others.

- *Access and rationing of health services.* The development of multiple levels of services for classes of people — the poor and uninsured, the "coach" class, and the first-class luxury services — raises many ethical questions about the distribution of health services as a social good. Who will decide who gets what?

- *The impact of competition and economic restraints on the practice of health professionals.* Economic constraints are restricting practice interventions of nurses and doctors. If this is compounded by standards imposed from the executive level, how will professionals accommodate? If productivity is defined as the number of patients treated and the number of nursing care hours per patient or minutes per visit, what changes will occur in practice and how will they affect the health care professional?

- *The demise of the public hospital and care of the poor and the uninsured.* Because of the reduction of Medicare and Medicaid reimbursement, a few innovative state and community programs are being introduced. Few studies of the patterns of individuals seeking health care have been made, but one study indicates that education, income and geographic location of the health service unit are factors influencing choice of source of care.[15] Who will assume the care of the poor and uninsured? And how will it be paid?

- *Conflict of interest.* The health professional's involvement in the health care industry as a stockholder or owner when the service is operated as a business is in question. Full consensus has not been reached on what constitutes reasonable compensation for services rendered and whether these services are rendered for the primary benefit of the provider or the client. The purchase of expensive equipment for group or personal medical business in order to capture a market has been cited as leading to unwise and costly practices such as unnecessary tests and studies. No solution has been proposed to control these costs or to monitor use of equipment and testing in group and individual practice settings.

- *The ability of an institution or subchain to meet the specific needs of a particular community and the assurance of the permanency of the arrangement.* Some people are concerned that the participation of the community in decisions involving the health care system serving them may become increasingly restricted. Because of the elimination of competition, no other health care service may be available.

The restructuring of the current health care system has been widely criticized. Fragmentation and impersonalization are often cited as byproducts of this restructuring. The expectation that the customer is knowledgeable about the product (service) to be rendered may be unrealistic. Further, the recipient may not be the direct purchaser or the contractor because the arrangements are made through a third party, the business that contracts for its employees, the government that approves fees and arrangements, and insurers. Is it reasonable to expect that recipients of services will have a greater voice in services rendered? Since provisions for health care services are often made through third parties, how will the individual recipient participate in selecting the provider of care?

A fairly large proportion of individuals will be more knowledgeable about health and about necessary services. The emphasis on palliative measures and treatment of pathology is giving way to an emphasis on health and fitness. The stress is on the individual's responsibility for his or her health and on the larger community's adoption of programs to produce healthier living or healthier environments.

I believe this concern about health is not a fad. More and more individuals are becoming aware that they are responsible for the condition of their bodies. This awareness is beginning to be reflected in governmental social policy, such as the change in the Armed Services policy regarding smoking and the recent program on drugs.

With these trends and countertrends, what will the health system look like? I believe it will be divided into four branches. There will be a branch concerned with health promotion, health education, self-help, and health evaluation. Another branch's business will be chronic disease management, serving a clientele that will be fairly stable except for episodic illness when an omission or digression of treatment occurs in the management of the chronic problem. A third branch will be concerned with trauma and with severe illnesses in which pathology must be treated with highly sophisticated medical interventions. The system's fourth branch will concentrate on care of the frail elderly, the physically limited elderly, and the dying.

The services provided by these branches will originate in several types of structures, located in a variety of institutions. The majority of the structures will be in the community and readily accessible to the clientele served. Ambulatory services, home care, hospices, and protected homelike environments for the elderly and physically limited will dominate. Schools, industries, and social clubs will provide settings. The expectation that families will assume greater responsibility for family members will persist, but that expectation will be moderated by various types of program assistance and family resource centers. The hospital will be present but will hold a less central position. It will continue to be seen as a dramatic and overwhelming environment because of the high technology and scientific research in which the staff will engage.

A challenge to the executive and professional staff of these branches will be twofold. I predict that the current multi-institutional systems will become repugnant to those served. The emphasis upon ability to pay, the perceived impersonality, the schedules and waiting time, the time constraints and pressures placed on professional staff will all lead to restructuring of services in the various settings. Smaller subgroups serving groups of clientele and providing more personal and continuous interaction between the health provider and the recipient of services will be formed. Autonomy of practice will be returned to the practitioners. In addition, the linkage system among the various branches will be very complex and require highly sophisticated communication. Each person will own his or her own data base and will control additional input to it. Problems of data confidentiality and access will require thoughtful planning and a special staff to manage the data linkages.

FUTURE NURSING ROLES AND NURSING PRACTICE

The organization of health care into four main branches will appear fragmented as a result of attempts to make it more effective and personal, but the scope and nature of nursing practice will reflect the populations served in those four branches. Nursing

practice will continue to reflect intimacy, helpfulness, and compassion. The knowledge base required for practice will be extensive, regardless of the branch of health care in which nursing operates. Further, I predict that the title *nurse* will be used for only one class, the *professional;* support personnel will assist the nurse. If one class does not emerge, the professional in what we perceive today as the occupation of nursing will possess a new title. Skills in administrative and clinical decision making, human relations, interpretation of data, scientific inquiry, and communication will be needed. Nursing diagnoses and interventions will be well developed, and research and development will continue on these topics as well as on programs of health education, promotion, and maintenance for various population groups. Research and development of nursing will be a major concern within each branch (health promotion, chronic illness, trauma and severe illness, and the elderly).

The future roles of nursing will emerge from the needs of the clientele and the structure of groups of nurses in the branches. The services may not be connected administratively. Some of the services may be offered by larger systems; some by smaller professional corporations, whose specific mission is limited; and some may be offered by individual nurses on contract. The provision of links among units of branches will be challenging. Ideally, clients would enter the total system of health care through the branch of health promotion and health maintenance.

Nursing practice in the future will include the use of a number of functions, such as surveillance, diagnostic reasoning, provision of personal needs, and the care of the environment. Surveillance will involve the use of technology, especially telematics and machines not yet designed, for tracking individuals, for collection of data, and for orientation of families and individuals. The use of artificial intelligence will assist in diagnostic reasoning. Provision of personal needs will be made easier by the automation of systems to dispense medications and give highly specialized therapy, and to prepare materials for sustenance. Robotic equipment will assist in the maintenance of the environment. Individual automatic systems will monitor personal business relationships, such as tracking, ordering supplies, and correspondence. Scientific and technological advances will result in the design of devices that will enable the physically and mentally limited to be more mobile. The major role of nurses will be the assurance of personal interaction, support for coping and refreshing, and education of individuals on how to use programs and technology, including machines and telematics. Individuals will need help in making use of the media provided them.

Within each of the branches, at least four classes of roles are needed: the provider of direct services to clients; the researcher and developer of new knowledge and techniques; the case or panel manager; and the executive. The provider of direct services evaluates the health status of clients and patients, makes nursing diagnoses and plans interventions, designs nursing orders, executes selected interventions, makes clinical nursing decisions, and uses and evaluates support personnel, who may come from several professions and occupations. The researcher and developer uses various approaches and other personnel to develop new knowledge, educational programs, technology, media, telematics, and the like. The case manager in the health promotion and maintenance branch, who provides entry into the whole system, serves a panel or group of patients or clients. This case manager assesses clients and plans interventions to keep them well or refers them to other professionals or units of service, if necessary. The case manager in the health promotion and maintenance branch is, in a sense, the primary care giver and manages the health care of individuals. The functions of the role are concerned with health status assessment, health promotion, and health maintenance. The role evolves out of the current nurse practitioner role with major emphasis on prevention rather than remedy.

Executives will be needed to administer groups of nurses in the units. Their role will be concerned with securing resources; allocating resources; policy development, evaluation, and revision; and distribution of services.

Case managers in each of the other branches manage groups or panels of patients referred to them from nurses and physicians in other branches. They assess clients and make nursing diagnoses, then refer them to direct-care givers. The case manager views the panel of patients as a collective and serves as both the major coordinator of the information and the liaison with nurses in units of other branches. Case managers and direct-care givers will be scholarly clinical practitioners and scientists. The collection of information for assessment, diagnosis, and planning will be obtained by highly sophisticated methods and devices, many of which have not yet been designed or even thought of. The transmission of data will likewise be much easier and much faster. Nurses will provide these services through four different arrangements:.

- Professional corporations headed by nurses who contract with populations or other organizations as a group to provide nursing services, such as intensive care, school nursing, hospice or home health care, or business.
- Nurse specialty practice groups that individually contract with clients or groups to provide special services, such as counseling, health maintenance, and technological services.
- Practice on an individual basis arranged by contracts to provide for highly specialized nursing service on a one-to-one basis or to give consultation to other nurses, professionals, and institutions.
- Employment in both profit and nonprofit health care systems operated by boards of directors. These will be chiefly oriented toward acute care.

STRATEGIC DECISIONS

Nursing practice in 2010 will be intimate, compassionate, empathetic and truly professional. The knowledge base of practice will be well delineated and unique; its use will enable the practitioner to offer services for which there is no substitute. Nurses will be well educated, highly skilled, and capable of managing their own affairs. They will practice in many types of settings and under varying contractual arrangements. Ethics and legal issues will be a major concern. Above all, nursing practice will continue to be directed toward helping others to live lives of the highest possible quality or enabling them to die with dignity and peace.

514 NURSING AND FUTURE HEALTH CARE DELIVERY

To achieve this preferred future of nursing, several strategies must be put in place now and in the near future. I am confident we can do the necessary work, but only if we have the necessary clarity of purpose and strong determination. Some of my proposals may be seen as elitist. That is my intent.

First of all, we must strive for clarification and understanding of the nature of the profession. Definitions and scope-of-practice statements are insufficient. A profession reflects the acquisition of knowledge and skills that no other group possesses. Consequently, there is no substitute for the professional. The knowledge of nursing must be exclusive. With our current egalitarian attitude and our eagerness to give content to others, we are impeding our drive to make our knowledge base exclusive and retain fully the skills that are needed to serve the public. We compromise our image, confuse the public, and most unfortunately, by default, make it possible for people to receive care, called *nursing care,* which is inferior and for which we are not responsible or accountable. But in the public's eye we are giving it. I am calling for a restriction on the practice of educating individuals to be less than professional nurses. In order to serve the public better, we need to garner our knowledge, refine it, and identify that which is exclusively ours. For example, I do not believe that the use of nursing diagnosis, diagnostic reasoning and nursing interventions should go the route of nursing process and be used by others. The professional in any field uses support personnel, but those individuals have a different knowledge base and different skills. Above all, access to those who are served is controlled by the professional. Further, the professional is accountable for support personnel.

Second, individuals entering nursing must meet high standards of intelligence and motivation. Public service motivation is paramount. Professions maintain control through admission to professional schools and through employment opportunities. I believe that we will not achieve the goal of excellence in nursing care for the public if we continue to be preoccupied by numbers and ignore standards. Neither can we attract talented individuals if we mix them with poor risks. For too long, nursing has been preoccupied with numbers. We are the most counted,

most tabulated, and best described occupation in the United States. I believe that we must concern ourselves with building a cadre of true professionals rather than expend our energies in other directions. Furthermore, we need to learn how to use support personnel. There is a great need for excellence both in clinical nursing and in administration.

Third, a remodeling of nursing education is long overdue. The future calls for a different and much more extensive education than that currently in place. More depth in the sciences, a greater understanding of economics, emphasis on ethics and legal issues, introduction to management and business, understanding of information technology and artificial intelligence, and greater clinical application are all indicated. The future, although exciting, will not be easy. The student entering a profession today and graduating at the age of 25 may practice for 40 years. Many changes in the health field will take place. The educational foundation of the practice should be sound.

Fourth, the professional of the future needs preparation in self-governance and self-management. How can we provide that outcome through our present educational programs and current work experiences? Does our approach to teaching, especially in the practicum, allow the development of self-regulation? Only mature students can be prepared for self-governance and self-management. Opportunities for more responsibility in learning and in continuity of clinical nursing experiences are required. Avenues for the development of clinical nursing judgment must be explored and made available to students.

Fifth, our relationship with the public and the power elite and power brokers must change. Political action must extend beyond the legislative arena; it is not the only arena in which power brokers operate. We must learn the subtleties of power-brokerage. It can be done. We should move nursing into every aspect of community affairs. I suggest that nursing leadership make a concerted and calculated effort to move into powerful circles. There is no reason why nurses cannot become college and university presidents and vice-presidents, leaders in community and business affairs, heads of corporations, and chairs of boards.

Sixth, because money controls and dominates, let us get on with the costing out of nursing services, gaining reimbursement for our services, learning the management of contracts and business, and attaching value to services and quality. Many will say that what I propose will be too expensive for society, that we will make ourselves too costly. I disagree. The avoidance of the loss of functioning of others, the reduction of the length and cost of illness, and the value of rehabilitation of the sick will more than meet any additional cost. Further, nurses have always earned income; it simply has filtered to others disguised as hospital room costs or payments to non-nurse supervisors. Let us recognize that a reimbursement system that pays directly to nursing services obtained by contracts may assist in identifying our worth.

These strategies are simply put, but they are not simplistic. To be effective, they need to be carefully fleshed out. Guiding us is a vision of nursing—a preferred future. Let us capture that vision and make it real, for not to do so places us among the oppressed. And it is time for us to carve out our own image and transform ourselves to that image. The public we will serve in 2010 will be better for it.

REFERENCES

1. Hacker, A. Women at work. *NY Rev. Books* 33(12):26–32, 1986.
2. Felton, G. Harnessing today's trends to guide nursing's future. *Nurs. Health Care* 7:211–213, Apr. 1986.
3. Pifer, A. *The Higher Education of Blacks in the United States.* New York, Carnegie Corporation of New York, 1973.
4. Health-care spending's share of the GNP reaches new high. *The Washington Post* p. A6, July 30, 1986.
5. Davis, C. K. The federal role in changing health care financing; Part I. National programs and health financing problems. *Nurs. Econ.* 1:10–17, Jul.–Aug. 1983.
6. Davis, C. K. The federal role in changing health care financing; Part II. Prospective payment and its impact on nursing. *Nurs. Econ.* 1:98–104, 146, Sept.–Oct. 1983.
7. Jones, K. R., and Kilpatrick, K. E. State strategies for financing indigent care. *Nurs. Econ.* 4:61–65, 88, Mar.–Apr. 1986.
8. Robert Wood Johnson Foundation. *Special Report.* (Updated report on access to health care for the American people, No. 1) Princeton, NJ, The Foundation, 1983.
9. Aday, L. and others. *Health Care in the U.S.: Equitable for Whom?* Beverly Hills, CA, Sage Publishing Co., 1980.
10. Reinhardt, U. E. Rationing the health-care surplus: an American tragedy. *Nurs. Econ.* 4:101–108, May–June 1986.
11. Bauknecht, V. L. IOM study of "for-profits" finds care costs not very different. *Am. Nurse* 18:3–5, Jul.–Aug. 1986.
12. Institute of Medicine, Committee on Implications of For-Profit Enterprise in Health Care. *For-Profit Enterprise in Health Care.* Washington, DC, National Academy Press, 1986.
13. Brown, M. Multihospital systems in the 80s—the new shape of the health care industry. *Hospitals* 56:71–74, Mar. 1, 1982.
14. Relman, A. S. The future of medical practice. *Health Aff.* (Millwood) 2:5–19, Summer 1983.
15. Kronenfeld, J. J. Organization of ambulatory care by consumers. *Sociol. Health Illness* 4:183–200, 1982.

CHAPTER 61

Obstacles to Nursing's Preferred Future

Geraldene Felton , RN, EdD, FAAN

I am not sanguine that nursing will be well positioned in 2010 A.D. unless we attend to certain current issues. First, without question, the history of nursing's growth and the development of authority over nursing practice must be principally the history of graduate education and university-based research and scholarship that nurture an astonishing advance and diffusion of knowledge in nursing. Moreover, the fortune of university research will depend heavily on funds from foundations, fund-raising drives and alumni contributions, and on undergraduate instruction in the arts and sciences — the historic focus of American higher education. Second, I believe that there are headaches of the moment that need to be addressed. These include equity and excellence, threats to affirmative action, and recruitment. We must deal with these issues if we are to maintain the orientation of the nurse as an educated person and as a truly national resource.

EQUITY AND EXCELLENCE

The Civil Rights Act of 1964 has so affected our society that it is difficult to remember a time when the protection it affords was not present. Actually, the "American way of life" is characterized by a delicate

Reprinted from *Nursing Outlook*, Vol. 35, No. 3, with permission of the American Journal of Nursing Co. © 1987.

interplay between equity and inequity. Inequity is less talked about but is in fact the more fervently practiced (in economics, professional specialization, intellectual superiority, for example).

There is no doubt that the educational system is not all it could be. A project sponsored by the Association of American Colleges that explored the question of coherence and integrity in undergraduate education agreed that collegiate education in this country is seriously lacking in both.[1] But in responding to the need for change and reform, higher education has to be careful not to lose sight of the system's objective — to provide citizens with as much education as they are willing to seek and are capable of achieving. If we lose sight of that goal, we will be turning our backs on a historical commitment to equity and opportunity that has given hope for advancement to families across the nation.

Just as the concepts of equity, excellence, and opportunity in higher education were reinforced by earlier waves of reform, current efforts to make the educational system more responsive to societal needs must be guided by an emphasis on quality and excellence. But now we are faced with the dilemma of how to reconcile the countervailing forces that may be perceived to exist between the goal of excellence and quality on the one hand, and the goal of equity and opportunity on the other. Educators, including nurse educators, are seeking ways to manage these issues so that we expand the boundaries of our educational system. Meanwhile, there are those who still agree that the most important distinction in collegiate nursing education is not between professional and liberal, or between general and special, but rather between serious and trivial, responsible and irresponsible, better and worse.

AFFIRMATIVE ACTION

Affirmative action means adoption of a plan to broaden access through goals (quotas) for hiring or promoting blacks, women, or persons of Hispanic descent. The quota system that is part of affirmative action is the opposite of the one established to support racism. The latter system existed as a device to limit strictly the number or proportion of specific groups of people in universities, professions, and so on. The quota system that is part of the present affirmative action effort seeks not to keep out but to open up, not to make entry impossible but rather to assure entry — in equitable proportion — to those who have been victimized.

Education is not divorced from politics. Only a fool would pretend otherwise. Some, in the name of affirmative action, try to make us believe that the merit principle is somehow only a minor conceit on the part of those who still feel it is worth defending, and that hiring the "best qualified" candidate for a faculty or administrative position should necessarily be subordinated to the politics of race and sex. That is bad politics. It leads to cynicism, demeans the process, and smacks of condescension.

During the early sixties, public consciousness and concern swung in favor of human relations, civil rights, and affirmative action. Action to correct the inequities of past discrimination against women and minorities became a high priority for human relations and civil rights agencies, and the public pendulum swung in their direction. Unfortunately, few compliance and enforcement agencies used this favorable climate and their successes to develop innovative processes to obtain the desired results with less adverse consequences for other groups. In part, this oversight paved the way for claims of reverse discrimination and cries of unnecessary preferential treatment.

Now, the public policy pendulum has swung in the opposite direction. The Civil Rights Act of 1964, affirmative action, and even Supreme Court decisions have been successfully attacked. Compliance and enforcement agencies across the nation now find themselves struggling to survive. Yet a change in public policy will not remove the need for civil rights and affirmative action. The survival of civil rights will depend on the ability of each agency and public institution to realign its methods and emphases and calm the fears of the majority population while retaining both its focus and its priorities.

There are new problems of educational access for our nation's rapidly growing minority population. The 1980 census indicated that blacks and Hispanics constituted 18.1 percent of the total U.S. population. There are predictions that by 2020 blacks and Hispanics will make up between 25 and 30 percent of the population. Yet the college participation rate of minority students has been dropping dramatically. A profile completed by the American Council on Education reports that the least represented groups among college students are blacks, Mexican-Americans, and low-income whites.[2] The number of high school graduates going on to college declined nearly 15 percent between 1977 and 1982, leading the Children's Defense Fund (CDF) to conclude that black children are "sliding backwards."

Moreover, a report of the College Board supports the finding that blacks are underrepresented in business and management, health professions (including nursing), and physical sciences; drop out of college with greater frequency than do whites at almost every point along the educational pipeline; and most cite financial difficulties as the reason for leaving college.[3]

Nursing needs to emulate model programs to expose minority youths to careers in the discipline. One program called Project Seed, sponsored by the American Chemical Society, admirably stripped of bureaucratic red tape, allows chemists around the country to receive approximately $750 for hiring a disadvantaged high school student for a 10-week laboratory job. More than 200 students took part in this program in 1984, and that number is growing steadily as foundations and private donors provide additional funds. A National Science Foundation program in the division of biological sciences allows professors to receive small grant supplements for the same purposes. These programs could be expanded to nursing with other sources of funds. Government agencies could well follow the NSF formula; private groups could pattern programs on Project Seed. The opportunity to give minority and educationally disadvantaged students exposure to science in a friendly environment can be effective at early and formative stages in their lives.

Quality in higher education has to do with institutions defining what an educated person is rather than letting people define it for themselves. Thus, expectations of what universities are about have caused establishment of all kinds of programs for minority students, economically and educationally disadvantaged students, and those who have culturally divergent backgrounds: precollege enrichment programs, better coordination between high schools and colleges, coaching for standardized tests, early admission and financial notification programs, better orientation for incoming minority students, and more minority faculty. Other programs include special recruitment, counseling and advising, remedial courses, extensive tutorial systems, cultural centers, and more constructive relationships with faculty and staff. Unfortunately, many of these programs were never institutionalized. However, creating an environment of positive expectation recognizes how vital it is to have a realistic view of how educational and other organizations actually operate if one is to forestall victimization by the system. Three commodities are necessary: information, resources, and support. Many minorities in higher education, whether faculty or students, fail to develop tactical skills and political savvy. None of this is intended to deny that there are some other very real problems with minorities and excellence in education.

RECRUITMENT

As the number of high school graduates declines, colleges across the country are scurrying to find ways to keep their classes filled with able students. An annual survey of colleges and universities reported that enrollment at both public and private four-year colleges dropped 0.5 percent between 1983 and 1984.[4] Some schools have turned to direct mail campaigns; others are relying on more traditional tactics such as offering scholarships to top students or bringing about planned shrinkage by cutting undergraduate enrollment. In some schools the decrease in undergraduates will be partially offset by an increase in the number of graduate students. Some universities plan to accomplish this by adding more doctoral programs in management and other fields that draw on the school's strengths in such areas as computers and the social and natural sciences.

The proposed restructuring of nursing programs to require baccalaureate concentration in academic areas with professional study largely at the graduate level has led some nursing schools to replace the BSN with the MSN as the first professional degree offered, develop five- to six-year master's programs; and develop master's programs for RNs and college graduates with non-nursing degrees who wish to earn an MSN. The effort to turn the problem of declining enrollment into an opportunity to emphasize graduate study and research may provide a model for schools that find they cannot maintain both size and quality. However, this action may also be seen as a threat to the educational mobility of disadvantaged and minority students and may create a wider spread between the haves and the have-nots. This may also be a threat to nurse executives' attempts to maintain professional nurse staffs.

A related concern is the paucity of minority teachers, which may be one explanation for the decreasing minority student enrollment. The consequences of the shrinking ranks of minority teachers in academia are that: all students do not come in contact with minority teachers; students do not see all kinds of people in positions of authority; there are fewer role models on whom minority students can pattern their own performance and career aspirations. The number of blacks and Hispanics on school faculties is the most significant predictor of success in recruiting minority students for professional schools and graduate schools.

Educators have suggested ways to reverse the decline in the ranks of minority teachers, such as programs to forgive the college loans of students who will choose teaching and salaries or career ladders designed to enhance the rewards and status of the teaching profession. Many are quick to add, however, that the problem cannot be solved without general improvement in the education that minority students get in college and earlier. Nonetheless, college nursing programs must reflect the transcultural and demographic characteristics of society at large as well as a commitment to equity and access as a social goal.

CONCLUSION

What we are doing in this discussion symbolizes imagination — a difficult intellectual task — and willingness to expose our ideas on the chance of obtaining coherence and integrity of purpose. A prodigious effort is required not only to meet our obligations to serve as arbiters of the social conscience of society, but also to be able to take informed and practical

positions on issues and the kind of practice we want. But that is what we must do. The life we have chosen as nurses, educated persons, and as a national resource is not for the fainthearted. It demands uncommon fortitude.

REFERENCES

1. The Association of American Colleges. *Integrity in the College Curriculum: A Report on the Academic Community.* Washington, DC, The Association, 1985, pp. 17–24.
2. Lee, V. *Access to Higher Education: The Experiences of Blacks, Hispanics, and Low Socio-Economic Status Whites.* Washington, DC, Division of Policy Analysis and Research, American Council on Education, 1985, p. 36.
3. Darling-Harvard, L. *Equality and Excellence: The Educational Status of Black Americans.* New York, College Board Publishers, 1985, p. 52.
4. *Peterson's Guides, Undergraduate.* Princeton, NJ, Peterson's Guides, Inc., 1985.

CHAPTER 62

The Final Frontier

Nursing in the emerging health-care environment

Rosalinda M. Haddon, RN, MSN

As I visit hospitals throughout the United States, I continue to hear two questions: What has gone wrong with health care? What do I do now to succeed?

I am astonished that these questions are still being asked because we only have to study the history of the U.S. health-care delivery system or ask practicing nurses to know the answer. What has gone wrong? We haven't changed. What do we do to succeed? Change! Change with the ever-changing environment.

Simple, right? Yet despite the fact that these answers are staring us in the face, we seem reluctant to confront the issues that will create the solutions.

One of our most popular television shows, *Star Trek,* began each segment with the following introduction:

> Space, the final frontier. These are the voyages of the Starship Enterprise. Its 5-year mission: to explore strange new worlds, to seek out new life and new civilizations, to boldly go where no man has gone before.

I would like to paraphrase that introduction and challenge nursing to establish this as our mission:

> Nursing, the final frontier. These are the voyages of the Starship Opportunity. Our 5-year mission: to

seek out change and innovation, to boldly go where no one has gone before.

Change and innovation are nursing's final frontier. A frontier is the outer limit in a field of endeavor, especially one in which the opportunities for research and development have not been exploited.

CHANGING CHALLENGES

Nursing can either accept the challenge of exploring that final frontier or continue to perpetuate the current system that is rapidly disintegrating around us.

Arnold Toynbee once described the rise and fall of nations in terms of challenge and response. A young nation is confronted with a challenge for which it finds a successful response. It then grows and prospers. But as time passes, the nature of the challenge changes. If a nation continues to make the same (although once successful) response to the new challenge, it inevitably suffers a decline and eventual failure (Kanter, 1988). Our health-care delivery system faces just such a challenge and unfortunately responds with old strategies.

The answers to the questions of yesterday and our once-successful methodologies for responses are no longer workable alternatives to the changes we face today or will face tomorrow.

Reprinted from *Nursing Economics,* Vol. 7, No. 3, with permission of Anthony J. Jannetti, Inc. © 1989.

Success will only be guaranteed if and when we decide to innovate, create new ideas and systems, and take new risks. This can and will happen only when we decide to enable our staff to attain their greatest potential. Our staff are our future hope. Our staff are the leadership of tomorrow; and we, the leaders of today, must encourage and mentor their growth and development to achieve the necessary changes. Thus we have two charges and two responsibilities: (a) to begin the change process and begin the journey into the final frontier; and (b) to develop the next generation of leaders and innovators who will continue our journey.

REFLECTING ON OUR PAST

Before we begin our imaginary flight into what may be our future, let us reflect upon where we have been and where we are now.

Health care has always had a sound tradition in the service of caring. Our mission has shown reverence for life with compassion the overriding value. Ministering to the ill and the poor was considered noble and a justifiable rationale for expending resources.

Science was young and had not yet supplanted religion. Man's concept of the spirit was far stronger than his concept of the physical universe. Care was an enabling process that appealed to the spirituality of man to become cause over his environment. Nurturing the soul or a person's "beingness" was as important as nurturing his body. Man was considered "unique," a creation of God in His likeness and the center of all things.

The 15th and 16th centuries changed much of this thinking. Human relationships with God and nature changed substantially with the emergence of experimental science and its manipulation techniques. "Relying on these achievements, humankind abandoned its former image of the world and itself . . . Because of science, humankind took a step forward and began to regard itself in a different way" (Gutierrez, 1971, p. 18).

In the 19th century, Darwin totally changed our ideas of man by his theory of man's development as a species. Based on Darwin's writings, science now views man not as unique but merely as the current endpoint in the evolutionary process.

The spiritual being was no longer supreme; the physical being was; and science became determined to learn all it could about this remarkable animal and machine known as man. Prolongation of physical life superseded a life-long commitment to the spiritual life. Unlike the Middle Ages when artists had to rob graves to study anatomy and the Victorian period when vivisection (even for scientific study by physicians) was illegal, experimentation and examination of a deceased body are almost prerequisites for burial today.

The changes brought about other changes. Ethical dilemmas ensued. Moralistic values clashed with religious mores. So came the separation of church and state. But where did and does health care fall? Is it in the realm of the state or the church?

In the late 1880s, government clearly assumed authority over mankind's health status as it began assuming responsibility for the health of its citizenry through the efforts of such notable persons as Florence Nightingale, who moved hospitals from church control to government control.

Not until the 1930s with the passage of the Blue Cross Acts did the U.S. government get involved in outcomes and payment issues. What the government began paying for, it wanted the right to examine.

However, until the 1980s, health-care institutions in the United States were relatively free of governmental interference. Caring was still considered the major mission of both lay and secular hospitals. The poor were expected to be cared for as well as the rich, religious and whatever resources were needed to provide the necessary services were acceptable. The government had no control over standards of care or standards of operation, and therefore institutions were accountable to their boards and their communities.

Each institution had a distinct cultural climate. Hospitals developed philosophies based on the beliefs and values of the institutional founders. Such values included education; research; care of the poor; and care of certain ethnic groups, religious or social classes, ages, or diseases. All, however, were based on a ministry of some kind. The purpose was to provide a needed service to mankind—one that would be valued as life-giving by the recipients of that service.

And because the prolongation of physical life was now the ultimate goal, resources were unlimited. No cost was too high to save a life.

Young men and women who chose health-care careers were carefully selected by schools and universities. The supply was great; rewards were more personal than material; and the calling was noble, respected, and inspirational. These careers were perceived as life-long commitments to sacrifice and service.

Technology still had not achieved great success, so caring was still the paramount product of health-care institutions. Because caring was so important, anyone who needed care was granted admission to the hallowed halls of hospitals. This provided a great sense of satisfaction on the part of the caregivers for their charges included as many patients who went home healthy in mind and body and pleased with their experiences as patients who died, lingered, or were discharged to a changed life status.

Caregivers were generalists who treated all kinds of conditions and diseases in all age groups at all levels of acuity. Patients remained in the hospital until caring was complete with discharge possible only when patients were better than when they arrived.

In those days, every hospital admitted every patient so access to care was never an issue. You simply drove to the nearest hospital or emergency room and were treated regardless of your ability to pay. The government subsidized those hospitals that had nonpaying patients. There was a time when admission clerks did not ask for insurance cards; they merely asked patients' names, addresses, and names of attending physicians. If a patient did not have a physician, clerks assigned physicians from lists provided by the medical staff.

Hospitals were considered cottage industries. Frequently, entire families worked at a single institution. All services were done on premises with nothing contracted to outside vendors. Hospital personnel made many of their supplies and equipment. Hospitals were isolated companies that depended on outside resources only for raw materials.

As little as 30 years ago, the hospital of 250 beds commonly had an administrator, often a retired elderly physician, and a director of nursing as its only administrative staff (Drucker, 1986). They acted not only as the leaders of the organization but the caretakers of staff. This type of paternalism was for many years applauded and characteristic of organizations that had high morale; a staff with a sense of family had greater affinity for the institution. This structure generated pride and longevity among employees.

Although these structures were male-dominated and the majority of staff were female, the sense of being cared for was the acceptable work ethic of the day. Communication and decision making were hierarchical; you had to get permission from "mother" or "father."

Staff were expected to "fit into" these nice family structures. Sources for staffing were unlimited with more people available for positions than positions available. Hospitals could select whom they wanted and did not want. Although staff were "cared for," they were often not "cared about" and therefore taken for granted because the organization was more important than its parts. Parts could easily be replaced. After all, who wants a disobedient rebellious child in the family? They could disrupt the false sense of harmony, peace, and calm.

With no external forces for change and organizations existing in stable environments with internal operations resembling clockwork and unvarying in practice, individuals could be ignored or dismissed. Success was an organizational prerogative and not an individual enterprise. People were merely units of error and potential sources of error. The organization was the asset.

Hospitals were designed to be predictable with predictable structures, operations, outcomes, and profits. They almost ran automatically. Management was there simply to handle the few unexpected events that might occur.

TURBULENCE OF TODAY

Within the past 10 to 20 years, however, things have changed drastically. And nothing today is as it was as little as 2 years ago.

Science has advanced at a rate never before known to man. Incredibly, 80% of all scientists that have ever lived are alive today and are producing. In less than one century, science has moved us from the horse and buggy to the moon, Mars, Saturn, and back. We have been witness to the development of cures for tuberculosis, syphilis, specific cancers, and the near elimination of diseases such as polio, smallpox, and measles. We have witnessed the discoveries of DNA, RNA, and micro-, cryo-, and laser surgery. We have witnessed enormous advances in public health thanks to microbiology and epidemiology and a simple little instrument called the microscope. We now have machines that can explore every body part to diagnose problems and computers that can analyze data faster than the human brain. We can transplant organs and replace some with mechanical devices. We can mechanize, computerize, and analyze every human component except the indomitable spirit of man, which is the core of his creativity. Only man can create; machines cannot and organizations cannot. Only individuals who compose organizations and who run machines can create.

And man has created change and innovation within our health-care delivery system. Man has also created change in our basic premises and values of health-care delivery.

CHANGING RELATIONSHIPS IN HEALTH CARE

Health care is no longer a noble mission. It has become an inalienable right of mankind; and as a right, now falls within the purview of government control and inspection. The government ensures and protects the rights of its citizens and therefore becomes the major determinant of the services necessary to sustain those rights.

The U.S. government began to truly exercise its role in health-care delivery with the advent of Social Security in the 1930s, increased its presence in the 1960s with Medicare, and increased it even further in 1983 with DRGs and again in 1988 with the catastrophic health insurance bill. All directly resulted from public demand.

American consumers created these changes. American culture and moral values changed dramatically between 1920 and 1980 yet corporate cultures, especially in hospitals, remained stagnant. This should not be surprising. Because hospitals believed (and

some still believe) that the organization is the key to success — not people — they continue to run their enterprises as they had successfully done in the past when the culture fit the ethics.

But American employees have changed. No longer content to be part of the family, they became part of a national change process. They no longer wanted to be cared for by their employers; they wanted to be part of the employment setting and to have some control over this environment. Two opposing forces then developed: management and staff. Unable to change structures internally, employees sought external changes that would force internal change.

Government involvement was and is one such external pressure. With scientific changes, technologic advances, and the increased life span and rise in chronic conditions, health-care costs skyrocketed. Consumers could not afford the quality of care they felt they deserved. So they enacted laws that would force hospitals to provide the latest services to all consumers at an affordable price. They wanted a guarantee that if and when they needed services, those services would be available.

The government was happy to oblige consumer wishes, but it then had to monitor the compliance with its regulations. Hospitals became not directly answerable to consumers but to the government who acts on behalf of its citizens.

PROBLEMATIC HOSPITAL STRUCTURES

Hospitals did change as a result of this external force. They added layers of management to oversee the compliance requirements and ensure fiscal well-being while frequently decreasing the number of caregivers. The buzz phrases became "do more with less," be more "productive" and "efficient." But this seemed to apply only to staff level positions as management grew fatter. This created more bureaucracy and moved management further away from both the employee and the customer.

Hospitals got bigger so that they could provide the ever increasing numbers of services that science was creating as well. And as Peters and Waterman shared, "Along with bigness comes complexity, unfortunately. And most big companies respond to complexity in kind by designing complex systems and structures. They then hire staff to keep track of all this complexity and that's where the mistake begins" (1982, p. 306). Drucker has added, "As a result, middle managements today tend to be overstuffed to the point of obesity . . . This slows the decision-making process to a crawl and makes the organization increasingly incapable of adapting to change" (1986, p. 200).

Hospitals continue this seemingly endless cycle: External pressure from government = Increased internal complexity = Increased administrative staff = Increased alienation of staff = Increased pressure for more external changes. Yet they fail to realize that the cycle can only be broken by change—internal change that is planned and chosen with staff input.

Today many hospitals are effect rather than cause; they are reactive rather than proactive. They are victims and followers rather than leaders and innovators.

Many hospitals reacted to the nursing shortage as if they were surprised. They couldn't believe it was happening to them and failed to take preventive actions like those of Boston Beth Israel and other magnet hospitals. Too many hospitals sat back, waited, and began wringing their hands and looking for someone to blame when the shortage hit. Guess who got the blame? Just consider the number of vice presidents of nursing filling placement offices today for the answer.

Hospitals simply did not want to change. They were successful with old strategies and expected them to continue working. Peters and Tseng described the situation as follows: "Hospitals are gripped by conditions of stability, continuity, persistence, and inertia . . . systems, once established, generate countless forces and balances to perpetuate themselves. Not only do systems tend to absorb small variations in their basic patterns, thereby continuing their own pace and direction, but most of the actions of their decision makers are simply adjustments to maintain the equilibrium of the system. A host of institutional safeguards, some of them vested with sacrosanct status or mystification, are built around stabilizing decision-making purposes. Outsiders and outside ideas are smoothly rejected" (1983, p. 23).

They forgot one important component: their people. The staff wanted a change. Everything was changing; and sometimes when changes come so fast and furious, the tendency is to put our heads in the sand and wait for the dust to settle or to try and stop the world so we can get off.

But once begun, change increases in velocity, especially as mass increases; it does not slow down or stop. Change gathers momentum, and our mass has increased. More people are pushing the system, and hospital entities are becoming larger.

What will it take, however, to awaken some of our institutions to change? Neither unionizing nor limiting dollars seem to do it. Increasing technology does not seem to do it nor bankruptcies, mergers, or restructuring. Increased competition, reduced lengths of stay, increased acuity, and an aging population aren't working either.

Consumers are increasingly aware of their health-care needs and concerns. They are also more aware of their legal rights and are litigating more than ever.

Even though consumers believe health care is better today due to technological advances, they are also more apt to request second opinions and feel that health-care providers are less responsive to their needs (Pokorny, 1988). Yet even this does not seem to have made a difference.

NURSING'S RESPONSES

Nursing, however, is making the difference. As early as 1981, Mauksch and Miller indicated that increasing numbers of nurses were willing to initiate changes, become more effective leaders, and implement more innovative ideas (Mauksch & Miller, 1981).

The 41 hospitals selected as magnet institutions by the American Academy of Nursing in 1983 were exceptional examples of nurses selecting change as a means to success, implementing change as a means of taking control from external forces, and creating change as a means of ensuring leadership status.

Organized nursing is changing both health-care delivery and the profession. Nursing is evolving closer to full professional status by increasing its science base through active research and continually improving its educational base by moving into institutions of higher learning.

Nursing is learning to speak with a united voice on issues ranging from professional standards to nuclear arms. And nursing is coming closer to a definition of its customer and its final valuable product.

Nurse executives have evolved from expert clinicians to expert business people who never lose sight of the customer, the product, and the mission of caring. Nursing vice presidents are no longer supervisors but the progenitors of tomorrow's leaders. They plan and develop programs and structures while planning for and developing tomorrow's innovations.

But there is a rub. Take a group of highly motivated change agents, and plop them down in the middle of organizations that want to maintain the status quo, and what do you get? Conflict!

OPPORTUNITIES CREATED BY THE NURSING SHORTAGE

Fortunately, in this dilemma, the scales are tipped in our favor. We have a very powerful ally that is helping us force the changes necessary for success today.

The nursing shortage is that ally. Whether we have fewer resources or more demand for nurses today is not an issue for debate here. Needless to say, beds are being closed and the quality of care is suffering because hospitals cannot attract and retain the number of professional nurses necessary to achieve hospital goals and objectives.

The shortage directly results from institutions' old beliefs that people are secondary to the organization. This is total folly for as external forces change and overwhelm smooth operations, change requirements increase and hospitals must rely on more of their people to make decisions on matters for which routine, predictable answers no longer work. As Kanter noted, "Thus individuals actually need to count for more because it is people within the organization who come up with new ideas, who develop creative responses, and who push for change before opportunities disappear or minor irritants turn into catastrophes" (1983, p. 18).

This creative power must be relearned by nurses who for years have been socialized to trust the paternalistic hospital environment. Nurse executives must develop both staff and other management personnel. We must teach them that future success depends upon the unleashing of the creative powers within our staff. We must all learn to trust that the ideas of our staff are the most potent weapons in the world for change and are necessary for continuity — not stagnation. Stagnation at best is mediocrity and, at worst, death.

CALL FOR NURSE EXECUTIVES

What we as nurse executives must create are what Tichy and Devanna (1986) call "transformational leaders." Fortunately, this process can be learned and consists of a purposeful and organized search for changes, systematic analysis, and the capacity to move resources from areas of lesser to greater productivity.

As American health-care institutions slip further into the doldrums, innovation and change are beginning to be recognized as national priorities. But there is still a clear and pressing need for even greater innovation because we face social and economic changes of unprecedented magnitude and variety that past practices cannot accommodate. Hospitals must make an investment in innovation through policies and practices that encourage staff to solve problems, seek new ideas, challenge established norms, and experiment. Indeed, when hospitals lead, they lead because of innovation.

In our present environment of scarce resources, low profits, negative growth, and pressure to increase services while decreasing costs, the capacity to invest resources and to promote broad innovation is even more sharply reduced than normal. Given the standard equation of innovation with risk, the usual propensity to be risk averse is now even more exaggerated. Yet under present circumstances, the status quo is even riskier!

And so we come to our final frontier: the mastery of change and the control of a chaotic, antiquated, and disintegrating system that has lost its mission. This is our challenge.

MISSION BEFORE US

Where do we begin? Thomas Paine once said, "A long habit of not thinking a thing wrong gives it the superficial appearance of being right." So first we must recognize that things are wrong and need to be changed. People facing change must come to grips with some hard realities. As they change their behavior, they must struggle to get closure on the old ways of doing things and develop new routines. Then we must not only diagnose our organizations' strengths and weaknesses and match them against environmental opportunities, but we must also find ways to inspire our staff to meet these new challenges. This vision of the future must be formulated so that the pain of changing will be worth the effort.

As leaders, nurse executives must both find and create a vision of an organization that is better in some way than the old one and encourage others to share in the dream. One method of achieving this is by using what we call the KRC Triangle with the sides representing knowledge, responsibility, and control, with each side dependent upon the other. You cannot have control without knowledge and responsibility. With knowledge, one can assume responsibility and eventually control.

Staff will not assume responsibility for change until they are knowledgeable of the vision. Our leaders, therefore, must provide this knowledge, this learning, this development. We must be certain that our staff know and understand the need for change and the inherent benefits both for them and the organization. Once this knowledge is internalized, the responsibility for creating the change is easily assumed. The responsibility for change becomes the focus of all activity and creates a tremendous desire to make it work.

Once the change has occurred and staff consider it theirs, they will feel a sense of control, ownership, autonomy, and pride. This, by its very nature, instills the confidence and desire to create another change and then another. Internal rewards come from self-actualization, and external rewards come from organizational success. Everyone wins — especially the leader who created and nurtured the process.

UNIQUE ADVANTAGE OF NURSE EXECUTIVES

Nursing occupies the most advantageous position in this change process. With the nursing shortage, the spotlight is on us. Everyone is poised and ready to see what we will do. Let's not disappoint them.

Nurse executives are in the pilot's seat. We can steer the industry to future success. Nurse executives are the only health-care managers in today's institutions who by generic education have both the technical expertise that keeps us close to the customer and the management and group dynamics expertise with which to enable our staffs. Both are keys to success.

Most administrators are lay people with no understanding of customer needs and even less understanding of the hospital product and how it is delivered. Physicians have the technical expertise, know the customer and the product, but are not socialized or educated in enabling strategies. They do not develop people, and this is not considered a priority.

Nurse executives by the very fact that they are nurses "care." This caring can be translated into activities that create the transformational leaders of tomorrow.

In a review of common characteristics of the magnet hospitals, one trait was pervasive: The nurse executive in these institutions "listened" as summarized in this advice, "Listen to the staff . . . The best consultants are on your own staff" (McClure, Poulin, Sovie, & Wandelt, 1988, p. 84). This is a form of caring that may not be unique to nursing but certainly is a cornerstone of nursing practice.

Nurse executives are, however, in a unique position to listen. They are not afraid to leave the confines of their offices and visit staff on their own turf.

An added benefit to this visibility is the closeness to the customer. Patients and physicians are hospital customers. Nurse executives can listen and communicate with both groups and meet both groups' expectations. No other administrator can make that claim.

And lastly, nurse executives care about the customer, not just the bottom line. We are the vanguards, the very last line of defense between the patient with needs and a health-care system that has too often become more concerned with quantity than quality.

LOOKING AHEAD

Where are we going? We know what lies ahead: more restrictions and regulations, fewer dollars, limited personnel resources, and more government control and bureaucracy. Hospitals will be run more like big businesses than service industries. There will be tremendous growth in high technology with increased competition for customers and resources. Consumer awareness will continue to grow with increasing emphasis placed on ethical issues and "caring" programs such as TRI-CARE and Planetree. There will be continued changes in nursing — education, autonomy, advocacy for consumers, unification as a single voice for health care, and movement from a practice based on the medical model to science/theory based practice.

Hopefully, the future portends a rediscovery of basic beliefs and values within which nurse executives can establish a new mission and a new corporate culture based on quality, caring, and outcomes instead of process. There will be a reestablishment of values such as honesty, open communication, customer importance, enthusiasm for risk, and a commitment to what works. Nurse executives will be the catalyst for these changes. They will be the creators and transformational leaders of the new age.

As nursing assumes its responsibility as this catalyst for change, we will embark upon our journey to the final frontier — a destination that will rightfully place nursing in the health-care delivery system as leaders. It takes only the vision of tomorrow, entrepreneurial spirit, and commitment to create the reality from the dream. The dream is within our grasp.

Nursing, the final frontier. These are the voyages of the Starship Opportunity. Our 5-year mission: to explore strange new ideas and new methodologies, to seek out change and innovation, and to boldly go where no one has gone before.

The journey will be exciting and wonderful. So bon voyage!

REFERENCES

Drucker, P. (1986). *The frontiers of management.* New York: Harper & Row.

Gutierrez, G. (1971). *A theory of liberation.* New York: Orbis Books.

Kanter, R.M. (1988). *The change masters.* New York: Simon and Schuster.

Mauksch, I., & Miller, M. (1981). *Implementing change in nursing.* St. Louis: C.V. Mosby.

McClure, M.L., Poulin, M.A., Sovie, M.D., & Wandelt, M.A. (1988). *Magnet hospitals.* St. Louis, MO: American Academy of Nursing.

Peters, J., & Tseng, S. (1983). *Managing strategic change in hospitals.* Chicago: American Hospital Association.

Peters, T., & Waterman, R. (1982). *In search of excellence.* New York: Warner.

Pokorny, G. (1988). Report card on health care. *Health Management Quarterly* 10(1), 3-7.

Tichy, N.M., & Devanna, M.A. (1986). *The transformational leader.* New York: Wiley and Sons Publishers.

SUGGESTED READINGS

Part III NURSING AND FUTURE HEALTH CARE DELIVERY

Beyers M: Future of care nursing delivery, NAQ 11(2):71-80, 1987.

Davis C, Oakley D and Sochalski J: Leadership for expanding nursing influence on health policy, JONA 15-21, 1982.

Goertzen I: Making nursing's vision a reality, NO 35(3): 121-123, 1987.

McBride A: Shaping nursing's preferred future, NO 35(3):124-125, 1987.

Moritz P, Hinshaw A and Heinrich J: Nursing resources and the delivery of patient care, JONA 19(5):12-17, 1989.

Pelfrey S and Theisen B: Joint ventures in health care, JONA 19(4):39-42, 1989.

Pointer D: Responding to the challenges of the new healthcare marketplace: Organizing for creativity and innovation, Hospital and Health Services Administration 30(6):10-25, 1985.

Sovie M: Redesigning our future: Whose responsibility is it? Nursing Economics 8(1):21-26, 1990.

Westbury S: The future of health care: Changes and choices, Nursing Economics 6(2):59-62, 1988.

Index